THE GATES OF HEAVEN

VOLUME THREE OF Seven Brothers

ALSO BY

CURT BENJAMIN

SEVEN BROTHERS

THE PRINCE OF SHADOW
(Volume One)

THE PRINCE OF DREAMS
(Volume Two)

THE GATES OF HEAVEN
(Volume Three)

THE GATES OF HEAVEN

VOLUME THREE OF Seven Brothers

Curt Benjamin

DAW BOOKS, INC.

DONALD A. WOLLHEIM, FOUNDER

375 Hudson Street, New York, NY 10014

ELIZABETH R. WOLLHEIM
SHEILA E. GILBERT
PUBLISHERS

http://www.dawbooks.com

First Printing, September 2003
1   2   3   4   5   6   7   8   9

DAW TRADEMARK REGISTERED
U.S. PAT. OFF. AND FOREIGN COUNTRIES
—MARCA REGISTRADA
HECHO EN U.S.A.

PRINTED IN THE U.S.A.

This book is dedicated to the usual suspects: Mom and Dad and Erik and David. "Ben's Groupies"—Barb and mom Charlotte—for their unflagging support and food for the soul. Bonnie, without whom this would have been written on stone tablets, and the Hoffmans whom I'm buttering up for their expertise on the next project. Tom and Cathy, who were there when Llesho was born and still give great advice. And of course the Free Library of Philadelphia, for slipping me the cool books.

PART ONE

LEAVING THE GRASSLANDS

Chapter One

IN LLESHO'S dream, Dognut the dwarf tilted his head, inviting him to consider carefully. "Who, among the thousands who follow you, would you trade for the life of your best friend?"

The dim light from false dawn hadn't yet brightened the red canvas of their tent, but it had dulled the light of the lamp hanging from the tent pole. In the aftermath of the battle that had defeated the witch-finder, Hmishi's murdered body lay on a pallet hidden in shadows with Lling an indistinct grieving heap at his side. Master Markko, through his lieutenant the witch-finder, had clouded Lling's mind while he tortured her lover to death. Lling's lover. Llesho's best friend through all the struggles that had brought them from Pearl Island to this. He'd searched for them across the length of the Gansau Wastes and into the grasslands themselves. And now he'd found them, too late for Hmishi and too late for Lling in a lot of ways, too. She would live forever with the memory of Master Markko oozing through her mind, something Llesho shared in common with her. Almost, he'd been too late to save his brother Adar who lay sleeping, thanks to Carina's potions, in a nearby tent.

In the haze of morning, the lamp still caught the gleam of Dognut's eyes. Llesho gazed deeply into them as the mortal god of mercy revealed himself in all his stern sorrow. Dognut was a tag-name dropped on him by the ignorant. Like a careful farmer, the dwarf cultivated insignificance in men's eyes. Uncounted years ago, however, some mother and father had greeted him newborn and named him Bright Morning. Had they known then that they gave birth to a god? Or that in age his warm lined face would promise rainbows and scudding clouds and blue, blue sky?

Llesho wanted to believe in Mercy, but the question—whose life in trade?—was a dangerous one. Hmishi had died in his service, one among the many who had perished to defend him since he'd walked away from the pearl beds with a quest laid on him by a ghost. Pearl Island and Farshore and Shan and Ahkenbad—he wore the names of their dead heavy around his neck like the pearls of the Great Goddess at his breast. He was supposed to be growing stronger under their weight, but he didn't feel at all wise or kingly.

He was just a boy, sad and weary, whose best friend had died of such terrible injuries that Llesho's heart squeezed in sympathetic pain. Not anymore, though. Hmishi's pain was gone. And Dognut—Bright Morning—was offering what? A trick? Choose a lesser life to die, and return your friend to merciless agony that would leave him crippled inside and out for the rest of his pain-filled life? Or did the dwarf offer something more seductive: the return of his friend to life and health in exchange for an innocent sacrifice and thus, Llesho's corruption. What kind of test was it this time, and how was this mercy of any kind?

"Who would I give, to see Hmishi alive?" he repeated in his dream, though the event had gone much more quickly in real life. His answer remained the same, however: "No one."

He remembered the Dinha's words—"Spend my Wastrels well"—and knew she didn't mean this. The gods and warriors who traveled in his company were his responsibility, not his property. He could spend their lives—had done so in this very battle—but their deaths had to buy more than a friend's laughter.

"It's just . . . He's one too many, you know? I need a reason to keep going. I thought that Kungol was it—home, and freedom, a kingdom—but they're just words and a world away.

"The cadre—Hmishi and Lling, Bixei and Stipes, and Kaydu—have been my only home for so long that I've lost the knack of imagining another."

When it had happened for real, his brother Balar had been there, and Master Den. Bixei and Stipes had stood guard at the entrance to the red tent. His dream had stripped the memory of their presence, and of his admission that he did not find in his brothers the home he sought.

As in life, however, Bright Morning agreed: "The mortal goddess of war did good work when she bound your cadre to each other, though its strength was never meant to last beyond its usefulness."

"A broken sword wins no battles." His own argument could go against him. He thought he had some value to these mortal gods because the Great Goddess cared for him as a beloved husband. But would she love him still if he were so easily broken? Would his guides and mentors abandon him if she didn't?

The dwarf dropped his hands into his lap. "You ask too much."

He'd said the very words himself, to no avail. The gods kept asking for more anyway; he figured it was time they knew how it felt. Bright Morning read the thought in his face and shook his head. In the end, it came to a simple truth: "Your heart needs rest." With that, the mortal god of mercy took up a silver flute and set it to his lips.

This time, the dream had been kind to him. The music had lightened his heart and stirred Lling from her sleep. "What's happening?" she asked, her eyes on Llesho but her ear cocked in the direction of the music.

"I don't know," Llesho began, but the silver tones of the flute lifted him with unreasoning hope. When he looked on his dead friend, Hmishi's breast rose and fell, rose and fell, almost imperceptibly at first, then growing stronger with each breath, until his eyelids fluttered and opened.

"Hmishi!" Lling fell to her knees, her arms enclosing him. Between her sobs she repeated his name, "Hmishi, Hmishi, Hmishi."

Llesho watched them. Although he stood close enough to

reach out and touch them, his heart no longer felt a part of the joy of his companions. The tent itself seemed to have grown as large as the khan's great traveling palace, and Llesho found himself in the lowest place near the door. He'd wanted this, asked for it, had thought himself the hero of this tale of sacrifice and redemption. In the end, it wasn't about him at all.

Hmishi's eyes roamed without focus or comprehension until they fell on Llesho, then his brows knotted. "Am I dead?" he asked.

Hmishi had asked him that before. This time, Llesho had smiled and answered, "Not anymore."

"Good." With a contented sigh, the dream Hmishi closed his eyes, which seemed like a signal for Llesho himself to leave sleep behind.

He rubbed his face with the palms of his hands and, as he did every morning on rising, checked his pack for the safety of the sacred gifts he carried as part of his quest. The spear he left for later, going first to count the scattered pearls of the Great Goddess' necklace, the "String of Midnights" that he hung in a small bag from a thong around his neck. Six, not counting Pig, who dangled from the silver chain of the Tashek dream readers. Everyone from the Jinn to the mortal goddess of war had insisted he find the pearls, each as big as the knuckle of his thumb and as black as its name indicated. Touching them usually soothed him, but their hypnotic mystery couldn't dispel the dream that lingered in the air of the red tent.

With the camp coming to life around him, he set the little bag of pearls over his heart where they belonged and drew out the jade wedding cup that the Lady SienMa had given him back before he knew she was the mortal goddess of war. It was a promise; he knew that at the end of his quest the Great Goddess waited for him. He wished she was here now, to take away the dreams that haunted him. This one had been milder than some. In the worst of them, Hmishi woke screaming in agony and Llesho knew, in the way one does in dreams, that his friend would suffer the terrible pain of his wounds forever. In another version, Lling had gazed up at Llesho with a look so near to worship that he squirmed under the heat of it.

"Don't thank me; I didn't do it."

"You interceded with the gods. I know you did."

He didn't want her thanks. He'd done it for himself; not for Lling or even for Hmishi, but because he wanted to hold onto the friends he had left. Lling's adoring gratitude, however, warned him that they were followers now; he'd already lost them as companions. Unlike the dream of never ending pain, this one was true.

Mercy had lived up to his name. Hmishi still needed time to rest and heal, but the mortal god called Bright Morning had mended the worst of his injuries when he'd brought him back from the dead. And his friends now treated Llesho more like a deity than they did the real gods who wandered among them. Dognut had watched him come to the realization with one of those deep, patient looks and Master Den had worn his teacher's face. Apparently that was the lesson he was supposed to learn out of this. It could have waited until he'd had a chance to savor the joy.

Even now, he didn't have a quiet moment to steal a might-have-been. The sounds of waking outside the tent had grown to include angry voices at the entrance. As he put away the jade wedding cup, he heard Bixei's greeting and the Harnish prince, Tayyichiut, shouting something back at him. Llesho couldn't make out the words, but the anger and hurt were plain to hear.

"Let him in," he called out to his guards—if Bixei was on duty, Stipes would be nearby—and climbed off his cot, braced for bad news.

"He's dead!" Prince Tayyichiut burst into the tent, his shirt and tunic disheveled, his braids coming undone so that his hair flew wildly as he paced. Word of Hmishi's return from the underworld hadn't spread in the camp yet, but the Harnish prince didn't know him. He hadn't been their only loss, of course. Tayy himself had lost a friend in the fighting. He'd grieved, but not like this.

This new loss had shaken Tayy to the center of his soul, however, which meant Llesho needed reinforcements. He snapped Bixei to action with the urgent command, "Get Master Den and Bright Morning. My brothers, too. And Carina." It might be too late for her healing services, but as a shaman she was an expert at unraveling the mysteries of the underworld. She would know what had happened, what was to be done.

Bixei gave a bow to acknowledge his orders. Before following them, however, he called on a pair of Gansau Wastrels to replace him in front of the tent. Taking up their station, the Wastrels reminded Llesho to take nothing at appearances. Once he'd thought the desert warriors his enemy, but they had fought and died for him, not only at Ahkenbad, but here, against the stone monsters as well. Dread shivered through him at the memory; he had a feeling he was going to need them again before long.

It took just a moment to set the guard, and then Bixei was gone. With a nod of acknowledgment, Llesho turned again to the distraught prince.

"Who's dead?"

"My father. Chimbai-Khan."

"Oh, no." Llesho sank back to his cot, stunned by the news. Balar had warned him the universe would demand balance for the return of his friend's life. How much harm had he caused to the Harnish people and their prince with his one selfish wish?

Tayyichiut heard only the concern of a friend in Llesho's exclamation. "Yes," he confirmed with a bob of his head, "Dead in his sleep of snakebite, Bolghai says. I will miss him greatly."

"What kind of bite?" Llesho asked, though he knew already.

"Bamboo snake." Tayyichiut spoke with the calculated gravity of one who said more than met the ear. "Somehow, it made its way into his bed while the khan slept heavily with fever. Serpents will sometimes do that, looking for warmth, though Bolghai says bamboo snakes are rare in this area and they are more inclined to stay in the trees than to visit sleeping men in the night."

No accident, then, but murder. In his dream travels Llesho had seen the bamboo snake resting on the khan's breast. She had spoken to him with Lady Chaiujin's voice.

"A tragedy," Llesho agreed. "And the Lady Chaiujin, his wife, mourns her loss, no doubt." He'd had his own encounter with the lady, who had offered the peace of the underworld in her arms and in the form of a snake had poised with tooth at his throat. He would have ended up like Chimbai-Khan if not for Master Den's timely arrival. He wished now he'd said something, but the khan had been safe from her tooth since their marriage and he hadn't seen the dream for the warning it had been.

"She weeps for the loss of her husband and for the unborn son who will never know his father," Tayyichiut said, answering the words with the ritual responses though he marked the irony of the sentiment with a knowing drop of his lashes. As the inconveniently full-grown heir, he would be next on her murder list. Then she would claim the khanate for herself in the name of her dead husband's unborn son. If such a son existed, which Llesho doubted in spite of her claims. As a snake, she'd shown no sign of carrying a human child. He didn't think the Harnish clans would follow a khan hatched from an egg, however valid his claim by descent.

Llesho's reinforcements arrived then and he welcomed the newcomers with a jerk of his chin. It said much about his adventures that he drew comfort from the trickster ChiChu, who traveled as the servant and teacher Master Den. The god filled the entrance to the tent with his huge bulk and set down Bright Morning, who had ridden to the war counsel in the crook of his arm. His brothers followed, except for Adar, who remained in the hospital tent. He had sent his blessings with Carina.

"I will be Adar's eyes and ears," she promised. "He chafes at his confinement but cannot hide his moans when he tries to move about. Still," she assured them quickly, "he is recovering, and will be on his feet soon enough."

Fixing a concerned frown on Tayy, who continued his agitated pacing in the crowded tent, she added the question they all had come to ask: "What has happened?"

"The khan is dead," Llesho told them. Since the lady could be anywhere in her serpent form, he carefully refrained from stating aloud the obvious conclusion. Lady Chaiujin had murdered her husband and would do the same to her stepson as soon as the opportunity presented itself.

"My uncle says, 'have patience,' but how can I?" Tayy exclaimed. "Between one summer and the next I have gone from the most favored son of my mother and father to a homeless orphan!"

"Mergen will protect you," Llesho assured him, though he wondered about that. Did the lady lay her plans alone, or did she scheme with her husband's brother to take his place on the dais of the khan?

"I know he will," Tayy agreed. "In fact, I have to go to him now. He awaits with Bolghai. The ulus will have to elect a new khan."

"I'll go with you," Kaydu offered, "Little Brother has missed you." Little Brother had traveled on the prince's back the day before and was notoriously fickle about his attentions to anyone but his mistress, so they all took her claim for what it was. Tayy had his own band of young followers who acted as his bodyguard, of course. Until they knew in which direction the khan's brother would move, however, the affection of Kaydu's monkey familiar for the Harnish prince would give her an excuse to stay close.

"I'll go, too," Carina offered. "Bolghai will need help to tend the body." She bowed her head in sorrow for the dead khan, remembering that the shaman's own son had lately died as well.

Llesho couldn't help but notice that death followed wherever his quest took him. He would have handed himself over to Master Markko on the spot to save the people around him from harm, but he knew that wouldn't work. Heaven itself was at stake, and the mortal kingdoms both waking and sleeping, if he failed. The magician would loose the demons of hell itself, releasing chaos from the gardens of heaven to the underworld, sweeping the worlds of men along in their fury. He had to believe that the khan had died to save all the grasslands from that coming storm or he would go mad.

Tayy, however didn't seem to blame him, and Llesho remembered that the khan's first wife had died suspiciously a season or more before their own band had entered the ulus of the Qubal people. Chaos stalked on more than one horse, it seemed. Perhaps fate had brought him here to save Tayy, not to cause his father's death.

The prince accepted Kaydu's offer of company with a courtly nod. "I won't be able to get away again until the ceremonies are completed, but Yesugei will explain the proper respects an outlander owes a dead khan." They left together, Kaydu sweeping the area with the fierce gaze of a hawk—or a dragon—on the lookout for a snack. The Lady Chaiujin would do well to keep to her human form or she would find herself trapped in an unlikely gullet.

Chapter Two

WITH the rituals returning a khan to his ancestors completed, Yesugei had called Llesho and his brothers to a formal audience at which strangers might pay their respects to the Qubal clans in their time of loss. Both sides would offer assurances of continued friendship, at least until a new khan was elected. The Qubal seemed unlikely to choose a leader who would move against visitors who had been granted the hospitality of the ulus, but the possibility remained a worry.

Kaydu had flown out at dawn to report to her father, but Shokar gathered Llesho's cadre and his brothers for the audience with the royal family. Since Hmishi still needed time to heal, he had called up as temporary replacement the Thebin corporal who had worked with Llesho in the recent battle.

"Tonkuq," Shokar introduced the middle-aged woman with the scar over her right eye. He had trained her with the other troops he had gathered for Llesho's cause, and added from his experience with her, "None better with a knife."

"He says that because he hasn't seen Lling work." She didn't mention Llesho's own royal skill with the weapon, but Tonkuq gave him a look that told him she guessed it. Llesho remembered her competence in battle and accepted her temporary presence beside them.

"And Sawghar." With a gesture, Shokar motioned forward

the Gansau Wastrel he had chosen to fill in while Lling recovered from her own ordeal. Llesho thought it no coincidence that his personal guard now counted in its number at least one representative from each place he had stopped since he had walked out of the bay to begin his quest. His brother had served as a diplomat to the Shan Empire before he took up farming in the aftermath of Thebin's fall.

"Welcome." Looking from one to the other, Llesho wondered how many of them would be alive at the end of the day. Shocked at the strange death of their khan, the camp had grown wary around mysteries. Not least of these they counted the wizard-king, as they had come to call Llesho. Word had spread about the magical spear he carried and the messenger who came and went in the shape of a bird. With the tales came whispers that he had used his unearthly powers to wrest a Thebin warrior from the clutching grasp of the underworld to serve him.

Llesho had given up his protests that he was merely the impoverished prince of a broken house on a mad quest. More than that he hadn't figured out, though, and suspected he wouldn't until he reached the gates of heaven in his mortal form and asked the Great Goddess herself what purpose he had on this her earth. Maybe not even then, if she decided he had to solve the puzzle of his existence for himself. In the here and now, however, Harnish warriors avoided the little valley by the Onga where Llesho's forces made their camp, and they made warding signs against the evil eye when their paths crossed one of his fighters. His own small band of fifty could scarcely hope to stand against the grasslands if that fear turned against them.

The trickster god joined the diplomatic party as they followed Shokar through their own camp. He uttered a long-suffering sigh when he saw where they were heading. To reach the ger-tent palace of the khan, they would have to climb the steep shoulder of the valley to the plains above.

"What are you going to tell Prince Tayy?" Master Den asked, knowing without needing to be told the road Llesho's mind wandered.

Llesho shrugged a one-shouldered "I don't know" but said nothing until they had moved a little way from the tents clustered around the commons at the center of the camp. He had to give Tayy some explanation, and he had too little information about the alliances shifting within the ulus—the gathering of clans under the khan's spear—to figure out the prince's position in all of this. Would he be sharing confidences with a friend, or demonstrating the powers he wielded among the mortal gods for a potential ally?

When they had drawn away from the curious glances, he pondered his lack of a ready answer. "I'd like to tell him that Carina made a mistake which we happily discovered when Hmishi sat up and asked for a cup of tea. It's happened before."

"That's why someone always sits with the body until the pyre is ready," Master Den agreed.

Llesho shivered in horror at the thought. Hmishi hadn't been alive, of course, until Bright Morning brought him back from the underworld. Carina *didn't* make mistakes like that. Still, it gave a soldier pause.

"But?" When he didn't continue, Master Den prodded with the less than patient tone he took when a student deliberately avoided the point of a lesson.

They were passing through a stand of spindly trees, and Llesho gave his surroundings a wary inspection. The bamboo snake had killed the prince's father in his sleep. As Lady Chaiujin, she'd tried to seduce Llesho to his death as well, and might have succeeded if Master Den hadn't found him just then and sent her off to do her mischief elsewhere. He didn't think for a minute she was done with him, however, and kept a wary eye on the reaching branches.

Before they began the steep ascent up the side of the dell, Master Den took the opportunity to relieve himself on a slender sapling with much contented sighing. Llesho kept his eyes carefully averted; he had come to know too much about his godly companions already. Wondering if the trickster god intended his relief as an insult to murderous Lady Chaiujin, Llesho decided to hold off on both question and answer. There were too many leafy hiding places where the lady might be slinking nearby, so he waited until they had climbed out of the little valley.

A chill dread pushed him ahead of his companions. Llesho reached the lip of the valley in the lead and he took a moment to look around. Here, on the high ground, the Harn had raised the white-and-silver ger-tent of the khan's palace. Lesser tents had grown up around it, dotting the rolling landscape with round white mounds among the stony outcrops. In the late morning light of both the Great and Little Sun, sparks bright as fireworks flashed off the chips of mica in the stone. He squinted, and sniffed cautiously at the air. It still carried the taint of flesh and other objects burned with the dead khan. On a pyre taller than Llesho's head, the Harn had stacked the most prized of their khan's personal possessions, including his favorite horses, and a flock of sheep to feed him in the underworld.

Spirits did not eat mutton, but Bolghai, the Harnish shaman, had spent most of yesterday afternoon in the ritual slaughter of the sheep anyway. "It's not important how useful the gift is to the one who receives it," he'd explained to Llesho. "What counts is how much it means to the giver."

In this case, one sheep from each clan plus horses and other goods demonstrated not only the loyalty of the ulus, but also the wealth of the respective clans that made up the gathering. "And wealth," Bolghai had added, "is just one among the many powers in competition here until the new khan is installed."

"There you are." Huffing a bit from the exertion, the mountainous trickster god crested the rise. Leading them a little away from the edge of the tent city, where they could talk without being overheard, he waved a hand to signal a halt at a curved sweep of stone cushioned with a thick mat of grass.

"Better," he declared, dropping heavily onto the stony seat.

Llesho doubted this heaving display of weakness. As Master Den, servant, launderer, and combat instructor, the trickster had walked most of the way from Pearl Island at his side, and had never drawn a labored breath. But if it bought him time, he was willing to give ChiChu even this small trick.

"But?" Master Den repeated, bringing him back to the matter of explanations. Friend or not, as the prince of the Qubal clans, Tayy would demand answers.

Llesho gave the grass at his feet a distrustful frown, but saw no creature who might be the Lady Chaiujin or one of her spies. "Prince Tayy knows his father's death was murder, and no accident," he offered his opinion. "He doesn't know how the Lady Chaiujin managed it, or what part I played in the murder. I'd rather he never did—at least the last part, about me."

"You had nothing to do with the khan's death, Llesho."

Master Den patted the grassy seat next to him, and Llesho climbed up, careful not to disturb the bluebells and the buttercups rising on slender stems at his feet. He was much shorter than his master and his dark legs hung inches above the ground. Shokar sent Balar and Lluka with his cadre to form a circle of defense to guard Llesho's privacy. For himself, he remained nearby in a watchful pose that did nothing to hide his agreement with the trickster god—or, Llesho noticed, to mar his dignity like a dangling child.

Dignity wasn't the issue, however. "Tayy's father died because I wanted my friend back. You heard what Balar said: the universe demands balance. If Mercy grants a life, another must be taken in its place. I wanted Hmishi back and Bright Morning, in his mercy, favored my desire for a friend over Tayy's need for his father. Now I have my cadre, and Tayy has no parent. Who will protect the prince from his stepmother now?"

"His uncle?" Shokar suggested, arms crossed over his broad chest. "Yesugei? The ten thousand Harnish troops who now stand ready at a word to do battle in his defense?"

"Bolghai?" Master Den added, with a wry little smile, "You?"

"Oh, me, right. The Lady Chaiujin asked for my life. I stood with arms outstretched and offered it to her, and I am supposed to save her stepson from the same fate?"

"You what?" Shokar came out of his slouch with fire in his eyes, and Llesho flinched at the rage he saw there.

"It was nothing. A moment's weakness . . ."

"And knowing how you reacted to Hmishi's death, you wonder why the dwarf felt you needed his mercy?" Shokar unfolded his arms and gripped the hilt of his sword as if he would slay the demons of Llesho's mind. He wasn't prepared for the eagle that swooped down and landed on it, and flinched when she wrapped her talons around his forearm.

With a flap of her wings, Kaydu rose again, just enough so that when she became human, only a little bounce on the balls of her feet gave evidence of her return to earthbound form. The distraction didn't save him, however. "He's taking the blame for killing the khan, isn't he?" she asked as she settled next to Llesho on the grassy outcrop.

He made a face at her. Jammed cheek to cheek and shoulder to shoulder on that rocky shelf as they were, he had the fleeting thought that they must look like three demons of misadventure in search of mischief.

Looking on with evident disapproval, Shokar answered Kaydu's question. "I thought he felt guilty because Bright Morning took mercy on his flagging spirits at cost to some other poor soul in the earthly kingdom," he answered with acid in his words, "but now I wonder. Balar said that the universe must remain in balance, but no one ever said that the Chimbai-Khan's death was the weight that countered Hmishi's life. In fact, it would seem likely that somewhere a butterfly stumbled, or a miner cracked a rock deep underground to balance the small spark of a lowly soldier's existence.

"It would take a larger price to balance the death of a khan. The life of a boy-king, for example. By the Goddess, Llesho, where do you keep your brain, because you clearly aren't using it today!"

"He's right, you know," Master Den slapped his hands on his knees to emphasize the point. "Hmishi hardly seems the equal to a khan, even if murder could restore the balance upset by mercy."

"It can't, of course," Kaydu finished the thought. "According to my father, murder by its very nature creates a void in the universe. One murder doesn't pay for another, and we've had two of them."

"Habiba is the servant of the mortal goddess of war," Llesho objected, "He would say that—believe it even—to free himself of the guilt of murders done in her name."

Kaydu glared at him. "Don't play those games, Llesho. War

is not murder, as you well know. And you, at least, have never killed except in honest combat.''

"So your death wouldn't have saved the khan,'' Shokar insisted, ''But think of the people who follow you, who would have died in a vain battle to avenge you with no hope of seeing Thebin free at the end of it. Think of the Great Goddess, your wife, and what will happen if the siege against the celestial kingdom wins through and the gates of heaven fall.''

"But what about Tayy?'' He whispered the question to himself as much as to his companions. He saw too much of himself in the Harnish prince, now an orphan like him and eager for revenge against the forces at work against his people. Like Llesho, his life remained in danger as long as his enemies lived.

"Good question.'' Kaydu bounded up and dusted off her butt before dragging him to his feet and giving him a push. "Isn't that what you were going to find out?''

They found Prince Tayyichiut of the Qubal people with his stepmother, Lady Chaiujin, surrounded by advisers in the crowded ger-tent of his father. The many guardsmen of the khan, who had failed him in his moment of greatest need, now watched the gathered clans with an alertness that begged to redeem itself. Llesho recognized Yesugei sitting in a traditional Harnish pose, with one knee propping up his chin and the other leg tucked under him, in deep but hushed discussion with Mergen, Tayy's uncle. Around them were ranged the clan chiefs and old women, the Great Mothers of the clans, gathered there. Bortu, Tayy's grandmother and the murdered khan's mother, sat among them as Great Mother to her son's clan. Llesho didn't know what a Great Mother was, exactly, but he figured he was about to find out.

As strange as it seemed, the Harnish chieftains would actually vote for the one among them who would lead the clans in their dealings with one another and in war with outside forces like Master Markko—or, he thought, like him. Would the new khan throw the clans behind the magician's Harnish Southerners? Or would he side with Llesho's foreigners, who had come into the grasslands in search of their companions and had stayed to forge alliances against a mutual threat? Chimbai-Khan had favored his cause, but Llesho was painfully aware that the next few hours could turn the tent city from a sanctuary into a prison.

Leaving his Wastrels to guard the door of the ger-tent, Llesho advanced through the crowd to the foot of the dais where Tayy sat with his stepmother accepting the condolences if not the fealty of the clans. Llesho had put on the sumptuous traditional Thebin coat, sleeveless and embroidered all over with fine needlework, that Master Den had carried for him all the way from Farshore Province. Under his coat, he wore a rich Thebin shirt and breeches, with soft boots on his feet. Shokar likewise wore the clothes of his princely station. Kaydu appeared in soft greens and blues and grays, the military colors of Thousand Lakes Province, home to the mortal goddess of war in whose service Kaydu marched. Even Master Den had added a red sash on which were written many characters of prayer and good fortune, though it bound only his usual knee-length white coat over a breechcloth slung low under his enormous belly.

The interior of the ger-tent had already changed in the aftermath of the khan's death, stripped of the personal objects that would furnish Chimbai-Khan in the underworld. The ornately painted chests remained, however, as did various objects that would count as family wealth or the property of the khan's own clan. As the prince and the lady, watching him approach across the vast expanse of the ger-tent, were themselves both the property of the clan and its potential leaders. Llesho noticed the bronze bust of his Thebin ancestor, carved ages past in Llesho's own image. Someone had moved it to the painted chest nearest where Prince Tayyichiut sat in his father's place. No personal object, this had come to Chimbai-Khan through his fathers, and would pass to his son regardless of the outcome of the coming vote. That Tayy displayed it so prominently at his right hand declared his intention to continue his father's alliance with Llesho's band. What his gathered clans would make of this, however, was impossible to guess.

When it came his turn to speak to the grieving family, Llesho left his companions and stepped up to the dais with a deep bow. He knew where he stood with these two primary contestants in the coming battle for the khanate. The Lady Chaiujin, widow of the late khan and mother, as she claimed, to his unborn child, wanted Llesho dead. She'd already made attempts on his credibility and on his life.

Prince Tayyichiut, his own age and stepson of the Lady Chaiujin, had become a friend. The two princes shared the ill regard of the lady, who had likely murdered Tayy's mother as well as his father, and would wait only long enough to allay suspicion before sending the son to attend his parents in the underworld. In Lady Chaiujin, they shared Tayy's enemy. As importantly for Llesho, however, Prince Tayy had seen the battleground of the stone giants raised by Master Markko. He'd lost friends to the monsters and understood the threat that the evil magician posed to his ulus. If named khan, he would fight alongside Llesho's other allies of necessity. So they shared this enemy as well.

The chieftains had no obligation to vote for a member of the khan's family, however. Any one among them could win the confidence of the gathered clans, moving his own clan into the fore of power and wealth. A stranger might soon gather in his hand the warriors of all the clans to hold tight or loose against his enemies as he chose. The heirs of Chimbai-Khan would recede into obscurity then, taking Llesho's negotiations with them. If it came to a change in rule, Llesho knew he might depend on Yesugei, who had found him on the borders of the Northern grasslands and brought him to his khan. Of the others, he had no clue.

The Lady Chaiujin held out her hands to him. "Prince Llesho of Thebin. You find the people of the Chimbai-Khan in grief and sorrow."

"Your grief is my own, Lady." Llesho took her hands and touched his forehead to them.

"And yet it is a lesson for us all, how the least of nature's creatures may bring down the mighty." She veiled the knowing mockery of her eyes behind the thick lashes of her dark-painted lids.

"Hardly the least of creatures, Lady." He felt the nail-edge of her forefinger scrape against his palm and drew away quickly, before she broke the skin.

"You would know, young prince. I understand you encountered a like serpent, and would have joined my master in death had it not been for the timely appearance of your servant." She raised her chin in a challenge directed at Master Den. "No wonder you give the lowly one pride of place at your side."

"Do we have a nest of vipers, then, in the ulus of the Chimbai-Khan?" Prince Tayy addressed his stepmother politely, with none of his emotion on his face.

"Perhaps we have come upon a mother among serpents." She considered the thought, seemed to like it. "She may strike with the intention only to protect her eggs against strangers who would destroy her own."

Pinned under her cold stare, Llesho wondering what egg she had planted in the khan's bed. His companions stood a little behind him and appeared not to hear, though Llesho doubted the innocence of the trickster god's expression. No one else would have heard the lady's low words as she alluded to the murder of her husband. With a shiver, Llesho turned to his friend.

"Tayyichiut," he said, and bowed his head over the prince's hands as he had done with the Lady Chaiujin. He did not use any title, nor would anyone do so until the vote had been cast and a new khan elected. Then, he would be Tayyichiut-Khan or simply Tayy until the next contest of the ulus. "I share the sorrow of your loss." The look they shared spoke of the understanding between them, of lost fathers and murder. Tayy gave a brief nod and frowned at Kaydu standing empty-handed at his side.

"Where is your familiar, Captain?"

"Little Brother spends the day with Bright Morning, the musician," she answered with a bow, referring to the monkey that traveled with her everywhere, except when she flew in the shape of a bird. Tayy knew this, and doubtless wondered where she had been and what she had seen. Answers would have to wait for later, however. "I would have him learn to play the sweet potato, to the indignation of his teacher."

Her droll explanation hid the truth of her travels but brought a smile to the prince's eyes. "We have become friends, Little Brother and I," he informed her, and added, "I wish to be kept abreast of his progress."

"And so you shall," she promised.

Their message of condolences delivered, Llesho made to leave, but the prince stopped him with a hand on his arm.

"Stay," he said, "as my witness in the voting."

Llesho wasn't certain what being a witness might entail, but Tayy looked at him with such anguish that Llesho couldn't deny him. They were both orphans now, a bond beyond politics or shared enemies.

"Of course," he said, and drew aside his companions to the lowest position just inside the door of the ger-tent to await the outcome of the vote.

Chapter Three

LLESHO watched, taking in every step in the process of electing a new khan. For something so important—the khan would lead the clans, including their army of ten thousand—the method proved disappointingly simple. As the ceremony progressed, however, he found himself drawn into the gravity of even the simplest act.

Bolghai was summoned and came at the call. He wore his hair in a mass of plaits from each of which hung a talisman of metal or bead or bone. His robes, cut to show their many layers, still bore the bloodstains of the sheep he had slaughtered for the khan's pyre, but he had cleaned the pelts of the stoats that hung by their sharp little teeth in a collar around his neck. He did not walk with a stately pace to the dais as a Thebin priest might do, but scampered and pranced like his totem animal, setting the pelts to kicking at his shoulders in a little stoat-dance. His clothing jingled at each step with bells and amulets that swayed on silver chains sewn onto them.

The first time Llesho met him, the shaman had shocked and repelled him. But Bolghai had helped him to find his own totem, the roebuck, and had taught him to control his gift of dreams for his own ends. Sometimes at least. Now, he watched with interest as the shaman hitched and hopped to the dais in the persona of his totem stoat. Bolghai carried a flat skin drum and the thighbone of a roebuck that he used as a stick. He wouldn't be creating totemic magic, so he wouldn't use his fiddle. Rather, he'd need the drum to set the pace of the coming ceremony.

When he had reached the fur-heaped royal dais, the shaman grasped the thighbone in the middle and tapped with first one end, then the other, in a rapid tattoo on his drum.

"When is a prince not a prince?" he demanded, confronting Tayy with more beating of his drum while he waited for the answer to his riddle.

If there was no khan, there could be no prince. Tayyichiut bowed his head, accepting the judgment dictated by custom and the sacred nature of the riddle. Allowing himself to be ritually driven off by the beating drum, he left the dais to sit with Bortu and Mergen of his clan.

"When is a wife not a wife?" the shaman asked next, subtly changing the rhythm of his drumming. It wasn't what she expected. Llesho, watching Tayy carefully, saw the surprise in his eyes as well. Bortu's features, however, relaxed in grim satisfaction. Her son was dead, but she was no fool.

"I am no barren tree, but bear the khan's heir in my belly." she clutched a hand below her unbelted waist and spat at the shaman's feet. So, the riddle had set her aside not as the widow, but as one who had not truly blessed the marriage bed of the khan. Llesho figured that much. Sort of. And she objected. He wondered not for the first time what, if anything, the Lady Chaiujin did carry in her womb.

Bolghai accepted her correction, more or less, with the smallest of stoatlike gestures and adjusted his drumming accordingly. "When is a queen not a queen?" he amended.

A wife remained a wife even at the death of her husband, but with no khan there could be no queen. Lady Chaiujin bowed, as Tayyichiut had done, but with less grace, and let herself be driven from the dais. She took a step toward her husband's clan, but Bortu turned her back, and the Lady Chaiujin hesitated, finally taking up a position alone, though closest to the dais. No one challenged her for the assumption of that right, but no one came to support her either. While few might guess her part in the death of their khan, she had made no friends among them.

Alone on the dais, Bolghai let the thighbone hang by a cord that tied it to the drum. Holding up his open hand, he asked another riddle: "Apart they are weak, together they smite their enemies." As answer, he closed his hand tight and raised it high over his head: the separate fingers were each fragile, but made into a fist, they made a powerful weapon. So, Llesho figured, the clans, joined in the ulus, became strong.

Bolghai's next words confirmed Llesho's guess: "Who here gathered would make a fist?"

A huge roar rose out of the gathered clans, aided by the shaman's drum. When he settled into a slower rhythm, the clans began the process of electing a khan. No one outside of the clans had ever been privileged to see the like before, and Llesho held his breath, his eyes darting everywhere to see everything, as two guardsmen came foward and set a low table down in front of the fur-covered dais.

Bortu came forward first and set a bowl on the table while Bolghai drummed and danced so energetically behind it that Llesho wondered how he managed not to kick it over. Bortu's bowl, of simple wood but inset everywhere with precious gems, he recognized for its great age. When she set it down, she raised her chin in challenge at her son's wife, who had no clan to bring to the ulus but must put herself forward as the regent of her husband's unborn child.

Bortu retired to sit again among the leaders of her clan, a signal for Great Mother to follow Great Mother, each rising to place her bowl before the drumming shaman. Every bowl was made of a precious material—worked silver or gold, porcelain, or alabaster, and each was elaborately decorated with some sign or sigil prominently marked to indicate the clan of origin. None showed the age of Bortu's, however. Chimbai's clan was the oldest, then, and Bortu, by chance or destiny, was the oldest of the Great Mothers. When he looked into her eyes, something moved, and for a moment the whites vanished into the hard black light of a bird of prey. Not a snake like her daughter-in-

law, but he wondered what magics lay hidden within the old
lady.

In a contest, he would have placed his bets on Bortu and he
wondered why she had not used her skills to save her son.
When he looked again, however, he saw only a sad old woman,
grieving for her precious child. He thought of Lluka, his brother
who saw all futures falling into chaos, and wondered if the old
woman sacrificed her line to some future that none of them
could see. He was pretty sure he didn't want to, all in all.

The procession of the Great Mothers had ended with seven
bowls placed upright on the table at the shaman's feet, and
three placed upside down as some sign to the gathered clans.

Master Den leaned over with a brief explanation that confirmed his guess: "'Up' means the chieftain will accept the khanate for his clan if he is chosen. 'Down' means the clan has no
wish to rise to khan right now. Not wealthy enough, or not
united among themselves enough, or perhaps just wise enough
to know they presently count no generals among their younger
men."

"Or waiting out the killing before stepping in to pick up the
pieces, and the wealth of the losers," Kaydu suggested. They'd
both seen as much in the far provinces of Shan, where Lord
Yueh had hoped to reap the benefit of Pearl Island's fall and
had been gobbled up himself by Master Markko. Llesho determined to pay more attention to those who had turned their
bowls down. But now the Qubal clans focused on those who
would be khan.

"One a hand may brush aside," Bolghai intoned to a slow
and steady drumbeat, "Many lift their heads to heaven with a
glittering crown about their brow."

Tayyichiut was the first to rise in answer to this riddle. In
his hand, Mergen had placed a pebble—easily swept away, but
many became a mountain with a crown of glaciers. He went to
the table and set the stone inside Bortu's bowl with a bow to the
shaman, who had stopped his dancing and shivered in place in
a fit of ecstasy, and another bow to the ancient bowl. After him,
Yesugei rose and, performing the same bows, set his stone in
Bortu's bowl as well.

Master Den let go of a little sigh as their friend sat again among his clan. At Llesho's raised brow of inquiry, he whispered, "Yesugei was the most likely candidate if the clans decided against Chimbai's policies. He has signaled his followers where his own allegiances lie."

Llesho nodded. He thought he understood, but Master Den seemed unsatisfied with his reaction and added, "It could have come to war among the Qubal clans, with enemies on both their borders waiting to fall on them."

Master Markko in the South, and Tinglut, the Lady Chaiujin's father, in the East. He looked at the lady, sitting with venomous poise, her head demurely downcast, but with calculation glinting from under lowered lashes. As soon as they were done here, he'd have to find Shou and warn him. Tinglut would sign his treaty with a pen in one hand and sword held in the other behind his back.

"Would you share the thought that wrinkles your brow like an old man?" Kaydu asked him.

"I just realized that I am starting to think in Bolghai's riddles."

She rolled her eyes in sympathy and added, "If you start giving orders in battle that way, I'll thump you."

He was so happy to hear her talk to him as his captain from the old days that he didn't even bother to point out he had never given the orders in battle anyway. That was her job.

The vote came to an end then, or so it seemed. The pebbles all looked alike. It would be harder that way to figure out who voted against the new khan once he took office, Llesho figured. That made retaliation less likely, though he was sure that some had done it in the past. His understanding of politics had grown that subtle at least. They hushed while Bolghai gave the count: three clans had stubbornly cast their votes for themselves, but seven had gone to Chimbai-Khan's line. The clans retrieved their voting bowls and each took a pebble from the little heap at Bolghai's feet.

When the table before the royal dais was once more empty, the shaman declared in riddle form, "Out of many, one. Out of one, four. Out of four, one. Out of one, many." Each part of the riddle was punctuated with a flurry on his drum.

The first part made sense: many clans had voted, one clan won. What the rest meant, Llesho couldn't fathom, until four figures came forward and faced the dais again. Chimbai-Khan's line, but who among the likely candidates would be khan?

If she spoke true that she carried the son of the dead khan, Lady Chaiujin might claim right to the khanate as the regent of the heir. That presupposed the truth of two potential lies: that she carried a child of the khan at all, and that the khan had chosen her unborn babe as heir over his grown son by the wife who had gone on before him. Bold as the serpent she was, the lady pushed her way to the fore all out of order of her precedence and placed an alabaster bowl on the table at Bolghai's feet. "For my son," she said, "in the womb."

Bolghai looked like he would speak some prophecy or judgment, but his trembling overcame him and the Lady Chaiujin made her escape without comment.

Bortu, who should have been first, followed with greater dignity and cold, bright eyes on the back of her rival. In the death of her son, Lady Bortu had a right to seek the khanate in her own person, but she set her bowl upside down on the low table, removing herself from the contest. Lady Chaiujin settled in her place with a little gloating smile at this. Bortu returned her only a slow blink of a predator hypnotizing its prey, before turning away. Llesho had a fleeting vision of a hawk with a snake's neck crushed in its mouth.

When he had cleared his eyes of the image, he found Bortu staring at him with the first emotion he had seen on her face since the death of her son: he had surprised her. *Read my mind, old woman,* he thought. *Know me. I come for vengeance and you are welcome to sit on my shoulder when I ride.* But she gave him a small turn of the head, an answer, "No," and a reason— she looked now at her other son.

As chieftain of the clan during his brother's reign, Mergen had a rightful claim to the khanate and he drew near the dais and set his jewel encrusted bowl upright next to the two that had gone before him. Tayyichiut followed, and like his grandmother, repudiated his claim upon the ulus. Instead of putting his cup facedown, however, he lifted Mergen's up and set his own beneath it. When Bortu saw what he had done, she smiled and returned to the dais to do the same. Now the four cups were gathered into two, Bortu and Tayyichiut showing that they stood with Mergen against the outsider with the questionable belly. The Lady Chaiujin raged behind her impassive demeanor, Llesho could see it in her eyes, but the chieftains nodded their heads in approval as the pace of the drumming grew more rapid.

The contestants had no vote, since each had made their choice in the position of his or her bowl upon the table. One by one the chieftains, smiling or grim, followed Yesugei again to the dais and cast their pebbles into Mergen's bowl. When the last vote had been cast, there was no need for the shaman to make his ritual announcement, though he did it anyway:

"When is a chieftain not a chieftain?"

To which the gathered chieftains replied in a rousing chorus, "When he is khan!"

After that came the swearing of loyalties, first, through their captains, the personal guardsmen who tended the khan and protected him. Then the chieftains, one by one, each dropped to one knee, fist clasped over his heart, to promise warriors at need and cooperation in counsel as was the custom of these Harnish clans. Not a king, but something else entirely. Llesho had known that with his head, but understanding shifted in his gut as he heard the chieftains give their conditional allegiance. Finally it came time for the heirs to swear their loyalty.

"I have lost my bravest son in service to the Qubal clans," Bortu mourned, and added, for Mergen, "The underworld will find my smartest son more difficult to bring home."

"I hope so," Mergen answered. By home, of course, she meant death, and Llesho suspected that Mergen would be a great deal more difficult to kill than his brother.

Llesho recognized the worry line that creased Tayy's forehead, but Mergen moved instantly to erase it. Taking his nephew's hands, he announced, "The son of my brother is my son. I beg you call him prince, and treat him as you would my own person."

"My father—" Tayy began, but Mergen-Khan stopped him with a finger touch of warning on the back of his hand. "Leave everything in my hands, Prince Tayyichiut. I am your khan."

To the gathered clans it sounded like a good-hearted reminder to a younger relative that he owed a greater deference to his uncle's new status. Llesho heard Mergen's words for what they were, however—a promise—and saw Tayy's embarrassment likewise as cautious hope and grief all roiled together. He waited to see where the ax would fall. Not on Tayy, for sure.

It came as no surprise that the Lady Chaiujin offered no allegiance but an insult. "Among the eastern clans, a brother would offer the safety of his own hearth as husband to his brother's widow and father to his brother's child. I expect no such comfort from a man who would take his anda for a bride, but beg a small tent and a servant to tend me until my time. When I am delivered of my dead husband's true heir, I would ask only the freedom to choose a husband from among the clans."

Mergen-Khan's face became thunderous. The slight was obvious. A Harnishman, particularly a man of position, made alliances in many degrees, but anda was the closest. Blood brothers for life, sealed by gifts and held in the heart, the anda was a cherished friend. Occasionally more, which caused no trouble in the tents of a man who also kept to his wives and his husbandly duties to his clan. But Mergen had no wife, and his anda, Otchigin, had died fighting the stone giants of Master Markko.

The Lady Chaiujin threatened civil war with Chimbai-Khan's unborn son as her instrument, but Llesho didn't think that Mergen had noticed that. She'd called his dead anda a coward and a thief, stealing Mergen's duties from his clan. The khan's eyes went flat. "Better my anda than the serpent who made my brother's sleep so permanent," he said, and raised a hand as if to strike her.

She flinched, but the action didn't save her. By prearranged signal, the guards of his dead brother, newly sworn to their elected khan, came forward. Two who had been Chimbai's oldest and most valued friends seized her between them, and Mergen's own swordmaster stepped up behind her.

"Strangle the murdering witch," Mergen said, and the swordmaster wrapped his hands around her neck and squeezed.

"You'll pay," she choked out. With a twist of her neck, she turned into a jewel-green snake. Her grin exposed bared fangs she sank into the meat of her strangler's hand.

"Ah!" he screamed, and dropped her as his hand throbbed with venom. Her captors struggled to hold on, but her arms had vanished. Slipping easily out of their grasp, the Lady Chaiujin glided quickly into hiding between the layers of rugs on the ger-tent floor.

"Everybody out!" Mergen ordered. And to his guards, "To sword! Find her and put an end to her." He reached out and grabbed a goblet from the chest that sat by the fire and raised it over his head. "This jeweled cup to the man who brings her dead body to me: snake or woman, I don't care which. Just find her!"

Chapter Four

MERGEN-KHAN'S swordmaster died with blood running from his nose while the Harnish women shook out the heaped furs and beat the rugs, rolling them afterward as if they were going to shift camp on the moment. Men searched the firebox and under all the chests and boxes, and looked in all the surrounding round white tents. They dismantled the ger-tent palace of the khan and checked in all its lattices before setting it up again at a distance that shifted the orientation of the camp. Then they had to move many other tents to keep everyone in their proper place according to their status in the ulus.

The Lady Chaiujin had vanished. Neither the Tinglut princess nor her totem form, the emerald-green bamboo snake, could be found anywhere on the great high plain.

In a moment of quiet, Llesho rode out with Prince Tayyi-chiut to exercise their horses and their own camp-restlessness. Two hounds followed them, a black dog with a lolling grin and a red bitch with bright, intelligent eyes.

"I didn't know you kept dogs."

"The Lady Chaiujin claimed a fear of their barking and had them banished to the sheep pens. Perhaps she guessed they might recognize her for what she was." The prince cast a fond glance at his hounds. A little bit of the weight seemed to have lifted from his shoulders since the lady's disappearance, another of many changes in the camp since they had arrived, just one of many things he had to think about.

When they had gone a ways from the camp so they wouldn't be overheard, Llesho hesitantly asked Tayyichiut about the Lady Chaiujin's claim against Mergen that gossip did not answer in his presence.

"About Mergen-Khan's anda—" His own cadre rode behind with Tayy's guardsmen, out of hearing but not out of sight or the range of a bow. The Harnish prince could answer the question in confidence between friends of equal rank if he chose to do so, but Tayy deflected the request.

"It's none of my business, or yours," he said with a dismissive wave of his hand.

"It's not that I disapprove." Llesho cast a glance behind them, where Bixei and Stipes both rode in his defense. "I'm trying to understand what the Lady Chaiujin was trying to do when she said that about Otchigin and your uncle."

"A treasonous suggestion that Mergen had reasons to wish his brother the khan dead." Tayy snapped, clearly unhappy with the question. Llesho waited out the scalding glower until the prince relented.

"Otchigin and Mergen were closest friends from the time they were fostered together as boys. After my father became khan, when the clan had named Mergen chieftain, Otchigin brought him gifts and swore his personal loyalty to Mergen and the Qubal people. Together they committed their lives to the service of the khan.

"Lady Chaiujin hoped to make the chieftains believe that Mergen had placed the personal relationship above the political. She hinted that my father wanted to seal a treaty but that Mergen refused any marriage. The clans were supposed to suspect that Chimbai-Khan sent Otchigin out to die so that his brother wouldn't have a reason to disobey him anymore. From there, it wouldn't be hard to convince them that Mergen killed the khan to avenge Otchigin's murder.

"She didn't have to prove anything; if she'd raised enough doubt, Mergen would have lost the confidence of the clans. Then she could have demanded a new vote to take the khanate in the name of her unborn child. My uncle was ahead of her, of course, but I don't think it would have worked out the way she expected anyway. Yesugei has held the clans to Mergen till now, but he'd stand for the khanate himself before he'd let the ulus fall to infighting between the clans."

"No one could have guessed what Master Markko would raise out there," Llesho objected, "It was supposed to be safe, a simple scouting expedition." But he wondered why someone of Otchigin's rank had ridden on a such a lowly mission. It began to add up in ways that raised question about Chimbai's motives.

"No one," Tayy agreed with a warning in it, not to let his thoughts run down that path. At his heel the black hound, fretful at the sudden change in his master's mood, added its own cautionary growl. "Nor would Chimbai-Khan have had such a need—Mergen obeyed my father's every wish. And the khan had decided that Mergen should have no wife."

"Are all Harnish relationships about politics?" Llesho asked. He'd thought they shared a growing friendship based on common age and rank, and even similar losses. Before the khan had died, he'd offered Tayy a place at his side, as part of his cadre. Now he wondered if the prince saw him, like Otchigin and his uncle's nonexistent wives, as a political agreement on horseback.

Tayy's answer didn't make him feel any better. "In the royal ger-tent, yes, I suppose they are. How else could it be?"

"Sometimes, people just like each other." Llesho felt stupid as soon as the words were out of his mouth, and he knew the answer Prince Tayyichiut would give him before he even said it.

"No one just likes a prince, any more than a prince—or a khan's brother—is free to make friends who do not serve the khan."

Tayy must have thought they were still talking about Mergen, because he returned to his uncle's case with an ironic laugh. "In any event, Sechule would have been surprised to hear that Mergen held an exclusive affection for Otchigin."

"Who's Sechule?" Llesho could figure that for himself, but

guesses could lead even a Prince of Dreams down a tangled path.

Tayy's predatory smirk was answer enough without his words: "A loyal woman of Yesugei's people, and the mother of two of Mergen's blanket-sons, born outside the ger-tent as we call it. They ride behind us now among my guards."

"Two of?"

"Marriage—even undeclared marriage—is political. But if a person wanders into a certain tent more often than into others, who is to say?"

And that worked out so well for Chimbai-Khan, Llesho thought, but didn't say out loud. Chimbai-Khan may have loved Tayyichiut's dead mother for all the politics of their marriage, but that left his second wife in a cold corner of the ger-tent. "Wouldn't the Lady Chaiujin have known that? About Mergen and Sechule, I mean?"

"There is nothing to know about Mergen and Sechule," Prince Tayy reminded him stiffly. The dogs had run off to chase rabbits through the flowers and he followed their progress with his eyes while Llesho worked that out.

A relationship would have meant a political alliance with Yesugei's clan. But. With a sudden, blinding grasp of the obvious, Llesho wondered how many other blanket-sons and -daughters Mergen had scattered through the ulus, and what political ties those relationships "weren't" binding to the khan. Tayy gave just a little twitch of an eyebrow to acknowledge the dawning light in his face, and then finished his vastly understated explanation.

"Tinglut-Khan sent his daughter in the spring. From the start she liked the Qubal no more than our hounds. Chimbai-Khan wouldn't have confided in her, and Mergen is hard to know even among his own."

She'd wasted no time eliminating Tayy's mother, her competition in the khan's ger-tent, which meant she understood the politics of her own marriage. Lady Chaiujin must have wondered why her husband hadn't given Mergen a wife, and she'd come up with the only solution available to her in plain sight.

Bortu had told them the answer, however, when she

honored her living son—the smart one, she'd said. Chimbai, too, must have recognized his brother's subtle mind. While making use of his brother's discreet attachments throughout the ulus, he'd assured that no legal heir gave Mergen ideas about securing a dynasty to his own line. In the true affection of the brothers for each other, the Lady Chauijin might have seen Chimbai-Khan's caution as a weakness, that he allowed his brother to slight his family obligations for his heart's desire— little knowing the politics long at work in the ger-tent of the khan.

When Llesho put it together himself, however, the Lady Chaiujin's veiled accusation made sense even if she didn't have all the facts. Chimbai-Khan had loved his brother, but feared his ambition enough that he had not permitted Mergen to marry or recognize an heir. As khan, he'd sent Mergen's anda on a mission that eliminated any political maneuvering under Otchigin's influence. Now, Chimbai-Khan himself was dead and his brother, who had denied any such ambition, sat alone on the dais of the ger-tent palace. Chimbai's son remained, as Mergen's heir rather than his khan, but for how long? Mergen-Khan could marry as he wished now, or declare his blanket-sons his heirs. Would his uncle disavow Prince Tayyichiut then, or have him killed to remove the threat to his own rule? All that Chimbai may have feared in his brother seemed to have happened.

Questions kept Llesho awake in his tent while the Great Moon passed overhead. Bolghai surely knew the answers, but wouldn't likely tell them to an outsider. Master Den might give him answers as well, but the trickster was no god to the Harnish people and his idea of a good match for Emperor Shou left Llesho doubting his expertise in matters of a royal heart. Shou, however, was older and a mortal man who understood the politics of the palace and the bedroom. As emperor, and as the human lover of the mortal goddess of war, he must.

Llesho considered a dream-walk, and groaned at the very thought of dragging himself back off his cot. He'd had lessons

in dreams before the shaman, however. The Tashek had taught
him to travel in his sleep, which seemed a much better idea in
the ghostly light of Great Moon Lun. He had scarcely thought it
when his eyes pulled shut, his limbs grew heavy.

His dream brought him to the governor's palace at Durnhag.
Llesho scanned the area, saw no one. But there—he tensed for
attack as starlight glinted off silver at the corner of his eye. Pig,
dark as the shadows except for the fine silver chains that
wrapped his black body everywhere, sat on a bucket as if he'd
been waiting for Llesho to come along.

"What are you doing out of bed?" Pig asked, "You have a big
day tomorrow; you need your sleep."

"A big day of waiting," Llesho grumbled. He'd relaxed as
soon as he recognized his guide in the dream world, but the
rush of fear left him edgy and overreacting to the taunt.
"Mergen-Khan has refused to honor the agreements we made
with his brother. He wants to ask his own questions before he
makes up his mind to help us and he won't hear us at all until
he's done interrogating the prisoners he took in the fight with
Tsu-tan. He's still mad that Lling killed the witch-finder before
he had a chance to interrogate him."

Pig made a sweeping gesture with an imaginary broom "Tsu-
tan's master would have seen his old minion dead before that
could happen, but not in time to save Lling, or your brother."

Tsu-tan had slipped his leash, driven mad like a rat in a trap
with his master's threat in one direction and his enemy's forces
in the other. Even Markko couldn't control his lackey's murderous impulses by then. Llesho didn't regret Lling's actions one
bit, but Mergen still had to wonder if they had removed his best
witness to keep some secret from their Harnish allies. Which
left them sitting on their hands until Mergen decided he trusted
them.

"In the meanwhile, we wait," Llesho finished.

With a smirk on his face that promised more, however, the
Jinn waggled his piggy eyebrows. "Ask, young king."

"I don't think so." He acknowledged the old joke between
them. "You can't fool me that easily, old Jinn."

A Jinn could bind a human who made a wish. Llesho didn't

think Pig would close that trap even if he fell into it. They both served the Great Goddess, after all, and the Jinn would never risk his place in her gardens. It was a point of honor between them, a game of matched wits. So he chose to understand it, to remain on friendly terms with his guide in the world of dreams. With a wry tilt of his head, therefore, he made his move:

"I do not *wish* to know what you are talking about, though I will be happy to listen if you *wish* to tell me more."

"Let it wait, then. You'll find out soon enough." Pig laughed, accepting his loss this round but not giving up his information. "I suppose you've come to see the emperor?"

"Yeah." He might even need her ladyship's advice, though he wasn't sure he had the nerve to ask. Face a charging army? Llesho had done that plenty of times. Discuss the marriages of kings with the mortal goddess of war? That took more nerve than any combat. With a shake of his head, he made for the wide central door.

"Not that way." Pig stopped him with a forehoof on his shoulder. "Unless this is a formal visit of state, which would raise questions of its own."

"It's personal," Llesho confirmed, though he might just as easily have called it spycraft. He remembered the secret ways of the palace at Shan and travelers arriving under cover of darkness. He could enter through the front door; he was a king, a trusted ally, and had that right. Having it, however, he found that he preferred to see Shou in the old way, before he knew he was a king making an ally of an emperor. "I just need to talk to him."

Pig nodded sagely. "Woman trouble," he guessed, and Llesho held a tight rein on the urge to smack him.

"Not woman trouble. At least, well, sort of. But not mine."

"Oh." Pig led him up a walled stairway carved into the thick palace wall, onto a narrow protected balcony, one of many that dotted the palace. "That explains everything."

Light shone through a pair of doors made of colored glass that left shadows thick in the corners. Pig reached for the catch with a flourish. "Here you are—" He gave a less than mystical yelp as a figure stepped out of the dark.

"It's you." Shou slid his sword back into its scabbard with an emphatic snick. "Trouble?" He didn't invite them in and Llesho didn't ask what Shou was doing out on the balcony in the middle of the night.

"Maybe." Llesho gave a twitch of a shoulder to emphasize his answer, or lack of one. "I'm not sure. You know about Chimbai-Khan?"

Shou nodded, enough to tell Llesho he didn't have to explain the khan's death. "Kaydu reported that the clans placed his brother in Chimbai's place. You don't trust this brother?"

It wasn't quite a question. If he'd trusted Mergen, he'd be in his own bed, not dream-walking to find Shou in the middle of the night. Llesho didn't bother to answer it except to say, "He doesn't care if we trust him, and he certainly doesn't trust us."

"I can see that would be a problem," Shou said. "I wasn't thinking clearly the last time we met or I would have left you with a larger force to lend weight to your arguments."

That was all he said about his torture and near-madness as the witch-finder's prisoner. Master Markko had crawled around in his brain and made him watch the torments of all the dead in his wars. For a little while, it had broken his mind. "Still, this new khan has accepted you as a guest if not an ally. Harnish rules of hospitality should keep you safe enough."

"I'm worried," Llesho admitted. "Prince Tayy loves his uncle. He believes the Lady Chaiujin killed his father on her own—" which raised questions about Shou's own treaty with the Tinglut—"but I'm not so sure now it wasn't Mergen."

"Then you'd better come inside."

He opened the door and went in, leaving Llesho to follow with Pig coming last in their little procession. The room was sumptuously draped in a richness of color and style that the Guynmer people would abhor, but which had suited their corrupt governor until his emperor removed him from his palace, his office, and his earthly existence. The bed lay empty now, its covers smooth except for the single untroubled indentation a man's still body might have made.

In a white robe richly draped and clasped in gold, the mortal goddess of war stood at a table covered with maps. Llesho remembered her this way from another dream. He would have wondered if she existed outside his dreams at all, except that her magician, Habiba, stood at her side. Kaydu's father. He said nothing, but searched Llesho's face for tragedy, relaxed when he found only confusion.

"What have you brought us?" The Lady SeinMa asked. Her eyes glanced off him, to Shou, who lounged against the doorjamb, but returned to Llesho with the full force of her gaze. He squirmed under the attention.

"I asked Prince Tayyichiut about his uncle today. He defended Mergen-Khan with politics, but I'm not so sure."

He explained the conversation, and his own political calculations, all of which led to Chimbai-Khan dead and a worrisome brother set in his place. He finished with the conclusion that troubled him most, that had sent him out looking for Shou in the dark of his night: "Did Mergen plot *with* the Lady Chaiujin to kill his brother?"

Habiba watched him out of hard dark eyes that reminded Llesho of the times the magician had appeared in the form of a roc. "According to Kaydu's report, he wants her dead, to avenge his brother's murder."

"It's what he said," Llesho agreed, "and Prince Tayy believes it. But what if Mergen-Khan really wants to remove the only witness to his conspiracy?"

"Or," Shou lifted his shoulders away from the doorjamb and wandered—casually, he would have them think, though some restless torment burned in his eyes—into the room. "He may be as innocent as he claims, and wary enough to keep secret the people he loves, who might still die for being close to him." His glance flickered off the Lady SeinMa's face, as if his point went to a different argument, one that tightened her ladyship's mouth into a cold frown.

"You're the emperor of Shan," she reminded him tartly, "One values your life for more than the entertainment it affords."

In the silence that followed, Llesho dropped the question he hadn't wanted to ask at all in front of the mortal goddess who shared the emperor's bed. "Has Tinglut offered you a daughter?"

"One serpent in my bed is enough." Shou bowed his head at the lady, who glared back. "I declined."

Llesho remembered another dream: Shou and the Lady SeinMa as a turtle and a white cobra. He *really* didn't want to be having this conversation. But they were waiting for him, so he plunged ahead.

"How can we trust a treaty with Tinglut here in the East when he's already murdered Chimbai-Khan and brought down all our agreements in the West? And how can we defeat Master Markko if all the Harn ally with him against us?"

The Lady SeinMa actually smiled at him. It didn't make him glow with pride. He wanted to curl up in a little ball under the table where, hopefully, her piercing eyes could not find him. That didn't seem like the kingly thing to do, however, so he locked his knees and tried not to shake.

"You are beginning to think like a general," she praised him, and he wished he could crawl inside himself and disappear. "But you base your conclusions on two assumptions that may not be true."

Habiba nodded support for his lady's argument. "You assume that Lady Bamboo Snake is the true daughter of Tinglut-Khan," he said.

With his gaze fixed on the Lady SeinMa, Shou added, "And you assume that a man of subtle ambition will betray his brother and his duty for the whispered promises of a serpent in his ear."

Llesho wondered who, besides Mergen, Shou referred to in that comment, but he grabbed for the part he felt safe to address: "You think that the Lady Chaiujin isn't Tinglut-Khan's true daughter?"

"More properly," Habiba corrected him, as a teacher might, "one must ask if the serpent is the Lady Chaiujin at all."

"Then you think Master Markko killed the real daughter, and put the snake in her place?"

"Only the underworld knows the truth of that," Lady

SeinMa said, "But it wouldn't do to underestimate Lady Bamboo Snake herself, who may have acted for her own reasons."

He'd come for answers, and they'd given him more questions. A huff of frustration escaped him and Llesho pressed his lips closed. Unthought reactions wouldn't serve him here. But the exasperation was still there. "Do you have any proof at all that I can take back with me?"

"Just this," Habiba told him, "that Kaydu, in her report, described the Lady Chaiujin as very beautiful and young. In the camp of her father, the aged khan, the lady has a reputation for kindness and plain features."

That certainly didn't describe the Lady Chaiujin he knew. Llesho felt as if he'd been set adrift in deep water, and without a paddle. "What am I supposed to do?"

Shou blinked, surprised. "Exactly what you are doing," he said. "Watch, evaluate, act as well as you can. That's all anyone can do."

Habiba nodded. "Leave the problem of Lady Bamboo Snake to Mergen-Khan, but see what he does. It will doubtless teach you something."

He would have objected, but Pig, who had said nothing during this conversation, moved toward the door. Llesho felt a tug at his gut, moving him away from Shou and toward the light of morning.

Chapter Five

HE AWOKE from his dream travels with more to worry about than when he'd gone to bed, and stumbled out into the false dawn of Little Sun for morning prayer forms. Their camp had followed the pattern of the Harnish one they had replaced in the dell. It had a clearing at its center where horsemen mustered for battle or to play the competitive games that honed their skills at mounted warfare. With Master Den to chivy them on, the space easily became a practice yard for the prayer forms of the seven mortal gods, first step on the Way of the Goddess. The forms had been a lifeline through all the turmoil and struggle that had brought Llesho from the pearl beds to the very brink of his own country again. With a sense of fitness that settled in his heart, therefore, he scrambled sleepily for his place in the ranks of the worshipers, and stretched into the familiar patterns as Master Den called out their names.

"Red Sun." Den moved his huge pale body with agile grace into the simplest of the fire forms.

Llesho followed his lead, stretching his body with arms raised in a high curve. Secure in his companions, with Kaydu on one side and Bixei on the other, with Hmishi in back of him and Lling in front, and Stipes a steady presence nearby, he reached for the zenith as the Sun might, chasing its lesser brother. Then down again, until the backs of his fingers almost reached the ground to represent the setting of the sun in the slow circling of the Way of the Goddess.

"Flowing River," Den called next, a water prayer to honor the Onga at their backs.

The present was a landmark passed in a never-ceasing flow into the future. But sometimes, as if around an unexpected bend in the river, you saw the past as well, the one you knew and the markers grown strange long before you were born. Llesho stretched and moved in the slow rhythm of the prayer form, letting his mind drift with river-thoughts flowing back into time. Ages drifted past his mind's eye. In all of them, he fought and died, and fought and died again, until he wondered how many lives had ended violently, and why?

No sooner had he thought the question than he saw, across a turning in the flow of movement, a man wearing his face but twice his age and more, worn down with battle. A bloody spear lay beside him—Llesho knew that weapon, carried it in his pack—and blood crusted on his skin grown pale with wounds and the poisons coursing through them. A woman wept for him, his head cradled in her lap. Llesho knew her from his dream travels. The Great Goddess, his wife, had appeared to him in the guise of a young girl and other times as a beekeeper. She had comforted him after Master Markko's torments, when the magician's potions had left him shattered and weak, and he knew his duty to rescue her from the siege at her gates. Her presence at this one of his deaths did not surprise him.

Watching the scene as if across a curving river, he saw the boundaries between past and present thinning in the way he had come to know under Bolghai's teaching. He stood on one side of the river bend, with the answers to his questions on the other, and centered his mind. The prayer form carried him deeper into his vision and—step, step—he stood above his dying self, looking into the grieving eyes of the Great Goddess, his wife in that life as in this. He saw, first of all things in her eyes, that she loved him as truly and deeply in age as he loved her in youth. And each of his deaths left its mark on her heart, which he regretted.

"Will it always be like this?" he asked, while the breath of his older self stuttered and bubbled in his broken chest. He recognized the wound, had seen it in dreams of other ages as the mark of the spear he carried, that now lay stained upon the riverbank. Llesho would have run away, afraid he saw his future in his past. This was his own fate, though like a dream he saw nothing to tell him how his former self had taken such an injury, or what threats waited just outside the boundary of his vision.

"That depends on you," the lady his wife answered with tears in her eyes, and he wondered if she meant he had failed the past, and would fail again in this turning of the wheel. But she gave no sign of blaming him, only mourning all the pasts in which he'd died as he was doing now, on the grass by a river that couldn't be the Onga.

The lashes of his dying self fluttered open, and for a moment, his own older eyes, dulled with pain fading into death, met his younger ones. His dying self gestured for him to draw nearer, and he bent to hear the strangled whisper,

"Remember justice. The world cannot endure without justice." Satisfied that he had said what he must, the dying Llesho's eyes clouded. A tiny frown marked his ravaged brow until the Great Goddess his wife leaned into his field of vision again. Then, with a sigh as if something had completed itself, breathing stopped.

He wanted to ask if he'd been so unjust in his actions that he needed a reminder, but the lady's eyes had closed and she rocked the body in her arms as if she could not hold the pain inside her. This was one of those moments that wasn't about him, he figured—or not about the present him at any rate—and he didn't want to intrude on her grief to make it so. But her Way had brought him here to learn something. His questions might save them all from going through the same again.

"What did he—I—mean about justice?"

"Remember," she said, while she pressed his dead mouth to her bosom, "your heart will guide you."

He'd gladly do as she bid him, if he had any idea what it was she meant for him to know. But she wasn't seeing him anymore, he could tell. With a step, and another step, he found himself among the ranks of his cadre again, with Master Den calling out the prayer forms. At his side, Bixei started, but quickly regained his place in the slow procession of the movements.

"Wind bends the willow," Master Den called out the air form.

Like the willow tree, Llesho thought, he must bend to the Way of the Goddess, accepting his fate in her service. His past had spoken to him of justice, but he didn't know why. He would die in battle in this life as he had so many times before, he thought, killed by his own tainted weapon or by the poisons of some secret enemy, shot through with flights of arrows, or cut down by sword or with a dagger to a kidney in the embrace of a false friend. So many ways had he died, and nothing he had seen promised an old age surrounded by grandchildren. When the prayer form returned them to the rest position he discovered tear tracks on his cheeks and a yearning powerful as the river current drawing his gaze to the distant mountains.

"To die in your arms," was all he had asked of the Great Goddess out of all his pasts. He knew that now, and felt her kiss in the breeze that lifted the hair from his brow. That did comfort him: wherever this turn of the wheel brought him, he loved and was loved in return, and gave his life in the service of that great love. It had, his vision told him, always been enough.

Master Den brought them back to rest. With a bow to the gathered students, and a bow from the ranks in turn, morning prayers ended.

"Where did you go?" Bixei asked him while his cadre gathered their gear.

Llesho gave a shrug. "I don't know. The past, I think." He wouldn't accept it for his future—not this time around.

"What did you see?"

Kaydu had returned, sword and dagger cinched at her waist and Little Brother perched on her shoulder. "You were there," she said, "and then you weren't."

Hmishi handed Llesho his gear. "And then you were back again," he finished for his cadre.

Llesho took the short spear and strapped it to his back. The sword he clipped to his belt where his knife already rode, never leaving him as was the way of Thebin royals. Settling his weapons about him gave him a moment to compose his thoughts, but only Lling and Stipes did not press him for an answer. Lling shied away from her own questions and Stipes, he knew, still felt as though he rode above his station in this company. He flicked a challenge at Hmishi, however, daring him to speak of where he had been before Bright Morning had raised him from the dead.

A soft smile told him this most gentle of his fierce companions would not take the bait. "How can we protect you if you insist on going places we can't follow?" Hmishi asked. And he added, "At least you could tell us what to expect of your sudden excursions out of this world."

Before he could come up with an answer, Master Den joined them with a wide grin. "Well done, young king," he praised Llesho with a pat on the back that nearly threw him to his knees. "I knew that with a little help you'd figure it out."

"Figure *what* out?" Kaydu insisted. She was their captain, and had the right to demand answers where it concerned the safety of their charge. More to the point, she was a witch like her father, and wanted to understand the workings of any magic she came in contact with.

"The Way of the Goddess," Master Den answered, "is the path to heaven. For some that means a life well lived in a manner that finds welcome from the Great Goddess. To others, who practice the forms with extraordinary skill, the Way is a more direct road which one may travel at will, or stumble upon in moments when need and proper form come together."

"There must be many roads to heaven," Llesho suggested the thought as it came to him, and Master Den applauded his perception.

"The Goddess honors the path of earth and air, fire and water, out of which all living things are formed. The spirits of the grasslands travel the underworld of dreams and spirit-animals and the dead who lately honored the living world and the ancestors who went before them. Between them roam the mortal gods and mortal humans who would aspire to the ranks of heaven, which must surely count among their numbers the beloved husband."

At this last Master Den gave a little bow. His cadre had fallen silent, half afraid even to hear the conversation between the trickster god and his royal pupil. For himself, Llesho didn't quite know if his teacher honored him or mocked him. Perhaps both: honored for reaching through the prayer forms to what lay behind them, and mocked for taking so long to discover what that was. He ducked his head in confusion, unsure whether to be proud or embarrassed, but still troubled by what he had seen.

"I died," he said.

"Often," Master Den agreed in a familiar tone that reminded Llesho he traded words with the trickster god. ChiChu had, perhaps, known him in those others lives and deaths.

"The Goddess wept," he added, and again his teacher nodded his agreement.

"Always," Master Den said.

"Then perhaps it's time to try a different way."

With that, Llesho drew his sword, baring steel, and he showed his teeth in a warrior's grin. His cadre understood. Kaydu met his grin with a like challenge of her own and Little Brother dived into the pack on her back as steel hissed from its scabbard.

"Defend yourself," she dared him, meaning in this practice contest and also to learn enough to stay alive in the battles that lay ahead.

They had, he realized, taken on another charge in their growing quest—to arrive at the end of it alive, and end the tears of the Goddess. And as he fell into a fighting stance, an echo of a feeling shivered down his spine. He lay dying, beyond pain, except for the breaking of his heart at the tears of his beloved wife who wept above him. "Don't cry," his own voice whispered down through memories he could not have, and he resolved that she would not, this time, weep for him.

* * *

"**E**nough!" Kaydu called out, and Llesho dropped his aching arm to his side, waiting for the trembling to stop before he tried to settle his sword in its scabbard. His knife went easily to its sheath, however. He wiped his brow with the back of his wrist and let the practice yard come back into focus while he caught his breath. Shokar, he saw, waited patiently for the warriors to settle battle reflexes before he spoke.

"Adar would like to see you," he said when nerves had calmed enough for Little Brother to venture out of his pack. Bixei and Lling had ended their practice as well, and along with Stipes and a still struggling Hmishi, came to achy attention.

"Tales of the Lady Chaiujin's challenge to the new khan and her transformation into an emerald bamboo serpent have reached the infirmary," Shokar explained Adar's summons. "Our brother has heard and needs assurance that you won't do something stupid."

Shokar softened the message with an ironic twist of his mouth. Adar never doubted what he must do, but if the story of Llesho's own meeting with the lady had reached him, his brother would surely have words for him to rival Shokar's angry lecture.

"I suppose it won't help my case to say I'm busy."

"You can delay the inevitable, but not for long. And he won't forget about it," Shokar pointed out. "It's not like he has anything else to occupy his mind."

He would have questioned that. Adar had the healer, Carina, to think about, something he did with fixed attention. She returned Adar's gaze with stars glittering in her eyes. Once Llesho had wanted her to look at him that way. He'd gotten past that and now hoped that their interest in each other might distract them from his own foolishness.

"Best get it done, then," Kaydu suggested as his cadre settled itself in defensive formation around him. Llesho never went anywhere without his cadre now, including Stipes. The man wasn't officially a part of the team as constructed by the Lady SeinMa, but he'd been an unofficial member since he and Bixei had found each other again in the midst of battle several countries ago in the flight from Farshore. Despite the loss of an eye

in Llesho's service, he fought for his right to be there and
refused to be left behind. No one tried to stop him as he fell in
beside them now.

They had all walked through the fire and come out
wounded in one way or another, Llesho figured, and each had
earned a place at his side at cost to heart or mind or body. Even
Kaydu's monkey-familiar, peering out of her pack at him, had
served his quest, bringing help when they would have been
murdered on the road without it. When the cadre sometimes
overlooked his newly acknowledged status and treated him
like a comrade-in-arms, he accepted their criticism or their
teasing, grateful for the momentary forgetfulness. With the
death of Chimbai-Khan and the elevation of his wary brother,
Mergen, to rule the northern Harnish clans, however, no one
was forgetting anything. They watched him like hawks—
sometimes *as* a hawk, in Kaydu's case. They were giving the
Lady Chaiujin no chance to send Llesho after the khan into the
underworld.

At the infirmary, Bixei and Stipes took up positions outside
the door while Hmishi and Lling went round to the back. He
would have questioned their fitness for duty so soon after their
ordeal but Master Jaks had shown him long ago that a leader
who wanted his orders obeyed didn't give commands he knew
would be ignored. The defiance in Hmishi's still-awkward
salute told him this time he didn't want to challenge his
friend's determination. Kaydu shook her head, but followed
him inside.

"You didn't tell me it was a family meeting." Llesho wondered why Shokar had failed to mention this important point.
Adar lay upon his bed. Healers, everyone knew, made terrible
patients, and this one was growing anxious to be up and about.
Only Carina's gentle insistence kept him in his place. He'd
expected to find Adar, of course, but not Balar, who sat in the
corner, one hand muting his lute at the neck while the fingers
of his other spidered idly over the strings. Balar kept his eyes
on his instrument when Llesho came in.

Lluka, however, stood away from his camp stool. "Blessed
Husband," he said with an ironic flourishing bow.

"You overstep," Llesho warned him with a frown in Kaydu's direction. He'd argued his status often enough with Kaydu and his cadre but that particular term was used only between husbands of the Great Goddess, and only at the exchange of most sacred oaths.

"Then don't bring strangers to a family council."

"Enough!" At Llesho's sharp tone, Kaydu came to fighting readiness, her hand on her sword.

The raised voices brought Bixei into the doorway, a pike held ready. "What?" he asked.

The company of princes gathered inside might fault the informality of his response; they did not doubt that his pike would find its mark in any one of them at Llesho's least gesture. Balar looked shocked. But Shokar, who had ridden with Llesho's witch-captain and his cadre, arched an eyebrow as if he watched the playing out of a game where the outcome was already clear on the board.

"You find humor in his threats now, Shokar?" Lluka demanded, his fury barely contained.

Shokar gave a little shrug. "His cadre *is* his family," he explained with subtle patience. "They are his temple of worshipers and his first defense against the worlds arrayed to oppose him. If they perceive you as a threat to him, they will kill you. Given what I've seen of his captain, I'm surprised she hasn't killed you already."

"Llesho is supposed to find *all* his brothers." Kaydu answered the question even though he hadn't asked her. Since she couldn't use her sword, she cut him with her words: "Not just the useful ones."

"And what are we princes of the same father to him, if these ragpickers' sons and daughters are his family?"

"Family again, someday, I hope," Shokar suggested, "But right now we are his dim past and little more to him than the stones he picks up as he crosses the board his master set him."

Not true, Llesho began to say, but it was more so than he wanted to admit, so he started again, with, "More than that."

Lluka brushed aside his protest with a careless wave, his

mind chasing a different conversational rabbit altogether. "And who would his master be?"

"Lleck, of course," Llesho answered with an edge in his voice. "The ghost of our father's minister. You know that."

"Ah." Lluka gave him a mocking nod. "Your adviser among the dead, and not the god of suds and linen who visited after prayer forms this morning, then?"

"Don't let him hear you say that," Llesho suggested with a tiny smile. He loved the trickster god best in his persona of laundryman, the hours they had spent together in the washtubs tipped with gold in his memory. But ChiChu, who went by the name Master Den in his mortal travels, suffered fools with little patience and malice not at all when directed at himself. Against others, he might give assistance, of course, which brought a laugh bubbling from Llesho's throat. What a mad quest he pursued!

Lluka didn't take kindly to his laughter, nor did he appreciate the weapons bristling in the tent.

"Oh, send them away. No one is going to hurt you here!"

"Pardon, Holy Excellence," Kaydu begged permission to speak, directing her request at Llesho in the full title due the god-king of Thebin. She had grown up in the court of the mortal goddess of war and knew how to offer the camaraderie of a friend when it was needed and to turn any rough tent into a royal audience with a word and a shift of posture. Llesho followed her lead in this as he had so many times in battle. Drawing himself up with a regal tilt of his chin, he gave a slight nod for her to speak.

"We cannot, in conscience, leave the chosen husband of the Great Goddess unguarded."

"Against his brothers?" Lluka gathered himself in a pose that mimicked deep offense.

Kaydu had grown up on easy terms with gods and emperors, however, and would not be cowed by a lesser brother. "Serpents are everywhere," she reminded him with a pointed stare that challenged him to reveal the schemes bubbling beneath his public display of indignation.

Balar brought their arguments to an end with a discordant bleat of strings on his lute. "Adar is falling asleep."

"No, I'm not," Adar insisted around a yawn. "But I am heartily tired of the quarreling. Can we get to the point?"

"Which is?" Llesho demanded of his brothers. "You summoned me—I don't know who called us together, or why."

"Master Den has been in to visit," Balar said, which explained much about Adar's growing fretfulness.

"The old trickster exaggerates," Llesho suggested.

It didn't help his case that he offered the excuse before hearing the outcome of the visit. Even held to his bed by a broken bone and a wounded spirit, Adar wouldn't be taken in by the lie. He said nothing, however, but waited for Llesho to continue.

"What has he told you?" Good start, Llesho applauded himself. Give away no advantage, but make the enemy come to you.

Adar refused to accept the role of enemy, however, and likewise refused to treat the discussion like a game. "That the Lady Chaiujin came to you with the offer of peace," he said, "and you would have gone willingly to the underworld in her scaly embrace, had he not come along when he did."

"That sounds more like a tale than you or Master Den talking." They all knew he was stalling. He wondered if he should tell them what his dream-travel conversation with Shou had suggested—that the Lady Chaiujin never had made it to Chimbai-Khan's great traveling city. The woman who counted herself the khan's wife was no such thing, but a demon snake who had taken her place in the khan's bed, and in his ulus. Before he could sort his thoughts, however, Lluka sucked in a breath to complain. Shokar took his lead from Adar and silenced their brother with a glare, but the moment had broken. Llesho decided to keep that bit of information to himself and watch, as Shou had advised him.

He wasn't getting out of this conference without telling his brothers something, however. Balar looked up at him with a gentle smile, letting his fingers wander over the strings of his lute. "We're not going anywhere," he said, a reminder not only that they would wait out his silence, but also, perhaps, that he would not lose them by his answers.

With a little shrug, Llesho decided to come clean, at least as far as his own experience went. "Carina gave me something to counteract the Lady Chaiujin's love potion, but a trace still lingered. I could feel it, like an itch under the skin. It made me think about all the other mistakes I'd made since I started out. It was my fault Hmishi and Harlol and Master Jaks were dead. Tsu-tan might have killed Adar, too, and all because Master Markko wanted me for some purpose I still don't understand. Now I seemed to have another enemy.

"And I was thinking about Shou and Lady SeinMa."

Adar's face had gone very bland through all of this, and Llesho should have worried about that. But the question, "Love potion?" gently asked, slipped right under his defenses. His brothers were holding out on the injured healer.

"She didn't want me." He'd been sure of that even when he'd wanted her. "I would have embarrassed our cause and made a complete fool of myself."

"And you know this because?"

"You know the wedding cup I carry, that Lady SienMa returned to me at the beginning of my quest?"

Adar nodded to indicate he knew the cup, but didn't speak. Llesho knew that was a trap, to draw him out, but he fell into it anyway.

"She served me in another, its match except for a symbol carved at the bottom, like a coiled snake. I was supposed to accuse the khan of stealing it from my pack, I think, but I recognized that the lip was thicker than my own cup. So instead of accusing her, I mentioned both the similarity and the differences."

She'd made him a gift of it; he had it in his pack, carefully kept separate from his wedding cup. Unfortunately, she'd also had a backup plan.

"When I didn't fall for the cup, she fed me the potion in the tea. That one did work, sort of."

He'd enough experience with potions to know when he'd been dosed with one, and managed to get out of the lady's presence before he committed a serious breach of etiquette, though the khan and those closest to him had seen the sudden longing in Llesho's eyes. They hadn't, he recalled, blamed him for his reaction to their queen, but allowed him his escape with good grace.

"Carina figured it out quickly enough and gave me an antidote that cleared most of the potion. But there was a bit of a residual effect I hadn't counted on. I wasn't thinking too clearly."

"I figured that much." His brothers seemed content to let Adar carry the gentle interrogation. Even Lluka had settled back into his chair and watched Llesho with eyes wide and nervous as Adar suggested another question: "Shou and the Lady SeinMa?"

"I wanted to see the emperor, so I asked my totem self where he was. I found him in Guynm Province. The Lady SeinMa had joined Shou in the old governor's palace at Durnhag. And, well, they weren't exactly interested in company when I showed up."

He kept to himself his most recent visit, which had left him more confused than ever.

"You've been getting quite an education while I've been away." Adar twitched his lips as if he had the bitter taste of unripe plums in his mouth.

"Oh, yeah. I'm learning to dream travel." That qualified, without going into areas he shouldn't have brought up at all. With any luck he'd divert their attention enough that they wouldn't ask him any more questions about Shou or his love life. "Of course, you can't guarantee what you'll find when you travel in the dream world anymore than you can in the waking one."

"I suppose the emperor of Shan tucked away with his lover surpassed the guarantee," Balar commented under his breath. Llesho could see his brother plotting more than chord progressions in his head and wished he remembered how much Balar knew about the Lady SeinMa. It wasn't any surprise that the emperor of Shan had a mistress, or even that he loved her. But the mortal goddess of war scared him more than Lady Chaiujin did, and with good reason. She was the embodiment in human form of all the chaos and bitter pain of war. Its strategy and gamesmanship, its sweep of courage and valor as well, but Llesho remembered mostly the chaos and the pain. He could not imagine loving that.

"So," Adar summed up the high points for him, "with a love potion in your veins, and worry for your companions mixing with thoughts of lovers—disturbing lovers—in your head, you wandered off without a word to anyone, right into the arms of the Khan's murderous wife."

When put that way, it seemed pretty stupid—even Little Brother had sneaked back out of his pack to grin his disapproval—but Llesho had his defense ready. "I didn't know about the murderous part, or the serpent part, then. Even Carina wasn't sure why Lady Chaiujin dosed me with the love potion. It seemed like a political move to discredit our party in front of the khan. Chimbai-Khan might have ordered me killed for the insult to his wife, I suppose, but Bolghai is a friend of Carina's mother and had trained Carina in the ways of a Harnish shaman. Master Den is pretty good at getting me out of the permanent kind of trouble and, on balance, it seemed more likely that the lady just wanted me to look foolish in front of her husband."

"You were wrong."

"Yeah," Llesho admitted. "Still. She didn't ask Mergen's swordmaster if he wanted to die when she bit him, and I suspect she didn't ask Chimbai-Khan if he was ready for the underworld either. So why did she ask me?"

"Not out of any romantic attachment," Adar suggested dryly.

"She didn't want *me*," Llesho agreed, "Not in that way, at least." He wasn't ready to offer his suspicion that the mix of powerful emotions he had scarcely been able to contain had drawn her like a jackal to the smell of blood.

Adar seemed to understand what Llesho was thinking without being told, however. His mouth, already drawn in pain, tightened into a thinner line.

"Don't wander out alone," he said. "She'll try again."

Llesho was on the point of objecting that he wasn't that foolish, but on second thought, wasn't sure anyone, including his own cadre, would believe him. A mission from the newly elected Mergen-Khan saved him from further debate on the issue.

"Prince Tayyichiut, of the Qubal clan, to speak with his Holy Excellence King Llesho of Thebin," Bixei announced just ahead of the Harnish prince.

Chapter Six

"TAYY," Llesho greeted the prince informally with a bow, as between equals.

"Llesho," Tayyichiut returned the bow, but with a distracted air. The dogs had not accompanied him, so his visit must be official, or secret. "My uncle the khan would speak with you on a matter of some urgency for your quest."

"I'll come right away." He'd have taken any excuse to escape his brothers' disapproval, but Mergen had been questioning the prisoners captured during the recent battle.

They'd seized a handful of survivors. As a guest, Llesho had no choice but to put their disposition in the hands of Mergen-Khan. From what he had heard from Tayy, they'd talked quickly enough. Tsu-tan, the witch-finder, had scared even these hardened bandits, who told tales of possession by an evil demon of the underworld. They'd have been even more frightened if they knew how close to the truth they really were, but the khan hadn't found anyone who had any useful information until now. Mergen-Khan's summons must mean that he'd uncovered something important.

"I have horses waiting Up Top," Prince Tayy added as they made their withdrawal from the unhappy brothers.

They had taken to referring to the two camps by their locations: the tent city of the Qubal clans "Up Top," on the grassy

plain, and "Down Below" in the dell through which the narrowed Onga flowed, the camp of Llesho's small force. Yesugei
called it Llesho's honor guard, though at the moment it was the
only army he had. Horses could manage the slope between the
camps at a pitched run, but for convenience they gathered
the animals Up Top, where the grazing and exercise were plen-
tiful.

Llesho would have walked the easy distance between the
infirmary tent Down Below and the ger-tent of the khan Up Top.
Prince Tayy, however, considered it demeaning to go on foot.
"Only slaves and servants would approach the khan on foot,"
he insisted. "Mergen-Khan will ask your opinion, but you will
have to convince him that your words are worth hearing. To
persuade him, your suggestions must carry the full weight of
your own position as a king. At the least that means a horse."

The Harn in their traveling cities of felt and lattice were
more exacting in the formalities than the emperor of Shan with
all of his stone palaces. Or perhaps, it was that those you didn't
trust had to announce themselves with their approach and
stand inspection before they reached the seat of power. Llesho
had come gift wrapped to the emperor, and after a trial run. In
the camp of the khan, he hadn't yet proved himself, so Llesho
readily agreed to Prince Tayyichiut's conditions.

With the prince at his side and his cadre at his back, Llesho
crossed the beaten common. As he passed, soldiers of Thebin
and mercenary volunteers from north of Farshore bowed in
salute. Out of the corner of his eye, Llesho noted that he'd
picked up his Thebin corporal and the Wastrel Sawghar again,
pacing his cadre like outriders, ready to cut off any assassins
hidden within bow range.

"I thought the prisoners had turned out to be a dry well,"
Llesho commented, meaning no source of information. He
hoped to draw Tayy out about the summons of his uncle, but
the Harnish prince wasn't filling his bucket any more than the
prisoners had.

"They did," he said. "My uncle the khan figured that out
pretty quickly and gave them to his guardsmen as spoils of
war."

"Oh."

Enslaving the prisoners made sense according to Harnish justice. The khan wouldn't put a warrior to death for following the orders of his captain, but he couldn't free him to fight again either. Slavery offered each captive some freedom of movement natural to the nomadic people while charging each slaveholder to control his new property with punishments as necessary. Llesho figured that he ought to be glad for anything the khan did to the witch-finder's followers. After all, Harnish raiders— perhaps some among these very captives—had laid waste to his country, killed his mother and father and his little sister, and sold him into slavery as a child. In spite of all his arguments to himself, however, the fate of the prisoners reminded Llesho too much of his own.

Tayy gave him a curious frown, but continued his explanation of Harnish ways. "If we've caught a firstborn by some chance, his family will probably ransom him, which would be good, because we need the horses. The rest will be stuck with the dung-work in their masters' tents for a year or two, but then they'll be adopted or marry in. War makes widows, after all, and widows need husbands. Down the long path, their families in the South will consider it a favorable alliance and our khan will work those connections for the benefit of the ulus as well."

Llesho wondered what Kaydu would say about the need for husbands, but for the Harnish it wasn't the part of the story that he doubted.

"That is not slavery as I have known it among the Harn."

Tayy bristled at the challenge, but caught something in the bleakness of Llesho's disbelief that stopped him in his tracks, thinking. "Bolghai told me a story once, when I was little," he said, and began walking again, "that he had dream-walked in the life of an outlander slave. Like cattle led to slaughter, he said, only Chimbai-Khan, who had asked for the tale, would never treat his cattle so badly. Bolghai wept at the telling, and wouldn't speak of it again. "

The Long March, Llesho thought, and shivered in weary dread of his own memories.

"These men are prisoners taken in fair battle. The Qubal

clans aren't raiders," Prince Tayyichiut insisted, "When we kid-
nap someone, it's to ransom him back where he came from, or
for marriage, not to sell to strangers for the highest price."

Llesho wasn't sure the Qubal's neighbors, paying ransoms
and weeping for their lost daughters, would appreciate the difference, though it apparently mattered to the khan who traded
only in "honorable" slavery. The Ulugar clans had committed
horrors on his people, however, had tortured Hmishi and
served the master who had driven the emperor of Shan mad.
For his own sake, he was glad that the northern clans he
counted as allies had no part in death marches or the sale of
their foes into perpetual servitude. But he would have no mercy
for the southern clansmen who had fallen into Mergen's hands.

"And Tsu-tan's lieutenants?" he asked. "What has your
uncle the khan learned from them?" Unlike the warriors sent to
work off their parole, battle commanders were held accountable
both for the orders they received and for the ones they gave.
There had been two, he had heard, taken alive.

"Nothing, yet. They had the usual choice. One talked. He
had no information of value to offer, but it saved him from a
worse fate. Mergen had the man's head cut off this morning.
The other will not, or cannot, answer the khan's questions, not
even to say he doesn't know. So we are come to the place where
the river ends."

Llesho frowned. "What river is that?" he asked, though he
could guess what the riddle meant.

Prince Tayyichiut gave a little shrug as if the answer should
be obvious, but explained in plain terms that Llesho couldn't
ignore. "Mergen-Khan has run out of options. Prisoners of military rank may choose to give up their master's secrets in
exchange for a swift death. If they prefer to take their knowledge
with them to the underworld, they do so with their bowels in
their hands and their enemies walking on their living graves."

Burial, Llesho had learned from Bolghai, was an eternal
prison for the Harn. In Harnish belief, fire sent the dead of the
grasslands to join their ancestors in the spirit life and to be
reborn into the world. A man put into the ground would remain
there, trapped body and spirit to molder and rot forever. But

Prince Tayy meant more than that. As they climbed the steep path that led onto the grassy plain above the dell, he explained his uncle's quandary.

"It will hurt the khan soul-deep to hand this man his liver and bury him alive. Mergen's a rational man and knows the value of fear when trying to extract information from an enemy. Once you've torn out his entrails and thrown the dirt in over him, though, your enemy can't tell you anything. So you reward the traitor with an easy death and punish the honorable man with unspeakable horrors, all for the hope that next time a fool tries to hold onto his honor, he will believe that you're serious and give in before you have to do the same to him."

"Does it work?"

Tayy gave him a defensive glare. "It's not like it happens every day."

Llesho had never dealt with this part of the aftermath of battle—interrogating prisoners—before. The Way of the Goddess allowed him defense both of self and subjects, and his training had turned killing into a reflex to save his own life or the lives of his companions. The Goddess forbid causing pain for its own sake, however; he had never used torture as a means to even his most worthy ends.

Thinking about it now, he realized that he hadn't wanted to know what Shou had done to the captives after the attack on the Imperial City of Shan, or how Habiba extracted information from the enemy. With a countenance as flinty as the stone that littered the plain, Kaydu climbed the side of the dell at his side and he wondered what acts of terror she had committed in her father's name, for his cause. By his silence he had lost the right to ask about that now, but he was done leaving the decisions to others.

They had reached the high plain where horses waited for Tayy and Llesho as promised. None for his cadre, however, nor had Tayy's young guardsmen-companions awaited them on the edge of the Up Above, which gave Llesho cause to wonder who really had sent the prince.

"Your uncle doesn't know that you've asked for my help, does he?" If he hadn't been distracted by his brother's more gentle interrogation, he might have guessed sooner that the prince had taken on himself this mission to save his uncle the khan from his prisoner's agony. He expected Tayy to look guilty when he confessed, but the prince raised his head proudly. "He doesn't know you the way I do, or he would have thought of it himself. But he'll listen if you go to him. I promise."

"What do you think I can do?"

"I don't know. You'll think of something."

That wasn't the answer he was looking for. In more than one sense, Llesho decided, it was time he took the reins for the Great Goddess in whose service he fought. He didn't think Tayy was going to like it, though.

"I can't let him do it," he said.

"That's the point, isn't it? To get the information out of the prisoner somehow, so Mergen doesn't have to gut him and bury him alive." Tayy left off checking the cinch that held the sheepskin saddle to his horse's back, waiting for Llesho to explain himself further.

"The Way of the Goddess is peace," Llesho answered, "I am that great lady's husband. Whether he speaks or not, I can't stand by while a helpless prisoner is gutted like a fish and thrown into a dishonored grave."

Prince Tayyichiut leaped into his saddle and looked down at Llesho where he stood at his stirrup. "If you fail, you won't have to stand for it; you'll be sitting on a horse."

Not a confusion of language friend to friend, but an uneasy warning from a Harnish prince to an outlander that reminded Llesho of an earlier conversation. Friendship, Tayy had said, survived among princes only as long as it served the ulus. As a deposed king, even a wizard-king of the Cloud Country, Llesho did not rank with an acknowledged khan in his own lands. He might attend the interrogation at Tayy's insistence, but he wouldn't get a say in the proceedings unless he came up with something more than a crown he didn't own yet to support his position. Tayy, and probably his uncle the khan, wanted magic from him.

Llesho looked more deeply inside himself. It had to be there, the core of what made him the god-king of the Thebin people and true champion of the Goddess. His brothers believed in it and grew impatient for him to show it. The mortal gods who trailed after him likewise insisted that he accept his nature and pick up his duty. And once, it seemed an eternity ago, he had felt it touch him in the camp of the mortal goddess of war.

Sometimes, he forgot that. But he remembered it now: that moment at the foot of the Lady SeinMa, and his words to her. He repeated them, more to himself than to the Harnish prince: "I *am* god."

Tayy blinked, then he grew more princely in his awe. "You've never done that before," he pointed out.

Llesho tilted his head, a question and permission to continue, while a secret smile tugged at his lips.

"You're glowing. Heaven seems to be shining through you. I've never seen—" He broke off, at a loss for what to say.

"Tell me about the prisoner." Llesho set a hand to the prince's stirrup, gentle insistence.

With a sigh of relief that they had not, as yet, committed some irredeemable act in the eyes of this creature out of the Cloud Country he suddenly didn't recognize, the prince spilled answers like a sacrificial offering. "He seems to know something, but hasn't opened up yet."

Tayy winced at the unfortunate choice of words for reasons Llesho well understood. Tsu-tan's lieutenant would be opened up soon enough, if he didn't talk. He let the error pass, though his own gut was cramping. It seemed to have a mind of its own as it tried to crawl more deeply into hiding than a soft belly provided.

"Let me see what I can do," he finally agreed. "Perhaps I can persuade him by less painful means."

Prince Tayy gave him a long, thoughtful look. "Mergen-Khan is no magician, but he says he sees in you divine powers." He mentioned this as if the notion had struck him as foolish before and he was still wary of accepting it as truth in spite of his own eyes.

"You may use any powers you have to persuade the prisoner to betray his master. Honor demands, however, that the prisoner retain the right to refuse."

Which meant, Llesho figured, that he could use any means he possessed to torment or terrify the man into submission, but Harnish custom prohibited reaching into his mind to draw out painlessly what he wanted. They might take the prisoner's life in any way they chose, so long as they left him his honor. If he had the skill, of course, Llesho would seize the man's knowledge in a heartbeat and leave him standing in his own skin. To a Thebin, honor did not include gutting his enemy alive or burying him to suffocate slowly while above him men walked across his open, dirt-packed wounds. Unfortunately, the Goddess hadn't gifted him with the ability either to read minds or to unseal men's tongues against their will.

"I don't have any such powers," he answered truthfully.

Tayy's frown told him his friend no longer believed that about him. "If you don't, that man will spend the next three days dying a horrible death. You will dishonor your goddess and Mergen will spend the rest of his life with this man's screams in his head."

"Wanting doesn't make it so. I have some skills, some gifts of my lady wife, but none that apply here. None that Bolghai can't do better." Growing into his gifts took time—that was the hard part about them. And they weren't always what you wanted or thought you needed, though they often turned out to be both in the end. Meanwhile, the khan had ten thousand Harnish warriors to bring against Llesho's handful. If he tried to stop the khan by force, he'd be throwing their lives away and Mergen would do what he felt necessary anyway. "I don't know what he expects me to do!"

"Convince the prisoner to give his honor into your hands while he speaks, so that Mergen-Khan can give him a painless death. At the least, your anguish should convince the fool that Mergen-Khan doesn't make idle threats."

Just when Llesho was beginning to hope that they *were* idle threats, Tayy added, "They always give in once the gutting begins, but by then it's too late. They're off their heads and can't get a clear thought past their own screaming."

He'd thought Tayy didn't know. Not every day, then, but he'd seen it, or heard enough.

"He'll have to kill me first." Well, that was one way, Llesho decided. Not the one he'd have chosen with time to think, but the first one out of his mouth and no way to take it back now.

Tayy didn't blink. "Uncle said as much. I think it would destroy him to do it. That's why he didn't ask you to attend from the start." He stopped, as if giving some thought his full attention, then added, "Perhaps, if you screamed enough, the prisoner would break. But you'd still be thrown with all your gaping wounds into a living grave."

It took one quick glance to realize Prince Tayyichiut was telling the truth. Like his uncle, he'd never show his feelings to the lieutenant of their enemy, but for his friend horror bled from his eyes.

"We'd better go, then." Llesho rose into his saddle with a command for his cadre, "Stay here."

"What are you going to do?" Kaydu had heard it all. She stood nearby with Little Brother cradled in her arms as if the animal had understood and sought the comfort Llesho would never have.

"I'm going to be a king," he said because she wouldn't understand "be a god."

"Then you'll need an honor guard appropriate to your station. I can muster the troops in moments." She unwrapped her arms and set her familiar on her shoulder. Little Brother knew this as preparation to ride and crawled back into his pack until only the top of his head peeked out.

Llesho shook his head, a sad smile meant at his own expense on his lips. "Fifty or a thousand guards can't make me more than I am in my own skin. If that's not enough, nobody else should die for my lack."

A protest marked her troubled frown. Then she took a closer look at him, and answered his crooked little smile with one of her own. "Holy Excellence," she said, the title of the Thebin king, with an emphasis on "holy" and a deep bow to go with it. "A king requires pomp and circumstance," she answered her own question, "a god carries ceremony within himself."

So. She understood more than he'd thought. He shouldn't have been surprised, but the notion didn't sit comfortably in his mind yet. It came as a shock that others saw and accepted more easily than he did himself, though Kaydu was the daughter of a powerful witch and a witch herself in the court of the mortal goddess of war. Consorting with gods presented no novelty to his captain or his cadre.

"Then just us, as witness," she decided with a gesture to include his cadre and he couldn't forbid that. They would have marched on foot behind him, but horsemen of the khan approached with Yesugei at their head. A perfect solution, though the Qubal chieftain might not think so.

"Little king!" Yesugei addressed him with a seated bow from the waist. "Mergen-Khan sent me to find you."

"I am at my host's command," he answered politely. "But will need your horses for my guardsmen—"

"Of course." The chieftain motioned his followers to give up their mounts. He carefully blanked his face, though his glance kept stealing to Prince Tayyichiut. Wondering, no doubt, if Tayy had anticipated his uncle.

When one cadre of riders had changed places with the other, Yesugei wheeled and took off, not for the ger-tent of the khan but skirting the tent city. When they had gathered sufficient distance from the palace, he cut through a cluster of modest white felt tents, bringing them out on the wide avenue that formed the axis of every encampment. A processional to the front door, then, as an honored guest or a questionable ally.

Yesugei didn't lead them to the ger-tent of the khan, however, but stopped instead at the playing field that opened out in front of the palace of white felt and silver embroidery. This, too, conformed to the plan the tent city followed at each stopping place. On a field almost the same as this, but a hundred li behind them, Llesho had played a Harnish game grown deadly when the ancient spear he carried at his back awoke with blood-lust in its flight. He'd conquered something in himself that day, and tamed some of the hunger for death in the weapon. Again, a crowd waited to see how the outlander would fight a different battle, for the honorable death of an enemy.

Yesugei worked their party through the waiting throng, past a raised platform set up beside a shallow grave dug into the

temporary playing field. The prisoner lay spread across the platform in his shackles. Llesho spared no closer look in that direction, however. Harnish raiders from the South had shown no
mercy when they attacked Kungol. They now made common
cause with Master Markko, who tortured and killed his friends
and had poisoned Llesho in the long days of his captivity.

The prisoner couldn't hurt him now, though. He'd followed
Tayy's summons to save a Harnish life from torture and end it
in dignity as the Way of the Goddess dictated. But in a secret
part of himself, he was afraid to look at the man who had followed Tsu-tan on Master Markko's business. His rage was so
vast that it waited only a glance, a word, to sweep away his
duty to his Goddess and her Way. So he didn't look, lest vengeance take the place of mercy in his heart, but let Yesugei lead
him forward until he faced the khan.

Surrounded by his guardsmen at the center of the playing
field, Mergen-Khan awaited Llesho on horseback. He wore the
richly embroidered silk coats and tunic of his office and, on his
head, the quilted-silk-and-silver headdress of the khan, covered
over with the silver helmet that served in battle as a crown. At
his right hand, in her massive headdress of silver horns draped
everywhere with strings of precious gems, sat the old woman,
Bortu, the mother of this khan and his brother who had preceded him. Prince Tayyichiut urged his horse forward and took
his place at his uncle's left, the heart-side for the heir. Yesugei
called a halt then, and announced, "I have brought the wizard-
king of the Cloud Country, may he serve the khan well."

With a low bow in his saddle, Llesho added his own polite
greeting to his host: "I come at your call, Mergen-Khan."

Mergen returned the bow with a courteous nod.

Those nearest him knew Mergen in all his moods, thoughtful
and whimsical, determined or grieving. None would have
doubted that cold judgment ruled him now. Llesho saw himself
in that shuttered emptiness, however. Like Mergen, he'd
learned to close away his distress behind the mask of a king; he
knew how upset the khan was by how completely he hid the
emotion.

"Ride beside me while your ally questions your foe,"

Mergen said, and nudged his horse into slow motion, his mother and his nephew still at his side. Llesho followed his lead, with Yesugei beside him and his cadre among the khan's own guardsmen. When they reached the platform on which the prisoner lay, Yesugei dismounted and strode forward on foot, drawing his sword. Kaydu followed, her face set as she prepared to act on Llesho's orders even if it killed her.

The raider locked eyes with his executioner, but Yesugei didn't flinch. The point of his sword rested lightly against the raider's belly; it hardly shook at all when Little Brother crept out of Kaydu's pack and swung himself onto the raised pallet.

Kaydu tried to rescue her familiar, but Little Brother whined and refused to leave the prisoner to his fate. Anxiously the monkey patted the man's whiskers.

"Have you anything to say, Southern Man?" Mergen-Khan asked with a glance at Little Brother that promised monkey stew for dinner.

With an effort the captive turned to face the khan. "I am not a southern man," he said.

He hadn't worn a beard then, but his voice echoed in Llesho's memory from the time before Farshore, when he'd trained in the gladiators' compound on Pearl Island.

"Don't let him send you to hell without your tip," he said out loud, changing only slightly the advice that Radimus had given him years ago, when he hadn't even understood what he'd been told. He'd been called up to the great house on Pearl Island. Lord Chin-shi hadn't tapped him for the usual reasons that a lord pulled a boy out of the training compound, though. He'd wanted information Llesho didn't have then, about the red tide killing the bay, but he'd paid his tip all the same.

"Fighting and dying you do for nothing, because they own you." Radimus repeated his own explanation from that long ago morning. "Anything else, they pay for. It's tradition. Llesho? I thought you were dead, boy."

"Not yet." Llesho dismounted and came to him while Radimus barked out a rough laugh.

"Glad to hear it."

Little Brother darted away in a panic at the sudden noise,

or so it would seem. The monkey curled himself on Kaydu's shoulder while the khan watched for signs and miracles, as if he hadn't already seen them.

"I'll take it from here." He held out his hand.

Shaking his head in confusion, Yesugei turned over his sword. "I—" he began, but he didn't seem to know what he'd intended to say. Llesho understood, and showed it in his glance so full of forgiveness that the chieftain fumbled at a loss and turned away.

When he had gone and Llesho's surroundings came back into focus, the khan was looking down at him like Habiba with an interesting specimen to study. "You do that very well for a boy," he said. "Can you teach it to Tayy?"

"First, you have to be born a god." He'd never understood that about himself, and meant it as a flip answer. The situation was too dire for him to manage irony, however. Radimus seemed not surprised at all.

"I'll keep that in mind," Mergen promised, though whether he took it for a boast or a joke was hard to tell. He didn't object when Llesho dropped the sword at his feet, so they had at least progressed that far.

Sweat slimed Radimus' torso and lay in glistening pools in the hollows of his orbits. How long had the questioning gone on before the khan had sent for him? Too long. Llesho refused to let old horrors sidetrack him.

"I think we need to talk."

"Would if I could, boy." Radimus rattled his chains, explanation enough for that answer. There was more to his silence—or less—than loyalty to an old and dangerous master.

"A spell?" Llesho wondered.

Terror and longing moved in the captive's eyes. "A—" Before Radimus could finish the word, his body contorted, conscious thought lost in a strangled scream.

Suddenly, after an endless, heart-stopping moment, the convulsion ended, leaving Radimus limp and with the life gone out of his eyes.

With a long sigh to compose himself, Llesho turned to the khan an expression of polite inquiry. "He's done this before?"

"Several times," Mergen-Khan answered. "Usually he makes no sound at all before the twitching begins. Is he possessed?"

"More likely a spell." He looked again at Radimus, who watched him warily through the exhaustion that followed his fit.

"He's told you the truth. He's not from the southern clans. We were slaves together in Lord Chin-shi's stable on Pearl Island, more than a thousand li north of where the grasslands even begin."

"Gladiators?" Mergen-Khan infused the single word with doubt.

Llesho gave a little shrug. "Novices. I was in my fifteenth summer. Radimus was older; he'd come to it fully grown. We trained together with Bixei. Stipes was ahead of us in the ring." He didn't mention Master Den, who had taught them hand-to-hand combat for the arena.

"And now," Mergen-Khan added coldly, "he rides at the bidding of this Master Markko, who also served the lord of Pearl Island. This same magician has swept a path of death and destruction through the Shan Empire, and now into the very heart of the grasslands. If Prince Lluka is believed, he will bring the universe down around our heads in chaos and nightmare."

Llesho knew the terrors of his brother's visions, had walked through their fire and smoke in his dreams, but he couldn't let the horrors of the future distract him from Radimus' plight in front of him. "None of that is the fault of your prisoner," he corrected the khan gently. "Radimus is a slave and had no choice of masters."

"Once a slave," Mergen agreed, who had apportioned out his own lower-ranking captives to tents not of their choosing. "But now? He wears the braids of command."

Or had, Llesho figured. Radimus' hair was as much a mess as the rest of him. Too exhausted to show even a glimmer of hope, Radimus stirred weakly on the altar of Harnish retribution.

"They're going to gut me," he whispered, as Yesugei muttered an apology and took up his sword again.

Llesho said nothing. Mergen looked unforgiving.

"Don't let them bury me alive, please—" Radimus moistened his lips with a furtive tongue. "When it comes time, wield the knife for me your own self, boy. I don't deserve a kindness, but I would see the face of a friend—"

"You'd do better with Yesugei. He's had more experience at this." The khan spoke to the prisoner, but his gaze never left Llesho. "He'll cause you less pain than the boy."

Now was not the time to make grandiose demands. He needed to think. Too much imagination, that was his problem. The weight of Yesugei's blade in his mind tensed the muscles clear to his shoulder. He felt Radimus' blood on his hands, and the slick glide of entrails. Suddenly, his skin was as sweat-slick as Radimus', his mouth as dry. The Harn would take advantage of any weakness they could find, however; a king with no stomach for the customs of Harnish warcraft might see his own troops slaughtered by the very men he had thought were his allies.

"He thinks you'll defy me and kill him quickly, as a friend," Mergen said conversationally. "The cut ends high, just below the heart bone. The blade is sharp, and a careless thrust might penetrate the heart itself, removing all temptation to give up his intelligence before he gives up his life."

"Master Markko has put him under a spell of discretion!" Llesho's temper strained to be let loose. "Prince Tayyichiut said I couldn't interfere if the prisoner didn't want to talk, but Radimus would tell us what he knows if he could!"

"But he can't. He's useless if we can't reach the information we need about his master," Mergen pointed out calmly. "In the meantime, we can't trust him. He may harbor secret instructions to murder any or all of us. If he's dead, at least he can't hurt anyone. And it sends a message to his master."

"With the blood of a man twice captive on your hands and no information to speak of for your troubles, you will tell his master that he wins." Llesho was sure about that, and equally sure that, "I've faced the magician in battle down all the roads from Farshore, and I haven't ever let him win."

That hit Mergen-Khan like a slap. "What do you expect me

to do, *god-king?*" Sarcasm edged his words, but there was an honest plea in the question. *How do we get out of this with all the Qubal clans of the East watching?* he meant, in true desperation. As the newly elected khan, his brother recently murdered in his bed, he could ill afford to show weakness.

"Bring me Carina," Llesho answered. "And Master Den. Ask Bright Morning, too, if he will come, and Bolghai. This is a matter for physicians, not torturers."

"And we need launderers for—?"

"We need our gods about us when we challenge evil men," Llesho answered softly the question that had troubled the Harn since his arrival. Yesugei seemed unsurprised, while Bortu looked pleased with him, a doting mother more impressed with his honesty than with Master Den's identity. It was impossible to read Mergen-Khan, but Prince Tayyichiut was plainly furious and holding onto his anger only in consideration of the crowd that hemmed them in. He wanted his explanation to go no further into that crowd, so he addressed a supplicant's bow to the khan and avoided meeting Tayy's eyes.

"In that case," Mergen said, "you must have your launderer and your dwarf as well." Which told him clear as a blue sky that Mergen knew all along what companions Llesho traveled with. No doubt his shaman kept him well advised. "Bind the prisoner to a horse and take him to Bolghai's burrow. Consult with your witches and tricksters, and return to me with this Radimus' secrets, or with his living entrails."

Which was as good an outcome of the afternoon as he could have hoped once Prince Tayy had shown up at the infirmary. Llesho bowed his thanks, rising only when the khan had departed with his retinue. Yesugei remained with a handful of his guardsmen to keep watch over the prisoner, and Llesho waited while he ordered the bringing of a horse. Bemused, the chieftain allowed Bixei and Stipes to direct Radimus into the saddle and raised no objection when they padded his shackles with strips torn from their own clothing.

"Where is Bolghai's burrow this time?" Llesho asked when they were ready to ride.

On balance, Yesugei decided to be pleased to have escaped

committing murder through an error in judgment. He answered with a wry smile and a play on an old riddle. "Where the river ends."

Tayy had spoken the same riddle. The answer was death, but Radimus hadn't died yet. Llesho figured the chieftain was speaking literally this time in a game of double meanings doubled. Beyond the dell, then, past the camp Down Below. Not where the Onga River ended, many li to the south, but where it grew more narrow as it rounded a bend. He had no doubt that Carina and the gods he had asked for would be waiting for him when he got there.

Chapter Seven

CHARGED as he was to keep watch over the prisoner, Yesugei led them to the shaman while Llesho's cadre held the nervous Harnish guardsmen to the outskirts of their party. Bolghai's burrow—a felt tent just one lattice in circumference—was set over a depression dug into a hollow where the river broke against a rocky spit. It proved less difficult to reach than Llesho had thought.

"Wait here," he instructed his cadre, with the explanation they could see for themselves, "There isn't room inside for all of us." He depended on them to keep the khan's men out as well for reasons having more to do with information they might hear that shouldn't go past the khan and his shaman.

Kaydu agreed, with one exception, "Where you go, I go."

Yesugei likewise agreed, and with the same exception for his prisoner, so four entered the tiny burrow—Llesho and Radimus, each with a representative from the party who guarded him. As he passed through the doorway, Yesugei stopped and took up a position at the right. Although he was himself a leader of a clan and not a guardsman, he knew how it was done and set himself ready to defend against attack from within or without. Kaydu fell in behind his lead and took the left, hand resting on sword hilt in an equally threatening posture. The way protected by his high-ranking guardsmen, Llesho brought his prisoner forward.

The burrow was much as Llesho remembered it from their encampment to the north. Felt batting wrapped the small lattice frame like snug blankets with just a hole in the umbrella roof over the firebox for the smoke to escape. Skin rugs padded the earthen floor and the pelts of stoats hung on the walls among the rattles and drums and the fiddle that Bolghai had played to set the pace of his running when Llesho had learned to dream-travel. Bunches of herbs still hung from the ceiling. Llesho never had figured out what they were for, but he remembered the brooms the shaman used for ritual sweeping—and dancing. He tried to pick out the one he'd partnered in the strange dance of discovery that led him to his totem animal, but it didn't call to him anymore. The narrow chest at the back of the tiny burrow had been covered with tiny skulls the last time he'd visited, but they had already been swept to the floor to accommodate the teacups.

Bolghai wasn't alone this time. Carina, at the firebox, flashed him a smile as the shaman rose from his nest of heaped furs. The little stoat heads of his ritual garb bobbed as if they were still alive, a matter which sent Little Brother shrieking up a broom to the umbrella-spoked roof. From there the monkey vanished out the smoke hole.

"My pardon." The shaman bowed an apology to Kaydu. "I don't bite." His smile showed a line of sharp teeth. "Not friends, at least."

"My pardon, good shaman, for my companion's discourtesy." Kaydu replied with an equal bow. "He imagined danger from your totem animal, I suspect, and so his good manners fled."

"Taking their hat and coat as they went," Bolghai summed up the monkey's disappearance. "Will your companion be safe on his own?"

"Bixei will take him up, or Lling," Kaydu assured him, and set herself once more in a posture appropriate to a door guard.

Bolghai accepted the end of the conversation and turned his attention to Llesho, who stood waiting with a hand on the prisoner's arm.

"Is this a social visit, or are you here to continue your training?" With a nod in her direction, he added, "Carina was just making tea—you will of course join us. And your friend."

In his own quarters, Bolghai didn't always speak in the formal riddles of his office. He had a way of phrasing the simplest question, however, that made Llesho certain even an invitation to tea hid a secret meaning when looked at out of the corner of the eye instead of dead-on, so to speak. Whatever the shaman's purpose, Llesho had come for his own reasons, and he refused to let his suspicions distract him.

"A matter of professional assistance." He urged Radimus the few paces forward with a dip of his head first to the shaman, his host, and second to Carina, who knelt at the firebox.

She wore, he noticed, her own shaman's costume hung everywhere with silver charms and purses filled with medicines and the skins of her totem animal, the little hopping jerboa. With the teapot in one hand and a cup in the other, she returned his bow with a smile and a nod.

"Butter and salt?" she asked, looking past Llesho to his prisoner. "Or Shannish-style, with honey? I don't think we've met—I'm Carina, daughter of Mara who would be the eighth mortal god and Golden River Dragon, my father."

"Take the honey," Llesho advised, "Bolghai's tea tastes like stale socks."

Radimus looked from one to the other of them as if he had fallen in among madmen. He was saved from answering, however, by a commotion at the door. Master Den strode in with two Harnish guardsmen dangling from his sleeves.

"Bright Morning has refused to come," he explained the absence of the god of mercy, though not the presence of the guards who let him go to untangle their hair from the hanging brooms. "He said to tell you that Mercy has no place at an execution."

The prisoner flinched at the message. It must have sounded to Radimus like his old teacher wanted to see him put to death. But how could he explain the grim disapproval Llesho heard in the words, or make clear the reminder from a god whose purpose must be served by others here?

Master Den left no room for explanations. "Radimus!" he

greeted his old student, only then noticing his presence. "What are you doing here?"

"Having tea," Carina answered. "He was about to tell me if he wanted honey or butter."

"Of course he'll have honey," Master Den answered for him just as Radimus himself got out, "Yes, please," with a gesture to show that his hands were chained. He could not easily take the cup.

"Don't tell me *you're* Mergen's prisoner?" Master Den asked, though Llesho thought the shock was a bit much. "Isn't it a small world!"

They had settled themselves comfortably enough, though the size of the small tent offended propriety by setting the high-ranked visitor next to his low-ranked prisoner below the fire-box. Now they shifted over once again to make room for Master Den, who lowered himself to the pelt-covered floor with much theatrical grunting that gave no true indication of the god's ability to fold himself into a Harnish position. With a smile, Carina reached over and placed the cup carefully into Radimus' chained hands before fixing one for Llesho and another for the trickster god. All with honey in them, he noted with heartfelt gratitude.

"My name is Radimus," the prisoner offered in polite response to Carina's interrupted introduction, though Master Den had made that less than necessary. "Gladiator-in-training to Lord Chin-shi, now deceased, traded in payment of debts to Lord Yueh, also now deceased, and come by right of capture to Master Markko, overseer to the properties of Lord Chin-shi, then Lord Yueh. Recently risen in the magician's service through no wish of my own. Is your father really a dragon?"

"Yes, he is," Llesho answered for her. "I've met him and, aside from swallowing my healer in one bite, he's quite polite as dragons tend to be."

"Hmmm," Bolghai commented. Llesho wasn't sure whether the comment referred to Radimus' story or to his own description of the Golden River Dragon. After a pause to appreciate his own steaming cup, however, the shaman added, "Do you see a pattern with this Master Markko, young Radimus?"

"I'd rather be his servant than his lord," Radimus answered bluntly. It seemed that he would say more, but his eyes grew distant with pain as they had before he convulsed on the khan's playing field. They approached an area under the spell, then.

Bolghai noted it as well and forgave the question with a dismissive wave of his hand. "Drink your tea. You're safe here."

Llesho couldn't guarantee that, not even from himself, but he said nothing, and Radimus drank. Almost immediately, he began to nod off.

"What did you give him?" Llesho asked Carina, who passed a hand over the prisoner's brow with a thoughtful frown.

"Just some herbs to help him sleep while we figure out what to do about him—that's why you brought him here, isn't it?"

"Yes—" She meant the doing something part, Llesho knew, and would have protested the sleeping part, but Carina hadn't finished.

"We know Master Markko can see across great distances, using the eyes and minds of his followers, even his captives. He did so with Tsu-tan, and for a little while with Lling."

Master Den agreed. "It makes sense that Radimus has survived this long because his master wants him exactly where he is—inside Mergen's camp. Markko can learn nothing from a sleeping mind, however."

"Whatever our needs for secrecy, Radimus himself needs the rest," Carina added tartly. "I do not dose my patients for the convenience of their captors."

If they couldn't figure out how to break the spell that kept Radimus silent against his will, Mergen-Khan would carry out the terrible execution they had delayed but not completely halted. It might be kinder to sleep through the deliberations that would decide his life or death, but Llesho knew he would want to know every step of that decision if it were him.

"When will he wake up?"

"Not for a while," Bolghai answered vaguely. "The cup heightens the dream state."

"Oh, no!" Llesho knew where this was going, and he didn't plan to do it. Nuh-uh, not in any way. "I thought this was about Radimus needing rest, not Mergen's need for answers."

"I offered the prisoner sleep. Dreams are a part of sleep." Carina didn't look happy with her own explanation, and Llesho figured she was having as much trouble with it as he was.

"I'm not going in there," he insisted, meaning Radimus' dreams.

"Of course you are," Bolghai assured him. "The Prince of Dreams rules in all worlds dreams take him."

"That's your word, old man, not mine. I am not so presumptuous."

Master Den interrupted with a huge sigh. "He's telling the truth, you know," he said over his tea cup. "Our young king resists every effort to convince him of his station. He would deny his wedding night while his head rests in the lap of the Great Goddess, his wife."

That brought Llesho's head around with a blush and a frown. Master Den raised his cup and eyebrows both, to claim the hit.

How much did the old trickster know of the dream he'd entered during morning prayer forms? How many of his deaths had the god ChiChu watched him die—how many times had he denied his worth to husband the Goddess, his wife? He was supposed to ask himself those questions, he figured, and if he knew anything about his old teacher, the answers were supposed to lead him to Radimus' dreams. Once again destiny had cornered him, this time in a round tent where all his excuses failed him.

Did he owe what Mergen demanded of the Prince of Dreams? No question of that. Master Markko was Llesho's problem, brought down on the Qubal clans when they agreed to help him. Even if Chimbai's death had come out of his own politics, the present khan had still paid in advance with the life of his anda. And Llesho asked for more, all his troops committed against an enemy who could raise the very ground they walked on as an army against them.

Did he owe Radimus? A memory sparked behind his eyes, of men sorted like cattle in the arena at Farshore. The will of slavemasters had put Radimus in the camp of an enemy that none of them wanted. If the Lady SeinMa hadn't moved faster to secure his own services, Llesho might have fallen to the magician right there. None of their fates had been Llesho's fault, but maybe he did owe Radimus something for breakfast rolls stuffed in his pocket and four silver coins in his hand, a lord's payment for services he hadn't rendered. That didn't make it any easier. The very thought of entering a mind where Master Markko already lodged filled him with such terror and loathing that he couldn't bear it calmly and leaped to his feet as if he had somewhere to run.

"We need to move him out by the river." Bolghai followed as if Llesho had given a signal and motioned Yesugei and Kaydu forward to carry the sleeping man. "Move the rugs there; you will find the carrying poles."

When they had shifted the rugs away, it turned out that Radimus had fallen over onto an artfully positioned litter. Arranging his feet and legs more comfortably, they lifted him easily.

"Did Mergen plan this all along? That he'd give me the prisoner, and I'd bring him here?" For some reason that he didn't quite understand, it made Llesho angry to think that the khan had never meant to kill the man, and that he'd anticipated all their moves.

"Mergen-Khan hoped—but didn't presume—that you would win the goodwill of the prisoner," Bolghai answered the anger Llesho gave voice to. "He hoped, too, that your own great flaw would not prove fatal."

"My flaw! What about his? He's the one manipulating us all!"

"To spare your friend a horrible death," the shaman reminded him, "and to uncover the reason why magicians wage war on the grasslands. But you don't ask what your flaw might be."

"I have so many to choose from," Llesho snapped.

"But only these will be the death of you: that you overestimate your enemies, and you underestimate your allies. Mergen-Khan is a wise and subtle man more given to thought than action. But when he acts, he has always acted well."

"I wonder if Chimbai-Khan would say as much, if you could ask him now."

The veiled accusation fell into a silence deeper than stone. Yesugei, a chieftain among the Qubal clans, said nothing, but his stern presence reminded Llesho that hasty words loosed in the world created their own mischief. Too late to call them back, he took a caution out of the expectant hush.

"A question for the Prince of Dreams," Bolghai answered when it seemed that no one would speak at all, and Llesho realized that he'd been drawn into another trap. The last lesson the shaman had to teach him, the one that circumstances had kept him from, would see his totem form dream travel in the underworld to seek out the dead.

He shook his head, knowing better than to follow that path. "I would find no welcome there. Let the khan's own shaman visit him in the underworld."

"The prisoner," Carina reminded them, breaking the uncomfortable pause. "The tea lasts only a short time, and by the motion of his eyes I believe that dreams have taken him."

With that Bolghai wormed his way between his guests and led them, ducking hanging brooms and catching herbs in their hair, out of the door. There they picked up Llesho's cadre on their short march to the river.

"Put him down," the shaman said. "These others of your guardsmen may wish to stand apart, where they needn't witness the mysteries of their king."

But Kaydu refused to leave him and Hmishi scoffed at any such concerns—"I've been dead; not much to worry about after that—" which Bolghai agreed was a point to consider.

Standing with their companions, none of the others would remove themselves from their post at his side, though Little Brother leaped for the smoke hole above Bolghai's tent-burrow again, watching with quick, wise eyes. "What will they see?" Llesho asked, meaning, would they see him transform into the young roebuck, his totem animal. He didn't look at his companions, or the shaman, but at Radimus, whose eyes darted after dream images beneath his closed lids.

"They will see what they are ready to see," Bolghai answered, which said nothing, or everything. He was used to tests and guessed that his companions were as well.

"All right," he said, and shivered. The sun had fallen below the zenith and a chill wind had set in from the south, Llesho assured himself, nothing more. Figuring the best way to do this, he bent his head, knotted his hands into fists and pumped his elbows forward and back, in the motion of running. Then he walked a tight circle around the litter on which Radimus dreamed, going faster and faster as he set his path in the muscle memory of calves and thighs, running, running, in that tight circle until with a toss of his head antlers nearly unbalanced him. Halfway there, he had gained his totem form. Then, with a kick of his heels, he leaped into the air over the sleeping prisoner, and into his dreams.

No surprise, the dream took him to Master Markko's yellow silk tent. Radimus stood guard at the entrance while voices drifted from the other side of the yellow silk curtain that divided the tent.

"You made a bad enemy at Ahkenbad," he heard his own voice say, and in reply, Master Markko's offhanded answer: "Of corpses and children."

The magician hadn't known that he'd wakened the Dun Dragon. Radimus, quaking at his post, knew only that something terrible had happened across an unimaginable distance and prayed to his own strange gods not to be called to the other side of the curtain he guarded. This wasn't what Mergen wanted to know, however. Llesho stepped gingerly forward in his totem shape.

"Are you real?" Radimus asked.

Llesho nodded and shook his head at the same time, the way a roebuck would with new growth itching at his antlers. "You are having a dream," he said in his own voice, which echoed him with different words—"I won't be staying"—"but this did happen once, and I have truly entered your dream on Mergen-Khan's business."

Radimus knew what that meant and he winced as his dream changed sickeningly to the present. Chains appeared on his wrists. He no longer stood at attention, but lay on the altar of the Khan's harsh justice. His eyes grew guarded as he asked, "Are you here to kill me?"

They both knew Master Markko had that skill, to kill in dreams. Llesho shook his head. "I don't know how, even if I wanted to, which I don't. We believe your master put a spell on you, to prevent you from speaking when questioned. I'm here to find the spell and remove it, or find the answers locked behind it and report to the khan the intelligence he needs to form his strategy against the magician."

"If you tamper with the spell, he'll know," Radimus confirmed Llesho's guess with the calm of his dream state. "He'll find us, and kill me, and seize your mind to take my place as a spy in the Qubal ulus."

Llesho shifted into human form. "He will try," he said, accepting that struggle though not its conclusion. "Show me the spell."

Radimus frowned, puzzled at the command. "I don't—" he began.

Llesho reached out and touched a fingertip to his forehead, that place where the brows almost meet below the hidden third eye. "Show me," he repeated.

Suddenly, the tent, and Radimus himself, disappeared. Out of a gray fog a shape grew more solid as Llesho concentrated on it: a knot, intricately tangled, with Radimus' beating heart at the center of it. It was a trap. If he pushed at the knot, like Mergen had done with his questions, the knot would tighten around the prisoner's heart and kill him. If he tried to untangle the spell, he might free Radimus, but the threads would weave themselves around his own heart just as quickly, leaving him in the magician's trap.

"Cut the knot," he thought, and drew his Thebin knife to do just that. But the spell throbbed with sentient power. If he didn't sever all the threads in one pass, those that remained would kill Radimus. And maybe, knowing Markko, cutting the threads would only cause them to multiply, not to let go at all.

As he watched, the knot seemed to grow until it drifted almost as large as he was himself and just outside his reach. This was all a trick; he knew that as well as he knew his name.

Somewhere inside that snarl of words and symbols, a part of Master Markko was daring him to do something stupid. Llesho had been here before, however. Not this dream, or this spell, but he remembered another time, dangling from a chain in a mist just like this one, with Pig for company. That gave him an idea.

Reaching into the leather pouch he wore at his neck, he pulled out not a pearl, as he carried in the waking world, but a bit of stone left behind when a stone giant plucked the heart from his dead victim. Llesho had gathered only the black pearls of the goddess on that battlefield, but the dream world allowed poetic justice, if not other kinds: once again, stone would stand in for a heart, but this time for his own. With more certainty than he had felt since finding Radimus on the executioner's platform, he held out his open hand, infusing the stone with the pulse of his own veins. And then, carefully, he began to untangle the threads of Master Markko's spell.

Words of power wrapped around a talisman tied to a sacrifice risen up in smoke. A living creature, burned alive to seal the spell. He trembled with revulsion as the links of the chain wrapped themselves around the pulsing stone heart he held in his hand. Each strand clung tenaciously where Master Markko had spun them, but Llesho loosened them with the promise of his own blood leaking from his fingertips and spilling onto the stone. At first he'd been afraid the spell would wrap his fingers together with the stone they held. In the dream state they seemed to want only the false heart, however. With his mind he lifted it so the inky strands might cross beneath, each pass wrapping the stone with the magician's whispered curses.

In shrieking fury the spell fell upon the stone, drawing itself tight and greedy around the false heart and sucking its own death out of the lifeless shard. When he saw that all of the twisted curses had wrapped the stone fragment in his hand and none remained in the gray mist of the dream place, Llesho closed his fingers.

"This man is free now," he told the thing in his fist, and squeezed until he felt the stone grinding in his hand.

The spell resisted, screaming its promises of torment, but

Llesho held on tight while the last dying wail of thwarted terror faded into nothing. He knew the spell was dead when the mist cleared, revealing the Onga River and the trees. Whether this was the river of their Harnish encampment or the dream river on which he'd seen his own death, he couldn't tell. It didn't matter. Peace had descended, and for a few quiet moments he let himself breath it in like an elixir. It would be so easy to stay here, in the dream world, but Mergen-Khan still planned to kill his prisoner—so far he'd won an easier death but no reprieve. He'd have to go back to do that.

With a last long look around him, Llesho spread his fingers. Only a handful of ash remained where spell and stone heart had lain. He pursed his lips and blew, scattering the harmless dust of the dead spell out over the river.

"Llesho! Llesho!" Bolghai called sharply to him as if he'd messed up a lesson.

"What?" He muttered, suddenly aware that on the waking side of the river a light rain had started.

They were all getting wet, including Radimus, who blinked rapidly at him as if he hadn't caught up to events going on in his own dreams.

"Llesho?" Radimus asked.

"Not now," he begged, brushing away explanations with a wave of a hand that wasn't as controlled as he would have liked. Suddenly, the riverbank tilted. He was still considering the strangeness of that when he felt himself swept off his feet.

"What are you doing?" he asked sharply.

"You fainted," Master Den supplied an answer from far too close, and Llesho realized he was riding in the trickster's massive arms. "I'm taking you back to the infirmary. Carina can keep an eye on you while she watches Adar."

Nearby he heard the voices of his friends: "Is he all right?" from Hmishi; and, "Did the spell catch him?" from Kaydu. Lling called his name, and even Bixei muttered angry oaths in the distance.

"I'm fine," he insisted, struggling to get down. "The spell is dead." But Master Den held onto him until their horses came into view and Llesho could be slung into his saddle. "I don't need the infirmary; I need to be there when Mergen-Khan questions Radimus."

"You are going to the infirmary, Holy Excellence." Carina mounted behind him with the superior authority of healers everywhere. "And though of less exalted rank, Radimus needs rest as well. Mergen-Khan will be informed when the prisoner is ready to answer questions."

Of course. Mergen wouldn't waste the time to treat Radimus just to kill him; he still needed answers. Carina gave him a reassuring pat on the shoulder. Radimus would require medical attention for as long as Llesho needed rest.

Chapter Eight

"**W**HAT word?" Mergen-Khan asked, a formal request for a report. He sat on the dais amid the rich fur pelts and knotted carpets of the ger-tent. Around him gathered the chieftains and Great Mothers of the clans, the men and women of wisdom, while his guardsmen stood at wary attention with their backs to the lattices. To the side, where Llesho had found them in friendly conspiracy in the past, Bolghai the shaman huddled in quiet council with Bright Morning, the mortal god of mercy. He'd expected Master Den to join them, but the trickster god stayed at his side, a keen light in his eyes, watching for some critical move in the game he played with the lives of kings and khans.

As he led Radimus to the dais, Llesho saw that Mergen had put off his outdoor coat for silks of yellow and blue, embroidered with gold and silver threads suitable to his new office. Bortu, mother of khans, sat at his right shoulder still in her mourning colors, though in fabrics as rich as he had ever seen her wear. Prince Tayyichiut, as elaborately dressed as his uncle and with a silver-beaded hat that turned up on both sides, took the place he had so lately claimed at the side of his father. His eyes still showed the mark of that loss, however, giving him a gravity that suited the heir of this grim khan. He nodded welcome to Llesho, guarded hope lifting a little of the weight of his expression.

With a quick glance around him, Llesho wondered where the Lady Bamboo Snake had gone and if more tragedies awaited the Qubal at her touch. He shook off the feeling with an effort. He had to stay focused or he'd lose everything he fought for right here.

Llesho had expected the formality. Mergen had been interrogating a captured enemy under conditions of internal security right up until the time he'd allowed a foreigner to intercede for the prisoner. Now, he engaged in statecraft with a Thebin king over the fate of a hostage. To show his respect for the khan, Llesho had come to this summoning with his whole force around him as an honor guard. Fifty men and women who had journeyed with him from Ahkenbad spread out along the back of the ger-tent, keeping to their place below the firebox but present in barely suitable numbers to honor their leader's station.

His personal guard followed him toward the royal dais, adorned with the rankings of the services from which he had borrowed them. As a record of the powerful allies who supported him, the varied uniforms might persuade the khan to join their number. Or they might tempt him to remove a danger with one sweep of a blade. Llesho couldn't allow that to happen, for more than the sake of his own neck. The chaos and death of Lluka's visions awaited them all if his quest failed, so he stepped forward with all the confidence he could muster, his brother-princes at his sides. Even Adar had joined them, though Carina had bound his arm tight under his formal court coat to brace the healing bones of his shoulder. Together, the princes bowed to the dais, though Lluka did so with less grace than he might have shown and Adar with more pain. For all the pomp of their entrance, Llesho was a ruler without a domain come to beg a favor of a khan risen to power under a shadow in his own. The khan's attention fixed more surely on the ragged prisoner who entered at Llesho's side than on the unlanded king of the Cloud Country himself.

"Your report?" Mergen accepted their bows with barely contained impatience, only repeating his question when Llesho had drawn Radimus forward. "Have you broken the spell that binds this fellow's tongue?"

"Yes, Lord Khan, I have." Llesho pointedly observed the formalities of address that Mergen had omitted, drawing an abrupt gesture of apology from the khan. They had made him wait two days for his interrogation, and he had run out of patience on the first of them. But he hadn't expected that answer. Tayy had, of course, and let his chin drop onto his fist with a little smile of satisfaction.

"This Markko's magic is not so formidable after all," he suggested.

"Oh, yes," Llesho answered with a level gaze. "It is. Ask Otchigin." Mergen's most-beloved friend, that was, who had fought the stone monsters Master Markko had raised up out of the grasslands and who had died in battle with a stony fingertip lodged between his ribs where his heart used to beat.

The khan's temper flared behind his eyes, and was quickly brought under control again. Mergen was no fool. "But you are more so?"

Llesho gave a little shrug. "I'm just a boy. But one does not set all his guards to defend an outhouse."

Mergen acknowledge the riddle with a wry smile. "And have you tested your success against this lesser challenge, excellent prince?"

Better than no title at all. "No, my Lord Khan. But Radimus has promised to answer your questions to the best of his knowledge, and I have promised to intercede with you for his life."

"His information is that good, then?"

Shou had taught him to negotiate before the markers went on the table, but Radimus had taught him something of bargains as well, and hinted at the dice in his hand to up the ante. "Yes, Lord Khan, it is."

"You already have my word, as painless a death as a blade can deliver, in exchange for information about his master."

Llesho smiled, more confident in the game now that he knew there was something in the pot. "Not for his own sake, but for the friendship I hold for him and our shared past, I would ask that you return him to me alive."

"And if I offered you one favor," Mergen suggested, turning the game on its head, "and you could have this old companion of your slavery returned to you, or the aid of the Qubal clans to fight against your enemies, which would you choose?"

Llesho studied the khan for clues. He knew a test when he saw one, was sick of them, but couldn't risk a life protesting now. Mergen gave away nothing of his own thoughts. A glance to the side showed him Dognut watching back, every twitching muscle bent on his answer. And Llesho knew then what it had to be.

"I would have Radimus."

"I knew it!" Tayy crowed.

"And that," Mergen assured his nephew, "Is why the clans do not elect boys of sixteen summers, such as your present self, to the khanate."

"It was a brave answer," Tayy objected, and his uncle rolled his eyes.

"He risks the lives of all his followers, and the lives of the people of the Cloud Country, and the very heavenly kingdom that he says lies under siege. And for what? The life of a slave he knew briefly while a slave himself, who in the years since their parting has risen in the service of the mortal enemy who is the cause of all his troubles. Only a boy could find romance in such a tale."

But Dognut was smiling, the tension gone out of the lines around his eyes. And when he looked to her for some sign that he'd not been as stupid as Mergen claimed, Bortu actually winked at him. He wasn't sure what he'd just proved with his answer, but the khan made a mockery of his own exasperation with a broad wave of his hand. "Oh, sit down, and bring your guest with you. Let's hear what he has to say before we do anything hasty."

Prince Tayy had turned red to the tip of his ears at his uncle's taunt. Llesho figured it for a not-wrong answer, if not exactly the one Mergen had hoped for, and took a seat where Tayy, with a grin made self-conscious under Mergen's dubious approval, made room beside him.

With a bow as overdone as the wave, Llesho drew Radimus down with him at the side of the khan. "What would you like to know, Lord Khan?" he asked.

"I'd like to know what in the name of all the ancestors this Master Markko wants with the grasslands." His tone made it clear Mergen expected no answer. Radimus didn't have the rank to carry great state secrets, but they might get an observation or two out of him that would make the whole thing less of a waste of time.

He was wrong about that.

"He wants power. Even with the resources of Farshore and Pearl Island he couldn't defeat the emperor of Shan. When we lost in the capital city he needed to find a base close to the source of his magic where his power might grow stronger. The South remembered him from a long time ago. There are still stories about the thing he set lose there, some demon that wiped out whole clans before it disappeared, off to lay waste to somebody else's world, they say."

"You scatter the secrets of your master like pearls at our feet, good Radimus." Mergen-Khan pierced him with a calculating stare. "I have heard the old stories, of course, but not your magician's part in them. How do you come by this valuable intelligence when a second of your same rank scarcely knew the name of the magician in whose service he fought."

"I would not lie to you, Lord Khan," Radimus swore to answer the khan's doubts. "I owe the magician no loyalty. He calls up demons and practices his spells and poisons on his slaves and prisoners. You've promised me an easy death in exchange for what I know, and that is more than he will give me if Master Markko gets me back."

"Your master does not seem a trusting enemy. How did you come by your information?"

And then Llesho remembered. "I know," he said, diverting the intensity of the khan's focus to himself. "I remember, in a dream-walk, seeing Radimus in the doorway of the magician's tent."

"I stood guard," Radimus confirmed, "And heard his conversations. When he muttered to himself in the throes of his
experiments or incantations, I couldn't shut my ears no matter
that I wished never to hear what went on there.

"I do not like magic," he added forcefully as an explanation.

"You are no friend to your master," Mergen-Khan repeated,
to make sure he had it right, "and yet I am to believe that he
trusted you enough to stuff your head full of his secrets and set
you over the Southern Harnishmen, and then sent you as a gift
to the hands of his enemies?"

"He rules by fear. Master Markko knows I hate him and that
I'm terrified of him. He likes it." Radimus admitted the plain
truth. "He doesn't trust anyone, certainly not me. He binds his
guardsmen with spells so we can't speak or raise a hand against
him, then he forgets us, as if we were no more than his tent
poles. Even if we could break the spell enough to slip a dagger
in his heart, we wouldn't dare act against him. We've seen what
he does to his enemies when they fail."

A quick glance at Llesho, who had experienced Markko's
treatment firsthand, then he finished, "As for why me, I've
asked myself that question often enough. He's known me
longest, though, and thinks he has my measure."

"Gladiators," Mergen snorted, as if he still didn't believe
that story.

Radimus nodded. "Lord Chin-shi's stable, until he lost us to
bad debts and a plague on the pearl beds. Then Lord Yueh's
until Markko murdered him and turned us into soldiers.

"I've thought you were dead half a dozen times since then,"
he turned to Llesho with a shake of his head. "Markko was certain they'd killed you on the road from Farshore, then up you
popped again and defeated him at Golden Dragon River. They
almost had you in the battle at Shan Province, but your defenders were braver and your tacticians smarter than he'd expected.
Master Den isn't just a laundryman and hand-to-hand instructor, is he?"

"Not that those things were ever just in themselves, but no.
I wouldn't say he's more than that, but certainly *different* than

we thought him on Pearl Island." Llesho couldn't help the wicked grin.

The trickster god returned it with a mock frown. "More respect," he demanded in a haughty tone, "or I'll set the priests on you. Let them debate my good qualities while you squirm under the boredom of their arguments!"

"Boredom sounds good," Llesho admitted. Aware Mergen was beginning to lose patience, he turned back to the prisoner with a warning, "The tales of my near death experiences may be entertaining in the peace of an evening fire, but I think we can forgo the list for now."

Radimus gave a little shrug, still with the wary question in his eyes, how had Llesho avoided death or capture so many times when so many others had not. Mergen was likewise adding up his qualities anew, and coming to a better notion of this beggar at his door.

"The night after Llesho made his dream visit to Markko's tent—" He stole a glance at Llesho, remembering a night when Master Markko had tortured the young prince, who had been hundreds of li away among the tents of the Qubal clans. "—he sent me to retrieve his prisoners from the witch-finder, and to find out where Llesho was hiding. He'd destroyed the Tashek mystics at Ahkenbad and knew Llesho had left the Gansau Wastes, but he didn't expect him to recruit a new set of defenders so quickly. If he was still alive, I was supposed to capture him, not the other way around."

The prisoner's eyes glinted with satisfaction. Llesho had freed him from his master's spells. "As for what you want, I know all of his secrets. All of them."

"Truth?" Mergen-Khan asked Llesho

Radimus gave a ghost of a nod, something he seemed scarcely to know he was doing. Everything Llesho remembered of Radimus urged him to believe, not least that he had seen this with his own dreaming eyes. "Yes," he said.

"Very well." Mergen had been sitting in the Harnish style, with one leg tucked under him, the other foot tucked up close so that his knee rested just under his chin. Until this point he'd sat back a bit, straight-spined and cautious, but now he draped

his arm over his knee and rested his chin on his arm. Slit-eyed
with concentration, he began his interrogation in earnest.

"You say he wants power, and yet he spends what power he
has amassed chasing a boy with nothing but a pathetic band of
deluded followers at his back. Why is that?"

"The magician follows the Way of the Goddess," Radimus
explained as if it were the most obvious thing in the world, "He
wants to be one of the mortal gods so that his living body may
enter heaven."

"That's not the way it's done," Master Den commented
softly, and Bright Morning, in his corner, agreed with a disso-
nant trill on his flute.

"I've never met a god, so I wouldn't know. I'm sure I don't
want to either." Radimus frowned at Master Den's bark of
laughter. "Who knows what a magical creature can do?"

Mergen, however, did not see the humor. "The prisoner
seems to have more sense than all the rest of my guests combined. Even the Qubal people can see that these gods seem only
to cajole their subjects into deeper trouble than they had managed on their own."

He challenged Master Den to deny it, but the trickster god
bowed to accept the hit. "In the battles waged between the
worlds, sometimes the gods' own favored warriors suffer.
Sometimes, the gods themselves suffer. We are not immune to
our own struggles. But the Way of the Goddess does not lead
down an evil path."

"He doesn't think he's evil." It took a great deal of courage
to speak up, but Radimus was fighting for his life. "He calls it a
shortcut, and blames Llesho for making it necessary. If you'd
stayed with him, he thinks, and gathered your brothers under
his banner, he wouldn't have had to hurt you or your brothers
or any of the other people he's killed for getting in his way."

"And you believe what he says?" Mergen clearly doubted,
but Radimus corrected that impression.

"It's what he tells himself. He's mad, but he thinks he's making sense. He talks about defeating the siege of heaven and taking the gates for himself. The Great Goddess will love him then,
he thinks, and make him a god out of gratitude for all he's done

for her. But he needs the princes of Thebin to do it, the prophecy says so. He has to have them all."

"What prophecy?" Llesho asked, while Tayy interrupted with, "If he needs the princes, why is he trying to kill Prince Llesho?"

"He's not." Radimus shook his head emphatically. "He wants Llesho to work with him, and he thinks he's preparing him for some great battle with the demon he set loose a long time ago. He's not strong enough to defeat it himself, but he thinks the prophecy means Llesho can do it for him."

Llesho wondered why the khan was letting the two princes he'd already dismissed as boys lead the questioning. Radimus seemed more comfortable answering them, however—maybe because they didn't plan to kill him at the end of it. Mergen would make use of that greater ease as long as it got him what he wanted. Or, like now, intercede when he needed greater clarity in his answers.

"Yet the young prince keeps escaping death at his hands," Mergen reminded him.

"It's the prophecy," Radimus explained. "Or he thinks it's a prophecy, though some say it's a song and others that it's just a tale. Master Markko doesn't have the exact wording, just hints and rumors that grow thick around the borders of Thebin. He knows he needs all the princes, but he takes that to mean however many princes are still alive when the battle comes."

"So, if he can't persuade the princes to work with him, he plans to kill them."

Radimus nodded. It didn't need more answer than that. Adar, however, dismissed this interpretation of the prophecy. "It won't work," he said. "The princes of Thebin will never serve an evil power. That isn't the Way of the Goddess. And even we know that Llesho is the key. If he dies, hope dies." He challenged even Lluka to deny it.

Their brother dropped his gaze, but not before Llesho saw denial in his eyes. *Does the magician speak to you in your visions?* he wondered. *Does he feed your despair with those images of death I saw in your dreams and promise your own rise to kingship if you follow him?* He looked to Adar to confirm what he thought he saw in Lluka's downcast eyes, but Adar had already looked away.

Mergen, however, had settled a thoughtful stare on Lluka's bent head. "You pose an interesting problem, Prince Llesho," he said. "But so far you have shown no evidence that it is *my* problem. The eye of the Qubal people must turn east to the Tinglut who sent murder among us."

"Ask questions in that direction," Llesho suggested. "There may be more than the Qubal people who have suffered losses through trickery. But the fall of heaven is a concern for us all."

"When the demon takes the gates of heaven," Lluka interrupted, his voice forced and rough, "all the worlds above and below will fall into fire and chaos. All worlds, even yours, Mergen-Khan." Something malevolent glittered hard and dark in the back of his eyes. Something mad. Llesho shuddered, but it had caught Mergen-Khan's attention, too.

"We need to know more," he said. "We need to find the lost Thebin princes, and uncover the secret of this prophecy. Then, we will consider how to proceed."

"Master Markko is looking for the lost princes, too," Radimus volunteered. "Among the rumors, he believes it true that one of the brothers is still in Kungol, leading a resistance force against the southern invaders. The whispers say that he defends a great jewel of power, but no one knows what kind of jewel it is."

Llesho didn't know about any magical jewels and his brothers didn't speak up either. It might have been a secret even from the oldest of them, who had been full grown when the Harn invaded, but he didn't think so. They either weren't letting on, or there wasn't any jewel. He kept his thoughts to himself while Radimus told them about the other brother.

"The magician says that brother will be easy to find once he enters Kungol, and he figures Llesho will bring the others to him when it's time. As for the last, there are stories about a blind poet, a slave in the household of a master physician in the West. None of the stories have connected the poet to the lost princes of Thebin, but it sounds like it might be him, and the time seems right. So Master Markko seeks the last brother in the

West. He says the battle will be on us soon and the princes must come together to fight it.''

Mergen nodded, accepting the truth, but not the need. "The last time I sent a scouting party on your mission, Prince Llesho, you returned their dead bodies to me. I won't stop you, but I cannot offer you the lives of more Qubal warriors to spend on an outlander's. Go, and bring back proof of danger to the grasslands if you find it. Then we'll talk about your wars and what aid you may expect of us.''

"I understand.'' Llesho bowed, accepting the khan's decision, but with a question still on his mind. "Radimus, Lord Khan?''

All eyes fell upon the captive, who knelt and touched his head to the ground in the way Llesho had seen the Harn do when they begged some mercy of the khan. Radimus, however, waited for judgment, saying nothing.

"And what do you deserve of the khan of the Qubal people, Radimus?''

"I've been a slave all my life, Lord Khan,'' he answered with the form of address that Llesho had used. "What does a slave deserve of his masters but what they will of him? If killed, however, I would ask to be set out to feed the birds, who will take me on their wings to heaven, if that is possible.''

"Your people have strange burial practices,'' Mergen commented. To which Radimus answered, "At least we wait until a man is dead,'' which seemed to amuse the khan.

"Men have died in battle with your master, Commander,'' Mergen chose to address his captive in his military rank rather than his more lowly status as a slave, which might have boded well or ill. His second, after all, had spilled his little knowledge and then his blood.

But then Yesugei led two women toward the dais. Ah. Prince Tayy had explained about the Qubal custom. Llesho kept his smile hidden behind tightly clenched lips and was glad he did. Mergen hadn't expected two, and he didn't look happy about it.

"I lost my husband to the stone monsters,'' one of the women said, and Llesho guessed from her age, and the anger that touched the words with which she demanded this captive slave, that she was Otchigin's wife. "My tent needs a man to tend the sheep and oversee the herd, and to stand between my children and the night creatures." Wolves, that meant, creatures howling on the outskirts of any camp, even one as large as the tent city of the Qubal.

"I have no husband," the other said, with a glare at Otchigin's wife. "Duty to a brother and a friend took the one who should have been mine. I need a man to tend the sheep and oversee the herd, and to stand between *my* children and the night creatures."

Mergen-Khan inhaled sharply, as if he'd been slapped. Then he turned to Yesugei, who watched him somberly. Llesho realized he wasn't the only one who had to put up with tests.

"Radimus," he turned to the prisoner. "A man of this ulus died in battle with your master. Will you take his place as a slave in his household, serve his wife as she would be served, protect what is hers, and ease her suffering in all things as she chooses?"

Radimus raised his head from the fur-draped floor of the dais, his eyes full of questions, but he said, "To the best of my ability I will serve the lady and defend her children, though I do not claim any power to easy the suffering of her loss."

"I think you'll be surprised," Mergen suggested dryly. Radimus was younger than the lady's former husband, and she seemed to be pleased with what she saw before her. Llesho suspected that her relationship with her husband had not been warm for reasons that had settled weariness into her bones but lit an angry fire in the other woman's eyes. The second woman wasn't young anymore, but she was still beautiful and carried herself with haughty defiance. Sechule, the khan's lover, he guessed.

Mergen-Khan confirmed it with a narrow-eyed nod in her direction. "As for you, friend Sechule, be free to enter any tent you wish. There is no claim on you, no blame will follow wherever you find shelter."

It wasn't the answer she wanted. Llesho saw the sharp recognition of betrayal twist at her mouth before she dropped her

head in submission to the judgment of her khan. Yesugei, however, seemed pleased with the decision.

"Fool," Llesho thought, with some compassion. Though he
had barely seen eighteen summers, he knew the feeling of wanting someone who wanted someone else. Lling had followed her
heart. For that matter, so had Carina. Mergen had closed off that
path for Sechule, however; perhaps it wasn't quite the same
thing after all. Which, Llesho thought, just made things worse
instead of better.

He took a hesitant breath as Otchigin's widow led Radimus
away by the hand. His old friend looked like a man who had
plunged his hand into a sack of burning coals and come out
again with a star in his fist. The widow's eyes were clear as
glass, but Llesho had a feeling the weight of a political match
had gone from her as well. A look of daggers passed between
Sechule and the khan. For a heart stuttering moment, Llesho
wondered what had become of the plain, kind Lady Chaiujin,
and who had introduced the serpent into the ger-tent of the
khan.

Chapter Nine

WHEN the public work of justice had been done, Llesho sent his troops away, all but a small cadre of guards as a dignitary would be expected to keep around him for the night watch. With nightfall, darkness had swallowed the vast empty reaches of the felted palace. Only a few scattered lamps on the brightly painted chests behind the dais shed their yellow glow over the circle of heads bent over the maps spread before the khan. At a sound out of the clotted dark, Llesho looked up sharply to see a shadow-figure approach. It took a moment to penetrate the gloom before he put a name to the shadow-figure.

Radimus. After a brief absence to introduce himself to his new mistress and her children, he returned to the ger-tent of the khan with an apology that he could not join the companions of his gladiator days on their quest. He understood his position as a slave of the Qubal clans only too well. Better this than service in the tent of the magician, he assured them all, in case they were thinking about rescuing him. Llesho suspected that Radimus was secretly happy with his fate and made a space for him beside them, accepted his offer instead to tell them everything he had learned about the enemy during his years in the magician's service. Mergen would head east with all his warriors to confront Tinglut over the death of Chimbai-khan. Llesho warned him of the vision he'd had in his dream travels: the

Lady Chaiujin whom Llesho had met at Chimbai-Khan's side was nothing at all like the lady described within her own lands. If some other hand had kidnapped the lady during her journey and put the emerald serpent in her place, then Mergen brought not only war but grief to Tinglut, who had made a powerful alliance with the emperor of Shan. None of them wanted to see the mark of the magician's work in the household of the khan, but Radimus warned it sounded very much like one of his schemes. He would set the ulus against each other and challenge the victor for all of the grasslands.

"He won't respect you," Llesho had said while the lamps burned low and went out, one by one. "He'll expect you to attack Tinglut for revenge for the death of Chimbai-Khan or to win over the Qubal clans who chose your brother over you when he was alive. For all that he thinks the rest of humanity are lesser beings, that's what he would do. It won't cross his mind that you would question what you have seen."

"Llesho's right," Radimus added. "When Master Markko thinks no one can hear him, he mutters that the Harn are unruly children and mindless weapons. But his own ambitions are no better than the worst of his enemies."

"That will be his undoing." Mergen leaned forward like a hawk sizing up its prey. A small, dangerous smile reminded them that the subtlety of his mind rivaled Markko's own. "I'll look for answers first and act only when—or if—I have proof of Tinglut's treachery in my hand." If there was something to find, he would uncover it and act within the honor Llesho had come to respect in the ulus of the Qubal people. The magician would not so easily drive the sword of suspicion between the clans.

As a token of his pledge to seek answers before war, the khan offered to care for the still healing Adar, who would travel in the hospital wagon for the long trek to the East. Then Shokar determined to stay and watch over their wounded brother. Bright Morning wished to find the emperor he served as musician and spy when not tending to his duties as a god. "For the times cry out for mercy everywhere, but always with the greatest need where the Lady SeinMa walks," he explained. Knowledge of the future etched sorrowful lines into his face, but he said nothing of what he saw.

Three great forces would come together at Durnhag—the Tinglut, the Qubal, and the empire of Shan. Llesho didn't need a vision to understand the hazards of Shou's path. His inner eye flashed on a memory of burning pyres and bitter guilt. If not peace, the god of mercy had offered him a moment of release from the responsibility of so many deaths in the name of his quest. He would have had that comfort with him again, but knew that, having chosen War as his consort, Shou would have the greater need of Mercy.

When Mergen's route had been charted, the khan rolled the map they'd studied and called to a guardsman hidden in the darkness to bring the maps of the Western Road. From the chest where the bust of Llesho's ancestor stood, the soldier opened a drawer and drew out several long rolls of parchment. Mergen took them and spread them on the furs that covered the dais, setting small lead weights at each of the corners. The company turned their gaze to the West, where Menar lay hidden from all but rumor in the camps.

"Beyond the grasslands are not one, but three powerful kingdoms. Thebin we know as the Cloud Country, with the Golden City, once a great center of piety and learning, at its heart. Raiders from the South put an end to that. Now a traveler finds only danger and misery in the South. The caravans go elsewhere."

Llesho flinched at the description of his lost home. Kungol would again regain its place in the world of honor and learning, but first he had to find Menar. For that, he looked to the second place on the map where Mergen tented his fingers.

"Bithynia is the "Door to the West," the greatest power in the world when it comes to trade, and second only to the former glory of the Cloud Country for its learning. From the little Radimus could tell us, I would guess you will find Menar here. The Bithynians are a people of two faces, it is said: one face looks to the stars and the sea, to the deep mysteries and the arts, while the other looks to the balance book and the armory. They say that the Grand Apadisha builds his roads and bridges and wages wars on his far borders so that his scholars may study in peace, but I have never been there to see for myself. If it is so, your Master Markko may have studied in the workrooms of Bithynia."

"Bithynia produces as many magicians as it does master builders or healers," Kaydu agreed. "My father attended the great school at Pontus for a time. He didn't know Master Markko then, but there are a lot of schools in Bithynia. Then, too, a lot of magicians learn a lesser form of the trade as pages and apprentices to the magicians of the great houses."

When Llesho first met him, Master Markko was the overseer of Lord Chin-shi's holdings on Pearl Island. His post brought with it wealth and power, but he'd been a slave like the rest of them. A page in a household with a lesser magician, perhaps, made sense of what Llesho had seen. An inferior education in the magical arts might explain Master Markko's obsession with arcane learning and the lack of control that had set a powerful demon loose to lay siege to the gates of heaven. Llesho gave a little shudder and cautioned himself against building a past for his enemy out of his own imagination. Only Master Markko knew where his path had led him, and none of it made his actions now less terrible.

The map beneath Mergen's hand showed a thick scattering of stars that represented towns and cities. "So many places to search," Llesho whispered, trying to keep the despair out of his voice. It was hard, and he wasn't sure he'd succeeded. He'd known where he was going when he found Adar and Shokar, and Balar had found Llesho, saving him a search, though at the cost of a great many dead. To find Menar he had only the name of a territory more vast than the grasslands, filled with crowded cities. "Master Markko is already ahead of us. If he knows the land there as well, how will we find Menar first? How will we even know where to begin?"

"Pontus." Kaydu tapped the star on the map with the point of her dagger. "There is a saying my father sometimes uses: 'Reputations rise in Pontus and fall in Iznik.' It's a warning that a servant who loses the favor of a king will find himself posted to an outlying district. But he says it's also true in its most literal sense."

An old saying didn't give them much to go on, but he would find Menar because he had to. Faith would take him there; his dreams and the mortal gods who dogged his steps would see to it, as they had seen to the finding of his other brothers. He just had to let himself follow the unguided path that made the Way of the Goddess.

"What is the third kingdom?" he asked, wondering how far this new road would take him.

Mergen shrugged, with no good answer to give. "Barbarians and bankers, or so the reports come back with the caravans. Their lands lie far to the west, beyond the borders of the Grand Apadisha. On any given sunrise, only he can say where those borders are, or where they will be when Great Moon graces the sky. If you want to know more, you will have to ask the Apadisha himself." Mergen returned Llesho's horrified stare with a wry smile. "Or the master of his caravans," he relented. "Pontus is where all caravans end. In the marketplaces of the city the merchants from the West exchange their goods for wares of the East, and then both return the way they came, their goods exchanged at the Silver Door, which is the name given to Pontus."

Radimus added, "I've heard stories of the West, that men live in huts made of sticks and wear the skins of animals untreated and unstitched as their only clothing. It seems an unlikely wardrobe for a kingdom of bankers." He gave a shrug. "Stories may travel like silk and wool, but they change more in the passage. The magician dismissed them as children's tales, but there is often a seed of truth in the most outlandish tale. Whoever they may have been in their own country, Bithynia has the say of it now."

Llesho nodded. It was a forbidding reminder of the vast power that held Menar in slavery. Llesho had met great powers before, however, including Mergen-Khan himself, and he'd come out of it with his life and his heart more or less intact. He'd do it again because he had to. Between the grasslands and the star-scattered realm of the Apadisha, however, lay a field of blue that began a few days march west of the khan's current position and stretched more than a hundred li in every direction.

"What land is this?" Llesho asked. It seemed by far the most convenient route, though he knew there must be some reason why the caravans had avoided it for the passes above Kungol.

"No land at all, but the Marmer Sea," Mergen said, sweeping his finger around the southern curve of blue. "Your Master Markko will doubtless take his men around the curve of the shore here."

Master Markko himself might choose to travel as a bird or in the shape of one of the horrific winged monsters Llesho had seen him transform into before. Though they had to learn the trick of it, magicians inherited that skill with even one drop of the dragon blood in their bloodline. His Harnish followers would have to travel more mundane paths, however.

"Why not by sea?" Llesho slashed a diagonal across the blue with his finger. The sea route from the southern grasslands to Pontus would save some distance.

"No Harnishman would willingly leave solid ground to risk his life on something as soft as water," Yesugei explained. "Any more than one would cross a fire by leaping from flame to flame. Fire and water can only be tamed so far. At any moment they may rise up against their master with soft power, dragging their victims down to their own level to destroy them."

None of the young warriors lost at the river in the recent battle had known how to swim, which hadn't made sense to Llesho. Now it did.

"The Marmer is well known for its storms," Radimus agreed. "They sweep up suddenly, demon-tossed, and crush a boat like a paper toy in the palm of a giant."

"Don't forget the pirates," Prince Tayy almost managed to hide his grin. "As deadly as the Marmer's storms, and just as unpredictable." In the grasslands, pirates were villains of tall tales passed around the stove late at night, and not the dread of seafarers.

"And dragons," Kaydu added with her own irrepressible grin.

"Still," Mergen-Khan objected with a frown meant to subdue

his nephew, "most ships get through, or there would be no sea trade at all." When he received a sufficiently meek bow of the head, he turned to Llesho. "I assume that's the route you'll be taking?"

"When the storms blow, do they drive boats back to shore, or hurry them on to Pontus?" To Llesho there seemed no point in taking the shorter route if storms would make the journey longer, but Mergen answered, "They rise in the grasslands and drive their prey onto the shores of Bithynia, though not always so conveniently as to bring them into port."

Llesho nodded, taking it all in. Danger, of course, but not more than facing the magician in battle, he thought. "How far?"

"Three days' travel." Mergen cast him a dubious look. "Two if you're eighteen."

The world was turning out to be much bigger than he'd dreamed when the ghost of his father's dead minister sent him out to find his brothers and save Thebin. He wondered if the Dun Dragon hadn't been right about biting off more quest than he could chew. If he faltered, however, Kungol would be lost forever. The very gates of heaven would fall under the onslaught of whatever demon held them under siege. So he bowed his head and prayed that Bithynia was as far as he'd have to go.

They talked long into the night and went to their beds exhausted for a short rest. Lluka and Balar would have traveled west to find their lost brother as well. In Llesho's dreams, however, Lluka was a hand tightening around his throat. Somehow his brother must be dealt with, but the khan had left him no time to discover what drove a blessed husband of the Great Goddess to madness or how to stop the growing torment of his visions. As the light of Great Moon Lun moved across the roof of his red tent, Llesho lay awake with images of a wall of fire out of Lluka's dreams sweeping over his weary head. Finally, he came to the decision he had known in some part of him that he would have to make.

On the journey they had to attract as little attention as possible. That meant disguises and speed, with only his cadre that the Lady SeinMa had gathered around him at the start of his quest. Their old disguises—as rambunctious cadets out to see the world—should work a lot better this time, since they didn't have the emperor of Shan along to complicate things.

Balar the musician they might have fit into the scheme, but Lluka had none of Shou's dubious talent for being other than he was. And Llesho had to accept that he didn't trust his brother's dreams not to betray them along the road. He would find a way to draw his cadre away from the camp on their own, therefore, and say no good-byes to alert anyone that they were leaving.

Decision made, he slept until Master Den called the camp Down Below to prayer forms. Eyes met eyes as his companions fell in around him in the beaten circle of dirt at the center of the camp. Even Kaydu joined them, her jaw firm with determination; they had each, he thought, come to the same conclusion. His mind was so fixed on the journey ahead that he rushed through the forms, paying only enough attention to hear the form and re-create it under Master Den's disapproving glare. But none of his usual disturbing dreams visited him, for which he was grateful. The path ahead was complicated enough without receiving more warnings from heaven. When they finished, he was not surprised to find Hmishi tugging at his sleeve.

"A walk?" Hmishi suggested, drawing him away from the dispersing gathering on the common.

They headed through the trees along a path the river had carved and abandoned ages past as it rose to meet the plain. Horses awaited them where the small dell ended. Llesho went to his own mount, friend of many campaigns across a thousand li and a thousand more of mountain and desert and grassland. He recognized the horses of his companions. Pack animals of Harnish breeding bore their supplies and fodder for the road beyond the grass. Which left one creature Llesho couldn't account for—a pale old warhorse so large that their own mounts looked like cart ponies next to it. A saddle fitted for a giant covered its back. Llesho tried to imagine how one would climb into that saddle without Dognut's ladder, but was saved from further straining his imagination when Master Den joined them. Bixei and Stipes followed him out of the woods.

"Kaydu has gone ahead to scout the way," Bixei greeted them with a quick nod of the head in salute. He gave his own mount a welcoming rub down the length of its long face. "She'll join us on the road."

Llesho was glad he didn't have to face her at the start of this journey. They'd all been through rough campaigns and knew the danger, but still he was afraid of the blame she wouldn't be able to hide—in his imagination, she never hid it at all. Harlol, the Gansau Wastrel and Kaydu's love, should be with them, but Llesho had sent him out to die.

"It wasn't your fault." Bixei hoisted himself into his saddle and reached for the reins of her riderless mount, looping them loosely over the horn of his saddle. He might have been reading his prince's mind, but Llesho figured he'd just let too much of what he was feeling show on his face. He'd have to stop that. If Bixei could read him, Master Markko would as well.

"I know." He didn't really, but he knew what answer they wanted to hear, and gave it rather than stand for more assurances that made him feel not one bit better.

Bixei and Stipes had been with him at Ahkenbad, however, and they passed a look between them that assured him of no peace on the issue. "You heard the Dinha's prophecy," Bixei reminded him. "She knew from the start that we would lose the Wastrels in this quest. She told you then that it wasn't going to be your fault. You saw what the magician did to the dream readers—to the whole city. It's not just your war. It hasn't been since Master Markko attacked Farshore."

"Shou's our friend," Lling added her arguments to Bixei's. She hadn't been at Ahkenbad, but she'd traveled with Shou and knew the emperor of Shan as well as any of them. "But do you think he'd have put the empire on the line for us? He fights because he sees Thebin as a warning, and he doesn't want to find his own people dead or in exile or on a slave block in Bithynia. I didn't know Harlol, but I've heard what happened at Ahkenbad. That's why he gave his life—to keep the dream readers safe from Markko ever attacking them again."

"Give in," Master Den advised him, "The longer we stand here arguing over the dead, the greater the chance we'll be found out before we have made our escape."

Hmishi, watching him carefully, saw the question when it rose into his eyes. "Tonkuq and Sawgher both wanted to come, but Kaydu thought they would serve better by keeping their eyes open and reporting to Emperor Shou all they see on the road. The only people who will be *surprised* that we have gone are the ones who wouldn't take good-bye for an answer. I think," he suggested, "we should be gone before they come looking for you."

It was true. He'd said his farewells to Adar and Shokar the night before, given the khan his pledge of good faith and his gratitude for his hospitality. That left only his brothers Lluka and Balar, whose good intentions hadn't stopped them from making a complete mess of his plans before. He'd have liked a word with Prince Tayyichiut, but they'd made their formal farewells and the Harnish prince had said it himself—statecraft left no room for the personal in friendships between princes.

"I'm ready." Llesho mounted up.

"Then let's be off." Master Den set his massive foot into the stirrup of the monstrous horse and hoisted himself into the giant saddle.

He should have figured it out for himself, but still the sight of his teacher towering over them on his horse shocked him. "I didn't know you rode," he stammered.

With a predatory grin that made Llesho wonder what lay ahead, or followed behind them, Master Den settled into the saddle. "When the army travels at a walk, I walk. When boys take flight, however, Bluebird and I travel together."

Bluebird. Mountain was more like it. Llesho wasn't sure what was more surprising, that his master had a horse who came when needed, or that the horse had a name. When the creature winked at him, however, he reordered his thinking. Not Master Den, but the trickster god ChiChu went with them, riding a steed as magical as himself. As they urged the horses carefully across the fording place to the far side of the river, Llesho wondered what other surprises he had waiting.

The answer to his question came flying after them, robes flapping and determination set in a frown of concentration on his face. Two hounds raced beside him, their tongues lolling. Whimpering, they stopped at the river, casting wounded glances at their master, who kept going. Llesho pulled up to confront him, but Prince Tayy refused to slow down. "Hurry up! There's no time!"

"What are you doing?" Llesho nudged his horse to a gallop and caught up with the fleeing prince.

"Going with you. I thought you'd have more of a head start—" The hounds raised a mournful, accusing howl behind them but didn't follow.

"You can't—"

"There's no time to argue." Prince Tayy drew his horse in a little, to stay with Llesho, but pressed the pace all the while. "Lluka is searching the camp for you!" He spared a quick glance at Llesho over the neck of his horse then bent into the motion and was off again as if he could indeed fly.

Llesho had a thousand questions—starting with "does your uncle know what you are doing?" He tucked them away for later. If the Harnish prince said they were out of time, he believed it. Crouching low in his saddle, Llesho urged his horse to speed. Then they all went, like a flock of ravens skimming the rolling grasslands.

Chapter Ten

THEY left any reasonable cover behind them at the dell where the Onga River flowed. A day out from the Qubal tent city, nothing broke the endless rise and fall of the ground, the swell of a sea of grass turning brown with the advance of autumn. Kaydu found them as Great Sun followed his brother over the horizon. In bird form she landed on her saddle, scratched with the talon marks of many such landings. The beast had trained for this maneuver, one which would have shied a less-accustomed mount. He steadied his gait and, when she transformed into her human shape, he accepted the increased burden with no more than a snort and a toss of his head. Prince Tayyichiut didn't take it quite as well, Llesho noted, but struggled to blank his face to match the unsurprised welcome that the cadre around him wore.

Kaydu located her weapons in their usual places and settled them about her. After a terrible moment when they all looked at each other and realized no one had Little Brother, Master Den reached into his pouch and produced their captain's familiar. "He refused to be left behind," the trickster god insisted, but laughter flavored his indignation. Llesho wondered sometimes if the monkey and the trickster weren't two of a kind, but he kept the thought to himself.

"There you are!" Kaydu took the creature in front of her on

her saddle and dropped a kiss on his furred head. Then she steered them toward a dip in the landscape a little way off their heading, where a natural formation of tumbled stones formed an uncanny circle of jagged white teeth. "There's no better cover between here and the sea," she said, "and the wind will grow stronger the closer we come to the shore. We should rest while we can and move again at dawn."

Llesho followed willingly. He'd ridden too many long days to be surprised at how much a day in the saddle could make him ache. Only the promise of a chance to walk on steady ground and sleep lying down at the end of it had kept him moving at all. Before rest, however, the horses must be tended, weapons seen to, and dinner put together.

"I'm a king," he thought, "I have more important things to do," the most pressing of which was curling up in his blankets and closing his eyes. But his companions were watching to see what he would do and Tayy had already begun rubbing down his own mount. Princely status among the Qubal did not, it appeared, free him from the care and feeding of his own horse.

Llesho knew he had to start as they would go on. Their disguises wouldn't work at all if he acted like a—but no. Shou was an emperor, and never broke his cover story to save himself from work. He was better at picking disguises that kept him out of the cook pot until the food was ready, of course. Llesho suspected that even the emperor had once had to work his way up in the ranks of spies before he took the imperial mask of Shan. "What is proper behavior for a king?" he muttered, and gave himself the answer he thought he'd hear from Shou: "Whatever it takes to keep his country free."

Imagining the emperor grooming the horses or stirring the pot wasn't as hard as he thought it would be. Soon he'd unburdened his own horse of its saddle and set it to graze on the coarse and faded grass outside the confines of the circle of white stones.

"What is this place?" he asked when he joined his companions at the cook pot. Lling had taken charge of Hmishi's horse so that he could start their dinner. He carefully nursed a low fire they would keep going only long enough to warm the way-fare in the pot.

"A holy place of the ancestors," Tayy said. Finished tending his own horse, he had wandered back with Kaydu, who laughed and shook her head at something he said. The Harnish prince showed no sign of discomfort from the long ride, but settled companionably on the grass next to Llesho with an eager eye to the first bubble in the pepper pot of millet and dried meat.

"There are gates like this, to the underworld, scattered all over the grasslands. The shamans know about them and guide the clans well clear when moving camp."

"Away?" Kaydu asked. Her father was a magician, after all, with dragon blood in his veins. Kaydu never ran away from knowledge. "Why away?"

"No one but a shaman wants to visit the underworld before his time," Tayy answered gravely, "or meet one who would come out of a gate such as this."

"Not all the dead wish ill of the living," Hmishi objected. It was the first mention he had made of his time in the under-world. "There are souls desperate to return because they have left something vital undone, and souls who were malevolent in life for whom death has come as no improvement. Most don't realize they are dead at all, I think. I know I didn't. I thought I had died when Bright Morning brought me back, but death itself seemed no greater a step than between the camps of Up Top and Down Below that we left behind us on the Onga."

Rumor in the camp had said that Llesho had gone to the underworld to bring back his most trusted warrior, so this was news to the Harnish prince. He made no comment about the powers of a dwarf musician from the court of the emperor of Shan having to raise the dead, however; the fact, accomplished in whatever manner, sat in front of them stirring the dinner pot. Instead he questioned the wisdom of raising the dead at all. "Are you sorry to return to this life when you had already moved on?"

"What does it matter?" Llesho really didn't want to hear the answer to that. Hmishi had set aside the cares of this life and Llesho had selfishly refused to continue his battle without him.

Bright Morning had made the selfish part clear even when he returned Hmishi to the living world. "There's nothing we can do about it now."

He wasn't sure it would matter if he could. But he didn't want his friends to know that. "Unless you plan to help him down that road with your knife."

"I don't think that's what he meant," Kaydu interceded on the prince's behalf. "We are all friends here, after all."

That had been Llesho's call. Back the other side of Hmishi's return and the death of Tayy's father, he'd made the offer in the rashness of the moment, "There is room in my cadre for a likely warrior," he'd promised. He'd spent too much time with the Qubal, and he'd forgotten, almost, that the prince was one of them. And Tayy had taken him at his word. For some reason, the fact that the prince was here by his own invitation just made Llesho madder.

Hmishi was reading him like he always had, though. "It doesn't matter," he agreed gently. "I'm here now, and I have no great desire to go back. I would soon enough have come to realize that Lling had not come with me, and I could not leave her to fight the coming war without me."

"I'm glad Bright Morning found you and brought you back," Prince Tayy conceded, though it was clear he hadn't known the powers of the dwarf and was handling the conversation not much better than Llesho himself. "But I'd just as soon avoid trouble with the underworld and all its places."

"Then why are you here?" Llesho asked with a gesture to take in the jagged circle of stone. He hadn't thought he was challenging Tayy's right to be with them at all. With the words halfway out of his mouth, though, he realized that he meant that very thing. Why had Tayy left his ulus and the ger-tent palace of his uncle to chase them halfway across the grasslands on an errand with no profit for the Qubal and little likelihood of success for any of them? Why did the Harnish prince enter a forbidden place and sit with them to eat where restless spirits prowled. That was a part of his question, too. Llesho wanted all of it in his answer.

Tayy, begging off with a look that pleaded friendship, received no encouragement from Llesho.

"What's the matter, Llesho?" Kaydu asked. His cadre was as confused as he was, only they didn't have the benefit of the argument he'd been waging in his own head.

"No one 'just likes' a prince," Llesho repeated Tayy's hurtful words from an earlier conversation, "any more than a prince is free to make friends who do not serve the khan. Or in this case, the king of Thebin. So I have to wonder why you are here."

Tayy paled, his hand frozen halfway to the pot. "I thought . . ." he began and remembered where he'd heard those words before. "I was talking about my father and Mergen-Khan, how life is in the royal ger-tent. Not . . . I thought it was different between us. That you understood.

"You're right, of course. There is no place next to his brother for my father's son. Mergen will make his own heirs and there is the matter of the murderous Lady Chaiujin, who seems bent on wiping out my family. I thought I might serve better out of the eye of the coming storm."

"With one who does not serve the khan?"

"Clearly, I was wrong. I won't bother you any further. My uncle must be worried sick, wondering where I have gone. It was foolish of me to leave camp with strangers and not even my personal guard around me." Tayy bowed his head, accepting his mistake, and withdrew into himself as he rose from the circle of friends inside the gate of stone.

All of whom, Llesho discovered, were glaring at him.

"What was that about?" Lling asked, more gently than any of the others might have done. She touched the back of his hand, reminding him that they were confused but still there.

"Something he said once. I thought we were friends, and he set me straight. Princes don't have friends. So I have to wonder what he's doing here.

"Somebody has to ask," he defended himself against their skeptical frowns.

Thick bubbles began to rise and pop in the pot. Master Den put out the fire with a handful and another of dirt, so that only a low glare of coals glinted through to light the night. "It sounds very lonely," he said into the darkness. "To ride out among friends and discover at the end of the day that they are strangers after all."

"How much better," Kaydu recited with a nod to the trickster god, "'to ride out with strangers, and find oneself among friends when darkness falls.' I miss the dwarf already."

"Mercy abandoned us for a more promising target," Llesho reminded them sourly. He really hated being wrong in an argument, and he was having a hard time defending himself against sacred verses of the god of mercy while trying to figure out how he might persuade Lling to act as his ambassador to Prince Tayy. If he put it just that way she would do it, of course, but this was the wrong time to substitute court manners for friendship. As Tayy had been trying to tell him, maybe.

"But," Master Den began with a wicked grin.

Llesho sighed. They weren't going to give him any kind of break. "But Mercy is never absent when he travels in our hearts."

Having won his point, Master Den was willing to end the lesson with a gift of compromise. "The greatest struggle all kings face is how to balance justice with mercy."

The words jangled like a memory struck by a gong somewhere deep in his belly. "Sometimes Mercy *is* justice." He answered out of bone-knowledge rather than a lesson learned. He was the king. It was his mercy, his job to offer it. Jealousy had no place on that scale. With a sharp tilt of the head to acknowledge his duty, he wandered out beyond the stones.

"Tayy!" he called. "I was being stupid, and I'm sorry! Come back!" But Tayy's horse was no longer with the others and the night felt empty around him. With a last call that startled the horses into their own skittish answer, he returned to the fire.

"He's gone." Llesho flung himself on the ground and shook off the brooding sulk that threatened to draw the trickster god's mocking disapproval. "Took his horse and left for home, from what he said at the fire. I called and called, but he didn't answer."

His companions weren't pleased with him, but not even Kaydu said anything. They were wondering, he suspected, whether the whole king-thing had gone to his head before he even had a throne to sit on. Which was less embarrassing than the truth. He'd wanted Tayy's friendship for himself. The cadre's easy acceptance of the prince had made him jealous, and then he'd been hurt by the prince's words.

A wolf howled in the distance, followed by the nervous cry of a horse just outside the circle of stones. Llesho pulled his coat more tightly around him. It wasn't safe for Tayy out there alone. Wolves and who knew what else prowled the night. Southern fighters might be on their way east, looking for the lost remnants of Tsu-tan's force.

"Maybe we should stir up the fire." With an ill-tempered grumble he gestured with a shoulder at the lightless fire pit. "It will keep the wolves away. And, if he changes his mind, Tayy'll be able to find us in the dark."

If Master Markko's southern raiders were prowling the area, their fire would serve the enemy as a beacon as well, or they'd have kept the fire going in the first place. No one objected, however, when Hmishi threw on more bricks of dried droppings. Kaydu snapped her fingers for sparks. "We should sleep now. If Prince Tayy comes back he can settle his own billet, and if he doesn't, we'll have to assume he made his own way home."

Home wasn't there anymore—the whole tent city had packed up and moved east, toward Durnhag. That fact went into the saddlebag with all the other issues they weren't talking about. Later, Llesho thought, when the wolves weren't nosing the outside of the circle of stones and the spirits of the dead weren't pressing on the gate of the underworld where they sat. They'd talk later. In the meantime, he said, "I'll take the first watch."

Kaydu nodded, allowing him this small penance. Settling Little Brother at her head, she rolled into her blankets and closed her eyes. One by one, the rest of his companions did likewise.

Llesho climbed up on the highest of the stones that made the circle where they rested. He brought his pack with him, cautiously checking the precious objects he carried, gifts of the Lady SeinMa and the pearls of the Great Goddess. With both ears listening for any approach, and an eye for the night held at a distance by their renewed fire, he drew the leather thong from where it hid beneath his collar. The small bag that hung from it had grown fat with the black pearls of the Great Goddess' necklace. Once again he regretted the loss of his teacher, the counselor Lleck. There hadn't been time to learn all he needed to know, like how Lleck had stolen the first of the pearls from Pearl Bay Dragon, who he had known as the motherly healer Kwanti. Or how the pearls would restore the balance between heaven and earth. Or how many pearls he had to find.

Three he had received as gifts before he ever left the empire of Shan—one from the hand of the lady SeinMa herself and one from Mara, Carina's mother and an aspirant to be the eighth mortal god. And the one Lleck had given him, stolen from the Pearl Bay Dragon. She'd told Llesho that she meant to give it to him anyway, so that turned out all right. He hadn't told her at the time, but he had grown to love the dragon who had treated him kindly in her human form and saved his life once in the sea.

Four more pearls had come to him like dreams. One bound in silver, had disguised Pig, the Jinn and chief gardener of heaven, who came to him as a guide in the dream world. Pig had never been entirely clear about the pearl or the silver that bound him. Was it part of the Goddess' String of Midnights, made use of by a vision? Or was it truly the Jinn, escaped as he said in the shape of the pearls lost to heaven in some great clash at the gates? He still didn't know, and wore it separately, hung from a silver chain by a ring in its back.

The last pained him most to look at—he had found them like the broken bits of finger the stone giants left behind when they stole the hearts of their murdered victims. In a dream he had gathered them from the breasts of the Gansau Wastrels dead in Llesho's own service, freeing them to continue on to the underworld. When the dream ended, the Wastrels were still dead, and the pearls remained as a reminder of his loss. He tucked them carefully away close to his heart again, wondering how many more he had to find. How much more suffering would they be a

part of, before he could return them to the Goddess? He didn't
know, and couldn't imagine how he was going to find out.

The short spear of the Lady SeinMa had drawn his blood
down through lifetimes he couldn't count, could only vaguely
sense at all. In all those lifetimes the spear had taunted at his
back until it had turned and killed him, but in this one he'd had
enough and wrested control from it. Like a conquered beast, it
waited in silence until he faltered. Llesho would have destroyed it, but his dreams told him the weapon had a part to
play in battles still to be fought before the gates of heaven. So
he set it aside and pulled out the two jade cups he now carried.
The first, a wedding cup from his own past lives that the Lady
SienMa had returned to him, had delicate carvings on a rim
thin enough that the light of the sun, or even a candle, would
shine through it. He checked it for damage before picking up
the second, its match in all except the thickness of its rim and
a strange spiral rune, like the coils of a snake carved at the bottom of the bowl.

The Lady Chaiujin had given him the cup, filled with the
potion that had made him desire her. She had known he carried
its match, the marriage cup of his past life: where had she gotten
the second, and what significance did it hold? He didn't want
to think about her now, with the wolves howling nearby and
the fire burning low at the center of their camp. Putting the cups
away in his pack, he sent a nervous glance over his shoulder.
No one moved. There could have been no breath at his ear, no
shift of a sleeve at his back, but he felt as if someone was watching him intently.

"Spirit, show yourself," he said, because they rested at a gate
to the underworld and could expect visitors from among the
dead.

No answer came to him, but a chill as if of distant, mocking
laughter made Llesho shiver. The cold of night, he tried to convince himself, but superstitious dread ran little mice feet up his
spine. "What do you want?"

He thought he heard a slithering in the grass at the base of
the stone he sat on but when he looked, he saw nothing.

Great Moon Lun rose and started across the sky, but Tayy

didn't come back. Llesho shivered in his coats and wrapped a blanket close around him, but he couldn't keep out the cold breeze that tugged at the edges of his clothes and blazed an icy trail up his sleeves. Even the wolves seemed to have departed for the warmth of their dens, leaving him only the ghosts for company.

"Want company?" As if conjured by the thought of ghosts, Hmishi appeared at his elbow.

"You're alive," Llesho answered, sounding foolish to his own ears.

Hmishi nodded, though, as if it were the most sensible greeting in the world, and between them, maybe it was. "Thanks to you," he said, answering one part of the surprise in Llesho's voice. He'd been dead, and now he wasn't. That fact had sparked the argument that sent Tayy off into the dark, but it had just been an excuse then. Alone in the dark, so near the abode of ghosts, it was hard not to wonder if he'd made a mistake.

"What was it like?" Llesho whispered, cutting a glance at his old friend out of the corner of his eye. They'd come close over the supper pot, but no one had quite asked the question until now. He wasn't sure it was safe to ask it here, where the ghosts could hear him. Too many had died in his short life, and his own past deaths haunted his dreams. With Prince Tayy out there alone with the wolves and the creeping mysteries he might have added to their number this very night.

Hmishi curled up next to him on the rock, huddled close for warmth so that Llesho felt rather than saw his shrug. "Peaceful, I guess. Mostly, I don't remember it at all. But when I think about it, it feels peaceful. It hurt so much, what Tsu-tan did, what he let his soldiers do to me. I'd been praying for it to be over for days. Lling needed me; I felt guilty wanting to escape before we rescued the princes and saved Kungol, but I'd come to the place where the river ends. I was ready to go."

Llesho nodded, letting Hmishi know he was listening, understanding, but not getting in the way if he wanted to go on. After a quiet moment, he did.

"I wasn't sorry to go. I remember thinking that I ought to be—sorry, that is—but it all seemed so far away, as if it didn't have anything to do with me any more. As if it never had. Then I heard Dognut playing his silver flute. It makes no sense, but I heard words in the notes, telling me to wake up, to come back to the world. The melody was so joyous, but the words were sad, as if the flute knew what it was asking, and regretted the need. I didn't want to come back at first.

"I was afraid of the pain," Hmishi looked away when he said it, as if it embarrassed him.

"It was horrible," Llesho agreed. "I still have nightmares that he brought you back all broken like we found you."

"I have some of those myself," Hmishi gave a little twitch of discomfort. "Anyway, I was ready to begin again with a new life, free of all that. Still, I wanted to see Lling, and I'd left so much undone that when he called, I came back. Better to face your burdens in this life than to carry them along into the next one."

"I'm figuring that out myself," Llesho agreed with a wry twist of a smile. The dreams had made it clear that he was carrying some major debt from his past life, and he didn't plan on lugging it along to the next. He just hoped that having Hmishi here beside him hadn't added more than he could carry to that burden.

"You'd better get some rest." Hmishi turned to face out beyond the rocky circle, signaling his turn at watch. "If we're going to find Tayy we're going to have to start early in the morning."

"Yeah," Llesho agreed, speaking of debts he was unwilling to carry forward. "He can't have gotten far."

With a last companionable nod, he unfolded his curled legs so that he could stand and wandered back to the dim glow of the fire. Lling, he noticed, waited only for him to settle in the place they'd left for him closest to the coals before she was tiptoeing in the direction of Hmishi at the watch. Good, he thought. No one should be alone with the wide and empty night. And with that thought, he closed his eyes and dreamed that the spiral rune at the bottom of the Lady Chaiujin's cup uncoiled like a serpent and slithered from the bottom of the bowl. As it reached the rim the leading part became the head of an emerald bamboo snake. The body followed, with scales like green silk, until the rune had left the cup completely and coiled itself against the heat of his body.

"Llesho!" the snake whispered in his ear with Lady Chaiujin's voice. "I am the goddess of the underworld, and I want you. Accept my kiss and come with me."

"No!" he said in the dream. "You are no god, and I don't want you!"

"Yes you do," she said, and Llesho felt her fingers, her lips, no serpent at all, but the lady herself, in human form.

"You're a demon," he accused her, and she laughed at him.

"So are you," she whispered. "So are you."

"No!" He woke gasping for breath, with the word still on his lips and the howling of dogs in the distance in his ears, smeared with the feel of her lip rouge where she had kissed him.

"What is it?" Kaydu had leaped to her feet, sword in hand and with Little Brother clinging to her neck. Bixei and Stipes followed not more than a pace behind her, while Hmishi sprang to greater attention on the rocks, and Lling circled their camp, leaping lightly from stone to stone.

"I saw nothing," Hmishi reported, and Lling added, "Nothing has troubled the horses."

"It was a dream." Llesho apologized for waking the company.

"A traveling dream?" Kaydu wanted to know. "What's going on?"

She meant elsewhere in the dream world, but Llesho shook his head. "Nothing like that. It was just a dream, and a stupid one at that."

"Oh?"

They weren't going to leave him alone until they heard the dream and judged it for themselves, so he told it, how the rune at the bottom of his cup had become a snake, and the snake had become the lady, that he'd known her for a demon, and she'd known him for the same. When he had done, Kaydu was watching him with the greedy eyes of a magician. "Have you checked the cup?"

"I don't need to check it. There was nothing here."

With one eyebrow raised in an expression of doubt, she reached over and wiped the corner of his mouth. When she held her hand up in front of her, the dull firelight showed a dark stain coloring her thumb.

Llesho swiped the back of his own hand across his lips, wanting to erase every sign that the dream had been true. If she could reach him past their guard, touch him in his sleep and no one see, she must truly be a demon. He wondered, sick with dread, if that meant the rest of it was true as well. Was he a demon, as she said, and no prince of Thebin at all? Perhaps the real prince had died in Pearl Bay at the very beginning of the quest, and he'd been going through the motions of someone else's life—

"Llesho! Snap out of it, you're scaring me now!"

Llesho came back to himself with the realization that Kaydu had been talking to him, and that his whole cadre had formed a worried circle around him. "I'm not a demon!" he insisted, though he wasn't sure he believed it himself.

But Bixei was looking at him like he'd lost his mind, not his soul. Stipes was shaking his head and Hmishi reached out a hand to check his forehead for fever.

"You're not a demon, Holy Excellence." Kaydu reminded him with his title of what he should never have forgotten. He was the beloved of the Great Goddess, who had cared for him when Master Markko had awakened the poisons in his body. He had received gifts of his past from the goddess of war and had been granted the gift of a life by the god of mercy. He had traveled with the trickster ChiChu almost from the first moments of his quest. A demon could not have tricked the trickster god himself, nor could such a creature win the love of the Goddess.

"But she was here," he explained away his confusion. "In my bed, as snake and woman."

Bixei gave his shoulder a little shake. "You recognized what she was and told the truth. She just wanted to scare you, and hasn't said a truthful word since the first time we set eyes on her."

"I know." And he did. But there was more to it than that.

Not a demon, surely. But she'd seen something about him. He wondered if ChiChu could tell him what it was. When he looked around, however, he realized that the trickster's blankets were empty and Master Den was nowhere to be seen.

"I didn't see him leave," Himishi admitted, though that didn't mean anything where the gods were concerned.

Lling gave a long look to the grasslands rolling in waves beyond their tiny circle. "Perhaps he went to look for Tayy," she said, and the shuffling that followed told Llesho that they'd all been worrying about the Harnish prince.

"We'll find out in the morning," Llesho said. He didn't, at heart, believe it, however.

With nothing more to be said, they wandered off to their separate blankets. Llesho sat with his legs tucked up and his back against a rock, watching the fire die out in fits of falling embers. He didn't think he was going to sleep any more that night, not with the Lady Chaiujin haunting his dreams, and suspected the rest of his cadre was pretending to rest as well.

Master Den returned as Little Sun was calling to his brother. He said nothing about where he had been, and Llesho said nothing about his dream. Secrets were deadly. Lluka was proof enough of that. But somehow he couldn't bring himself to ask, or to reveal his own secrets while the trickster god was hiding something from him. Instead he rubbed his face in his hands to brush away the sleep, wondering if he hadn't just set their quest on a road he'd regret, while the mountainous mass of his teacher turned his back and went to sleep.

PART TWO

EDRIS

Chapter Eleven

THE LADY Chaiujin did not return to him during the night in her form as woman or as emerald bamboo serpent. No dreams came to him at all that he could remember, but Llesho woke with exhaustion dragging at him so that he thought his body must have spent the night wandering while his mind slept. His companions looked no better, except for Master Den. The trickster god rousted them out for prayer forms with a bounce to his step, as if he had not just crept back into camp with barely time to close his eyes before starting the day again.

Llesho followed his lead through the forms, scarcely noting what he did until his teacher called him to attention with a sharp reminder that the earth they honored in their prayers deserved better of him. It did, he realized with a jolt. The sun cast spears of yellow light around small, puffy clouds drifting low in a sky of blue so brilliant it brought tears of wonder to his eyes.

Those clouds would release no drop of rain, would drift no lower to brush their cheeks with mist, until the spring came again. Already the grass around them had turned the color of old Dun Dragon, drawing back to reveal the dusty bones of the earth as the dry season passed its arid hand over the land. Still, the day was beautiful in an unforgiving way.

A jerboa watched him from the shadow of a boulder in the

circle of their camp for a moment before hopping away. Llesho thought of Carina mimicking her totem animal's skipping gait in the shade of Bolghai's den and the way his brother Adar watched her when she moved around the hospital tent. He thought about Balar playing his lute and Dognut his silver flute, and wished that he'd remembered to sing more when he'd been with them. A harmless black snake slithered by on its own business, and in the distance a herd of wild horses ran like a dark cloud come to earth. They were too far away to see clearly, but his mind's eye supplied the tails flying out behind them and the manes rising like gleaming halos around their supple necks. Their own mounts whickered to join them.

The wild run pulled at the spirit of Llesho's totem animal, the roebuck. He felt the change start in him, the weight of antlers on his head. But Master Den called him back to his prayer forms and his companions and the burden of kingship. Menar remained ahead of him and Prince Tayy was out there somewhere, maybe hurt, or lost. There was too much to do before he could indulge the call of freedom. As he finished the "Wind through Millet" form, returning to the rest position, he felt the wildness settle a little. He might be a roebuck in the grasslands, but his heart belonged to the gardens of the Great Goddess, and to the high sweet call of the priests and priestesses in the Temple of the Moon. If he had to be a king to win back those things he loved, that's what he would do.

But first, he had to find Tayy and repair the damage he'd done there. No one had friends enough to throw away.

"We're going for him, aren't we?" Kaydu lifted Little Brother out of his pack and settled him on her shoulder. She looked more tired than any of them, having taken the last watch. As a bird, she'd spent much of the day before in the air, scouting the way to the sea.

He nodded, and a tension drawn fine as wire seemed to let go of his cadre. Somehow, Tayy had become one of theirs. Of them all, it seemed, only Llesho hadn't noticed until it was too late. Master Den heaved a deep sigh, but said nothing. Just as well, since he had no intention of listening to any objections.

"We go," he said, with an eye to the horses playing in the distance. "And we start there."

They didn't find him, though their search grew more determined after they circled in on the wild horses. Prince Tayy-ichiut's mount was among them, free of its saddle and trailing its reins. Hmishi and Lling tried to catch it to bring with them, but the horse shied away when they drew near and the chief stallion of the herd challenged them with teeth and hooves to defend his new prize. They wouldn't capture Tayy's mount without fighting the leader, and Llesho decided he'd rather lose to the animal than cause it any injury. Cutting among the herd he kept the beast distracted long enough for Lling to clear the escaped horse of its bridle and then he drew his companions away again. With a toss of its head, the creature left them, returning to the life it had known before the Qubal had put their saddle on it.

After that they watched the ground for signs of where Tayy had fallen or been thrown. As the shadows grew longer than the rays of the sun, however, the truth became too pressing to ignore. They weren't going to find him.

"It's time to stop," he admitted to Master Den, who rode beside him on his dusty old horse.

"Maybe," Den agreed, but Stipes interrupted his reply with a cry and a frantic wave of his arm.

"A trail!" he called. "Dismount before you come any closer! Horses have passed this way." Crouching close to the ground, he added, "Their feet were covered."

Llesho leaped from the saddle, as they all did. In matters of tracking, however, whoever found the trail took the lead. Therefore he deferred to Stipes, suggesting only, "Two hands or more of horse," as he tested his own eye against those of his cadre.

"I'd say." Stipes agreed as Bixei joined them, followed by Hmishi and Lling. "One is carrying a double burden."

"Tayy's horse got away," Lling reminded them. Tayy hadn't been so lucky. They all figured that.

Stipes reached out and measured with his finger the depth

of the print left in the dirt. "Rear hooves," he said. "Dug in really good." The horse had carried a dead weight slung over its rump. Tayy was hurt, knocked out in the struggle at least, though Llesho saw no evidence of a fight.

"They found him when he was sleeping," he said, and thought, *alone, without anyone to guard his rest.* "But who took him? Not the Southern Harn, they don't wrap their horses' hooves like this. And they'd be taking him south, to their own camp, or east, to bargain for ransom. These prints are heading West."

"Pirates," Master Den suggested with a tone of certainty that made Llesho wonder again where'd he'd been the night before and what he'd seen or been a part of. "The sea is no more than a day's ride; they'll have been scouting for slaves."

"So we'll find him." Llesho gave a shrug more casual than he felt. "We can trade the horses, use part of the money to buy him back and the rest to pay our passage across the sea. If he even needs our help. When he tells the pirates who he is, they'll ransom him back to his uncle. Tayy said that's what they do with valuable captives on the grasslands."

He knew what they did with conquered royals of no particular value but didn't think a Harnish prince would suffer the same fate. Reluctantly, Kaydu shook her head. "The pirates aren't from the grasslands. They come from everywhere, but mostly from Bithynia."

Master Den added his own grim intelligence: "Pirates usually sell young female prisoners as concubines or servants in the marketplace. The old they murder outright, throw them overboard at sea or strangle them on land. Men of an age for hard work they put to the oar."

Now that they knew where Tayy had been taken, Kaydu had the best chance of following. "I'll find them," she said, and handed Little Brother in his pack to Bixei, who slung it over his shoulder.

"Behave yourself," he warned the creature. "If you give me any trouble, your mistress will find you in the stew pot when she comes back."

No one believed him, of course, least of all Little Brother.

They all watched as Kaydu leaped into the air, changing into a hawk as she rose. When she had reached flying altitude, she arrowed away in the direction of the sea.

Llesho turned his attention back to the god who stood watching him the way Habiba studied an experiment. "What part did you play in this, trickster?" His voice fell dangerously low. If he knew for sure . . . he didn't know what he would do, but murder came to mind. Even the gods would answer to him if they had used him to harm the Qubal boy.

"It hardly takes a trickster god to create a falling out between princelings who jump to conclusions as quickly as they leap into their saddles." Master Den sniffed indignantly and smoothed the sleeves of his coat as if he actually had feathers to ruffle.

The rebuke hurt almost more than Master Markko's poisons. His fault. Stricken with guilt, Llesho turned an eye to the path in the dust. *Why didn't you tell me?* It was on the tip of his tongue to ask, but he knew better. As a teacher, the trickster god had always believed he learned best from his mistakes. So he said instead, "No lesson is worth Tayy's life."

"See. You've learned something already." Master Den gave an encouraging nod and grinned at him.

Llesho turned away, impatient with his teacher's mood. "I think Shou must need your advice," he said. "For myself, I have no appetite for your lessons." He walked away, mounted his horse, and rode after the pirates who had too much head start.

Presently he heard the sound of horses following, but none had the thundering sound of the monstrous creature the trickster god had ridden. Good. Let him find someone else to torment with his smug tricks and hurtful lessons. Llesho didn't have time for it anymore. And if he remembered, from step to step, that he had done this and not his teacher, he pushed the thought down deep and looked ahead to the sea. His cadre would free Tayy from the pirates who had taken him for the most evil labor known to a seafaring people.

* * *

Mergen had been right about the distance. They had lost the morning searching for Prince Tayy, but made up some of the lost time by resting only in the deep dark and riding again when Great Moon Lun rose in the sky. As they rode, the ground fell away from the heights of the grassy plateau. When they came to the sea in midmorning of the third day of their travels, they had again passed into lands on the very brink of summer, the air rich and thick with moisture. Or rather, when they reached the outskirts of the strange port city of Edris. Spread around a protected inlet, the city blotted out any glimpse of the Marmer Sea.

Kaydu joined them as they completed their descent to the coast, reverting to her true form as she landed lightly in her saddle. "Nothing," she reported, as Little Brother screeched a welcome.

The monkey climbed out of his pack on Bixei's saddle and leaped from one horse to the other as they rode. Her mount, accustomed to its rider coming and going in great leaps, chuffed indignantly but didn't shy as she lifted the monkey onto her shoulder. It seemed to give them both some comfort against the bad news.

Together, their newly regathered company pressed forward, through a familiar circle of carts, to a cluster of round tents set in a series of half-moon curves around the landward side of the city. Black felt roofs washed like angry waves up against the city walls that rose in the distance. The Uulgar clans, who had sent raiders against Kungol and driven Llesho into slavery on the Long March, had come to market.

The Uulgar had aligned themselves with Master Markko's mad purpose, though what they hoped to gain from the fall of heaven and the destruction of the living worlds in fire and chaos Llesho could not imagine. He wondered grimly, however, how many enemies he would have to fight for the life of one Harnish prince. Only the thought of Tayy, abandoned to pirates and a living death in slavery to the oar, kept him from turning his horse and running in the opposite direction.

His companions had their own memories of the black tents of the Uulgar. Hmishi had been tortured to death in one, and Lling had suffered her own captivity of mind as well as body.

Kaydu and Bixei and Stipes had all fought with him in Tsu-
tan's camp to rescue their captive friends. They knew what the
power of the magician could do when joined with the blood-
thirsty ruthlessness of the Harnish raiders. As if of one mind,
they drew closer to each other. For Tayy, whose unhappy plight
lay on their consciences, they drove on.

Down the center cut the wide avenue that Llesho and his
band had come to expect of a Harnish tent city. This was not a
massing of warriors under the war banner of their khan, however, but a smaller gathering for trade and commerce. Llesho
had never actually seen shops in the Qubal ulus, though he
knew they must trade for the many foreign goods he had
noticed in the camp. Here, however, wares of Harnish make
were laid out on blankets at the side of the road. An old woman
sitting in the style of the clans presided over each blanket, hag-
gling with passersby and shouting gossip and prices from one
to the other. Llesho saw worked leather and beaten metal buckles, and woolens made from the fleece of the sheep that grazed
the grasslands. No silver or gold seemed to change hands at the
blanket bazaar, but buckles went for beads and leatherwork for
embroidery silk.

Farther on, they found Harnishmen with their horses. The
Harnishmen watched the small band of riders with calculation
in their eyes. They were selling the culls of their herds, however, not buying, and had no use for the outlander saddles and
tack. Llesho's cadre pressed on.

The road through the camp ended at a gate in a high wall of
plastered rubble that carried on out of sight in the distance to
either side. Since it was morning and well into the trading day,
the gates stood open. At the center of a sweeping arch over the
passway, a watchman noted the comings and goings into the
city with a keen eye for trouble. Enclosed like a covered bridge,
the arch had arrow slits and lookout windows cut at random
along its length, from which the city guard might defend the
gate.

For a moment, the watchman seemed to catch Llesho's gaze
and he wondered if the gates would suddenly swing closed on
them. Would an army spill from the garrison to seize them

when they passed and turn them over to the Uulgar traders pressed up against the defended city? That was long ago, he thought at the man, the Uulgar have no claim on the princes of Thebin. Whatever had been in the gatekeeper's glance, he turned away and gave them no more attention as they passed inside.

Llesho's experience with cities, from Kungol to Farshore and then back to the Imperial City of Shan, had all led him to expect spacious thoroughfares gracious with trees or banners or ribbons dancing on the wind. He knew about the poverty of cities as well, of course. In Shan, hidden out of the sight of the broad avenues, he had sidestepped slops pitched out of upper windows in buildings sagging in on one another like drunken revelers over streets so narrow a donkey cart would not pass. He wasn't sure what to make of Edris, however. The streets were narrow and winding like the poor sections of the imperial city and like them too, water trickled thinly over slops dumped in open ditches.

The day was warm and the smell of ripening ordure overpowered the newcomers. Llesho cut a sideways glance at Kaydu, to find her wrinkling her nose in distaste just as he had. Bixei had handed over the pack where Little Brother usually rode, and the monkey had hidden himself away in it, indignant at the smell, so that he didn't even show his face as they rode.

Behind the steaming ditches, however, whitewashed terra cotta walls showed the pale blush of their blank faces to the winding streets. Protected by their walls the houses were hidden, roofs the color of burnt umber rising in lofty disdain well back from the noise and odors of the streets. Narrow windows high under the eaves peered mysteriously down on lush secret gardens with just the crown of a tree or a spill of bright blossoms on climbing vines visible on the street below. Llesho figured even the most highly perfumed flowers behind those walls couldn't entirely protect the aloof residents from the smells of the ditches.

Visitors from every nation Llesho knew, and some he didn't,

filled the narrow avenue leading into the city. He was jostled by a Shannish merchant and bumped with more deliberate insult by a Harnish trader, while a camel drover in the coats of the Tashek people passed through the crowd without looking in their direction. There were men in half a dozen different styles of turbans and some in round little caps and women dressed in everything from veils to soldier's pantaloons. He would have enjoyed the novelty of it, but the constricted passage reminded him too much of shuffling down the chute to the auction block at the now-banished slave market of the Imperial City of Shan.

Much as Llesho hated the feeling, he understood a bit of the reasoning behind the rabbit warren craziness of it. Any invading force would find a pitched battle in the narrow streets impossible to fight. Llesho had lived through two such attacks—in Kungol, and in the imperial city—and thought that was a pretty smart idea, especially given Edris' neighbors on the grasslands. But even a cart with a broken axle could dead-end the way into the city, causing panic as traffic continued to press in from the gates. Once that thought had planted itself in his head, he couldn't shake the cold dread it fostered.

Eventually, however, the road emptied them out into a wide square paved with blocks of stone round as dinner plates, a fountain at its center. At each of the cardinal points rose a long building open at the street level. Kaydu flung her arm in a wide sweeping circle to take in every compass point. "The Edris market," she declared. Their party dismounted, staring about them The space after the confines of the streets stunned them, and the market buildings themselves—

Llesho was impressed, as newcomers were intended to be. Arches held up by pillars—hundreds of them marching like paired soldiers down the length and breadth of the market—roofed the open street level while supporting the enclosed stories above.

"That's where the real money changes hands." Kaydu had followed his gaze to the upper stories of the north side market, each level decorated with its own motifs of arches and screened windows looking out over the square. "Legend says that countries have changed hands in the trading houses above the market at Edris. Kings, surely, have risen and fallen as the needs of merchants dictated.

"Perhaps that is why Kungol fell," Llesho mused aloud while his companions watched him nervously for prophecy. It wasn't that, just common sense facing a market where Kungol would have temples. "The Uulgar wanted the riches of Kungol. The merchants would have wanted to attract the caravans away from the high passes and down to the sea. So it might have been arranged."

"Worse now," Kaydu figured, "with Master Markko looking to the gates of heaven in the mountains. You don't take on the easy quests."

"So Dun Dragon said." He gave Kaydu the lead since she seemed to know the city She directed them toward the south end of the square, where the sound of cattle lowing and chickens squawking told them livestock was sold. "We can sell the horses here, and probably our tack as well."

Llesho drew his horse after him, under a set of vaulting arches. Even though there were no sides to the market, the heat of animals and their buyers and sellers combined in an unwholesome stew that raised the sweat on Llesho's brow and made it difficult to breath.

They passed by selling booths where chickens and geese flapped squawking in wicker cages stacked against the walls while frantic vendors shouted out their prices. Small yards housed pens of rabbits and other small animals offered to the wives and servants on their own quests to bring back dinner for their households. Voices ebbed and flowed with the bargaining; hands flashed with the exchange of coin.

"What will you take for the monkey," a woman dressed in bits of finery from all the peoples who traded here shouted out as they passed.

"Not for sale," Kaydu let her know.

"This is Edris market," the vendor insisted. "Everything is for sale." Her hand reached for Little Brother, who peeked solemnly back at her from his pack.

"I said 'no.'" Kaydu emphasized her reply with the point of her sword. "Not even in Edris market."

"No harm meant." The vendor tucked her hands into her front pocket to show she meant no harm but gave their party a measuring look. As they walked away, Llesho heard a curse at his back. "Everything's for sale at Edris market," the woman muttered when he turned around.

"Not today." As she led them away from the greedy vendor, Kaydu nudged a warning at the monkey. Veteran of many battles and no few spy missions of his own, Little Brother quickly ducked out of sight, sacrificing his curiosity for safety.

They went on in silence for a while, each occupied with his or her own thoughts. As they passed deeper into the market, however, Llesho noticed many empty stalls. The lingering odors of horse sweat or cow dung attested to the presence of the larger animals somewhere in the building.

"The auction block is down here, at the center of this market," Kaydu led them forward until they could follow the sounds of the caller for themselves.

The missing cattle were being paraded around a sawdust-covered corral with bids following them through their paces. A tall man made even taller by his high turban was keeping a reckoning by turning down the brightly colored bits of paper that he had slipped between his fingers. A sign posted on a nearby column had a painted word on it in a script Llesho didn't recognize. The roughly drawn outline of a horse beside the word made clear to outlanders what came next. In the distance, he heard the heartbroken wail of a child and knew with a chill in his heart that the slave auction would follow soon after.

Kaydu flinched at the sound, but she didn't let any of her distaste show in her voice. "We can sell the horses here," she said, "and probably our saddles and tack as well."

Without horses, they had to lighten their load to what they could carry on their own backs. Like the others, Llesho went through his pack, gathering the basics of survival from his gear. Unlike them, he also drew out the strange gifts that he had brought with him through his travels.

If all went well they'd have money for passage by boat soon enough and be on their way. By putting their horses up for auction, however, they exposed themselves to more public attention than he would have liked. Master Markko's spies or any of their enemies might recognize them. They could find themselves fighting a pitched battle in the marketplace. Or they might be followed and set upon in some rat-infested alley on the way to the docks. He trusted his cadre to win such a contest, but would rather not put it to the test.

And they still hadn't found Tayy. "I don't trust this place," he said.

Hmishi darted quick glances around them as he emptied his own pack. "Neither do I."

"We're bound to call attention to ourselves if we stay together." They still wore the uniforms of young cadets out to see the world that they had chosen as their disguise, which worked well enough on the road. Their presence in the market would seem a greater curiosity and gossip had a way of traveling faster than a dream-walk. Llesho cast a nervous look at the buyers and sellers gathered around the corral. Any one of them might be a spy.

"It's time we split up and took the measure of this place," Kaydu agreed. "I'll need someone to help me with the horses and the tack." She singled out Bixei for the task. "The rest of you, pair up and scout out the exits. Note where the aisles are blocked and where we'll find good cover if we need it."

"We aren't likely to find the Harnish prince here, since the pirates don't sell anyone they can put to the oar." Bixei had started to gather the abandoned gear together. He dropped a saddle on the heap as if to emphasize his words.

"But they'll know in the stalls if the red trousers have been buying or selling in Edris." Kaydu must mean pirates by that, Llesho figured, though he hadn't heard the term before. She went on with her instructions, "Ask for news of work for a young soldier. Say you'll work for passage to Pontus—that should draw out any news of pirates.

Lling and Hmishi worked best together as a pair, so Llesho chose Stipes to accompany him. Bixei puffed up his chest with pride for his partner.

Stipes himself seemed less than gratified with the honor.

"You might trust one of the others more to watch your back, two eyes being better than one." As a reminder, he touched a hesitant finger to the eye patch over the empty socket.

Stipes had lost an eye in battle, but he saw as much with the one remaining to him as most men did with two. In spite of his injury, he remained an able soldier and Llesho refused his offer to stand down with a firm shake of his head.

"We have all survived the same number of battles, and each with our own injuries. I'll trust to your instincts—and to your one eye for danger—as quickly as to anyone's."

"If you see trouble, don't take it on by yourself," Kaydu insisted, including them all in her glance. "Find us, and we'll handle it together."

The reminder that he didn't guard the husband of the Great Goddess alone seemed to reassure Stipes, who straighted his shoulders to a military correctness. "Best get on with it, then," he accepted the task, and with that they broke up, each to his or her own assignment.

Chapter Twelve

THE SOUTH Market traded only in livestock, but that they had in plenty and with a variety of sizes and shapes that Llesho had never seen collected in one place before. Horses and cattle had gathered at the auction block, but camels, with one hump or two, restively pulling against their tethers still spat disgusting gobs as they passed. There were cages with chickens for roasting and roosters for fighting, each in a rainbow of colors. Dogs and sheep and strange small lizards sold alongside hummingbird tongues and monkeys considered a delicacy for the sweetness of their brains. Llesho shivered, thinking of Little Brother.

Here and there they paused to ask about work, but each time they met with a shake of the head and another rant about the hardness of the times. Then, in a stall filled with baskets of rabbits, a woman answered their questions with a buyer's eye. "No work," she said, "at least not the paying kind." She dismissed Stipes with scarcely a glance, but examined Llesho with more interest. "I know as some might be looking for a strong back, if a coin or two would see a bed under you at nightfall."

He'd seen that look in the slave markets and it made his skin crawl. It was the first hint of pirates, however.

"I think I'll keep my eye open for more honest coin," he answered with a sneer appropriate to the suggestion. It would look far too suspicious if he asked for information himself, but

Stipes could do it. He dropped back a pace so that Stipes blocked her view and pinched him hard on the arm.

The guardsman twitched, but his training kept him from reacting more obviously. "Where would a man look if he wanted to do a little buying or selling in that market?" He didn't sound enthused about the prospect, but Llesho did a fair job of acting out his outrage at the suggestion.

"And who did you plan to offer in exchange for a plate of meat?"

"I meant nothing by it," Stipes assured him, almost as good at the part as Llesho.

The vendor cackled and pointed a thumb toward the corner most deeply hidden in shadows. "Ask the doorman at the Gate of Despair." Another joke, or perhaps no joke at all, which she found more humorous than otherwise.

She'd given him an idea, though. As soon as they were out of sight of her little shop, he pulled Stipes into an empty stall smelling of large animals. The sides were high and made of wide planks with only the narrowest of chinks between them. With Stipes blocking the front, no one could see him and he quickly stripped off his military coat and trousers.

"What are you doing?"

"Sell these for me," he answered, holding out his uniform and his pack, all except for the Goddess' pearls, and the gifts he had carried since Farshore Province. "Or trade them for a pair of farmer's drawers, since we are in the wrong market for even road-worn finery."

"You're not making plans behind Captain Kaydu's back, are you, Holy Excellence?" Stipes whispered with a pointed stress on his title; kings were supposed to weigh their actions.

"No one else has any plan at all for getting Prince Tayy back!" Llesho knew he had to be careful. Lord Yueh had taken Stipes when the rest of them had gone to Farshore. He'd come to be a part of the cadre later, as Bixei's companion, and had always doubted his position among them. The Lady SienMa hadn't chosen him for the task, after all. The trick would be to win his cooperation without bruising his soul, but they didn't have time for discussion and debate. Even now, the pirates might escape them.

"It's my fault this happened." And it felt like ice in his belly when he thought about what he'd said that drove Tayy into such danger. "I have to fix it, but I need your help to do it. I'm not asking you to keep a secret from Bixei or the others. In fact, I'm going to need you to tell them. But right now we need to hurry."

Stipes looked at him with pleading in his one remaining eye, as if that alone might soften Llesho's resolve. Finally, with a defeated sigh, he gave in. "What do you want me to do?"

"I need a better disguise. I'll explain when you get back."

Shaking his head, Stipes made his way back out into the market while Llesho hid himself in the straw. He had only a few moments to wait, however. Stipes was back almost before he settled himself.

"They thought I was a black crow who had stripped the uniforms off the dead on some battlefield," he grumbled, dropping into his purse the few small coins he had made on the deal. "I could have traded all our uniforms and made a list for next time!"

Llesho took the farmer's pants. They fit as well as such things ever do, which he realized wasn't very well at all. At least Stipes' garb could pass for that of a retired fighter turned farmer. "I suppose it's the eye patch. Most fighters who have lost an eye are happy to retire to their rocking chairs, trading stories instead of blows"

"More sense they," Stipes muttered as he handed over the shirt. "Now, however, you said you would tell me the plan."

"Thank you." Llesho's head popped through the neck of his secondhand farmer's shirt. "And, yes, I will.

"The rabbit-vendor gave me the idea, actually," he explained as he worked his arms through the sleeves. "The 'Gate of Despair' she mentioned must mark the slave market. She thought that you might sell me there for the price of a night's sleep."

"I won't," Stipes cut off that direction with a sharp slicing motion of his hand. "I know you are smarter than I am, and higher above me than the sky above the sea. How can one as low as me pretend to sell you in the marketplace!"

"Not pretend, Stipes. It won't work unless it's true. You will sell me to the pirates who will in turn take me to their ship. When they move, follow them until you find out what ship we move out on and where they are going. Then you go back and tell Kaydu, who will lead the charge to rescue us. Simple."

"Begging your pardon, Holy Excellence, but that's the stupidest idea I ever heard!" Stipes managed to sound like he was shouting even though he kept his voice below a whisper. It cost him, though, as the vein pulsing at his forehead attested. "It's bad enough we've lost one prince. How will I explain to Bixei and Kaydu, let alone Hmishi and Lling, that I've lost the other one to the same damned pirates!"

"Does anybody else have a better plan?"

"Yes! You can sell me instead. The cadre can rescue me more easily than you, since I don't have a magician trying to make me his prisoner at every turn, and you will stay safe among your guardsmen. You're the one who knows the plan anyway— they'll need you to lead the rescue."

"It won't work." Llesho shook his head, determined. "How long can you hold your breath underwater?" Stipes shrugged a shoulder. It wasn't something a gladiator or a soldier was often called on to do. But he'd trained on Pearl Island and knew about the pearl divers well enough that Llesho's next words came as no surprise: "It has to be a Thebin."

"You're not the only Thebin on this quest, though. Hmishi could do the same, right? Or Lling. Either one is Thebin."

And expendable like himself. He didn't say it, but Llesho saw it in the set of his guardsman's jaw and the spark of hope in his eye. Unfortunately, that wouldn't work either.

"It has to be me. Tayy won't take orders from anybody else."

"I have a feeling I don't want to know this," Stipes said, "but what do you want him to do?"

"When the time comes, he'll have to jump overboard. You'll be waiting to rescue us in the boat that Kaydu's supposed to hire."

"I was right, that's a horrible plan."

"I've heard better myself on occasion," Llesho admitted. He didn't much like it, he just couldn't think of anything else and, as he pointed out again, "No one else has any plan at all."

"They died like flies caught in honey when battle took them into the Onga River," Stipes remembered. "Not a one of them could swim. Do you think Prince Tayyichiut will throw himself into the sea even for you?"

"I'll find a way to get him in the water." He'd figure out that part later. First, Llesho had to find him. He headed for the shadows where the Gate of Despair was waiting.

Stipes, however, wasn't finished. "How are you going to keep the others from noticing their king on the auction block?"

"Not the auction. We'd have no control over who bids or who wins. No, we find the pirate captain and make a private deal." He could handle a private sale, had played that part before with Emperor Shou. His courage failed him at the thought of the auction block, however. He couldn't live through that again. This way had to work. "You can say that you don't like the way your wife looks at me so it's not enough to get rid of me, you want me far away. Or that I tried to escape and the sea will prove harder to run away from."

Stipes didn't like it. Now that he'd he agreed, however, he had suggestions of his own. "If you are seen to follow me through the market untethered I can hardly try to sell you cheap because you tried to run away." He tugged the leather belt from his waist and tied a loop in it that he slipped over Llesho's head. "That should convince the customer." He tugged the knot up snug against Llesho's throat, then slung his own pack at him. "Until the money changes hands, they'll expect you to carry the burdens."

Llesho sucked in a quick breath, fighting panic and the grim foreboding that he wouldn't escape the noose as easily as his plan dictated. Necessary anyway, he reminded himself. He couldn't ask the khan for help in the coming battle for Kungol if he lost his nephew to the pirates. That wasn't his real reason, of course. Even if it gained him nothing but the life of his comrade, he couldn't leave Tayy to that fate. But it seemed more kinglike to back the plan with a political motive. "Let's go."

Stipes gave him a last worried frown. "I have a bad feeling about this," he said.

"Give me choices," Llesho countered.

As he knew, there were none. Stipes took up the end of the tether and led him by a roundabout path through the market to the corner where slave merchants had their holding pens.

In the distance the auctioneer called for the horses in a language very like Thebin. "Get a good price," he muttered, his mind blessedly on Kaydu and the horses as he followed Stipes through the marketplace. "This plan doesn't work without a boat."

Underwater, he could breath into Tayy's mouth long enough to convince the pirates they had both drowned. But they'd be out of reach of shore. Without a boat to rescue them, he and Tayy both would die at the oar.

It wasn't as bad as he'd thought it would be, Llesho decided. It was worse. The last time he'd tried this particular ruse, Shou had accompanied him to the market in the guise of a jaded merchant looking to buy slaves rather than sell him. He hadn't known Shou for the emperor back then, but he'd had the comfort of knowing the man for a general of the Imperial Guard should the situation get out of hand. It had, of course, and he'd nearly died in the battle that followed in the streets of the imperial city. But he hadn't had to worry about Shou bending to the pressure of a slave trader intent on separating him from the Thebin boy he claimed as his property. This time the plan called for Llesho's pretended owner not to buy the freedom of his brothers but to sell him into hard labor.

He followed Stipes at the limit of the leather belt tied around his neck as he circled in on the shadowy quarter of the market. There they found a section separated from the rest by a tall privacy shield of woven lathing.

They didn't dare to exchange even a word of encouragement as they hunted out the gate that would gain them entrance to the slave pens beyond. Stipes tugged on the leather thong and glowered at him with a sharp word of warning to make the masquerade more convincing.

"Hurry up there, before the trading is done. You were quick enough under my wife's skirts when I was away at market." He started grumbling low enough that only those nearest them could hear his words. Gradually, he raised his voice as if overcome with anger, until he ended at a near roar, "At the oar or with a stone around your neck, you are for the sea tonight!"

Rude snickers followed them, but Stipes merely glared and flailed his arm in a pantomime of rage. "Laugh all you want, jackasses, all of you. Then ask yourself who is sneaking into your wife's chamber while you're here making a joke of an honest man!"

Stipes pushed through and presented himself at the Gate of Despair, a simple construction of wicker and rice paper covered everywhere with the images of wailing bodies in torment. The gate stood open, a plump guard with dead flat eyes sitting cross-legged on a dusty carpet with his back against the fence post.

"Wishing to sell." Dragging Llesho forward by the noose around his neck, Stipes showed him to the gatekeeper.

The man didn't let him in at once but set down the stick that he'd been using to scratch under his wrapped head covering. He rose ponderously to his feet and shook out his thin linen coat over voluminous pants. Taking Llesho's jaw in his hand he looked deep into his eyes, as if he could read his mind, or his soul, through them.

"He's very frightened," was his conclusion. Not a hard reach, Llesho thought, though the man added the observation, "Caught in the wild, I take it—" a captive taken from his village or clan, that meant, "—and not born under the yoke."

Stipes shrugged. "Don't know where he came from. Needed help with the farm and his price was cheap. He tried to run once or twice, but I beat him and he seemed to settle in. Turns out he wasn't so cheap, now that he's cost me a wife, but what can you do?" Llesho had accumulated plenty of scars in his short life. He wondered how many of them would pass for the discipline of a harsh master, but Stipes had thought of that.

"He'd been cut up a bit when I got him. Healed and all—

hasn't seemed to affect his heavy lifting or bending to the plow, but he doesn't exactly put himself out for his master." And Llesho hoped the calluses on his hands would support that lie with the gatekeeper, who might not be a guard after all, but something else entirely.

The man turned his attention from Llesho's face to his hands, turning them over and inspecting both the fronts and the backs. "Too small for my use, I'm afraid." He dismissed Llesho with a flutter of manicured fingers. "Will you be putting him to the block?"

"Not any chance of that." Stipes shook his head, emphatically. "I don't want him washing up at my door ever again. Private sale I'm looking for, someone just passing through on their way back where they came from. As far from here as a boat can take a man."

The merchant, as it now seemed, released Llesho's hands with no comment about the pattern of his calluses, but heaved a sigh. "Not much market in that," he said. "Most who come in before a voyage are bent on ridding themselves of their excess baggage, not buying for the trip. Still, if you don't care what price you get, you might find what you're looking for inside. The red trousers came in a little while ago and they are always looking for muscle. He doesn't have much of that in the way they measure a fighter in the ring."

A hand wrapped around Llesho's upper arm demonstrated his point. While his fingers did not meet his thumb, they came closer than they ought for an arm with any power in it. As a slave, Llesho had no status to speak, and Stipes kept quiet about his training as a gladiator. He had an eye for a different buyer, which the slaver seemed to understand.

"He seems wiry and strong for all that if you're looking to put him to the oar. They won't pay much, but you'll get something for him, and of course the satisfaction of knowing he won't be sniffing under skirts any time soon."

Their story had made it clear that they had come from the countryside, and the merchant or guard gestured them forward as a host might. "This is the market just for working stock," he called after them with a wave of his hand to take in the whole building. He talked equally of the human and four-legged kind. "Quality trade you'll find with the luxury items across the square."

Stipes gave a knowing nod to signal his understanding but declined the invitation. "We have women at home," he told the man, "but I would take a boy in trade to do the chores of this one. Do you know if the red trousers have brought in any such?"

"Maybe, but I wouldn't want you to speak ill of this market in your town, sir. I would be cautious of that trade and take my money to a local vendor who hasn't put as much use on any boy you wish for labor."

The red trousers, who Llesho thought must be the pirates, weren't likely to sell the strong young men they seized to row their ships. A slave near his own age offered for sale must already have broken under the oar. He'd be no use for heavy labor of any kind. With a companionable nod that he would heed the warning, Stipes tugged Llesho after him into the slave market.

The auction would take place in the same corral where Kaydu and their companions were selling the horses, but the slave market sheltered an array of booths and corrals like the ones they had seen filled with lesser creatures on the outside of the Gate of Despair. Each merchant displayed his wares, shouting out his trade to drum up interest for auction or to complete early private sales. A trader in an elaborate headdress of many-colored scarves braided and wound into a tall turban with ribbons hanging down his back displayed his human merchandise in mating pairs crouching in cages too low for them to stand and too narrow for them to sit.

Another in stark white from his tall round cap to his slippered feet showed half a dozen children with glazed expressions in their eyes tied by ropes to the support post of a shadowed booth. Llesho wondered if he read the sign above their heads correctly. The script was very like Thebin, but its advertisement, "for religious purposes," made no sense.

Or he hoped it made no sense. Bolghai the shaman had sacrificed sheep and horses to fuel the khan's pyre, and his burrow had been littered with the skulls of small animals. Without con-

sciously willing it, he moved toward the booth with some half-
formed idea of rescuing the innocent victims of this fearful
place, but a warning tug at the noose around his neck pulled
him up short. "He's buying, not selling," Stipes explained
under cover of a warning glower. "It's a rescue mission of sorts.
The priests pay a small sum for them and raise them in the
mission school. They'll do more praying than a free man would
put up with, but they stopped feeding children to the burning
god long ago."

Llesho wondered how he knew, but a slave didn't ask questions, so he kept his mouth shut and his face blank. As they
passed still more vendors with their human misery huddled in
the backs of stalls or shivering cattle pens, Llesho heard a familiar accent in the crowd. Harnish, from the South. When he
looked around him, he saw that they had passed into a corner
of the market dominated by the raiders. In a smooth glide honed
with long practice Llesho's hand went to his sword, remembering too late that he came unarmed to the market as a farmhand
and not a soldier. Quickly, he shifted his hand to rub at his hip
with an aggrieved glare at Stipes, who marched ahead of him.
With luck, any who had seen the move would mistake it for
nursing the ache of a beating.

"Cut out the auctioneer's fee; you won't do as well if you
wait," Llesho heard a customer say, pointing out the flaws in a
trembling man of middle years with no flesh on his bones to
speak of.

"You're right." The raider sized up the huddled slaves
crowded in the pen he guarded. "Maybe you'd like to take his
place."

The customer drew back in horror and departed at speed
for the more "civilized" corners of the market while the raider
laughed at his back. "I've sold his kind before—" The slaver
had caught sight of Llesho and followed the noose back to
where the belt ended in Stipes' hand. He swaggered over with
a gait calculated to set the long hair of his murdered victims
swaying on the scalps sewn to his shirtfront and planted his
gruesomely decorated chest in Llesho's face. "This isn't the best

market for his kind, but I can get a good price for him if you're interested."

Llesho's hand squeezed into a futile fist at his side. With no sword, not even his Thebin knife, he had no chance against this walking horror from his nightmares. He would die before he ever reached his target and that would put an end to their plan to rescue the Qubal prince from a slower death at the oar. It was just the memories that kept his mind leaping like a jerboa to act on his most fatal desires.

Stipes was shaking his head in a friendly but determined way, as if it didn't matter that this man wore the skin and hair of his victims on his shirt. "This one's going on a sea cruise." He laughed as if he'd made a witty joke and pulled the noose tight when Llesho didn't do the same. "Aren't you, boy? A sea cruise, courtesy of old Red Trousers, hahaha!"

Llesho thought he was starting to enjoy the part a little too much, but even the raider wasn't ready to contest with pirates for a scrawny Thebin slave boy.

"If you change your mind, we will be here until the end of business tonight, but you'll get a better deal in trade before the auction starts."

"I'll keep that in mind," Stipes promised, and resumed his search for the pirates.

"We must be close," he muttered. "We're running out of places to look."

Llesho heard the words, but they didn't come together to make sense in his mind. In the background, the cries of children rose above the murmuring roar of commerce to die abruptly again. Lost in his past, he remembered his own raw voice worn to silence on the Long March, so that he made no sound in the pens at all. The captain of the slavers had put his keepers on notice: "Shut him up, or I'll cut his throat."

The woman who carried him had handed him over to a man who had once been a soldier. That one had covered his mouth and his nose until, unconscious, he made no noise. After that, when he cried, the man always found them, and with his face wiped clean of feeling, would cradle Llesho in his arms and cover his face until, so near death that he had passed beyond the care of his mortal existence, he did not weep. Llesho had been a wise child, however. It hadn't taken long to learn not to cry at all.

So entangled had he become in the horrors of his past that he didn't realize they'd come to a halt in front of a corral with a small kiosk in its center. A small group of boys and men stood or sat at the limit of their bonds around a tall post set like a guardsman in front of the kiosk. "Is he touched in the head?" A woman reached out with a horny hand and grabbed him by the shoulder. With a hard shake, as if to rouse him to his senses, she added a caution, "If he is given to fits, we can't have him among the oars."

"No fits," Stipes answered the question for him as his owner had the right to do. "But he's slow-witted."

Well, he had to be pretty stupid to come up with this plan, Llesho agreed. The slave dealer had skin like leather from the sun and the harsh winds on the water, and her lips were stained bright red from the nuts she chewed while she talked. A scarf aswirl in bright and clashing colors did a poor job at holding back her hair, a mix of brown and gray that seemed to be making a brave effort to escape the knot tied at the nape of her neck. She might have been any seafaring short-hauler from the clothes that any passerby could see. Llesho knew she was a pirate, however, because he was looking down as suited a humble slave. Beneath her homely skirts peeked satin cuffs where wide trousers with red-and-yellow stripes were gathered in tight above her greasy slippers.

He had a feeling this one knew how to wield the short curved knife she wore at her hip and maybe practiced with it on slave boys who were a bit dull-witted. Did Kaydu knew that women roamed the Marmer Sea as pirates? His mind skittered away, down its own odd trails as it often did in times of peril. He tried to imagine his captain in red-striped trousers, swarming the side of a fat freight hauler. It scared him that the image came so quickly and fit so well.

"He doesn't look very strong." With the back of her wrist she wiped a trail of ruby-colored drool from her lip and then, like the merchant at the gate, she took his hands in hers. Turning them to look at his knuckles and back again, she ran rough fingertips over the calluses on his palms.

"He's stronger than he looks," Stipes bargained. "It's the southern blood, off the mountains, that makes him look so scrawny, but his kind have a name for endurance."

"Looks like he's done a day's work of some kind," she agreed, and released his hands. Llesho wondered if she recognized his skill with weapons in the pattern of his palm and the ridges on the side of his hand, the horn on his fingertips and knuckles so very like her own, but she said nothing of it.

"Take off his shirt."

That drew Llesho's head up, the spark of resistance in the tilt of his chin which he had enough sense of self-preservation to point at her out of a very unkingly slouch. She had a sharp eye, and he had a feeling that she'd read the scars on his body like a map of his battles even if she hadn't credited the calluses for what they were.

The pirate took his defensive bristling for a different meaning, however, and snorted rudely out of an overlarge nose. "You're a bit old for that trade, boy." Without further explanation, she grabbed the hem of his shirt and pulled it over his head to slip down the leather belt that Stipes still kept a grip on.

Reflexively Llesho's hand came up to cover the scars on his chest. He didn't want anyone to see, didn't want the evidence of what had happened to him out there for the world to make its own conclusions about him. The pirate wasn't giving him a choice, though. In front of anyone who traversed that part of the slave market she tugged his arm down. Tapping her foot thoughtfully, she examined him like a butcher assessing his value on the hoof.

"Somebody did a clean job on that arrowhead." She poked at the scar on his shoulder. "Odd, in the front though." She turned him around, inspected his back. "You'd think a running slave would have his scars here—" She swept a hand across his back, where he carried just a few light marks from his days in slavery. The worst of it had come in Markko's workroom and didn't show on the outside.

"Neighbors helped round him up. The local constable caught him in an ambush."

The pirate nodded, accepting that for an answer. "I'm surprised you didn't just leave it."

"He would have been useless for the work. My wife had some skill with herbs and we thought to save the price of a replacement." Stipes gave a hunched shrug, indicating much that wasn't true. Llesho kept his mouth shut while the pirate peered over his shoulder with a knowing wink.

"Now this—" She turned Llesho around again, trailed a callused finger down the scar over his heart, his belly.

The marks told a story, of the claws of a giant bird that was no bird at all but the magician, Master Markko, tearing him open on the steps of the Temple of the Seven Mortal Gods. But he had no intention of recounting the tale for pirates.

"Does it pull much?"

"Hardly ever," he lied, the first words he'd spoken in the bargaining. He couldn't tell whether she believed him, but she signed away the evil eye with casual superstition.

"He reeks of dragons."

"Not dragons, goodwife, but the hunting eagle of a great lord, who mistook the boy working in the fields for a coney stealing grain. The lord feared for the safety of his bird and would not call it off until it had satisfied its rage on the boy. But he healed well, and is as strong as he ever was."

"And afforded your goodwife another opportunity to act the tender nurse," she mused, as if his words had confirmed something she had already guessed. "Been covering himself in his master's feathers, has he, and cockle-doodle-do-ing in the henhouse? He doubtless appealed to her sympathy. I suppose that explains why you'd like to rid yourself of him.

"Very well," she decided. From a purse that hung from the scabbard of her sword she drew half a dozen coppers. It seemed too low a price.

He had no experience with the buying and selling side of slavery, having only been on the bought and sold side when a small and shattered child, but Llesho knew the price was low enough to make her suspicious if Stipes didn't haggle. Fortunately, Stipes had his story ready.

"Not so fast, now. I don't know much about city ways, and so I don't know to haggle over the price for boys in the marketplace. But this one has already cost me more than he's worth in trade. So I'll take your coppers, if you make as part of the bargain that he is gone from this port by morning, and he never sets foot on dry land again."

Llesho thought that was a bit strong, but the pirate shook her head as if the agreement Stipes demanded made a sorry kind of sense for the cuckolded farmer he pretended to be. "All right. He's young for the work and not likely to survive past the first storm anyway, but he's cheap enough. You've got your bargain. I claim him bought and paid for the Bayerenin."

Llesho figured that must be the local name for the pirates. He was already thinking ahead to the next step in his plan. He scarcely noticed when the pirate stuck out her fat tongue and licked a bright red streak across her thumb. When she pressed the sticky thumb to his breast, right above the arrow scar, he twitched away in surprise.

"None of that, boy." She tightened the noose threateningly around his neck. "You've got my mark on you now. I will not be best pleased if I lose my six coins for nothing, but the market guards have little care for that. They will kill you if you try to run and present me with the carcass when they are done."

Stipes took a step with mayhem in his eyes, which would put them back to where they were when they had begun the search for Prince Tayy, but this time without a plan. So Llesho bent his leg and groveled in the dust at her feet.

"Sorry," he croaked out of his constricted throat, and she let up on the noose with a righteous sniff.

"As you should be."

When it seemed that he might survive long enough to reach the sea, Stipes took up both his and Llesho's packs, and turned to leave.

Chapter Thirteen

DON'T GO! As if he heard the unspoken words, Stipes turned around one last time. The pirate woman read it as easily as Llesho did.

"Too late now, young farmer." She spat a fat red gob of slime onto the sawdust covered floor to emphasize her point. "Coin has changed hands, the deal is done. I can maybe trade you an old fellow for him, or a girl, but that's only because I'm a good-hearted soul and hate to see a customer go away dissatisfied."

Hate to strangle the merchandise when you can sell it, Llesho thought, but he dropped his gaze to the sawdust lest the evidence of his fear sway Stipes into doing something foolhardy.

"What's done is done," Stipes agreed, and with a heavy tread, he walked away.

Do something foolhardy. Get me out of this. Tayy must be thinking the same, with less hope, Llesho thought, and reminded himself that Stipes wouldn't be far off. He knew the plan and he'd follow the pirates. Kaydu needed to know where they had taken him; not, however, before he found Prince Tayy-ichiut.

"I don't suppose you've been fed or watered since morning," the pirate muttered under her breath. It was clear she was talking to herself and not to Llesho. She took up the belt that Stipes had looped around his neck and tugged on it to get his attention.

"Come on. No food; food gives strength and strength gives a new slave ideas. But I can find a drop of water to keep you on your pins at least until we reach home. Then you can have something to eat, and all the ideas you want for whatever good they will do you." She laughed then, and though she had said nothing of ships and the sea, Llesho knew the joke all right. With any luck at all they would turn the punch line back on the pirates. But he kept his expression humble and managed a quiver in his chin.

"Don't lay it on too thick; there's none but me to see it, boy. Keep it for a more gullible audience. You're saucy enough when it suits you, I reckon."

Llesho didn't say anything, which was what she expected. "Drink, and don't make trouble. I'll wring your neck and mourn the loss of six pennies if you give me any trouble."

"Yes, ma'am." He took the cup and drank, then let her lead him to the post where she tied him among the handful of young men who sagged dispiritedly around it. They gave him an incurious glance but said nothing. Sliding his back down the pole, Llesho sat in the way of the pearl divers taking their rest in the shade of a palm tree on Pearl Island, letting none of his time in combat show in his posture. The woman had made it clear that the pirates kept a watch for slaves plotting together, and he didn't want to give them a reason to separate him from Tayy in the boats. In fact, he decided, it would be best to pretend hostility when they met again. What better cure for escape plans than distrust? He refused to consider that they might not be the same pirates, or they might not put him to oar on the same ship.

"Alph!"

Called by the pirate's sharp cry, a man with a wide-sashed coat over his pirate pants bustled out of the kiosk at the center of the corral. A hand of women trailed behind him on a lead. The pirate woman gave him a nod of greeting and took the lead. "Keep the boys quiet while I'm gone," she said, and hauled on the rope to set the women in motion. "It shouldn't take long to dispose of these, and then we head for home." None of them were young enough or fresh enough to sell for wives in the luxury market, but they'd go for washerwomen or cooks, perhaps. In spite of their weeping they'd been fortunate to survive their encounter with pirates at all.

The man with the coat over his pirate garb nodded an acknowledgment. Like his companion, he said nothing to give away their destination or their identity. Anyone might know, however, who thought to look down at the ankles of their yellow-and-scarlet pants.

Left alone with the slaves destined for the oar, he sat on a stool and bounced the flat of a scimitar against his knee as a warning. When one of their number wandered too close to the end of his tether, their guard snarled threateningly with a yawn in his voice. Even here on land he expected no resistance. At sea, Tayy's rescue from within the ranks of the slaves themselves would come as a complete surprise. Or so Llesho hoped. But Tayy wasn't anywhere in the corral, and he hunkered in on himself, saving his energy for the night ahead.

The pirate woman came back as the market was closing up for the day.

"About time, Moll," her companion grumbled. "A man needs some relief from time to time."

"Tie a knot in it," she answered him back. One way or another, she'd rid herself of the women she'd left with, bringing back one man about Bixei's age but with a darker tan to his skin and a sneakier look around his eyes. "It will have to wait until we reach the docks."

Instead of putting the new man into the corral, she hauled on the ropes and thongs that bound her earlier purchases, tying them together in a line that her whining cohort shoved into order. Llesho found himself toward the middle, tied by the neck and one ankle far too close to a much taller man in front and with another tied up close behind him.

"Left!" Alph the pirate called the cadence and Llesho tried to raise his foot at the same time as the man in front, put it down to the same rhythm. He was the only one among them who had gladiator training, however, and had learned to match the rhythm of an opponent. Their line was soon tangled again, since most of the slaves didn't know what a "left" was.

"This one," Llesho gasped out, tapping the left instep of the man who'd been to his rear a moment before. Then he'd lifted his right foot and knocked Llesho and himself down with it. All along the line nooses had yanked tight around the slaves' necks, and they all pulled at their bonds as they struggled to breath.

"Fools!" The pirate, Moll, ranged up and down their sorry line, clipping at this one and that one with a shortprod meant as a reminder and not punishment. They had to be fit to work at the end of the day.

This time, when Alph called out the cadence, "Left!" they all managed to lift the same foot, if not at the same time. The line was learning to work together. Llesho recognized the method if not this exact version of it.

Still, panic threatened to rob him of the breath he needed to walk. He couldn't, couldn't, do the Long March again. Better to lie down and die where he stood. He considered doing just that, falling to the pavement and letting Moll mourn the loss of six small coins while she strangled him.

But ahead he heard the sound of the sea lapping against the stone of the wharf and the gentle slap of wavelets against the wooden prows of boats. Once or twice he caught a glimpse of Stipes matching their pace in the shadows. The pirates had no reason to suspect a plot, however, and paid no attention to what might be following. Alph called them to a halt and lined them up along the stone edge of the wharf. Looking down onto the dark water gentled to a soothing lap against the piers and jetties, Llesho wondered if they were supposed to swim out to the pirate vessels, but Alph shifted his coat and his trousers and let a bright yellow stream arch out into the water below.

"Don't take all day about it," he ordered the men and boys who stared from the pirate to the waiting sea.

In his long travels, Llesho had learned never to waste an opportunity to eat, sleep, or relieve himself on the march, and Alph didn't have to make the suggestion twice. Before long there were six streams arching into the night. And soon, they were done watering the sea and had settled their clothes again.

Moll had faded into the shadows while all of this was going on. As they prepared to march again, she reappeared, more impatient than ever with her prod and her cursing. "Come on, you lubbers! What do you think this is, a picnic? We sail on the falling tide if we ever reach the ship!" In fact they had only to walk a hundred more paces to reach their destination, a ship far larger than he'd thought any pirate ship to be. And this one had a gangplank resting on the shore with a name, *Guiding Star,* on an arch above the landing.

"Property for my master on the Islands," Moll called out to the customs official standing under the arch. Not a pirate ship, then. He doubted they'd grown so bold, even in Edris. The pirate in disguise handed over a sheaf of papers and drew the new slaves forward, one by one, to have the thumbmark on chest or arm or shoulder checked against the one that filled the official circle in the documents. All legal, and Llesho wanted to kill somebody for it, to tear the market down and put it to the flame. The customs official, knowing nothing of these thoughts of blood and murder, held the papers up to Llesho's breast and measured the prints one against the other.

"All watertight and seaworthy," the official handed back the papers and turned to his next customer as Moll led her property up the gangplank. They'd meet the raiders of the sea somewhere between Edris and the Islands.

Stipes had vanished, going back to find the cadre and report, he hoped. In the meantime it was down, down, into a hold with water ankle deep on the floor and the light from a single lamp to find their way. Moll stopped halfway down the ladder, leaving Alph to slosh through the bilge to a long beam set low to brace the hull of the ship. Into the beam were set metal shackles and the same hung from the rafters over their heads. The pirate grabbed a loose chain draped over the Y of an upright supporting the deck over their heads and used it to fasten the slaves to each other by a metal leg ring. Only the last of their line, the one closest to the hatch, did he shackle to the beam.

Prepared for a quick escape. Llesho figured they'd never

reach the Islands where the *Guiding Star* was heading, and Alph would only have one lock to deal with when they made their hasty exit. If the ship were breached in the hold, they'd all still drown, as they would if they hit the water so burdened with each other and the heavy chain. Most ships didn't sink, of course. The knowledge would have comforted him, except that he didn't think the pirates planned to off-load their cargo on land.

Then Alph was done with them and headed up the ladder after Moll. In his hand, he carried the lantern. Too soon, he had cleared the hatch, taking with him the last of the light. Above, hinges shrieked in rusted pain and the hatch slammed down with a crash of timbers meeting timbers. They were well below the waterline and so had no windows or vents for air or light. Llesho found himself in a dark more complete than he had ever known.

Not silence, though. They did not speak to each other, each as ill disposed to conversation as the next. But the soft sound of one man's prayer mingled with the sibilant curses of another and the moans and sobs of yet another. Llesho tucked his legs up tight under his chin and clasped his arms around his shins. *I will count the days of the season before I weep*, he bargained with himself. When he had counted his way around the seventy-seven days of summer, he made a new deal for the days of spring, and so on into winter.

Halfway to midwinter's day the boat lurched at its mooring and Llesho heard the shouted chant of sailors dragging in the lines. So they were on their way. Somewhere out in the night Tayy was pulling an oar under a sky thick with stars that offered him no hope but Llesho, who lay chained at the bottom of hell. For about the hundredth time since Alph had dumped them in the dark, he wondered what had possessed him to come up with such a stupid plan.

In spite of his terror, however, the exhaustion of the day and his almost-forgotten familiarity with the motion of the boat on the sea worked against him. He'd barely made it round to summer again when he lost his place in his count. Soon, to the rise and fall of the waves at his back, he fell asleep, only to wake again to the harsh thud of a boat ramming them amidship.

Another. Another. Llesho roused up to the shouts and sobs of his fellow slaves crying out in terror of being holed. The boats that had come alongside seemed to be nudging them along but were making no attempt to damage them, at least not yet. Pirates, Llesho figured, and unlikely to sink them while their own cargo rested in the bottom of the ship. Still, he huddled with the others in fear for his life and waited for a sign that they were rescued—from drowning, if not from the pirates—or left to die.

Confirmation of his guess came quickly. Above them, the hatch slid open with a heave. Sticking his head into the abyss, a stranger with a thick dark beard and his hair held up in a brightly colored turban held out a lamp to light the way. More pirates, their wide red-and-yellow pants billowing to the narrow cuffs at their ankles, started down the ladder. In the lead, Alph carried a scimitar between his teeth. One hand guided him down the ladder and in the other he carried a key.

By the dim light of the lantern, Llesho noticed that the newest of the slaves, the one Moll had brought back from her sale of the women, braced himself in a way Llesho recognized. He was going to attack the pirate and try to take the scimitar, which might have worked if Alph were alone, but would get them killed now.

Under cover of scrambling out of the way, he fell against the man and grabbed his arm with a muttered warning in Shannish, "If he drops that key, we will lie here until we die." Then he tried again, in the few words of Harnish he could string together. While pleading for Radimus' freedom he had learned the word for "shackles" and "release" but he couldn't be sure that he'd strung them together in a way that made sense. The man might not speak either language, but there was still Thebin to try. Llesho sucked in a breath. Before he could get out the words, however, he felt the tension leave the slave's body.

A slight nod, and the man gave him a thoughtful look, taking in more than Llesho wanted him to know. How another soldier in the mix affected his plan would take some thought. For the moment, the man had settled into a waiting mode. With any luck, Alph would never know how close they had all come to disaster.

The pirate had waited until they sorted out their apparent clumsy tangle before approaching, which he did with a grunt of distaste. On the open sea they had taken on more water—not enough to endanger the ship but too wet for most stored goods. Llesho figured that's why they put the human cargo down here. Human flesh took longer to rot than flour or salted fish. The shackles by which the lead slaver had tied them all to the keel beam was now underwater and Alph reached for it with his nose pinched and a snarl around the scimitar in his teeth. Finally, the key turned in the lock and the leg ring fell open.

Quick as that, he moved the scimitar to his hand, waving it at the ladder. "This way, or die with the ship," he said, and waded away.

Though free of the ship's beam, the slaves remained bound to each other. Llesho curbed his panic, knowing if they rushed the hatch they would tangle and maybe die down here. With all the self-control he could summon, therefore, he waited for the sorting out that set the last man into the hold first in the line that followed Alph up the ladder. It seemed like forever, but in moments they were out of the bottommost hold. Through another hatch they found themselves on the lower deck, a long gallery that had once been a gun deck. The guns were gone. Between the cradles, passengers with their belongings in sacks and bundles had marked out spaces in family groups. Now they huddled together, clutching at each other in terror.

"Pirates!" went the whisper through the *Guiding Star,* and already the red trousers were moving through the clustered knots of cowering passengers, roaring curses and waving their scimitars. They were on their way out of port and had no need of market slaves, but sorted out the men who might be useful at the oar.

As they went, they opened bundles and scattered property in a careless search for valuables, though they were finding little worth their effort on this deck. A little girl began to cry. Horrified, Llesho watched helplessly as a pirate snatched her from her parents by one leg and tossed her out a gun port. Chained as he was, he could do nothing to stop the rampage.

Alph ignored the looting but gathered the new captives as he went and led them all up the next ladder, where open sky and chaos greeted them. Under the white glow of Great Moon Lun, the crew of the ship had closed in hand-to-hand combat with the overwhelming forces of the pirates. A dozen or more small galleys surrounded the larger but less agile *Guiding Star*. The merchant sailors did not give quarter easily but fought across a deck washed red with the blood of pirates and seamen alike. Metal clashed against metal to the cries of the wounded and the gurgles of the dying.

Smoke that began as a trickling irritation at the back of Llesho's nose soon billowed over the deck in dense black clouds. He'd fought fire before and knew the devastation the flames could wreak in just a short time. If he were going to die, he preferred the sea to the flames. Better not to die at all, though, and Alph kept them moving in spite of the panic of the slaves and the carnage around them. Llesho crouched low under the smoke and followed as quickly as the boy in front of him could move.

Then the dead weight of a murdered seaman crashed into them. A single pass of a scimitar had severed his head from his neck, which bled out the last beating of his heart in great squirting gouts over the chained slaves. The boy ahead of Llesho stopped with a horrible scream, his bloody hands raised as if to cover his eyes until he noticed what they were covered in. Then he froze, pale as Great Moon-Lun herself.

"Come on!" Alph had continued moving and Llesho gave the panicked boy a shove before they were all strangled by the chains that linked them neck to neck. "Stay down and stay moving or you'll wind up like that sailor!"

He didn't know if the words sank in, but his hand on the boy's arm seemed to calm him enough to follow where he was led. Llesho got him moving, realized the new man had done the same behind him. Keeping low and skirting the worst of the fighting, they scurried across the slippery deck. A thick rope with knots tied at regular intervals served as a ladder down to the pirate boats. With one leg over the side, Llesho scanned the deck littered with dead.

When he'd been imagining his plan, the pirates had taken them down to the docks and piled them into their own boats and rowed them out to sea. But the city was full of guards and customs officials who would seize the small boats and put them all in prison if they came openly to port. As with most of the plans that had brought him across half the known world, this had been almost a good one. The trickster always struck between the details, however. As if thinking of the old proverb could call up what it spoke of, a familiar voice called out of the gray mist.

"Ahoy, there, get those boys into the boat before the fleet sees the smoke and comes calling!"

Master Den, in the wide striped trousers of a pirate and a sash tied around his naked head, strode toward them with with a gleaming sword flashing in his hand. When he drew closer, Llesho saw that he wore a gold ring threaded through a hole in the side of his nose.

"Down you go, boy, by ladder or by air. Unless you can fly, I'd start climbing." Not a flicker of a lash gave a clue that the huge figure was anything but what he seemed—a giant among pirates—or that he recognized Llesho.

"We have to help put out the fire!" Llesho called to him. Flames were leaping into the sky from amidships, and already smoke curled from just above the waterline.

"The fire will go out on its own soon enough," Master Den the pirate said, as if this were an obvious fact.

"Magic?" Llesho asked hopefully.

"Water," the trickster scoffed, "When the ship sinks. Now go before I change my mind about you and feed you to the fishes."

There couldn't be two of them. Master Den's warning, so like the threat of becoming food for the pigs on Pearl Island, told him this must be the teacher he knew. As he began the long climb down to the pirate ship bobbing below, however, Llesho wondered. Could the trickster have an evil twin? Or had he grown so used to Master Den the teacher that he'd forgotten the nature of a trickster god? What was he supposed to learn from this, or had all the time from Pearl Island to Edris been some elaborate prank? Would he pay for his adventures not only with Tayy's life, but with the lives of all aboard the *Guiding Star*? With the freedom of all Thebin, too, if he didn't get out of this in one piece?

He doubted anyone less familiar with his moods would notice, but it suddenly struck him that the trickster god looked more nervous than Llesho had ever seen him. He glanced over his shoulder as if to hurry his fellow pirates to their work, but his eyes strayed to the bridge of the ship. Llesho stole a glimpse in the same direction and felt his heart stutter in his breast. The fighting had moved on and Master Markko stood alone above the fray, looking down on the clash of swords on the deck.

Reflexively, Llesho ducked his head below the rail, letting his mind process the information as it could. What was the magician doing here? The answer struck him as forcefully as the mind of the magician. Pontus, of course; Menar was on the other side of the Marmer Sea. It had always been a race to find him first. If Kaydu was right, Master Markko was going back to the place of his own first enslavement in search of Menar and the prophetic rhyme that would tell him how to win the gates of heaven.

Master Markko wasn't looking his way, but seemed to be focused on the fire burning amidships with a combination of frustration and anger that made him wonder how the fire got started in the first place. The magician had the power to conjure flames, but he'd never seen him put a fire out, by magical or any other means.

Master Markko had always been capable of mistakes. Llesho figured setting fire to your own boat had to be one of his smaller ones. That didn't help the innocents who huddled together at the stern, unsure where their greater danger lay—the sea or the burning ship. When he turned back, Master Markko had disappeared, but in his place a monstrous bird rose out of the flames. No phoenix, he guessed, but the magician himself escaping his own fire in the shape that had nearly killed Llesho in the battle of Shan market. With a blood chilling cry the horrible creature wheeled overhead. Catching sight of Llesho, he dove to the attack.

Llesho pulled at his chains but bound to his companions, and with no weapon but the chains that held him, he could do nothing to protect himself.

"Ahhhh!" screamed the boy who had lately stood in shock at the blood of a dead sailor on his hands. Llesho grabbed his shoulder and pulled him down to make a smaller target of them all. The stranger who moved like a soldier narrowed his eyes as if measuring an enemy in combat, but weaponless against the magician he was as helpless as the rest of them.

Master Den had to do something, however; why else was he here? From the trickster's direction he heard a whistle, as master might call a favored hunting bird. Across the looming disk of the moon the sleek shadow of a great-winged osprey passed. Kaydu! It had to be, and he watched as she dove at the awful half-bird, half-beast creature that Master Markko had become.

"Awk!" The great sea eagle screeched her terrible battle cry. With talons extended, Kaydu dove on the creature's neck, shaking him in her beak as he lashed about him with his scaly tail. He escaped her hold on him but left a bleeding chunk of flesh which she spit out onto the deck below. Llesho ducked as the steaming flesh fell on the hot planks.

Master Markko advanced his own attack, but Kaydu, in her osprey form, stayed just out of reach, harrying the monster when he dove for Llesho who watched from below. It might have gone on longer, but each bird had suffered wounds in the battle that sapped the strength they needed to hold their magical shapes. With the ship in flames below and hostile pirates everywhere in the sea around it, there could be no safe landing place. Soon Master Markko broke off, heading back in the direction from which the *Guiding Star* had come. When it seemed that he had been vanquished for the moment, Kaydu likewise made for shore.

Llesho wished that she could have delayed for a word before leaving him again to fate, but he knew that was impossible. Her father might have taken on the shape of a dragon and plucked him off the ship in his talons, but Kaydu didn't have that skill or that strength yet. He was stuck here until his cadre came for him in a boat, and only now did he begin to wonder if he'd live until that help came.

But the string of chained slaves was moving again and Llesho had to move with them or take the whole line down in a heap. Slowly he made his way down the knotted ladder to the high prow at the front of the pirate galley. The little boats, he saw, had decking only at the two ends. At the stern, the helmsman and the beater sat. The high prows on their galleys acted as a bridge over which the pirates could swarm their prizes like an army of ants rising out of a dozen tiny anthills. From there, pirate captains directed the boarding and as was happening now, the return with loot and slaves.

"Not there." Master Den leaned over the rail. With his sword he gestured directions at his fellow pirates. "I want the young brown one—no, not him, the other one. Right," he said when Alph grabbed Llesho's shoulder. "And that one, with the scar." He pointed to the man Moll had brought back with her after selling the women at market. The one with battle-tested nerves.

"Aye, Captain ChiChu," Alph answered with as much of a bow as he could manage in a bobbing boat. He held Llesho steady long enough to unlock his chains, then he gave him a shove in the direction that Master Den had indicated with his sword.

It wasn't the next boat over, but the galleys were set with their sides one against the other. Old reflexes learned on Pearl Bay took over. Llesho measured the roll of the swell and the movement of the boats. At their closest point he stepped down with his right foot and up with his left, matching the pitch of the sea. He reached the boat that was his goal without incident while the second man followed him over. His new companion had the sea legs of a native sailor and moved from boat to boat as if crossing the unmoving floor of some rich mansion on shore.

The pirates herded Llesho and the new man onto the foredeck, pushing them down to sit out of the way of the slave who beat a drum to set the pace of the oars. Suddenly, a shout went up, "Captain, 'hoy!"

Llesho looked around him, trying to find out what the warning was about. What he saw left him slack-jawed and speechless: Master Den—Captain ChiChu to the pirates, who might know the trickster as a god or as a man named after the patron god of pirates—stood on the burning deck of the *Guiding Star*. When the shout went up, he hooked a loop of rope around his foot and swung far out on it, over the sea. More precisely, Llesho realized with horror, over the boat he himself sat in. The rope was attached to a boom, and as ChiChu the pirate dropped toward the boat, a burning sail rose on its mast behind him, slowing his fall. A second before his foot touched down Den slipped from the rope and stepped lightly to the deck.

Freed of his massive weight, the rope whipped back up again, releasing the sail which bellied and fell with the sound of strained rigging and beating canvas.

"To the oars!" Captain ChiChu called out. The galley slaves didn't ship oars, however, but instead used them like punts to nudge their light, swift vessel away from the burning ship. When they had cleared their own boats as well, the beater set up a flurry of sound on his drum that signaled the order of the stroke. Oars rose and fell in sequence and the boat leaped forward, paused, leaped again. If Llesho hadn't been sitting down, he'd have fallen. With only a hand resting lightly on the side to steady him, however, Master Den shifted his weight into the motion, as unmovable where he stood as a lighthouse.

"We can at least save the people in the water!" Llesho cried as the galley moved into the night. In their wake, the burning ship shed an orange glare over the black water. "You can't just leave them to die!"

He stretched his arm to the hapless few who had escaped the massacre by leaping into the sea. The desperate passengers splashed helplessly in the water, calling to their loved ones over the thunder of the flames and the deceptively gentle sound of the surge striking the wood of ships.

The pirates near enough to hear him snorted at his distress but said nothing. Master Den, however, turned a cold eye on him. "Pirates are not known for their mercy," he pointed out in icy tones. "Nor could we take on any more if we wanted to. We would sink under the weight of those we tried to save. Or their fellows would overturn our boats in their desperation to board us themselves."

The trickster god stared out into the night of terror with a look that had no mercy in it—that was the province of a different god—but something more than indifference.

"Some lessons are harder learned than others," Master Den finally said. "When the fighting is over, the innocents have always paid the highest cost."

His teacher seldom gave him the answers to his lessons, leaving it to Llesho to figure out the meaning. This time, however, the cost for his tutelage was too steep to leave to the usual methods. "This will, I think, prove an educational voyage for you, oarsman."

With that, Master Den turned away. But Llesho wasn't finished. "And what of Justice?" he demanded of the trickster god. In his journeys he'd found traces of the seven mortal gods wherever he looked. Some, like ChiChu himself, and the Lady SienMa, mortal god of war, he had met in person. Others he felt only in their touch on the land and people that crossed his path. In all this traveling, however, it seemed that this one god, the avatar of Justice, was marked most by his absence. Where was Justice?

"When you know that," Master Den answered with a glint in his eyes of secrets and lessons still to teach, "you will have solved the puzzle of your quest." So much for confidences.

They were well out from the wreck now. The beater struck a flurry on his drum like a warning to his rowers and then lifted his padded drumstick to his shoulder. As if each represented a single arm of one body, the rowers raised their oars in place. Suddenly, the boat was still except for the gentle rise and fall of the sea and the lazy movement of unseen currents. In the lull, Moll came rolling toward them. The disguise of her skirts gone, her pirate trousers hung about her thick legs in folds in the still air.

"Last found, first claimed," she said, jerking her chin at Llesho and her most recent purchase. "You owe me ten copper coins for the boy, old pirate. The man cost more—I had to trade a strong young woman and her crone for him at the market and transport him all the way from Edris. If you want him, it will take a plump and comely girl for the concubine market in trade, the next from the ship's allotment."

"A fair price," Master Den agreed. Llesho would have told him that she'd cheated him on his own price, and the other slave's as well. Moll gave him a warning glare, however. He kept his mouth shut, remembering that she would mourn the loss of six coppers but not the loss of his sorry life if she felt the need to pitch him overboard. When it was clear that she would get her price, she added, "Where do you want me to put them?"

"Set the youth to work next to the Harnish boy—" which explained what Llesho was doing on this particular galley. "I recognize his kind. Thebin, they are called, rare enough in the marketplace but stronger than they look. And he knows his way across a deck. At least he won't capsize us when he drops his load over the side."

"You're the expert." Moll gave a noncommittal shrug. She wouldn't sink a sale by naming her doubts, but he clearly hadn't shown any signs of this Thebin strength to her.

"His people have a grudge against the grasslands, so they are unlikely to conspire foolishness together," Master Den added as if he were working out the placement at the oars as he spoke. "But they are of an age and well graded for height. Put him on the outside position, next to the block, the Harnish boy in the middle, and an older, more experienced hand to guide them on the aisle.

"This one will take more watching, I think," he added with a nod to the other man he'd brought aboard. "But he seems resourceful and strong. Not too resourceful," he added a sharp warning in the glance he cast on the stranger with the eyes of a soldier. "Put him on a short chain, between two experienced hands. That will keep him from disappearing when the wind is ripe."

That meant, when the smell of land beckoned. The new slave looked back at the trickster god with cold calculation in his eyes, but said nothing. Llesho wondered who the stranger was, and why Master Den had wanted him nearby. It seemed unlikely he would find out until his old teacher wanted him to know, so he followed Moll down the narrow center aisle of the galley to his place on the bench.

Chapter Fourteen

Llesho had never seen a galley ship before. Lord Chin-Shi had used fat wallowing sailing boats in Pearl Bay, with oars on board only for the rare days when they found themselves becalmed by a freak of the weather. Most days the boats rode with the prevailing winds which blew out with the tide of a morning and in with the tide at night. His journeys since he left the pearl beds had been mostly overland, with the exception of a memorable river crossing on the back of Golden River Dragon.

He'd heard of galleys, of course, but in stories they were great longboats each manned by hundreds of rowers pulling on oars long enough and thick enough around to form the corner posts of a seven-story temple. The narrow, sleek trim of the pirate galley seemed dangerously unbalanced and he walked cautiously, as if a misstep would overturn the small boat and land them all in the water. Moll had no such worries, however. She pushed him along, past a slim bronze gun affixed to the forward deck, into a cradle that took the recoil down a center aisle just wide enough for one to walk with caution.

On either side of the aisle were benches of rowers resting at their positions while the pirates settled the newcomers. There were more rowers than pirates, but not the hundreds that rumor claimed. Across each bench the pole of a single huge oar was drawn, holding the blade out of the water at a pivot point off the side of the boat. The stories hadn't lied about the size of the oars. Llesho tried to imagine the giant from which such a monster might be cut; only in the oldest forests might one find such a tree.

Under direction of the pirates, rowers at the front carried loot from the *Guiding Star* to the rear, disappearing into what he assumed to be a shallow hold. A second gun amidships divided the groups of rowing benches across the narrow width of the boat. This gun was smaller than the forward artillery, since the cradle could only manage a lesser recoil on firing. Llesho knew about guns. The principle was similar to the fireworks of Shan, except that instead of explosions of colored lights, the guns hurled balls of iron or stone. He wondered if he might get a closer look, but Moll stopped just past the forward deck and nudged at the rower on the aisle.

"Wake your center." She pointed to the rower in the middle. When he had roused from his dazed stupor, she gestured to the rear with her thumb. "You to the back," she said, and leaned over to unlock the shackles that chained his right leg to a small step in front of the bench.

At first, the man didn't move, as if he'd been stunned by a blow to the head and couldn't hear for the ringing of his ears. Llesho could see the bones standing out on his arms and across his throat. The rower's ribs showed through the laces on his tattered shirt like the steps on a ladder. There were open sores on his hands and blood on the oar he had held. *This will be me, if we don't get out of here*, Llesho thought. *This will be Tayy.* He wondered how his teacher could be party to the anguish that had passed beyond expression on the man's face, into the numbness that preceded death. He wanted to believe that Master Den wouldn't let it happen to him or to Tayy even if his plan didn't work. But he wasn't as certain of ChiChu the pirate.

"Put this one in the middle for a shift or two," Moll shoved Llesho forward. "When he has the knack of the oar, I'll move him to the outside as suits his size."

The slave on the aisle seemed to have a higher status than those who manned the inner grips on the huge oar. Sensible, when all their lives depended on the rower who controlled the pace and the power of each stroke. The oarsman seemed to have that in mind when he turned a disgusted eye on Llesho.

"This bank already has a new fish." He snorted, a sound wet with snot, and thrust his jaw to the side where Prince Tayyichiut of the Qubal people huddled in his chains.

"They are suited by size and too clever by half." Moll took the time to answer his objection, but made it clear she would hear no more about it. "This one will pick up the pace quickly enough or Cook will grind him up into pies for the captain's table."

He guessed that she exaggerated the punishment for failure. The man he replaced had looked like walking death, however, and Tayy's shirt bore the scars of a struggle earned during his capture. He also wore the bloody stripes of the lash. If the plan worked, those open wounds would make his time in the water that much more painful. But the Harnish prince didn't look up when his bench mate departed, and he didn't look up now, when Llesho sat down next to him. The Harn avoided all bodies of water larger than a teacup and Prince Tayyichiut, for all his bravery on land, kept his eyes on his feet as if not seeing it could keep at bay the terror of water lapping at their sides.

It wasn't going to be easy getting him over the side. He'd live, though, if the plan worked. Determined to learn the trick of the oar and save them both from further lessons drilled into their flesh by the lash, he slipped into his place.

"How about a look under my skirts, boy?" Moll laughed at him as she snapped the shackle around his leg. "Not so full of spit and vinegar now, are you?"

Llesho knew the old pirate didn't mean him to answer the question. He kept his mouth shut, looking as much as possible like the cocky youth who had finally discovered the wages of sin were more than he could pay.

"Singer will show you what to do. Mind him and you may survive the trip." She gave him a good-humored pat on the shoulder, as if she had not just condemned him to slow death as a galley slave, and left them to make her way to the rear, shouting, "Stow that barrel before you kill somebody with it!"

"I'm Singer," the head rower on their bench introduced

himself with a warning: "Do what you're told and keep your head down or it will be the lash for all of us."

Llesho gave him a brief nod. "So what do I have to do?"

That did bring up Tayy's head, astonishment widening his eyes. And then he caught sight of the pirate captain newly arrived on the forward deck. At first, it seemed that he did not trust his eyes, or his surmise, since Master Den had his back turned to them. With a shout to bring them about, however, Master Den scurried to the side, showing his profile clearly to the rowers at rest on the forward bench. There must have been another captain when ChiChu was crossing the grasslands with Llesho's cadre, but the trickster god was clearly in command now.

Prince Tayyichiut closed his eyes, but when he opened them again, Master Den still called out the orders to set to. No dream, then. Llesho sympathized with the feeling. He wasn't happy with where he found himself either.

"So it was a trap all along," Tayy said. "Pointless, though. My uncle will never pay ransom to get me back. I am at best an inconvenience to him."

"Ransom!" Llesho snapped with all the contempt he could fake in his voice. He had to stop the prince from saying anything that would give away the fact that they knew each other.

"Who would pay ransom for Harnish scum! Old Stipes said he would see me pay for pleasing his lady wife, which was more than he could do. I was ready for death, but this is more than insult! I'd rather feed the fish right now than share a bench with damned Harnish scum!"

That did it. Tayy's head snapped back as if he'd been struck, but it stopped the hasty words for a moment. They communicated in silent glares and speaking frowns for a long moment. Llesho wasn't at all sure what the prince made of his desperately rolled eyes, but Tayy only said, "I didn't think it could get any worse."

"I don't know anything about it. I've got problems of my own," Llesho retorted gruffly. He ducked his head between his shoulders, hoping the pirates hadn't heard them argue while he tried to figure out how he could explain it away to Singer, who watched them with ill-concealed contempt.

"You two know each other?"

"He's Thebin," Tayy answered with a superior sniff. "If there's trouble, you're bound to find a Thebin at the heart of it." His grim expression may have passed for race-hatred in front of the rower, but Llesho read it rightly as a warning. He had, after all, come on board in the company of Master Den, his own trusted adviser, who now wore the breeches of a pirate. Tayy finished with a wary glance at their captain. "I know him, though."

"We are lucky," Singer agreed, though Prince Tayy hadn't meant it that way. "The trickster god himself favors our boat with his presence."

Fortunately, Tayy asked the question that burned on the tip of Llesho's tongue: "You know him for the god ChiChu?"

"Of course. The pirates honor him for bringing them good fortune on their raids, which is no good fortune for us at the oar. But no boat with ChiChu on board has ever lost its oarsmen to the sea. This trip was a risk. The monsoons will be rising soon. With storm season upon us, I'm happy to see the old trickster on our decks."

"Huh." Llesho looked over at his teacher wearing pirate garb instead of his usual loin wrap and simple coat. This man could be a stranger. He'd assured Tayy that he'd had no part in whatever scheme the trickster had up his voluminous sleeves, however, which was all to the good. Now they just had to survive long enough for Kaydu to rescue them both.

The beater had set up a flurry on the drum and Singer rose to his feet, grabbing onto the handhold at his position on the oar. "Set oars!" he called in a singsong voice that explained his slave name. The oars came forward with a snap on the benches, all but their own.

"Grab hold!" he cried, and powerful muscles pushed on the great timber oar. "Right foot up!" he called out the pace. Llesho fumbled for a moment, watched what Singer did, and found the footboard. He set his right foot on it and lifted.

"Left foot up!" Singer called again and Llesho paid attention as Singer pressed forward, raised up on his right foot and set his left down on the narrow band of another footboard, this one across the back of the bench in front of them. Tayy had no sea legs and the motions were foreign to him as even a small boat would have been. They heaved forward on the great oar and he stumbled, struggling to keep up. Llesho took the weight of both their positions on himself and realized that Singer, too, was pulling more than his weight.

"Pull!" With a mighty heave against the oar, the rower threw himself backward, falling down onto the bench and dragging the oar after him.

Llesho did the same, discovered the bench wasn't hard as he'd expected but cushioned against the repeated rise and heavy fall as he rowed. He soon felt as if he'd been beaten with a stick, but years in the saddle had toughened his behind and he didn't think he would blister where he sat. At least if he managed their escape when night fell. He didn't have another day to find their way out of the chains, he realized. Tayy was a skilled horseman, well versed in a variety of military arts. He had no aptitude for the sea, however, and his dread of the water tightened all his muscles into rigid bands, doubling the effort it took for even the simplest action of the oar.

Llesho and their lead rower could only do the work of their comrade for so long. It took all the self-control he had not to rail at his teacher. Master Den stood at the prow with a glass trained on the horizon and spared not a glance for his pupils suffering at the oar.

Sometime during his duty shift the pirate galley slipped into a prevailing current that ran through the sea like a river through the land. The rowers to the front and behind his own bench sat down to rest in a pattern that reduced the number of working oars to a quarter of their full strength. If they'd continued to row as they had in the pirates' escape from the vicinity of their prey, they would have hit the men in front of them in the head. Singer showed them a new pace that was easier on all their backs, however. At quarter strength on the oars, the current carried them forward at much their former pace, except the boat no longer paused on the forward stroke. Old reflexes learned under sail on Lord Chin-shi's boats snapped back into play and Llesho adapted his balance to the new motion.

Prince Tayyichiut struggled with the change in their conditions. Unable to keep to his feet on the forward motion, he fell against the oar and would have driven it into the heads of the men in front if Singer and Llesho hadn't pulled back on their handholds. In saving the men in front of them, they missed the beat for dipping the blade of their oar, however. Alph was there, suddenly, with a lash to their backs to remind them of their jobs while they waited for the next beat of the drum to fall into the rhythm the beater had set. Tayy, who had never suffered the abuse of angry overseers, cried out in surprise, but Llesho kept his head down and put his back into the stroke.

"Hush!" he muttered under his breath. "Don't draw attention to us!"

Singer threw his full weight against the oar, but he looked at Tayy like he was dead already.

Llesho pulled at the oar until his shoulders burned and his back screamed for rest. Then he pulled some more, but he wasn't strong enough or expert enough to make up for a missing oarsman. Blood speckled the footboard in front of him—travel on horseback hadn't prepared him for the shift and beat of his feet as he pushed off, pushed off. When he thought he would lie down and die from the pain, a whip cracked over their backs and he snapped to, pulling with arms that felt like they were on fire. It went on, forever it seemed, until his mind fogged and he felt the part of himself that measured things like pain and exhaustion grow distant.

Then, suddenly, it stopped. Tayy fell into a heap at the bottom of the well between the rows of benches, but there was work still to be done.

"Help me with this!" Singer pivoted their oar against the thole pin so that the shaft dipped low in the well. "Grab that chain and lock it down."

Llesho did as he was instructed, locking the oar to a stanchion set in the bottom of the well for that purpose. With their station secured, the blade of the oar rode safely out of the water.

Sagging to the bench with a weary sigh, Singer grabbed Llesho by the shoulder and hauled him off his feet as well.

"Rest."

"No problem with that one," he acknowledged the welcome order. He ached all over. His hands were bloody, though not as bad as Tayy's, and his feet looked like someone had been pounding on them with a stick. Which he sort of had, he figured.

Callouses would take care of the problem eventually, if he planned to stay, which he didn't. But he needed water, he realized with a sudden sweeping desire that would have knocked him off his feet if he'd been standing. His mouth was dry right down to his sandals and his teeth felt gritty. Not since waking up slung over the back of a camel in the middle of the desert had he been this thirsty. Half-drowning in Pearl Bay had taught him what would happen if he drank any of the seawater just beyond his reach, though. Not a good idea.

Just as he had decided to ask about the problem, Singer reached under the bench and rolled a barrel into the well.

"Water." The oarsman filled the dipper he took from its side and poured it into a cup which he handed over to Llesho. "Drink it all, or you'll die of the heat."

Llesho did what he was told without thinking, the way he'd trained as a slave child to respond to Lord Chin-shi's overseers. He wanted more, but knew better than to ask. The water revived him, however. Surfacing from the darkness of his own exhausted mind, he found that Prince Tayyichiut had curled as far from the side of the galley as he could get.

"I can't do this!" Tayy cried. His hands were callused from weapons practice and the reins, but the new work still found bits of soft skin to shred. Blood dripped from the handhold carved out of the side of the secured oar.

"Take it." Singer pressed a cup of water on him, but Tayy brushed it aside.

"Just let them kill me and be done with it! Who cares whether I take days to die like the last person in my seat or die immediately? He curled his blistered fingers into loose fists and tucked them protectively up under his arms.

"And what do you think they will do with your sorry carcass if you can't row?" Singer jeered at him. "I thought you didn't like the water."

Tayy was a Harnishman, the son of a people well known for their dread of deep water. The wandering clans would walk the length of a river to avoid wetting their shoes in the crossing of one. No Harnishman had ever learned to swim and dozens had died when the battle with Tsu-tan had pushed them into the Onga River. Nothing could be more terrifying than the sea washing the side of the boat at Tayy's shoulder. At Singer's goading, however, he gave a shuddering glance over the side, as if he could not yet believe that a man of the Qubal clan had wandered out of reach of land. He quickly turned away, braver if he didn't have to look at the water under their boat.

"I would prefer to die in my own ger-tent of old age with a proper funeral pyre and a good shaman to guide me to the underworld. But there is only one way to get off this boat, and it's clear even to me that I'm bound for a watery grave sooner than later."

Turning his gaze on Llesho, his face was void of expression in a way that had become all too familiar. After their last argument, Tayy wouldn't have expected Llesho's cadre to travel for days to find him, or that they would set a rescue plan in motion. He'd given the Harnish prince a clue, but Master Den, Llesho's most trusted adviser, walked free as the captain of the boat that enslaved them. So he must wonder what truth he might find in the pantomime being played out on the pirate vessel, and if it had anything to do with him at all.

Tayy wouldn't parade his shattered hopes for the world to see, not even the tiny world of their small bench. In case he was wrong, he waited for a sign to tell him what he should do. Action was still hours away, however. At the moment, they had a more pressing problem. If Llesho didn't find a way to tell his friend that they *had* a plan, he was going to get himself killed.

Fortunately, Singer had his own method for keeping his young bench mate alive. He sneered in a way that seemed calculated to make the newly enslaved young grasslander angry. "If they made it easy to die, everyone would do it," the oarsman said. "You foolishly assume that the pirates who rule your life on the bench would waste the energy it would take to kill you with a knife or a sword."

"I have seen men tortured before." Tayy firmed his chin, but his skin was very green, whether from the sea, which had become choppy while they talked, or from the memory of Radimus' torture at the hands of his uncle, Llesho couldn't tell. In spite of the memory, he seemed ready to endure the attentions of his slavers if it would end the misery of his waterborne existence.

"Torture, too, takes energy our pirate captors are loath to spend on the wind," Singer pointed out.

Llesho figured the rowers, in the absence of sails, were the wind that moved the galleys. No torture seemed like a good thing to him, but the punch line must be coming. Apparently Tayy had the same thought. He cast a baleful glare at their head rower and waited for the explanation.

"If you will not work, some enterprising pirate, or perhaps your rowing mates, will pitch you overboard to sink or swim."

Singer gazed out toward the pale gray clouds that obscured the horizon, leaving little doubt as to the likely outcome if one should land in the water. Land lay under the mist, more distant than the mainland had been from Pearl Island. Even with all the skills of a pearl diver, Llesho had almost died trying to reach his own far shore. He wondered how many others on the galley were like Tayy and couldn't swim at all. They were all chained to the footboard, of course, and could neither leap over the side nor be thrown over until the pirate with the key unlocked the chain. Or until somebody picked the lock.

"I don't want to be here!" Tayy shivered miserably and huddled at the bottom of the boat.

"Nor do we all," Singer agreed. "But between the sea or the boat, we generally choose the boat."

"I don't want to die," the prince admitted.

"Then see that you don't," Llesho instructed him tartly. With luck, the sharpness of his tone would alert Tayy to be cautious. "There are worse things even than the sea."

He meant it as encouragement, but the mist that hid the

horizon seemed to stir, clotting into clouds before his eyes. Edris lay in that direction. Llesho felt the whisper of a familiar, dreaded consciousness moving in the distance and wondered. Storms were worse, especially magical ones, and a magician whose ship had burned out from under him might take that shortcut to his goal. He kept the thought to himself.

"How much time do we have for rest?" Llesho asked. They couldn't escape during a work period or while daylight showed their every move to the watchful pirates. When they did go, they'd need to be as rested as possible. To have any hope of success, he had to know the rhythms of the boat and their own cycle of sleep and rest.

"Count on the same period of rest as of work."

The situation could have been better, but Llesho thought they could live with that. Singer had his gaze turned away from the land, however, and stared out over the water as if measuring something the rest of them couldn't see. "We are at quarter shifts right now, but I think we will leave this current before long. Expect the rowing to go harder in the next shift."

A slave was passing down the aisle, feeding the rowers on rest break. Llesho held out his cup while the slave filled it with a runny soup of beans and rice and topped it with two hard biscuits. He ate them, scarcely noticing their bland flavor, staring into the same distance as their lead rower. When he squinted, he could just make out the ripple of the current running inexplicably faster than the general run of the tide. It would loop them back toward land if they rode it much longer.

Come nightfall, both tide and current would pull toward shore. If their rescuers didn't find them in the dark, they might still float in with the tide. He turned to warn Tayy to conserve his strength. The Harnish prince was already asleep, curled where he had fallen in the bottom of the boat, his dinner scarcely touched.

"You'd better do the same, boy," Singer admonished him. He scooped up the abandoned food, tucking the biscuits in Tayy's pocket and finishing off the soup for himself. He wasn't cruel, just practical. Tayy wouldn't survive another day as a galley slave and there was no point wasting any more food or time on him. Singer'd left him his biscuits in case he decided to live, but more than that just hurt their own chances of survival. If Tayy were a stranger, if they didn't have help coming, Llesho might have felt the same way. He hoped not, but he might think differently after a few more shifts at the oar.

"I get the bench."

The oarsman's voice brought him out of his silent contemplation. Briefly, among his own followers, Llesho had been a king. With a notable breakdown of good sense where Prince Tayy was concerned, he had been learning measured judgment with a mind to his subjects and those who looked to him for leadership. But Llesho didn't even consider disputing Singer's claim to the most comfortable bed. Some things learned at an early age come back quickly when they mean life or death.

In the hierarchy of the slave pens he was lowest of the low. Newest to the bench, he needed sound advice and the goodwill of his fellow slaves if he wanted to stay alive. And in the politics of their bench, Tayy was even lower than that, written off in the accounting books of a slave's head as drowned already. He wondered how long it would take chained to an oar before he was eyeing Prince Tayyichiut's biscuits for himself.

Tayy was taller than Llesho, but neither of them were tall by Singer's standard. There was plenty of space in the well between the benches for both of them to sleep if they curled up a bit. Worn out by the labor and his terror of the sea, Tayy had already wrapped himself in a tight ball and was sleeping fitfully with his back pressed against the side of the boat. Llesho shifted around a bit, trying to get comfortable, but decided that wasn't going to happen. He had worried that his mind, abuzz with plans for their rescue and anxious about Markko following somewhere behind them would keep him awake. But the impossible weight of his lids dragged them down over his eyes almost before he had settled his arms and legs about him.

Singer's voice followed him into sleep: "You did well, boy."

Exhausted from his labors at the oar, Llesho longed for deep, dreamless sleep. In his days as a pearl diver, the rise and fall of the swell had often soothed him, but it wasn't working now. He was pretty sure he'd only dozed off for a few minutes when his eyes popped open. He tried to close them again, but they stubbornly refused to obey. Logically, his restlessness shouldn't have surprised him. Tayy was in bad shape, and Llesho hadn't caught sight of a rescue boat since they'd left Edris.

To make matters worse, the mist over the harbor city was growing darker and more ominous. Even at a distance the storm, in its birthing, stirred up a choppy sea that cut across the current in which they ran. With the tug and hesitation of the oars, it seemed like they were being pulled in three different directions at once. More frightening to Llesho was the restless mind reaching out from within it. Master Markko was in there somewhere, and the magician was looking for him.

Llesho gave up on sleep. He sat up and looked out over the water, wondering where Kaydu was with their rescue and fretting at the absence of the pearls he had carried at his throat for so long. He was just wondering if his crowded mind could handle even one more crisis when a strange sound at the side of the boat shocked him to attention. Something was out there, climbing out of the depths and scrabbling determinedly to board the low pirate galley.

Terrible monsters inhabited the sea, fearsome creatures with rows of teeth in lines one behind the next like a phalanx of skeletal soldiers. The overseers on Pearl Island had encouraged tales about them as a warning against escape: they would snap a man in two and grind him up like pie filling between those terrible teeth. Or vast, shapeless horrors with snakes dangling from their heads would crushed a man to paste, feeding gobs of entrails into their great huge mouths like the most devoted servants. His own attempt to flee would have ended in his death if Pearl Bay Dragon hadn't rescued him, but not all dragons were as friendly. Certainly a dread of such beasts had stopped many an escapee from ever setting out.

He was on the very point of waking Singer to alert the ship to their new danger when Pig popped his head over the side.

"There you are." The Jinn climbed into the boat and shook the water off the silver chains that wrapped his bristly black hide. "I've been looking for you. I see you've found Prince Tayy-ichiut."

"What are you doing here? I'm not asleep and I'm not dream-walking!"

"Of course you're asleep. You need it, too, but we don't have any time to waste. There's a storm coming."

Chapter Fifteen

"**W**HAT are you doing in my domain, Jinn?"

Llesho whirled at the sound of a voice behind him. No one had seemed to notice that he was standing in the well of his bench talking to a soggy black pig wrapped in fine silver chain. Undetected, however, the slave whom Master Den had chosen to accompany Llesho from the *Guiding Star* had stepped up behind him. He looked much the same as he had in the waking world, both competent and dangerous. As proof of both, he had escaped his shackles.

"You know each other?" the slave asked Pig, who ducked his head as if he didn't want to answer.

"Not if it displeases you, Master Dragon." The Jinn bowed, but not before Llesho caught the shifty slide of his eyes.

"Dragon?" Llesho saw no changes in the captive's features that would prove the conclusion, but he didn't doubt Pig's word. He'd met enough dragons in his travels to be cautious in their presence, however. Particularly over water.

In his human form, the dragon inclined his head in the affirmative. "Permit me to introduce myself," he said, but his deep, silvery gaze never left the Jinn. "I am Marmer Sea Dragon, king of this sea and the shores that mark its boundaries."

Llesho accepted the introduction, inclining his head with diplomatic precision in the same degree as the dragon-king had done. "Llesho, King of Thebin in exile and husband of my lady the Great Goddess."

"You are welcome, young king. Your companion, however, is not."

Pig shuffled his two back feet uneasily and rubbed at his nose with a forefoot in a display of nerves that Llesho had never seen in him before.

"You were thrown out of the Beekeeper's gardens for your actions, beast." The dragon-king growled his displeasure with a rumble in his throat that made Llesho glad the magical creature couldn't spit fire in his human form. "What makes you think you are welcome in the domain of the very one you have injured beyond measure?"

There could be only one beekeeper a dragon would mention in that company. The Great Goddess. Pig had told him a very different story about his departure from the heavenly gardens.

"Thrown out?" He wanted the Jinn to deny the accusation. The thick silence that followed was more damning than any words. First Master Den, and now Pig. The harrowing disappointment of one more betrayal fed Llesho's anger. Did he have any friends in this wide world, or was he a fool, trusting in his enemies as they used him like a dupe for their purposes?

"You said you escaped to bring help for the Goddess. What other lies have you told me?" He kept his voice low, but even Pig must hear the iron in it.

"No lies." The Jinn gave a phlegmy snort, his version of an indignant sniff. "You didn't need all the details and my lord dragon's version isn't exactly true in all its particulars either."

The sea itself had grown still as lamp oil beneath them: waiting, it seemed, for the tale to erupt in storm and fury.

"Did my lady, the Great Goddess, expel you from the heavenly gardens or not?"

"She was displeased with me, yes. I departed her company by mutual agreement, to seek redress for the wrong I had done by my actions. I've returned twice in your company since then—did I seem unwelcome?"

He hadn't, but that could owe more to the need of the moment than the status of the Jinn. Llesho turned his head, looking from Pig to the thunderous dragon-king and back again. When he thought he was braced for the worst the truth might bring, he asked, "What did you do?"

Pig didn't answer, so the dragon-king did it for him. "The magician who follows you," he said, "who would take all of heaven for himself."

"Master Markko," Llesho agreed. "What about him?"

"He was but a mountebank doing tricks for coins in the market square when he met our friend the Jinn."

"You released the demon from the underworld!" The air went out of Llesho's lungs with a whoosh. He couldn't believe it. Wouldn't believe it. "It's your fault that heaven is under siege!"

"No!" Pig drew back, rattling the fine links that wrapped him. Llesho had wondered about them before, but now they made sense. The Jinn had escaped heaven but not the chains that had bound him there.

"Not exactly. And that's not the whole story. If I'd known what Markko intended, I'd have done it all differently."

Lluka's dream swept over Llesho with heart stopping intensity. He saw the fireball rise again in the sky, felt the flames sweep over him, consuming all the worlds in destruction and chaos. He remembered the seductive question— "Is that a wish?" Pig had asked it so many times that Llesho had come to look on it as a game, which it had never been. His country in ruins, friends facing death yet again, his brother Lluka driven mad by the future Master Markko intended for them, a future that would see the end of all creation: had it all happened for the twisted pleasure the Jinn took in playing games with human hearts? With their greed? And not only humans. Marmer Sea Dragon had his own grievance.

Pig had denied that he released the demon that held the gates of heaven under seige, but he still hadn't answered the question: "What did you do?"

"Markko was born the child of a slave girl in the court of a minor dignitary on the outskirts of Pontus." The Jinn gave a little shrug, mimicking, perhaps, the way he had dismissed their most feared enemy in the past. Kaydu had guessed he might have had his training there.

"This official never acknowledged his parentage but kept his son in the household as an educated slave. Growing up as the property of his father, he trained himself in the dark arts—for revenge, I thought. I'd have been happy to help him out there; his father was a petty tyrant and deserved any retribution his son might concoct. But Markko wished to be a great magician. He had some romantic notion of wooing the Great Goddess with the hope that she would grant him eternal life. For a price, I could have granted even that wish, but his mind was twisty even then."

Llesho'd had more than a taste of slavery. He wondered if that long-ago Markko the mountebank had made his wish out of pride and vanity, or because he could see no other escape in the life he'd been given? Too late now to know if a different turning then might have saved them from the end of all their worlds; Markko the magician had done too many loathsome things since to feel sorry for him. Questions still begged for answers, however.

"And how did a lowly slave with romantic dreams of winning the attentions of my lady wife become a magician with the fate of all the kingdoms of heaven and earth and the underworld in his hands?"

"You need dragon's blood in your veins to be a real magician," Pig explained with a little shrug. Llesho knew that.

"Markko had none."

"That can't be so," Llesho objected. He'd seen for himself the scales that mottled the magician's skin.

"There was this young dragon—" The sea rocked the pirate galley as if the water had a mind of its own and, like a horse with a blanket of nettles, wished to throw them off. Llesho grabbed hold of the oar secured by its stanchion to steady his balance.

"My son," the dragon-king said.

Pig had the courtesy to look dismayed, but this had come as no surprise. He maneuvered his great bulk so that Llesho stood between the dragon-king and himself, keeping a hold on the oar against the pitching of the boat. On the bench, Singer had started to snore. Tayy frowned in his sleep and curled a little tighter in on himself. Neither woke. The fate of worlds might hang in the moment, but on the bench in front of them the rowers stepped up and fell back, stepped again in the quarter-pace stroke.

"This young dragon," the Jinn persisted in his tale, "fell in love with a girl and wished to be human. It seemed a perfect solution for them all."

Llesho had known Pearl Bay Dragon as the healer Kwan-ti for most of his young life among the pearl beds. He had only seen her in her dragon form twice: once when she had saved him from drowning, and again, when she had come out of the sky like a silver arrow in the battle against Master Markko in the capital city of Shan. The dragon-king himself appeared before them in the shape of a man. "I don't understand," he therefore said. "Dragons can appear in any form they want, even human."

"And so would my son, if he had waited. Shapes are a gift of a dragon's maturity."

"Which comes slowly as humans measure such things," Pig explained. "The young dragon did not feel this lady had such patience in her."

Llesho figured that meant she'd have died of old age before her dragon-lover had the power to approach her as a handsome young man. A tragedy for the embroideries of storytellers, but something you were supposed to accept and get over in real life.

"What did the dragon-boy do?" He didn't really want to hear the answer but knew it must figure in his own saga somehow. Otherwise, why this particular dream?

Pig avoided his eyes when he answered, "He wished to be a man."

"And so to kill two birds with one throw, your friend the Jinn fused the dragon who is my son with the man who wished for dragon blood, and made them into one being," the dragon-king answered, and tears stood in his human eyes. "My son is trapped inside that madman, who used his stolen powers to call forth a demon-king of the underworld. No more can a young dragon control such a thing than he could become a man for the love of a girl!''

"Merciful Goddess!'' Once, when Llesho had just begun his training in dream traveling, Master Markko had snatched him off his path and held him captive in his command tent. The magician had awakened the old poisons in his blood and Llesho'd had the satisfaction of being sick all over the the magician's robes. Markko had held his head until he settled, then changed his soiled robe for a fresh one.

In those moments with his skin exposed, Llesho had seen Master Markko's great secret—thick patches of dragon scales mottled his sickly flesh. At the time, he'd thought the magician an unfortunate child of a mating gone awry between a dragon and a human, driven mad by the strangeness of his own body. Now, the truth made him ill. No wonder Master Markko was insane!

"I have given up hope of rescuing my son.'' The dragon-king choked out the words through a throat clogged with tears. "I wish only to end his misery.''

"Would you care to repeat that?'' Pig hunched his shoulders as the dragon-king's shape flickered and changed. Llesho kept his eyes on the blurred form through the dizziness of mind and eye rejecting what they saw. If the creature settled in the shape of a dragon, his great size would sink them on the instant, unless he burned them to a cinder with his breath first.

Pig made no excuse for his untimely offer, but told the truth that Llesho hadn't wanted to hear: "It is in my nature to ask.''

"It would be worth the price to wish you dead for what you have done,'' the dragon-king replied, settling firmly into his human form again, "but no, I do not wish it so.''

They were saved, if one could consider it that, by the sudden appearance at Marmer Sea Dragon's elbow of Master Den in his full pirate garb. "Ah, I see you three have met at last. Good, good.''

"I see no good in this at all!'' Llesho exclaimed. "Pig, whom I trusted as the loyal servant of the Goddess sent to guide me, now proves to be the enemy of my lady wife, banished for his crimes.''

Visions of chaos and fire filled his mind, and he turned on
the Jinn, shouting into his woebegone piggy face, "Do you know
what you have done? Can you imagine the destruction your
actions have brought down on all our heads?"

"I've been remiss in my hospitality," Marmer Sea Dragon
said with an ironic bow to Llesho. "Are you fond of ham for
dinner, or perhaps ribs in barbecue sauce?" Pig he snubbed, a
dangerous thing to do to a Jinn. Unless you are a dragon-king.

Pig glared at Master Den. "This is your doing, old fool. What
in all the kingdoms of heaven and humans and the spirits below
did you think you were doing by bringing the boy here, to meet
him!"

"I wasn't fast enough to stop a foolish tongue," Master Den
admitted, "though for a change it was not my own."

Llesho flinched at the reminder. His hasty words to Prince
Tayyichiut had put them on this path.

"We had to cross the sea anyway." The trickster gestured to
his own billowing scarlet-and-yellow pantaloons with a flourish. "And no quest is complete without pirates. As for our
friend Marmer Sea Dragon, he was on the trail of a prophetic
rhyme that would put in his hands the power to stop Master
Markko and release his son from his torment. It seemed only
logical to bring him along."

Something about Master Den's sly innocence made Llesho
wary of hidden truths in that introduction. Dragons, after all,
could take the shapes of many things.

"Have we met before on this quest, my lord dragon? Do I
know you by another name?" he asked with a polite bow as
befitted a supplicant in the halls of a great king. The Marmer
Sea was the dragon's domain.

With an exasperated sigh, the dragon-king let his glance
slide sideways, where Master Den waited with mischief curled
in the corners of his grin. "I had to think of something quickly,"
the trickster god apologized. "I looked down and there they
were right to hand. Or foot, actually. Bluebells. The word just
popped out of my mouth, and then we were stuck with it, so to
speak."

"One of us was, at least," Marmer Sea Dragon shook his

head. In the shape of a great horse, he had carried Master Den on his back for a time. And had suffered the indignity of a flowery alias. "Avoid the company of Jinns and trickster gods," he warned Llesho, "They are nothing but trouble."

"I had noticed that." Bluebell. Llesho had traveled in the company of kings and gods for a long time now, and knew to keep his smile to himself.

The dragon-king studied Llesho thoughtfully. "Plots within plots, I see, Master Trickster," he murmured. "Is he truly the one?"

Intruding upon the conversation at great peril, Pig answered the question. "He is, and late for an appointment. Her ladyship, SienMa, the mortal goddess of war, sent me to fetch him."

"And what are we to do about the young heir who lies dying at his bench, or this magician who holds my son prisoner within his own body?"

Master Markko! "He'll follow us. He wants that rhyme, and my brother Menar, as much as we do." Llesho stared out at the sea, wishing he knew what the magician was up to.

Marmer Sea Dragon followed his glance with more purpose, as if he could be everywhere at once upon the watery surface and below. Which perhaps he could. After a moment, however, the life returned to his eyes and he shook his head.

"He is searching for you. He knows, of course, that you are on the water, but his fight with your friend the osprey has sent him back to shore to find another way. His main purpose seems to be to reach Pontus ahead of us, but I don't know how he plans to do that on the land, which is outside of my own kingdom. For whatever reason, he now conjures a storm which may be more powerful, I think, than he knows."

From the start Master Markko had set into motion powerful spells that quickly spun out of his control. That weakness had released the demon bent on destroying all the realms of mortals gods and spirits that had started Llesho on his quest. Storms were tricky business, and it seemed likely he had done the same again, reaching for magics just beyond his grasp.

Llesho wondered if this time his lack of control was all the magician's fault. Marmer Sea Dragon ruled here, over the waters above and below, and had an interest in seeing Master Markko fail. He didn't want to risk offending his host with the suspicion, however, but instead offered a gentle reminder that friends rode before that wind as well as enemies.

"What of my cadre?" he asked, thinking of Kaydu and Hmishi and Lling, of Bixei and Stipes somewhere out on an angry sea. He wondered if Little Brother got seasick.

"I see all that passes within my domain." The dragon-king confirmed what Llesho had suspected, but then revealed a limitation, "But not what will happen in the future. Someone has trained your witch well, and the blood of dragons runs true in her veins. She is young and inexperienced at weather working, however. Her familiar has powers of his own, but he won't be able to help her there. If your enemy loses control, as I think he must, then your friend stands little chance of success."

He didn't ask how the dragon-king knew of the plan; he'd already said he knew of everything that took place upon these waters. Llesho hoped the dragon was wrong about Kaydu, though. She was even stronger than their watery host suspected, but he'd never seen her try to work a magic that powerful before. Wasn't sure he wanted to see it, but knew he had to find her before he met with her father. Habiba would have questions.

"I have to find her and then report to Lady SienMa. But I'll come back," he insisted. "I won't leave Prince Tayyichiut to die alone in the company of pirates."

"I'll make sure our young king gets back in time. You have my word." Pig sealed the oath with a solemn bow. No one trusted his promises, least of all Llesho, who had just lately discovered the depths of the Jinn's deceit.

If Prince Tayy woke to find that Llesho had gone, despair would surely kill him. "Help them if you can," he begged.

"I'll see what I can do." The dragon-king didn't seem happy about it, but he, too, gave his promise.

Llesho accepted with a grateful bow. Dragons always honored their word. "Then I am off with our villainous friend."

With that he shook his head, imagining into being the antlers on his brow, and leaped into the sea . . .

. . . which disappeared from under him as he ran.

Llesho had dream traveled to places he'd never been in the waking world before and he knew to center in on something or someone familiar where he wanted to go. As he'd been trained in her ladyship's service long ago in Farshore Province, he looked to his captain for direction. Kaydu stood on the deck of a small ship with two masts stripped to a minimum of sail. At her back, the cloud bank he'd been watching from the pirate galley boiled more ominously on the horizon. Wind blew her hair in manic tangles and snapped the full sleeves of her uniform like the pennants racing from the topmast to the bowsprit in front of them. She seemed to be staring abstractedly out to sea, but concentration drew tight lines around her mouth and her eyes. In her arms, Little Brother stared into the same distance. The same air of concentration gave an almost human cast to his wizened features. Once again, Llesho wondered what powerful secrets hid behind that monkey face and what Marmer Sea Dragon knew about them.

The clatter of his hooves on the deck distracted her from whatever magics she was controlling. "Llesho!" she cried even before he had returned to his human form.

Slipping into his pack, Little Brother gave a last enigmatic monkey look that took in all of the deck and Llesho lying on it before hiding his head. Llesho wondered what that meant, but Kaydu gave him no opportunity to discuss the thoughts of her familiar, or Marmer Sea Dragon's opinions on the subject. Taking advantage of her suddenly free hands, she knotted them at her hips with the air of a village scold and tapped her foot just inches from his nose where he had fallen. "What are you doing here?"

"I'm looking for you," he explained as he struggled to his feet. The little ship pitched angrily and Llesho wondered if Marmer Sea Dragon had been wrong about Master Markko. The eye of the storm had not yet moved out to sea, but even at a distance it didn't feel like anything had control of it. He grabbed hold of the rail, afraid of tumbling off the pitching ship or merely falling on his backside again in front of Kaydu.

"You found me." She gave a furtive look behind them, where a line of rain marked the edge of the shore. "Look, I can't really talk now. Hmishi and Lling are belowdecks and they can report if you want, but I'm worried about this storm." With that, she turned her face into the wind and reached an outstretched hand to hold back the rain with a staying gesture. Llesho felt unseen forces clash out beyond the ship as the storm pressed to leave the land behind and Kaydu pushed it back. For a moment the wind stuttered and paused. Llesho felt the whisper of a mind he knew too well, and at his peril. Then their few sails filled and the ship surged forward on an angry swell again, more steadily but still at a headlong pace.

"Marmer Sea Dragon says that Master Markko raised the storm but won't be able to control it," he shouted over the sound of the wind snapping in the sails. "It's getting too big!" He left his question unasked. Could she do what the magician couldn't? She answered it anyway, in Kaydu style, with no surprise that Llesho had turned up another dragon when most people went their whole lives without even meeting one.

"Then tell Marmer Sea Dragon to get his ass over here and stop the damned storm himself! I need a calm sea and a steady wind, not a critic grading my skills."

Llesho considered explaining his own conclusions about quests and tests, but figured with Habiba as her father she already knew. "I'll tell him," he said, and left her to her contest with the sea.

Ducking down the ladder to the gangway below, he met Lling on the way up. "Llesho! Is this a dream?"

"It was a dream when I left the pirate ship, but I don't know what it is now," he admitted. "Pig is around somewhere."

Lling nodded, accepting that answer. They'd met like this before, when Markko's henchman, Tsu-tan, had held her prisoner. "Did you find Prince Tayyichiut?"

"Yes, and Master Den, too, who captains the pirate ship and

seems to think that rowing a galley should be part of every prince's education."

"Never trust the trickster god," she agreed, though they had both put their lives in Master Den's hands in the past. "We're on our way, as fast as we can move, but a storm has complicated things."

"Master Markko's doing." He kept to himself that Tayy was dying in bondage on the pirate galley. Kaydu's ship had to stay in one piece to rescue them. If his cadre knew how bad things were, they might take chances that would endanger them all.

"Where's Hmishi?"

"He's below, in the quarterdeck cabin, trying to calm the ship's captain. She seemed capable enough of coping with a normal blow at sea, but fears magic on principle and magical interference with the weather in particular. Your appearance on board won't improve her nerves, but it would help if you could get rid of the antlers."

"I forgot," he admitted, shaking his head to focus on the weight of the branches. In a moment he had his senses centered on the itch just above his forehead and then the antlers were gone. "I was just talking to Kaydu and she never said a thing about them."

"Kaydu is a witch. She has ridden with gods and kings, and has seen you in antlers before. Our captain, however, is a simple sailor with only the blood of human ancestors coursing through her bones."

"The world isn't simple anymore, not even for sea captains." Remembering the pirates' attack on the *Guiding Star,* he wondered if it ever had been. Certainly not since Master Markko had called a demon from the underworld to hold the gates of heaven hostage. He didn't ask if Kaydu could control the storm the magician had conjured. For all their sakes, they could only hope their captain was as powerful a witch as her ladyship, the mortal goddess SienMa, seemed to think when she put them in her captain's command.

He found Hmishi in a cabin that extended the width of the ship's stern, with tall windows looking out over a gallery protected by an elaborately carved rail. Brocaded fabrics draped the walls and the furnishings, falling in folds where they were pulled away to let in whatever light the windows gave them. On the right, tucked into a protected corner of the cabin, feather cushions covered in bright silks were heaped luxuriously on a bed rack. Two matching chests in dark, satiny wood were clear of breakables in the high seas. Nevertheless, they showed the captain's taste in the carved and painted scenes that decorated their tops and sides.

Under the windows at the center of the cabin stood a spacious table covered with charts. Five chairs were set around it, all occupied but one. Bixei, Stipes, and Hmishi sat at one side of the table. A muscular woman Llesho didn't recognize sat on the other, gripping the table with white-knuckled fingers.

"She hasn't let us down yet," Hmishi said as he stared out at the storm moving on the horizon.

Bixei and Stipes nodded their support, but the stranger gave an emphatic shake of her head. "I am a simple merchant sailor and have no business with secret missions or witches who control the wind and rain."

"No evil will come to this ship." Llesho stepped into the cabin with a little shake of his head just to reassure himself that the antlers were gone. "I have it on the word of Marmer Sea Dragon himself." That wasn't quite what the dragon-king had said, but Llesho had taken it for his meaning.

"Llesho!" His companions leaped to their feet, careful not to give away his title but unable to entirely still their bows.

"More magic!" The sea captain made a warding sign which had them all speaking at once to reassure her.

"He's a friend."

"Llesho won't hurt you."

"You can trust him."

"Safe, he says!" the captain remained unconvinced. "If by safe you mean swallowed down the gullet of a dragon and digested in the fire of his belly. For myself, I choose not to call that safe, if it is all the same to you, young master. And I'd like to know where you came from yourself. If a stowaway, you owe passage on this ship. Her few cabins are full, so you will bunk on the deck or with the seamen.

"If you are some magical creature like yon witch and the dragon from whom you claim promises, then you can find your way off this ship the same way you got on it. And you can take that girl with the uncanny way with a storm as well. I won't have any more magic on my ship!"

"Pardon my intrusion, good captain." Llesho gave her a low bow as to one of greater station, but it did little to pacify her. "The witch on your deck didn't raise the storm. Even as we speak Captain Kaydu strives against the evil forces that rise against us in that wind. If she leaves her post, you'll likely lose your ship and all hands aboard her before long."

The captain was already as pale as her skin would go, but she blinked several times, as if the news had snuffed her mind like a candle. Llesho waited as, her jaw clenching slowly, she came back to herself.

"So, then." Pause. "I suppose I had better get Cook to send up something warm to eat."

Hmishi gave her a brief smile and a suggestion: "Captain Kaydu requires a hand free at all times for her working."

The sea captain didn't like the reminder of the magic on her deck, but she acknowledged the need with a curt nod. "And you, master messenger?" she asked of Llesho.

He decided to leave her in ignorance of his true identity, which could serve only to heap more wonders on a mind that rejected all that was not ordinary.

"I left certain property with my friends, and I've come to retrieve it. Then I will be off your decks." She would wake in the night with the memory of a strange dream, he thought, though his presence on her ship was as real as the sea.

When she departed, Stipes looked uncomfortably to his companions to speak up, but they glared him down and he was forced to offer his own defense. "Those items being of importance to Thebin interests, I handed them over to your own countrymen as seemed fit." He mentioned nothing of his own troubles, but Llesho knew they must have been considerable.

"I'm sorry if I worried anyone—"

"Anyone!" Hmishi snorted indignantly. Having spent some time dead in the underworld, he felt more freedom to speak his mind, even to the Holy King of Thebin. "Whatever possessed you to go off on your own on such a cracked-brain scheme! Kaydu takes it as a personal failure that she could not protect you from your own foolishness. And as for the rest of us, we hardly know how we will greet the Lady SienMa, having lost the one hope we had to save the world from disaster!"

"I'm sorry—"

Bixei had been quiet until now. Bound to the quest only by the luck of his servitude, he had neither the tradition of family service to the mortal goddess of war nor the fealty a subject owes a king to hold him. That and his attachment to Stipes, who had joined their cadre in spite of his injuries because they didn't want to be separated again. For him, Llesho's disappearance had caused a private injury.

"How could you do that to Stipes? Did you ask for him to accompany you to the market because you knew he couldn't say 'no' to you? You must have known he would be blamed for your actions, though there was little he could do to stop you."

"You can't think I meant to deceive you from the start!"

Looking from face to face, he realized that they believed just that, though Hmishi admitted, "Kaydu never did. She thought it was one of your harebrained spur-of-the-moment ideas that look good until you get into them and then turn out to be quicksand in every direction."

Which pretty much described it. He wasn't sorry he'd done it, though. Not yet at least. "The plan will work," he insisted. It had to work, or Prince Tayy would be dead. "But my rest period will be over soon. I don't have time to argue the matter."

They seemed unwilling to let the matter go. Lling, however, remembered Llesho's dream visit to Tsu-tan's camp during her own rescue. She understood the urgency of speed and rose to find her cabin and the objects she and Hmishi had hidden there. "What do you need?" she asked. "Everything?"

Llesho stopped her with a shake of his head. "I will need my knife and my spear, and that which you wear around your neck for me." He didn't want to mention the pearls—most particularly the one he was most worried about at the moment—where a seaman might be passing at any time.

"I'll bring them right away."

Hmishi followed her, a wise precaution to guard all their movements in a strange ship. At the hatch, however, Lling turned around and asked again, "Are you sure you don't want the cups?"

"Why?"

"They give me strange dreams," she answered uncomfortably. "In the night I hear a woman weeping, and sometimes the slither and hiss of a serpent—"

Llesho knew who that was. His dreams had been blessedly free of her presence since he'd sent the cups away in other hands. He didn't want to put Lling at risk, but he didn't dare carry the false Lady Chaiujin with him into the court of the mortal goddess of war. Not when he still had Tayy to rescue.

Lling read both of his concerns—over leaving the cup and about taking it with him—in his hesitation and waved off the request. "I can carry her a while longer. But she must be dealt with eventually."

"I know. Just not today."

With a nod that accepted his decision she disappeared after her partner.

Settling to wait, Llesho took a chair at the table. "Her ladyship SienMa has called me to attend her in my dream travels," he told Bixei and Stipes, counting on them to fill in Hmishi and Lling. "She will want a report of all our doings."

Bixei still hadn't let go of his anger, but he leaned forward, his hands between his knees. Between those two he always did the talking. "Kaydu thinks we'll catch up with the pirates by tomorrow afternoon. If we can outrun this storm, we'll stand off until dark. If the storm proves stronger, we will all need rescuing, I think."

"That's what Marmer Sea Dragon says." Falling silent, Llesho stared off into a broody distance.

"We won't fail you," Stipes promised. He seldom spoke up except at need, and Llesho wondered how badly he had hurt all his cadre, how they must have interpreted his rashness as their failure.

"You never have," he assured the two, knowing they would

pass the message along. "I trust you with my life, and with my honor, as I trust the air to be there when I breathe. But Marmer Sea Dragon is right. It's a risky plan. The storm has a strange character to it. Master Markko had a hand in its birth, but it grows a wild and powerful soul of its own, I think." The enormity of the task that remained ahead bowed him for a moment.

"If Kaydu manages to tame that wind, we are still far from completing our quest," he cautioned them. "Wars will be fought over our bones if we fail."

"Then we won't fail," Bixei said, as simply as if offering tea. Stipes added, "What do you want us to do?"

They were so sure, so solid, that he found a smile creeping onto his lips in spite of how close to despair he had fallen over the betrayals of this voyage. If he gave it a moment's thought, no one had surprised him in all the mess he found himself. Master Den was the trickster god, after all, and Pig was Pig. Though he put the safety of the Great Goddess and the heavenly gardens he tended before all other things, in matters to do with humans he would be what his nature made him.

If Llesho's own lady wife forgave her servant, as it seemed the Goddess had done, he could do no less. He'd take a lesson from the experience, however. Pig was his guide in the spirit world and a devotee of the Goddess, but the Jinn had never been a friend. It was a mistake to think of him that way. If he'd relearned wariness around the magical creature, so much the better. As for Pig's actions in the past, while horrific, they didn't change the present. Only Llesho could do that.

"Do you really think Master Den has betrayed us?" Bixei asked him.

Since he'd seen the trickster god crossing the deck of the *Guiding Star,* Llesho had thought so. But the conversation with Marmer Sea Dragon had made him stop and think.

"I'm not ready to trust him completely, but he probably means us no permanent injury." His teacher hadn't kidnapped Tayy or carried him off to the galleys. He hadn't sold Llesho back into slavery in a plan that was looking less well thought out by the stormy minute. As the patron of pirates and also the teacher of young kings, however, he had put himself in a position to watch out for both Tayy and Llesho. Not to see that they came to no harm, perhaps, but to see that they came out of the experience with a lesson well learned.

That part wasn't working any better than Llesho's plan at the moment, but he hoped, by the time he'd pitched Tayy into the sea and breathed into his lungs to rescue him, that they'd both have learned something. With a sigh, he wondered why none of his teachers believed in writing his lessons on a slate.

When he came out of his reverie, he discovered that Hmishi and Lling had returned and his companions had continued their conversation without him.

"Where do you suppose he's been this time?" Hmishi asked.

Lling answered with a little shrug. "He gets that look when he's deciding what not to tell us. Which happens right before he gets into trouble for keeping things from us."

"You're right," Stipes agreed. "That's the look."

"It's nothing worth telling." At least, not until he figured out what it meant.

It seemed they had learned that cynical twist of the mouth from each other, because he saw it in every direction he looked.

"Whenever you're ready." Hmishi pulled the thong with the small bag of pearls from around his neck and handed it over.

He didn't really need the true pearls, but didn't trust Pig around somebody else's neck. The thought of Hmishi turned into a creature like Master Markko made him ill. Llesho didn't know what Master Markko would do to his friend to seize the pearls for himself, either. Hmishi had already died for him once and he didn't want it to happen again.

Next, Hmishi drew out the silver chain around his neck and stared at it with sick dismay. The pearl in its wire setting was gone. "I had it, I swear," he cried. "I haven't taken it off since Stipes put it in my care, and I check the slide every shift to make sure it is secure."

"No one can hold Pig when he goes wandering. He's around here somewhere," Llesho assured them, and slipped the empty chain around his neck, next to the thong that held the bag of pearls from the Goddess' necklace, the String of Midnights. "You haven't found any more of these by any chance?"

Hmishi shook his head. "I prefer to leave the adventures to you."

Llesho took the knife and the spear that Lling handed him with a wink. It would be their little secret, that Hmishi was having an adventure, at least until he figured it out for himself. But Llesho could well understand the impulse. One day, if he completed his quest to save his country and free the gates of heaven, he hoped only for a quiet life at the side of his lady wife, the Great Goddess. He was lucky he didn't see Pig, or he might be tempted into just such a wish.

"Her ladyship, the goddess SienMa, is waiting for me." Llesho rose to depart, and then added, "Habiba will want to know how Kaydu is faring."

Hmishi made a face like he'd eaten something sour.

"She is my captain and I trust her," Bixei gave a helpless shrug and grabbed the edge of the table as the ship heeled over in the heavy seas. "I don't want to think what will happen if Master Markko proves stronger in controlling this storm."

Llesho didn't think Master Markko would prove strong enough to control the building typhoon, but he wasn't sure Kaydu could do it either. He remembered Marmer Sea Dragon's offhand comment about her familiar. He'd had his own suspicions about Little Brother—and hoped the monkey's hidden depths were of practical use to his mistress as well.

No time to question it now, though. He shook his head, feeling the buds of antlers rising above his forehead. When he reached the upper deck, he let his hold on his human form start to slip. And then, as he crossed the open expanse amidships, he began to run. A step, another, sharp hooves clacked across the wooden deck and he was up, up, rising above the tossing sea. In his totem form, the roebuck that Bolghai had taught him to find, he made in his mind the image of the mortal goddess of war and flew to her.

Chapter Sixteen

"**Y**OU'RE WET."

That was Habiba's voice. Pig usually had the good sense to bring him to her ladyship's witch first. It gave them a chance to sound out the situation before they went blindly into whatever crisis currently simmered around the court. Llesho remembered when he'd accidentally traveled into the dreams of the mortal goddess of war on his own. In her dreams the Lady SienMa wore the form of a great white cobra, which scared the life out of him if he admitted to such unheroic feelings. From their first meeting, when Master Jaks and Master Den had tested his aptitude for weapons, he had learned to fear her as much as he had later learned to honor her. He never wished to have her undivided attention.

Habiba was, if not safe, at least not so visually disturbing. He had the power to take the shape of great and mystical creatures, but he seldom bothered except as needed during battle. Llesho had seen him fight as a great mythical bird and in the shape of a dragon, easier since witches and magicians all had a dragon somewhere on their family tree. Except for Master Markko, of course. He still didn't know what to make of Pig about that. Even given that the Jinn could not know where his foolish actions would take them, it had still been an evil thing to do.

Pig had disappeared again. The silver chain Llesho had reclaimed from Hmishi still lay empty at his throat, next to the Great Goddess' pearls. He'd felt naked without the pearls; their presence comforted him in spite of the trouble he would have explaining them if his pirate captors caught sight of them. He wasn't sure how he felt about Pig's absence, though. Didn't know what to say to him after the dragon-king's revelation, but he wasn't sure he could get back to the galley without him either.

"Ahem." Habiba was looking down his nose at him across a familiar lab table laden with bubbling equipment that oozed smelly vapors. He was awaiting an explanation for the seawater dripping on his marble floor, but somewhere nearby, her lady-ship demanded Llesho's presence.

"Stipes sold me to the pirates. I've been rowing in a slave galley for the past day or so."

Habiba gave one slow nod to show that he'd heard but made no comment about Llesho's return to slavery or Stipes' part in it. "And my daughter?" he asked.

That was why he hadn't already been hurried off to see the mortal goddess of war. Llesho had expected as much, and was ready for the question. "On her way to rescue us, as planned." He didn't mention whose plan, though her father would figure it out easily enough. "Master Markko is raising a storm that threatens to overwhelm us all, however."

Llesho considered passing on Marmer Sea Dragon's opinion, that she wouldn't be able to hold back the storm for long, but decided against it. Kaydu seemed to know what she was doing when he left her and he didn't want to keep the mortal goddess of war waiting. He shook his head like a lion, sending a spray of seawater flying into the room. Droplets spattered Habiba's robes with a dark, fine spray.

"Was that really necessary?" The witch combed a hand through his beard, all that he would show of his exasperation.

"Pardon." Llesho bowed low to show the humility of his apology. "Her ladyship wished to see me?" He hadn't mentioned Prince Tayyichiut's fate, or why Stipes had sold him to the pirates, preferring to make his case only once for the mortal goddess herself. That suited Habiba as well, except for the sea water Llesho had brought with him in his dream travel.

"You cannot go to her ladyship in that condition. Take those clothes off and get into something dry."

Llesho wondered first why a magician who could turn into a dragon at will and reappear with his clothing intact couldn't dry out a few drops of sea spray. Then he wondered where he was supposed to remove his clothes, and where the dry ones were to come from. Before he had a chance to ask any of his questions, however, Habiba gave an annoyed wave of his hand. Suddenly, Llesho found that he was naked, but still dripping on the floor. Habiba made another gesture and a cloth of soft cotton fell over Llesho's head and across his shoulders.

"I don't know why you didn't just dry the clothes I had," he grumbled. He had burrowed into the towel and hoped his mumbling would go unnoticed.

In addition to the powers that dragon blood imparted to a witch, however, Habiba was graced with excellent hearing. "Clothing falls within the domain of man," he replied tartly. "The sea, which you brought with you into my workshop, is the domain of Marmer Sea Dragon. Even in a dream, only he or his offspring can command it, to the finest of its drops.

"We've met." Llesho emerged from the towel to discover Carina had joined them and, with Habiba, was staring at his back. The healer's presence meant his brothers must be nearby. The princes were not on his mind when he hurriedly draped the towel to cover his front, however. Under Carina's professional scrutiny, embarrassment had turned his skin a deep burgundy from his toes to the top of his head. Once he'd had hope of attracting her attention, but this wasn't what he'd had in mind.

"Let me treat your back before you put on new clothes."

"Pirates use the lash." He'd almost forgotten, but his shrug set the angry welts complaining again along his ribs. The discomfort made it easier to bear her troubled gaze.

"Have they broken the skin?" He wouldn't refuse a bandage if he stood in danger of infection, or of spoiling dry clothes with bloodstains.

Carina wrinkled her nose with distaste, but shook her head. "No blood, but you should have bandages to protect the welts from the rub of your clothes until they heal."

"Moll would know something was up if she caught sight of them," he decided, "so I'd better not."

Habiba had been silent while the healer tried to persuade him to have his wounds treated, but now he stepped into the discussion with his own persuasions.

"A fresh cut would open your shirt, revealing treatment you wouldn't have received on board the pirate vessel," Habiba agreed. "But a little salve won't hurt. Something to prevent infection, at least."

"I have just the thing." Carina had set up her small shop in the adjoining room and she returned quickly with a dark crock and unsealed the wax that protected it from air and moisture.

In fact it did hurt, first burning like fire, then freezing like ice. But in a matter of moments, Llesho decided that he could hardly feel the welts on his back at all. His hands remained curled around his towel so she couldn't see the damage there and he didn't offer them up for treatment. They, at least, must look the way they had when he left. When the salve had seeped into the skin, Habiba offered him dry court clothes in the Thebin style. He couldn't quite bring himself to release his towel with Carina still in the room, however, even if giving up his towel didn't mean showing her the bloody blisters on his palms.

"I'll be nearby if you need me." With a graceful bow and not a single comment about his foolish modesty in the presence of his healer, she left the room.

"You can let that go now." Habiba maintained a studiously blank expression as he handed over a shirt and drawers. Llesho was glad for the slide of fine linen on his skin again. He thought he'd escaped comment from the magician, but Habiba was waiting for him with a raised eyebrow when his head emerged through the neck opening of his clean shirt. Llesho drew a breath, though he wasn't certain what he would say.

The magician put up a hand to stop him. "A difficult situation handled with discretion, but now we must hurry. Her lady-

ship and the emperor await. Mergen-Khan of the Qubal clan
has arrived within the hour; he demands words with you, and
possibly your head. His nephew, Prince Tayyichiut, disappeared soon after you departed his camp.

"He has sworn blood feud against your party, which grieves
him as much as the loss of his kin, he says, for the debt his
family owes your own. Since you are an exiled king, however,
he has come to declare war against the emperor of Shan, who
guaranteed your actions in the grasslands, if the boy is not
returned to him."

"Nobody forced Tayy to travel with us. I tried to send him
home from the beginning."

"I believe the first part of that, but suggest you work on
sounding more convincing when you try to persuade his uncle
of the latter part of that statement," Habiba commented before
adding, "Mergen-Khan would likewise declare war against his
neighbor, Tinglut-Khan, for the murder of his brother by the
Tinglut princess, Chimbai's wife."

Llesho had paused to listen to this summary of events and
Habiba hurried him with a wave of his hand. "Finish dressing.
Her ladyship awaits."

A king obeyed the mortal goddess of war as quickly as a
common soldier. He put on the fine woolen overshirt and slid
the breeches up over the linen smallclothes. A servant came
forward with a sleeveless Thebin coat embroidered in gold-and-
crimson thread crossed with blue silk. Llesho slipped his arms
into the slashed openings. The luxurious cloth drew his touch
but he curled his fingers away from the shimmering decoration,
afraid that bloody streaks from his damaged hands would spoil
the work.

As Llesho dressed, Habiba continued the briefing: "For his
own part, Tinglut-Khan would have words with you about the
disappearance of his daughter, the beloved Lady Chaiujin. He
has declared war on the Qubal, but her ladyship has asked for a
truce until the facts can be judged, perhaps again with your
testimony to the injured party. And I see, by the guilty conscience that marks your face, that he may have cause for his
complaint against you."

"I had nothing to do with the Lady Chaiujin's disappearance," Llesho began. His guilt had much to do with his dream
in which the lady had come to him in her bamboo snake form
and as a woman, whispering enticements in his ear, but he had
no wish to share that intelligence.

"Do you by any chance have my boots here as well?" he
asked, turning Habiba's attention from where he didn't want it.

The witch knew what he was up to, but conceded with a
little smile. "By no chance at all, we do. And a belt for your
knife and sword as well."

The servant brought out a pair of soft leather boots encrusted
at heel and toe with gold filigree. Llesho pulled them on and
buckled the belt at his waist. The scabbard for his sword hung
empty at his side, but the knife slid easily home in its own
smaller sheath. He settled the short spear at his back. Then Habiba opened a flat box that had rested hidden on his lab table.

"The others will be wearing their own crowns of state," he
said, and held up the silver fillet of a prince of Thebin. "We
have yet to win back the king's corona for you, but this will do
for now." When Llesho had settled the silver band at his brow,
Habiba led him into a long corridor he thought perhaps he had
seen before.

"Are we in the governor's palace at Durnhag?"

"It *was* the governor's palace. Now it is the emperor's headquarters at the front. We may be on the march soon, but that,
too, is a matter for her ladyship to discuss." Habiba made it
clear that he would say no more, and so they proceeded in
silence to the audience hall where the gathered dignitaries
awaited them.

In the past, Llesho's visits to the palace at Durnhag had
occurred in secret and under cover of night. Pig had disappeared during those visits, too, he remembered. He'd seen the
roof and the courtyard, various balconies, Habiba's workroom
on several occasions, and the private chambers of the mortal
goddess and her chosen consort, the emperor of Shan.

The last time he'd seen Shou, the man had been sharing her

ladyship's chambers, but he had seemed to take no joy in his place by her side. Rather, it had seemed as though he had hidden away in this shell of a palace to brood over the smoldering coals of his wounds. And her ladyship, he would almost say, fluttered around the glowing heat of his agony as though she needed his pain more than she needed the pleasure he might bring her. Not for the first time he wondered at her marriage to the governor of Farshore, who had been a man of peace until his murder at Markko's urging.

Such thoughts made him extremely nervous, more so than he was at the summons itself. Never before had the mortal goddess of war called him to a formal and public audience. It might bode well, but it didn't get his hopes up.

Chapter Seventeen

GUARDSMEN bristled dangerously in front of the massive, elaborate gilt doors to the audience chamber. Their chief moved to stop the newcomers.

"No weapons beyond this point, Master Witch." The guardsman bent his knee and bowed his head as he spoke, no doubt fearing some terrible magical retribution for doing his duty.

Habiba touched him lightly on the shoulder. He flinched, but settled under the gentle touch. "The knife is a ritual object of the Thebin court. As for the spear, her ladyship gifted him with it. She will want to see for herself how these two have fared together."

The chief of the guards spared a glance filled with dread for the weapon and Llesho wondered for a moment if the man could hear it whispering in his ear. *Let us go on*, he willed the guard. *For it will not be left behind.*

The guard lost the focus of his gaze for a moment. When he came back to himself, he seemed to have come to the same conclusion. Stepping aside, he signaled his men who swung the huge doors wide for them. Habiba swept Llesho into the audience chamber and followed in his train to the echoes of the crier announcing their names.

As he'd noticed about those parts of the palace he'd seen before in his visits, Llesho observed that the audience chamber was crowded with the wealth that the governor of Guynm Province had extorted from his neighbors and had stolen from his own people. He remembered Shou's horror at the torture chambers in the governor's cellars. The corrupt official was dead now, and no loss to anyone. His legacy remained in this overheated room aglitter with gold and silver and sumptuous with carved rosewood thrones upholstered in satin and draperies of heavy beaten silk. The floor was set with glass tiles colored like jewels, each no bigger than the nail on Llesho's thumb. Overhead, chimes in the shapes of birds and butterflies made endless music of the breeze that sifted through the slotted windows cut in the walls high above them.

There were five thrones set in a semicircle, Llesho noted. Mergen-Khan, in the cone-shaped hat heavy with silver threads that served the Qubal people as a crown, sat on the throne that would have been the farthest right if they'd been set in a straight row. Mergen seemed to have aged since they'd last met. He'd lost a brother to betrayal and he believed that once again trust had cost him dearly in his nephew. His hooded eyes followed Llesho's approach with predatory intensity over a set mouth made grim by the lines that etched themselves on either side of his nose.

He sat with his back straight and his legs tucked up as if he rested on the dais of the ger-tent on the grasslands, in a caftan of red-and-yellow brocade under a dark blue sleeveless coat with the sky and the sea woven through it. Chimbai-Khan had worn those very clothes at Llesho's first audience in the ger-tent palace that, like the clothes and the crown and the lost boy, belonged to Mergen now. Llesho met his eyes as openly as he could, but still he flinched at what he saw there. How many people would die if he didn't get Tayy off that boat? Too many, and he figured their number would start with him. It wouldn't happen, though. He couldn't do anything about Chimbai-khan, but they'd get Tayy back. He'd already promised that.

A man Llesho didn't know sat in the throne that would have been the farthest left if the line had not curved in upon itself. The stranger was old in a human way, with iron-gray hair and a seamed face pale with some great anguish. He had a cone-shaped hat like the one Mergen wore, but with gold threads instead of silver, and a costume of caftan and coat as elaborately woven as that of the Qubal Khan. Even in less identifiable clothes, however, the strong, sharp features would have given him away as a Harnishman. Tinglut-Khan, grieving the loss of his daughter, Llesho guessed. He had seen enough of grief and battle to know they had the makings of a war sitting in those opposing chairs.

The throne next to Mergen-Khan was empty. Shou sat next to the stranger, watching as Llesho walked across the jewel-tiled floor with Habiba at his back. The life had returned to the emperor's eyes, which focused unflinchingly on Llesho's approach. Little else showed of his face, however. Like the others, he had dressed for a state occasion, including the huge gold helmet that covered most of his features. Llesho had only seen the helmet once before. Shou had passed through the streets wearing it and the golden clothes of state in the celebration that followed the defeat of the Harnish raiders in the Imperial City of Shan. Then, Llesho had thought that the emperor looked like a god. Time had passed and he'd grown at least a little bit wiser. He wondered, now, how Shou managed to balance the heavy burden on his slender neck.

Her ladyship, SienMa, the mortal goddess of war, sat at the center of the gathering with Shou at her right hand. Her ladyship had dressed in the colors of Thousand Lakes Province, blues and greens drifting into one another like the lake grasses floating under the water. At her waist she wore a girdle of embroidery stiffened with buckram and held by a series of buckles worked in precious metals. Her face was white as snow. White as death. Blood-red tinted her lips and the long curved tips of her nails. She wore no ornaments of hair or throat to draw the eye of the beholder from the glistening blue-black fall of her hair or the brightness of her eyes. To make her interest clear to all who saw them, she rested her blood-tipped fingers delicately against the back of Shou's hand, which lay on the arm of his tall throne. He didn't look at her, but settled under her touch. Just so, she showed both her favor and her control.

On a step below the five thrones, four lesser chairs had been placed in a row and on each chair sat one of the princes of

Thebin, each in the court clothes of the Palace of the Sun, and each with a silver coronet around his forehead. Adar's arm and shoulder lay bandaged tight along his side, but he had lost some of the purple weariness that recent injury painted under his eyes. Balar watched him as one might who walked a narrow bridge over a deep gorge with rocky teeth reaching out for him from below.

Shokar made as if to rise, but thought better of it, given the kings and the goddess at his back. He settled back into his chair though he followed Llesho's every move with an intense protectiveness that shook him to his soul.

"I didn't realize," Llesho thought to himself, shocked to see his brother's love written so starkly into taut sinews. Seeing that love, he would have distanced himself from it to protect his brother, but knew for both of them that was impossible. Lluka didn't look at him at all. It seemed, in fact, that Lluka saw nothing of the room where he sat, so inwardly did his gaze turn. Llesho knew what images he saw behind his eyes and shuddered, horrified at the thought of being trapped inside those annihilating images as he was himself so recently trapped behind an oar. They had to find a way to stop it before Lluka passed beyond their reach into his madness.

He hadn't noticed the stool at the foot of the goddess until a silver trill drew his attention. Bright Morning the dwarf, who was the mortal god of mercy, announced Llesho with a flourish of silver notes he played on a sweet potato that fit in the palm of his hand. At his back rested a quiver of flutes, and he had wedged a small drum between his knees.

"Welcome back," he said with such warmth in his eyes that Llesho had to blink back his tears. He had missed the dwarf's quiet understanding, and the greeting brought all the feelings for his brothers gathered here, for Shou and even the Lady SienMa, dangerously close to spilling from his eyes. If he had come to account for his failure with Prince Tayy, the gathering of princes, kings, and deities reminded him of his successes as well.

"I trust we find you well, King Llesho of the Thebin people, beloved of the Great Goddess who suffers in heaven as we strug-

gle here in the mortal realm.'' With that reminder of the urgency
of his quest, the mortal goddess of war reclaimed the hand that
had rested on Shou's wrist and extended both slender palms for
Llesho to lay his forehead on.

"As well as can be expected, my Lady SienMa." He placed
his own hands beneath hers and bowed his forehead low over
them as she had invited him to do.

Having completed that formality, she addressed him more
familiarly. "My gift has served you faithfully, boy-king?" She
tilted a brow at him as she pointed one blood-tipped finger at
the spear peeking over Llesho's shoulder.

"It has not, of late, tried to kill me," he reported with a grim
smile more answer than the words. "I decide the direction of
its flight, and the spear limits itself to the occasional muttered
complaint. So far, our agreement holds."

"Then perhaps there is still hope." For the first time since
they had parted company in her yellow silk tent at the outset of
his quest, her ladyship showed him her true emotions. She
smiled with tears in her eyes, and he saw hope struggle with
such despair that he would have fallen to the floor of glittering
glass tiles except that his knees locked, keeping him upright. In
Shou's steady gaze Llesho saw that he shared her foreboding
and would fight to the last to hold back the terrible fiery dark
that awaited should Llesho fail in his quest.

With a flutter of her fingers to signal that they should move
on, her ladyship motioned him to the empty throne at her side.
Llesho would have preferred a seat next to his brothers, or better yet, to sit by the dwarf at the foot of the goddess. He had lost
that choice long ago, however, and took his place among the
kings. As was his practice, Habiba went to take up his watch at
the side of the mortal goddess, ever in her service. She gave him
no overt notice, but a little of the tension seemed to go out of
her.

"Your hands are bleeding and rough with blisters, Llesho."
She nodded at his lap, where he had locked all his fingers in
one tight fist to hide the damage. "What have you been up to?"

"Rowing a galley, your ladyship." Llesho took the question
as an introduction to the matter of Prince Tayy. He ignored

Adar's gasp of dismay and humbly bowed his head to offer his apologies to Mergen-Khan as he knew she meant him to do.

"Your nephew, Prince Tayyichiut, joined our party as we parted ways with the Qubal people, Lord Khan." The circumstances, which included the delivery of bad news in front of a room full of kings and the goddess of war herself, made him more formal in his speech than he found comfortable. Comfort, of course, had nothing to do with his present situation.

"We tried to persuade him to stay behind, but he felt it a point of honor to join my cadre's quest. There was a misunderstanding between us. I took something he had said as a rebuff. With my own feelings wounded, I fear that I offended him deeply. When I realized what I had done, I tried to find him, to make it right with him, but he had already left our company to return home. In the morning we found signs that pirates had taken him in the night."

At the mention of pirates, Shokar tensed as if he would draw a sword he did not carry in an assembly of kings and in the presence of the goddess. Mergen closed his eyes, as if he could will away the terrible news. After a moment, however, the khan gestured to Llesho to go on. A glance at her ladyship gave him permission to proceed. Llesho took a deep breath and began his tale.

When he reached the part where Marmer Sea Dragon lost his son to an ill-thought wish, her ladyship stopped him with a mournful sigh. Llesho agreed with the sorrowful sentiment.

"I would see this injustice repaired, if it is possible, my lady." He asked with a bowed head, as a supplicant.

"Give this token to Marmer Sea Dragon, with my promise—" From her girdle, the goddess SienMa took a buckle and put it into Llesho's hand. "—We will do what we can. It may not be enough, but that is a risk we all share."

"Yes, my lady." The weight of it against his open blisters hurt, but only a little. The copper circle had been worked in the shape of a dragon coiled in a loop. He hoped the blood that already marked it from his rough hands did not portend an evil outcome for the young dragon. When he had tucked it into his pocket, her ladyship motioned him to go on.

There was little more to tell. He finished with the news that Master Den now traveled among the pirates as their patron and king.

"You bring us news of brave and worthy deeds," she said of Llesho's tale. Musing, she added, "One never knows the intentions of ChiChu, the trickster god, but it seems to me he wanted you on that ship."

Lluka, who had seemed unaware of the conversation taking place around him, chose that moment to speak out. "Proof again," he said, "that only fools put their trust in the trickster god."

Catching his breath in a stifled gasp, Llesho waited for the retribution the mortal goddess of war would rain down on his brother for speaking so in her presence. The tense silence told him the whole room did the same. The Lady SienMa, however, bowed her head to acknowledge that the mad could sometimes speak the truth others would not see.

"In my experience as his pupil," Shou offered with an ironic drawl, both accepting and dismissing Lluka's complaint at the same time, "Master Trickster often chooses the hard lesson learned once over the gentle one which must be repeated many times. For example, this business of offering oneself to slavers. As I recall, the last time we used such a ruse in the Imperial City of Shan the point was to free the castle without losing the foot soldier. That lesson might need relearning."

Shokar coughed to smother a bark of laughter. Llesho never had the time to learn the game of chess, but he understood Shou's meaning as well as his brother had. Shou had dangled him as bait to find Adar's owner and buy the prince's freedom. It turned out that Shokar had already freed his brother, but Llesho had managed to stay off the block that time.

"He might let the pupil in on what the lesson is supposed to be," Llesho grumbled. "I learned I didn't like being a slave when I was seven and I don't know what pirates have to teach me about it that I couldn't have picked up with a word in the ear instead."

Mergen-Khan might once have questioned such magics interfering in the lives of men, but he had seen more than he wished in the ger-tent of his brother. His own shaman trusted this trickster, ChiChu, and the Lady Carina, who had learned at Bolghai's knee as her mother had before her, had traveled with both the Thebin kingling and his tricksy teacher. "The honorable emperor probably has the right of it," he agreed. "What we are taught is perhaps not as important as what we learn."

Llesho gave that a moment's consideration. He had convinced himself he'd learned nothing, but if he accounted for all the time since discovering that Tayy was missing, he'd figured out a lot. He'd thought he already knew most of it, but it turned out that he needed it driven into his head like Shou said.

"I knew Tayy was my friend, but mistook his confidences for rejection of my friendship. So I learned to listen more closely to the actions of a friend than to hasty words, and to question my own understanding when words and actions contradict each other. If I'd questioned him right then, Tayy would have been safe."

"Quests are never safe," Shou reminded them all. "You have ridden with danger as your companion since before I knew your name, young king. Prince Tayyichiut would be no less a warrior. He will test his skill against the blades and arrows of our mutual enemies just as your cadre has."

Stipes had lost an eye. Lling had suffered grievous wounds and Master Markko had controlled her mind in captivity. Hmishi had died and returned as a gift of Mercy, but Harlol had joined his ancestors, murdered by stone monsters who left a black pearl in place of his heart. Llesho carried that evidence of the cost of his quest among the pearls of the Goddess he had collected in a little bag he wore at his throat.

Even Shou had broken, for a time, under the magician's torments. And Lluka . . . Lluka was a warning of what would happen to them all if they failed. Llesho dropped his head, humbled by the suffering endured in his cause. Her ladyship raised him up again, however, with a finger crooked under his chin.

"It appears to me that you have learned more than this," she said.

He nodded slowly, conscious of her fingers rising with the

motion. With a slow smile, he lifted his hands to show his bloody palms to the gathered rulers and the mortal goddess of war. "I have learned the price of my honor," he said. "I will bring Prince Tayyichiut home safely, or die in the attempt."

"It seems you would aspire to be the mortal god of mercy," Bright Morning teased him gently.

Llesho knew he intended it as a compliment, and returned the smile with a shake of the head. "Not mercy, but justice." He meant only to say that his actions were no more than Tayy's due, but the words resonated through him like a forgotten memory.

Bright Morning seemed to recognize more than he ought about how Llesho felt all of a sudden, because he gave a knowing wink that puzzled Llesho as much as the feeling had.

Mergen-Khan studied him like one of Habiba's specimens, as if the khan was working out some puzzle meant for Llesho himself. Then he let all his breath out in one great release of tension that had held the room in suspense since long before Llesho had arrived.

"Justice. Perhaps," Mergen-Khan agreed. "A hard-won lesson nonetheless. For myself, I find the pupil has become the teacher. I have learned that true friendship has no limits, even to the sacrifice of life and freedom. And I have learned that the honor of our Thebin ally likewise knows no bounds."

Mergen rose from his chair and faced Llesho, bowing deeply to show his respect. "You humble me, Holy Excellence. I am in your debt."

"There can be no debts between loyal friends acting in good conscience," Llesho corrected him. "I will bring Tayy home safe because he is that friend."

"That may be a lesson you have to learn as well as teach," Mergen-Khan suggested. "Free my stubborn nephew to follow his heart because it is your duty to do so. After that, it is up to Prince Tayyichiut where his honor takes him."

"I guess safe is out of the question, then," Llesho conceded. For the first time since he had arrived in Durnhag, he saw smiles light the eyes of the gathered company of kings, though his brothers looked worried with it. What they didn't know about the Harnish prince they could guess by the company he kept.

This would, in normal times, have called for a commentary on Bright Morning's flutes, but the dwarf kept his hands still and his lips closed. His questioning gaze he turned upon Tinglut-Khan, who watched them all as if he would call up a ward against demons.

"You have said much of monsters and gods and the loyalty one owes a friend, young King Llesho." The old khan of the Tinglut clan nodded his head to emphasize each point of his argument. "And yet, you say nothing of my daughter. Does your honor stop at the well-being of a friend and useful ally in your coming war with the South? What of a woman who leaves her home to forge alliances with her kindness and her love? What of such a woman, lost in the vast sea of grass, and the brink of war to which her loss brings an honored friend and a potential ally?"

"I would speak of your daughter and cherish her honor as my own, Tinglut-Khan, but I never met her." It pained Llesho to speak his fears to the father of the missing Harnishwoman, but he could not, in conscience, withhold what he knew. "The woman who sat next to Chimbai-Khan as his wife was no Tinglut but a demon of the underworld with some plot of her own."

Tinglut-Khan's face grew red with fury. "And how do you know this, young man?"

"Because she told me so, while I slept on the grasslands on my way to Edris."

"And you spoke to this demon during your dream travels, as you say you are doing now with us?" Tinglut-Khan asked with disbelief clear in his voice.

Llesho shook his head. "No," he answered. "In a dream, I knew that the emerald bamboo snake had uncurled from a spiral rune at the bottom of a cup with which the lady had once poisoned me. When I awoke I found that in her serpent form, the lady had wrapped herself against my belly. She hissed my name and in the shape of the false Lady Chaiujin she offered to make me a king among her own kind if I would join her in the underworld. We argued."

He didn't tell them what she'd said. "You are a demon, too." Didn't want anyone to know until he'd figured out what she meant, or if she'd been lying to draw him under her spell. "She would have killed me where I lay, except that I refused her. Then she slithered away into the grass. I couldn't find her again after that."

"This is serious," the lady SienMa interrupted him. "Did you bring the cup with you?"

"No, my lady. Lling carries it for me until I have freed Prince Tayyichiut." And now he wondered why he had refused when Lling had wanted to rid herself of the miserable thing. What danger had he left among his cadre because he did not wish to bring it into this company?

Her ladyship accepted this with a thoughtful nod. "Bring it next time. In the meantime, I will ask my witch to discover what he can about this bamboo snake demon."

Llesho accepted the gentle rebuke. Knowing that Habiba was on the case gave him some measure of reassurance. As he expected, however, Tinglut-Khan dismissed the tale. The Harnishman expressed his disgust with a hawking sound deep in his throat. He looked around for somewhere to spit, and gave up with an irritated growl.

"This is all nonsense. Gods and demons do not consort with homeless kinglings in the light of day. I do not believe half of what you have said. If I did, I would order my armies into this city and burn it to the ground to cleanse the earth of these unholy monsters.

Bright Morning watched as if he attended some play or entertainment, but the Lady SienMa found his discourtesy unpleasing. Tinglut did not have to believe, Llesho thought, to bring the wrath of the mortal goddess of war down on his head.

"If you are speaking of Master Markko or the demon who has taken the Lady Chaiujin's place to murderous advantage, all here in this room would support you, and join in your grief." Her ladyship spoke with compassion. He was, after all, a father suffering a great loss.

Then she added a sensible warning, "When in the house of

strangers, however, one cautions a proper respect for the company one finds there."

It seemed for a moment poised upon a knife blade that Tinglut would object to her ladyship's rebuke. The khan saw something moving in her eyes, however, that stilled his tongue. *War,* Llesho thought. Even Lluka kept still.

Tinglut bowed his head. "Like Mergen-Khan, the Tinglut join the young king in learning something new today."

Her ladyship accepted his apology with a gentle incline of her head.

"I have to go back. Marmer Sea Dragon says that the storm Master Markko has raised will soon grow out of his control and Kaydu can't do much more than slow it down. The dragon-king has agreed to help us, but he hasn't yet said how, or if his aid will be enough to turn the tide."

Llesho asked permission with his eyes and received it when her ladyship held out her hands to be kissed. He rose and bowed to all the gathered dignitaries. Shokar seemed on the point of pleading with him, that if he stayed he might escape the fate of his comrades. Even he, with anguish in his eyes, held his tongue, however.

Rather, Mergen-Khan asked, "Will you do us the honor of leaving from our presence, or do you require privacy for your transformation?"

Mergen had studied with Bolghai the shaman and knew what Llesho must do to return to his ship. For the rest, they had traveled with wonders for many cycles of the seasons now. Tinglut-Khan, however, might need a demonstration to prove the story he had heard. Lives surely depended on the khan believing that the Qubal people had not murdered the daughter sent to be Chimbai's second wife. With a last bow, Llesho stepped away from the company of thrones into the center of the jeweled room. Slowly he began to run in the tight circle that Bolghai had taught him, gaining speed as he focused on his goal.

Like an anchor the place where he'd begun his dream travel tugged at him and he tossed his head, irritated at the itch of antlers breaching the skin on his forehead. A gasp behind him followed by Tinglut's guttural voice swearing, "It's a demon!" almost threw him off his course. He righted himself and lifted, to a litany of Tinglut's curses and prayers to the ancestors while Bright Morning played a cheerful jig to speed him on his way. As his hooves cut the sky, Llesho figured that the old khan would need assurances, but at least he had seen something of the magical parts of the tale for himself.

In the twilight world of dream travel, he felt the pull of a familiar, malevolent power. Master Markko, his inner vision ever roving, latched onto Llesho and pulled.

"No!" Llesho thrashed against the tug at his soul, felt himself surrounded by the turbulence of the distant storm.

"No," A deep, calm voice from outside of the dream world agreed. Something scooped him up and tucked him into a pocket of calm, away from the storm and safe from the magician's madness.

Then he was falling, his shabby slave's clothes flapping in the fresh wind and his arms and legs flailing as he returned to his human shape. The galley appeared beneath him and he fell toward his rowing bench.

"By the Goddess!" Just in time, Singer rolled off the bench where he'd been sleeping.

Llesho fell onto the padded surface with a bone-jarring thump. The spear remained strapped to his back and the knife at his belt, and beneath his shirt the pearls were a familiar weight. But . . . a moment later, her ladyship's buckle fell out of the sky after him. No pockets. Somewhere in his trek across the dream world, he'd lost his court clothes and landed back where he began in the slave clothes he'd left in. Which had no pockets. He made a grab for the copper token, but Singer, who was shocked but not knocked senseless from his fall, reached it before him.

Chapter Eighteen

THE GALLEY bobbed with a gentle warning of the coming storm, which seemed farther away now than when Llesho had left. He figured Pig had kept his promise, returning him to the pirate galley before he left it. The absence of his court clothes seemed to confirm his suspicion. That was good news. The bad news was Singer standing over him with the Lady SienMa's token in his hand.

"What are you?" The oarsman shook the copper buckle in Llesho's face. Fear made him dangerous. When he'd gone to sleep, the newcomers had been chained to their bench like the rest of the galley slaves. Even Llesho had to admit that waking to find his bench mate falling out of the sky on top of him was a bit much to take lying down, so to speak.

Common sense warned Llesho to tread cautiously. While his bench mates had managed some rest after their shift at the oar, he'd spent the missing time dream traveling and doing the heavy work of statecraft. He'd had no sleep at all, he was exhausted beyond measure, and Singer had her ladyship's token. He made a grab for the buckle, but Singer held it out of reach.

It was turning into a really bad day, and Llesho just wasn't up to any more diplomacy. "I'm the king of Thebin and you've got my property there—who're you?"

He knew his answer would rub a raw spot on his fellow slave. He didn't have the energy to worry about anything more than getting back the gift her ladyship had sent for Marmer Sea Dragon. Singer didn't seem inclined to cooperate.

"Well, I'm the king of Shan." Sarcasm didn't hurt as much as a punch in the nose, but Llesho still winced.

"Really?" Tayy stirred from his sleep in the well between the benches. "You said the emperor was back in Durnhag, Llesho."

"He is," Llesho heaved an irritated sigh. "Our good friend Singer is trying to say he doesn't believe me. Which is just fine, because I hadn't intended him to."

"It's true, then?" Singer fell to his bench and grabbed hold of his oar as the galley tipped into a small trough. Time and Master Markko's storm would catch up with them soon.

"Not really." The rest he'd managed had revived the Harnish prince. Discovering the biscuits in his pocket helped even more. He pulled one out and took a bite.

Relief flashed across Singer's face as Tayy struggled up out of the well. Anger replaced it quickly, though, at having been made to look a fool with all the talk of kings and emperors.

Then Prince Tayyichiut finished his sentence. "He used to be a prince of Thebin, until the raiders overran the city of Kungol and killed his parents. He was on his way home to reclaim his father's throne when he was captured by pirates."

"Not captured," Llesho corrected him. "I came to rescue you."

"Nice of you, considering it's your fault I was captured in the first place," Tayy answered tartly. Now that it had become clear that he hadn't been abandoned to his fate he'd cheered up considerably. It seemed he might even be inclined to live.

At that moment, as if to remind them of their situation, the beater changed the pattern of his drumming with a flurry of sound before settling into his rhythm again. Llesho twitched as if he'd been struck by the tip of a lash. He'd become so accustomed to the regular pattern of the drum that it had blended with the sound of the sea and the creak of the oars. He hadn't really heard it at all until the change reminded him of his position here.

"The call to the next quarter," Singer explained. He looked off to the horizon, where Master Markko's magic stirred the haze over the land. "I don't think we'll have a full shift of rest. It looks like a storm may be coming."

"There is." Llesho followed his gaze, remembering Kaydu standing on the deck with her hand out, holding back the wind. If he expected Marmer Sea Dragon's aid, he would need to get her ladyship's token back.

Tayy was familiar with dream travel and in the way of a Harnishman who spent more time than was completely healthy tagging after shaman, recognized the signs of it in Llesho's answer. "You've been travelling again," he deduced. "Where have you been while the rest of us slept?"

"Durnhag." He didn't ask for a bite of Tayy's biscuit, but Llesho wished he'd thought to grab a snack before he left the palace. Time moved strangely in the dream world. He knew it had been a lot longer since breakfast for him than for the rest of them. "The emperor is doing better, but I am in big trouble with your uncle. And Singer here has her ladyship's buckle, which is not meant for him."

"Durnhag? Wow!" The mortal goddess meant little to the Harnish prince. He believed in a different religion and had never met her, but he'd never traveled farther than the grasslands with the Qubal before either. "I wish I'd talked Bolghai into teaching me how to dream travel."

"He'd have done it if you asked."

Tayy twisted his mouth up in distaste. "Only if I agreed to train to become the next shaman, which wasn't an option even if I'd wanted to."

"I suppose not." It would have made rescuing him a lot easier, but princes didn't get such choices. Llesho knew that as well as anybody.

"Uncle?" Singer had listened in stunned silence while they repaired their friendship, but now he brought them back to the point where their story had set him back on his heels. He'd turned an unpleasant shade of green in the meantime, which might have been the effect of the increasingly choppy seas, but seemed more likely the result of the present conversation.

Llesho wondered what shade he'd turn when he discovered who "her ladyship" really was.

"Is this some sort of outlander game?"

"No game," Tayy assured him. He'd met few people in his lifetime who didn't know who he was, and so he didn't understand Singer's disbelief. "Mergen-Khan is my uncle, since my father's death, the leader of the Qubal people, the greatest clan to wander the grasslands." His tone of voice said the oarsman really ought to know this last bit at least, but Tayy skittered on to his next thought without looking back:

"If you saw my uncle, were the princes there as well?"

"All four of them." Llesho thought about what he had seen. "Adar is looking better, but Shokar would like to take me back to his farm and set me among his children, I think. And Lluka—" He stopped, unsure what to say about his brother. Tayy had no such hesitation.

"Watch yourself around that one," he warned. "His mind travels a dark and dangerous path."

Llesho didn't need the warning. Didn't know what to do about it, but he knew better than to get sucked into Lluka's reality again.

"If he's a king, what are you?" Singer interrupted the exchange of warnings with a barely whispered question. His throat seemed to close up around the thought, strangling the words. The rower shifted her ladyship's token nervously from hand to hand. He probably didn't want to hear the answer, but Tayy gave it to him anyway.

"Prince Tayyichiut, son of Chimbai-Khan, now dead but during his life the greatest warrior chief of the Qubal clan. Also nephew to the present khan, Mergen, my uncle, as I've already mentioned." He gave a little seated bow to acknowledge the introduction.

"The plan didn't call for making a public announcement for the pirates to hear," Llesho complained. With a wary glance at the oarsman, he tucked his weapons out of sight under their bench.

Tayy seemed undisturbed. "We can't very well keep our

escape a secret from him when we are chained together on this bench," he reasoned, but Llesho wasn't reassured.

"We could have kept it quiet until we were ready to go. Then he wouldn't have time to warn the pirates."

The oarsman, however, had paid no attention to their argument and telling the pirates was the farthest thing from his mind. "I share an oar with a prince and a king?" He shook his head, still unsure whether they were playing a game at his expense. "I would cuff you both on your heads for making fun of your lead rower, except that this one just fell out of the sky on top of me." He pointed his thumb at Llesho in a contained gesture that took their conversation no farther than their bench.

Llesho responded with a little tip of the shoulder in apology, for what he wasn't sure except that it did seem to be his fault. Tayy seemed to be pacing his thoughts along a parallel track.

"Did you explain to my uncle it was my fault?" he asked, dropping the thread of what Singer should or shouldn't know about their escape plan. "Some hero I turned out to be, running off instead of fighting for my place in the quest. And then I allowed myself to be captured by pirates! I should have fought them off—there were only five of them, after all. You were right to refuse my company."

"I don't think even Kaydu could take on five armed warriors alone, not and win." Llesho thought she probably could, actually, but he wanted to salve Tayy's wounded pride. It seemed the sort of thing a friend would do. "I told your uncle that I overreacted to a misunderstanding and got you in trouble. He seemed to think you were equally at fault, however, and has forgiven everything because of my efforts to repair the damage my foolishness has caused. He'd appreciate it if I got you back out alive, of course."

"Good of him." Tayy sniffed. "I still haven't decided whether I've forgiven you."

He finished his biscuits and looked around for more, but he'd missed his bean soup back the other side of his nap. Singer gestured with her ladyship's token at the barrel in their well, and Tayy drew himself a cup and drank it down with a satisfied slurp.

"You mentioned a plan," he reminded Llesho. "When do we escape? I really don't like all this water." he gestured over the side to indicate the vast salty body of it, and not the cup in his hand.

At the mention of a plan, Singer scanned the deck nervously, but the pirates had their eyes turned to the stern, gauging the cloud bank moving off the shore. "Don't even think it," he warned them. "Since this one arrived," he palmed the copper buckle and gave Llesho the thumb again, "we have been watched constantly by the pirate king among our captors, and by the new slave who came on board with him after the raid on the *Guiding Star.*"

"The slave will get along much better if you return that buckle, since it was meant for him." He didn't mention the dragon-king's identity. The reminder of their danger had Llesho craning his neck, however. "It's Moll and Alph we have to worry about," he warned them, but he saw no sign of the pair on deck. "Moll paid Stipes six copper coins for me, and she won't be happy when we slip away."

Tayy took a quick look around as well. Though Moll had come aboard with Llesho and he couldn't know her, he had his own experience with the pirates to make him wary.

About Master Den, however, Llesho thought he could reassure them both. "Unless I have been mistaken these past three cycles of the seasons, your pirate king is in disguise as well, and I suspect he'll have a lecture waiting for us when we are done here."

"The trickster god is Llesho's teacher," Prince Tayy explained to his bench mate, "and even worse than Bolghai about learning by experience. Or I hope that's the idea."

"Unless it's been a trick all along." Llesho conceded the possibility. "Shou seems to think not, though. The emperor seems pretty sure this is another one of those awful tests the gods are always springing on us." He didn't mention Lluka's opinion which Tayy would have taken contrarily as a good sign.

"Now I know you are yarning stories to pull an old rower's tail," Singer objected. "Next you'll be telling me that you know the dragon who resides at the bottom of this sea."

Llesho didn't want to tell him any more than he already had, at least not until he got that buckle back. The stranger who had lately introduced himself as Marmer Sea Dragon had left his bench, however, as if there was nothing unusual about chained slaves wandering about the galley at will. No one was looking in his direction, not even Master Den. With each step the sea itself seemed to calm beneath his feet.

"My Lord Dragon," Llesho greeted the man with a proper bow, which he returned.

"This isn't happening," Singer whispered, burying his head in his hands.

Llesho had no time to comfort him, and Tayy, while willing, came from a straight-talking people. "Of course it is!" the prince insisted. "I never thought I'd meet a dragon in real life, but Llesho always knows the most interesting people."

"Not for long. Without some help, we'll all be too dead to know anybody." Llesho turned to Marmer Sea Dragon, still in human form, with his appeal.

"Holy King of Thebin," the human form of Marmer Sea Dragon said, "how fares your witch?"

"As well as she can," Llesho admitted, then explained using the polite form of speech that reminded him to be nervous around such creatures. "Captain Kaydu holds back the wind for the moment, but soon, I think, it will overtake her ship. She stands to lose all hands."

His cadre would drown, taking with them the only chance he had to rescue Tayy and himself from the pirates or the sea. "I have been in counsel with the emperor and the khans, and her ladyship, the mortal goddess of war, who has sent you a token."

He didn't want to tell the dragon-king that Singer had stolen the gift of the Lady SienMa. Fortunately, he didn't have to. The oarsman dropped the copper buckle as if it were on fire.

Quick as a blink, the dragon-king reached out and snatched the ornament out of the air. He held it to the uncertain light, in which the copper coils of the dragon design stood out sharply. "This is from the mortal goddess of war?" he asked, though he seemed to know what it was and where it came from. His face alternately suffused with color and drained of it, so that he was by turns pale as a ghost and an inhuman shade of green.

"On the other side of my dream, you promised to help Kaydu, the captain of my cadre, who is the daughter of her ladyship's chief adviser." He almost offered his guess at the reasons for the gift. On balance, he wasn't certain they had anything to do with Kaydu or her father at all. He did have her ladyship's promise, however, which he gave in place of suppositions.

"The Lady SienMa bade me make this promise in her name, that she will do what she can." For what, he wasn't certain, though remembering the image worked into the buckle, he might have made some guesses of his own. "She further bade me to warn you that it may not be enough. But, she says, that is a risk we all share."

Marmer Sea Dragon nodded, though it seemed that he listened to something far off and not her ladyship's promises at all. Then he flung the copper buckle high out over the water, well beyond reach of the galley. Something deeper than thought stirred Llesho into action, and he would have leaped after it. Tayy caught him by the shoulder, however, and tugged him down into the well between the benches. His eyes never left the copper token, however. He saw it blur and grow like a copper-colored mist, uncurling from its frozen coil of metal and filling the sky as it tried its gossamer wings.

"Father!" the copper-colored mist cried in a voice out of another world, filled with anguish and pain. Then the mist slowly broke up, and with it the image of the young dragon. The buckle, for so it had become again, fell into the sea.

"By all the gods, he *is* a dragon!" Singer skittered to put as much distance between himself and the dragon-king as his chains would allow. His leg remained shackled to the footboard, however, giving him no way to escape their company. Even Tayy gave a nervous hitch of his shoulder, but he refused to show more fear than Llesho did.

"I'm sorry," Singer began with a trembling voice, "I didn't know—" But Prince Tayyichiut, who had survived in the court of the Qubal-Khan, Llesho reminded himself, silenced the oarsman with a warning shake of his head.

With his soul fixed on the distant patch of sky where lately her ladyship's buckle had become the image of his son, Marmer Sea Dragon had paid their conversation no attention. "What would you have me do?"

The dragon-king turned a set face on the companions in the well. He seemed unaware of tears the slaty blue of the troubled sea falling from his eyes. Llesho would have given him more time to mourn, but he felt the pressure of the storm building in the distance. They didn't have time to wait.

"As king of the world below the sea you must have the power to block even Master Markko's raising in your realm," he suggested.

"I don't know." His silent tears had dried, but the dragon-king stared out to sea with the same fixity. Llesho thought his mind must still be reliving the vision of his son released from the copper buckle. Then he heard it. The sound of the wind had changed, growing higher in pitch. Angrier. The galley rocked on restless green wavelets that painted her sides with white foam. The storm crossed the shore in a darkening mass, gathering water as it spiraled out to sea.

"Think of the waves as wild horses and the sea as the herd." Marmer Sea Dragon explained what they heard with an example familiar to the grasslands. It was easy to picture with the white foam flying like manes streaming out across the gray-and-green backs of the choppy waves. Llesho knew the water, but he figured Prince Tayyichiut would better grasp the nature of the problem that way.

"Imagine that your Master Markko has called down lightning and thunder to stampede this watery herd. The tools he uses will certainly set all in motion, but will the herd go where he wishes?"

"Not *my* Master Markko. His quarrel is with Llesho." With the waves bucking under them like a horse trying to unseat his rider, Tayy did grasp the example, however. So did Singer, who sat stonily looking out to sea as the young prince shook his head.

"Not likely to go where you want," he agreed. "Not easy to get them stopped again once they're spooked, either."

"Now you see the problem," Marmer Sea Dragon nodded his head and Llesho noticed that his hair was the murky red of seaweed and his eyes the heavy gray of the stormy sea. "The witch has slowed the wind a little and rides ahead of the storm with a firm hand on the reins."

Llesho heard it as "rains," which seemed as accurate. In the distance, ominous dark clouds scraped their green-and-purple bellies on the rooftops of Edris, blotting out the horizon.

Marmer Sea Dragon followed his gaze. "Until it runs its course, there is little even I can do to halt it."

Prince Tayyichiut had spent all of his life on a horse. Llesho had spent most of the past three cycles of the seasons that way, and he'd ridden out many a storm on Pearl Island before that. So it surprised neither of them that the solution came to them both at the same time. Grinning like a madman, Llesho deferred to Prince Tayy with a bow.

"You can't stop a stampeding herd," Tayy agreed, "but a good herdsman who knows his way around a horse can turn it."

"Yes, he can," Marmer Sea Dragon agreed. "It's a dangerous maneuver, though, and requires that your witch ride at the very edge of the storm. Even then, it won't necessarily work.

"If, between us, your witch and I do manage to turn the storm, it will still run very close to her ship and to this galley, which is the course she set."

"And Master Markko?" Llesho feared the magician would fight them for control, bringing them all to disaster.

The dragon-king shook his head. "He's too unpredictable. I can't say what he will do."

"He won't stay and fight for control. If all else fails, he'll escape in the shape of a bird and leave his ship to die." Llesho had seen him do it before, and he had no doubt he would do the same again if his plan failed.

"No doubt," the dragon-king agreed. "Many birds fly before the storm and not all of them have feathered souls."

That sounded like Markko. "What bargain would you make, Lord Dragon, to help Kaydu turn the storm, to save the lives that follow us and the lives on this ship?"

Marmer Sea Dragon looked at him out of eyes of stone, letting his form flicker and melt into scales and horn. "Her ladyship has already made the bargain for my services."

For his son, though Llesho wasn't sure if the goddess of war offered the peace of death or knew some way to release the young dragon from his prison of distorted flesh. But he would not have his debt paid by another.

"That is her ladyship's promise," he pointed out, "and does not pay the debt I incur on myself."

Marmer Sea Dragon acknowledged the honor of the request with a tilt of his head in a bow. "Where is Pig?" he asked.

"Pig is here?" Tayy asked, risking a glance over the low side of the galley as if he expected to find the Jinn swimming in the sea. "Will I get to meet him?"

Llesho tugged on the chain at his neck, pulling it free of his collar to show the pearl wrapped round with silver wire.

Marmer Sea Dragon recognized it for the Jinn's disguise, or his punishment. "Keep him there," he bargained.

"I'll try," Llesho agreed, though he couldn't promise to succeed. "I don't command him; Pig comes to me at need, or at the beck of the gods. Until he has undone the terrible harm he has inflicted on you, however, he will have no moment of peace. That I can promise on the honor of my lady wife."

"That will do." Marmer Sea Dragon sealed their pact with a deep bow and leaped into the sea. Freed of the constraints of their small boat, he soon reclaimed his dragon size.

"There he is!" Tayy cried out, pointing down into the water. Llesho saw the flash of gleaming green scales alongside the pirate galley, but Singer refused to look.

"Wife?" he asked. And Tayy answered, "You really don't want to know."

They were interrupted by an urgent flourish on the drum then, and Llesho escaped the necessity of explaining his promises to the dragon-king. Since he didn't quite trust Singer with the truth yet, Llesho almost welcomed the emergency.

"Storm warning!" came the call. "All oarsmen, ship oars!"

Most of the benches had kept an eye on the darkness growing in the distance and each immediately snapped to his post.

Chapter Nineteen

"**W**E'RE going to race it for landfall," Singer said. "Our pilot has decided on a course that will take us away from the eye of the storm." Pointing out what they were to do, he instructed them to bear down with all their weight on the handholds of their oar while he released the stanchion. Free of its chain, the great oar pivoted on the thole. They were off their count; Singer grabbed hold, pressing down on the oar so the blade raised up out of the water.

The beater had set a rapid pace with his drum. Singer held them steady until the bench across the gangway from their own was in position. At the next beat he threw his back against the oar. Since Llesho and Tayy were both new and might lose their pace in a panic, he called the count for them: "Step, step, pull! Step, step, pull!" Llesho would have found the pace torture for his already abused back and arms, but his knowledge of the storm that followed them gave him renewed strength.

"Starboard, hold!" came a call from the stern and all the oarsmen on their side of the galley held their oars out of the water while all the benches on the port side dipped and raised, dipped and raised. "All pull!" came the next command, and Llesho watched Singer, followed his lead to step, step, pull.

The order had turned the galley and they fought their way out of the current that would have dragged them back to shore north of Edris, through the deepest part of the blow. The sea was higher at the boundaries of the current and the work of rowing across it grew harder still. Then they were through and the beater sounded a rest for all hands, chance for a last breath before striking out on their new heading.

During the lull in the galley's struggle, Singer took a moment to let his young rowers know what was going on. "There are islands all around here. Our pilot will find a sheltered cove where we can lay up until the blow passes."

Though it was midday, they were beginning to lose the light behind those ominous clouds. The storm was gaining on them, and Llesho didn't see any islands. He didn't think they were going to make it. There wasn't time or breath for more discussion, though; the drummer had picked up the pace again. To lose the beat would mean death—at the hands of the pirates if not the storm—so Llesho straight-armed the oar out over the bench in front, taking the giant steps from footboard to footboard, and fell back again onto the padded bench until he thought the bones of his backside would be pounded to rubble.

Even here, well beyond the gray line of rain as they were, he knew they were losing the race. A fresh wave higher than the rest hit them broadside and the galley heeled over, dropping their port side almost flat to the water. Llesho heard the thunderous crack of an oar snapping under the strain. Men shouted in terror as the oarsmen who had lost their hold flew through the air, caught up sharply by the chains around their ankles. One man, thrown against the thole braces, fell unconscious to the bottom of the boat. His bench mate was flung with such force that he spilled overboard, leaving a severed foot dangling from his chains.

Llesho held on tight. The pirate galley rode high in the water at the best of times and the next wave might turn her over. If that happened, they would be trapped underneath and drown. His first instinct had been to pick the locks on Tayy's shackles and free his companion. The chains had saved one man on the port side, however; he was already stirring from where he'd been knocked insensible by the wave. It hadn't been enough to save his companion, however.

There wasn't time to do anything about it anyway. Already the horizon had disappeared again behind a cresting wall of seawater that swept inexorably down on them ahead of the storm. They had managed to turn their nose around and the galley rose on the great wave's back this time. Llesho clung to his oar as the sea fell away below them, leaving the bow suspended in the air for a terrible moment. Then they pitched forward, grabbing at their oars while the galley dropped with a dizzying plunge into the trough. The thick spray tossed up by the crashing sea washed over the side, soaking the rowers and leaving behind a wash of seawater to slosh at their feet in the well between the benches.

Llesho shivered in spite of the sweat he was working up at the oars. The low sides of the galley had seemed like a blessing from the god of Mercy himself for the success of his escape plan. Suddenly, however, they had become the greatest danger. Without their shackles to anchor them to the galley, they might be washed away in the next wave.

He'd experienced that contradiction of chains before, so it didn't surprise him that they might owe their death or their survival to their bondage. Unfortunately, he hadn't thought to put the chains back on his own leg when he'd fallen out of the sky onto Singer's bench. The next wave might well sweep him away. He could probably dream travel himself out of danger, but Tayy didn't have that option. The prince would die in the water he hated and feared.

Escape was out of the question if it meant leaving a friend without even a familiar face for comfort at his death. Sometimes, being a king was harder than others, he had long ago come to understand, and this was one of those times. So he stepped, stepped, pulled. Beneath his feet the well filled up with water while next to him, Tayy, with his reserves of energy already gone, moved only because his hands had clenched in knots around his oar hold and he couldn't let go.

Overhead, flocks of birds raced ahead of them in long, ragged vees, all following the same road in the sky. Their pilot made corrections to their course, following the winged scouts who must, Llesho thought, find land when sailors searched in vain for any sign to lead them. They pulled, pulled on their oars, afraid that the birds would leave them behind when, suddenly, a great winged beast crossed the sky, heading back into the storm and painting a long dark shadow across the deck as it passed.

"The ancestors fly to battle," Tayy remarked with a superstitious glance upward.

"Somebody's ancestor," Llesho agreed. Neither Mergen nor Shou had such powers of transformation. He didn't know how the Lady SienMa might travel, whether she could turn herself into a bird or follow the dream-road through time. But she wouldn't leave in the middle of negotiations, when an ill-considered word might see the grasslands at war with the Shan Empire.

Habiba had traveled both the dream-road and the road of magical creatures before, though, and he wouldn't leave his daughter to fight the storm alone. Llesho took comfort in the knowledge that Kaydu would have powerful magical assistance from her father as well as Marmer Sea Dragon. Maybe even from Little Brother, if the suspicions he had formed proved true. A monkey god, if such he was, had more of a reputation for mischief than for rescuing hapless travelers, but for Kaydu he might make an exception. Their own fate was not so well provided.

Another of the giant oars snapped in the heavy seas, this time to starboard and far to the stern. Llesho saw the rowers flutter like birds with arrows in their breasts, though they seemed to come to rest with all their limbs intact.

"Stow oars! Stow oars!" The wind had risen so that they couldn't hear the call from the stern. Pirates stationed at short distances from one another along the gangway passed the order down the ship, however, and gradually the oars came to rest. Llesho thought that they would tie the oar above the waterline using the stanchion as they had during their break, but Singer showed them how to tuck the oar up along the side and lash it out of the way.

This had to be done in order, so that their oar would rest above that of the bench in front of them and below that of the bench behind. Then Singer grabbed onto the stanchion chain and told them to do the same. Together they huddled on their bench, trembling with fear that they would be cast into the sea with a leg torn off at any moment, or capsized and drowned as they fought against the chains that dragged them down.

"We're not going to die, are we?" Tayy's voice shook, and Llesho flung an arm around his shoulder, as much for something to hang onto in the galley as to offer comfort.

"I don't think so," Llesho said, but inside he was wondering about Master Markko, with the greed of a failed magician and the captive spirit of a dragon-lord twisting his flesh out of true. They were still on the outer edge of the typhoon, but it felt like they were plunging into the very heart. He tried not to think about how much worse it must be where Kaydu was.

"Can you find out?"

"I don't exactly have a silver bowl of still water handy." He didn't mean to snap, but they'd just plowed through another trough and he was feeling sick as well as terrified.

Tayy looked at him with misery and threw up at his feet, too paralyzed with fear of the violent seas to hang his head over the side. Which was probably smart and made their bench smell no worse than the one in front of them, where the rowers were taking turns emptying their guts. Llesho figured in about ten seconds he'd be in the same position, with his head between his legs. It had been a lot longer since he'd eaten, but he expected the last water he'd drunk to make a reappearance real soon.

Tayy was persistent in spite of his illness, however, and he made Llesho listen. "If Kaydu doesn't turn the storm, it's coming right down on top of us, isn't it?"

"Probably." He was swallowing seawater in big unwelcome gulps, praying to all the gods he knew that they wouldn't head down one of those troughs and not come up again.

"Then don't you think you ought to go and help her?"

"I came to rescue you."

Master Den's huge frame loomed over them suddenly. The trickster god looked ragged and waterlogged. His red-and-yellow-satin pants, rimed with salt, clung to his tree-trunk legs and salt water dripped from his lashes onto his thick lips.

"I think he should go to Kaydu," Prince Tayyichiut informed the trickster god. "If she fails, we all die!"

"Of course, you're right," Master Den agreed.

"I don't know what you expect me to do there!" Llesho shouted over the wind.

"If you don't think of anything more useful, you can always bail water."

With that, the trickster god picked him up under his arms as if he were a toddler and threw him into the sea.

"Llesho!" Prince Tayy's watery voice came to him from above the sea, but Llesho was sinking, sinking. Under the surface the sea moved in restless undulations, but he remembered old lessons and rode the surge effortlessly. He held his breath as if he'd never left the pearl beds and looked around, orienting himself by the movement of the seaweed and the direction of the fish who passed him indifferently on their fishy way. Then, underwater, he set his destination in his mind and started to make the motions of running on the land. He barely held his own against the sea pushing him away from the land, but he could feel the change coming and he leaped, scrabbled, found the deck and skittered across it. A rope snaked across his vision and he grabbed it as he slid down the wet and tilted surface until he caught up hard against a hatch cover that dug into his ribs like a knife.

"Get under cover!" Bixei appeared at the hatch and grabbed at him, pulling Llesho through and latching it tight behind him. They stood in a patch of calm belowdecks while the wind howled like a mad thing over their heads.

"What are you doing here?"

"I came to help."

Bixei shook his head, but opened another hatch that led them deeper into the bowels of the ship. They dropped through into a hold knee-deep in water and lit by one dangerously swaying lantern. Sailors milled in the darkness, sorting themselves into a line.

"Take this." Hmishi handed him a bucket full of water and when he turned around, Bixei was already gone.

"Where's Kaydu?" Llesho shouted above the sound of the sea and the wind pummeling the ship. "I came to help turn the storm!"

Lling took his bucket. "Do you know how to do that?"

Without breaking the rhythm of the bailing line, Hmishi thrust another bucket into his hands. Llesho passed it off to Lling, who handed it to a sailor who handed it to Stipes. He didn't, actually, know how to help Kaydu, so he took the next bucket Hmishi slapped into his hands and moved it along.

"I saw Habiba on deck, but he looked exhausted just from fighting the storm to get here," Bixei mentioned as he sloshed by with half a dozen empty buckets slung by their handles over his arms.

Llesho grabbed a full one from Hmishi, moved it on, took the next one. "Marmer Sea Dragon has offered to help, but the storm is out of control. He says that Master Markko started it."

"As usual," Hmishi growled. "He spends all of his time scheming about how to create a disaster, but he never bothers to figure out what to do with it, or how to calm it back down when he doesn't need it anymore."

Which did about sum it up. Llesho moved another bucket up the line. As far as he could tell, they weren't making any progress lowering the level of water in the hold. Good seamanship kept them running ahead of the wind, but heavy seas washed over them, spilling through the chinks in the decking to the holds below. Gradually, in spite of the bucket brigade, the ship settled lower in the water.

"Here." He handed off his bucket and slipped out of line. Wiping the blood from his reopened blisters on his pants legs, he headed for the hatch. He wasn't sure what he could do on deck, but it had to be more than this.

The wind nearly took him over the side when he stepped out on the deck. As he skittered down the slope of the listing ship, he reached for a handhold and missed. His legs went over the side and he scrabbled frantically for something to grab onto. Whipping by the deck rail, he managed to get an arm around it before he went flying out over the water. He hung on tight with his legs dangling in the air.

"Pig!" he called. "Pig!"

A set of piggy fingers wrapped around his collar while another set grabbed him by the seat of his pants and hauled him back on board the ship. "What do you want?" Pig asked. Neither the wind nor the thundering waves that washed over them troubled the Jinn's easy stance on the canted deck.

"Where's Kaydu?" That wasn't what he'd meant to say when he called out to the Jinn, but he'd already accomplished his main purpose; Pig had prevented him from washing overboard. The Jinn had missed a good opportunity to blackmail a wish out of Llesho, but the idea didn't seem to upset him much.

"The good captain is at the stern, lashed to a mast. Her incantations have held the storm at bay. She would not have held much longer, as her strength was failing, but help has arrived to save the day."

Llesho didn't know if that meant Habiba or Marmer Sea Dragon, or even Pig himself, but the question of "who" came second to the warning he had come above decks to issue. "We're taking on water," he shouted over the howling of the wind and the crashing of the water. "I don't know how much longer the ship will stay afloat!"

"That is a problem," Pig agreed. He was turning a sickly shade of green, which was a strange sight on a large black pig. "Nevertheless, this is just the very tip of the storm, which will wash us all before it as if we were mere specks in the maelstrom."

That seemed a bit more elaborate an explanation than the moment required, but Llesho got the point. Why worry about the water in the hold when they would be washed off the decks or smashed to splinters up against some reef? They were all going to die.

Not if he could help it, though. Determinedly, Llesho made his way to the stern, clinging to Pig as to an anchor. Habiba had moved out onto the gallery. He stood exposed to the sea with

his hands spread wide, calling down his spells and incantations
to the wind and the water and the earth itself.

As Pig had described, Kaydu stood on the deck, frozen in a
position of supplication, her hands also held wide. The ropes
that held her fast to the mast had stretched with repeated soaking from the waves, so that she was battered against the spar
one minute and flung off the mast at the next. She held her arms
out steadily, but her eyes had lost the sense of an intelligent
presence behind them. She chanted her spells mechanically,
the way a clockwork blacksmith might hammer out the hours
on an automaton.

At her feet, Little Brother clung to the mast, his wizened face
solemn, his eyes bright and alert as he took in all the surrounding chaos. With the wind and the high seas, he should have
been swept from his perch the moment he set himself down
there, but the sea seemed never to touch him.

As if he felt the weight of Llesho's thoughts on him, Little
Brother pulled back his lips in a wide monkey grin. By a trick
of vision it seemed that two creatures sat in the same place, one
the monkey that had traveled with them from the reaches of
Farshore Province to the very brink of disaster on the stormy
sea. The other, an old man, seemed to sit huddled at the foot of
the mast. His eyes were dark as Little Brother's. A bristly gray
beard covered his chin and his long, flowing gray hair fell from
a topknot almost to his elbows. The avatar of the monkey god
met Llesho's gaze and grinned, becoming again the monkey that
remained at the foot of the mast even while the graybeard had
appeared like a ghost around him.

Llesho shook his head, afraid that the near spill into the sea
had damaged his eyes, or his perception. The old man was
gone, however, leaving only the mystery of how the monkey
escaped the perils of the storm. It seemed unlikely that he
would solve the puzzle while the ship threatened to sink at any
moment, though, so he stepped out, hazarding himself to the
wind, and called upon Marmer Sea Dragon.

"Lord Dragon!" he called, "I have come to help turn back
the storm!"

No answer came, and Llesho felt the cold touch of despair

freezing his heart. They would founder under the great mountains of water that rose up around them. He had done this,
bringing his friends out on the terrible sea to die. With their
deaths, the quest would end in failure. Thebin would remain
under the despotic rule of the Harnish raiders and the very gates
of heaven would fall. All because of an unthought word spoken
in hurt and in haste to a friend. The enormity of the outcome of
so small a mistake stole his breath and drove him to his knees.

"No!" he shouted, and recalling that a failure of manners
had brought him to this place, he replaced the angry words he
would have spoken with a plea. "Please! I know you are doing
all you can to help. But they don't deserve to die for what I've
done."

"No, they don't," Pig agreed.

Llesho had forgotten the Jinn's presence, but now he
weighed the cost of another, potentially dreadful mistake. Pig
had great powers, but they were held in check by one condition.
He couldn't do anything unless someone made a wish.

No one had ever confused a Jinn with the mortal god of
mercy. Wishes came with a price every bit as dreadful as the
wish was grand. He figured that wishing away a storm of this
size was a pretty grand wish, and didn't figure he'd survive the
price. On the other hand, it didn't look like he was going to
survive the storm either.

He turned, took a deep, wet breath to shore up his courage,
and Pig said, "Don't do it. My lady, the Great Goddess would
have my head boiled for her dinner if I gave you a wish. She
would bar me from her gardens forever, and they need me."

"Is there any other way?" he asked. Llesho knew the difference between the instructions that a spirit guide might rightly
give and the exercise of a Jinn's powers to grant wishes. Once
before, Pig had led him into the hills where he had freed the
Holy Well of Ahkenbad and gained the pearl that was Pig in his
disguise—or banished form. It hadn't been the working of a
wish, but it had served the purpose.

Pig, however, shook his head. "You are where you need to
be," he said, which was information at least if not more help

than that. "I can't do anything else without jeopardizing my own position in heaven."

Llesho stared back across the sea to the shore from whence they had come. He was thinking not of Edris or the grasslands, but of Thebin and the gates of heaven hidden in the mountains high over the Golden City.

"I need to save my wish," he realized. "I'm going to need it on the mountain." To fight the demon Master Markko had raised, he meant. Pig understood, gave a lift of a shoulder in a shrug as if to say he didn't know, but wouldn't risk his own fate for stakes as small as the lives of Llesho's friends.

Marmer Sea Dragon was there, however, sliding like moon-glow beneath the water. Llesho knew the way of dragons, that they might appear as small as a human being or large enough that four armed soldiers might walk abreast down their backs. So it didn't quite surprise him that the sleek worm gliding across their stern was longer by far than their little ship.

There was a hatch on the aft deck as there had been amid-ships. It opened against the wind, so that it opened only with difficulty. Llesho slid through and the storm slammed it closed tight behind him. He managed to secure it with only a brief spill of water following him onto the quarterdeck and made his way to the captain's cabin. There the shutters were closed tight, but a door let onto the gallery where Habiba had taken his stand against the storm. Llesho joined him on the narrow walk. He said nothing to distract the magician, but found the gate in the rail and passed to the outer side. Nothing protected him from the sea now but his faith in the dragon-king.

As if he'd been waiting for this very act of trust, Marmer Sea Dragon glided to a halt and raised his immense green head. Llesho craned his own head back on his neck, watching Marmer Sea Dragon rise and rise and rise out of the sea until the worm towered over the ship's naked masts.

The dragon-king's body created a little oasis of calm between them in the stormy sea, and Llesho bowed with appro-priate respect to the great green king.

"My Lord Dragon," he said, confident that the creature would hear even a whisper in his own domain. "I am no great

herdsman, but I have ridden from Farshore Province across half
the known world to this place, and I would ride in defense of
my comrades and the great Marmer Sea that is your home."

The dragon smiled, a terrifying sight in such a creature.
Standing rows of teeth big as glaciers stood guard in a mouth
from which smoke lazily drifted past a red carpet of forked
tongue. Llesho held his ground, however, and bowed to show
that he meant no disrespect by the request.

"We will see how good a seat you have," Marmer Sea Dragon
agreed. He didn't reduce his size, but dropped into the sea so
that his great snout sat level with the gallery. For a moment
Llesho wondered if the dragon-king meant him to walk down
his gullet and ride to battle against the storm in his belly the
way Mara the healer had traveled in Golden River Dragon's gut.
But Marmer Sea Dragon dipped his nostrils into the sea, making
a gangplank of his nose.

Llesho walked up between the dragon's eyes, clambered
over his great eye ridges, and reached the top of the monstrous
dragon's head, between sharp curved horns like a gate of bone.
Looking around him, Llesho found a hump like a third eye pro-
truding out of the dragon's forehead. He remembered the
dreaming-room between the horns of Stone River Dragon,
where the dream readers of Ahkenbad had read the future in
the sleep of pilgrims.

Green scales, each longer than Llesho was tall, overlapped
in a protective glittering pattern that covered the head and back
of the dragon. Llesho's trust had been abused on this leg of his
quest, first by Master Den and later by Pig, making him question
his judgment in allies. But he did trust Marmer Sea Dragon, at
this moment and in this situation. The great worms had their
own sense of time and purpose, and they could hold grudges
long enough to wear down mountains. But if a dragon-lord
made a bargain, you could trust him to keep to it. Llesho pushed
at a scale until it shifted enough to expose a hollow depression
like the cave he remembered at Ahkenbad.

"Be my guest," the dragon rumbled.

Tumbling inside, Llesho found again the strange veins of
light that crossed everywhere in the bony knot that formed the

cave. In Ahkenbad, the dream readers had placed a pallet against the rocky wall, but here a bed of seaweed spread a thick carpet between the horns of the dragon. At the center of the cavity, a spur of bone like a saddle rose out of the cavern floor.

Llesho undid his belt and wrapped it around the base of the bone spur. Then he settled his feet on both sides, using his belt as reins, to keep him in his place. He had no illusion he could control the dragon's flight from here, but he hoped not to fall into the sea.

"Take a deep breath." The words rumbled through the cavern of bone. With no more warning than that, Marmer Sea Dragon dived.

Chapter Twenty

WHEN Llesho came up with his big rescue plan, he'd expected to use his skills underwater to save Tayy's life. This wasn't what he'd had in mind. Water was pouring into the tiny cavern of bone above the dragon-king's forehead, though, so he held his breath and clutched his makeshift reins until his knuckles whitened. The dragon plunged deeper and deeper into the sea.

They were diving below the storm. When they reached a layer of calmer water, the dragon turned in a great curve and headed back toward Edris. Vivid images flashed through Llesho's mind: the sea boiling in angry rivers up the narrow streets turned the city square into a deep salty lake. Swift-running currents swept away buyers and sellers along with all their wares: priceless silks clung to cheap tin pots caught on the horns of cattle trying to keep their heads above water. Human hands reached out of the flood, begging silently for rescue as the torrent carried them away to their deaths. Little boats that might have helped them lay shattered against upper-story windows, now even with the flood.

Far inland, roof tiles torn off by the wind fell many li from where they had started, amazing the terrified horses who fled across the grasslands to escape the storm. And everywhere Llesho's gaze fell, the rain tumbled like an angry quicksilver wall.

"It's too late to help them now," a voice echoed in his head.

Llesho couldn't answer without breathing, and he couldn't do that while the cavern in which he traveled was full of water. But the questions formed and clashed inside his head, created equally of surprise and guilt. "How?" he thought, the dragon's words clear in his head.

And, "Why?" In his dream travels he had visited Durnhag and returned before he left with the idea of turning the storm. Why hadn't he traveled farther back, before Master Markko had shaped the storm with his mind and the sea? Llesho could have stopped all that death . . . though he didn't quite know how.

"We don't always get to choose." The voice of the dragon echoed in his head, resonating to something that Dognut had told him just weeks ago, though it seemed like forever since they had bargained over Hmishi's life. Fate ran a certain way, and changing it always had consequences down the line. Maybe Master Markko had played with fate when he raised the storm, or maybe fate had used him to do its will. Llesho was about to take the same risk in turning the storm. He didn't think he was meant to die now, however, when the end of his quest seemed within reach. Edris would suffer through the terrible storm. Many would perish on land and at sea, but he had to believe fate intended him to stop the end of the world or he would give up and breathe water where he sat.

"Good choice," the dragon-king approved his decision to keep his mouth shut and stay alive. They were rising now, and Marmer Sea Dragon warned him, "Hold on tight," as water started to drain from the bony cavern.

"Now!" the dragon's voice boomed through the cavern. Llesho clamped his hands over his ears and realized that he hadn't just imagined that the sound came from outside his head. A driving wind rose from unseen passages blocked off during their dive. Suddenly water exploded through an iris at the front of the cavern, forced out in a geyser that must reach high into the air as they neared the surface.

"Help!" Llesho grabbed the bone spur he had used as a saddle, but he was lifted out of his seat, flung aloft by the powerful wind whistling through the cavern.

"Hold on!" Marmer Sea Dragon snapped at him.

Llesho tightened his hands around the spur while the wind swept him end over end, so that his legs stretched out in front of him, drawing him into the storm with the water spout.

"I can't!" he screamed. He'd lost all sense of feeling in his hands. Already bloody and blistered from his time at the oar, they couldn't hold him any longer. One finger slipped, another, another. He felt the air go out of him in a defeated sigh as strength failed him. His hands opened, the wind took him, and he flew, out of the cavern, into the air.

To be plucked out of the spume by a hook of horn growing out of the joint on the dragon's wing that would have been an elbow in a human. They had come to the surface behind the storm which was moving slowly away from them now. To their rear, Llesho could see the shattered wreckage of the port. Ahead, the relentless lashing of the wind raised the sea into great towering mountains that met the banks of evil green and blue-black clouds on every side. Rain pounded at the troughs in slanted sheets, blending air and water in one turbulent essence. Only the angry white foam that capped the waves and ran away down their sides marked the dividing line between the sky and the sea.

"Try to stay put this time," Marmer Sea Dragon advised, and dropped his passenger back into the bony cavern between his horns.

Llesho caught hold of his belt, which had remained fast to the bony outcrop where he had tied it. Then the dragon-king stretched out his great, scaly wings. They flew, so high that they soon looked down on the violent, many-armed disk of the typhoon. It was quieter up here. Amazingly, Great Sun still chased his brothers across a blue-and-yellow sky while below the clouds turned in a huge spiral dance of death.

Over the many li his quest had carried him, Llesho had seen a myriad of things that had frozen him right to his soul in horror. Magicians in the shapes of mythical creatures had made war above his head. Golden Dragon Bridge had come to life, throwing Master Markko's troops into the river and swallowing whole his healer, the aspirant Mara. Master Markko himself had raised stone monsters from the very ground, murderous, unkillable creatures that ate the hearts of warriors and left bits of stone in their places. Nothing, however, had inspired him with as much awe and terror as that great, ferociously wheeling storm.

"By the Goddess," Llesho whispered, overcome by the sight spread out as far as he could see. "How can we stop such a monster!"

"We can't," Marmer Sea Dragon agreed, "but we can, perhaps, turn it a bit."

Llesho shook his head as if he could clear it of the terrible sight and deny his part in it at the same time. He would do whatever he must, of course, but for a moment, he gave in to the human need to deny the enormity of what he must do. The dragon-king couldn't see the gesture, of course, but read the answer as he had read all of Llesho's thoughts and moods in the chamber between his horns. He didn't say anything about Llesho's part in bringing such violent death to the Marmer Sea, however. Rather, he cautioned Llesho against taking on too much blame.

"However it happened, you were bound to cross the Marmer Sea in search of your brother-prince, and the magician was bound to follow you," he said. "Blame yourself for the suffering of your friend Tayyichiut, whose back has felt the lash by your actions. But this storm, and the upset that it brings to the sea and the shore, belongs to him who follows you, and to the Jinn who set the madman in motion to reward an ill-considered wish."

Llesho felt in his bones the truth of the dragon's words, but they didn't make him feel any better. *I could have stopped this,* he thought, and imagined Master Den's response to such a claim. The trickster god would smack him on the back of the head and warn him against using guilt as false pride. Which was probably true and didn't change anything.

"What can I do?"

"Pray," the dragon-king answered.

It sounded, at first, like an insult, that Llesho could be no help but must stay out of the way. Dragons were a respectful species when it came to the spirit, however. They were, after all, creatures of the sky, where the celestial kingdom lay, as well as of the water. Marmer Sea Dragon wouldn't taunt him with the Way of the Goddess. There was something . . .

Llesho closed his eyes and began to move through the motions of the prayer forms. "Red Sun." He stretched to honor Great Sun, which shed a golden light on the tops of the billowing clouds. As he stretched his arms in the up-reaching circle, he shaped in his mind the memory of the gardens of heaven. The light there flushed the sky with a diffused glow that never changed. Moving into the "Twining Branches" form, he called to mind the wild profusion of plants and tangled weeds that had overrun the heavenly gardens. And in this moment of great need, it was the plain and graying beekeeper he conjured in his mind.

Suddenly, he was there in the heavenly gardens. Disoriented from the shift across space and dimensions, he sprawled on his knees in front of a tree with a bees' nest in it. The Goddess had appeared to him beneath this very tree on his first dream visit to the heavenly gardens. She was waiting for him now in the same place, with the netting tucked out of the way over the crown of her wide-brimmed hat.

"Llesho?" She bent to touch his shoulder, lifting him up. "What has happened?"

"I don't know how I got here," he answered with a deep bow from the waist. "But the quest is in grave peril."

Briefly he repeated the story of Tayy's capture and their ill-fated struggle with the storm. When he had finished with Marmer Sea Dragon's instructions to pray, she nodded as if none of his words surprised her.

"I know the lesson Master ChiChu wished to teach with this prank, and you have surpassed all our hopes. This time, however, our trickster friend risks too much."

Master Den seemed the chief target of the Goddess' anger. She brushed aside Llesho's own confession with a gesture as of a broom sweeping away his objections. "You have learned your lesson from that mistake and taken action that cost you dearly to correct it. What point in belaboring it now?"

Mergen-Khan had said as much, and honored him for his sacrifice. It humbled him to know that he had not fallen in the eyes of his blessed wife, the Great Goddess. For himself, however, only success would free his heart of the burden it carried. That meant defeating the storm before anything else.

"Marmer Sea Dragon seems to believe I can do something to help him turn the storm. I think he sent me to you to find out what it is."

"I've seen this storm from my window." For a moment sorrow clouded her brow, and he wondered how much she knew of what he had seen, and what he had begun to guess. He didn't ask that question—figured he'd have to survive to find out the answer—but waited until her terrible, bright eyes cleared.

"It's simple, really." The beekeeper briskly dusted off her hands, as if she could dismiss the worries that bloomed on her brow as easily. With an encouraging smile she touched his shoulder. He was back with Marmer Sea Dragon again, looking out on the terrible circle of devastation below them with her voice still in his ear: "Follow my Way, and the storm must do likewise."

"Where have you been?" the dragon-king asked.

"Praying," Llesho answered, and moved into the next form, "Flowing River." He felt the currents of the sea in his bones, and the way the storm seemed to touch and lift, touch and lift as he skittered along its flowing path.

"Wind through Millet" followed. Arms even with his shoulders, legs bent, he felt the wind pass through his limbs as he swayed, sweeping his weight from the back leg through his body and onto the forward leg, then farther, carrying the back leg through the move so that it became the fore. He envisioned the wind as it passed through him and answered the call of it, drawing him down into the storm. The wind and the rain and the clouds became a part of him. The wildness, the violence of it, took root in his heart and with it the need for motion and speed and the flex of muscles, gripping and tearing and turning end on end everything in his path. As he swept along with the storm, he felt stronger than he ever had, more powerful and more free. He rebelled against the memory of Pearl Island and the reality of the past day at the oar, and more shockingly, he tore and shrieked against the demands of his quest that bound him more surely than any shackles.

He felt the stamp of Master Markko's mind somewhere in the sprawling arms of the typhoon, feeding the great spinning disk with the press of his fear and desire. The magician became aware of his presence, clutching at him in desperation. He had lost control of the storm, but still he rode within it, carried along as in a herd of stampeding horses. He would have pulled Llesho in with him, but already he had exceeded his reach. His prey slipped out of his grasp.

Habiba's touch brushed against Llesho's senses, and Kaydu's. The storm paid them no heed. Its vast disk turned faster and faster as it closed on the tiny ship. Llesho shared its longing for the splintering of masts and the crashing of spars into the sea—a longing that the magician fed with his insanity.

Chaos. The storm reached to gather chaos in the curve of its vast spiral arms. Llesho turned in its grip, no way out, wanting none, and found an eye of quiet. At its center, Marmer Sea Dragon rested with his head propped up on the coils of his body.

"Is this what your Lady, the Great Goddess, intended of your working?" he asked, curious, it seemed, but not judging.

Llesho stared at him out of the storm's eye, as if he'd never seen the dragon-king before. "What do you want?" he asked. Even the storm knew its king.

"My son," he said. "For the moment I'll settle for a hope that the world won't end tomorrow."

That meant nothing to the storm, but Llesho reached for the worm's presence in the world outside the storm. "My Lord Dragon?" he said.

"King Llesho?" The dragon-king asked back.

"Yes," Llesho realized. And then he knew what he had to do.

Neither witch nor dragon, he had no power to command a

storm, nor did any of the prayer forms he had learned address such a need. But he could create a new form, following the Way of the Goddess to a new place on her path. Slowly he began to move in the paces of "Wind through Millet" again. Where the form called for straight arms even with the shoulder, he curved his arms toward his body, gathering the power of the storm within them.

Releasing the new shape of "Wind through Millet," he stepped out, as if performing "Flowing River" but then folded his knees so that he almost rested on his heels. Instead of shifting his weight from side to side, he turned in a tight circle. From this low crouch his foot lashed out. Ah. Here was the point at which the turning of wind and water had become a combat form.

Master Markko, who wished his way into his powers, had little knowledge of the Way of the Goddess, or how that way was an echo of the natural world. He had no understanding of the form or power of the typhoon he had set into motion but called on the stolen magic of the dragon-king's son to raise the storm to still greater heights, as if he could overwhelm Llesho with the pure might of wind and water. Llesho, however, had come into his own power with careful training and the grace of the Goddess, his wife of many lifetimes. Khri, his bodyguard, had taught him as a tiny prince in the Palace of the Sun in the Golden City, and he had learned at the foot of his mother's throne. Lleck had taught him as man and ghost and bear cub. And Master Den had added the formal style of the prayers to the inner knowledge he had gathered from everyone he had touched from the day he was born.

To set against the raw anger of the storm, Llesho created a new prayer out of his body and his soul and the teachings of a lifetime. In the shaping of the prayer he learned the nature of the spinning wind and the greater forces that propelled it forward across the sea. Now he had to find a way to change that course.

Marmer Sea Dragon read his mind and his touch, returned a satisfied "hrmmm, hmmm" whuffling through the passages of his long snout. High above the storm he turned toward a breeze that pressed with no great speed against them, showing Llesho what he knew. The gentle-seeming wind banded all the world of men, never restless but always moving. Storms might cross it, sunlight might stir it, but the breeze was always there. Gentle clouds of midsummer and the storm that circled in on itself were both propelled forward by this breeze.

Llesho understood. In the prayer form he created, "Gentleness turns the storm," Llesho touched here, there, and the breeze shifted. At its heart, the storm continued its rampage, gobbling up the ocean in its path and emptying it back again in angry torrents. But gradually, gently, and from a distance, the breeze turned the storm.

At first the new path seemed no change at all, a single footstep off its former route that Master Markko, caught in the violence circling outward from the calm center, didn't notice. Then, the typhoon seemed to take another step, and another. The gentleness of the breeze, aspiring not to destroy the storm but to guide it, succeeded where the force applied by the contesting wills of magician and witch could not. The great wheeling disk veered away from Kaydu's ship. Its new path would take it more li out of the way of the pirate galley.

He sensed the easing of Kaydu's spells, and those of her father, as they felt the changing direction of the storm. Master Markko, too, felt the shift. Screaming with rage, he seized upon the storm and called upon the young dragon bound into his flesh to set the typhoon back on course. Caught within the prevailing pattern of the world currents, however, even a dragon-prince could make no change in the path of the storm. Instead, he fed the storm with his desperation. Its far-flung arms spiraled faster, gathering so much water in its embrace that a man of Edris could walk a li or more onto the sea-bed and never dampen his sandals.

From high above the storm, Llesho watched that writhing, skyborne sea obliterate all distinctions between earth and air and water. In that onslaught, the malevolent consciousness of the magician vanished, swallowed by the very storm he had conjured. Not dead—that would be too much to hope—but Master Markko was gone, and sorely weakened, at least for now, by his struggle. The storm would carry him far out to sea, where Llesho's prayer form had sent it. With a weary sigh, he fell onto his back in the cushioning seaweed bed that lined the bony cavern between the horns of the dragon.

"You did that well," Marmer Sea Dragon informed him. "Better than I expected, better even than I had hoped."

"Don't you people ever get tired of tests?" It seemed petty of him to be arguing the point while the storm raged harmlessly out to sea. They'd just missed death by a whisper, however, which made Llesho short-tempered.

"I tired of them long ago." The dragon-king snapped his answer, revealing much of his own temper and pain. "But you can't expect all the powers of heaven and mortal beings to put their faith in your hands until they are sure you have the courage and the strength to use them properly. And that doesn't even mention the intelligence to know when to use them and when to keep still."

Llesho was exhausted and not in the best mood for arguing the fate of all the worlds. It made him snappish as well. "If you had anyone else, you wouldn't need me, so it seems a bit pointless to pretend there is any choice about it." Master Markko hadn't left any of them a lot of options.

"Some fates are worse even than the end of all creation."

Marmer Sea Dragon went very quiet all of a sudden and Llesho figured he'd said more than he was supposed to. Something to do with worse choices.

Then he knew, and oh, by the Goddess, he was too tired to consider it, but he'd figured it wrong all along. He had assumed that the demon laying siege to the gates of heaven would raise the terrible firestorms in Lluka's dreams, the chaos that ended all the worlds of men and heaven and the underworld. But what if that weren't so?

What if the gods and spirits had determined to bring an end to all of creation rather than allow the demon to enter the gardens of heaven? He had to figure that the powers of the universe knew as well as he, or Lluka, what awaited the execution of their plan. What could be so much worse than what they them-

selves intended? And what would they do to him if they realized he knew?

Llesho decided then and there he didn't want to find out.

He thought he was safe for the moment, but the discussion
left him feeling like a dragon snack.

"We need to get back to the ship."

PART THREE

PONTUS

Chapter Twenty-one

MARMER Sea Dragon vented a puff of warm air and salty water through the cavern where Llesho lay in boneless weariness. "Tell ChiChu, if you please, that I'll be around," he requested politely. Then he added the assurance, "I don't forget my promises, especially not to her."

"Tell him?" Llesho groaned. "You're not going back?" That meant another run for the dream world. Only he didn't think he could make it. Exhaustion seemed to be leaking from Llesho's marrow into the seaweed bed he lay upon, taking muscle and sinew with it, and leaving him no more strength than a fading corpse.

He ached when he considered even standing on his own. The thought of focusing his mind and his legs on the skills Bolghai had taught him left him stunned, as though he'd taken a blow to the head. Since they'd been exploring the matter of choices anyway, Llesho admitted that he seemed to have none here either. So he rolled to his side and pressed his hands beneath him to push himself up.

A gentle breeze drifted through the cavern as the dragon-king sighed through his broad dragon snout. "Lie down, boy." The sonorous voice gently soothed like a lullaby. "Remember, you had lessons in dream travel at Ahkenbad before you ever set foot in the grasslands."

In a cavern very like the one in which he now lay, Llesho had traveled in dreams to the gardens of heaven and back. He'd thought it a natural formation of rock carved into the shape of a dragon's head when he'd first seen the abode of the dream readers. Then Master Markko attacked and the Stone River Dragon woke up.

"Most people sleep and then dream," the dragon-king gently reminded him. "I think you can spare the time to do it the old-fashioned way."

"Tayy . . ." Llesho started to object, but the dragon shushed him with a soothing hoo-humm through the cavern.

"There is little you can do without a rescue ship," Marmer Sea Dragon pointed out. "Your Captain Kaydu must see to the storm damage her vessel has taken before she can come to your Harnish prince's rescue.

"I don't think Tayy has that much time." Hope had give the prince renewed strength, but Llesho knew that wouldn't last long with the galley receiving such a beating from the sea. He had to get back, if only to reassure the prince that help was coming.

The dragon-king dismissed his concern with a whuffling breath that nearly flung Llesho into the sea. "ChiChu has a use for him yet, I reckon. He may not be comfortable or happy, but he'll stay alive as long as the old trickster wears the red-and-yellow pantaloons."

The dragon's voice eased its way into his thoughts. As a pirate captain, Master Den could see to Prince Tayy's safety until help arrived. He had to believe Shou was right about Master Den's intention—a lesson, an adventure, but not murder. It made sense, just like sleeping did. The seaweed bed held him like a soft nest and he was so tired. Llesho felt his eyelids grow heavier still. Suggestion drew him further into the leaden drowsiness that called him to sleep. He found it impossible to resist the low rumble vibrating through the bony cavern where he lay.

"Master Markko!" The thought set his heart to drumming as if he'd suddenly fallen from a great height. His eyes popped open. "I have to find him."

"Gone for now, driven on the same winds as all the ships before that storm." The dragon-king answered in the low thrumming tones that were doing awful things to Llesho's concentration. "Leave that fight for when you have a hope of winning it."

Which was good advice. Llesho didn't stand a chance against an angry sparrow in his present state. The magician should be in no better state, though he'd never lacked for allies. What creatures had the magician gathered around him? What powers might they bring against Llesho's own followers? He didn't ask the questions out loud, but he'd forgotten that the speaking part didn't matter with dragons.

"Few," the dragon soothed, reading his mind as his kind did when a human being rested in the crystal cave between their horns. "Fewer still serve the magician by choice."

Which was meant to reassure him, Llesho supposed, though it reminded him not only of Marmer Sea Dragon's power but also of the bargain he'd made. His help in exchange for Pig's continued bondage. How free were the allegiances of his own company, which included a cadre formed in slavery and allies who bargained for the lives of their families?

"It's not the same." But there was doubt in the mind that sought to reassure him.

"I know." Llesho did know. He just wasn't sure the difference mattered. In the long run, he and Master Markko both used blackmail to get what they wanted. The difference was the magician held out the threat of death as a punishment for opposing him and Llesho held out the hope of life for those who helped him.

Bitter laughter hummed quietly in the cavern. Llesho got the point. Given a choice, he'd picked life as well. It was a good thought to fall asleep on, so he did.

He expected uneasy dreams to carry him back to the galley immediately. Like Stone River Dragon at Ahkenbad, however, Marmer Sea Dragon had the power to give him dreamless sleep and then to calm his travels in the other realm. It seemed like only a passing reverie at the edge of consciousness that brought him to wake in the well of his rowing bench. As awareness came back to him, he realized that his exhaustion had passed, leaving behind the grogginess that follows a deep sleep. He didn't remember how he'd gotten there but figured as dreams went, this one, in which he felt comfortable and rested, was better than most.

The heat of Great Sun fell on his eyelids but he wasn't ready yet to admit he was awake. Hoping to delay the inevitable questions, he kept his eyes closed and listened to the activity around him. Nearby, he heard Tayy speaking to someone in hushed but determined tones. "He's to sleep until he wakes, and I'm to watch over him. Captain's orders."

"And what's a six-penny slave to do with the trickster god and patron of all pirates, when this ship needs all hands ashore?"

That was Moll, and Llesho was curious about what Tayy would answer.

Master Den, however, intervened. "He's a special project of mine who fell into your hands through a combination of bad timing and worse judgment," the trickster god said. Llesho had a suspicion that his teacher knew he was awake and was using the opportunity to chastise his pupil under cover of the explanation. He was fair enough to add, "Still, it all worked out in the end. Or it will."

"What end?" Moll had a querulous tongue that grew sharp when others might withdraw into caution. She turned it on the trickster god now. "The *Shark* is beached well off her heading and you've pulled two able-bodied young slaves off water duty. We've a far way to go before we can call this voyage ended— their hands would see us on our way that much sooner."

"The *Shark*'s tale has a good way to run yet," Master Den answered agreeably. "But this is where our young princes part company with it. They have their own tale to spin, and it leads them away from here on their own path. Or it will do as soon as yon laggard greets the morning."

"Princes? Hah! Every slave's a prince stolen from his cradle or robbed of his birthright by a sinister uncle. If we start bowing to every scrap with a story, we'll have no time left for rowing at all!"

"My uncle is not sinister!" Tayy objected. "And he's robbed me of nothing. The clans elected him fairly because they chose his wisdom over my youth. To gain some wisdom for myself, I'm on a quest."

"Bah! Quest indeed!"

Moll raised her voice in derision, but Tayy held to his position, admitting only in the spirit of full honesty, "Well, it's Llesho's quest, really, but I am determined to help him gain his throne back and repay the debt of honor the Qubal clan owes his line. And so I will guard his life or his sleep, as Master Den says."

"Fine words for a fine fool," Moll grumbled.

"But true," Master Den assured her and laughed. "And a fine job you're doing, too."

Llesho could hear the sound of a hand slapped companionably on a back. The grunt that followed was definitely Tayy losing his breath to the trickster's exuberant approval. It was time to wake up, before anyone said anything else about him. He had a report to give as well, he figured, and though he wasn't up to dream traveling to Durnhag quite yet, Master Den would do in a pinch. He figured Habiba would tell her ladyship what had happened, but he needed the reassurance of his teacher that he hadn't messed up along the way.

As he'd guessed from the heat beating on his eyelids, Great Sun shone brightly, chasing his pale brothers through a clear blue sky. Sitting up, Llesho stared stupidly around him, trying to get his bearings. As Moll had complained, the ship had backed itself onto the strand with its bow facing out into the flat blue water of a sheltered lagoon. Low hills covered in dense green growth surrounded them, blocking the wind and gentling the tides.

He licked his lips, realizing he was parched and sore from the sea salt that had dried on his wounds. They wouldn't fester that way—salt cured more than barrel-pork—but he could have used some of Carina's salve right about then. Looking around, however, he felt a more pressing need for answers than for physical comforts.

"Where are we?" was the first question that came to mind, though perhaps not the most important he could have asked. As it was, Moll seemed unwilling to provide an answer anyway.

"That's for us pirates to know, and no business of yours," she answered him warily. "You cost me six copper pieces," she added for effect, "I suppose, if you're a prince, you'll be worth more than that in ransom."

"Probably not." If they were speaking plain truth, Llesho had to admit that she'd paid too much and wasn't likely to get even that back for his hide. When it came to money, he had none. "My country is in the hands of the raiders from the South," he explained, careful not to insult Tayy by damning all Harnishmen for what he now knew to be the work of the southern clans.

"What's this, then?" Alph, who seemed to be Moll's partner in matters of the galley slaves, had worked his way to the forward bench where the current conversation was taking place. He carried a short whip, flexing the long thin handle in an unspoken warning. Overhearing Llesho's words, however, his mouth pinched in around the idea of ransom while his eyes widened round as gold coins.

"Two worthless princes littering our decks," Moll filled him in, but a sly smile had creased his slippery features.

"This one isn't worth a silver penny to the Thebins." Alph had heard some of their conversation and he nudged Llesho in the chest with the handle of his whip. "But the Southerners would likely pay a good bit to get their hands on him."

"They didn't place much value on me when they sold me to work in the pearl beds in my seventh summer," Llesho pointed out.

The wily pirate burped, which seemed as much opinion about the young slave's worth as it was indigestion. At the mention of pearl beds, however, Moll brightened.

"And might you remember where to find those pearl beds now, young apprentice?" The pirate flung her arm companionably around Llesho's shoulder, leaving him in no doubt about the trade in which Moll considered apprenticing him. Pearls were worth more than most of the plunder they could gain by boarding the trading vessels that plied the Marmer Sea. If you had someone who knew where to find them, and if that someone had the skills to raid the beds.

"Pearl Bay," he told her, and because he knew that answer would mean nothing here at the other end of the world, he described its whereabouts: "Pearl Island lies off Farshore Province, on the other side of the empire of Shan."

"You've been to Durnhag, then?" Alph seemed to measure his answers for a lie. Durnhag, the capital city of Guynm Province, was the most southerly inland trade city of the empire. It seemed unlikely that he would know his geography beyond that point. Even Durnhag must be a place out of tales for the rovers of the Marmer Sea. With the trickster god at his side, it seemed a good time to strike a little wonder into the pirate's heart.

"I have," he therefore answered. "Once by caravan, and several times again in dream travel to the governor's palace." He did not say that the emperor himself now took up residence in that palace. Shou's business was his own, and didn't bear discussing in the open.

Alph seemed on the point of dismissing this for a tale constructed out of wishes to buy a moment free of the lash, when Llesho offered a detail out of his memory of that recent occasion: "The floors are made of colored bits of glass that glitter like many-colored jewels in the sunlight falling from the windows high overhead."

"So I heard once from a lady who had visited that court in her travels." Something about the way he said it discouraged asking what had happened to the lady in question. But the pirate's eyes widened as he realized Llesho had indeed seen the inside of Durnhag Palace.

"As far south as we are from Durnhag, that is as far south as Durnhag is from Pearl Island. I'm on a quest set me by the Lady SienMa, mortal goddess of war, and the ghost of my own adviser, Lleck, to free Thebin and defeat the demon that lays siege to the gates of heaven."

"Such a quest requires money," Alph poked at Llesho's hip

as if he might have a purse hidden there, which he knew was impossible. He'd been searched before boarding the *Guiding Star,* and had dropped his drawers to do his business over the side like the rest of them. If he didn't get the pirate off the idea that Llesho must have some source of income on his person, however, he was likely to discover the pearls of the Great Goddess that now hung around his neck.

He couldn't let that happen. Giving a falsely casual shrug as if it meant nothing to him, Llesho brushed the lash away and launched into the relevant conclusion of his tale:

"When I have needed the aid of troops, armies have been given to me. Emperors and khans have counted me a guest in their palaces of stone and felt. But I haven't seen any money since I left Pearl Bay."

For some reason, while this answer seemed only to confirm something that Alph had been thinking on his own, it outraged his consort, Moll. "You've come all the way from the other side of the world with not a penny in your pocket?"

"That's about it."

"And that fellow who sold you into my care for six copper pieces—he was no outraged farmer but a companion pulling a con to finance your quest?" she continued.

"Not exactly." Llesho refused to feel guilty for the deception. They were pirates, after all, and did what they accused him of on a regular basis. He still wanted it clear that his plan had called for nothing so like their own tactics.

"Kaydu, our captain, sold our horses at auction for the funds to buy passage on a ship. We made up the story about Stipes and a farmwife to get me close to Prince Tayy so I could rescue him."

"So you mean to abscond not only with your own person, for which I paid hard-earned money, but with this wretched excuse for an oarsman as well!" Moll cuffed Tayy on the back of his head, but neither he nor Llesho made a move to protest. They still hoped the trickster god's presence meant they would escape their current situation without bloodshed. Especially their own.

Master Den said nothing, though he watched this give and

take as avidly as the pirates themselves. Tayy did the same while Singer listened with his head studiously turned forward, trying his best—with little success—to look smaller than Llesho. Doubtless, he wished to avoid the scrutiny of these powers who argued around him. His ploy didn't work, however.

"And you!" Moll cuffed Singer as well. "I suppose you have been plotting with these destitute princes to rob me of my honestly acquired property?"

"I knew nothing," Singer protested, "until the dragon appeared to take the young king off to herd the storm." He glanced up at the sky, shaking his head as if he still couldn't believe the clean-scrubbed blue above him.

This came as further news to Moll, however, whose eyes opened wide with suspicion. "Dragons!" she complained, anger pinching her eyes into slits. "Dragons and princes and storms turned aside by magic! That's what comes of allowing the trickster god on your decks! You've cost me enough this trip, Master ChiChu; you can find your own way home from here!"

"If it weren't for Marmer Sea Dragon, and for the young kingling, come to think of it, you'd be having this conversation with the fish and not breathing on dry land!" Master Den seemed to grow even larger, puffed up in his most offended dignity. "Who do you think turned the storm?"

"I reckon there'd have been smooth sailing if I'd left the lot of you where I found you," she threw the answer over her shoulder, having dismissed them from her mind with a toss of her scarf-wrapped head.

"Does that mean we can go?" Tayy asked in a small voice from where he huddled in the well between the benches.

"And as quickly as possible," Master Den stressed his meaning with a shooing motion to get them up and over the side.

As usual, however, Tayy balked. "We've washed up on an island in the middle of the sea." He flung his arms wide to take in the whole of their surroundings: sand, water, hills, and trees. "We need water and food and a way *back off* again. How are we going to do that if we leave the ship? That old pirate is stranding us here, not freeing us. We might as well be behind walls for all the good the sea does us!"

No Harnishman tolerated walls for long. That he made such a comparison said more than any speech he might declaim about his feelings for the sea. Fortunately, things were not as dire as the prince made them out to be.

"I expect Kaydu will be here shortly. Right, Master?" Llesho cast a glance at his teacher to confirm Marmer Sea Dragon's parting words. "We'll just wait up on the shore until they arrive and continue on to Pontus with the rest of our cadre."

Master Den scanned the horizon with a worried frown, though Llesho saw nothing to trouble him. Off in the direction of the rising sun he saw a speck growing larger in the sky, an osprey, he thought, but not Master Markko, whose questing mind sought Llesho from a greater distance. He thought it might be Kaydu on a scouting mission.

The trickster god agreed, squinting off in the direction of the rapidly approaching seabird. "Help is on the way," he said. "If you want to be here when your rescuers arrive, I'd suggest you get off this ship before it leaves for less crowded climes."

Llesho was thinking the very same thing. He picked up his weapons from under the rowing bench where his dream-self had laid them.

"Hey, then!" Alph tapped his wrist with the handle of the small whip he carried. "What's this? And where did it come from?"

"You don't want to mess with the spear," Tayy warned the pirate with a too-casual air. "It's magic and it likes to kill people. He sometimes has trouble controlling it."

Alph took a breath: to scoff, Llesho figured. He'd been deadly with the knife long before he'd ever met the short spear, but Tayy was right. He didn't always control the spear. Right now, however, he did. It was easy enough to will the weapon to life in his hands, and he let the blue lightning flicker faintly along its length.

"Is that from a dragon, then?" The pirate seemed more curious than frightened by the strange effect. He reached a finger almost to the point of touching the spear, then pulled away again, wiping his hand on his red-and-yellow pants as if the thing had burned his fingertips.

"No," Llesho answered with the same false casualness that Tayy had used. "Her Ladyship SienMa, the mortal goddess of war, returned this heirloom of my family at the start of my quest. Sometimes I rule the spear, and sometimes the spear rules me."

He gave the man a dire smile that made even Tayy shiver. It had its intended effect on the pirate, however. "Did anyone ever tell you that you travel in unlucky company, boy?" Alph asked Tayy with no real expectation of an answer. "Best get the thing off this ship, then. We want no bad-luck magics on this voyage."

Alph backed away with his hands open in front of him to show he meant no threat. He tracked with a flicker of his eyes as Llesho wrapped his belt around his waist with his Thebin knife hanging by its small scabbard. If the pirate noticed the bag bulging with pearls that Llesho now wore around his neck, he wisely decided to keep the information to himself.

Sheathing the spear, Llesho gave him a nod to acknowledge that he intended to do just as the pirate instructed. Then he slid the strap carefully over his shoulder. It hurt where it rested against the lash marks on his back, but he couldn't very well swim with it between his teeth. When he had it secured, he clambered over the rowing bench to lower himself over the side.

This far forward the galley was still in the water, which was deeper than he expected so close to the shore. He plunged in over his head and came up sputtering again, bobbing in place as he called for Prince Tayyichiut to join him. Tayy, however, remained where he was, blinking down at him as if his eyes couldn't decide whether to widen in surprise or narrow in expectation of something nasty at the end of whatever had pulled him up short in the middle of the rowing well.

"Our cadre?" Prince Tayyichiut asked as if he suddenly found himself in the dream world without quite knowing how he'd gotten there. He'd always been the outsider before. This was something new and he half expected to have the words snatched back if he reached for them.

"Your uncle seemed to think you'd want to come along." Llesho treaded water, hoping that Tayy would take as given the part missing from that statement, but the prince seemed to be having more trouble processing the unstated apology than he'd hoped.

"I'd scramble, if I were you." Master Den urged Tayy forward with a little nudge between the shoulder blades.

Llesho remembered his own less than dignified entry into the sea at his teacher's hands back the other side of the storm, and apparently so did Tayy. His long hours at the oar and cowering under the near approach of Master Markko's storm hadn't helped the Harnish prince's fear of the water, however. He peered over the side with a grimace. Llesho waited patiently, but offered the encouragement, "Pinch your nose closed with your finger and thumb, like this—" he demonstrated with his own nose. "—close your mouth and your eyes tight, and just jump. I won't let you drown."

"I'm sure Moll would be happy to have you if you wanted to stay," Master Den answered the hopeful look passed his way.

The day before, he'd been ready to die quickly in the sea rather than linger slowly on the bench. The reminder of his fate if he remained on the galley was all it took. Prince Tayyichiut of the Harnish people, who for all his life had avoided all water wider than a teapot, clambered over the rowing bench and onto the side. Then, with his hand over his nose and his eyes tight shut, he took the last small step and fell, splashing, into the sea.

"Glug!"

It sounded something like that. Tayy hadn't waited until he surfaced to scream. Llesho found himself holding the Harnish prince up by his collar with one hand while he pounded on his back with the other, all while treading water to keep them afloat.

"Stop thrashing around! You're going to drown us both!" Tucking an arm under the prince's chin, he gave a simple two-part command: "Shut up and stop moving. You can't sink while I've got you this way."

Which wasn't entirely true, not if Tayy kept windmilling his legs and arms that way. Llesho figured assurances would work better than threats, though, so he took the positive approach, if not an entirely truthful one. "It's impossible to sink in salty water. I promise. Relax your arms. Watch what they do."

Tayy did what he was told. "Wow!" he said as they floated to the top.

Llesho gave him a smug smile. "Now relax your legs."

He had the idea now. Tayy didn't fight when he found himself tilted with the back of his head in the water. Slowly, his knees and upper legs floated into view on the glassy surface.

"That's it. Now just lie there and think dry thoughts. Are you coming, Singer?"

The question seemed to take the oarsman by surprise. He looked over the side, then back toward where Moll and Alph had their heads together in fierce discussion. "It's not the work," he said. "The oar or the plow makes little difference. The conditions, however—with more food of better quality, and more rest. With a wage at the end of the day, or a share of the takings . . ."

"You'd rather be a pirate than a hero?" The trickster god, Chichu, asked. He was the patron of pirates, Llesho remembered, so wasn't as surprised by the questions as he might have been.

Singer, however, seemed more amazed at his own answer. "Yes," he said, "I think I would."

"It can be arranged. I'll be leaving the ship with our young royals; the *Shark* will need a new captain. You've protected my interests well enough so far . . ."

Llesho didn't wait to hear any more but took off for the shore with Prince Tayyichiut in tow. The sea was warm and the storm had stirred up the bottom very little in this protected cove. Comfortable, Llesho would have thought, if he wasn't escaping from pirates while towing a prince of the Qubal clans, on his way to a soon-to-be-deserted island. That the pirates had agreed to let him escape took some of the danger out of the occasion. The presence of the Harnish prince and his fear of water balanced that scale however. Llesho almost would have preferred the arrows of the pirates, which he could avoid by diving, over the prince, who could drown him with a thoughtless grab at his throat. But if the prince stayed calm, he'd have to admit the day seemed to be improving.

Beneath them, fish darted on their own business through ribbons of seaweed that reached for them from the bottom. Tayy couldn't see what was going on below, which was for the better. It was impossible for him to forget that he was floating in water deeper than the river that had killed both Qubal and Southerner during the battle on the banks of the Onga. When he didn't instantly drown, however, the Harnish prince started to think beyond his fear of water. When he had lost hope of escaping the pirates any other way, Tayy had considered drowning himself in the Marmer Sea. To convince him not to seek his own quiet death in the water, Singer had threatened him with sea monsters. At some point, the prince would remember that threat.

Llesho could have told him that sea monsters were often very nice people. Pearl Bay Dragon and Marmer Sea Dragon were two such creatures who proved the point. He couldn't be sure what lay beneath them in the caves that honeycombed the hills where they plunged into the sea, however. He kept quiet on that point and so they came to the shallows.

"You can stand up now." Llesho dropped his feet to the shelf to demonstrate. When he stood, the water came only to his waist.

Tayy did as he was told, thrashing and sputtering as the rest of him sank with his feet. He managed to right himself in short order, however, requiring neither a thump on the back nor assistance getting his legs under him in the knee-deep surf. Overhead, the sea osprey Llesho had sighted before wheeled in a great sweeping circle overhead then banked in a slow glide to return in the direction from which it had come.

"Chewk! Chewk!" She was a female, as Llesho recognized from the markings, and it seemed that in her cries the sea eagle was laughing at them. Definitely Kaydu, he decided, and he'd hoped to keep this tale out of her ear until it was old news.

Now that they had almost reached the shore, Tayy was regaining his cocky assurance. He watched the osprey with a hunter's appreciation of a great hunting bird, but he hadn't put together yet that he might know her in another form. "What about Master Den?"

Too soon, Llesho allowed his guard to fall. "He'll be up on the beach." They both looked toward land, and that was when Tayy noticed what Llesho or Master Den could have told him from the start. The *Shark* had grounded with her stern up on the beach. That way her bow guns faced outward to the sea for defense. Her lowest and most vulnerable aft section stayed out of reach not only of attack, but also of storms like the one they'd just escaped. Pirate galleys were made for just such a maneuver, and offered easy escape to dry land for her pirate crew.

"There's a gate," Tayy said.

"It appears so," Llesho agreed.

"And a ladder." Tayy pointed to the sturdy ship's ladder by which pirates and slaves alike left the stern for the shore.

"I suppose that's how they bring on supplies and water."

A search party returned then, bearing supplies scavenged from the island and confirming Llesho's guess. He didn't feel it was necessary to add that Master Den awaited them at the foot of the ladder. Or that the trickster god had reached the same beach without a drop of the lagoon touching even the cuffs of his billowing red-and-yellow breeches.

Moll watched from the deck above. She'd planted her hands on the rail so that she didn't fall overboard as she craned her neck to watch them soggily drag themselves to shore.

"Did you have a nice swim?" Her laugh bounced off the hill-sides, echoing in the air. Even the slaves hauling water from the stream hidden among the trees could hear, and their own laughter rippled back as the story was passed along.

"He tricked me!" Prince Tayyichiut had shown little of the haughty temperament of a royal since leaving the camp of the Qubal ulus on his adventure. Now he spluttered in outrage, his face growing very red under the streaming water from the lagoon that dripped from his hair. "I can't believe he tricked me into jumping into the lagoon!"

Llesho figured he'd have to calm Tayy down soon or they'd find themselves chained to a rowing bench again. "He's the trickster god," he pointed out. "That's what he does."

He let Prince Tayy figure it out for himself, saying nothing about his own shaken faith in his teacher. Deciding a young prince needed a lesson in sinking or swimming was one thing. But the pirates had killed innocent travelers, children. He couldn't forgive the old trickster for being a part of that, especially as he'd been present during the attack on the *Guiding Star.*

"That makes it all right, then? We are nearly killed, and the only answer you have is that he just does that?"

Stalling for time to sort his thoughts, Llesho reached down and scooped a bit of sand from the beach. Drying his hands on it, he gave the only real explanation he had. "It's his way as a teacher. If you ask yourself why he played that trick at this moment, you will come to understand a little more of what he has been doing to me for the past three cycles of the sun, and to Shou before us, for that matter."

"Well, not to me, he doesn't. My people have fought wars for insults less grievous than his."

"The pupil doesn't choose the lesson." They hadn't been in danger of death at any point in their swim to shore, of course, but that wasn't the part of Tayy's rant that grabbed hold and refused to let go.

"Going to war over an insult put your clan in my debt!" The accusation brought Tayy's chin up on the defensive, but slowly the meaning of the angry words they had said to each other sank in.

Tayy let go of his frustration with a long sigh. "I'm all wet," he said.

"So am I. I never said he was an easy teacher."

"The tales make adventures sound like so much fun," Tayy complained, though with considerably less heat. "Storytellers never mention the cold and wet and hungry part, or the drowning part."

"If they did," Llesho pointed out reasonably, "no one would go on quests. Then where would the new tales come from?"

"Well, when they tell this one, I hope they leave out the falling in the water bit."

"Don't worry," Llesho assured him, "Once they polish up

the adventure with embellishments for art's sake, you will have risked your life overboard in high seas to save a princess. There's always a princess in tales. The embarrassing parts will be forgotten forever."

"You'd better be right."

"There you are!" Master Den slogged toward them through the sand, but Prince Tayy was in no mood for conversation with the trickster god just yet. He set his gaze on the trees above the sandy shore with distaste. "We're going to need food and water." He didn't wait, but headed for the line of palm trees that marked the start of the forest.

"Was it something I said?" Master Den asked, innocently enough, though he had that twinkle that always made Llesho nervous.

"He'll survive," Llesho asserted. Tayy already had, but he wasn't ready to tell Master Den that yet. "Others on this journey, innocents who did nothing to deserve their fate, have not. I need to think about that. Alone." Throwing a disgusted look over his shoulder, he followed Tayy. He hadn't gone more than halfway up the beach, however, when a ragged shadow dark as the deep of night blotted out the light of Great Sun. The creature, for Llesho could make out the line of outspread wings and the trailing darkness of its tail, let go a cry that thundered off the hillsides and rattled among the trees. Pirates fled in terror, or fell on their faces in the sand, as if they could escape the terrifying presence that had invaded the island. Even the birds in the trees and the insects chittering beneath the carpet of rotting leaves fell still as if in silence they might escape notice of this terrible invader.

In a moment it was gone, but Llesho guessed what it must be and started to run toward the forest where it had disappeared. Master Markko, blown across the vast sea as they had been themselves, had fetched up on the same hopeful shore. And Llesho had sent Tayy alone into the forest to look for water.

"Ahhh!" A high, shrill, pain-filled cry startled the birds out of the trees who added their own dismayed calls to the afternoon. Tayy screamed again, a sound so terrible that it cut through the sudden cacophony of birds and pirates like an icy wind.

"Ahhh!"

Almost without thinking, Llesho drew his spear with one hand and his Thebin knife with the other. He started to run.

"What's happened?" When the shadow didn't return, oarsmen escaping the watchful lash of the pirates burst from the woods. They dropped their water kegs and their nets full of fruits and small animals as they ran, seeking the protection of the ship.

Master Den was running, too, faster than someone his size ought to be able to move. Llesho picked up his pace. Prince Tayy was his responsibility, and he would not let the trickster god arrive first at the site of whatever had befallen him. Because he wasn't certain what Master Den's intentions were.

Chapter Twenty-two

INTO the forest Llesho followed that terrible sound. Animals had made a sandy path and he followed it, leaping over trailing vines that crossed his path and swatting with his spear at low-hanging branches that brushed his temples as he dashed by them. He'd done this before on Pearl Island, once trying to run away from his own life and then in long training sessions for the arena. The terrain was rockier here and the hills climbed more sharply, but he didn't let that slow him down.

Visions of Tayy attacked by the magician filled his head. All his fault. He'd taken Tayy away from the protection of his people and lost him first to slavers and now to the deadly clutches of his own personal nemesis.

"Too late, too late." His feet pounded the rhythm through his body until it hummed in his teeth and in the scars that still pulled sometimes when he moved the wrong way.

It's just been minutes, he reminded himself, though it felt like he'd been running forever. Prince Tayyichiut would be all right, he just had to reach him in time. Master Markko didn't want Tayy anyway—he wanted Llesho, and if Llesho was there, he'd leave the Harnish prince alone. Llesho ducked a branch and tumbled into a clearing broken by shattered rock from which hardy beach grasses grew.

Tayy lay with his back against a jutting boulder spattered,

like his clothes and the sandy grass beneath him, with blood oozing from a dozen or more razorlike slashes scoring the prince's belly and ribs. A bedraggled monster, half bird and half beast, loomed over him: Master Markko. Attacking with beak and claw, the horrifying creature opened a deep gash across the prince's gut. Llesho saw the pulsing of his entrails until blood filled the gaping wound.

The prince had already screamed his throat raw. The sound this latest wound tore from him rattled with despair as he gazed in fixed horror on the bedraggled creature out of nightmares. Holding him in its obsidian stare, the creature used its beak to pick a bit of dangling human flesh from its talon.

Llesho's palm ran with sweat around the knife hilt clutched in his left hand. In his right, the spear of the mortal goddess of war sparked lightning all along its length.

"Kill him," the spear whispered in his mind. Normally, he didn't listen to the weapon, but this time it had a point. His grip on his knife relaxed, ready for the explosive unfolding of the ritual defense moves that would leave his opponent dead. The spear he clutched more tightly, lest it lead instead of follow his action. He knew better than to show any sign of fear. In fact, however, he didn't feel any fear, except for Tayy. Markko's powers were at a low ebb, sodden and tattered, while Llesho felt fresh from his untroubled sleep and calm in his purpose.

"Leave him alone!" he shouted, waving his arms wildly to distract the magician from his helpless prey. Then he charged.

The creature fluttered its waterlogged wings, raising itself only as high as the lowest branches of the palm trees that surrounded them. It was enough to evade the initial attack, however, and to counter with its vicious talons. Llesho shifted to the left to avoid a slash, jabbed with the spear, drawing blood that burned to blackened ash on the blade, and leaped back to avoid a blow from still-powerful wings.

The spear had ideas of its own. Without a thought or the twitch of a muscle, Llesho brought the weapon up and thrust for the great bird's eyes. He missed, but blue lightning snapped between them, throwing the magician off and shaking his hold on the magical shape he had taken for the battle. With a convulsive shudder, as if he were settling his ragged black feathers, Master Markko regained his human form, coming to rest lightly with his sword over Tayy's heart. The Harnish prince was helpless to save himself, and Markko would kill him before Llesho could move against him.

"Is he one of yours?" the magician asked with mock civility. "I thought I knew them all. Still, it brought you. That's what matters."

"You failed," Llesho commented. "We're still alive." One eyebrow raised meaningfully. Of the two of them, Markko seemed to have had the worst of the storm as well as the battle. His face was gaunt and ashen, his hair streaked with white and tangled in a great matted nest from which bits of flotsam peeked like the treasures in a bird's nest. His dark robes, though made of rich brocades, were torn and showed the wear of salt water and the wrack of seaweed and other, less wholesome stains. He was making an effort to look imposing, but Llesho noticed that he leaned a bit on an upthrust spur of stone. Tayy was in danger from his wounds, but the magician seemed hardly strong enough to hold up his sword to inflict another.

"No failure," Master Markko corrected with a haughty smile. He gave Tayy a nudge to remind him to stay still. The prince whimpered back, but slowly the magician seemed to cave in on himself. He spoke as if his battle-weary state meant nothing, however. "It was a test, and you passed with flying colors. As I knew you would. And in the end, the storm has put you where I wanted you—where, as you can see, I have been waiting for you."

"You can't even lie convincingly anymore. You were thrown up on this island the same way we were—tossed here by the storm." The spear crackled in Llesho's hand, but he willed it to stillness. "It's all been a lie, hasn't it? You're not even a magician; you're a fraud."

High on Master Markko's cheeks, spots of color stained the ashy gray. "A fraud? Ask your friend about that." He brought his hand up and twitched a finger at the prince lying in a puddle of his own blood. Tayy whimpered, responding to some torment that Llesho couldn't see. He seemed to be trying to draw himself into a ball around his exposed entrails, but his body wasn't cooperating. They needed a healer, and soon, or Prince Tayyichiut was going to die.

But Bolghai was with Mergen at Shou's temporary court in Durnhag. So were Carina and Adar. They were all far away, and Tayy had never learned to dream travel. Wouldn't have been able to do it in his current condition even if he'd studied the art, Llesho figured. He couldn't have focused on moving between the realms himself with his gut in danger of spilling from his body like that.

Lightning leaked back into the spear at Llesho's side. "If Prince Tayyichiut dies, I'll find you wherever you go, however you hide. Then we'll kill you." He meant by that the short spear as well, whose whisper had become a persistent moaning in his ear since Master Markko had cast his shadow on the island.

"You won't kill me. You can't. We mean too much to each other." Master Markko sheathed his sword and held out his hands, as if to embrace him. Blood and bits of flesh still clung to his fingernails. "If you intended to see me dead, you'd try it right now, wouldn't you? But you won't."

He was right. In the heat of battle, with a friend's life at risk, he could have killed the magician and given it not a moment's thought. But he hadn't fallen so far that he could kill in cold blood, over a conversation. There would be other meetings, however; Tayy needed him now. Llesho ripped the hem from his shirt. Blood still dripped from the pulsing wound in the prince's gut and he packed the cloth into it to stanch the flow.

"I know what you are."

The magician waited with his mad, patient smile for Llesho to reveal himself.

"Marmer Sea Dragon told me what you did. What Pig did."

He hadn't expected to hear that. Rage blurred his features. At his feet, Prince Tayy keened a high, panicked whine as the monstrous bird showed through the human form of the magician, and the shape of a lion-headed creature more horrible still. Llesho had seen both before and carried their marks on his body.

"I won't kill you now," he repeated, "because I owe the dragon-king of this realm a debt. But all your futures look bleak. If I can, I'll find a way to free his son from his prison in your flesh. You'll be powerless then, and I'll see you face the justice of those you have harmed.

"If I can't free the dragon trapped within your flesh, I'll kill you to protect Marmer Sea Dragon. A father shouldn't suffer the blood of his child—even in this perverted form—on his hands.

"If Tayy dies, however, I won't be concerned about justice. You'll have my vengeance to fear then. And the spear of the Lady SienMa likes vengeance."

Blue flame blazed along the length of the weapon. It sparked azure fire up and down Llesho's body and filled the clearing with an unearthly light unbearable to look at. For the first time in all of their encounters, from Pearl Island to this hideout of pirates on the other side of the world, Master Markko looked nervous.

"You'll come around," he said, but he didn't sound as assured as he wanted to appear. "And while we are apart, remember. I can reach you any time I want."

As if to prove his point, the magician raised a talon-clawed hand. Although the broken clearing lay between them, Llesho felt a touch on his shoulder, a stroke that brushed the hair from his forehead.

"I chose you," a rusty voice whispered in Llesho's head. "I made you as a father makes a son, in the raising. You won't escape the path I've laid for you."

The transformation was not as smooth as Llesho had seen in the past, but slowly the magician faded from view. In his place squatted a huge bird with a predatory gleam in its eye. With a lumbering flap of its wings the bird rose awkwardly into the air and circled, found a thermal updraft, and wheeled away.

"Well done."

Llesho jumped at the sound of the deep voice. It hadn't come from inside his head, which was an improvement. But where? Ah. Master Den stepped out from among the trees with a satisfied smile. "You did that very well. I liked the bit about Marmer Sea Dragon's son particularly." He'd shed his pirate garb for his more familiar dress of loincloth and coat, but it was going to take more than a change in his clothing to trust him again.

"I meant it." Llesho dropped to his knees at Tayy's side, but he didn't know what to do, where to touch him that wouldn't cause him more pain. They had to close that wound, but how, without sealing up the poisons that festered in hiding? The thought of maggots in that huge wound made his own gut crawl.

"You were right about the false magician. He did lie." He didn't dare ask the question, *What are we going to do?* aloud because he didn't want Tayy to hear it. But his whole soul cried out in dismay at the growing pool of blood. The prince's lips had grown as pale as his skin, and his eyes drooped half-closed already.

Master Den squatted down beside him and rested a huge hand lightly on his shoulder. "This is no test. Not for you, not for Tayy. This is the war. I'd protect you from it if I could, but it's your war. I can only watch, and guide."

Which was more real information than the trickster god had ever given him before and it made him wonder about all the other gods he'd met along his way. They could help, of course. Hmishi, alive, was proof of that. But Dognut had explained the cost of such a boon. Even once was more than you could ask in a lifetime, the god had made that clear. He hadn't been able to get Harlol back and he couldn't ask for Tayy.

Master Den had trained warrior kings and gladiators for more lifetimes than Llesho wanted to think about, however. "Get my pack for me," he said. "I left it there in the trees."

The pack, wrapped in a clean cloth, was right where the trickster god told him, hidden behind a rock jutting up between the trees. The trickster took it without looking and continued his instructions as he pulled from inside it a small pouch of what looked like tea and a small length of clean white cloth.

"Go to the beach," he said, "And bring back some of the nets you find there."

"What nets?"

His teacher had his mind on Tayy. "Go, quickly," he urged before turning back to his patient. He wiped gently at the many wounds on limbs and body. The prince was semiconscious, but sounds of distress escaped his slack lips.

Llesho ran for the beach. He would force Moll to take them to Pontus, where they'd find doctors and magicians for Tayy—

The pirate galley was gone. Singer was a good rower, and he'd make a good captain, but he had no taste for the magical. He'd headed out to sea, far from the the presence of a magician in the shape of a huge raptor with an eye for human prey.

As Den had known, however, the pirates scavenging for supplies had dropped their bundles on the shore when Tayy screamed. There were drag marks in the sand where they'd retrieved most of them, but a few nets remained, bursting with their booty of fruits and meat. Moll would have more bolt-holes to visit for food and water; safer hideouts. He didn't know what Master Den wanted with the nets, but he grabbed two of the loads and raced back to the clearing.

"Here."

"Ah. Better than I thought." From among the small lizards and the breadfruit, Master Den pulled a coconut and cracked it on the sharp end of an upturned boulder.

"Drink up." He handed one half to Llesho and gulped down the rest himself.

"What about Tayy?"

"You know better than that."

He did, of course. Gut wounds were chancy. If you fed one, you ran the risk of horrible infection that killed faster than the wound itself. Without water, however, the patient would die of thirst. Already Tayy had the pinched, almost powdery look of one who had gone too long without drink.

Master Den had straightened the prince's body so that he lay flat on the grass with the cloth from Llesho's shirt packed in his wound. With his own belt the trickster god had tied the prince's hands to his sides, but still Tayy reached mindlessly to pluck at the curling edges of the wound. Llesho had seen the like in battle; without the restraints, he'd tangle his fingers in his own entrails. His lashes fluttered weakly when Master Den spoke, but he seemed unaware of what was being said.

"We can keep him alive if you don't lose your head," the trickster reminded him sharply. "When you've drunk that coconut, you're going to find the spring where Moll's crew were drawing their water and you're going to bring some back in the shells.

Water—that made sense. He drank the coconut and took the other half of the shell. "I'll be back as soon as I can."

"I know. Take a bit of net with you to carry the shells in. You may need to keep your hands free."

Llesho did as he was told, snugged the broken halves of the coconut shell into a net that he tied over his shoulders. Then he looked back, unwilling to leave the clearing for fear that Tayy would die while he was gone. Squatting next to the prince with his elbows on his knees, Master Den made a shooing motion with both his huge hands before tackling the nets with their booty of food inside. "Go, go. We won't leave without you."

Which hadn't been Llesho's fear, or maybe the trickster didn't mean on the ship Kaydu was bringing. With an abrupt, single nod to show that he understood, Llesho left the clearing for the forest.

As before, he followed a path already beaten down by the animals that lived on the island. They would know better than he where to find water, and the shortest routes to it. He met with no large predators, though small scavengers skittered in the undergrowth on either side of the path and some strange creature with tall, slim horns on its head leaped out of the way as he came upon it nibbling bark from a pine tree.

Not more than a few hundred paces from the clearing a tumble of fractured rock blocked the path. And from a crack in the rock high over his head, water trickled in a thin stream. It would have been impossible to capture that water, which drizzled through tiny grooves and cracks in the stone. At the base of the spill, however, water collected in a shallow basin made of the fallen rock. On the far side of the path, the water overflowed the basin into the sandy soil. Quicksand, he figured, and creatures with too many teeth that lived in the marshes and fens. He kept to his own side where countless animals had laid the safest course and climbed the stony wall of the pool. Filling the coconut shells, he settled them on his back again and climbed down off the rocky pile. Careful not to spill a drop, he headed back down the way he had come.

It turned out there were more than human predators on the island after all. A tawny she-cat whose head came only to his hip, but with teeth longer than the fingers on each hand, barred his path. The thick hair around her neck bristled threateningly.

"Nice kitty." With cats, it was simple. Whoever intimidated the other more would have the right of way. Or so he had heard. On the other hand, she was female and looked ready to drop her young. That made it more complicated to know how she'd jump.

Llesho was taller and he glared down at her, eye to eye, declaring his dominance. "Is this your own special route to the spring? That's okay." The creature couldn't understand his human language, but his tone would communicate his confidence. "You can have it. After I'm gone."

This was the tricky part. Stepping off the path for either of them meant backing down. The she-cat could walk away, submitting to Llesho's control of the path. Or they could fight. If Llesho stepped aside, he'd be prey again, and she'd try to kill him for sure. He might win either fight, but not without killing the cat.

He'd had enough of bloodshed for the day, however, and would rather not murder a mother defending her own ground. There was always the chance she'd beat him, too, in which case he'd be dead. Slowly he drew the knife from its sheath at his side. Lifting his shoulders away from his body, he made himself look bigger and held his ground.

"Raowr!" She tilted her head, spreading her jaws so that he could see all her sharp, shiny teeth.

"No!" Somehow the spear had come into his hand, flickering the blue sparks it gave off when it wished to strike. That was enough for the she-cat. She shook her head, ceding the territory, and padded away into the forest.

This time, Llesho had won their little game of dominance and power. Even now, however, he didn't dare let himself be afraid. The cat would smell the emotion on him and stalk him, waiting for her chance. Then she'd be on him before he knew she was there. The back of his neck prickled with unease, as if his skin already felt the heat of her breath, the pressure of her jaws snapping fragile bones. Whistling a cheery tune to convince both himself and the cat that he was just fine, he continued at his former pace to the clearing where Master Den waited with Tayy.

"There are predators about, we can't stay here long." He carefully set the net with the coconut shells down before joining his teacher at the prince's side.

"We have to get to shore to hail Kaydu's ship anyway," Master Den agreed.

"Cover your ears—there's no time to warm it properly. This is going to hurt."

Llesho thought he'd lost his mind. The prince was unconscious, or close enough to it to make no difference. He fretted mindlessly against the soft bonds that held his hands out of his wounds, but otherwise showed no sign of awareness. Then, the teacher upended the coconut shell over the vast open wound across Tayy's belly.

"AAAAHhhhhhh!" The scream that followed echoed from the hills and reverberated in Llesho's ears, in his head, in his gut. Prince Tayy lifted physically up off the ground in one convulsive heave as his body reacted to the cold touch of the spring water against his tortured flesh.

"Oh, gods and ancestors! Stop!" Tayy whimpered, reaching for his wounds. His hands remained tied to his sides.

"Please!" he gasped, his breath coming in short, sharp gasps.

"Stop!" Llesho balled his fists at his sides, scarcely noticing that his left hand had clenched around his knife. "What are you doing to him?"

"We have to keep the wound clean." Master Den rummaged around in the bits and pieces from his pack that he'd spread out next to the patient. He took up a piece of gauzy white cloth and poured more of the water on it, then laid it gently across the wound.

Tayy scrabbled at his sides with his fingers, as if he could walk them up his body and snatch away the wet cloth. He was sobbing openly, though apparently not aware that he was doing it.

"Ssshhh, ssshhh," Master Den soothed. He held out his hand. "The other shell?"

Llesho handed it over, watched as he tilted it first to moisten Tayy's lips, then, when he had the prince's attention on the water, lifted his head to the shell. "Drink," he said, "But slowly." He pulled the makeshift cup away again and Tayy craned his neck to follow it.

"Shush, shush," Den continued in the warm soothing tones that Llesho remembered from long ago, at a hospital in Shan. "You can have more in a moment."

Master Den settled Tayy's head back against the tussock of grasses where he lay surrounded by broken stone. A worried frown creasing his brow as he studied the contents of his pack spread out before him. Taking up the pouch of herbs, he deftly gathered a pinch of leaves and shredded them between his fingers. "Here, boy, let me put this in your cheek." He tucked the bundle between Tayy's teeth and the flesh, complaining, "This would work better in a tea, but we haven't time to build a fire." The prince twitched his head away, moaning, but Master Den lifted him again, crooning, "Drink, there's the thing. Let the water soak the herbs. It will help with the pain."

Llesho thought he'd been forgotten, but the trickster god had another request, which he gave without looking away from his patient. "We need two strong sticks as long as your two arms spread wide." He lay Tayy down again to demonstrate his need, opening his own arms so that they stretched from the prince's head to his feet.

"You're going to make a litter with the nets," Llesho deduced. He didn't need an answer. "I won't be far, if you need me."

As promised, he didn't stray far from the clearing. Nearby, however, a stand of young bamboo grew to just about the right height. Drawing his knife, he went to work on the woody stems. It took longer than he'd hoped to free them. By the time he had finished, soft padding feet were coming nearer, rustling in the undergrowth. The she-cat, drawn to the smell of fresh blood.

Llesho hurried back to the bare campsite, remembering another time, other predators. On the Long March, Harnish raiders had led their Thebin captives on a brutal journey across all the grasslands to the slave markets in Shan. Predators had prowled beside them every step of the way, picking off the sick and the weak and the children, anyone who fell behind. His people had saved him, passing him hand to hand, carrying him across a thousand li and a thousand more. He'd do the same for Tayy if that was what it took.

Bursting into the clearing with a long bamboo pole in either hand, he announced, "We've got company."

"I know." Master Den tied up his supplies in their white wrap, which he knotted over one shoulder.

"Leave me a knife," Tayy begged. The herbs had dulled his pain, but his eyes were dark with the terrible knowledge of his condition.

"Don't be a fool. We aren't leaving anything, least of all you." While Master Den tended to his patient, Llesho carefully wove the bamboo rods between the knots of the netting.

"It's ready," he said when he had finished. The litter had a bamboo handhold on each side, separated by the width of the nets Llesho had used to form the sling where Tayy's body would rest while they carried him to the shore.

"Come, help me load him up. And don't drop him when he screams." Master Den had already taken up his end of the litter. Llesho slung the net filled with fruit over his back and picked up the other end of the bamboo rods. They carried the litter over so that it lay next to Tayy.

"This is going to hurt, but we'll have you comfortably tucked in bed before you know it."

"They're here?" Llesho tilted his head, listening for the sound of a shore party, but heard only the sounds of the birds and the skulking cat pacing in the trees.

"Soon. Very soon." Master Den lifted the prince in his arms. The herbs had helped with the pain, but not enough. An agonized growl rumbled deep in Tayy's throat and he tugged at the belt that held his hands out of his wounds. The mountainous trickster god just held him more securely, as if he were a child, and bent to place him on the litter.

"Now help me get him out on the beach, where they can find us."

The shore seemed farther away with a wounded burden to carry, but they reached it in a fairly short time. At the edge of the forest, their hungry escort left them to go in search of easier prey. Setting down their burden on the cool, damp sand, both master and pupil looked out to sea. There was no ship waiting for them.

"They're not here," Llesho stated the obvious. The lagoon lay placid and still, a mirror in which no ship reflected. Beyond the headlands all the way to the horizon the sea was empty. Not a sail, not a pennon dotted the vast expanse of empty sky.

"Wait." Master Den dropped to his haunches and took one of Tayy's hands in his own. Gently, he stilled the restless wandering toward the wound moistened by a cloth laid over it and dampened to translucence.

There didn't seem to be much else that he could do. Llesho sat himself down on the other side of the litter. Like his teacher, he took Tayy's hand in his and stroked it to soothe his friend. "I'm so sorry," he whispered, "I never imagined Master Markko would come after you."

When he looked up again, the ship had appeared, sailing out from behind the hills that enclosed the lagoon.

"Impossible." He blinked to clear the mirage from his eyes, but the ship remained on course around the headland and into the protected cove.

"Not impossible," Master Den instructed. "Not even magic. Just a shift in direction to come up undetected in case there were pirates still about. Our friend Habiba would have seen to that."

Habiba. The ship had come as near as it dared, and someone had let a small boat over the side. Llesho hoped that Habiba was in it. Her ladyship's witch would know what to do. He could let go. Three figures climbed down, but they were two small to identify at the distance the ship was forced to keep. The osprey that rose from the deck, however, had watched them from above when they made landfall on the island. In moments, the bird had scrambled to a landing on the sand.

"What happened?" Kaydu asked.

Chapter Twenty-three

"THE WINDS that drove the *Shark* onto these shores carried Master Markko in the same direction. He found Prince Tayy alone and attacked before I could stop him." Llesho pulled the gauzy covering away to reveal the wound. It had begun to stick, so he poured more water on the cloth. Tayy moaned and his knees bent as if he would draw them protectively around his middle, but the effort left him gasping in pain.

"Hush, hush," Master Den smoothed the long, thick hair from the prince's brow, lulling him with the hypnotic sound of his voice.

Kaydu ruffled as if she still had feathers. "And the pirates?" she demanded, and he thought she would rise on the next thermal and attack the galley in her sea eagle form.

"The pirates stranded us here, but they knew help was coming." He gave her a wry smile. "Their new captain has no fondness for the uncanny."

She settled then, waiting for the rest of the tale. Llesho explained as briefly as he could while keeping a watchful eye on the advance of the longboat. When he got to where he allowed Master Markko to escape, Kaydu glared darkly at him. "Why didn't you kill him?"

"I'm not finished with him yet. I'll know when it's time." He didn't mention Marmer Sea Dragon's son or reveal his intentions to free the dragon-prince. He was pretty sure she'd damn him for a fool if she knew, but he hoped that wasn't his reason for keeping the information from her.

It wasn't his story to tell. Pig had taken everything else the dragon-king held dear. Llesho could leave him his privacy. Missing that key intelligence, however, Kaydu arrived at the wrong conclusion. "Don't tell me you've already forgotten the second rule of a soldier!"

"Never."

Not a rule in the strict sense, Kaydu was talking about the common sense that soldiers sometimes needed to remember, "Don't let revenge get in the way of a clean shot." Llesho had heard the complaint it addressed, that death was too easy for this enemy or that. He'd have said the same about the raiders who had invaded Kungol. The truth was, though, that while you were stewing over how to cause the enemy more pain, he was usually sneaking up on your flank. So said the hardened campaigners, that a dead archer can't shoot you in the back.

"That isn't why I let him go," he answered the question she asked in the speaking of the proverb. For himself or his captain, he wasn't sure which, he added the reminder, "I hate all this. Hate the fighting, hate seeing my friends die. I don't know how people do this for a profession."

He was thinking of Master Jaks, who had once led his troops in battle and who now lay in an unmarked grave on a battlefield a thousand li away. And Shou, who had suffered a broken mind in the camp of the enemy. Kaydu already knew that about him, of course, that hatred of the waste of lives to death and memory. He spoke his fears aloud now for Tayy, who had lived for the war games of his people and might die on this beach of his first battle. Rules didn't matter when you made war with magicians. The Lady SienMa, mortal goddess of war, had tried to teach him that. She moved them all like pieces on a board, he thought, and shied away from the notion that sometimes he hated her as well.

The longboat had grounded its nose on the shore and Lling jumped out, arrow knocked, bow drawn. Bixei and Stipes finished stowing the oars and then they, too, leaped into the shin-deep water, dragging the boat higher on the beach so that the tide didn't wash it away.

"Over here!" Kaydu stood up, waved a hand to alert the rescue party to their presence. While they waited, she rested a hand on Llesho's shoulder. "We all know how you feel," she said, "It's why we follow you. But sometimes even the most honorable soldier falls to dark thoughts. Master Markko has given you more burdens than a reasonable man might expect to carry. We might worry less if you let us carry more of the weight."

Any clearer and she'd be inviting a confrontation over the secrets behind his reasoning. Llesho shook his head, grateful she'd left him room to refuse. "It's not about revenge." He gave her that much. "It isn't even about me."

She laughed at that. "Haven't you figured it out yet, Llesho? It's *all* about you."

He returned her laughter with his own ironic twist, pretending she hadn't meant it. They were saved from further discussion by the arrival of their companions.

"What should I be looking for?" Lling swept a glance over the trees at the edge of the shore, her arrow pointed where her gaze fell.

"There are some hunter cats in the forest, but they seem to avoid the beach," Llesho reported for his guard. "They have kept their distance while their prey is so closely watched anyway."

"Pirates?" she asked.

"Gone," he confirmed. "They don't seem to have left a lookout behind."

Bixei had turned his gaze to the hills above them on either side, and he added a caution to that. "I don't see anybody keeping watch, but it won't hurt to get out of here as fast as we can. Who knows when they'll come back?"

There was more than one reason to hurry. "We need to get Tayy to a doctor, fast."

The wound was visible through the damp cloth. Lling winced, her vision closing in around memories they all shared. Llesho had nearly died of his own wounds inflicted by the magician. And Hmishi—she'd been there when Master Markko had tortured him. The god of mercy had returned his life to them, but he hadn't wiped away the memory of his death at the magician's hands.

"Let's go, then." Bixei picked up one end of Tayy's litter, and Stipes, in perfect step with his own partner, lifted the other. Surrounded by the company on the shore, they carried him to the longboat and settled him on the bottom. Together, they pushed the boat into the water.

Bixei and Stipes took the oars—Llesho knew better than to offer, which was just as well. He'd be happier if he never had to row a boat again in this lifetime. He found a place toward the bow and settled himself, felt the bump and shimmy as his companions joined him.

"How are we going to get him over the side?" Llesho asked. Almost as round as a washtub, the sailing ship Kaydu had commissioned for them rode high in the water. Her hull rose well above their heads even standing in the longboat, which Tayy couldn't do. He wouldn't survive a seat hoist either.

"Simple," Kaydu told him. "The rest of us will use the ladder, then they'll hoist the boat."

It did seem simple enough—as long as the sailors didn't drop the boat on the way up, which they did pretty regularly. This time, however, it worked as well in the doing as it sounded in the planning. Hmishi joined them on deck and they soon had Tayy off-loaded and in the captain's cabin. Stipes swept the luxurious coverings off the bed to reveal the simple linen beneath. They tried to be gentle moving the prince from the litter, but even half unconscious he moaned in pain.

"Where did Master Den go?" Llesho asked. He'd done this so much more smoothly before, but he was nowhere to be seen now.

"I saw him heading toward the galley," Stipes seemed as confused by it as the rest of them.

"Well, somebody fetch him."

A noise at the hatchway drew their hopeful glances, but it was the captain of the little ship who popped through it. Lling gave a nod of courtesy as she brushed past on her way out.

"I heard you were bringing a wounded boy on board," the ship's captain announced, "so I've brought up our own surgeon to tend him."

Llesho wondered where she had brought him up from, until he appeared in the hatchway behind her. The man was almost as big as Master Den, and as dirty as the other was neat. Sweat glistened on his brow and across a chest that looked more like a fortress than mere flesh and blood. His arms were brawny, ending in huge hands that looked like they'd last had a wash on shore before the voyage began. If then. In one of them he carried a hammer the size of Llesho's head, and in the other, a leather bag that clanked when he put it down.

"He needs sewing up, is all." The man dropped his bag on the table and took out of it a needle used for mending sails and a length of cotton thread. "It was wise of you to tie his hands. Now if someone will sit on his legs, and two more hold down his shoulders, we can get him closed before you know it."

Adar would be having a heart attack about now, Llesho figured. Still, he didn't want to abuse their captain's goodwill. "Do you think it would help to wash up, and maybe give him herbs for the pain?" he suggested as graciously as he could manage under the circumstances.

"No point," the blacksmith/surgeon licked the end of the thread and aimed it at the eye in the needle. "That there is what we call a mortal wound. Means he won't live through the night, if he's lucky. He might linger a few days more, to all of our regrets, but he's not getting up from that bed except sewed in a sailcloth to go over the side, and you can lay your money on that.

"No, we'll just stitch him up for tidiness' sake. And if he's still alive at the end of the sewing, I'll have Cook fix up a nice porridge to keep his strength up. But it won't do no good."

The surgeon bore down on the bed but stopped short as Llesho's cadre formed a wall between the patient and the dirty needle.

"Where's Habiba?" Llesho asked. He'd hung all his hopes on the magician being aboard to take over. He would know what to do for Tayy.

But Hmishi was shaking his head. "He left when the boat was sent to fetch you off the beach. He said to tell you he'd meet you in Pontus with a doctor."

"Doctor won't do you any good." The surgeon gave a shrug as if to say he took no professional slight from their preference for a foreign healer. "That's a gut wound. I've never seen a gut wound survive."

"His name is Prince Tayyichiut," Llesho objected. "He's not a gut wound; he's a Harnish prince wounded in the gut. And he will survive. I've promised his uncle."

Mergen had absolved him from that promise, but Llesho held himself to his word. At least until Tayy recovered enough to make his own decisions, now that he knew the danger.

The surgeon shrugged again, clearly at a loss in dealing with these mad strangers. "Suit yourself," he said. "I'll send the porridge up anyway. But open or sewed shut, he's dead by sunset." With that he left them to their vigil.

When he had gone, Llesho collapsed into a chair. It seemed inconceivable to him that he was among friends again, that they might, if not for Tayy's wound, have been safe. For all that he refused to believe the surgeon's prognosis, he was afraid he might be right. "We need to do something before Pontus," he said.

With perfect timing that usually escaped the trickster god, Master Den chose that moment to enter the captain's cabin. "We shall, boy, we shall," he advised.

"What?" Llesho bounded from his chair, finally secure enough to let his temper explode. "Where did you go, and why are you running around with a teapot in your hands when the crown prince of the Qubal clans—our allies against the South in the Harnlands, mind you—lies dying with no one but a grime-besmirched blacksmith to tend his wounds."

"You didn't let—"

Master Den had the good grace to look horrified at the mention of the ship's surgeon, but Llesho had no intention of letting him off the hook.

"Of course not! For all the good that it did Tayy. He needs help now and what do you do? You disappear, just like Habiba, who is off to Pontus to find too little help too late to do any good. I don't know why I put up with any of you. For all that magic is supposed to have its benefits, it has done nothing from start to finish but cause pain!"

His own cadre stared awkwardly at the deck under their feet, nervous to confront him while he raged. Master Den, however, smiled benevolently. "You're getting better at that," he said, and set down the teapot. "The tea is for Tayy. It will help with the pain until we get him to a doctor. If someone will bring me a clean basin and some clean cloths, I'll see what we can do about the wound until we reach port."

Grateful for something to do that would take them out of Llesho's way, his cadre scattered in search of the items Master Den had requested. All but Lling, who joined then at the table where their teacher had set the fat iron pot.

"I brought this," she said, and carefully unwrapped the jade cup.

Her ladyship, the mortal goddess of war, had given Llesho the cup at the start of his quest, a gift from another lifetime with a challenge to repair the love and honor it represented. He had entrusted it to Lling while he rescued Tayy on the pirate ship. Now he took it in his hands, watching the bowl brighten with the diffused light that poured through the wide windows of the captain's cabin.

"I thought that, being magical, it might help," Lling suggested. "I left Lady Chaiujin's cup in my cabin. I'll be happy when you take it back—I've had enough of the lady haunting my dreams. But this didn't seem like the place." That was for reassurance. The Lady Chaiujin had murdered Tayy's parents, had poisoned Llesho himself once with a love potion in a cup very like the one he now held in his hand. Except that one had a spiral rune at the bottom of the bowl. Llesho looked anyway, but of course Lling was right.

"Thank you." He handed the cup to Master Den, who wiped it with a corner of clean cloth torn from the bandaging material Bixei had brought. He filled it, then poured an inch of the clear tea into the basin Kaydu set on the table.

"First a drink to dull the pain," he said, and lifted Tayy's head, made him drink a sip, another, another. Then, when some of the tension went out of the muscles of arms and legs clenched with pain even in his semiconscious state, Master Den began to moisten the cloth that had lain on the open wound. Gradually, he was able to loosen it and remove it without causing more bleeding. "This is going to hurt," he warned them all, but asked for no help to hold his patient down. Then, slowly, he poured the remaining tea into the wound.

Llesho knew how that felt, like a knife slicing him open all over again, and his own gut fluttered with sympathy as Prince Tayyichiut screamed. Instinctively, he wanted to cover his ears, but he held his hands at his sides. If Tayy could live it, Llesho could listen. The herbs in the tea did their work, however, and soon the cries fell to murmurs and ended on a sigh. It seemed too much to hope, but Master Den confirmed his suspicion.

"He's gone to sleep," the god said. "He'll rest now." With that he lay the dampened cloth over the wound and lowered his own considerable bulk into the chair that Llesho had pulled up by the bedside.

"Sit down," he instructed Llesho. His chair creaked when he moved, pointing to another at the table. "You look like you are about to faint and it is making your cadre nervous."

Llesho wanted to object that he was fine. He wouldn't have fooled anyone, however. When Hmishi drew the chair over for him, therefore, he sank into it without further argument. "Habiba's gone to Pontus," he said. "When will he be back?"

"He's not coming back. He'll be waiting for us on the docks. He trained in Pontus and says he knows a physician who will take us in."

"How much longer? He needs a proper surgeon now!"

"It's less than half a day's journey," Kaydu assured him, news that would, perhaps, have put a stop to his show of temper before it had begun. "I thought you knew—" She cast a reproachful frown at Master Den, who hadn't told him as much.

Again, a nod. Llesho heard her voice, but it seemed to be growing more and more distant with every word she said. The ship was on course, he'd done what he could, and there was nothing else to do but wait. With the need to keep moving gone, his eyelids wouldn't be denied.

Vaguely he heard some hushed argument, to leave something where it was or move it to a more comfortable location, but his weary mind wouldn't process that they were talking about him. Eventually, the "leave him" faction won and a weight fell across his shoulders, his knees. Someone had covered him with a blanket. He realized from the fringes of sleep that while he didn't need the cover for warmth, it made him feel safer somehow. Safe enough that he didn't need even that much awareness anymore. So he let it go.

The cry, "Land ho!" wove itself into his aimless dreams and left them again as fleetingly as it had come. When Llesho next became aware of his surroundings, it was to hear Habiba's voice, and that of a stranger directing the off loading of their patient. The scuffling of litter bearers followed. In the silence that followed their passage through the hatchway, the rustle of heavy silks almost drew him to open his eyes. But his lids were so heavy . . .

A gentle hand rested on his shoulder, "Llesho? Are you hurt?"

Habiba's voice, he recognized it even though the man whispered close to his ear. Not the voicing of a secret, but the calming of a wild creature. Llesho wondered what he must look like for her ladyship's witch to take such care in his waking.

"What's the matter with him?" Habiba asked someone. "Why doesn't he wake up."

"He's awake," a stranger's voice said, "or nearly so. Give him a minute to think about joining us."

He didn't know the voice, knew he'd never met the man who owned it, but it stirred comforting memories anyway. A warmth he hadn't felt in a long time told him he could trust that voice, so he slowly let his eyes drift open. The magician crouched at his side, his brow furrowed in a worried frown. Standing at Habiba's shoulder, the physician watched Llesho with warm and understanding eyes. He wore a white linen skirt both long and wide with a short square jacket. On his head he had a tall felt hat and on his feet slippers of the same color. In between, he wore a gauzy open coat with long, deep sleeves. His eyes were dark, his skin was pale and he wore a neatly trimmed mustache and a short, pointed beard. Between the two, a warm smile showed a neat row of even, white teeth.

Llesho had seen a priest dressed the same way buying children in the slave market of Edris. Stipes had called the man a missionary, saving the children, not harming them. Which might have been the truth, or might have been a quick lie so that Llesho didn't break their cover to do some rescuing himself. This man didn't look like a slaver of children, but still he pulled away, groping reflexively at his side for his knife.

"Welcome to Pontus." The stranger gently plucked Llesho's fingers from his belt and held them between his two hands. "My name is Ibn Al-Razi and I'm a doctor. My carriage is waiting on the docks to take you to my hospital. Do you need a litter, or can you walk as far as the carriage?"

A doctor. That made sense. Adar used to hold his hand the very same way when he wanted to check his energy points for vitality.

"I can walk." Llesho stretched and looked around, but his other senses hadn't failed him. They were alone in the captain's cabin. He remembered hearing the ordering of Tayy's removal, but realized suddenly what had been missing from that scene. Tayy had made no sound, though he'd been jostled surely getting him out of the bed and onto the litter.

"Prince Tayyichiut—"

"Still alive," the physician-priest assured him, though his expression took a downward course. "I make no promises for the future until I have had a chance to treat him. He's had some syrup of poppy to put him to sleep until we settle him in my infirmary."

Llesho nodded, grateful for the update. He'd heard of syrup of poppy, how it dulled the mind to pain more surely than any of the other herbs he knew, but hadn't seen it in use before. He felt all dull around the edges and curiously incapable of greater motion so that he wondered if he'd been dosed on poppy himself.

"What's the matter with him?" Habiba had noticed as well.

He took Llesho's other hand, found the pulse point at Llesho's wrist.

Ibn Al-Razi, more angry than concerned, denied any part in Llesho's condition. "What did you expect? He's been charming storms and warding hunting cats, all without proper training in the arts or any magical support."

Llesho didn't realize that Master Den had returned until he spoke up from the hatchway. "That's not entirely true. I may have miscalculated the resources he'd already expended in the galley, but Marmer Sea Dragon was with him when he worked the storm. No one knows these waters, or the working of them, better than the dragon-king himself."

Al-Razi glared at the trickster god, waiting for the part of the explanation he was unwilling to say. Habiba was the one who gave in, however. "Worse awaits him in the mountains. Her ladyship, whom I serve, had to know if he could do it."

"The fact is," Master Den interrupted, brushing away the witch's explanation, "We expected the boys to spend a few days as oarsmen on a pirate galley before their companions caught up and rescued them. It seemed a good experience for the Harnish prince, who had yet to be tried in adversity.

"Weather working wasn't in the plan at all. Markko should not have been able to raise a storm of that magnitude. We miscalculated the effect the dragon-prince would have on his abilities in the realm of the dragon's birth, however. Fortunately for all involved, the boy proved adept at taming storms, or they'd all be dead of our miscalculation."

Throughout this telling of the secret plans of gods and magicians gone astray, the physician from Pontus was shaking his head. "For whatever reasons, he's been working well beyond his capacity to protect himself for far too long." Al-Razi chastised the trickster god and Habiba, the representative of the mortal goddess of war, as well. "It's drained his resources to a dangerously low ebb. You will be lucky not to end this adventure with two dead princes on your hands."

"I know." Master Den came forward then and swept Llesho up into his arms, blanket and all. "But talking about it isn't going to keep them alive."

"No, it isn't. Bring him."

Ibn Al-Razi swept from the cabin with Master Den following and Habiba in the rear. Llesho struggled to escape the trickster's firm grip, but was shushed like a child. "Can you even feel your legs, let alone walk on them?" his teacher asked.

When he thought about it, he found only pins and needles where his legs should be. With an ill grace to be caught at such a disadvantage, therefore, he settled into the massive arms and let himself be carried to the docks.

Chapter Twenty-four

IT WAS raining in Pontus, but wrapped in his blanket on the padded bench of the physician's carriage, Llesho scarcely noticed. Somehow he was brought into a courtyard, and from there into a large airy room with a harmonious combination of architecture and furnishings to create a setting at once peaceful and conducive to healing. He rode in Master Den's arms, but how he got there or why he traveled that way he couldn't quite gather the energy to question. For whatever reason, the journey soon ended in a comfortable bed with a soft mattress and cool white sheets. Windows were open nearby, and curtains fine as gauze floated in the breeze that brought the smell of rain into the room.

Master Den stepped away, but another form took his place at the bedside. "You're safe now." The man with the pointy beard crouched low so that his patient could see him clearly without straining his neck. "We are in the infirmary of the physician Ibn Al-Razi. I am that physician, and I will see that you are well taken care of."

"You told me your name before." Llesho felt uncommonly pleased to have remembered, though the conversation had occurred no more than an hour ago. All his thoughts were light as butterflies, however, that skittered away whenever he reached for them. So he felt a certain satisfaction to have got his hands around this one. He knew the doctor's name.

"Yes, I did." The physician smiled as if he'd accomplished some great feat. "And hopefully you will remember it again after your nap."

"I just had a nap." Llesho struggled to rise, though it seemed every bone in his body rebelled against the act. "Where are my cadre? Tayy is hurt—"

With a thumb to Llesho's forehead, Ibn Al-Razi pressed him back down until he lay once again deep in the feather bed. "Your cadre is banished to the house until you've rested. As for the young Prince Tayyichiut, you did well to keep the smith away from his wounds. I go to tend him as soon as I am assured that you will not leave this bed. So, you see, your own promise will speed the healing of your friend."

Between the determination of the physician and the rebellion of his body, it seemed clear that he wasn't going anywhere soon. "Very well." Llesho gave in with as much grace as he could muster under the circumstances. "But please, keep me informed about Prince Tayyichiut's condition. I owe him more than his life, and I've promised his uncle—"

"More than you have the power to deliver without the help of a good physician. So go to sleep and let me prove my skills on your friend." Ibn Al-Razi rose from his crouch with a final warning, or blessing. "I know of the one who guards the wandering of your sleep," he said, brushing the backs of his fingertips across the silver chain at Llesho's throat. "If your dreams carry you from your bed, instruct our mischievous friend that your doctor orders peaceful travels only."

Llesho gave his promise with a nod, almost too tired even to answer. "Why do I feel like this?" he asked, while the infirmary blurred around him. He hadn't been injured, he'd shown no signs of illness. He'd just taken a nap in a chair by Prince Tayy's bedside, and yet he still found it difficult to stay awake. "What potion have you given me?"

"No potion," the doctor assured him. "But a story. In the center of the town of Pontus there is a well. The water from the well pours out freely for all who come there, citizen, slave, or traveler. All their animals are likewise welcome to drink from this well.

"From time to time, however, a great caravan comes through the town, or many pilgrims will descend upon the square at once. They draw and draw from the well, each according to his need and no more, but in so many numbers that the well runs dry. At these times our Apadisha, in his wisdom, builds a wooden house around the well. No one may draw until the water returns."

With a smile, the physician turned in a light-footed circle, his hands held out at an angle to indicate the walls of his infirmary. "Today you are this well, run dry from too many demands upon your inner resources. And this, my infirmary, is your wooden house. No one may burden you until your strength, like the water to the well, returns."

"How long?" Llesho asked around a yawn that cracked his jaw. He was, for the moment, willing to concede that perhaps he had drawn too often and too deeply from the well of his own inner strength. A nap couldn't hurt, and Tayy needed the doctor . . .

"We'll see," Al-Razi said, and laughter lurked in the voice that drifted away on sleep . . .

For a while, Llesho was aware of nothing. His sleep was deep and dreamless, like the bottom of that well Ibn Al-Razi talked about. And then, so slowly that he scarcely saw it happening, gray light crept in around his lashes.

The moss under his nose gave off a familiar scent, and he curled himself into the lush velvety cushion of its embrace. Memories covered him like a blanket. He'd been here before, under this tree. Safe in the arms of his Goddess. His heart yearned for her while his body dragged him back into sleep. When he woke again, she sat calmly beside him, a book in her hands and a pitcher and cups at her side.

"What are you reading?" he asked. It seemed a mundane question for one who had gone to sleep in a feather bed in Pontus and awakened in the gardens of heaven. He felt warm and sated with sleep, however, and distant from the cares that had propelled him across all the known world to collapse at a foreign doctor's feet. He was safe and warm and cared for. That other life could wait.

"It's called 'A Life of Prayer and Battle,' by four teachers of Farshore Province." She set the book aside as she gave the title, and Llesho knew without being told that the life in question had been his own, and that the book had not yet been written.

"Water?" She poured from the pitcher and handed him a cup. The water was cold and crisp on his tongue, reminding him of another time when a yearning for home stronger than Master Markko's poisons had brought him here.

He returned the cup with an apology, "I am a sorry excuse for a husband. It seems I only find my way here when I need you, and never the other way around."

"Your every step since you left Kungol as a child has been in my service." She brushed the hair from his forehead with fingers cool as the water he had lately drunk and smiled in spite of the tears in her eyes. "Through lives uncounted I have never had cause to doubt you, husband."

"My Lady." He took her hand in his and held it to his cheek. He had never moved so boldly toward her before, but her palm, her fingers, felt perfect against his skin.

"My husband," she answered him. As his eyes slid closed again, he felt her lips touch his. Husband. More than a word or a promise, for the first time it felt like the truth.

When he woke again, the sun had come out in Pontus. Golden light poured in through the open windows with a breeze that blew the curtains like streamers into the room. Beyond the windows, Llesho saw the city washed clean in the sunlight and dressed in all her bright colors. And, on a balcony he hadn't noticed when he was brought in, a man in a wide white skirt and boxy jacket danced in circles, his arms raised over his head, which was itself tilted in a dancer's pose. The dance looked nothing like the prayer forms Llesho practiced, but still it reminded him of the Way of the Goddess. He'd learned from the

Gansau Wastrels that many cultures trained their bodies to seek perfection and the goodwill of their gods and spirits. Watching the hypnotic motion of the dancer, he felt himself drawn up, as if he could float to heaven on the dance.

Presently, however, the dancer noticed his attention. He stopped his turning and entered through the long windows. Now that he'd drawn closer, Llesho recognized him as the physician, Ibn Al-Razi.

"You're awake. Hungry, too, I would guess."

"Starving," Llesho admitted. "It must be past dinnertime."

The doctor smiled down at Llesho with satisfaction sparkling in his eyes. "Breakfast, actually. Your companions have been worried. I told them you'd wake up when you were ready and sent them away to their duties."

"Worried?" A memory niggled at the back of his mind, of lying in the moss at the feet of his Goddess, but it seemed very distant now, clouded with the sticky darkness of sleep.

"You've been asleep for three days."

"Three days!" Llesho bounded up out of his bed, only to find that his legs refused to work and his head objected to the sudden change in orientation. Dizzy, he fell back down upon the feather bed. Someone had cleaned him while he slept, had taken away his rough clothes and covered him in a soft bed shirt that came to his ankles. Fine for sleeping in, but he couldn't very well stroll around Pontus dressed like that. Once he was able to stand on his own, which he was determined to do any minute.

"Prince Tayyichiut—?"

"Struggles still with his terrible wound." The physician shook his head, overcome by sadness at the horror that had been done to the young prince. "Syrup of poppy helps him to rest, and some of the medicines I compound in my workroom help when the wound suppurates."

Infection. Llesho'd seen enough of that in battle to know the danger. Working with the oysters in Pearl Bay as well, for that matter.

"Kwan-ti, the healer who tended us on Pearl Island, made a paste of molds and seaweed that calmed the redness of a wound," he suggested. She was far away, however, and he didn't mention she was a dragon-queen when not tending to the wounds of the children who had harvested the bay for pearls.

"I, too, know of such potions," Al-Razi assured him, "And my poets are able to recite the compounds for many of them."

Medicine in the empire of Shan made little use of poetry, and that of the Harn seemed mostly composed of riddles. But much of Adar's Thebin medical knowledge had been imparted in prayers. The notion of medicines and compounds reduced to poetry did not surprise him as it might, therefore. It did cause him to wonder why Habiba had sought out this particular physician.

"I would like to meet your poets, if I may." He didn't mention his suspicion, that Ibn Al-Razi harbored a Thebin prince among his poet-slaves.

"And so you shall after breakfast, when you are examined and your case is rhymed for the record books."

That wasn't quite how it was done in Kungol, but Llesho let that pass. He would soon have the answer to his question—did his brother Menar reside in the house of the physician Ibn Al-Razi? In the meantime, he was still worried about Prince Tayy.

"Have your poets given the prince any of these potions?" he asked. He knew that some people responded poorly to them. Had heard of injured divers who died of the potions though their wounds were slight. Al-Razi assured him this was not the case for the Harnish prince in his care.

"Prince Tayyichiut responds well to our unguents and potions," he said, "but a wound of such horror injures the soul as well as the body. How well he recovers will depend on his spirit and his will."

Llesho nodded his understanding. He didn't like the answer, but he remembered the time, several cycles of the seasons past now, when he lay wounded after the Battle of Shan Market. He would have died but for the presence of his brothers. Adar and Shokar, his cadre, and even the emperor himself, had pulled Llesho through the hard times in a way that potions alone could never do. He would have to do the same for Tayy. Flinging aside the clean white sheet that covered him, therefore, he tried once again to rise from his bed.

This time the physician let him stand. "The privy is in that direction." He pointed down the length of the room. "Can you make it on your own, or do you want a chamber pot?"

The privy hadn't been his goal when he stood up, but Llesho quickly changed his mind. Privy first, then Tayy's sickroom.

"I can make it," Llesho insisted. He wasn't ill, after all. Just worn to the bone. "Then I want to see Prince Tayyichiut."

"Privy first," the physician agreed only so far. "Breakfast second," he substituted his own schedule. On consideration, breakfast seemed like a good idea, too.

"And an examination of your own condition. Then we will see about visiting." Al-Razi sounded pretty final about the order of his day, and Llesho found he didn't have the energy to object. His legs did work, however. More or less. He could find Tayy on his own, later, if the doctor didn't want to cooperate.

Al-Razi motioned forward a servant who took his elbow and his weight, guiding and supporting him. They made it to the privy without incident, though Llesho wondered at how much longer than it looked the room became when he walked it. The way back was longer still, and the servant was nearly carrying him by the time he reached his bed, which was now mounded with soft cushions. When he was settled propped up on the mountain of cushions, the servant rested a tray with short legs on the bed over his knees.

Llesho wished for a plate of eggs and ham, a slab of bread or a bowl of porridge, but none of those appeared on his plate. Instead he found a variety of delicacies for an invalid. Sherbets and boiled fruits were spread out before him, along with thin squares of flat bread toasted until they were crisp and a yogurt sauce to dip them in.

In spite of his desire for heartier fare he took up a crisp of bread and dipped it, admitting that it was better than he'd expected. The fruit was tasty as well, and he discovered, to his dismay, that the doctor had been more accurate in his breakfast choices than Llesho himself. Half of the food remained on the tray when he stopped, unable to finish even the small amount put in front of him. He was glad he hadn't protested the tray out loud since he now had to apologize only in his own mind. Al-Razi seemed to read this in his eyes and smiled knowingly as he gestured for a servant to take the scraps away.

"It will take just a moment for my poets to join us. Then, if you have the strength, I will examine you."

"All right." Another servant took away all but two of the cushions and Llesho gratefully lay back again, exhausted by even the small effort of tending to his physical needs. In spite of his weariness, Llesho's heart beat faster, and nerves raised the hairs on his neck and his arms. In just a moment—

"Master Al-Razi." A man curiously tall and thin as a reed entered first, carrying a book of linen paper in his arm. With his free hand he touched his forehead and his heart in a respectful greeting. He was very pale, with chiseled features and strange blue eyes that saw keenly. Nothing at all like Menar, who was both Thebin and blind.

Llesho tried to shake off the disappointment. There were so many places Menar could be in Pontus. They had heard of the blind poet as far away as the grasslands, so he must be something of a public figure. He couldn't stay hidden for long, not with such a reputation. Once he recovered from this strange weariness, Llesho would go out into the city and find him.

A dark hand rested on the elbow of the first poet, however, where it was crooked to cradle the medical book. In a matter of two paces, the second poet followed his fellow into the infirmary.

"Master," the poet said. He looked a lot like Balar, but slimmer, more fragile. His eyes were scarred and filmed with cataracts, no natural failure of vision but the remains of a terrible injury.

Pain squeezed at Llesho's heart at the sight of his brother. Who would inflict such a horrible wound on a poet, even one who was a slave? Surely not Ibn Al-Razi, who tended him with such gentle care. The answer to a different question came easily, however. Who would torture a Thebin prince? The Uulgar clansmen. Remembering what the raiders had done to Hmishi, he trembled to imagine the wounds he couldn't see on his brother.

"Menar," he whispered, afraid to believe that he had found the prince. "What have they done to you?"

"I'm sorry, do I know you?" The poet cocked his head uncertainly in the direction of the voice. Llesho had seen only seven summers when the Harnish raiders came. He'd had the high, piping lilt of a child then, nothing at all like his voice now, deepened with maturity.

"It's me. Llesho." Struggling with his covers and with the failure of his strength, he dragged himself to the edge of his bed, but the physician kept him seated with a hand on his shoulder.

"Llesho? What Llesho is that?" Grief and anger crossed the poet-slave's face. "You ask what they have done to me? Only this: my brother Llesho is dead, murdered when just a child with the rest of my family by the same men who burned the eyes in my head."

A low moan escaped Llesho's throat. "Menar, it's me! I didn't die. The raiders carried me into Shan and sold me as a slave in the pearl beds. I've been fighting to get back home ever since." Which was the truth of his heart if not the start of his quest.

Ibn Al-Razi patted Llesho's shoulder encouragingly. "If your brother is the young king of Thebin, then this Llesho is he," the physician assured his poet-slave. "And if you are his brother, then I have sheltered a prince in hiding in my infirmary all these years."

"It can't be—" Menar shook his head, refusing the hope held out to him lest it tear his heart out when it was taken away again. Llesho knew the feeling, saw it in the working of Menar's jaw.

In spite of his doubt, the poet let himself be guided to the bed. Delicately, with fingertips grown sensitive to seeing with touch, he traced Llesho's brow, the curve of bone around his eye. When he had drawn the chin, the nose, the curve of an ear, he hesitantly withdrew his hand.

"The face of our father," he whispered, his own face a mask of awe and confusion. "Can it be? Llesho?"

"Yes, it's me." Llesho reached for his brother, and Al-Razi moved aside, guiding his blind slave to take his place at the bedside.

When their hands met, Menar sat down heavily on the bed and wrapped his arms around his brother. Pressing Llesho's head to his heart, he choked out a great gasping sob. "Oh, Goddess," he cried, "They have burned out my eyes so that I cannot even weep for you."

"That's all right," Llesho answered, his tears falling on his brother's jacket like a morning rain. "I'm crying enough for both of us."

"What's going on?"

Kaydu pretended to wander by coincidence into the infirmary at just that moment, but battle-ready tension underlay the casual words. Little Brother remained tucked away in the pack on her back, ready for battle even in this sheltered place. Llesho raised his head from his brother's shoulder and wiped at the tears with his gauzy sleeves.

"This is Menar," he explained, "my brother."

"The blind poet?" Kaydu sauntered closer, took a better look. "He does look a lot like Balar."

Little Brother, sensing the change in her mood, crept out of hiding and clambered to his preferred perch on her shoulder. He wore in miniature the uniform of Thousand Lakes Province and on his head a cap with the button of office on it. With a warning screech, the monkey leaped from her shoulder to the bed. There he stretched on tiptoes to touch an inquisitive finger at the corner of Menar's damaged eye.

Menar froze, afraid to move in the presence of some assault he could not see or rightly interpret. "What is it?"

In answer, the monkey whimpered his own distress and wrapped his arms around the prince's neck.

"It's Little Brother. My familiar," Kaydu explained. "Your injury has upset him and he wants to comfort you."

Llesho held his breath. He had grown used to traveling with wonders and for a moment let hope overcome reason. But the monkey's touch didn't heal the scarred wound. Menar remained blind.

Kaydu made no move to collect her familiar, but watched both princes with calculation in her glance. "I thought my father brought us here because of Ibn Al-Razi's other patient, but things seem to be moving toward a crisis in all directions on this quest."

"What other patient?"

The physician answered this question. "Your captain, who has not received visiting privileges yet, probably is speaking about my royal patient in the palace."

"He's the personal physician to the Apadisha," Kaydu confirmed. "My father has gone to pay his respects at the magician's college, but when he returns, he has promised to explain the next part of the plan."

Llesho waved away her explanation. He wasn't interested in Habiba's plans. Or rather, there remained little choice in what they had to do. "Of course I'll consider Habiba's advice in securing the aid of the Apadisha. But the quest remains on my shoulders, whether I want it or not. I won't see anyone else hurt by it."

He was thinking of all his friends wounded in battle, and those that he had lost. But Menar stroked his face with a sad and knowing smile. He was, after all, the source of the prophetic verse they sought in Pontus.

"I never thought, when the god of Pontus spoke through me, that he meant the brother I had thought lost all these years ago. But if you are the one foretold, you bring us war.

"People are hurt in war and the Apadisha knows it. He won't expect to escape unscathed. Rather, he will ask, 'Is the goal in this battle worth the cost in lives and homes and hearts?' And, 'Is this the star who will lead us to that goal, or a false light in a murky sky?'"

Llesho took that for a poet's way of asking if he was likely to lead them to victory, or to take the Apadisha with him into defeat. Mergen, Prince Tayy's uncle, had asked the same questions Menar predicted for the Apadisha. So far, he'd brought the Qubal people only the death of their khan and possibly the death of their prince as well. He didn't know if he had a better answer for Pontus. He did know the nightmare of Lluka's visions, however. The alternative to war was the end of all the worlds of heaven and earth, though the underworld might survive only to welcome the damned.

"War knocks on the Apadisha's door," he therefore said. "His choices are to fight, to risk death in battle so that the world he knows will go on, or not to fight, and watch his world burn. I will fight. So will Mergen of the Qubal people who roam the grasslands. The Tashek people of the Gansau Wastes have fought and died in this quest, and will do so again. The emperor of Shan is also with us, and Shokar has trained Thebin soldiers who will fight to return Kungol to Thebin rule. The Apadisha may join us, or he may stand aside and watch. But I have seen Lluka's visions. If we lose, he will die as quickly as the rest."

"Important questions, and weighty answers all," Ibn Al-Razi interrupted, "but the sickroom is no place to decide the Apadisha's business. Particularly since the Apadisha isn't here. Matters of state can wait until our young king has rested and can present his case at the Divan."

"Master." Menar bowed his head to accept the gentle rebuke.

Outrage stirred in Llesho's heart, to see his brother bend his neck to the yoke of his slavery. How could he trust the attentions of a doctor who held his brother in servitude?

But Ibn Al-Razi bowed his head to his slave with a smile that Menar couldn't see but must hear in the words the physician spoke. "I have always known you were a prince among poets. Now I find you are a prince among mortal men as well. When your brother, the young king, has rested, we will discuss the price of your release into his hands. For now, let me enjoy one last afternoon of your talents. Will you recite for us, something soothing to ease your brother's way into sleep?"

"Not yet," Llesho reminded them. "Prince Tayyichiut first. Then rest. If you put us together in the same chamber, we'll both be easier to keep track of. And I will rest more easily knowing how the prince fares."

"It may distress you, to see your friend so brought down by his injuries," Al-Razi objected. Then his eyes swept the scars at Llesho's breast.

"But I am reminded that you are no stranger to the terrible wounds of war. Perhaps." The physician dropped his gaze, contemplating some image behind his lashes. "Your friend sleeps deeply. He will not know you are there—the poppy robs the patient of his will to rise out of his slumber. But if you will rest more easily in his presence, it can be arranged. At least for a little while."

He gestured with a flick of his wrist and servants came forward, making a chair of their locked hands for him to ride in. Llesho would have protested that he could walk, but his journey to the privy had robbed him of his adventuring spirit. He let himself be guided to the human chair and carried into a nearby room identical to his own, where Prince Tayyichiut lay in restless dreams.

"His mind struggles to make its way back to the land of the waking," Al-Razi explained as Tayy's head tossed on his pillows. "For the sake of his stitches, however, he must remain quiet."

With that, the physician left him to take up a thin silver rod pierced through its center from end to end like a blade of river grass. He put one end into a vial of dark glass and put the other end to his mouth, sucking, Llesho supposed, until a dose of the poppy had traveled up the rod. Releasing the straw from his mouth, he capped it with his finger. Then he took the open end and inserted it between Tayy's lips, nudging it past his teeth, until so much of the straw had disappeared Llesho thought the prince must have swallowed it. When he was satisfied at the positioning of the silver straw, Al-Razi took his finger from the end.

Prince Tayy gurgled and choked while the physician soothed his throat with his thumbs. "There, there, it will be better soon," he said, and Tayy quickly settled down again, beyond the reach of pain or dreams that had caused the restless motion on his bed.

"I'm sorry," Ibn Al-Razi said. "But he must be kept quiet until the wound begins to heal."

"I remember," Llesho agreed with a bitter twist of a smile. He'd had no syrup of poppy in Shan and the herbs his brother had to offer were only of slight help in calming the fire that had torn his belly. "Whatever you can do for him, I'm grateful."

The physician returned his smile with a gentle one of his own. "And now your own examination, young king?"

"All right." But he said it around a yawn, as his mind wandered off on vague and meaningless questions, like, "Why does everybody I meet call me 'young king' instead of using my title? And why am I still sitting up?"

The answer to this latter came with the doctor's careful hands on his shoulders pressing him back into a feather bed that seemed to reach out to enfold him.

"Stay with him, if you wish," he heard Ibn Al-Razi whisper as he tiptoed away.

"Thank you." That was Menar's voice, accepting his posting at the bedside of his brother. And then the poet began to recite.

> "A king with morning in his eyes
> Walked out of the sun . . ."

Part of Llesho's mind made the connection to the sun and recognized that the poem spoke about the king of a new day. But another part, lost in the confused jumble of his undirected thoughts, saw a king in mourning with his losses etched into his weeping face. Neither understanding would be wrong.

Chapter Twenty-five

"Father of thunder! Daughter of heaven!
You, from whom all gifts are given!
Spare this son of war and strife,
Give him back his youth and life!"

IT HAD grown so dark that Llesho wondered for a moment if
he had lost his sight while he slept or, by some power of dream-
walking, had taken the place of his brother's spirit in the body
of the blind poet. Which would, he thought, explain why the
poem he heard seemed hardly the stuff to build a legend on.

"It's a mother's prayer for a child at war," a voice spoke to
him out of the darkness. Menar didn't need the light to see that
he'd awakened but used the senses of the blind. The change in
the sound of Llesho's breathing, or the shift from the paralysis
of sleep to the stillness of the wary, would have told his brother
everything. "I've run out of poetry, and fallen back on the simplest pleas of the common folk."

They'd been little more than children when his cadre set out
on his quest, so the prayer seemed apt. He wondered how his
companions were faring. Banned from the sickroom, they'd be
fidgety and quick to the knife or the sword as boredom and
worry made war on their training. They'd manage, of course—
they always did. Since he'd left the ship, however, he'd neither

seen the trickster god nor heard him mentioned by either of his names. And that made him seriously nervous.

"Master Den?"

The question must have seemed unrelated to Llesho's earlier conversation, but Menar replied with the patience one shows to the ill. "He's in the town. Master Ibn Al-Razi could not bar his doorway while your companion carried you in his arms, but he won't abide the presence of false gods as guests under his roof."

Llesho trembled to hear a prince of Thebin speak so about the trickster god. "How can one deny the existence of a being who walks through the door and gives a proper bow?" Admittedly, ChiChu had never picked Menar up by the scruff of his neck and set him on his path by the might of his tree-trunk arms. But the seven mortal gods made up the greater part of the Way of the Goddess and Menar was a prince of her holy house. He was afraid to ask the next question, so he posed it as a reproof. "But you know the truth. You could have told the physician otherwise."

Menar heaved a small sigh. As Llesho's eyes adjusted to the dim starlight, he saw a shift in the shadows. The bulk of the poet's shoulder moved in a shrug against the darkness. "I no longer follow the Way of the Goddess," Menar said. "We don't deny that Master Den exists, or that he may be a powerful magician in his own way. If we met the Lady SienMa, who holds our own Habiba's service, we would respect her skills as a worthy magician as well. But we do not honor any mortal being as a god. Master Ibn Al-Razi could not in conscience offer the hospitality of his roof to one who makes such claims about his person.

Llesho didn't know what to say to that. "Do you mean you don't believe in the Great Goddess, or in heaven either?"

That seemed impossible. Somewhere in the course of his journeys, Llesho had stopped thinking of the Goddess as an unreachable goal. The heavenly wife who fed him water when he was thirsty, who comforted him when he was in pain, who had mourned him through many lifetimes, was as real to him as his own cadre but more precious even than those companions.

"Once I did." Menar raised a shoulder in apology. "But no longer."

She kissed me. He thought to offer his own experience against his brother's loss of faith—*I have been to the gardens of heaven, and they are in need of our help.*

Another possibility came to mind, and though it pained Llesho even to think it, he couldn't leave it unspoken. "Or is it that, knowing the gates of heaven are imperiled, you *choose* not to heed her plight?"

A candle or a lamp would have helped him read his brother's feelings in the nervous twitter of his fingers or the play of emotion across his face. But a blind man has no need of light, so Menar hadn't lit one. Afraid that asking would break the tenuous mood, Llesho closed his eyes, determined to rely on the senses that Menar used to read the world every day. The poet's voice would tell him much. And the rhythm of his brother's breathing, now that he was paying attention, sounded strained with distress.

"The Bithynians are very strict about their religion," Menar explained. "A slave must accept the Father and his Daughter as his gods or die. A blind slave, even a poet, has few choices in such a place. A blind infidel has only the mines or public stoning. Or beheading, if he has a merciful master."

That isn't Mercy, Llesho wanted to tell him. *Mercy is a dwarf who plays the flute in the court of the emperor of Shan.* Menar had fallen deeply into his story, however. He kept his objections to himself while the poet-prince who had become a slave to gods as well as men continued with his confession.

"For a long time I resisted." The rustle of cloth brought Llesho's eyes open. Menar had raised a hand—perhaps reaching out, perhaps a gesture of helplessness—and let it fall again, no more than a shift in the patterns of darkness. "Faith had a part in my resistance, of course, and tradition. But I was freshly wounded as well, and preferred death to my new blindness.

"Ibn Al-Razi, however, refused to let me die. He brought me home to this place. Even in the perpetual darkness of my new condition, it reminded me of Adar's clinic in the mountains.

And he offered me a new life in the arms of the Father and his Daughter."

"But the Goddess—"

Menar stopped him with a sigh. "It's different for you, for Adar and the other chosen husbands. For those of us to whom she did not come, faith is a harder thing."

"Shokar says he had the greater gift, to be set free to live a normal life."

"The Father and his holy Daughter have been good to me, Llesho, when all the world seemed turned to ash in my hand. I honor your quest, I'll even follow you, but in the name of my new gods."

Llesho had always thought that faith couldn't be forced upon a believer but flowed from the hidden experience of the heart. It seemed that he'd been wrong. He wouldn't use the tactics of the slavers against his brother, however. As a true servant of the Great Goddess, he could only offer his own experience in exchange for his brother's story.

"She's real, you know, not some ideal turned into a philosophical parable. She fed me water with her own hand and held my head when I thought that Master Markko's poisons would kill me."

"I understand," Menar said. "Your companions have talked about this Master Markko. I am only a poet, but I would pierce this villain to the heart with my pen before I would let him touch you again. I have learned in my master's workrooms, however, that when we suffer great terror and pain, our imagination sometimes supplies what our heart needs."

"Is that how you explain your own prophecies?"

"Sometimes," Menar admitted, humor and something more coloring his voice. "Mostly, I just open my mouth and let others decide where the message comes from. But no god has ever given me a cup of water."

Llesho remembered his own days of doubt. Not that the Goddess existed, but that she could find worthy an exiled prince, an ex-slave and a former gladiator, all things that must fall below the expectations of the queen of heaven. He'd been wrong. So was Menar. He just needed time to find his way back.

Llesho was silent for so long that someone else might have guessed he'd gone to sleep. Menar, with the senses of the blind, knew better.

"Although it's heresy among the Bithynians to believe so, I can find it in my heart to accept that the Great Goddess exists in her own heaven, while the god of Pontus rules his separate domains of sky and earth. But don't ask me to abandon the god of Pontus and his Daughter. Try to think of it this way. What the Goddess discarded, the Father and his Daughter picked up for their own use. I would not desert them."

"All right." Llesho lay back on his bed. They would have this conversation again but, then as now, he had to respect his brother's choices. The matter of the prophecy, however, couldn't wait that long.

"What about the Apadisha?"

"He will not lift a finger to help a goddess whose very existence is heresy and an abomination in his eyes." Menar stated what Llesho suspected, so it came as no great shock. "Since the Marmer Sea separates the Harn from Pontus, and since the Harnish are notoriously afraid of water, he loses no sleep over the fate of Kungol becoming his own fate either."

Again, the news disappointed but didn't surprise him. Thebin was a long way from Pontus. They shared no gods and competed in trade, each at the pinnacle of a different road by which goods traveled west and east. Kungol's misfortune just made Pontus richer. Menar wasn't finished, however; he had held the turning point to the end, like the storyteller he was.

"But to fulfill a prophecy handed down by his own god, which his astrologers and the magicians in his service assure him most certainly will sweep all Bithynia before it, for that the Apadisha would do much."

Ah. The prophecy. Llesho still didn't know what it said. He took a breath to ask, but Menar quieted him with a hand crossing his forehead. In a gesture so like Adar's that his heart yearned to bring the brothers together, Menar drifted fingers over Llesho's eyelids, bringing them down with no force but the suggestion of sleep. "Later," he said, "when the sun has come up . . ."

* * *

"... another death of snakebite in the town," Lling whispered. "Bamboo snakes are rare anywhere in Bithynia and unheard of in the city. It has to be Lady Chaiujin, but how did she follow us so closely? It's not like there are forests or mountains to hide behind on the ocean. We would have seen a ship out there."

"It seemed pretty mountainous to me," Prince Tayyichiut answered in equally hushed tones. "I lay you odds that wretched cup of hers has something to do with it, though."

They hadn't noticed he was awake yet. Llesho let the quiet voices wash over him as he came back from the silent place in his dreams. He felt like he'd slept for just a brief moment this time, but the last time he woke up his whole cadre had been gathered in the sickroom. Kaydu was gone now, and so were Bixei and Stipes. Lling was reporting to Tayy the most recent disturbing news from Pontus, leaving Hmishi to watch over their king's sleep. He was doing so with a peculiar intensity that worried Llesho.

"You're back," Hmishi said. "The physician Ibn Al-Razi says I'm to ask you what you recall since you've been here."

"Kaydu was here. She said Marmer Sea Dragon is with Master Den, who is not allowed in to see me." He remembered that intelligence from the other side of sleep. "Menar said that is because he doesn't believe in the eight mortal gods and won't have as a guest any mortal who claims to be one, though he accepts Master Den as a great magician." Kaydu hadn't been there when he'd talked to Menar. It must have been two different conversations.

At the sound of their low voices, Lling and Tayy glanced over. Some question passed between his Thebin guards, and some decision. "Master Ibn Al-Razi has put the cup in the care of the college of magicians for safekeeping." Lling picked up her story again. Reluctantly, Prince Tayyichiut let his attention be drawn away.

"That's good." Hmishi tried to look pleased with him but ended up looking uncomfortable instead.

"What has put that expression on your face?" Llesho asked, keeping his voice down. Lling would hear later from her partner. And maybe, when he knew what was going on, he'd tell Prince Tayy himself. But for now, he'd humor his guardsman's quest for as much privacy as he could manage in the sickroom.

"I asked Ibn Al-Razi why you didn't wake up." Hmishi watched him as he spoke, gauging Llesho's reactions. "He said he couldn't help you. That you were moving far away from us, beyond even the realm of dreams, and that the dark of sleep offered peace you wouldn't willingly abandon. You needed to find the will to go on when strength had finally failed you."

That sounded too close to how he was feeling for comfort, but Llesho didn't say anything. Hopefully, he kept the truth off his face, but he didn't have as much control as he would have liked. Tears threatened and he didn't even know why, except that he was awake now and maybe didn't want to be.

Hmishi didn't wait for an answer, though. "I didn't right away, but the longer I'm alive, the better I remember dying," he said.

It wasn't about him, so Llesho felt safe in giving an answering nod. He remembered that time. Too vividly. It still visited his nightmares.

"I felt bad for Lling, but Tsu-tan had destroyed not only my body but my soul as well. I knew that even if flesh and bone mended, the wounds to my self—to who and what I was—ran so deep that they would never heal. So death came as a relief. I didn't have to hurt anymore. I didn't have to remember what his soldiers did to me, what he did to me. I could let it all go. Then you brought me back."

Llesho refused to apologize. "I still needed you," he said, though it sounded petty in his own ears. "Lling still needed you."

Lling had suffered as well. Losing Hmishi was one burden more that they had spared her, he and Dognut. That mattered almost as much as his own need to have his companions around him in his struggle.

"I know. I have a sworn duty here, in this life, to your service and to Lling's heart. I wouldn't have wished to carry the betrayal of those obligations into the next." A little smile cracked his otherwise somber expression. "Lling is fully capable of making me sorry the next time we meet on the wheel."

Which was true enough. Hmishi had put him off his guard with this talk of his own death and his connection with Lling, so the guardsman's next words struck him like an unexpected blow.

"You moved the realms of heaven and earth and the underworld to bring me back from the dead. Imagine how it is for those of us who have followed you across half the world, who have risked fire and storm for you. Who have entered the camps of our enemies as prisoners and diplomats in your service. Imagine how we feel to watch you drift away into the dark, abandoning the quest that brought us here where we are strangers and powerless.

"And what of the armies that gather at your back?" As he talked, Hmishi's voice gained volume. Lling and Tayy interrupted their own conversation, watching with mounting concern as Hmishi called his king to account:

"Do you understand what you have set in motion with your actions? And what now waits, losing patience, while you decide whether your quest is worth living for? From what I've heard, the Way of the Goddess has carried you down a similar path before; you've died in her service before. But that was in battle, or betrayed by your own weapon. How will you answer to the lady in your next life, knowing you left her to the mercy of the monsters raised by your greatest enemy while you *slept away* your life in Pontus!"

Hmishi ended with a roar that brought the rest of his guards running, Bixei still brushing the sleep from his eyes but with a sword in his hand. Ibn Al-Razi entered on the heels of the cadre. With a gentle but insistent hand on Bixei's wrist, he urged the sword point down, where it could do no harm in the sickroom that was suddenly boiling with people.

"What's happened?" Kaydu's sharp gaze covered the room, but found nothing amiss. She hadn't drawn her sword, but her hand never left its hilt.

Llesho dropped his face in his hands, too embarrassed to

face the anxious crowd that had suddenly transformed Ibn Al-Razi's hospital into an armed camp.

"Hmishi was giving a pep talk. He got a little excited, but everything seems to be all right now."

Lling answered the question in a tone that made Llesho certain not only that she'd been listening the whole time, but that the whole thing had been a setup. If he'd had any doubts, a quick look at Tayy's guilty expression settled them. Ibn Al-Razi just raised an eyebrow in a way Llesho was more accustomed to seeing on Habiba's face. A universal response, it seemed, but to *what* he hadn't quite figured out yet.

"Now that you've 'encouraged' your young king, perhaps you would let him rest?" Al-Razi suggested.

Hmishi, however, had other plans. "I think he's rested enough," he said. "I respect the rules of your house, honorable physician, but if his teacher is prohibited from entering here, it's time Llesho went to Master Den."

"The world would be a safer place if kings chose their teachers more wisely."

His companions waited for Llesho to defend his teacher, but Al-Razi only spoke the truth. Or part of it.

"A king who doesn't use his wiles in the defense of his people doesn't remain king very long. I learned that lesson in the Palace of the Sun in my seventh summer. Swords can support a canny king, but they can't keep an innocent in power." His father had been such a king, innocent in the ways of subterfuge and brutal attack. "Fortunately for Thebin, I return with a master of trickery at my beck. We will see a different outcome this time."

He didn't mention the mortal goddess of war, didn't want to offend his host more sorely than he already had. But Hmishi was right. He needed to see Master Den. And he was right about other things as well. Llesho had slept away the exhaustion of his travels and remained asleep only to escape the struggle ahead. It was time he woke up in more ways than one.

"I need my clothes."

Smiles bloomed on the faces of his companions. Even Prince Tayyichiut looked relieved. Hmishi ran to do his bidding, anxious, it seemed, to be out from under Llesho's gaze now that he'd decided to return to the land of the living. While he waited for something to wear, Llesho turned his attention to the physician.

"You have my gratitude, and that of my people—those who travel with me, and those who follow behind us. I will be further in your debt if you will continue to watch over our companion, Prince Tayyichiut, whom you have brought back from the brink of death with your excellent care." And someday he would have to trade stories with Tayy, find out how far down the path to the underworld he'd actually journeyed, and what stories he had to tell about the way back. But not now, when death still hovered too close in the air.

"As for myself, it is time I declared this particular well open for business again."

Ibn Al-Razi stroked his short beard thoughtfully, but a smile crinkled at the corners of his mouth, and made crow's-feet at his temples. "You will wish an audience with the Apadisha, then."

"First I have to meet with my counselors. Then we must pay our respects to the Apadisha of Pontus," Llesho agreed.

Hmishi returned with his clothes then and Llesho was unsurprised to discover that he carried not the rags of slavery, the clothes he'd come ashore in, but the royal garb of a Thebin king.

"Master Den?" Llesho asked, though he knew the answer.

Kaydu shrugged. "He said you'd need them."

"When did he say that?"

"This morning."

He didn't know why it surprised him. Or why he wasn't angrier that he'd been ambushed by a plot hatched among his guards and the trickster god himself. But they'd all signed on for a more important mission than the pleasure of Llesho's personal whim.

"Your father and Master Den are still at the school?" Llesho dressed quickly as they talked.

"With Marmer Sea Dragon," Kaydu assured him, while Ibn

Al-Razi made a warding gesture in the air to protect himself from the offense against his own gods.

"Is it far?"

"About a li, though the way is twisty." She gave him the grin that used to announce her intention to wipe the practice yard with his backside. "It'll be a good test of your recovery."

Llesho settled his embroidered sleeveless coat on his shoulders, wishing with a last backward sigh for his sleep clothes. Court dress was heavy and cumbersome in the warm climate of Pontus. He allowed Bixei to help him with his boots and then Hmishi set on his brow the silver fillet that marked a prince of Thebin. Master Den had been thorough, as always.

Ready to go, he looked around for the one face he hadn't seen since he'd awakened to Hmishi's rebuke.

"Where is my brother, Menar?"

"Here." Menar followed his voice into the room. He moved fluidly, knowing the way in his blindness as a sighted slave might find his way in the dark. He had set aside the attire of a slave and wore more elaborate clothes in rich silk, blue for the pantaloons and red for the shirt, with a cream-colored coat that fit tightly at the waist and flared in a wide skirt to his calves. On his forehead he wore a circlet of silver which he fingered with a questing hand at his temple, and over his eyes a rich purple cloth was bound.

"I have grown out of the habit of crowns," he confessed with an awkward smile. "But Ibn Al-Razi informs me the Apadisha will expect some such sign."

"But no Thebin court dress?" Llesho asked, not chiding his brother, but curious about the clothes he wore, which were nothing like the simple whites of his master.

"In the house of my master I am a recorder of medical poems, but the Apadisha often asks my presence for my skills as a teller of tales. This is what I wear to perform for his gracious majesty. The other slaves assure me that I cut a dashing figure, except for my eyes, of course, which are covered so the sight of them doesn't offend the Apadisha's company."

Llesho had spent so much of his life as a slave that he almost didn't notice Menar's reference to his own servitude. "Not a slave anymore," Llesho insisted when it struck him that they had not yet discussed his brother's condition. "I would dispute your master's right to own a prince of the royal house of Kungol."

"You need the Apadisha," his brother warned him.

"Then we will discuss with the physician Ibn Al-Razi the terms of your freedom. I wouldn't leave you here, a possession in a foreign land, under any circumstances. Under these, it is impossible. Lleck told me to find all of my brothers, not just the ones it was convenient to make away with."

"I know, better than you think," Menar assured him. "But wait, be patient. Hear the prophecy. Then we will see what we will see."

Llesho didn't mention that he'd come all the way to Pontus to hear the prophecy and, weeks after his arrival, had yet to find out what it said. He was about to hear it and arguing would only delay things. Instead, he untied the cloth that bound Menar's eyes.

"These are not times to hide the consequences of our actions, or our lack of actions, from our allies," he said. "If the Apadisha would hear the prophecy, and decide upon a course of action based on what he hears, he should see what the cost of doing nothing is."

It sounded harsh, but Hmishi had stirred him to action and he found that he had little patience for himself or anyone else who would avoid knowing the consequences if he failed to act. So he didn't apologize, but firmed his chin and, with a glare that dared anyone to test him, he swept out of the sickroom, leaving Prince Tayy wide-eyed in his bed and Ibn Al-Razi staring after them.

"My father is waiting for us," Kaydu said when they were moving. "I'll lead the way."

A single nod, and Llesho followed his brother. The physician arranged for sedan chairs to carry the princes, and Llesho's cadre fell in around them. Bixei and Stipes ranged out ahead and behind while Hmishi and Lling stayed close to the brothers in defensive mode. In that way they entered the streets of Pontus.

Chapter Twenty-six

PONTUS was larger than Edris, with a more varied architecture. Llesho could see the roots of the one city in the other, however. The streets were wider in Pontus, but the houses that lined them still hid behind high walls gleaming whiter here than those of the city that faced it across the sea. Gates were more prominent, with elaborately decorated arches over them and a view of the flowery gardens visible between the great hinges. Unlike Edris, Pontus was a city of towers: graceful slim minarets and clusters of thick, bulbous domes raised their heads high over the mansions and more modest houses at their feet.

Kaydu was leading them toward a huge gate of carved wood bound in bronze. As they approached, a wizened face peered at them out of a small slot and then disappeared. A moment later they heard a bolt sliding in its keeper, and a portcullis door opened in the gate.

"Come in, come in," The old man gestured them forward, reverting to the mysterious liquid sibilance of the Bithynian tongue spoken in the city. Kaydu quickly translated with a whisper in Llesho's ear: "The masters await!"

Inside the high, white wall, Llesho found a self-contained little city of its own, more than a dozen buildings, the smallest no larger than a cottage. The largest stood twice the height of the wall that enclosed them, with six towers rising into the sunlight around a central dome shaped like a giant onion. Between the lowest, nearest the gate, and the tallest, at the farthest reach of the walled city-within-a-city, buildings of varied sizes and shapes lay scattered along sweeping pathways among lush gardens. Some of those had towers of their own.

As they passed down one of those sweeping paths of raked pebbles, Kaydu pointed out scholars and musicians and poets and soldiers and bakers, each of whom she identified by their style of dress and the color of their pantaloons. Llesho was not surprised to find their chosen path took them toward a large, centrally located building crowned by one large dome. He figured this for one of the main teaching facilities, where Habiba had come to visit with the professors of his own days as a student at the school. He did not expect the greeting that met him when he entered the great hall beneath the central dome, however.

Hundreds of students sat in an ascending circle that reminded Llesho of the bleachers surrounding the arena where the gladiators had fought in Farshore Province. Here the central auditorium was covered in carpets, not sawdust. Masters in brightly colored robes that indicated their special fields of interest sat in chairs gathered in two rows beneath the colored dome. Habiba rose from the front row to greet them, with Master Den at his right hand and Marmer Sea Dragon, in his human form, at his left. A man and a woman, both wrinkled with age, held hands as they waited to greet him. Llesho sensed that they clung to each other for courage. He wondered what could frighten two wizards who sat untroubled by gods and dragons, but his own party were the only newcomers.

"Prince of destiny." The old man bowed to Llesho, making it clear where the title was meant to go.

"Prince of prophecy," the woman added with her own bow. "Come, sit. And Prince Menar, who is the poet-prince, and a prophet for his brother's coming: we hope to hear you recite the prophecy once again so that our students and masters can refine their interpretations."

"It will ease my heart to do so," Menar replied. "His Holy

Excellence, King Llesho, may have many answers for us, though I think we will none of us take pleasure in them."

"Prophets seldom have good things to say," the old man agreed. "Good news can wait for tomorrow. Bad news requires warning."

"Wise, as always," Menar acknowledged, bowing to show respect for the teacher. Llesho wondered how a follower of Ibn Al-Razi's more ascetic practice of belief in the religion of the Father-and-Daughter gods must view the Apadisha's school for magicians. The physician had recognized the working of dragon magic in Llesho's illness, however. His servant, Menar, seemed to have no difficulty with the more esoteric practices of the faith that included the training of witches and magicians and the welcome of gods and dragons into their school.

But the school wasn't Llesho's main concern. "The Apadisha has summoned us on the matter of the prophecy," he said with a proper bow. "I honor your school and your students, but I've come to beg leave for my companions to accompany me to the palace."

"Ah." The old woman smiled brightly at him, her cheerfully glittering eyes almost lost in a sea of wrinkles. "I have not introduced myself. I am the chief astrologer for the good fortunes of Pontus and all Bithynia, adviser to the Apadisha and teacher in his school for the great magicians. You may call me Master Astrologer.

"And this is my husband, our Apadisha's chief numerologist. You may call him Master Numerologist."

An astrologer read the stars for an understanding of past and future and interpreted that knowledge for guidance in the present. A numerologist predicted the mathematics of future events. Dates and the calendar were important in the plotting of the future, as were the seeming accidents of numbers as one measured the path of a lifetime. Pontus, Kaydu had told him, enjoyed a reputation for producing the most skilled in these as well as other magical arts. Llesho gave a slight bow suitable from a youthful king to those of greater wisdom and years.

"We have been apprised of your summons," Master Numerologist assured them. "Our sages and their students have been hypothesizing on the Apadisha's question all day. But we can make no formal determinations until the poet announces his prophecies of doom in the presence of the Apadisha. And, of course, we must observe the one who claims to be the chosen king of said prophecy."

At that, Master Numerologist stopped with a bow to his companion. Master Astrologer completed his thought as if they were but one person speaking with two mouths. "His Excellency, our most sagacious Apadisha, will then make such inquiries as will uncover any duplicity of the false prophet working in conspiracy with these barbarians from the East to deceive the sultanate. Or he will establish that the promised savior has appeared to assuage his troubled sleep."

The professors of the magical arts spoke in high-flown accents, using a language Llesho had never heard before. A high-court form of the tongue the gatekeeper had used, he guessed from the cadence and the sibilant flow of the sentences. Suppressing a little smile, Habiba translated both for content and for the style of address. Llesho understood the smile well enough, though he couldn't say as much for all the words. Unlike his own plain-spoken teachers, these courtly scholars used words to obscure as much as to enlighten. When he'd sorted through it all, he realized that, however the matter settled out, the astrologer and the numerologist could claim to have accurately predicted the outcome.

"So, Menar will tell his story, then I will tell mine," Llesho said to Habiba, confirming his understanding of the conversation as it was translated to him. "Then the Apadisha will decide whether or not we are telling the truth."

"That's about it," Habiba agreed, and hastily translated this into an elaborate description of Llesho's excellent comprehension.

"And if the Apadisha decides against us?"

Habiba gave a little shrug, as if the consequences were minor. "Stoning, or beheading. I would be disappointed if the day goes against us, but even more dismayed if you stayed to see sentence carried out against you."

The magician expected him to summon the avatar of his

dream travels, and in the shape of a roebuck to leap out of mortal danger. His companions might die, but he would remain to carry on the fight with the armies Shou had already gathered at the edge of the grasslands.

"According to Lleck's ghost, I need all my brothers, not just the ones easiest to keep alive." That was a warning. Menar was no more expendable than Llesho himself, though how the blind poet would be of use in the coming battle he hadn't figured out yet. For that reason if for no other—what he hadn't accounted for in his plans invariably rose up and bit him on the nose when he wasn't paying attention—he wouldn't abandon his brother to the wrath of the Apadisha. It wasn't the only reason, or even the most important. He didn't want to get into an argument with Habiba about family loyalty, though. Or, even worse, about the love he felt for his brothers—even the most exasperating of them.

The advisers to the Apadisha had left out one important detail, but Llesho had picked up on the clue. "The Apadisha has dreams."

Habiba blinked once, the only sign that he had understood the meaning behind the simple statement. He didn't translate, which was all Llesho needed to confirm it. The Apadisha dream traveled, or perhaps had his own prophetic dreams that woke him with the same fear and dread that Lluka suffered. If he had experienced those baleful visions, there would be no question of truthfulness. For all their sakes, Llesho hoped the dreams hadn't driven him mad.

"Shall we go?" Master Numerologist asked.

Llesho didn't understand the words, but the gesture was plain enough to follow. A student came forward and took Menar's elbow as they sorted themselves out in the correct diplomatic order. First came the two head masters of the magical arts, who would introduce the prophet and his prophecy. Then came Llesho and his brother Menar. Habiba, Master Den, and Marmer Sea Dragon followed as his court, with the rest of the teachers and then their students behind. Llesho's cadre, with no assigned positions, flanked the hastily assembled column on both sides.

In a procession of over two hundred souls, they made their way to an inner door guarded by two women in armor, each with a tall spear in one hand and a sword in the other. "You may not pass," the guardswoman on the right said, and tilted her spear so that it crossed that of the guard on the left side of the door.

"We come at the whim of the Apadisha," the astrologer said with a deep bow. "Delay us at your peril."

This seemed to be a formula of admittance rather than a genuine challenge. The guard took no offense but gave their party an assessing examination that would have fit right at home in the eyes of his own cadre. When the guardswoman's glance fell upon his companions, her formal posture gave way to battle readiness.

"No one may enter the presence of the Apadisha with weapons on their person," she said, and added, "no foreign soldiers may pass this door, in any state of arms."

"Of course." They'd had the same rule in the Palace of the Sun. That hadn't stopped the Harnish raiders. But who knew how many foreign spies would have slipped a knife between his father's ribs before then, if their mercenary guards hadn't made the same demands of guests and supplicants? Llesho, therefore, did as he was bidden. He took the scabbards from his belt and the sheath that held the spear at his back, putting them both into Kaydu's hand.

"Stay here," he said, "but stay alert." He didn't want them captured if things went badly on the other side of the door.

Kaydu gave a deep bow in salute, unhappy to be left behind but not surprised at the regulation. As a student of her father, she might have followed the others of the school, but that was neither her position in his cadre nor the uniform she pesently wore. She joined the others who followed him as they took up watchful positions around the perimeter. Llesho reclaimed his place in the procession. The Bithynian guardswoman struck a gong taller than she was that echoed through the hall and the door swung open.

Llesho had expected a room, but more gardens awaited them on the other side. This time an inner courtyard lay before them, surrounded by open and airy pavilions topped by the fat round towers he had seen in the distance on his arrival. A fountain gushed from the center of an intersection where half a dozen paved walkways met. From that center the paths wandered through stands of date trees and tall ferns. Thick vines raised themselves along white trellises, flowering with large red blooms that released a heady perfume as the procession passed.

In state, their party, with the whole school behind them, walked slowly past the fountain, down a path that snaked between hibiscus and oleander, to a set of doors the like of which Llesho had never seen before. They stood three times as high as Llesho's head and four times the width of a normal door. Elaborate patterns of flowers and trailing vines covered the surface that was made entirely out of gold.

"The Divan of the Grand Apadisha of Pontus and all the surrounding lands of Bithynia and the Marmer Sea that washes his shores in the east," Master Astrologer said. She smiled proudly as she announced the lands and holdings of the Apadisha's rule. Marmer Sea Dragon bristled at the mention of his own realm among the possessions, but did not raise an objection. The gleam in his eyes warned Llesho that more remained to be said on the subject. For the time being he kept his peace, while the doors in front of them glinted in the afternoon as if the sun itself blazed with the glory of the Grand Apadisha.

"Leaf," Habiba muttered in his ear. Gold leaf, that was. Artisans had beaten thin sheets of gold foil into the material that made up the bulk of the door, giving it the luster of gold but not the cost or weight. A solid gold door would have been impossible to move even if the Apadisha had wished to display his wealth in such a way. Gold leaf in such quantity itself spoke of overwhelming riches, however. Pontus was not just the center of magical education for witches and magicians. It was also the last stop in the East for goods passing into and out of the West.

Master Numerologist stopped in front of the magnificent doors and pulled on a thick silk rope that hung down from the center of a tubular chime. At the sounding of the chime, the doors began to heave slowly outward. Whatever they were made of, they were heavy. Three slaves on each side heaved against the thick crossbars, muscles bunching in their shoulders and veins straining in their necks. Slowly, the doors opened on soundless post hinges set into the ground and the lintel arch. When the doors had opened enough so that Llesho's party could enter three abreast, the headmasters of the magicians started forward again.

The governor of Guynm Province must have gotten his decorating ideas from the Grand Apadisha's Divan in Pontus. Everywhere the walls glittered with a million jewellike bits of glass worked in the same motifs of vines and flowers that had adorned the golden doors. Gold foil molded the leafy decorations that banded the ceiling from which rose the greatest of the bulbous domes that towered over the city. Stealing a glance overhead, Llesho saw a densely complex geometric pattern built of brilliantly colored tiles that covered the dome. Bits of colored glass let in shafts of painted light all around its circumference.

The Divan itself was a room so large that the two hundred students forming themselves in rows behind a hand-carved screen at the right of the door seemed to be tucked out of the way. Behind a matching screen to the left of the gold door an orchestra of boys played strange discordant music on their instruments. The masters led Menar and Llesho and their small party of advisers forward, with all the faculty of the magicians' school at their backs.

They came to the foot of the sumptuously draped dais at the center of the great room, where a reclining figure awaited them on a low couch.

"Health and long life!" Master Astrologer proclaimed the greeting. She fell to her knees, as did Master Numerologist, both dropping their foreheads to the floor, awaiting the pleasure of their sultan. All the faculty and students that had followed them did likewise. Llesho and his company bowed their respect, but did not kneel or knock their heads on the floor. Menar might have done so, but his blindness absolved him from the awkward duty. As for the others in their party, they either were themselves or represented equal monarchs in their own right, and owed the Grand Apadisha no greater abasement.

From her position on her knees and with her face still turned to the floor, Master Astrologer introduced the newcomers: "My lord Grand Apadisha of Pontus and all the lands and waters surrounding it on which his hand has fallen by the Grace of the Father and the Sword of the Daughter, I bring you the blind prophet and a king in exile who claims to be the foretold one."

Fortunately for them all, the old teacher ran out of air at that point, or they might still be listening while she awarded to the Apadisha all the lands from here to Pearl Island. The part about the Sword of the Daughter caught his attention, however. This was the first he had heard of a military aspect to the religion of the Father and the Daughter. Suddenly, he wondered how friendly this audience really was, and how seriously the Apadisha did take his claims to the property of his neighbors.

The Apadisha watched with bright, birdlike dark eyes. His gaze reminded Llesho of Kaydu, but he didn't think it was a good idea to inquire about the presence of dragons—or eagles—in his lineage. He was very thin, with dark circles smudging his cheekbones and sagging flesh, as if he'd recently lost a great deal of weight to worry or illness.

Dreams, Llesho thought, *could eat at the body as they ate at the soul.* A moment of unspoken understanding passed between them as the exiled king of Thebin and the Apadisha of Bithynia recognized in each other the terrible burden they carried. But even that connection of mutual understanding must be proved in front of the many witnesses.

"In truth I make no such claim about myself," Llesho corrected Master Astrologer. "I came to Pontus following rumors of the exiled poet-prince of Thebin, said to have been blinded and enslaved in the attack on Kungol, our home. I hoped to find my brother Menar, and I did." He couldn't help the smile that sneaked across his lips. Menar, injured but alive, stood at his side.

The Apadisha responded to his contentment with a formal reflection of his smile, but his eyes narrowed. "You travel with disreputable companions." He looked to Master Den when he spoke, letting his glance slide over Marmer Sea Dragon as if he wasn't sure what to make of this guest. "In both of the worlds open to men. But one is missing."

Many had stayed behind, he could have said. But the reference to two worlds meant the dream world and the waking one. The Grand Apadisha knew of Pig even if he didn't believe in the Great Goddess or her gardens.

"One follows the guide who knows the way," Llesho therefore answered.

"But not too far, or with one's eyes closed," the Apadisha warned him.

Menar, the poet and master of lore and story, joined the argument with a knowing little smile. "Even the blind keep one eye open in the land of the spirits."

Which offered Llesho the opening he needed to reassure his host, "Can I, with two eyes, be less wary than my brother?" He knew the Jinn's crimes as well as anybody, after all.

The Grand Apadisha raised an eyebrow. "Is that a question?" he asked in an ironic drawl that Habiba refrained from copying in his translation.

Llesho wondered who had been whispering in the sultan's ear, and what they'd told of his more hair-raising adventures in ignoring good sense. Still it was a fair challenge.

"Maybe it should be. Fortunately, I have other advisers—" At this, he made a small gesture with his hand to take in Habiba at his side. "—to keep me from falling too far off my proper course."

The Grand Apadisha could have no objection to the magician, who had trained in his own royal school in Pontus.

Indeed, the sultan accepted this answer with only the briefest glance at Habiba. "The Father finds favor in one who, like himself, has had the raising of a Daughter of the Sword," he agreed, calling upon the name of his god as witness. Then he added as a caution, "But for the Daughter's mind, we must ask his sages. It is her prophecies, after all, that will lead us into war or bar the way of our enemies."

"That is the other reason why I've journeyed to Pontus."

Llesho took this opening to plead his position. "The rumors that reached the grasslands, about this blind poet who might be my brother, claimed that prophecies spilled off the blind poet's tongue like water gushing from a fountain.

"My advisers suggested that I might find answers to further my quest with this poet. Even if he turned out not to be the Menar I lost as a child, I was honor bound to seek him out. But I know nothing of Bithynia's troubles nor can I claim any part in its prophecies until I know what the prophecies say."

The Grand Apadisha listened carefully and when Llesho had ended his little speech with a bow, he turned to Master Numerologist and Master Astrologer, who had remained on their knees, with their heads to the ground. "What do you have to say about this prophecy? Are we called to war in the East, or do we face the West for battle season? You have my permission to speak."

Master Numerologist rose from his position of abasement and dusted fussily at his immaculate robes, to win a moment more for thought before he must speak, Llesho thought.

"As Your Excellency knows, the sages of the school have studied the prophecy of the blind poet for three cycles of the seasons to no avail. In this young king from afar we have, at last, a key of sorts. It is time, we agree, to listen anew to the words of the blind prophet, but in the presence of the king of which it speaks."

"Master Astrologer?"

She rose as well, advising with fewer hesitation tactics but no more particular direction, "Let the young king explain what he can, and perhaps out of his tale we can find the star on which to set our course, and the numbers that mark the appointed time and day."

The Apadisha considered the advice of his sages. "Vague enough to keep your heads on your shoulders if things go badly," he remarked, to make it known that he hadn't fallen for the trick before he went on. "A blind man to set the course of the season's warfare. Hmm. Better than a pin in a map, I suppose, though barely."

Habiba hesitated just a moment before he translated in tones as hushed as he could make them. Understandable, that nervousness. *So,* Llesho thought, *we do not bring war to this Apad-*

isha. We just give him a direction to point his soldiers during hunting season. He tried to imagine what Shou would say. Not difficult. The emperor who now sat in the palace of the provincial governor he'd executed for plotting treason would warn him to be cautious. This sultan who played with real armies like other men played at Go might send his forces into Kungol at Llesho's behest. Getting them out again might prove more difficult than asking them in, however.

Shou would tell him not to invite an army he'd have to fight as soon as the common enemy had been routed. Especially when their leader was giving him that look that said, "It's snack time. And you're it."

In fact, however, the immediate message in those hungry eyes was a simpler version of "snack time." The Apadisha clapped his hands, summoning servants who had waited for his signal to begin their own procession. Breads and sauces, fruits and roasted meats, passed in orderly assemblage on great silver platters.

"Sit, sit." He waved Llesho's party to cushions scattered before the dais. "Deciding the fates of nations is hungry work. It's time we calmed the beasts in our bellies before they start making demands of the map."

When he put it that way, it sounded like a good idea. Llesho sat, with Master Den on his right and Marmer Sea Dragon in human form at his left. As a servant, even so exalted a one, Habiba remained standing. He placed himself between the Apadisha and Llesho's party as an arbiter. The sages, Master Astrologer and Master Numerologist, likewise did not join them at the feast. And since each had one of Menar's elbows, he didn't sit either.

When the Apadisha had taken a plate from a servant and helped himself to the delicacies there, he nodded his head at the masters awaiting his command.

"Let's hear it, then. This prophecy has set armies in motion and washed up on my shore an exiled king demanding aid and armies. What can this young king tell us to shed light on the words of our blind poet?"

Menar stepped forward and spread his hands in the way of

all poets, to show that he carried no weapons. In the market the gesture would also invite coins from the audience, but here it was form only. Menar gave a respectful bow and set his chin in the manner of one who looked into the distance in spite of his milky eyes. Slowly, in hypnotic cadence as if a force outside himself had taken control of his throat, Menar, prince of Thebin, began to recite.

Chapter Twenty-seven

"What is that sound?"
   The Father of all things asked.
Looking out his window, the day was clear
The sun shone brightly, but a cloud
Marred the distance.

Cries of grief rose from the darkness.

"It's only death,"
   The Daughter of the Sword answered,
Setting aside her blade to pour him tea.
"A war pauses in its path, destiny
Awaits a new coming."

And cries of anguish rose from the darkness.

"When will that be?"
   The Father of all things asked.
He drank his tea. The day had darkened.
The sun had fallen behind the clouds
Blotting out the heavens.

   Cries of terror grew closer in the darkness.

   Seven lost princes each find the others
Six heads crowned with stars a gate have hidden

Five armies, like one hand, close around them
Four worms breathing fire rise above them
Three bitter gifts must teach a bitter lesson
Two paths are offered, one is chosen
One jewel alone, to each of seven brothers.

A king is called to turn the sacred key.
Return to heaven that which heaven lost—
Justice brings both light and darkness—
Then heaven will have peace.

Cry, cry, for justice howled in the darkness.

MENAR stopped then, to the puzzlement of many. "Is that all?" the Grand Apadisha asked him.

"As far as I have been given, Your Excellency." The blind poet managed to shrug his shoulders and bow at the same time, no easy feat, but it said much of his own feelings on the matter.

Llesho wasn't sure about the structure of the poem. The numerological portion, of which he understood a good amount, seemed dropped in from a different poem altogether. He didn't know if that was the mark of prophetic poems in general or just the intrusion of the prophecy in what was otherwise a narrative poem about the gods of this land having tea, perhaps a preamble to an epic of war and battle. He'd heard enough of them in his time, across all the length and breadth of the road west.

The final verse should have had a reference to the daughter god at least, and a verse to follow, he thought, that summed up the reaction of the father in the poem.

As if his brother had read his mind and spoke to confirm the unstated question, Menar added, "I have tried, using my humble talents as a poet, to complete the verses. But it seems that whatever will happen next awaits what we do here, and will not be written until the path is truly chosen."

"This talk of paths is troubling," the Grand Apadisha grumbled. "One wonders if the poet is falling into pagan ways."

Llesho didn't know what the going penalty for idolatry was in Pontus—no matter that the Way of the Goddess didn't actually have idols—but he didn't want it getting in the way of his dealings with the Apadisha.

"Perhaps the gods of Pontus have been troubled by events happening elsewhere in the realm of spirits and gods," he suggested, "a realm far from the dominion of the Father and his Daughter of the Sword, where other heavenly beings on the side of right prevail for the moment but suffer attack by a mutual enemy."

Habiba was quick to agree. "The prophecy makes sense as a warning of battles waged within and without the kingdoms of the gods, which arise elsewhere to threaten the Father and the Daughter in their heaven and in Bithynia below."

It seemed as if the whole Divan held its breath while the Apadisha considered the witch's appeal. The sages were a conservative lot by nature and seldom risked their necks on any controversy. And yet, the school had brought these strangers forward, had presented Llesho and his struggle for a different heaven—strange and heretical to the Bithynians—as explanation for the prophecy.

If their ruler took offense, he might order the beheading of every master and student in the city. So they waited, breath held, until the Apadisha's narrowed eyes drifted from the poet to his Master Numerologist.

"What scientific proof can you present that this young vagabond is the king foretold by the Father and the Daughter?"

"That is the troubling matter," Master Numerologist admitted. "Some parts of the prophecy seem clear enough. This exiled prince is one of seven brothers. In another land, a spirit told him to seek out those he had lost, which he has done."

"All but one. I haven't found Ghrisz yet," Llesho corrected this small error. He had faith that the Way of the Goddess would take him to the last of his lost brothers. He didn't have to wait long.

"Ghrisz is in Kungol, leading the rebels," Menar said, as if this was common knowledge.

Apparently it was, because the Apadisha perked up at the reference. "Ghrisz the Ghost-Warrior of the Golden City?" he asked.

"The same," Menar confirmed.

"Then our brother is dead?" Llesho couldn't believe that he

had come so far to find his brother gone and his quest come to an untimely end, but Menar shook his head, to dispel the idea.

"Not dead, but very good at hiding, until he strikes at his Harnish invaders as they go about their ruinous business. There are many stories of his exploits. They say his lair is hidden within the very walls of the Golden City of Kungol, that he preys upon the raiders and escapes before they can catch him."

Ghrisz was alive! Llesho grew light-headed with relief. He hadn't dared to hope that he might actually succeed. There was, for one thing, a dreadful enemy to meet at the end of that road, and a more desperate demon if they succeeded that far. For a moment, discussion went on above his head while he tried to settle the piece of the puzzle that was Ghrisz in its place in his heart.

Time had passed and the corners that had fit so well when he was a child had grown chipped with wear. Even so, he felt a lack that all his brothers did not fill. Ping, their sister, dead after just two cycles of the seasons on the mortal world. He hoped for his own sake that she returned quickly to the mortal world. He wanted to meet her in her new form and know that she would grow up happy and safe in this life with all the joy and laughter that she'd lost to early death in the last—

But Habiba was nudging his elbow, and he became aware again that Menar had continued speaking.

"The tales also speak of a beautiful woman, who is called the sapphire princess because she is as priceless to the Ghost-Warrior's cause as the greatest jewel. I've made some of the stories into poems suitable for an audience myself, so I know that not all said of him is true. But it seems well known that he exists. His presence is felt wherever he leaves the wounded and the dead among his enemies."

Ghrisz, a legendary hero, and with a beautiful consort, it seemed. Such a pair might not welcome a younger brother returning to supplant them at what must seem the end of their long battle. Still, if the prophecy had reached even to the Harn, Ghrisz must have heard it as well. What if he believed the prophecy was meant for him? It struck Llesho that he might be bringing civil war to a country already devastated by invasion.

He didn't want that. Didn't want to be king, for that matter, but saw no way out, not even for a brother ready to take on the job. He already had one of those in Lluka, he reminded himself sourly. Why couldn't anything be easy?

Master Numerologist had made a bow to the Apadisha, however, and Llesho brought his thoughts back into line. He knew better than to wander in the presence of emperors and sultans.

"So the seven princes are accounted for in the prophecy," the numerologist counted off. "And the blind poet, Menar, has told us in council that the six heads crowned with stars must be the mountains that surround the city of Kungol."

"I would agree," Llesho said. "In the grasslands, many riddles are phrased like this prophecy. Bolghai could tell you better than I, but heads crowned with stars would seem to mean the mountaintops crowned with glaciers that glitter like stars in the sunlight."

"Five armies, like one hand." The Apadisha held out his fingers, then closed them into a fist. "Where are these armies?" So coolly did the question float on the air that one might almost have missed the menace in it. Llesho had entered Pontus as a wounded slave, with no armies at his back but his small band of guardsmen. The sultan must wonder, did his armies follow to attack once the beggar-king had allayed suspicion? Or, equally possible, was this exiled prince who washed up on his shores a madman whose accidental relationship with the poet had caused the sages to interpret the prophecy around him by mistake?

Llesho knew the answer, as did all of his advisers, who waited for him to speak. With a little smile, and an almost imperceptible bow to show that he meant no threat by it, he did.

"In Durnhag," he said, "or they were when I put to sea. I expect by now they are on their way to Thebin. A difficult run, but not so far as the Long March, and they carry no children into battle. Well, if you don't count us."

With that he showed he understood one part of the Apadisha's concerns, that they were too young, too inexperienced. Llesho could have told him of all the battles that stood between

Pearl Island and Pontus, all the dreams and nightmares and deaths, the wounds that still pulled over his heart and the wounds that his companions carried as well. Having the experience, they could scarcely be counted as too young. Though he said nothing of this, some of his reflections must have shown in Llesho's eyes, because the Apadisha's expression grew more narrowly considering.

"Still, a distance to travel," the Apadisha noted, "with many enemies between there and Kungol, which I believe is your goal?"

"Not so many enemies as there were a season ago," Llesho demurred. "And an army suitable to meet them."

"An army of children." The Apadisha allowed a smile to show as if he tried to suppress it.

Llesho had expected no less. He returned the smile, felt the clash as steel met steel in the duel of wits. "The children have all washed up on your doorstep, Excellency. But the emperor of Shan sends his regards to the raiders who have enslaved Thebin, and among their number the Dinha of the Tashek people has sent her Gansau Wastrels, great warriors all." He paused, lost for a moment in grief for the absent Harlol and his companions murdered by the stone monsters of the grasslands. "My brother, Prince Shokar, leads a band of Thebin recruits to make the second. Mergen-Khan of the Qubal people has brought the clans under his rule to join us, for three. And the Tinglut-Khan himself sends a party of his warriors to observe in the field and seek the answer to a puzzle that troubles the Tinglut clans. I count our armies as four. Discovering the prophecy in Pontus, I thought to find the fifth army here as well."

"Or, if not, your princely outlaws in Kungol will do to fill out the numbers, eh, Master Numerologist?"

The sage dithered, hoping that his sovereign spoke in jest, but the Apadisha waited, one eyebrow cocked, for an answer.

"That is for the future to tell." Master Numerologist gave as vague an answer as Llesho had ever heard. Did the Apadisha's advisers ever offer useful interpretations? Which was unfair, he chastised himself. His own presence was a dangerous enough answer.

"So." The Grand Apadisha waited long enough to make the Master Numerologist wish himself far away, and then he turned his dark and piercing gaze on Llesho. "Is it as easy to gather up four fire-breathing worms as to gather a hand of armies?" he asked mockingly. Llesho would have wondered if the sultan believed in the prophecy at all, except for a glint of desperation deep in his eyes. The condescending smile meant nothing, then. What had he seen in his dreams to terrify him so? This wasn't the place to ask. Maybe, if they met inside a dream . . .

But he hadn't answered the question yet. As it happened, he didn't have to. Marmer Sea Dragon gave a little bow, but let the green fire light his eyes to show that he was more than the man he might have seemed.

"The Holy King of Thebin has met four of my kind, all of whom have urged him on his way in hope and trepidation. We don't well understand the notion of cooperating toward a common goal. It is more our way to divide this world into our separate realms and abide where we rule, finding peace and harmony by ignoring our neighbors. The coming battle, however, may devour us all, and so we throw our lot in with the young king's armies. If the prophecy calls upon four of our kind, then they will be Pearl Bay Dragon, and Golden River Dragon, and Dun River Dragon. I am myself the dragon-king of the sea which you have lately claimed as your own," he added his own identity for the gathered sages and their Apadisha, as much a warning off his territory as a polite introduction. "Though I have my own sworn vendetta against the young king's supernatural guide, to free my son from the unholy embrace of the false magician, I shall aid his battle as well."

"Wonder upon wonder comes before me today," the Apadisha remarked with an acid tartness in his voice. "What am I to make of it all?"

Llesho couldn't tell whether Marmer Sea Dragon's revelation came as a surprise, or even if the sultan believed any part of the tale they related. He had little time to ponder the matter, however.

"Three gifts?" the Grand Apadisha prodded, stroking his

beard with one jeweled hand. It might almost have been a nervous gesture.

"I have those gifts, but with discretion I may not mention them here." Llesho bowed to show respect but his jaw was set, his eyes cool. He shared the knowledge of his blessed gifts only with his closest companions and advisers—the Apadisha was not yet even an ally. And then there was the other matter, that gifts of goddesses and spirits must offend the Bithynian religion. He would not budge on this one thing.

"Two paths?" the Apadisha asked instead, and Llesho had to ask himself how much he already knew from his dreams.

"I have no answer to that part of the prophecy," he admitted. "Since I left Pearl Bay I have followed just one path, the Way of the Goddess, though it may displease you to hear it. It would dishonor my lady wife to deny her place in the heavens and in my heart. If there is another path, I don't know what it is, and wouldn't choose it if I did."

"Foolish to reject what you do not see," the Apadisha warned, and for a change even Habiba looked concerned about his answer.

"Two paths lay before the young king," Habiba said. "At the behest of my mistress and with the aid of his many advisers, including the emperor of Shan, I have endeavored to guide him upon the path the gods of Thebin and Bithynia have set for him."

The magician carefully skirted the fact that he served two sets of gods. The Bithynian school of magicians, of which he was a part, honored the Father and the Daughter. The Way of the Goddess, on which he served the mortal goddess of war, promised the heavenly gardens of the Great Goddess at the end of struggle. From what Llehso'd heard about the Daughter of the Sword, he thought the paths of gods must cross. In his own world, the Lady SienMa might be this warrior daughter who stood with weapon drawn at the right hand of her father. But Dognut bore no resemblance to the father that the Bithynians worshiped, and neither did Master Den. The Apadisha didn't mention this careful blurring of the magician's loyalties, but nodded for Habiba to go on. "Another, darker path awaits at the call of the false magician, Master Markko,'' Habiba explained with a sign to ward against evil. "It is to his credit that the young king sees no path at all down that dark way. The Daughter teaches, however, that sometimes we can only reach the light by passing through the darkness."

That was disturbing. Did Habiba mean for him to fall under Master Markko's spell after all? It hardly seemed likely, given all the efforts they had taken to free him from Markko's clutches in the past. But there was no time to argue the point. He resolved to consider what Habiba might mean later, when he was free of the Apadisha's scrutiny.

"So, we come to this one jewel, to each of seven brothers."

"I don't know what that is," Llesho admitted. "My mother had jewels, but she took no interest in adornment for its own sake, and I can think of no ring or bead or necklet with special meaning."

"It wasn't our way," Menar agreed. "Jade objects, and bronze and silver and gold, brightly colored ribbons and precious embroideries were valued at court. But our mother had a saying, that Great Moon was her pendant, and Great Sun the only crown our father needed."

Master Numerologist considered the lack of a jewel with the rest of them. Then, tentatively, he offered a solution. "If we look to Kungol for this jewel, then perhaps it is no frozen gemstone at all. Didn't you say, holy poet, that the tales speak of a beautiful woman whom the people call the sapphire princess? Perhaps she is the jewel mentioned in the prophecy."

It seemed unlikely that the gods would burden Llesho's prophecy with his brother's consort. Unless the poem referred to Ghrisz all along, of course. He tried to fit the label on his relationship with the Great Goddess, but when he thought of her, it was the beekeeper who came to mind, easing his soul like a caress. Llesho couldn't come up with any better answer, so he let Master Numerologist's solution to the riddle stand.

The Apadisha, too, seemed less than convinced with the final part of the puzzle, but he passed over it with a wave in Llesho's general direction.

"So we are left with a king. I don't suppose you know what the sacred key is?"

"A metaphor, no doubt," Llesho guessed. "I've always found prophecies to be most helpful after the fact. The pieces all seem obvious in hindsight. Unfortunately, no one has handed me a key with 'gates of heaven' engraved on the shaft."

"No key at all, I suppose." The Apadisha looked hopeful, but not surprised when Llesho respectfully denied all knowledge of such a key.

"None whatsoever, except as knowledge may be a key. But even that comes slowly, and at cost."

The Apadisha's eyes seemed to grow darker, the irises consumed by the dark fire at the core of his inner vision. Llesho couldn't look away, couldn't hide anything. Discovered that he couldn't even move until, released from that intense focus, he felt the muscles in his shoulders ease back into his control.

"No small cost," the Apadisha agreed. "The mark of your struggle is there for all to see. But what knowledge has it bought, I wonder?" He gave Llesho a sardonic smile. "I doubt you could tell me even if you wished to. Soon, though. Very soon.

"Justice brings light and darkness?" He emphasized each word like pronouncing a spell.

Justice. Llesho felt the word like a cry right to his soul. *I should know this,* he thought. Like the word that fails the tongue, or the book just out of reach. It teased at his awareness until he tried to look at it, then skittered away just as it seemed he must catch it, there. But Light and Darkness, that he had carried with him since he left Pearl Bay.

"I mean you no harm," he said as he slipped a hand beneath his shirt.

Guardswomen he hadn't noticed until then came to attention, spears at the ready, but Llesho kept his eyes on the Apadisha, who watched him with eyes dark and hungry as a crow's. Llesho bowed his head and drew the thong from around his neck. He left the silver chain in place, willing Pig to keep quiet and out of the way, though he'd never had to worry about the Jinn in the waking world.

From the pouch that hung from the thong, however, he drew the pearls that he had gathered during his journey. One from Lleck's ghost, stolen from the Pearl Bay Dragon. She would have given it to him as her parting gift anyway, she had told him. One from her Ladyship, SienMa, the mortal goddess of war, who had plucked him from the arena and set him on his path. One from Mara the healer, Carina's mother, who aspired to be the eighth mortal god. Pig, who might or might not be part of the Great Goddess' necklace, he did not reveal.

His Wastrels, dead on a Harnish battlefield, had yielded the remaining three and he looked on them with grief and yearning. He would not have given up a single life to regain a trinket, not even for the Great Goddess. But to restore the balance of heaven, he would sacrifice many. All who followed him, he would give, for the lives of the millions who slept unaware, and for all the realms of heaven and earth and the underworld which would fall in the coming chaos if he didn't win.

The Apadisha's crow's eyes gleamed with the reflected light of the six black pearls, darkness shining on darkness, giving back black light. "Master Astrologer?" By the question, he signaled that he knew what he looked upon.

Pale and shaking, Master Astrologer stepped forward with a warding sign to protect herself from heresy. "So many," she said with a quaver in her voice. "I dare not speak. The heavens do not fit in the palm of a young man's hand. Such things do not exist. If they did, I dare not speak the consequences."

It seemed that words did fail her. "Beg pardon, Excellency. Beg pardon." Though a scientist of the heavens, she did not in all the time of her protestations reach out to touch the pearls in Llesho's palm. Rather, she curled her fingers in on one another and tucked her hands into the deep pockets of her magician's robes.

It was enough for the Apadisha, however. "Master Geomancer," he called, and a short, round woman came forward with more confidence than the Master Astrologer, but some hesitancy nonetheless. "Can you tell me where each of these was found?" she asked. "The pattern they scattered on the earth may tell us much to further our studies."

"Shan," Llesho told her, "Far to the south. Pearl Bay, and Farshore Province, and Thousand Lakes Province, perhaps. And the grasslands, halfway to Durnhag."

The geomancer's eyes grew distant with mathematical calculations, and Llesho guessed that she saw maps behind her eyes, as he did himself sometimes when plotting the course of a journey in his head.

The Grand Apadisha permitted her to disappear into her own head only briefly, however. "Do you have that which you have been studying these last three cycles of the seasons?" he asked.

Master Geomancer bowed, and drew from her ample robes a small carved box. Opening the puzzle catch, she held out the contents to the sultan, who took them in his hand and held them out to Llesho. Two perfect black pearls.

"They were found in a copper mine outside of Iznik after a night of storms that drowned a work crew and set fire to a quarter of the town. Accordingly, the overseer took them for an omen, and had them sent to the school at Pontus. Can you explain how they came to be where they were found, and what caused the terrible storms that accompanied them?"

"Heaven is under siege," Llesho answered. "Day and night no longer come to her gardens." The Apadisha might decide to have him beheaded for heresy, but he doubted it. The man knew too much.

"As I thought," the Apadisha agreed. "As did my Master Astrologer, who would not offend me with the truth." He put the two black pearls back into their box with a heavy sigh and handed them over to Llesho. "An unlucky number, eight, young king. I hope I do not damn your quest with this gift."

"Not eight." He didn't show the ninth, but ran a finger over the silver chain that showed at his throat when his hand brushed his shirt. "Ahkenbad, in the Gansau Wastes," he added for the geomancer.

The Apadisha didn't ask to see more. "Terrible things await us if you do not succeed, young king," he said. A small part of his burden seemed to lift from his shoulders in spite of his warning, however.

Llesho knew they shared the dreams of chaos and destruction that awaited them. He could offer no solace but the knowledge that what he knew was shared. "A gift of prophecy gives
no comfort."

To those who watched, it seemed that he must speak about
Menar's poem. Between the two of them, however, passed a
darker knowledge. Seeing the future in a dream didn't mean
you could change it in the waking world, or even rightly understand it. "What does not drive you mad sounds mad to anyone
who hears it," he added, thinking that having company in the
knowledge maybe helped a little.

"Is your brother mad, then, young king?"

The Apadisha's question stunned him for a moment. Lluka
surely was mad, or nearly there at least. Then he realized the
Apadisha meant Menar. Did they follow the babbling of a madman, which would make them mad as well for the dreams that
troubled their sleep?

"His eyes may not see, but his mind is as clear as yours or
mine." He offered no real comfort on that score. They might yet
all of them be mad. Master Den would tell him if it were so, he
thought. Then again, depending on the trickster god seemed
more proof of madness than otherwise.

"I agree." To what, the Apadisha left between them. He
clapped his hands twice and two of the guardswomen came
forward. One, Llesho noticed, bore a striking resemblance to the
Grand Apadisha himself.

"Take with you two hands of my guard, the Daughter's
picked swordswomen, and all who follow them. Boats will be
made ready for you.

"Now go. I have spent too much time on the puzzles of
strangers already."

Llesho accepted the dismissal. He had at least ten soldiers
from the Apadisha's picked guard to accompany him. Not an
army to bring against Master Markko, but it might, in a pinch,
satisfy Menar's prophecy. Llesho gave a proper bow and, in the
manner of one who has been granted a boon remained in the
abased position as he backed his way out of the Apadisha's

presence. As soon as boats could be made ready, they were going.

But first he had to see a magician about a jade bowl. He'd rather have left it behind, but had long ago concluded that any gifts of mystical inclination that came to his hand in his quest were there for a reason. He would not leave any of them, even the most deadly, behind.

Chapter Twenty-eight

As IT happened, the Apadisha would send ten thousand soldiers, women all, dedicated to the Daughter of the Sword. A thousand to each of his picked guardswomen, each of whom commanded her own hierarchy of officers. All fell under the spear of AlmaZara, a taciturn warrior who wore in addition to her weapons and armor the Apadisha's nose and his intense dark eyes. The gathering of such an army, with all their provisions and ships to carry them to Edris, took the greater part of a month.

Habiba, in the shape of an eagle, returned to his mistress, the Lady SienMa, to alert the gathered army when they might be expected on the other side of the Marmer Sea. Among the allies were Mergen and Tinglut. In their mutual grief for loved ones lost at the hands of the Bamboo Snake Demon, the two khans had come to an uneasy alliance. Each put down his suspicion of the other with great difficulty. Tinglut-Khan had no reason to trust Llesho's word, a new and uncomfortable ally.

As for Mergen-Khan, personal observation had shown him little to comfort him about Llesho. To make matters worse, Habiba carried news of Tayy's injury at the claws of Master Markko, a foreign and magical enemy. Coming so soon after the death of the prince's mother and his father, who was also Mergen's brother and the former khan, the new leader of the Qubal had little cause for trust. And yet, Habiba reported on his return, the khan continued to honor the agreements made before his brother's death.

This was partly Bolghai's work, Llesho knew. Close contact with those who understood him best must speak for him in some way; surely one who stood in the good graces of three gods on earth and the Great Goddess in her heaven must command respect, if nothing else. He wondered if even the gods knew what they were doing, though, to put so much on his shoulders. He seemed to stumble in the dark more often than he followed a straight path in the light.

All this stewing over events he couldn't control was giving Llesho a headache when he could least afford to be at less than his best. During Habiba's absence, the physician Ibn Al-Razi suggested that his hospital was no fit place for young kings or princes grown healthy in his care. Since they no longer needed his attention, he could serve his religion best without magicians who claimed kinship with false gods under his roof.

While their ships were made ready, therefore, Llesho and his company moved to the school for magicians. In a room that was part schoolroom and part laboratory, with a high table full of little drawers at the center and benches for the students on all sides, he was subjected to intense examination by the scholars and magicians. They determined that indeed he had no dragon's blood in his veins and agreed among themselves that unwittingly Marmer Sea Dragon must himself have influenced the storm according to the wishes Llesho conveyed with the empathic communication possible with such beasts.

Marmer Sea Dragon, in his human form, objected to the name of beast and assured them that he acted only as an observer. While the magicians apologized for besmirching his name, they shook their heads at his description of events.

"It's not possible," Master Astrologer explained with a simplicity surprising in her speech, "and therefore it cannot have happened that way."

Finally, they were left with disagreeing on the topic. That brought the debate to Llesho's greatest concern: Lady Chaiujin's jade bowl, which he had given into Lling's care. She had endured the strange and terrifying dreams of the Lady Chaiujin for her king's sake. When the emerald-green bamboo snake began to commit its murders in the town, however, she had put the bowl in the keeping of the school. They all now hoped to discover whether it was indeed the source of the lady's power in snake form.

While dismissing as a fairy tale the notion that a mortal boy might receive heavenly gifts from a Goddess wife, the masters found no reason to doubt that the bowl might be possessed by a demon. Picking it up from the high table where the instruments of their professions lay scattered in profusion, Master Numerologist studied the rune at the bottom of the bowl.

"I know of no computational symbol or representation of the numerical world corresponding to this mark. I would guess that it must be magical, however, since evil creatures usually are."

Master Astrologer took the bowl next. Since no such alignment of stars occurred in the night sky, she could shed no light on it either.

Master Geomancer, however, took the bowl gingerly in her hand with a grim and knowing frown. "The sign of the snake," she said of the spiral carved into the jade. "Though it's not an emerald, the color is suggestive, don't you think? But why give the bowl to this boy?"

"I don't know," Llesho answered, "I would have thought that she was some part of my quest—a test, or a battle—but she was working against the Qubal clans before I ever reached the Harnlands."

"Not everything is about Llesho," Tayy complained. "It just seems that way when the stitches pull. The Lady Chaiujin was moving against the clans seasons before we ever heard of the wandering Thebin king. She had already murdered my mother to raise her station in the ger-tent of the khan. Gradually she must have come to understand that my father the khan would never name her khanesse, and so she killed him as well. But that is a matter of the clans, not Llesho."

"You may be right." Master Geomancer cocked her head to study him. "It seems likely, then, that having lost her position among the Qubal, she sees Llesho's quest as a way to attach herself to a victim she is better able to control. Llesho is young and his quest would leave him with a crown on his head. To one such as the false Lady Chaiujin, a crown is a crown, perhaps. Any one will do to drop her eggs in."

The very thought made him shudder and when he looked to Prince Tayy, he was doing the same.

Kaydu, however, laughed. "What an absurd idea. Llesho is married to the Goddess. She is not so easily set aside as a human queen."

"Llesho loves his Goddess." Here was a notion that Tayy seemed to find perfectly normal. "He has the same look on his face when he talks about her as my father used to get when he looked at my mother. Only more so, because of the whole heaven and religion part of the marriage. How could she not see it?"

An image of Shou in the deadly embrace of a White Cobra with the Lady SienMa's face rose out of a memory of a dream. Not easily set aside, surely, but love? His own love was nothing like that. He didn't understand how Shou could love the cold white mortal goddess of war, even in her human form. But they did share a kinship of sorts: they both loved far beyond even their exalted stations. In past lives, that love had been the death of Llesho, and he wondered if loving the Lady SienMa would be the death of Shou.

With a knowing little smile, Master Astrologer took the hand of Master Numerologist. "One who *knows* nothing of love would *see* nothing of love in the young king," she suggested as an answer to the puzzle. "He seems a mere boy, inexperienced at such things and easily tempted into betrayal. It takes someone who has known love—of a husband or wife, but also of a parent or child, or even a beloved familiar, to recognize it in another."

"Of course!" Master Geomancer said, scratching behind Little Brother's ear to emphasize the last point. The monkey grinned back at her.

Hmishi had kept quiet in the company until now, but he knew better than most the boundaries of Llesho's loyalty. The king had called him back from the dead, after all. "Lady Bamboo Snake was wrong on two counts, then," he said, but Llesho stopped him.

"I would not knowingly betray my country or my friends. And I do love my lady, the Great Goddess." He thought of her at times as my lady beekeeper, and did so now, when he needed comfort. "But the Lady Chaiujin tempted me. If it were not for Master Den, she might have had me by the river the day that Hmishi died."

"You were attracted to the lady's fangs at the time, as I recall." Master Den spoke softly, but the heads of his cadre came up as if a drum had sounded. Only Tayy seemed to understand how he had felt that day, which Llesho figured was a bad thing.

"Even kings and the blessed husbands of goddesses are sometimes weak," he confessed. Perhaps he had more in common with Emperor Shou than he had thought. They both had flirted with the grave.

"You mustn't ever give up that way again," Hmishi insisted. "In serving their kings, soldiers die sometimes. If you choose to follow us to the underworld, our deaths are wasted!"

"I understand that now," Llesho said. "That doesn't give you permission to die either."

"I'll see what I can do."

"The bowl," Master Geomancer said, bringing them back to the topic in her hand. "If that is the source of her power, I doubt that we can break her hold on it."

Master Den took the bowl from her and held it up to the light as if the soft beams passing through it would somehow reveal the lady within.

"When accompanying a king on a quest, it is never a good idea to dismiss any magic one meets on the way as coincidence," he reminded them. "Mischance is not one side of a coin, with strategy on the other. It is one face of a many-sided box. The Lady Bamboo Snake may have had plots of her own in the Harnlands. Llesho passing within her reach may have been an accident or fate playing a part. But we cannot dismiss the suggestion that once he fell within her reach, the lady abandoned her former schemes to influence the greater struggle which would play out in the mountains above the Golden City."

"You mean it's all about Llesho after all?" Tayy asked mournfully. At that moment, the comment struck the company as funny. Llesho thought it was hysterical laughter, but he joined it anyway.

"Not in all places, at all times," Master Den assured him. "But in this place, and in this moment, one should hardly be surprised that it might prove so."

"It's an honor I would gladly forgo in favor of a quiet life. I didn't ask for this."

"Well, actually . . ." Lling gave a sly lift of the eyebrow. "I recall a certain pearl diver—with a very quiet life—on his knees before the overseer, pleading to become a gladiator."

Hmishi smiled at her. "Who would have thought we'd come so far?" It wasn't really a question, just a measure of his amazement at their adventures. But she smiled a challenge back at him. "I look forward to tasting the air of Thebin again soon."

Having come to a decision, Master Den handed the bowl back to the geomancer. "I think we can assume that any magical item that has come into Llesho's possession during his quest has done so for a purpose, whether we now understand that purpose or not. Until we do know what part this bowl is meant to play, we can't destroy it. Neither can we allow Lady Bamboo Snake freedom to use the bowl against us in our travels."

"We need a spell—isn't that obvious?" Kaydu asked. "Something to lock her up so we don't leave a path of dead among our allies." As a student she should have withheld her opinion until the masters had finished their discussion. As the captain of Llesho's royal guard, however, her opinions on the matter of his safety came before any more arcane discussion. Fortunately, Master Geomancer agreed both with her conclusion and her right to state it in front of the Apadisha's great mages.

"Exactly," the master said. Taking the bowl from Master Den, she held it up as he had done, examining the jade in the light. "If we cannot destroy it, we must contain it. So, this box of possibilities between strategy and mischance—we must set the bowl inside it and lock it with a key of our own making."

"A numerological spell." Not surprisingly, that was Master Numerologist's suggestion. "I'll weave dates and times and the latitude and longitude together in a spell that will trap her in confusion. If Llesho's time and place are here and now, we must make it so that she never finds the coordinates of his conjunction again."

"A star spell," Master Astrologer volunteered. "If we lock Lady Bamboo Snake's magic in the heavens, she cannot influence the coming battle in the mortal realm."

Llesho shuddered. He knew it wasn't the astrologer's intention to set the demon snake among the gardens of his lady beekeeper, but he could not escape the possibility that if she broke the spell she could do more damage in the heavens than even the failure of his own quest.

But Master Geomancer gave up the bowl to no one. "She is an earth demon, I believe, since she takes the form of a snake in the waking world as well as in the dreaming one," she said. "She will be bound only by an earth spell. Be careful, however, that you don't release her. Captivity will do little to improve her disposition."

He nodded his agreement. The distinction she had made took a great burden from his mind. Lady SienMa, he believed, had never turned into a snake when she was awake. He didn't think a demon could become a mortal god, but sometimes he had wondered.

"All right, then." She set the bowl back onto the table and rolled up her sleeves to work.

"This takes concentration, so the rest of you, out! I want the boy who will carry the bowl—our young king in exile. And a student assistant—you will do, if you can remember you are a student and not a general, young lady."

Llesho had never heard anyone talk to Kaydu like that, and her humble bow to the round, stern magician shocked him even more. But the geomancer accepted the bow as a promise and

turned to the rest of the company flapping the skirts of her robes
as if she were shooing chickens in a farmyard.

"Go!" she instructed his cadre. To Llesho's great relief,
Prince Tayyichiut fell in with them as if he had always been a
part of the quest. Together, they turned to their captain for
orders. Kaydu had taken on the role of student, however, and
gave them only a shrug for an answer. She would neither over-
rule the master nor set her own orders over those of the geomancer. They would have been at a stalemate, but Llesho added his
own wave of dismissal to the geomancer's.

"Kaydu is here; I'll be fine."

When they had filed out, the other magicians gathered
around the table. Master Den came with them, but the geomancer raised her hands to bar his way.

"We respect your skills, Master. And you have brought this
boy not only through a thousand li of danger and a thousand
more, but from childhood to a manhood of strength and wisdom
as well. For that you have our respect. But your religion is not
our religion, and your methods not our methods. We cannot
trust our secrets to one whose ends are always in doubt."

It seemed for a moment that Master Den would challenge
the geomancer for his place at the table. That battle they waged
silently with their eyes, however. When it was over, the trickster god bowed humbly and departed. Kaydu looked after him
with amazement, but it didn't surprise Llesho.

"Even now, do we know he means us well?" he asked her.
"He's the trickster god—it appears that he wants us to succeed,
but we could be no more to him than a tool he carries to a place
where he has other interests altogether. Then we may find out
that our failure is more to his advantage than our success."

"You don't believe that, do you?"

He'd shocked Kaydu, but that didn't change his mind. "It
doesn't matter what I believe. I don't know."

"Good answer!" Master Geomancer applauded him. "Now,
shall we set a trap for Lady Bamboo Snake, or shall we let her
kill another innocent citizen of Pontus while we argue the nice-
ties?"

Duly chastened, they turned to the jade bowl on the table.

From a long, narrow slot below the table, Master Geomancer slid a thin slice of marble. "A purified surface," she said, and wiped the jade bowl carefully before placing it on the marble.

"Now, for a nice earth spell, we need some dirt." Dusting off her plump, capable hands, she opened one of the many little drawers under the table, sorting among a dozen or more vials of soil.

"Not Bithynian," she muttered under her breath, "No known affinity here. Harnish soil might do—we know she has some connection to the grasslands since you found her there.

"But no, I think we will go with this." She pulled out a vial and emptied it onto the marble tablet. By the color and texture, Llesho knew it for Thebin soil, from high in the mountains.

"I'm making a guess here, but we'll set the spell with the destination. The spell's power will be strongest where you will need it most.

"Now, hmmm . . ." she continued to mutter ingredients while her fellow magicians Master Astrologer and Master Numerologist rooted through the little drawers to provide what she required. Dried herbs and saffron, small vials of oil, and something that smelled so badly it made Llesho's eyes run quickly took their places on the table.

None of the ingredients went inside the bowl. "A spell already resides within," Master Geomancer explained as she kneaded the ingredients into a paste. "We don't know what effect a second spell would have upon the first. Our spell will go outside the vessel, surrounding it so to speak, like a magical fence."

Kaydu stood quietly at her side, cleaning up each grain or leaf that fell onto the tabletop, outside the perimeter they had created with the marble tablet. When Master Geomancer waggled her fingers, Kaydu ran for water to wash the master's hands. When she smacked her lips, Kaydu brought water in a cup for her to drink, and followed that with equal service to each of the other magicians. Master Geomancer never gave Kaydu a word of instruction.

At first, the workings of the masters brought back memories of serving Master Markko as he compounded his poisons.

Kaydu would never aid evil so willingly, however, and the room had a familiar light and smell about it, of sunshine cutting through the gloom. It reminded him of Habiba's workshop, where his dream travels frequently took him when he visited Shou. When he let go of his fear, Llesho was able to appreciate the subtlety and skill of the magicians. He watched with fascination as the three masters communicated their needs with little signs they were scarcely aware of giving.

Kaydu worked tirelessly, silently, and accurately. He had always known and valued her skills as a soldier, but now he had a chance to see the other part of her training. It felt strange, but made him proud, as if he'd chosen her as his champion himself. The Lady SienMa, who had set Kaydu to guard him, knew soldiers as only the mortal goddess of war might. But he remembered, too, the water gardens of the governor's compound at Farshore Province. Somewhere along the line he'd forgotten the promise of those gardens. His captain, however, had remembered: after war must come healing.

He knew what Kaydu was doing among the magicians, but Llesho couldn't figure out why they hadn't sent him away with the others until Master Geomancer dusted off her hands in a habitual gesture that signaled a shift in her thinking. Master Numerologist had disappeared behind the table to rummage in a drawer as wide and deep as a spice chest. When he appeared again, he held in his hand a square wooden box covered all over with arcane symbols.

"Just decoration," he explained when he noticed Llesho's curious look. "And it scares away the curious."

Inside, the box was empty. Master Geomancer lifted the cup from the tablet while Master Numerologist carefully scraped the spell-stuff into the box. When he had done, the geomancer carefully wiped off the bottom of the cup so every grain went into the box with the rest. Master Astrologer then took a knife and cut a square of satin from the geomancer's sleeve. She set the satin on top of the soil in the box, and only then did Master Geomancer put the cup in its container. If he hadn't seen the whole process, Llesho would have noticed nothing unusual at

all about the package. Just a precious jade bowl in a carrying
case with no visible sign of the spell beneath the satin.

When the cup had settled in its place, Master Geomancer
closed the lid. "And now to seal the spell," she said. "Young
king whom those of the faith of Pontus may not call Holy Excellence, we need your blood now."

Oh. Well that explained why they hadn't sent him away with
the others, then. "I don't have much to spare," he reminded
them. He had suffered only minor injuries as a galley slave, but
lately he felt as though he had been drained of more than the
few drops the lash had taken.

Master Geomancer took no notice of his objection but put
out her hand. When he hesitated, Kaydu whispered her own
plea, "It's important."

She was his captain and he had followed her orders all the
way from Farshore. No point in changing that now, he figured,
and put his hand, palm up, in the outstretched hand of the geomancer.

"Not your sword hand—smart boy."

He was watching her for a sign of her next move so he didn't
notice when Master Astrologer reached over with the knife that
had cut the satin sleeve. So quickly that he didn't notice she
was moving until blood welled like a string of garnets, the magician slashed a shallow wound across his hand.

"Good." Just as quickly, Master Geomancer turned their nes-
ted hands over so that the blood dripped on the box. One. Two.
Three drops fell onto the wood. When she decided that there
was enough of his blood beaded onto the wood, the magician
freed his hand. Kaydu was waiting, silently, with water to wash
the wound and a clean bandage. As she worked, the Apadisha's
masters gathered around the box. Llesho didn't understand the
words they chanted, but Kaydu paled over her bandaging.

He didn't have to know the meaning of the words to feel the
impact of the spell. The air in the schoolroom thickened and
grew more difficult to breathe, as if it were tightening around
his heart. He remembered Master Markko's spell on Radimus
and the hearts of the Wastrels plucked away and replaced with
stone. He though his own heart would explode. Then, between

one breath and the next, the pressure vanished. When he looked at the box, the blood was gone.

"I think you are ready to go now," Master Geomancer said, and dusted off her hands one last time.

PART FOUR

KUNGOL

Chapter Twenty-nine

THEY were on their way, heading out of port with all the fanfare that had been missing upon his arrival. The Grand Apadisha himself had come to the docks to see them off, not a single, limping vessel this time but thirty war galleys flying the banners of Bithynia and Thebin and Shan and the Qubal. They had no Tinglut on board and had made no agreements with them concerning Thebin, so rode with no banner displayed. They would have carried the colors of the Gansau Wastes in honor of the fallen Wastrels and those who now traveled to their aid with Shou, but the Tashek had no banner. The warriors of the Wastes rode like the wind, like smoke, uncounted and unobserved.

As their galley slipped away from its berth, Llesho came to attention with his companions around him. Habiba was already on his way to find Shou and the Lady SienMa, but Master Den stood at his back, a hand on his shoulder and another gathering in Prince Tayy. AlmaZara, the Apadisha's daughter, had joined them on the poop deck for their departure. She stood a little apart with several of her fellow Daughters of the Sword at her side and Kaydu like a bridge between Llesho's band and her own. Over their captain's shoulder, Llesho saw Little Brother's head peeking out of his pack. The monkey clung to his mistress with a suspicious, unhappy glare for the sea on which they rode and the ship so like the one that had almost taken Kaydu and her whole cadre to their watery graves. *Smarter than the rest of them,* Llesho thought. If anyone among them shared his own fears for the coming voyage, they didn't show it.

From a bandstand set up on the dock, the Apadisha's orchestra of youthful musicians played until a military band made up of soldiers left behind took its own turn. Farewell songs and martial anthems alternated between them. The magicians of Pontus had turned out in all their finery. Master Geomancer had wished to go with them, to observe for herself the lay of any further pearls they might find. On stepping aboard, however, she found that the ebb and flow of the sea did strange things to her earth-bound stomach. With tearful regret she had debarked, and now stood among her fellows with her possessions in a forlorn sack at her feet. Since neither Master Astrologer nor Master Numerologist wished to take her place, they carried with them no scholars to represent the magicians' school but their own captain, Habiba's daughter and an apprentice witch in her own right.

Llesho had grown stronger, and Prince Tayy had healed a great deal since they had come to Pontus, but still they were glad to hear the call to oars at their backs that would mean the formal leave-taking would be over soon. With a roar like thunder the oars hit the benches in a showy display of rowing skill for their departure. Almost unconsciously, Llesho counted the beats. Muscles tensed under newly healed skin as his body responded to the demand of the beater to step, step, pull. The boat surged ahead in that leaping manner of a galley under oar. He kept to his feet, casting a sidewise glance at Prince Tayyi-chiut and receiving a shrug of one shoulder in answer. Tayy was twitching to the rhythm of the drum as well, but he wouldn't sacrifice his dignity to acknowledge it.

When the dock had grown so small that they could no longer make out the bands playing their clashing instruments, the travel party broke from its stiff pose.

"Pardon, Holy Excellence." AlmaZara had picked up the court-formal title. She approached him with the slight bow for almost-equals befitting the daughter of the Grand Apadisha to a foreign king. "If it would not cause offense, I would stay with my own swordswomen. I will, of course, come to your call under the light of the Father or the Daughter should you require my services or my counsel."

By night or day, she meant. Bithyninans, he had learned, saw Great Moon Lun as male instead of female, giving a stern, cold light. Great Sun's furious heat, the physician Ibn Al-Razi had told him, must belong to the heavenly Daughter of the Sword. And so the people of Pontus reversed the order of the Thebin universe. The pledge that AlmaZara meant by it, however, was the same.

"As you wish." In the normal course of things, he wouldn't agree with her decision to travel with her guardswomen, apart from his own company of advisers. Much of his decision-making went on in the informal give and take of the cadre. She would miss out on that if she separated herself from them. But it made what he had to do a lot easier. He could avoid at least one uncomfortable explanation about abandoning his guards to travel alone and unprotected in the dreamscape.

"I would also, for my peace of mind and the comfort of my father, set two Daughters of the Sword to guard your safety at all times. Not that I doubt the intentions of your own picked cadre—" She did not say that she distrusted his male guards. Her glance at Prince Tayy's middle, however, indicated that she'd formed her own opinion and it did not cast a favorable light on the ability of his companions, male or female, to ensure his safety.

"I would not wish to impose on your privacy, of course," she added, gesturing to take in the guardswomen in question, who stood watchfully at a distance. "They have orders, however, to keep you safe, even against your persuasive arguments. The pirates who roam this sea make poor hosts."

That last she said with a disapproving frown in Kaydu's direction. Her guardswomen didn't owe this king of Thebin any loyalty except as it served the will of their sultan. They wouldn't be trusting him to his own devices while he went off on one of his dangerous schemes involving, oh, selling himself into slavery, for example.

"No more pirates," he assured her, but kept his current plan to himself. He had an army moving on land as well as by sea. AlmaZara seemed to take his promise at face value, however, and with a formal bow, left him to find her own troops gathered belowdecks.

When she had gone, Bixei glared over at the foreign guardswomen, who glared back, weapons bristling. "What does she think we are?" he grumbled under his breath.

"Men," Lling stated the obvious. She kept quiet on the matter of how many times their charge had escaped their benevolent watch to get into more trouble than they could handle. But, with a knowing little smile, she pointed out, "She'll find out soon enough."

They all understood what she meant, and Llesho rolled his eyes at her. "I'm not that bad."

"Yes, you are," Prince Tayyichiut retorted. "It's just that no one else on this ship has the rank to tell you so."

"That's not true! Master Den . . ."

They laughed. Even his teacher had a twinkle of humor in his eyes, not an unusual sight, but still . . .

"That's right." Tayy didn't need to remind him, but he did anyway. "You are depending on the trickster god to guide you away from foolish risks!"

"Should a king run away and hide when his people are dying under the yoke of invaders and tyrants?" Llesho asked with perhaps more indignation than necessary. He didn't think they were going to like his next plan any better than they'd liked the last one, and he was setting up his defenses early.

"It depends on the king," Tayy answered, but he lifted his chin a little, a reminder that he, too, followed a dangerous path to pay a debt his people owed to the royal family of Thebin.

"The worst of the danger is over anyway," the Harnish prince added hopefully. "You defeated Master Markko at his own storm and sent him running when he tried to kill me. You're stronger than he is and now he knows it. He'll be afraid to come after you."

Kaydu looked nervous at that, and Llesho figured she'd been talking to her father, who would know better. "I'm not stronger," he corrected the misunderstanding before it took root in the minds of his company. False confidence could kill them all.

Tayy was right about rank; his captain couldn't call the prince's conclusions into doubt. For an ally to do so might, under other circumstances, have brought their nations to war. But this was Llesho speaking, a friend beyond rank, and about his own weakness.

"Master Markko raised the storm and threw it at our heads. The strength of that blow measures the growth of his power and learning. He couldn't control it, but I couldn't have raised it in the first place. I didn't control it either. With Marmer Sea Dragon's help, I shifted its direction just enough to protect our ships. The storm continued its destruction on a slightly altered course—it may still be out there.

"I'm no magician, just a man favored by the gods with certain gifts in the dream world." He knew that wasn't quite true even as he said it. Echoes sounded in his heart, something he was supposed to remember but couldn't quite grasp. *Later,* he thought. It didn't have anything to do with the current point, though it felt like it was going to be important later on.

"You heard what Marmer Sea Dragon said. Master Markko is as much dragon as human. The question isn't how powerful he is, but how well he has learned to control the dragon that has become a part of him. If we're lucky, Marmer Sea Dragon's son will resist Markko's efforts to turn his powers to evil. But I'm guessing they're both mad as loons by now because of what Pig did to them."

In the course of his argument with Tayy, he said a lot of things he hadn't told his cadre before. They listened in a silence unnatural to them lest he remember that he'd meant to keep the dragon's conversation a secret. Tayy had been present to hear it all the first time, however, and hesitated not at all to argue right back.

"Then how will we defeat him?" Prince Tayy had grown pale during the farewell ceremony, and now he gripped the rail as if he might tether himself to the world that way.

"Not with my powers as a magician, because I don't have any." But he hadn't given up hope. "The thing about being a king, though, isn't how strong or how powerful he is at doing all that needs getting done, but how well he leads others who have the strengths he needs.

"We have Habiba on our side, and Kaydu, and Marmer Sea Dragon and the seven mortal gods, or at least some of them, each one of them more powerful than I can even imagine. We have the emperor of Shan and the khan of the Qubal and the Tinglut and the Dinha of the Tashek people, who has given us her Wastrels. We have the Daughters of the Sword from Pontus, and the mortal goddess of war chose my cadre. And in the dream realm I am defended by a servant of the Great Goddess herself."

"A pig with more mischief than good sense," the prince reminded him about the last. They had met during a storm-tossed dream at sea and Tayy hadn't been impressed.

Llesho had to smile. The Jinn seldom made a good impression, even after long acquaintance, but somehow, he managed to bring Llesho home safely from his dream travels. Which he mentioned, adding the point of his list-making:

"Who does Master Markko have behind him? How long do you think the Uulgar raiders would stay there if they weren't terrified of his dreadful powers?

"If we win, it will be because all the powers of all the realms of heaven and earth and the underworld have thrown in with us against the terrible chaos that awaits if Master Markko has his way. It's a better chance at winning than you can imagine, but it doesn't offer any guarantees for the safety or survival of any of us. Not even me. The one thing we know for sure, though, is that if we don't try, all the realms will end in fire and chaos."

"But what if you die?" Prince Tayy challenged while his companions looked on with the same question in their eyes. "Who will all these powers follow then?"

"They'll follow the person who picks up my sword." Llesho didn't say who that might be, but Tayy got the message.

"Oh, no! Don't you put this on me! I'm not even from Thebin! I have my own problems and they don't include the mortal gods of Thebin or a heavenly garden I don't even believe in!"

"Hopefully, it won't come to that," Llesho tried to reassure him.

Kaydu might have been more successful with her, "I should think not!" But they all knew by now the tale of the spear Llesho carried at his back. It had killed him before, and while it rested quiet under his control now, in the past it had been his fate to die before his battle was won. Even Little Brother stared his accusation at Llesho, as if he meant to die on purpose, just to leave them all stranded in the middle of the fight. Which he had no intention of doing.

If he could help it.

He hadn't thought Tayy could look any paler. By the end of the debate, however, he had turned as white as the mortal goddess of war herself.

"Discussion of my successor can wait. You need rest," Llesho said with a hand to the prince's shoulder.

Tayy looked as if he might resist, but Llesho made a gesture that only he could see, a drift of fingertips that traced the scar of his own terrible wounds beneath his formal Thebin coat. Prince Tayyichiut would understand that and the challenge in the tilt of Hmishi's chin. He would be judged on this deck by soldiers who had suffered through their own terrible wounds, and they were looking for good sense and not bravery. A solder took rest when he could grab it, figuring he'd want to stockpile the healing for the days when there'd be no rest at all. Prince Tayy dropped his head, conceding the point.

"You can find me belowdecks in my bunk if you need me."

"I'll be heading to my own bunk soon enough," Llesho assured him. Tayy gave him a dubious look but seemed to remember diplomacy and kept any comment to himself. With a careful bow, his hand discreetly resting over the healing wound in his belly, he left the poop deck.

Master Den watched the departing Harnish prince with a slight tilt of the head. "He'll be fine. I'll just see that he makes it to his hammock," he said. With a final "Be careful" to signal that he understood Llesho's intentions, and approved, the trickster god followed Prince Tayyichiut from the deck.

Llesho watched them go, thinking that this time he'd actually told the truth. Sort of. He'd recovered completely from his confrontation with the storm but hadn't dream traveled since coming to Pontus. It was past time to see what was going on in the world. He had to check in with Shou; Habiba had doubtless reported already, but Llesho wanted to see how things were for himself. In particular, he wanted to know if Mergen and the Tinglut-Khan had settled their differences. He didn't want to show up on the battlefield to discover a war in his own ranks.

That was the easy part. They still had to find out where Master Markko had gone to ground. Moving through the dream realm, Llesho could orient on a place or on a person. Shou or Markko, the only difference was his reception on the other end. That made him the person best able to find the magician. He had a feeling that it all came down to the Golden City. Kungol. Markko would know that, too. It wouldn't take much effort to find him; doing it without getting caught made it a lot harder. With Pig's help, though, he'd finish the task and return before he'd left. He could rest then. And his companions would never know he'd been gone.

Looking out to sea, he shivered, wishing he could call Marmer Sea Dragon. Dangerous thought, that. When had riding to battle in the third eye of a dragon come to represent safety and comfort? He'd forgotten that his cadre still surrounded him until Bixei interrupted his musing with a long-suffering sigh.

"He's got that look on his face," Lling agreed.

"What look?" Llesho didn't pretend innocence. They knew he was planning something, they knew he knew they knew. But he was sincerely curious about how it showed. Oddly enough, they had even followed that convoluted thought.

"The little frowny thing," Hmishi supplied.

"And the faraway look you get in your eyes at the same time, as if you were trying to see something that was too far away to make out." That was Lling, who had commented in the first place.

"At least when I sold him to the pirates, I knew I could follow and get him back eventually," Stipes added, a surprise since he seldom spoke up in councils. He still placed himself below the others of his cadre. Not a thinker, or a courtier, he'd often said, but a simple gladiator who had become a soldier to follow his heart. But Master Markko's storm had brought their most recent plan to the brink of disaster, and he still smarted from his part in it.

"My father will be back soon with a report. Then you can decide what you have to do." Kaydu's tone was cool, logical, with none of the pleading he saw in her eyes. Even Little Brother looked worried.

So they knew what he intended, more or less. He didn't have to tell them, but perhaps Llesho owed an explanation of some sort. "The dream travel is my gift, and my one greatest weapon in my lady's defense. I have to believe she meant me to use it."

"And no report can relate as much as you can see with your own eyes." Kaydu had flown far in the shape of a bird. She did understand at least that part of it. He didn't think any of them would understand his need to confront Markko in his own lair, however. He wasn't sure he understood that himself.

Hmishi wouldn't look at Llesho, but followed his gaze out to sea. From the start he had protected his prince even to the point of dying in his place. He'd never been able to accept being left behind. "When are you going?"

"Now." Llesho stepped away from the rail and started to run in a tight circle. He noticed the Daughters of the Sword left to guard him pass troubled frowns between them, but he didn't have time to explain and wasn't sure how they'd take his answers if he gave them. That was Kaydu's job; she would know what to say.

He leaped, lifted, stretched with hooves that found purchase in the clouds. Marmer Sea fell away behind him and when he reached again for the waking world, he found a dream.

He knew it was a dream in the first place because it was dark, and he'd left Pontus in the morning. Time sometimes moved strangely in dream travel, of course, but one glance at the bed told Llesho he didn't want to take a second glance. This was definitely not his own dream.

He was in a yellow silk tent as large as the audience hall in Durnhag. Rich tapestries hung from thick silk cords strung between the tent poles dividing the space into several chambers. A single lamp rested on a simple wooden chest. Its soft glow illuminated a close circle around a low couch in the sleeping chamber where Llesho had landed. Shou's bedchamber, he thought, since he'd set his thoughts on Shou when he left the waking realm. With a glance at the low sleeping couch, however, he realized that he wasn't sure about anything except the sudden powerful desire to run as far as possible as quickly as he could.

Two shapes writhed at the center of the bed, covered to what would have been the shoulders if either had been human. But they weren't human, either one of them. Cobras each as thick as his own body had so looped their coils together that only the contrast of their colors told where one began and the other left off. The white cobra Llesho had seen before, and knew to be the Lady SienMa, mortal goddess of war. So he wasn't exactly terrified when she raised her head on a long, flared neck and stared at him out of eyes black as onyx. She said nothing, but collapsed back onto the bed, nudging at the brown snake with her nose and flicking a darting tongue over his face to wake him.

Llesho fell back in dismay as the brown snake turned, writhing under the blanket. Coils slipped and settled again; the cobra raised its head, watching him out of Shou's eyes, Shou's face. Terror and desire passed mindlessly across the emperor's face. He didn't seem to notice Llesho but focused inwardly, instead, on the shock of finding himself armless and legless with the fangs of a cobra stretching his lipless mouth. The white cobra heaved a loose coil over the emperor's snaky body, dragging the covers down to reveal more of their squirming lengths and Llesho looked away. His mind could scarcely grasp what he had seen, but he knew he didn't want to see any more.

"My Lady SienMa," he whispered, hoping that she didn't hear the terror in his voice. "I'll wait outside . . ."

"Mine," the snake hissed, bringing Llesho's head around with a snap. In her human form he trusted her completely to protect Shou. This strange creature, however, made the flesh creep on the back of his neck. *Don't turn away,* a voice of caution whispered in the back of his mind. *Don't trust what you see.*

Flaring her hood, the white cobra bared her fangs. Llesho screamed as she sank them deeply into the emperor's throat.

"Ahh!" Shou's eyes opened wide, clouded with confusion and the coursing of venom in his veins. "Llesho?" he asked, surprised. "You shouldn't be here."

"I'll go . . ." He began to back out of the room. Shou had closed his human eyes as if waiting for death.

Despite his terror, Llesho stopped in his flight, unable to leave the emperor in such danger. "If you kill him, he won't belong to anyone," he pointed out with a low bow to the great white snake.

"Mine," she hissed again, but withdrew her fangs.

Shou's head fell back on the pillows, eyes opening slowly as his body became once more the human shape of a man tangled in the bedcovers. "My lady," he murmured and reached a questing arm for her. "Come back to bed."

"Mine," a voice whispered in his ear, and then the tent vanished and with it the sleeping couch. That last voice, however, hadn't been the Lady SienMa. It had been Shou, and Llesho had the uncomfortable feeling that this time he hadn't entered the lady's dream, but the emperor's. What it meant, he wasn't sure, apart from the obvious. That had taken no more than the sight of her hand on Shou's thigh in the governor's palace at Durnhag to understand. He needed to talk to Habiba, though he didn't know quite what to say, or how he could say anything. Shou hadn't invited him into his dream and he had a right to his privacy. But Llesho had to do something.

"I agree." That was Pig, wandering out of the nothingness with a nod of greeting.

"To what?" Llesho asked him.

Pig just smiled and gave his body a little shake to settle the silver chains that wound around him.

"I need to talk to Shou," Llesho decided, "And in the light of day." Since he was already in the dream world, it took no more than the thought and a toss of his antlered head to place him outside the tent he had lately escaped. Great Sun was peeping over the horizon. Even in daylight, however, the guards in front of the tent made warding signs as he came toward them.

Pig, walking on his hind legs a few paces behind, whispered a reminder in his ear: "The antlers."

Ah, that explained at least part of the soldiers' dismay. Llesho shook his head again, composing his features into his own face. His transformation didn't seem to calm the guardsmen, and Sento popped his head out of the tent to see what the commotion was. When he saw Llesho, he motioned him forward, holding the tent flap aside while Pig entered after him.

"Holy Excellence, enter, please." The soldierly servant backed his way into the public audience portion of the great silk tent and brought a chair for Llesho to sit in. "His Highness the Emperor has been watching for you. We have all been worried."

Llesho did as he was bid. The tent was much as he'd known it to be in Shou's dream, with carpets and tapestries dividing the rich silk space into its various chambers. Llesho recognized this outer chamber from more than his dreams, however.

Long ago, at the start of his quest, he had knelt at the feet of the goddess and studied a map of the known world: the many provinces of the empire of Shan, and the grasslands, which had made no distinctions between friend and foe then but swept a single green march of fear and anguish across the map. The Gansau Wastes had appeared as a question at the edge of the known world and Thebin, far to the south, had glowed in golden threads that symbolized the Golden City at the country's heart. The map lay hidden somewhere in one of the many travel chests, but Llesho would never forget that day when he first came to understand that great powers moved behind his quest and worlds balanced on his actions.

"His Highness has just awakened from his rest," Sento continued with his greeting as Llesho reacquainted himself with his surroundings. He showed no sign of having noticed Pig, who chose for himself a bit of carpet off in the corner. Tossing a few pillows about to make himself a comfortable wallow, the

Jinn lowered his great bulk to the floor as the servant made his master's excuses: "He will join you shortly; I'm just setting out breakfast—" Sento bowed his way out before disappearing behind the hangings that divided the tent.

"It seems we are expected," Pig said.

In answer, the trill of a melody skittering restively from the throat of a silver flute.

"Dognut!"

"Llesho!" The dwarf, who was also Bright Morning, the mortal god of mercy, rose from a chair cut down to his small stature and crossed the space between them. "How fare our comrades? Have you been having many adventures?"

"Oh, the boy always has adventures," Pig answered grumpily as he snuggled down in his borrowed pillows. "Pulling honest people out of their hard-earned sleep."

"I see no one by that description hereabouts," Dognut greeted the Jinn's answer with glee. "Tell me everything," he insisted, "or I'll be reduced to writing love songs!"

Pig just snorted. The dwarf had said nothing of the love about which he might write, but the ample wrinkles at the corners of his eyes crinkled with the lively enjoyment of secrets shared between them. Llesho wondered what entertained the dwarf more—the strange affair of the emperor of Shan and the mortal goddess of war, which made an epic of itself, or the nest of cobras that filled the lovers' bed in their dreams. Or maybe, he simply enjoyed the discomfort of a young king from a country where they did not practice such sophisticated pleasures even in their sleep.

Llesho chose to believe it was the former, and aimed his comments at that target: "What in the name of all the realms of heaven and earth and the underworld do they think they are doing?" he whispered urgently. He couldn't free himself from the image of Shou's face above that snaky body, Shou's terror. None of the strangeness of the dream had shaken the emperor's desire for his goddess, however, in any form she took.

"Is that what loving above one's station does?" he asked, not alone about Shou, but for his own case and the Great Goddess who waited for him.

"It depends upon the lovers," Dognut mused, no help at all. He didn't say what it was about the lovers on which the shape of their affection rested.

One of the pair in question, the Emperor Shou, strode out from behind the tapestries that defended the privacy beyond. He wore the armor of a general in which Llesho had first met him and strode to the map table to oversee the arrangement of more domestic forces on the table. Sento followed, a heavy tray carried in his arms, and arrayed the fare as his emperor directed. Eggs boiled in their shells and steamed dumplings with red beans and stewed fruits held their positions amid the cups and plates while the steaming pot of tea marshaled reinforcements from the center of the spread.

"Breakfast?" Shou invited him.

Pig had perked up at the mention of breakfast, and his great turned up snout sniffed the air shamelessly, hinting at an invitation. Neither Shou nor his servant seemed to notice the presence of the Jinn, however. With a disgruntled sigh, Pig finally subsided into his silken wallow, his chin resting on his forehoofs. If no one noticed him, he could gobble down every word between the kings and gods gathered under her ladyship's silk roof. For a Jinn, that was almost better than food. Pig wriggled himself a little lower among the pillows, trying, Llesho thought, to make himself invisible. Which would have been impossible with a pig so large, except that no one could see him anyway.

"Her ladyship will join us shortly," Shou informed Llesho with a smile. "We can make plans and fill our bellies at the same time."

No other sign of the dream Llesho had invaded marked the emperor's features, though he would have sworn it was Shou's dream, and not her ladyship's. Something of his confusion must have shown in his eyes because Shou stopped, arrested in midgreeting. A half-remembered image notched a crease between Shou's eyes.

"I saw you . . ." The emperor blushed like a schoolboy. This was so unlike the assured commander and spymaster Llesho knew that he wondered if Shou still suffered the effects of his captivity. Markko, using his lieutenant Tsu-tan, had tortured Hmishi to death. His torments had left the emperor of Shan a broken man for months. Shou didn't look broken now, however. Just embarrassed.

"It's just a dream," he finally stammered out. "I'm not . . . she's not . . ."

Her ladyship joined them then, gliding across the thick layer of carpets in a many-layered gown dyed the colors of Thousand Lakes Province. Her face was as white as the glaciers on the mountains above Kungol—and as cold—her mouth the red of fresh blood on new snow. Her eyes, however, glowed with richness and warmth as she went to her lover and threaded a slender hand through his arm.

"I trust you slept well," she bade him before gracing Llesho with her attention. "Holy Excellence. Welcome."

She inclined her head in a mark of respect that brought a deep burgundy glow to Llesho's own bronze cheeks. Such a greeting, from a lady of her station, added the weight of her regard to his claim of a holy kingship in the realm of the spirit as well as that of the living. He'd grown accustomed to such deference among mortals, but felt he had yet to prove himself to the gods.

He was here, however, a thousand li and more from where his companions doubtless waited in seething frustration for his return. And without a drop of dragon's blood in his veins. That had to mean something. He returned the lady's greeting with a bow, and took his place in the camp chair at the table.

Shou's servant and guardsman returned with an extra plate and a cup for Llesho to join his hosts for tea and breakfast then. Her ladyship thanked him with a graceful drift of fingers.

"Would you ask Habiba to join us?" she said. "And the others who make up our councils as well?"

With a low bow to her ladyship, Sento departed, leaving them to break their fast in privacy. Or nearly so. No one would question the presence of the emperor's fool at his table, least of all those who knew the dwarf as the mortal god of mercy. As for Pig, only her ladyship seemed to notice his presence and she made no indication that he should remove himself. So Pig stayed, content to gather what information he might, while Dognut plated a small selection of dumplings and grains for himself and returned to his own specially-built chair in the corner.

Chapter Thirty

"**D**ON'T stand on ceremony with us," the Lady SienMa bade him with a gesture at the food spread on the table between them. "You must be very hungry from your travels."

"Always," Llesho agreed, gratified that he had drawn the smile he had hoped from her ladyship. As he tore off a bit of steamed bun and popped it in his mouth, however, Llesho wondered if he was really there at all. Was he still inhabiting a dream? And whose dream was it? Trying to figure it out was giving him a headache, so he decided to ask.

"When I leave here, will this visit have happened?" he asked in a low and musing tone, one that his hosts might politely choose not to have heard. "Will anyone remember it but me?"

In answer, her ladyship took an egg and held it up by the fingertips of one hand. With a short curved knife she sliced off the top, shell and all, to reveal the rich golden center. "I remember everything," she told him, holding the egg between them.

Their eyes met, his own filled with questions, hers offering answers he might never understand. Ages passed in the depths of her gaze, and memories of war and death past counting. His own bloody death: how many times had he fallen in battle, defending the Great Goddess, his wife, through countless lives? She had seen them all, and he read in her glance both the sorrow of those memories and the hope for a better outcome this

time. He took the egg, which seemed like a promise between
them. Spring coming, life renewed. They would hold back the
fire and the darkness together.

With a little nod to show that she had understood all that
had passed unsaid between them, her ladyship picked up a second egg and again she sliced the top off. This time, however,
she cradled the egg in her palm, which she held just below her
heart for a moment before offering it to Shou. Had she been
capable of it, he thought that she might have blushed herself,
an idea that boggled the mind. So many ages, so much she had
seen of slaughter and pain and the uneasy peace that fell
between struggles that he wondered what gentle emotion could
remain to unsettle such a heart.

Shou's eyes grew moist. He took the egg with a tender smile
so full of joy and protectiveness and fear that Llesho dropped
his gaze. *Too much*, he thought, *I don't want to know that much
about you.* After the first bite the emperor offered a spoonful to
her ladyship, who swallowed the creamy yellow center with
downcast eyes. Llesho was on the point of excusing himself
from the private moment when Habiba entered the tent.
Instantly the magician sized up the situation and, with a bow
so low that his beard almost touched the ground, offered his
congratulations.

"A fertile union casts its blessing on us all," he said, rising
once again to show not pleasure but doubt in the tight purse of
his lips.

"Can the hope of life bring anything but light to the darkness
we face, magician?" the Lady SienMa chided her adviser with
a hand resting defensively over her womb.

Llesho sealed his lips tightly, while questions swirled in his
mind. Somehow he'd gotten the idea that the mortal gods didn't
reproduce. They were too old, too much of the spirit world to
reap that which they planted in the mortal realm. Gods usually
left the harvesting to others, whatever the crop. He wondered
what kind of curse or blessing was born in a child of war con-
ceived amid the greatest struggle for the survival of all the
realms. Would the kingdoms of heaven and earth and the
underworld survive long enough to see the birth of a god's

child? With a shiver of superstitious terror the question he feared to even consider snaked its way into his thoughts: what sort of child—human or serpent—would the mortal goddess of war and the emperor of Shan produce between them?

He'd wondered much the same about the emerald bamboo snake demon who had entered the Qubal khan's bed as the Lady Chaiujin. But Chimbai-Khan had been deceived. Shou had joined the mortal goddess of war in serpent form. But that had been a dream. Shou was neither serpent nor magician. The dream readers of Ahkenbad might have found meaning in the shapes the emperor took in the dream world. But there was no evidence that the lady or her human consort carried into the waking world the physical properties of their dream-selves. No evidence that they didn't either, but he decided not to give that thought credence.

"I asked Sento to gather the others," Habiba reported blandly. He had schooled his features to show none of his emotions. Llesho strove to do likewise, but with less success. He wished he'd sent Kaydu in his place, as any reasonable king would have done. With any luck she would have kept all the personal stuff out of her report to him, and he'd never have had to know any of it.

His brothers began arriving quickly at Sento's summons, so he didn't have to wait long in a company that had become so strained that Dognut refrained even from any musical comment. Balar, with his usual enthusiasm, noted Llesho's presence with a wide grin and a hug. "Dreaming again, brother? It's been a long time since you included us in your travels!"

Shokar followed with a hug of his own. "It's so good to see you again, and unscathed, for a change." Neither brother stood on the ceremony due a king.

Lluka hung back, however, correcting his brother with dire warning in his voice. "He hasn't been traveling. At the moment of greatest need, his strength has failed him." *We are all doomed* fell between Lluka's words, but his fellow princes understood them anyway. Llesho closed his eyes for a moment of solitude before he entered the fray. He'd forgotten how taxing it had become to deal with Lluka's madness.

The healer-prince entered then, a little apart from his brothers but with the healer Carina and Bolghai, the Harnish shaman. They seemed distracted among themselves, as if interrupted in the middle of some deep conversation about salves or elixirs. Adar, however, had heard enough. He gave Llesho the slow, wise smile that had soothed him as a child. His words he reserved for his brothers, "At the last, perhaps his strength did fail. But not, surely, at greatest need, or he wouldn't be here at all. Nor, I think, would the rest of us remain to debate the point."

In spite of their brother's reassurance, Shokar was quick to remorse. "Did I hurt you?" he asked, and stepped away as if even his close presence might do further harm to unseen injuries. "I should have asked before cracking your ribs like that."

"No injuries," Llesho promised, though he knew he skirted the truth with his answer. His physical injuries, healed now, had been slight among the pirates. They'd been no worse at the end of that adventure than they had been the last time he'd seen his brothers, so they seemed to require no mention now.

As for the weariness of the spirit that had gripped him after his contest with the great storm raised by Master Markko, he didn't know what to tell them. Lluka had sensed something, however, and he'd need to address it soon. All his gathered brothers but Adar looked to him with worried frowns.

The healer-prince brushed the hair from Llesho's forehead, fingertips finding the nubs of antlers beneath the dark strands. His arm had mended since they'd parted on the plains of the Qubal people so long ago, it seemed. But Adar still read him as clearly as the recipe for any potion. "You've been through a lot," he observed softly, as if he held a frightened bird in his hand. "Not, I think, however, so much that you come to us in defeat."

"Less than victory, but more than rout," Llesho assured them. "But where are Tinglut and Mergen? Not gone to make war on each other, I hope."

Mergen joined them in the Lady SienMa's tent then, an entrance so opportune that Llesho wondered if he'd been listening at the tent flap.

"Still here, young king." Apparently, he heard at least the

last of Llesho's remarks. His next words made that clearer still: "And Tinglut-Khan, who raised his tents at an aloof distance, follows close upon my footsteps."

The khan raised both his hands in greeting to show they were empty of weapons. In so doing he acknowledged the rank of those in attendance without accepting any authority over him as a bow might have done. "At the risk of seeming discourteously abrupt, may I ask about that scamp, my nephew?"

"Well, or nearly so," Llesho reassured him.

They had but minutes to share the more frightening details. Sawghar, the Gansau Wastrel who had on occasion served in Harlol's place in Llesho's cadre, soon joined them to represent the Tashek in council. Then, with the jingle of silver medals on his silken coats, Tinglut brought their number to its full tally.

"I have had my breakfast, and look for none from your ladyship's table," Tinglut announced, his hands raised in a more abrupt version of Mergen's greeting. "This one—" he pointed an elbow at Sento, who had followed him in and now set about gathering cups and fresh tea for the newcomers,"—this one said we are called to council. I had thought we were finally to ride, and now I see that we are again to dangle from the tails of this young shaman-king."

"Dangle from my coattails or not, I do call upon those who would follow to ride now, or lose everything." Llesho stiffened his spine, his chin raised in the way that Master Jaks had warned him against so long ago. Then they strove to hide his rank from assassins who would have murdered him before he learned the statecraft to stay alive. Now his steady gaze, deep and dark with decisions made and consequences survived, matched the resolute tilt of his head.

The Tinglut-Khan read all of that as a leader of long practice must. If he continued to harbor doubts, he kept them to himself for now. "And my daughter? Any further news of the Lady Chaiujin?"

Reflexively, Llesho's hand went to his Thebin knife. "As Mergen-Khan and his advisers have reported to you, to our regret none of the Qubal people or any of my followers have ever met your daughter. The Emerald Bamboo Snake demon stole her name and her place among Chimbai's clans, who took their own terrible losses at her fangs."

Mergen gave a slow nod to remind Tinglut of their own conversations. "And is there any word of the false Lady Chaiujin who has caused so much pain to so many?"

"The lady followed us to Pontus, where she continued her murderous habits. The magicians of the Apadisha determined that her demon spirit somehow attached itself to the jade cup she gave me in the tent of Chimbai-Khan. They were able to contain her within it, so for the present, we are free of her influences." With his thumb he stroked the new decoration set into the butt, a signet as it seemed, carved out of wood. Those among the party who had advised and urged him on his path took this information as the sort of intelligence they expected of a king who must fight demons for the gates of heaven.

Tinglut-Khan, however, had his own agenda. "Where is it?" he asked, meaning the cup. He examined Llesho from head to toe with a greedy eye. Llesho thought he might snatch the cup out of his possession and release the demon to demand an accounting if he knew where he kept her hidden.

"He can't help you," Mergen deflected the Eastern khan from his interrogation. "He is here only in a dream."

"Is that so?"

Llesho answered Tinglut with a guilty shrug. "Afraid so."

"Enough," Shou said. "He cannot help you now. Be content that something has been done to curb the murderer of your daughter, sir. This holy king has traveled far by magical means to join our council. Let us hear what he has to say."

With her own hands, her ladyship offered Llesho tea. "Our trusted magician advises us that you have found allies in Pontus."

He took the cup as gingerly as if it held one of Markko's poisons. He trusted her ladyship with the success of his quest, but had grown wary long ago of the dreams she inhabited.

She had brought him to the purpose of his travels, however, and Llesho bowed his head to acknowledge the truth of Habiba's report.

"At Pontus we found Prince Menar a slave in the house of a

physician who practices a strict sect of the Bithynian religion. It suits his beliefs to treat his servants well. As with the rest of us who found ourselves in hostile lands, Menar kept his identity a secret."

"And are the stories about his sight also true? Is Menar blind?" Balar asked.

His brother's gifts balanced the universe. Llesho knew by the sorrow in his eyes that Balar had already seen the answer. "Yes," he said for those who hadn't already tallied up the costs, wondering which of his own escapes Menar had paid for with his sight. He'd been around that argument with Master Den already, though, and knew he couldn't add every ill of the world to his own account.

Each of the Thebin princes reacted to the news of their brother as their tempers dictated. Adar remained a calm center, though sorrow deepened the lines around his mouth and between his brows. Shokar, who had once claimed to be no soldier, clenched his hand on his hilts and Llesho felt the same impulse to fight the long-ago enemy who had so hurt his brother. Balar took Adar for his model and tried to compose his face, but tears ran a trail down his nose and clung woefully from his upper lip. From Lluka, there was a mad smile.

"You've seen it, too," he said to Llesho. "There is no escape."

By that his brother meant the dreams of devastation, fire, and wind and the worlds of gods and men in chaos. Llesho didn't believe it had to end that way, though, and paraphrased Master Den's reminder to the magician-scholars of Pontus. "Prophecy is not a coin with two sides but a box with many faces. We have to see around the edges to a brighter face."

He was meant to stop the destruction that Lluka dreamed, and finding Menar even in his wounded state fulfilled another part of Lleck's quest, showing, in his metaphor, another face to the prophecy.

"So, brother," he agreed, "the prophecy may speak true that we have no escape from the dire consequences of events set in motion long ago by a miscast wish and a foolish Jinn."

Then he added with the grim determination that had driven

him across the wide expanse of land and sea between Farshore and Pontus, "Victory, however, is possible. And I will have victory. The Grand Apadisha sends ten thousand of his Daughters of the Sword. They sail for Edris as we speak. I've come to count the armies we bring to meet them on this side of the Marmer Sea."

"Ten thousand from the sultan," Mergen said. "When do they count landfall?"

"Two weeks, maybe three, depending on wind and weather. Can you match them with an equal number from the Qubal clans at Edris?"

"That very number of horsemen await the word to ride," Mergen assured him with a knowing smile. The number had been decided long ago.

"An equal number from the Tinglut," the khan who took his name from his people contributed, unwilling to be bested in the matter of warriors under his banner. "But I will want vengence for my daughter at the end of this great battle of yours."

"Justice, surely," Llesho agreed. "I would not carry the consequences of vengence through another lifetime."

"The Tinglut have different beliefs in such matters, young king. But theological discussions can wait until we can debate them at our comfort in the Palace of the Sun."

Llesho bowed to accept this compromise and turned to the emperor for his tally.

"Twice that number from the empire, and more." Shou threw in his own armies, giving credit where due: "We have Wastrels among us, and a contingent of Thebin freedom fighters follow our banner. Another of mercenaries ride to reclaim their honor in the Golden City."

"And we are not so far from Edris as all that," Habiba assured him with a knowing smile. "You will find a familiar river flows not a day's ride from camp."

The Onga, where he had traveled briefly with the Qubal people. Llesho returned the smile.

Her ladyship, the mortal goddess of war, had said nothing while they made their reports, but called Sento with a sign to clear away the table. For security's sake, no other servant was present. They waited, therefore, while Shou's attendant cleared away teapots and cups and dishes covered with crumbs and bits of egg and fruit. When he had done, he spread a map where the breakfast had been.

"You sail to Edris?" Her ladyship traced the route from Pontus with a finger, but her brow knotted with the question.

"Not quite," he answered, understanding her concern well enough. Success depended on giving the enemy as little time to prepare for attack as possible, which meant moving in secret. Not even the best of generals could transport an army unnoticed through the center of a port city like Edris.

"There's a private cove a little to the south of the city where the ships of the Sultan will make landfall." Llesho pointed to a place on the map just below Edris that looked like some great sea creature had taken a round bite out of the land. "When we get closer to shore, Kaydu will scout ahead to track Markko's armies and report back."

He didn't mention his plan for a little dream travel scouting on his own, but Habiba guessed something. "I do not count my daughter expendable," he qualified what he was about to say, "but she's sworn her allegiance to a holy king sacred to the Great Goddess herself." Llesho himself, that meant. "If I may advise: were I such a king, I would reserve the greater risks to my own life for those occasions on which the fates of all the known universes rest. Let others take the risks at lesser moments according to their stations."

Llesho dropped his chin to show he understood and valued the gift of Habiba's wisdom. But he couldn't take the magician's advice, at least not this time. "Sometimes the fate of worlds rests in large battles spread across great bloody battlefields. Sometimes it rests on a single word, spoken at the right moment."

Her ladyship had listened with her finger resting on the map, where Edris met the sea. Now she moved her hand to cover Llesho's where it lay over the sultan's private cove. "Words seldom work on the mad," she reminded him.

The point sent nervous glances darting in Lluka's direction, but no one made any comment about Llesho's mad brother.

With a sigh, however, he had to disappoint even the goddess of war.

"I have to try," he said. Thousands would die in the coming battle. Tens of thousands. He knew Markko was mad, but the magician had always wanted to talk. Maybe he would see, if not reason, at least a less bloody path.

"Then take Pig with you," she insisted. "And remember what he is."

A Jinn, in spite of his piggy appearance, and the head gardener in the gardens of heaven. Which of these would serve him in the confrontation to come? Her ladyship had returned her attention to the map, however, with no more advice on how to use the Great Goddess' rascally servant.

"We are here." She pointed to a bend in the river that Llesho remembered well. He'd met the Chimbai-Khan in this place, and had learned how to travel in waking dreams from Bolghai the shaman. And here he had taken control of the spear that rode watchfully at his back.

"And the Uulgar are here—" She sketched a reach of grasslands that stretched upward to meet the high plateau from which Thebin looked down on its neighbors.

Habiba had already scouted the enemy; he supplied the intelligence of his own expeditions as a giant bird high over the grasslands. "With Master Markko riding at their head, the gathered army of the Uulgar ulus was heading toward the Golden City. Away from our forces who follow at speed. I think he means to lie up behind the city wall and wait out our siege."

It didn't change what Llesho needed to do, but it was good to know where he'd be going at least. Home, much changed as the Uulgar clans had made it. Kungol hadn't had walls when the raiders had carried him away all those years ago. He wasn't surprised to hear there was a wall now, however, built by the slave labor of his own people. The Harn had learned a lesson from their own attack and wouldn't be taken as easily themselves.

He remembered the form of the praying woman high atop the city on the tower of the Temple of the Moon, however. His mother was long dead, along with his sister. He didn't know what other woman might brave the staircase to the bridge of moonlight, but someone had. The sapphire princess, perhaps, that Menar had mentioned from the tales. Not of the royal blood, but Ghrisz's consort? Except that she had looked too young to be a wife, and he thought that he had heard her calling him in a dream. Not everything was real in the dreamscape, and not everything was now. Perhaps it was his mother, but from a time before the Harn came, when she was younger even than he was now. It comforted him to think that she might be reaching out to him across time.

His brothers had by this time figured out what Llesho intended, and they joined their objections with the magician and her ladyship's. Shou, however, said nothing until, with a cutting gesture that silenced the gathered advisers, he brought an end to the discussion.

"If all generals fought their wars between themselves, our farms would surely suffer the lack of fertilizer—but our farmers would not complain, I think." A raised eyebrow accompanied the reminder of land made fertile with graves of the rotting dead and watered by the tears of those left behind.

Llesho gave a bow of thanks that Shou again waved away. "Don't thank me, young king," the emperor said, with such weariness in his voice that Llesho wondered if the dream he'd visited earlier was a sign of a continued sickness of the mind. Shou had turned away, however, with a sad shake of his head. "It never works," he muttered, "But if you care at all, you have to try."

Which explained much that Llesho had wondered about in Shou's behavior. It was more than he wanted to know. Not more than her ladyship did know, it seemed, and Habiba's sigh was more long-suffering than surprised. Adar stopped the emperor's retreat with a hand on his shoulder, which was rejected with a bleakly warning glance. Only Mergen seemed wholly to understand the path of the two kings. He'd lost a brother to battles fought with magical forces and his nephew now stood with Llesho at the center of the coming storm. His dark and thoughtful glance moved from Shou to the young king.

"Be careful." He offered not so much a warning as a prayer.

"As you learned to be a king, so Prince Tayyichiut learns from you. Think about what lessons you wish to teach."

"I'm not his only teacher," Llesho reminded the khan. He meant Mergen himself, but an ironic twitch of a smile from that direction, with a sweeping glance of the tent and all its occupants, reminded him of another teacher. He'd left Prince Tayy behind with Master Den, the trickster god ChiChu.

"Then I don't dare die," Llesho promised. There was a lot more he could have said, but not with his brothers and all of their advisers and allies watching, so he turned his attention back to the maps. "Wait for us here." He pointed to a small outpost on Thebin soil, to the north and east of the Golden City.

Time was running; he felt the pull of it, needing to be away from the argument and debate. Events were moving "I have to go now—"

A disturbance in the dreamscape caught him as he made his good-byes. He let it sweep him away, into the maelstrom of the dream realm. Screams echoed from a distance that had nothing to do with his own life course and he let them go. The cold touch of Master Markko's interest reached out to him like a chill finger tracing the line of scars across his breast. He would have flown past in the chaos, but he caught onto that dread presence and used it like a line to track its source. When dreams spit him out again, he lay sprawled on his back on the carpeted floor of a familiar yellow silk tent.

Master Markko stood at a table lit by a single glowing lantern. A silver bowl filled with clear water rested before him and he looked up from peering into it with a mockery of welcome in his evil grin. "Welcome home, dear son," he said, "I wasn't certain you would accept my invitation—"

That touch, in the dreamscape, he meant. Llesho got his feet under him and shook out his coats, trying to rid himself of the sense of a clinging evil he always felt around the magician. *Not your son,* he thought, but kept the words to himself. It would gain him nothing to anger Markko before he'd stated his case.

There were several elaborate camp chairs scattered around the tent, richly carved wood that seemed all of a piece but folded on cleverly concealed hinges for traveling. Llesho's whole body yearned to fall into one, but he dared show no weakness before his enemy. So he stood his ground and made his offer.

"We can stop this," he said, ignoring the false cheer of the magician along with the trembling in his own legs. "I know about the thing you let loose from the underworld, the demon that sits at the foot of the gates of heaven. We both know what will happen if it somehow breaks through."

"Ah, the good Lluka's visions. All the demons of the underworld set loose to prey upon the worlds of heaven and mortals. All the kingdoms destroyed in fire and wind and chaos—"

Master Markko stepped away from the scrying bowl and clapped his hands for a servant. "Tea for my guest," he commanded when the slave answered the summons. The servant brought cups and a steaming pot and left again at a careless wave of dismissal. Markko filled the cups before answering Llesho's indirect question with a question of his own.

"But whose dreams are they? Surely they belong to the demon who sits on his mountain brooding over his failure. I wonder why the good prince Lluka credits the *creature's* dreams as reality and my own plans as nothing more than wishes? My power raised that beast; my power can control him."

"And all you have to do is find him." The demon had risen from the underworld in the shadow of the gates of heaven, which stood somewhere in the mountains that encircled Kungol. But no mortal man had ever set eyes on them. Not even Llesho, the beloved husband of the Great Goddess, who had passed through the gates in dreams, knew the way in the waking realm. Finding the demon would be question enough without an army of Harn raiders to defeat along the way.

Master Markko shrugged that off as an obstacle of no consequence. "With the right . . . incentives . . . all will become clear." He offered Llesho a cup with a smug smile. "It's taken longer than I'd expected to get you all here, but I will have my way."

"I don't think so." Llesho refused the tea. Made a peace offering of his brother's desperate truth. "Lluka has a gift. He sees the future in all its possibilities. The dreams you invade speak of more than the sick desires of the demon at the gates of heaven. All futures end here.

"Kungol, Shan, the Harnlands, heaven, and the underworld and all the kingdoms of mortal men who never heard of any of us will fall to fire and storm if the demon wins through. The demon and all his creatures will fall in the chaos they bring, but it will be too late for the rest of us then. With no heaven or underworld, no mortal realm for returning, the souls of all the dead will wander the darkness in despair forever.

"That's the vision that rides Prince Lluka's sleep and drives him mad when he's awake. In none of his raving does he make an exception for the souls of magicians, not even yours. But we can stop it. Together."

Master Markko gave no indication that he'd taken insult from the refusal of the tea from his hand. Setting the cup down gently, he gave Llesho a long and searching look from under a fine line of eyebrows. "You say that Lluka sees all futures truly, and all end in death," he said. "It stands to reason, from your own argument, that nothing we can do will stop the terrors to come. Why do you feel the need to try, knowing as you must that your efforts are futile?

"And," he added, a finger raised in warning as Llesho took breath to answer, "if you believe, as I do, that Prince Lluka's dreams are indeed mutable, and the future can be changed, how can you imagine I would abandon my own ambitions to follow you? Haven't I already proved, by raising him, that I am more powerful than this demon that stands at the turning point of all creation?"

"More powerful? Or a dupe used by the demon king to invade the mortal realm?" Llesho answered with his own question, and reminded the magician of what they both must know: "I have looked down your road and found nothing but death at the end of it, just as Lluka's visions predict. A different road offers at least the hope of a different outcome."

"Ah," Master Markko chuckled as if they shared a joke between them. "You seem to think I care about living. But you're wrong. Without winning, what's the point of any of it?"

He saluted Llesho's health with the small round cup in his hand and drank the tea which, this time, seemed to be a harmless brew.

"If losing means death," the magician set down his cup, finishing his explanation as he dabbed delicately at his lips with a silk square, "there is some consolation in knowing that I'll take the rest of you with me. And I could, for example, start with you—"

The silk square disappeared. Master Markko reached out an empty hand and slowly closed his fingers. Llesho watched, unable to move, choking as if the magician's fist had wrapped around his throat and squeezed. Black light sparkled behind his eyes and he seemed to be drifting, drifting. Vision narrowed to a tunnel down which he saw the magician raise a knife. Behind him, Pig frowned and adjusted the chains that wrapped him everywhere.

The sound of link against link broke Markko's concentration. The pressure around Llesho's throat eased for a moment, tightened again.

"Ahem."

Master Markko whipped around, ready to attack in the direction from which the voice had come. Instead he turned pale as a ghost, or the Lady SienMa, and screamed as if his own throat might be torn out with the sound.

"Let the young king go, please. We still need him," Pig requested politely, but he reached out with one huge black hoof that blurred into the rough shape of a hand. The Jinn grabbed the magician by his beard and lifted him over his head, slippered feet dangling like a puppet with tangled strings.

Master Markko released Llesho, but even as he hung there in Pig's grasp, kicking to be let go, he cursed and swore against the gods who denied him the destiny he sought. "Mine!" he cried. "You can't have him; he's mine!"

"Never," Pig answered. Then he gently set the magician down again. "I'm sorry for what I've done to you," he apologized with a deep bow. "I've learned a lot during my exile, not least the damage of a misspoken word. I would change it if I could."

"And I would roast you on a spit and serve you to my raiders to celebrate the fall of the gates of heaven. Neither of us is likely to get our way this time; but soon—"

The magician seemed very confident in himself, but Llesho read death in the Jinn's eyes. "No!" he shouted, his own arm raised to stop murder. "If you kill him, the dragon-king's son buried inside him will also die. What will happen to your gardens when that crime is added to your account?"

With a careless wave, the Jinn shifted them outside of the magician's reality. They could still see Master Markko, but he couldn't see them. He whirled around in a fury of summoning while Llesho watched dispassionately only inches from his face. For himself, Pig's thoughts had all turned inward. Something about that mystical separation cooled the temper as distance in the waking realm might. For that moment out of space, the magician had become less important than the puzzle he presented.

"If we live," Llesho reminded the Jinn, "if we vanquish the demon king and rescue the gates of heaven, my lady's gardens will need you."

"Yes," Pig answered slowly, hesitant to agree to something that might bind him to a promise he hadn't planned to make.

"When that time comes, and you stand before my lady the Great Goddess, she will ask you what you did to repair the damage you have done with your mischief in the mortal realm."

Pig squirmed uncomfortably, knowing already where that was going. "But—"

"I know. There is no way out of the mortal realm except death." Markko's death. Llesho sighed, sharing the sorrow for all who would fall in battle before that day came. "But this murder will not balance your scales."

"Because it's my fault," Pig realized. "I brought this on us all."

It was true. Llesho had no comfort to give him. A tear ran down the Jinn's round snout, but he accepted the judgment with a solemn lowering of his great black head.

"Do you have anything else you want to tell him?" Pig

asked. Master Markko still raged at their disappearance, though they stood no more than an arm's length from his foaming fury.

Llesho shook his head. "I had to try," he said.

"I know." The Jinn patted him on the shoulder, too dispirited even to ask him for a wish. "Now it's time to do it the other way."

War. He'd always known there was no way out. But he'd told the truth to her ladyship and to Pig. He'd had to try. Setting his sights on the ships he'd left behind on the Marmer Sea, Llesho took a step . . .

This time it didn't surprise him when the girl's voice called him. "Not yet," he whispered in his passing. "But soon."

Chapter Thirty-one

STEP . . . another, and he was tumbling onto the deck of the galley the Grand Apadisha had given him to be his flagship.

"He's back!" AlmaZara's guardswoman peered down at him, calling to his companions. They soon gathered in a worried circle around him: AlmaZara herself, with a Bithynian Daughter of the Sword at her right hand and Lling at her left. Hmishi came next, flanking Lling, with Bixei and Stipes. With a scuffle of running footsteps, Tayy joined them with Master Den looking curiously over the Harnish prince's shoulder.

That seemed wrong to Llesho. Master Den belonged with him, not with Prince Tayyichiut. A crinkling smile in the corner of the trickster god's eyes did nothing to reassure him. Llesho stuck out a hand, but no one offered to help him off his back. They waited, instead, for Kaydu to push through to the center.

"Where have you been?" She squatted on her heels to talk to him on a level, pushing him back again when he tried to get up.

"I had to confer with Shou and our allies among the clans." He didn't think his conversation with Master Markko would go down well, so he kept that to himself.

"My father said you left the emperor's tent weeks ago. You've been lost in the time stream." She glared at him with an exasperated frown before giving him a boost to his feet. "We've been frantic, but his scrying bowl couldn't locate you in the dreamscape or any place in the living realm."

"I was here and there." Llesho brushed himself off and took a good look around him. The galley stood out a bit from landfall with ten others of their kind resting at anchor in a harbor that, in person, looked more like a half-moon carved out of the mountainous landscape than a dragon's bite. Llesho recognized it for the sultan's private landing anyway. There wasn't room for all the fleet he'd brought from Pontus. Since no one seemed concerned about the missing ships, he figured they must be awaiting word to advance from outside the enclosing arms of the cove.

With no crisis but himself currently in progress, they could all focus on his answers. Llesho wondered if he could come up with something else to distract them, but it didn't look promising. The situation called for evasive maneuvers. "With Pig's help, a little more there than here."

"You know," Kaydu pointed out, "you are starting to sound more like Master Den every day." The sniff that accompanied this conclusion made it clear that she didn't think that was a good thing.

"Sometimes it frightens even me," Llesho admitted. "Have you been waiting here long?" On the shore a cluster of buildings remarkable for their elegant filigree work and the many slender towers that rose above them reached almost to the water's edge. He would have liked to stop there for a while, to enjoy the beauty and the calm lapping of a sea he didn't have to fight with an oar or a spell. Maybe on the other side of battle . . .

"We came to anchor this morning," Kaydu confirmed what Llesho had already begun to suspect: there was no coincidence in his sudden reappearance. He had wanted the whole thing over with, and Pig warped the time stream to carry him to when he needed to be.

"We didn't want to land before we'd found you." Kaydu didn't mention their worry that he'd arrive back at the ships to find them gone, or the realization crossing her face that he'd arrived just as they would have debarked if he'd been there all along. He wasn't sure if she was happier to see him or angrier at him for giving them such a scare.

"It's going to get worse before it gets better," Master Den warned her with a wry shake of his head. "As a daughter of the witch Habiba, and one who has served her ladyship, the goddess of war, for all of her life, you should know that not all battles are fought with swords and armies."

The trickster stood a little to the side, with Prince Tayyichiut under his wing. That development troubled Llesho the more he thought about it, and on more than one level. A pang of jealousy struck like a blow to the heart for one thing. It could mean nothing, of course, or it could mean the trickster god had abandoned him for another prince to raise in the tricksy ways of kingship. He didn't think he was ready to take on Master Markko and the demon without his teacher, but it was starting to look like he'd be doing exactly that.

"Habiba said you were going to try to talk to Master Markko into surrendering without a battle."

Llesho smarted under his captain's acid tone, which told him exactly how foolish she thought that idea was. Standing among his usual friends and advisers, the sultan's daughter AlmaZara watched him squirm uncomfortably under her sharply measuring gaze. She'd been raised among magicians and his explanation didn't surprise her as he thought it might. He found he was uneasy before that particular audience, however. His cadre had earned a certain degree of familiarity, and his teachers were in a regular habit of praising and criticizing at the same time. As Master Den's new apprentice king, Prince Tayy received no better treatment than he did and understood well enough the camaraderie of the trail. But the Daughter of the Sword reported to the Grand Apadisha, who looked at war as a sport.

As a king, Llesho had first to regain his kingdom. Afterward, he required the respect—if necessary, the fear—of his neighbors to hold on to what he had reclaimed. He didn't want the Apadisha measuring himself for clothes to suit a Thebin crown. So he wondered what report the daughter would make to her father, of a king without a home who disappeared at will and reappeared weeks later with no explanation for his absence, other than the vagaries of the time stream—

"And he took you prisoner?" AlmaZara asked, a hand to her spear. "Even in the camp of the magician we should have been able to find you—"

"He didn't." Llesho shook his head, trying to slow her down a minute. He was still feeling disconnected from his body and his surroundings, as if he'd returned in a dream and slept on somewhere in the puzzle box of his own crossed realities. "I needed to try one last time to stop the bloodshed before it began."

Bixei, who had known Master Markko longer than Llesho himself, tsked his disgust at this notion. "I could have told you that wouldn't work. I'm amazed you managed to escape him after a stunt like that."

"Pig helped."

This time Prince Tayy snorted his amazement. "Not like he helped the magician, I hope."

"No wishes," Llesho agreed. He settled his shoulders in his sleeveless coat and sharpened up the gaze he fixed on his captain. "Report, if you please. What's been going on here since I left."

"There's been some movement in the mountains," Kaydu snapped to attention, knowing that Llesho had reached the limit of scolding he would take from his worried friends. It was time to take up his kingship.

"The gates hold, but more demons are leaking through the barrier between the mortal kingdom and the underworld. Habiba doesn't know how much longer heaven can hold."

Llesho remembered the sounds from Master Markko's scrying bowl; it figured the evil magician wasn't the only witch with his eyes to silvered water.

Bixei peered into Llesho's face as if he were afraid this wasn't Llesho at all but some imposter put among them by the magic of their enemies. "We were afraid the demon snatched you out of the dreamscape."

"Nothing happened to me." Llesho shook his head, denying the terrors of his friends and followers.

"Sometimes, the time stream slips," Master Den suggested, and that sounded like what he'd experienced.

"I was anxious to make shore, and overreached my landing by the time between."

"You mean you managed to skip all the boring, nerve-racking parts." Prince Tayy had kept his peace until now, but he spoke up with a wry fit of jealousy of his own. "No boring days waking up to nothing but water and arguments about where we were going and what we would do when we got there? No nerveracking nights while Kaydu practiced her scrying and nobody could find you anywhere in the kingdoms of the living?"

"More or less," he admitted, then shifted Tayy's attention off himself with a report. "Your uncle was well when I saw him, by the way. For the time being, at least, he and the Tinglut-Khan have agreed not to kill each other over the Lady Chaiujin, though there will have to be some accounting for the losses there soon. Not before Master Markko is taken down, however."

"Sensible of them," Tayy agreed. "I assume you sent them somewhere to meet us?"

Llesho cast a glance skyward, reminder that their enemies might spy on them from anywhere, in any shape.

"Under cover, then," Kaydu led them belowdecks, to the only cabin that the galley afforded. Low divans took the place of chairs here, and cushions on the floor, but the table on its short legs held the usual array of maps and charts.

"We're here," she pointed to the familiar bite on the map.

Llesho gestured to a point farther inland. "This is where the emperor is bringing his combined army. When we meet, the assault on Kungol will begin. There's just one problem."

"Just one?" Bixei asked in mock surprise.

Kaydu made a face at the two of them. "I assume you mean the wall and not Markko or the demon we have to defeat after we've routed the Uulgar raiders and captured the magician?"

As he was meant to do, Llesho winced. "One more problem than I already had on my list," he amended. "But yes. The Uulgar have built a wall around the city."

Tayy was frowning and shaking his head over the new intelligence. "It seems a strange thing for grasslanders to do," he pointed out. "We don't like fences of any kind. Don't like staying in one place long enough to build a wall as a rule, even if we could endure living inside of one."

"Their own attack on the city proved the need, however. Habiba says they used the Thebin people as forced labor to construct it."

"I've seen it in my father's scrying bowl," Kaydu confirmed Llesho's report. "But we haven't been able to see past it, into the city. Habiba thinks Markko has set some magic about it to keep prying eyes out."

"I don't think he's in Kungol yet. Heading that way, but the sounds around us were those of a Harnish camp rather than a city of mud walls. Besides, he met me in his tent. I think, if he'd entered the city he would have installed himself in the Palace of the Sun. So we have that much time, at least. But he has the advantage of us in the shorter distance he still has to travel and in the plain fact that city gates held against us will open at his voice."

Master Den had listened in silence, but he now spoke up with a gleam in his eyes. "I presume you have made a plan . . . ?"

Llesho met his teacher's challenge with a level gaze. "At Kaydu's command, AlmaZara will lead the Apadisha's army to the meeting place. That will take, how long?"

"A week, maybe ten days," AlmaZara answered for her army of foot soldiers.

Kaydu gave nodding agreement. "Sounds right, assuming the troops are hardened to such distances."

"It's battle season," AlmaZara answered with a shrug. "We meant to march north to fight the barbarians, but one direction or another matters little to a soldier."

"That gives me ten days to make my way into the city and find Ghrisz," Llesho concluded.

You're going to do what? He saw the thought in the suddenly widened eyes of his cadre, but Kaydu pressed her lips together. When she had regained control of her reactions, she questioned his decision more diplomatically than her first impulse had dictated.

"I assume you aren't planning to ride up to the gates with your personal bodyguard around you and look for a breach in the Uulgar defenses when you get there."

"We would hardly arrive before the armies that follow us," Llesho reasoned. "If I travel through the dreamscape, I'll have a week or more to find my brother and see how things are before we have to attack. The resistance fighters in the city might have their own secret ways around the wall. If I can find a way to ally with them, we may be able to open the gates from the inside. Working together, we might save the thousands of lives that will be lost trying to batter their way past the Uulgar defenses."

"You can't go alone." Kaydu rubbed her head. "I might . . ." Something about her distress reached Little Brother who rode in his sling at her back. Carefully, he crept onto her shoulder and began grooming her hair in a comforting way. "It isn't my skill," she finally said. "I would follow you into the dream world and guard your back while you search for the last of your brothers, but I'm as likely to get lost and cause you more trouble than help."

"I know," Llesho bowed his head, not ready to admit he was too tired to do what he had to do, but heartily weary that he had to do it alone.

"If there's trouble, Habiba can find me. He's done it before." Reaching through the dreamscape the magician had brought Llesho home from his first dream-journey to the heavenly gardens. The dream readers of Ahkenbad had helped. They'd also died, but he didn't think it was a good idea to mention that now.

Finally, Hmishi surprised them all. It was he who spoke up in defense of the plan. "It's not just a matter of getting anyone at all into Kungol ahead of the armies or finding a way for our armies to pass through the wall the raiders have built, or even contacting Prince Ghrisz once our spy makes it into the city. The prince who leads the resistance will have to trust our envoy enough to listen.

"He won't believe another magician means him well, or another Harnlander. Lling or I at least look Thebin, but we have country accents and farm manners, both tainted by the ways of the North where we have lived most of our lives. No Thebin would believe we had the ear of a long-lost king. At best Prince Ghrisz would consider us spellbound hostages, at worst turncoat spies."

"He's right, of course." Master Den gave Hmishi a smile with too many teeth in it that seemed to make Llesho's bodyguard more nervous than pleased. But it was the truth, and even Kaydu had to accept it.

"When are you going?" she asked Llesho

"Now," he answered, with a nod that summed up "goodbye" and "good luck" and half a dozen other things that would have taken the rest of the daylight to say in words.

Dream traveling had become easier with practice. Tired as he was, Llesho had only to set a place in his mind and step . . . step . . .

Chapter Thirty-two

MOST of the time Llesho traveled through the dreamscape with only his dream-self visible to those he visited. He could talk and walk among those present, eat and drink and even suffer among them, but only as a dream. Before he left the Qubal encampment, however, Bolghai the shaman had taught him how to cross the river Onga with his body as well as the dream-self. He did that now.

Reality wavered, taking form and weight around him. Llesho fell to his hands and knees, his head hanging between his hunched shoulders. Shaken and exhausted from his travels, he gasped for breath in the thin, cold air, gathering his rattled senses about him. He was alone—hadn't startled any Uulgar guardsmen or frightened a cook out of a year's growth with his sudden appearance out of nowhere. When his chest had stopped heaving like a leaky bellows, he pulled himself back on his haunches and took stock of where the dreamscape had dropped him. A sharp wind cut through him like a knife; he knew the feel of that wind, knew the landscape spread out around him like a dream. Kungol: still so beautiful washed in the gold of late afternoon sunlight that he wept to look at it. The mountains rose up around the city, six taller than the others with glaciers at their crests that glittered like six crowns of stars.

More than a marker in a prophecy, those peaks were a place out of memories he'd almost lost in the years of his absence.

He wondered if he still wandered in dreams. But no, the wind was chilling him to the bone and hard stone bruised his knees. Llesho staggered to his feet, remembering. He'd never been allowed up here as a child, but he knew where he was: the king's pavilion at the very top of the Palace of the Sun, across from the Temple of the Moon where he'd seen in his dreams the shadow of a woman praying the forms of the Way of the Goddess by moonlight. Far below lay the great square. He remembered a festival to welcome the spring from long ago when he was small, before the Harnish raiders came. Ribbons flying in their own royal version of peasant dress, his parents had led a thousand dancers through the spritely steps to a simple peasant tune. How many of those dancers had died, like his parents, at the hands of the Harn?

Another celebration he'd welcomed with less pleasure, though he'd give his life to take back that childish anger. The priests of the Great Goddess in their brightly colored robes had sung the birth of his sister in this same square. He'd only seen five summers then and had resented the competition for his parents' attention, his brothers' affection. The Harn had murdered Ping, had thrown her body on a garbage heap, they said. Still, he remembered the sonorous many-voiced chant of praise that his mother had delivered a daughter for the Goddess.

Llesho himself had stood in that square next to his brothers while the first caravans of the season had passed. He'd wanted to ride a camel then, wanted to go where the caravans went and see the strange places where all the mysterious goods came from. Since leaving Pearl Island, he'd done all that and more; Llesho would have given it all never to have left home.

Tears froze on his cheeks. Turning away from the great square, he looked out on the city that once had thrived in the light of the gates of heaven. Temples to a thousand gods, a thousand different religions once had spread their banners across the city. Merchants and priests and guildsmen and caravanners had mingled on streets washed with the golden glow of sunlight on Kungol's unique mud plaster. Untended now, those mud buildings crumbled where war hadn't razed them completely. The banners were gone, the priests dead, the merchants fled. Guildsmen with nowhere else to go had hidden their skills if not their very existence. There weren't enough Uulgar in the city to fill it with life, just enough to beat back the life that once had flourished here.

In the distance, like a dark shadow, the wall the Uulgar had built—had forced the Thebin guildsmen to build—pressed in on the city like a glowering god, a serpent king strangling the city in the coils of its great body. He wondered how they stood it. Yesugei, a clan chieftain among the Qubal, had once told him that "Harn" was a name the Tashek gave to the clans. It meant the wind blowing on the grass and referred to the way the clans were forever picking up their tents to follow their horses across the grasslands. So how could they stand to live behind that wall?

And how was Llesho going to get his armies over or around or through it? He couldn't, and knew it. Not from the outside, not without sending his followers to wasteful deaths against the Uulgar defenses and Master Markko's magic. But if he made contact with Ghrisz and his resistance fighters, maybe they could find a way from the inside. It had seemed a reasonable idea before he had seen that dark and looming monster of a wall closing in the city. Now, he didn't know. Didn't know how he was going to find Ghrisz. Couldn't, for that matter, figure out how he was going to get away from the Palace of the Sun without being seen. The Uulgar might avoid this most exposed of Kungol's sacred places, but they wouldn't have abandoned the palace completely. They would surely kill him if they caught him. But they wouldn't look for him up here.

With his eyes carefully averted from the one sight he desired most, Llesho studied this aerie of Thebin kings for a way down. He stood on a bare stone platform in the shape of the sun. Nine tall pillars circled the outer rim, each too slender to hide a staircase. Between them no screen or parapet defended the king from stepping off the platform, but only death awaited that misstep. Above, a stone roof carved with the symbols of the zodiac rested on the capitals of the pillars. No escape there. One of the flagstones that made up the floor of the pavilion might conceal a secret catch that would reveal a hidden staircase, but the surface seemed unbroken by any seam or depression that might hide such a device.

Grit spun in little windswept eddies around his feet but gave him no answers. There had to be a way down—a flash of light at the corner of his eye brought him spinning to confront it. Not a glint on a drawn sword or the head of a spear as he had feared, but little moons Han and Chen rising—Great Moon Lun would follow soon. Some things were immutable in this universe. Unchanging, like the Goddess herself.

If he believed in the lady who waited for him among her bees and her gardens, and if he believed in her way, then he must believe that he had come to the place where he was meant to be. And, if he put his faith in the Way of the Goddess, it would take him to where he was supposed to go. Slowly he moved into the first of the evening prayer forms, "Setting Sun." In the circle of his arms he held the world and thought of warmth fading in a blaze of crimson flame on the horizon. Day gave way to night, the prayer reminded him, as summer gave way to winter and clarity to confusion.

When the circle opened, releasing all he held too close, Llesho said good-bye to fear and desire, to pride and friendship, to revenge and anger. The day ended, the sun would disappear. Holding on wouldn't make it stay or bring it back any faster. So the form taught. And finally, at the top of the world, he learned its meaning.

Kungol was no place of butterflies or bending trees, but Llesho shifted into the form of "Twining Branches," twisting in on itself like the plots of conspirators. Like the gnarled fingers of an old healer, or the stunted trees that dotted those few places on the deserts he had crossed where water sometimes coursed beneath the surface. Strength flowed not only in the straight and smooth and young, but in the stubborn refusal to surrender to the seasons and harsh weather. He found beauty in survival and moved on to the next lesson.

So many forms he had learned to honor the wind: over

water, over grass. None of them spoke to the unyielding heart of Kungol. Llesho thought and let go of thought, listened with his heart which whispered to him in a form all his own, "Wind over Stone." The mountains that rose around him, the platform that he stood on. Stone. Less yielding than those forms he had known, he made this new prayer the meeting of two equal powers. Softly insistent power, unbendingly immovable power, danced together, wearing each other through the ages to a gentler peace. He felt the touch of the Goddess in the wind at his face and knew he was the stone, enduring.

As the form came to a close he continued without stopping into the Goddess Moon form, honoring the Goddess in Great Moon Lun. At the height of the form, Great Moon Lun peeked out from between two mountains where they crossed low on the horizon at his back, slanting moonlight across the Temple of the Moon on the far side of the public square. Awestruck, Llesho brought the prayer to an end with his face lifted to the wondrous sight. The Temple glowed like molten silver; Great Moon's light, flowing with that cold heat, pierced him like a silver arrow through the heart.

"Oh, Goddess," he whispered: a prayer, a wish.

"She's not here."

"I think you're wrong about that," Llesho told the man who stepped out of the shadows cast by a pillar brandishing the sword in his hand. Uulgar by the look of him, and older than Llesho by a decade, though he wore no bits of human hair sewn to his shirt. He hadn't been there a moment earlier, but he looked too shocked by Llesho's presence to have dream traveled to that place. They studied each other for a moment, the guardsman the first to break that gaze with a confused sweep of the platform.

Llesho asked the first question. "Where did you come from?"

The guardsman's eyes darted to an opening in the floor that had looked like unbroken stone when Llesho had examined his aerie earlier.

"It only opens from the inside," the Uulgar clansman said.

"And the only way to reach it is past my post. So how did you get up here without my seeing you?"

"I came here in a dream," Llesho said. He drew the short spear from its sheath at his back and let the unearthly light flicker along its length. "Ask your shaman."

The Uulgar guardsman's eyes opened wide so that the whites showed all around but he didn't back down. "I've seen few wonders in my life, and fought with none. I'd like to keep my record unblemished in that regard. If you will come quietly to my master . . ."

"The magician?" Llesho asked.

The man paled, answer enough. Llesho slid his sword from its scabbard so that he had a weapon in each hand: one to counter the guardsman, the other to press the attack.

Llesho had fought in tight spaces before, but then he'd been hemmed in by enemies battling all around him. He knew how to clear room to move with great sweeping swings of his sword while jabbing away at anyone who came inside the reach of his blade. This was the opposite of his experience in the battlefield, however. He had all the empty space he could want, as long as his opponent stayed in the center of the king's pavilion. If they strayed to the edge, however, they'd be over it and dead an instant later when they hit the ground.

If his goal had been to slay his opponent, it would have been easy enough to press him to that edge. He didn't want to kill the Harnishman for performing his simple duty, though. It was clear that the Harnishman didn't want to kill him either, if for different reasons. Master Markko would want to see anyone found on the king's pavilion with no explanation how he got there. Llesho figured a guardsman who lost that prize would soon follow his hapless victim over the edge.

The guardsman brought up his sword and Llesho engaged with a clang of steel against steel before backing off. Circling warily, he took the measure of the stone platform as well as of his opponent. This far, no farther, he counted his paces. Pressed the advantage, then retreated in a flurry of sword and spear.

If they'd been fighting by arena rules, the fight would have been simple enough, except for that straight drop, of course.

He'd learned from his first days in Lord Chin-shi's compound how to put down an opponent without doing too much damage. But the guardsman didn't know those rules.

Attack, parry, retreat.

They circled each other cautiously. The guardsman had greater strength as befit his years, but his stance and the nervous glances he cast about him said the man had little experience at hand-to-hand combat. The Harnish had war games, of course, but in their own land they trained mostly on horseback. Standing guard on an abandoned building in a subject city gave little opportunity to sharpen skills at closer combat. Even so, the guardsman must have come in from the grasslands of his clans quite recently; he fought awkwardly on his feet, with little sense of swordwork in a confined space. The man's skills couldn't be counted on to keep either of them alive.

Llesho was faster and better trained for a sustained single combat. He darted inside the man's reach, jabbed with the short spear, drew blood from a scratch that by design did nothing more than trace a line of blood along his opponent's rib cage. Out of reach again perilously close to the drop, then away, he circled back to the center. The guardsman pressed the attack, scored. Llesho felt a wet trickle run down his sword arm. The muscles still worked, so he ignored it.

As sometimes happened in battle, his own blood rushing in his ears blocked out other sounds. He found the stillness at the core of his own technique, where his dead weaponsmaster Master Jaks still called out the moves from the governor's compound in Farshore Province.

Slash, parry, retreat—

He paced himself to the pounding of his heart, let that pulse measure his steps from the edge. He didn't have to think; an unconscious alarm seemed to alert him each time he strayed too close to disaster.

So he spiraled the battle inward on that high stone disk as he wove a tapestry of blows through which even his own spear could not slide. Back and back he pressed the Harnish guard until, wide-eyed with terror and gasping for breath, the man teetered on the brink. Llesho didn't want him dead, so he took a step back, let the man do his own circling away from a deadly fall.

Victory came with a simple trick. Llesho pressed him, the guardsman parried. Llesho counter-parried, sliding his blade under his opponent's and circling it up, away, more quickly than the dazed Harnishman could follow. Momentum carried the weapon out of the guard's hand, arcing off into space. Dismayed, he watched as his sword spun far out beyond the edge of the king's pavilion and fell, fell, until it clanged into the square below.

"Give." Llesho pressed the point of his spear to the man's breast. The man fell to his knees, the sword following him down, but he hadn't surrendered yet.

"There is only one way . . . down from this tower." The hoarse voice rasped painfully as the guardsman wheezed for breath. Blood ran from his nose and he spat a bloody gob of it at his feet. Llesho wondered if he had wounded the man more seriously than he'd intended. He half expected to see bubbling red froth at the corners of the Harnishman's mouth, but it didn't come. The man wiped his nose on the back of his hand, unsurprised at the red streak the action left in its wake.

Not his wound, then. The cold thin air on Kungol's high plateau punished those not born to her heights. Llesho waited while the man struggled to catch his breath. "There are many more . . . of my kind . . . between here and freedom. If you kill me, you will die."

"And if I let you take me to your master, I'll die anyway."

He saw the truth of that in the Harnishman's eyes. It wasn't the only truth between them on that windswept platform, however. He couldn't kill this man for doing his duty. Perhaps, if he'd worn on his chest the badges of Uulgar brutality, hanks of hair torn from the living scalps of his victims, Llesho might have been able to do it. But the more he thought about it, the more he realized that his decision had nothing to do with the man on his knees in front of him.

Battle had brought him no reward but to return in blood and pain to try again, over and over and over through ages so lost in time that he could scarce imagine them. For Llesho, the Way of the Goddess could no longer lead through fields of the dead. Finally he understood that.

He wasn't out of it completely—didn't see any way around killing the thing that held the gates of heaven hostage. For the rest, others could carry the sword from now on. It was time for him to step away from that life. So he threw his sword down between them.

"Go," he said, and looked up to the mountains where the Goddess waited for him. It felt like justice, to free this man who had done nothing but his duty. The guardsman could kill him where he stood, but Llesho didn't think he'd do it. Why would the Way bring him to this point, this understanding, just to die? If he believed, and he did, then there must be another way out of this. A just way.

A low moan of terror escaped the guardsman's throat. Llesho turned slowly, in no great hurry to see what horror crept up on them now. Not a horror, though; he saw a miracle.

Great Moon Lun had climbed higher, as if scaling the star-crowned mountains of Thebin. Her glorious light pierced the eye of the needle that was the tower of the Temple of the Moon. Between the earthly Palace of the Sun and the temple, symbol of the Great Goddess in her heaven, a bridge of molten silver had suddenly appeared out of moonlight. Forgetting the Harnishman, Llesho took a step, another. At first he seemed to have no control over his feet. Then he was running with all his will toward that unearthly light.

His foot felt air, nothing, but he didn't fall. He ran, not out of fear or to escape the Uulgar guardsmen who awaited them inside the Palace of the Sun but joyously. In his heart he knew that all he might desire at road's end awaited him on the other side. He had only to cross that mystical silver bridge.

The light held him, held him, until his foot found stone again high above the city on the far side of the square. He had reached the Temple of the Moon. He stepped onto the pavilion that returned the palace's gaze across the square.

All around the aerie atop the temple ran an elaborately carved parapet, protection on this side of the square against an accidental fall. Two breaks in the figured stone aligned with each other to allow the light of the rising Great Moon to cross the high platform, forming the eye of the needle through which Lun gazed upon the palace. Llesho remembered being here by daylight, remembered the balustrade guarding an open staircase that spiraled down into the center of the temple. Stone benches set at propitious angles allowed for comfortable viewing of the palace and the mountains in daylight. By moonglow they looked more ethereal than his memory supplied, with shadows more substantial than the stone itself.

Llesho took a step away from the edge but turned at the sound that echoed across the square in the darkness: boots running on stone, then a bloodcurdling scream. The Uulgar guardsman had followed Llesho out onto the bridge of light. He had taken no more than a single step, however, when he realized the gossamer structure wasn't going to hold him.

Overhead, Great Moon Lun moved higher in the sky. Her light crossed out of the eye of the needle, rising along the mountainside. The bridge of light disintegrated. Too far from the platform to save himself, the guardsman tumbled, screaming, to his death in the square below.

"Oh, Goddess."

Llesho closed his eyes, as if by shutting out the sight he might erase the memory of the man falling in terror. It didn't work, as he knew it wouldn't.

"Why couldn't you let it go?" he whispered to the dead man broken on the paving stones below. He knew the answer, of course. Duty. Knew, maybe, why the guardsman had to die. If he'd told his captain, and word had reached the magician, every raider and Uulgar clansman in the city would have been looking for him. He'd never find his brother.

The dead man made him question all his new assumptions about himself, about the reasons he had come back to relive a life of battle and death again and again. But he couldn't figure what else he was supposed to learn from it. All he knew for sure was that the death of this man he'd never met before cut him to the heart in ways that he had never felt a loss.

With Master Jaks, and when Hmishi had died, it seemed as though a fate larger than himself had stolen something from him. He needed them, and what he needed was taken from him. In Hmishi's case, the god of mercy had even seen his need and brought him back—for Llesho, not for Hmishi or for Lling. He hadn't, when he thought about it, given any concern for how Master Jaks or Hmishi might have felt about it in themselves, as the course of their own lives and not an extension of his.

Master Jaks had chastised him for trying to bring him back and had taken his own path into death in spite of Llesho's efforts. He hadn't given Hmishi a choice. Even now he couldn't say he was sorry for that, but he knew the pain he felt for the Uulgar guardsman was for the man and not for himself. He was sorry to have had any part in the Harnishman's fall.

Master Den would have given a smack to the back of Llesho's head for taking credit for it, of course. The Uulgar had his own path to follow; the thread of this mortal life ended here atop the Palace of the Sun. It really *wasn't* all about him, Llesho reminded himself. What a thought! Sometimes, it wasn't even about Justice. Which felt, when he said it that way even to himself, like the spirits were laughing at him.

While Llesho pondered their relative places in the cosmos, the guardsman's companions came running, calling to each other in dismay and amazement to find him dead on the ground. Llesho pulled away from the edge. He felt bad, but not bad enough to want to follow the man or let Markko's raiders catch him.

Great Moon Lun had climbed higher, leaving the temple once again in shadows that hid him from his enemy below. Llesho curled himself deeper into the darkness, crouched against the doorway to the staircase that led down through the center of the temple. In the silence, he heard dry and ancient voices calling him down that long spiral passage. He tried to ignore them, concentrating on not being seen as Uulgar guardsmen poured through that narrow door onto the roof of the king's pavilion across the square.

Quickly, they fanned out in a circle lit by the red glow of their lanterns, looking for evidence to tell them what had happened. Someone found the sword he had dropped there, and they poked their feeble lamps into every shadow. When they found nothing else, they drew back again, returning through the hidden door into the tower.

Soon all the light atop the Palace of the Sun came from that one small square as the Harnishmen descended the tower stair. Then the light disappeared completely as the last guardsman drew the cover back into place. They'd station an extra man below it, Llesho figured. But doubtless their captain concluded that whoever had pushed the man off the pavilion had escaped in the commotion. Like the dead man, however, the guardsman might well poke his head out again to survey the territory he was meant to defend. He'd have his eyes mostly on the tower he guarded, but he might look across the square as well. Llesho decided to wait a bit longer to find his way down.

The low stone wall gave the aerie atop the Temple of the Moon some protection from the wind or a fall, but still it was bitter cold up there. As he huddled in the windswept night, Llesho gazed up into the mountains. The gates of heaven lay hidden somewhere in those heights and he followed the path of Great Moon in her flight, wondering if Lun knew the way. As he gazed upward into the silvered mountains crowned with stars, something flared so brilliantly that he had to close his eyes against it. An answer to his question? He wondered, prying his lids open again. The cacophony of whispers from the tower fell silent, then rose again in wordless song as though the tower itself had become a reed flute.

The brilliant flash of light passed, taking the singing of the tower with it. In its place appeared a sight that drew his soul like filings to a lodestone. An arc of brilliant white light, like the waning sliver of Great Moon brought down to earth, reached out from the mountains to touch down on the opening in the low stone wall that faced its mate across the queen's aerie. It made sense now, or part of it did. He'd thought the Temple of the Moon had been named for the sheen of light that set it to cold fire in the light of Great Moon Lun. But this, as if Lun herself reached a hand to the temple, he had been too young to see and had never guessed: a bridge to heaven.

It seemed to be all about bridges: the palace to the temple, the temple to the moon, the mortal realm to the heavenly. He wondered: could the gates of heaven lie at the end of that cold white bridge of light? Llesho rose from his hiding place and walked toward the edge that looked away from the square, into the mountains. Toward that bright arc of light. He'd risked one insubstantial crossing that night and survived. And now the Way stood open with a step of stone reaching out beyond the rest, a pediment on which to anchor a bridge that bore no weight. So, this great light shone not for him alone. He'd discovered one of the great mysteries of the temple and wondered if his father had known, or if this was a secret way the Goddess used.

Standing between the stanchions that marked the boundary between the stone of the temple and the insubstantial light of the white bridge, Llesho hesitated. Was he ready? Was it time? Did he have a choice?

He reached a foot for moonbeams.

Chapter Thirty-three

THE BRIDGE vanished.

"Ugh!" Llesho gasped and threw himself backward. The mysteries that surrounded him high atop the Temple of the Moon had not so dazed him that he would have followed the Uulgar guardsman to his death on the stones below. The bridge might have held him if he'd crossed before Great Moon Lun left the gates of heaven. Or maybe not. He did know that when he brought his whole being through the dreamscape and into the city he became as vulnerable to mishap as any other mortal. Dream travel took a bit of planning, something even an adept might find difficult to do while falling from a tower. So he raised himself on his elbows only far enough to scoot farther back, away from the edge.

When he'd gained some distance from disaster, he pulled himself to his feet. He had to get away while the guardsmen were busy searching the palace. The mystical path to the mountains would have served that one purpose, but it wouldn't have put him any closer to his brother, so it hadn't been the best option anyway.

The staircase at the center of the tower would have been the most obvious way down, except that it was also the most obvious way up for the Uulgar guardsmen. Which left dreamwalking. That wouldn't get him any closer to his brother—he'd been looking for Ghrisz when the dreamscape brought him here—but it would get him down off the tower, hopefully without being seen. He could look for his brother on the ground, something he couldn't do on top of the Temple of the Moon.

Slowly, Llesho dragged himself to his feet. His legs still felt like water from the night's exertions against the guardsman and, if he were telling himself the truth, from his sudden terror when the bridge of moonlight had disappeared from under him. It was more than the physical exhaustion that slowed the pace of his running circle, however. The memory of voices beckoned him to the inner tower with soft whispers. His mother had lived here when he was small, with her priests and acolytes. Worshipers and diplomats had passed through the great audience hall below, and on special occasions the queen, his mother, had stood on this platform high above the city to greet her husband who waited on the other side, at the Palace of the Sun.

His mother and his grandmother, aunts and uncles who served the Moon, had trod those steps through all the ages that Kungol had stood among these sacred mountains. Their ghosts called to him out of all his lives, both past and present. He hadn't had the time with Bolghai to take the last test of his dream-walking skills, to visit the underworld in dream. This wasn't quite the same thing, of course, but he thought it just might do. And he did have to get to the street below somehow. Holding onto the balustrade to steady his way, Llesho moved into the shelter of the tower.

He'd thought the way must be dark as a moonless night inside the temple, or that guardsmen must stand in wait at every turn. But at his first step, a soft glow, like moonlight on white pearls, pulsed from the walls. It brightened ahead of him with each turning of the spiral staircase while above the way grew dark again as he passed. Llesho listened past the darkness for a sound that would mean discovery but heard no guardsmen on patrol.

He should have realized that no Uulgar would enter the temple to find the dead man's assailant: spirits whispered in the dark, growing more pronounced as he descended the staircase. Moving away as the light came nearer, the gentle sigh of their voices never faded wholly out of reach, never came close enough for Llesho to make out exactly what they said. As he descended from one level to the next the sounds faded away, replaced by new voices. Ancient laughter reached for him out of the distance of time. He heard song in a language he knew as Thebin but couldn't understand. The words had changed, the accent, though he recognized the sound and tone of it as the high-court tongue.

Down another level and weeping greeted him, the high keening wail of mourning and, beyond the ritual of grief, the inconsolable sounds of pain. Some long-ago queen had suffered a great and terrible loss here. He remembered his own dear Goddess, weeping for him in visions of lives past counting and blood upon his own breast. The thought that he might be listening to the weeping for his own dead self in those other lives sent a superstitious shiver from his heels to the top of his head.

Not again. He had tamed the spear he carried and had further determined not to draw it again, regardless of the peril in which he found himself. The spear itself would always be the greater threat.

"Not again," he whispered to the voices echoing out of time against the glowing stones of the Temple of the Moon, and around again. Another turning of the spiral, another age. The temple was wider at its base by far than at its top, and each circling on the spiral of the stairs grew longer. Distant sounds of battle came to him, the cold, sure voice of a queen of Thebin defending her temple.

Another round, more whispers. His face brightened to the color of old burgundy. Love cries, and murmured caresses. He didn't want to think about what other things went on when the king of Thebin visited his Goddess-wife in her temple. Too human sounds, the slide of flesh on flesh, a grunt, a sigh. He closed his ears to it and went on, wished it back again at the next turning.

Screaming. Terror, panic, pain. Boots and battering rams and curses in a language Llesho knew for Harnish, a higher, shriller version than the Qubal spoke. He had reached the base of the temple and with it had come to the most recent of its history.

The crash of swords, the warm voice of his mother, forgiving her murderers in the name of the Goddess while her priests and priestesses wept softly around her. Llesho froze, paralyzed by the soft hiss of a sword leaving its scabbard, so familiar that he felt the sympathetic shift in the weight at his own side as a memory of steel moved from hip to hand. And then the gentle voice of the queen his mother was cut off in mid prayer to the horror of her courtiers.

"Her head! Her head!"

"Don't let it fall!"

Llesho's legs refused to hold him. He slid down in a curled-up squat with his arms wrapped around his knees and his forehead pressed against the balustrade, trying to keep his stomach where it belonged while he listened to the death of his mother and the high, terrified shrieks of a child being carried away to her death. His sister, his mother, had died here and he hadn't been able to stop it. The fact that he'd seen only seven summers at the time, hadn't even been in the temple when it happened, didn't enter into it. He should have found a way to be here, and he would suffer her death over and over again until he found a way to make it right.

Except that he was fairly certain that he was going as mad as his brother Lluka. Perhaps that was the fatal flaw: a madness that ran through the Thebin royal family that had brought down the kingdom and all that it had protected in the temple and in the mountains. Or had their failure broken them? A gentle hand swept the hair out of his eyes. Llesho jerked his head up, saw no one. The cool fingertips soothed as they passed across his brow, not the sinister threat of Master Markko's touch or the rough attack of an Uulgar raider. For a moment, the weeping had stopped.

"Mother?"

"Champion."

Not his mother, who remained irretrievably dead. He recognized the voice, though.

"My Lady Goddess?"

"Champion," she repeated.

Llesho felt a touch as of a kiss at his cheek. He remembered a conversation long ago, when Kaydu had asked a loaded question: *Who are you?* He'd wanted to put off the question, hadn't been ready, back then, to share the secrets of his birth and the deaths that had followed his seventh summer, so he'd answered with more irony than he knew. "Just another Champion of the Goddess."

Half priest, half knight, the champions wandered from kingdom to kingdom performing deeds of chivalry and daring in the name of the Goddess. They were seldom presentable and generally considered mad. Which fit him as descriptions went, Llesho figured.

"Your champion," he answered back, not knowing if she heard him or not. The gates of heaven remained closed and under siege while her voice traveled through what ages down that terrible staircase he couldn't guess. Or perhaps, the whole temple had been possessed of ghosts and spirits all along and he hadn't heard them as child because his mother had protected him from that knowledge.

It didn't take a magician to know that he didn't belong here now, that he'd go truly and completely mad if he didn't escape it soon. So, up again, to his feet. He tried to remember if he'd ever seen this particular staircase when he had visited with his mother in the temple, but no memory came to him of any such place by sunlight. He wondered if the temple shifted into some other realm by moonlight, so that it abided only partly among mortals, while part belonged to the realm of heaven or of spirits. If that were true the staircase might exist only on the moonlit side of reality.

He could become trapped on the wrong side of that reality forever if he let himself dither about it. Better to keep moving, which would at least give him distance from the voices that had returned to whisper defeat and heart stopping sorrow in his ear. Off to the left, the dark seemed less dense and he went in that direction as if a beacon called him. He stumbled once over a piece of furniture that went over with a snap of fragile wood, and once he bumped into something that didn't move at all but left a bruise the size of his fist on his hip. But the light grew stronger, and soon he could see that the worst of the broken furniture had been piled up along a wall, and that someone had righted the candlesticks, though they remained dented and empty of candles.

And there, in front of him, was a door. Not the great front doors that had stood open like two arms waiting to receive the palace—or the king who resided within it. He recognized this small side door as the one he'd used as a child. Accompanied by his bodyguard Khri and a priestess nursemaid, he had often come this way to spend the day with his mother. Now he stumbled through and turned his face to the faint light of false dawn. A weight lifted from his heart, as if he'd just awakened from a harrowing dream. And yet, a longing more powerful than pain called him back to the inner temple and its whispering voices. He wanted his mother back, even if all he had of her was the sound of her voice at the moment of her death.

The sense of what he was thinking hit him like a blow to the gut. "No!" he groaned. "Oh, Goddess, nooo!"

As he curled into the pain, both arms wrapped around his gut, the shadows stirred and came to life.

Chapter Thirty-four

A FIGURE of rags and shadows raised out of the darker depths of the doorway. "Are you some ghost out of legends?" it asked in a lightly husky whisper.

Llesho would have said the same thing back. For a brief moment that sped up his heartbeat he thought that Ghrisz somehow knew they were on the way and had sent someone to meet him. His brother's name was on his lips but he bit back the words. Who knew what Harnish spies might hear? He was glad he did when the dim gray light of false dawn brought the blurred face of a young girl into sharper focus. This beggar who held her ground in front of what she took for wonders might have been a ghost herself, some ancient ancestor out of the darkness of that terrible staircase. Her question made that unlikely, of course. Llesho's experience in the temple had him jumping at shadows everywhere.

"Not a ghost," he therefore answered, keeping the bit about legend in reserve. He had returned to Kungol with a face out of history to follow a prophecy, after all. It wouldn't help his cause to start out here with a lie to his own people.

The beggar didn't look convinced. On closer examination, as the light grew stronger, Llesho decided that the girl didn't look like a beggar either. Her clothes were rags and tatters, her face smudged with real grime from the streets, and she had the

smell to go along with her fallen state. The disguise might even
have worked against an enemy she knew the shape of. Faced
with wonders, however, the stranger's eyes calculated angles of
escape and attack, and the longer odds that this wonder out of
a night steeped in mystery might be of use to her. A spy, then,
which wasn't hard to figure. But whose? And why did he get
the feeling he'd seen her before when he hadn't been back to
the city since his seventh summer? Llesho came up with no
satisfactory answer to any of his questions.

"Not a ghost. A legend, then?" the spy prodded.

The girl—she didn't look even as old as he was, though it
was difficult to tell what was under all that dirt in the gray
morning light—was sharp. Thebin, by the look and sound of
her, and posted at a door the importance of which only someone very high in the confidences of the royal family would
know. Master Jak's clan of mercenary guardsmen had known,
but the Harn had murdered them in the attack. The priests and
priestesses whose death cries he had heard on the stairs had
known. Was she a ghost after all?

Or had Ghrisz posted her here to keep watch? For what? Was
his brother expecting his own answer to the prophecy to turn
up here? Master Markko had the skills to scry his whereabouts.
The magician might have set a watch for him when he recognized where Llesho had landed. But he didn't think Markko
would trust a Thebin girl as his lookout. Wouldn't expect anyone else to trust the job to a girl either, which made her the
perfect choice if she was working for the resistance.

Llesho was used to taking risks on himself. Now, he decided,
it was time to take a risk on another person. "Some might say I
am the answer to a prophecy," he answering the beggar-spy's
question, more or less. Legend seemed a bit more than Llesho
was willing to claim, so he left it for her to determine.

"I'm looking for a jewel, a sapphire." The sapphire princess
of stories, he meant. It was sort of a test. Would she know the
truth behind the story?

The spy denied any knowledge of such a treasure. "The
Harn stole every trinket before either of us was old enough to
fight them. There are no jewels in Kungol now." The pupils of

her eyes tightened to pinpoints, however. Llesho's explanation of his presence had rattled the girl, no matter the deliberate way she failed to take Llesho's meaning. Hoped for, he figured, but he hadn't been expected.

Great Sun had touched the mountains while they talked; they had no time left to stand around and debate the issue. Someone would spot them and then there would be questions from the Harn. With the light the beggar-spy saw what Llesho was wearing. She managed to control her reaction quickly enough, but Llesho looked down at himself, wondering what she saw that sent that look of mingled disbelief and yearning crashing through her carefully blank expression. When he saw his coat, he remembered—he'd taken this dream-journey dressed in the riding clothes of a long-dead royal court.

"I'm not looking for a trinket," he said, referring to the girl's claim that the Thebins hid no treasure from their oppressors. "Your master will know what I'm talking about."

There it was. "Take me to your leader" as clear as he could make it. He thought the spy must have noticed that he wore the face of long-dead kings as well as one of their coats. Hoped as well that he hadn't just invited himself into Master Markko's clutches again. But the spy had made up her mind.

"Take off your coat," she gritted between clenched teeth.

Llesho did as he was told.

The spy took the coat with a quick, disgusted glance at the empty scabbard at his side. She didn't entirely come out of her cringing slouch when she saw Llesho's Thebin knife, but the look became more frozenly blank after that.

"I hope you have another one of these somewhere," she said, and with a deft twist turned the coat inside out and slashed it down the back with her own knife.

"Master Den will have one somewhere, I am sure." Llesho had never figured out where he got them, but the trickster god always seemed to have the proper clothes at hand when he needed them. He took the spy's point, however; running around the streets of Kungol in early daylight wearing an elaborately embroidered court coat would draw more attention than they could possibly handle. Inside out and badly torn the coat became just another rag on another street beggar. He slipped into it, noted that it didn't do a thing to protect him from the wind anymore.

He rubbed his boots in the ugly dirt caught up by the wind and gathered in the doorway to the temple and managed to get some of it on his chin and across his forehead as well. Only a handful of the Harn who controlled the city—the raiders who had murdered the royal family—had seen the king, his father, so he wasn't worried about being recognized for who he was. But he didn't want to stand out in the thin crowd of impoverished, dispirited countrymen. When he had reduced his appearance to match her own, the spy gave him an approving nod and led him out into the city.

As a child Llesho had seldom traveled on foot in the city. He had few memories to compare with the sight that now greeted him but he knew that even the worst of the city's poor had never lived like this. Many of the houses were abandoned, their walls cracked and crumbling to rubble that trickled in untidy heaps into the streets and thoroughfares. Those buildings that still showed signs of life—clothing draped out in the sun to dry on the heaps of rubble, piles of trash and slops both fresh and ripened in the street—were in little better shape, with windows broken and doors unhinged in toothless grimaces. They passed a street of temples leveled by fire that had passed from building to building. The mud walls didn't burn, but the fire had consumed the wooden beams and emptied out the rubble fill. With the supports gone, the mud plaster tumbled inward of its own unsupported weight. Each took down the next like a row of toppling dominoes.

Llesho remembered how the smells of Kungol had delighted him as a child: incense and spice and excitement. This new foul smell of a city dying amid its own excrement bore no relation to that long ago pleasure. *It's a dream*. He tried to convince himself it wasn't real. But Lluka's visions mocked him with the truth, that the dream world held worse for Kungol and all the realms of the living and the dead and the Great Goddess who ruled the gardens of heaven. Kungol at least they could rebuild. The world after that great cataclysm would die forever, unless he killed Master Markko's demon. That future sickened him and he faltered.

"This is no time to fall apart. Come on." The spy took his arm, not roughly, but with some urgency. She couldn't be seen offering support in a way that would alert their overseers to his presence. "This way."

One step at a time. Llesho roused himself from his brooding. First he had to find Ghrisz. Then he had to alert his armies. More than that would have to await events as they unfolded. The spy ducked past a broken door, into the last standing niche of a public building—countinghouse or shrine, there was no telling anymore—that had long ago succumbed to fire and conflict. Llesho followed, drawn through by an insistent tug on his elbow, and nearly tumbled down a ladder hidden in the shadows.

"Ah! What the—" The spy caught him up short with a firm hand raised to his collar. Suddenly, he returned to his senses and had to wonder where this stranger was taking him. What did she plan to do with him when they got there? And more pointedly, why had he followed the girl in the first place? Not memories of a long-dead childhood, but something more recent. A dream.

"I saw you in a dream-walk." He had it now. "You were praying by moonlight on top of the temple."

"You're mistaken. Down, and careful about it, if you please, my lord." The spy dismissed his assertion and punctuated her order with a nudge in the right direction, which Llesho had come to expect in his dealings outside his own camp. She finished with a court-mannered politeness to a noble visitor, if not a prince, however, which left all her meanings up in the air. Llesho puzzled over the contradiction while he groped for the ladder in the dim light from the shattered doorway.

They climbed down into the dark below. Kungol never had dug cellars or secret tunnels like the Shan, but sometime in the past eleven turnings of the seasons the city had sprouted tunnels and more, like the roots of trees growing in secret while their crowns shed their leaves and went to sleep. The Harn seemed unlikely to have done it, though he'd have said they didn't build walls either, before he'd seen the monstrosity that circled Kungol these days.

Master Markko had lived in the North, however, and knew the ways of the empire of Shan, where the capital city was surrounded by a wall riddled with tunnels like this. Still, it seemed unlikely the Harn, even under the magician's less than tender command, would have had the time or inclination to both build a wall and dig a tunnel system to subvert it. Which left the resistance. "You did this," he tested out the conclusion. "The Harn don't know these tunnels exist, do they?"

The girl examined her broken, dirty fingernails with exaggerated thoughtfulness. "Tunnels? What tunnels?" Llesho wasn't going to learn anything from her, at least not until she had taken him to her leader and they decided what to do about him.

A door blocked the way ahead. She knocked in a pattern of raps, to which a tiny window opened at eye level, closed again without a word. The sound of a bar being removed came through the thick wood, and then the door swung inward. A small, firm hand at his back propelled Llesho into the murk. Their coattails had scarcely cleared the entrance before a guardsman with the look of the mercenary clans who had served in the court of his father pushed the door back into place.

The man had iron gray hair and a face seamed with hardship more than age. He reminded Llesho a little bit of Master Jaks; all that clan shared a certain likeness, even Khri, who had died when Llesho was seven. He thought he looked enough like his father that the mercenary wouldn't kill him right off. Getting them to help might be more complicated, but he was probably safe for the moment with these resistance fighters.

"Mgar," the spy greeted the doorman in the high-court dialect. He responded with a quick nod of greeting and put his shoulder into the door.

"Help me with this," the mercenary grunted at Llesho. Between them they set a thick bar in place across the center of the door. When they had secured the secret entrance, the door-man turned the flame up on a lamp hanging from a chain at the turning of their tunnel.

"Is he here?" The beggar-spy, whose name had not come up in the exchange, asked. The doorman gave a single dip of the chin, answer enough for Llesho's guide.

"Then he'll want to see this one. He came out of the temple, but I didn't see him go in."

The mercenary's eyes widened slightly, then narrowed again around a long memory of disappointments. "I'll need his weapons."

The girl shrugged one shoulder and left it to the doorman to disarm him. Llesho's sword was already gone, abandoned on the king's pavilion atop the Palace of the Sun. He showed the guard his empty scabbard, but refused to give up the spear or his Thebin knife.

"If this is the headquarters of Prince Ghrisz, he will under-stand. If it is not, we had best begin now—" Llesho set his hand to the spear at his back, but the doorman raised both hands in a placating gesture.

"Let it be, Mgar," the girl-spy said. "If he's who I think he is, Ghrisz will want to see those things. But watch him."

Llesho turned to acknowledge the girl's intervention on his behalf, but she had disappeared down one of the branching tun-nels that ran away from the entrance.

"This way," Mgar said, and prodded Llesho ahead of him.

Lamps scattered at intervals through the tunnels gave enough dim light so they didn't trip as they made their way underground. But there wasn't anything to see except the rough dirt that nearly brushed his shoulders on either side. To keep from panicking, Llesho concentrated on figuring out the spy. When they left the surface for this dank hole in the ground the girl's posture and step had subtly shifted. Her back had straight-ened, her head came up, and her slouching shuffle became a swift light gait carrying her away from him just as he wanted to ply her with questions.

She'd left him in the hands of a mercenary guardsman. Lle-sho'd thought they'd all died in the invasion, but he would have known this Mgar for what he was even if he had never seen his face or heard him utter a word. Master Jaks had moved like that and so had Llesho's bodyguard Khri. Lately Bixei had grown to do the same. Sometimes, Llesho did himself. Mgar was a soldier, well trained and seasoned in combat of one sort or another.

Raiders of the Uulgar ulus had taken Kungol and held it by force of their army's savagery. They had no need of tunnels to hide in or secret knocks at hidden doors. All the evidence pointed to the resistance, who might see salvation in a returning king or a threat to their leader's autonomy. If it was Ghrisz, of course. If it truly was his brother—

"Wait here."

They had entered an open space carved out of the cold dry earth. The single lamp hanging from a support beam gave a feeble circle of light that extended no more than a pace or two in any direction, but the flow of air felt different. Mgar's voice didn't bounce in the hard bright way it had in the tunnels. So, a larger space, but not empty either. Anything could be waiting for him beyond that coin of light, which made the light itself more a danger than a comfort. Llesho gave a nod to indicate he understood the order. Mgar turned and walked away, back the way he had come. And Llesho took one step to the left, out of the light. And then another, soundless, back toward the wall.

When his hand came in contact with the rough surface he drew his knife and cut a mark into the hard-packed dirt at shoulder height. Keeping his free hand in contact with the wall, he moved away from the mark he had made, counting the paces that measured off the perimeter of the chamber. Ten ahead before he came to the corner and had to turn right. He had gone ten more paces when a tinder flared. A lamp came up, then another, and another. Enough to shed light on the room he'd been measuring with his feet. Enough to recognize the figure who sat watching him from a chair not five paces from where Llesho had stopped in his circuit.

Prince Ghrisz of Thebin examined him with an arched brow but made no immediate comment. Ghrisz had been away much of Llesho's early childhood and, of course, they hadn't seen each other since the Harn invaded, but Llesho recognized him by the family resemblance to their brother Shokar. Ghrisz must have seen the family resemblance as well, but he gave no sign of it.

The prince sat in an artfully carved chair covered in richly embroidered fabric, one of a dozen such around a conference table. The luxury of the chairs should have looked absurd in the roughly dug cellar. Ghrisz should have looked like a madman playing at being king. But only one of the twelve chairs was empty. The rest each held a man or woman with an air of fallen grace and ragged desperation. This was the power center of the resistance; Llesho felt sure of it. Their rescued furnishings seemed more a reminder of what they had lost than any comfort.

Still, Llesho could have used the doubtful ease of one of those chairs about now. He'd slept so much in Ibn Al-Razi's hospital in Pontus that Llesho had thought he'd never have to sleep again. That quiet time seemed like an eternity ago to him now.

"He's resourceful, I'll give you that," an elderly man commented from the bottom of the long table. "And he looks very like the king, your father."

"Perhaps." The prince leaned forward in his chair. "What are you doing here, boy? How did you get into the Temple of the Moon without any of my guards seeing you enter, and how did you get out again with your sanity intact? Or was Mgar wrong about that last?"

Llesho scarcely heard the questions. "Ghrisz?" he asked. Now that he had reached his goal he was afraid to believe it.

"Mad after all, then," Ghrisz said, though he didn't deny his identity. "No one in this city speaks that name. Who are you, boy?"

"Llesho," he said. With a little smile and a wave that took in the city above them, he added, "They tell me I am king of all this." He wanted to say more, but the lamps seemed to dim around the edges.

"He's bleeding!" A voice called a sharp warning out of the descending dark.

Who? Llesho wondered. But the ground was coming up at him very fast . . .

"It can't be the prince. Prince Llesho died on the Long March." Ghrisz's voice, a little above him and to the right, brought Llesho back to his senses. Or, from the sound of it, the prince had been talking for some time and Llesho had regained consciousness only for the last of his argument: "Don't you think I would have found him if he'd survived?"

That was a question worth contemplating. Slowly, Llesho returned to awareness. He had one of those padded chairs under him and someone had wrapped a bandage tightly around his arm, where the guardsman had marked him in the fight on the king's pavilion. He'd forgotten the wound, until he'd dropped like a stone in front of his brother's council. Now it throbbed in a dull, insistent way that didn't quite penetrate the lethargy that clung to him from his faint. He was safe for the moment, and he'd found the last of his brothers. If he'd had something to eat the moment would have been almost perfect. As his brother's words penetrated the haze of well-being, however, the dangers of his position unsettled his fogbound peace. If not himself, who did Ghrisz think he was? No one seemed to notice the hitch in his breathing as he shifted an aching rib off the arm of his chair. He kept quiet, hoping if they thought he still slept they would continue to talk about him as if he wasn't there. His answer came even sooner than he'd prayed.

"You can't deny the family resemblance," an aged voice Llesho didn't recognize objected. "You didn't know your father when he was as young as that boy. The likeness is uncanny, as if your father himself had returned in the blush of youth."

"Do you think he's a ghost, sent from the temple to warn us of some new danger?" The spy who had brought him here, that was. He was pretty sure she hadn't been at the table when he'd fainted in the middle of Ghrisz's questioning. Her tone had the steel of command in it in spite of her age and he wondered if he'd underestimated her status on his brother's council. He wished she'd call out his name to be sure, but he thought he'd heard her calling to him in his dream travels as well. What was she doing in his dreams?

Cracking his eyelids, he hoped no one would see the gleaming slits of his eyes but the table itself blocked his view of the advisers who sat around it.

"Ghosts there may be." Ghrisz's tone made it clear that he believed in no such thing, though he gave the suggestion his grave consideration in spite of his own doubt. "If they should exist—"

"They do," the girl insisted.

Ghrisz conceded with a nod to accept the rebuke before finishing his analysis. "It seems unlikely, however, that they would suddenly quit the tower they have haunted all these turnings of the seasons. Less likely still that they would bleed themselves away into a dead faint at our feet before delivering their unearthly message.

"No, he's human enough. But who sent him? And where did they find a boy who looked so much like the king?"

"He says he *is* the king," another voice chimed in. Llesho thought he recognized that one from somewhere, too. Likely his own father's council chambers, where they'd stolen this table from the Harn, he realized.

"So you, too, believe in phantoms?" Ghrisz again, irritated with his counselors.

"Perhaps. No living man has come out of the temple since we set a watch on it. None of our spies saw anyone enter by their own posts. But someone threw a Harnish raider off the king's pavilion last night."

Another voice, deep with years, added support to his fellow councillor: "Rumor in the marketplace confirms our own reports that no one went in or out of the temple. Only Uulgar clansmen entered or left the palace, and that only at the changing of the guard—except the guardsman who took the short route to the ground during the night."

"He strayed too close to the edge," Ghrisz countered that

argument. "Or one of their own dispatched him, in some argument between thieves."

Llesho was on the point of revealing himself to defend the honor of the soldier. The man had fought wonders in the performance of his duty on that tower, and had died of wonders, though not at ghostly hands. But Ghrisz picked up the thread of his argument, and Llesho listened.

"No, the boy is clearly a living being. Note the rise and fall of his ribs as he breathes, and the fact that he rests with his face on the council table rather than passing through it like a vapor. That leaves us no closer to understanding who he is or why he has come, however.

"If he truly is the prince, who has held him in secret all these cycles of the seasons since Kungol fell to the Harn? If he's an imposter, who went to the effort to find a Thebin boy with such a striking likeness to Kungol's dead king?"

"He doesn't necessarily look like the king," another voice objected. "Someone may have set a glamour on his features to deceive us with his appearance."

"But why have his captors—or his makers—sent him to us now?" Ghrisz wanted to know.

No one at that table hazarded a guess, but the first who had spoken from among Ghrisz's advisers did make a suggestion. "If we knew how he got into that tower, we'd have some of our answers," he suggested, bringing them back to the center of the argument.

"I don't know how he came to be inside the Temple of the Moon," the girl who had brought him here gave her own testimony to the council. "But I know how he left it. And I know that since the priests were killed no man has survived the descent from the tower. If he's not the king, then why is he still alive?"

Llesho wondered the same about her. Why had he seen her in a dream on the queen's pavilion above the Temple of the Moon? Did she pray regularly in the ancient place of the queen, or had he seen her there in another life? Who was she?

Llesho had the answers they debated—or some of them— while he pretended to sleep. He wasn't quite ready to ask his own questions, but figured Ghrisz was onto him and wanted him to hear their deliberations. But it was time to wake up and start talking before they'd argued themselves into believing their own speculations. So he yawned and stretched in a broad display of rousing from his collapse.

Chapter Thirty-five

As LLESHO expected, Ghrisz showed no surprise when he stretched and blinked himself awake at the council table.

"And do you have anything to add to our councils, my young lord?" the resistance leader asked with exaggerated politeness.

He didn't offer to explain, which told Llesho his brother had a good sense of when he'd actually woken and started to listen. That was fine with Llesho. He didn't want to deceive his brother; he'd just needed time to get a sense of where he stood. Which wasn't in good shape, but he figured he could talk his way through that.

"I'll answer any questions you want about myself," he offered. Honesty compelled him to add, "By your own arguments, if I were a stranger picked up on the streets because I look like a dead king would I tell you the truth? If a magician had laid spells on me, would I even know the truth?"

That was a question that woke him up at night in his own camp, surrounded by gods and kings. Master Markko had poisoned him and could evoke those poisons even now. What else had he done that might make of Llesho a weapon against his own allies?

"I can only tell you what I've seen and what my teachers and allies believe about me. Which is that I am his Holy Excellence, King Llesho, the seventh son of my father the king, and his chosen successor.''

"And so you would take my throne, boy?" That was the first time Prince Ghrisz had admitted his identity, though he looked to the girl when he spoke. She gave no sign that she had noticed but focused her wide blue eyes on Llesho, as if she could weigh the merit of his soul in his answers.

Now that he was here and had found the last of his brothers, impatience got the better of him. Llesho heaved a sigh, thinking of how many times he'd been tested and judged by gods and kings. Not by his brothers, though. He hadn't always appreciated their greetings—Balar had hit him over the head with a lute and carted him off flung over a camel—but they had never doubted who he was.

"At the moment, Master Markko holds the throne." Llesho's eyes lifted of their own accord in a telling glance at the dirt ceiling over their heads. He didn't know yet if he could defeat the magician but he was pretty sure his brother couldn't.

Ghrisz bristled at the insult, which Llesho hadn't intended as such but which struck the entire council a blow. They didn't deserve that of him. While Llesho had battled his way across the vast expanse of empires, they had fought a hidden war in these tunnels and caves. He didn't want to make enemies of the very people who might find a way for his armies to enter the city undetected. Time to make his play, therefore, before they answered the rebuke with rising tempers. But first he had to convince them he was the real thing.

"You asked who sent me. It was her ladyship SienMa, the mortal goddess of war. I'm here to throw out the Uulgar raiders and take the throne of our father away from the magician who leads them. Who sits in it when I'm done can wait for a later discussion.''

That could have been more diplomatically stated. It wasn't even completely accurate, but he had an army cooling its heels while they debated the question. Llesho tried again. "Lleck, our father's minister, set me on a quest to find my brothers and take Thebin back from the Harn. The Lady SienMa took an interest and has helped me on my long road from Pearl Bay to the Palace of the Sun."

He didn't think mentioning the trickster god would help his cause. Shou and Mergen would take some leading up to, let alone Marmer Sea Dragon, so he kept quiet on those allies and advisers.

"Lleck died during the sack of Kungol," a woman told him with a cold voice and sorrow creasing her face. No one at that table addressed the others by any name or title, as if afraid that hostile ears might know them and single out their targets by the level of respect their fellow councillors afforded them. It was a sensible precaution and he followed their lead in it.

"He didn't die in the attack." He wasn't sure if she'd consider the news he brought the good kind or the bad. "Somehow he escaped and found his way to Pearl Island, where he taught me and cared for me until his death in my fifteenth summer. It was then he sent me on my quest." Lleck had died again, as a bear cub fighting monsters in the battle for the Imperial City of Shan, but he didn't think that story would add to his credibility with Ghrisz's court. The part he still had to tell was bad enough.

"A dying man's wish for home," an adviser to his brother suggested with a shake of his head. "The likeness must have addled his brain."

"A dead man's quest," Llesho corrected him. "His ghost appeared to me while I worked beneath the waves of Pearl Bay."

Ghrisz was not convinced. He looked at Llesho as he might at any false claimant. "So you said. To rescue your brothers. Another lie—my brothers are dead." He made no exception for Llesho, who stood before him accused of being an imposter. "And so you appear on my doorstep with an empty scabbard and a ragged coat, telling tales of wandering the length of the known world.

"Why don't you give up and just tell the truth? You must know your story has fallen apart. You populate your tales convincingly enough with names you've heard out of legend or gossip, never thinking that the people at this table knew intimately as friends these characters you weave into your lies. Except for those you create out of children's stories and legends, of course.''

By that Llesho figured his brother meant the Lady SienMa. He forgot sometimes that everyone didn't call upon the gods as their personal advisers.

Ghrisz wasn't finished, though. "Your story suits a madman more than an impostor set upon treachery! So I will answer you in kind: I will do as you bid and gladly when these magical creatures make their request of me in person. But I find their emissary singularly lacking.''

The gathered ministers stirred in their seats, voices rumbling at what they saw as the upstart's insult. But Llesho smiled. His brother didn't want to believe, but he was in for a lot of surprises.

"I've traveled not only the length of the world, but it's breadth as well. In Pontus I found a prophecy which is said to have reached even as far as Kungol.'' He gave a moment's pause to gather his thoughts, then began to recite:

> *"Seven lost princes find their brother*
> *Six heads crowned with stars a gate have hidden*
> *Five armies, like one hand, close around them*
> *Four worms breathing fire rise above them*
> *Three bitter gifts must teach a bitter lesson*
> *Two paths are offered, one is chosen*
> *One jewel alone, to each must be another.''*

"I've heard it,'' the girl-spy, who had kept quiet for most of the discussion, spoke up now. As he'd guessed when they'd crossed the city together, she was younger than he was—surprisingly young, really, to be sitting in on the decision-making of the resistance. "A little differently and in the common tongue as you'd expect on the streets. Once even in Harnish. Until recently I thought as we all did that my brothers were dead and was unwilling to have the last of them join the others. We needed you alive, so I kept the verse to myself. Now, I think, we have to question what it means all over again. And, by the way, where did an impostor who looks like the long-dead king learn to speak the language of the court?"

Ghrisz clearly hadn't thought of that. Hadn't, from the shock that crossed his face, noticed that they were speaking a language which should have been alien to an impostor's tongue.

"He's well trained for his role," he grumbled. "Lleck might have done it, if he truly had been fooled by a passing likeness."

Llesho knew how closely he resembled his father and their ancient ancestor. The face he wore had called in debts to history owed by the Qubal clans, and he'd seen himself, older and dying in some past life across a river of time. But the girl who had brought him here from the temple had a more pertinent question:

"Why send an impostor now? If we had the power to seize the throne we would have done so already and put our own prince on it. The appearance of someone we don't know claiming to have some special right to the throne doesn't put us any closer to winning it back than we were before. The best he can hope to gain is the same beggar's dinner the rest of us eat. That and a cold place to sleep."

"A spy," the woman who had thought Lleck dead in the raid on Kungol spoke up. "One part of his tale may be true. The Harn took many slaves before and after the invasion. As a slave they may have trained him to spy on us. If we let him go he will surely report our movements to his masters."

"He isn't going anywhere."

Llesho kept quiet about the abilities that had brought him here, and that would take him away again at will. Ghrisz had a deadly look in his eyes; complete honesty about his gifts could get him killed. He didn't want to leave anyway—at least not until he'd convinced his brother that help was on the way.

"I didn't come to ask your help. Well, not the kind you think. I'm here because of the prophecy. 'Seven lost princes find their brother'—that was the first part of the quest: find my brothers— alive. You're the last, Ghrisz. I've found the others: Adar and Shokar in the empire of Shan, Balar and Lluka among the dream readers of Ahkenbad in the Gansau Wastes, and Menar last before you, blinded and a slave in the house of a physician in Pontus."

"An easy claim to make when you are standing in front of us alone and in rags no better than our own," Ghrisz challenged him.

Oh! "Just a minute." Llesho dragged his coat off, turned it right side out and slipped it on again, this time with the elaborate embroideries of Thebin court clothes on the outside.

Eyes widened around the council table. No one of them retained the finery of the palace, and even in this light they could see that his own coat's tears had happened recently.

"I was afraid someone would see us and recognize the coat," the girl said.

Llesho remembered something else. "I left my sword on the king's pavilion, but I still have my knife."

With that he pulled aside the front of his coat to show the blade in its sheath at his side. Except for the wooden signet afixed to the butt that held the Lady Chaiujin prisoner, it looked like the knife that Ghrisz wore on his own belt.

"How—?" A man old enough to have been an adviser under his father's rule spoke up with a querulous resistance to wonder in his voice.

Ghrisz silenced him with a raised hand. "You threw the Harnishman off the tower in the palace?"

"No." Llesho shook his head, half in denial and half to rid his mind of the image of the guardsman stepping after him on that bridge of light. Falling. With a shiver, he repeated the denial. "We fought, but I left him with just a small wound, like my own." He touched the bandage on his arm to demonstrate. "He tried to follow me and stepped off the edge." It didn't seem the time to tell them about the bridge of light. It felt like one of those hidden mysteries you weren't supposed to talk about. They didn't believe anything he'd said yet anyway, so he let them think what they wanted.

Ghrisz had moved from outright rejection to reserving judgment, however. "This prophecy. You say you found our brothers alive. I'll take that statement as the first verse in a story. Go on."

Llesho picked up where he had stopped. "The first was the easiest line to understand because Lleck had already sent me looking for the princes and I'd already found all but you. The rest of the rhyme was harder, but Menar put his head together with the Apadisha's magicians and we worked on it together. Once we figured it out it seemed pretty obvious."

"Obvious?" Ghrisz lifted a dubious brow while around him his advisers muttered, "Magicians!" with fear and loathing, and, "the Apadisha!" with doubt and calculation.

It had seemed a lot simpler to figure out once he'd stood atop the Temple of the Moon than it was in the Apadisha's Divan, but Llesho didn't mention that. "More obvious if you've spent any time with a Harnish shaman," he did admit. "They speak in riddles all the time."

"A Harnish shaman, a slave—no, wait," Ghrisz bid him with a wave of his hand, "Two enslaved princes and a Harnish shaman gather to discuss a prophecy about Thebin with the magicians of Pontus. This tale grows stranger and stranger."

"It didn't happen quite that way." Llesho didn't think the truth—that Bolghai was busy with the emperor of Shan, and so had no time to consult with the Apadisha of Bithynia—would help him out here. "I met this shaman. He used Shannish words with me, but he spoke in riddles just the same. To understand what he wanted, I had to figure out his riddle-speech. When we were trying to figure out the prophecy, I remembered about the riddles, and then it became easier. 'Six heads crowned with stars' are the six mountains around Kungol covered with glaciers. As for 'A gate have hidden'—what gate lies hidden in the mountains above the city?"

The gates of heaven. They all knew it, but no one spoke the words aloud.

"That gate is under siege." That was Llesho's real battle, but first they had to take back Kungol.

"Five armies?" Ghrisz asked. Something fired his eyes, as if he had guessed some part of what must come next.

But that would serve better at the end, after all the evidence was given, so Llesho shook his head. "That line and the last were the hardest to figure out. I'm still not sure we have it right."

"Four worms breathing fire, then," Ghrisz prodded, moving to the next line of the prophecy.

"Dragons," Llesho answered, "Four of them."

The snorts and sniffs about the table let him know well enough what the Thebin court in hiding thought of such mythical creatures.

The young girl, however, watched him with wide, unblinking eyes. Blue eyes, he noted. Ping had had eyes like that and he wondered if the girl was a cousin or some distant relative he'd forgotten. With a little sigh she finally freed him from the captivity of her gaze. "You've seen them, haven't you? The dragons. What are they like?"

Her elders looked askance at her, but Llesho couldn't hold back the little smile that sneaked across his mouth. "There is no one way for dragons. I knew Pearl Bay Dragon Queen for many years in human form as a lowly healer who tended the divers on Pearl Island. I've seen her only once since then, but I count her one of the creatures I love most in all the world."

"On the other hand, the first time I saw Golden River Dragon I thought he was a stone bridge carved in the shape of a beast. I had barely crossed when he sank into the river, drowning many of my enemies and turning others away in terror at the shore. Then he ate my new healer, Mara, who aspires to be the eighth mortal god. Fortunately he swallowed her whole and so he was able to let her go again when she insisted."

An old man at the table, one who had not spoken yet, pursed his lips as though judging the tale of a marketplace storyteller. "You recount more exploits already than most adventurers can claim in a lifetime, and yet we still have two dragons to go, boy. When did you ever have time to sleep?"

"In Pontus," he answered with a low, rueful laugh. They didn't understand his answer of course, but then, neither did he, really.

Ghrisz still didn't believe what he heard, but he seemed to appreciate the extravagance of the telling. "Come, finish your tale so that we may doubt with the full amazement it deserves. What of the third worm?"

"That would be Dun Dragon. He thought I had taken on more than I could manage as well."

He paused in his telling to get control of feelings that tried to overwhelm him. What to say about Ahkenbad, dead of Master Markko's attack on the dream readers? What of the Wastrels dead in the war that Llesho now brought to Kungol? What of Kagar, forced to take the Dinha's role too early amid the death and destruction that toppled the mountains of the most sacred city of the Tashek people?

Ghrisz led a handful of followers hiding in tunnels and caves beneath the city from which his father had ruled from the gates of heaven to the Harnlands. He'd probably understand Kagar better than Llesho did himself. But his feelings were still too raw about those losses to expose them to the doubt of his brother's council. So when his brother prodded, "And?" Llesho gave a little shrug, and answered with a voice as devoid of emotion as he could make it.

"I met him only briefly at the fall of Ahkenbad. He told me to learn to say 'no.'"

"The *fall* of Ahkenbad?" a voice muttered at the table.

Ghrisz watched him with a focused hunter's gaze that reminded Llesho of Kaydu in her eagle form, stalking prey. "That is very bad news indeed, if even a part of your tale should prove true."

His brother released his gaze with a sly nod of his head. "I can see the value in Dun Dragon's counsel, even as a narrative device. You seem to leave a trail of destruction in your wake. It certainly doesn't warm the next potential ally to your cause. A shorter trail might at least mean fewer dead allies."

Llesho wished he knew why Ghrisz was mocking him. If his brother took him for a braggart hoping to challenge his place among his cave dwellers, then they were all in trouble. But if Ghrisz was starting to believe him, and hid his own unease behind a caustic wit, then perhaps his mission would succeed after all. He chose to take it as the latter.

"I'll let our brother Lluka explain the stakes we fight for. His visions of the future have driven him mad, but even his madness is enlightening if you pay careful attention."

At the mention of Lluka's madness Ghrisz dropped his air of mocking humor, anxious, it seemed, to move quickly from the subject. "And the fourth worm?" he asked, weighing Llesho's words in the stillness of his perfect attention.

"Marmer Sea Dragon. I met him while I was working as the slave of pirates on the Marmer Sea. He helped me defeat Master Markko in a battle with storms at sea." Unconsciously, Llesho twitched at the remembered touch of the lash across his back.

Ghrisz saw it, and knew it for what it was. "Take off your shirt," he said. "This, at least, we can test."

His advisers looked at him as though he were mad, but from the shadows Mgar held out his hand for the coat. By the bleakness of his expression Llesho knew that the mercenary believed, even if his betters didn't. Llesho gave him his coat, stripped off his linen shirt, and turned his back on the table.

The old woman took a lamp and held it up to study the ridged flesh. "He's seen the lash, all right," she confirmed, "The wounds seem to have been recent, but well tended. Why someone felt the need to beat him, however, remains to be proved. Could be payment for a lying tongue more easily than the torment of a hero."

After a quick glance at the wounds, Ghrisz looked away. "Give him his shirt," he said, and added, "How did you convince this sea serpent to help you in your quest, then?"

"We sought a common enemy." Llesho kept that story to himself, however. It wasn't his to tell.

Ghrisz rubbed both of his hands over his face with a sigh.

"You shake my doubts," he said, "when I am least inclined to trust you. No one believes in dragons anymore. And yet, you seem to know more than you say, and say more than I'm comfortable knowing. If you're telling us any part of the truth. And so we come to three bitter gifts."

"I'm not sure of all of them, but I think I've got it worked out." Llesho had figured from the start that it would take the next part of the prophecy to convince his brother of the truth.

From the sheath at his back he drew the short spear that had taken his life so many times in the past. Just for effect, because he needed them to believe, he willed sparks to shiver up the shaft of the weapon as he placed it carefully on the table. "Don't touch it," he warned Ghrisz. "It burned Adar's hand and has tried to kill me on numerous occasions. We've come to a sort of truce, but I wouldn't want to risk any of our lives on the goodwill of the thing."

They might have thought him mad, but a trickle of smoke rose from the table where it lay.

"That is one," Ghrisz accepted with a nod. "Another?"

"In the keeping of my cadre. A jade wedding cup." No need to explain it; Ghrisz knew the legends as did his advisers. The spear and cup represented the beginning and end of the story. The cup, given in love by the hand of the Great Goddess herself, and the spear, cursed gift that murdered the hand that held it throughout the ages. The prince studied Llesho's face, the unanswered question clear in his troubled glance. Did this stranger with the look of his father tell the truth, or use a story he'd once heard to wriggle his way into their good graces?

The answer lay on the table shedding sparks. Ghrisz stole a glance at it before returning his gaze to his brother. "And the third gift?" he asked.

The first two had been easy to figure. Llesho had puzzled over the third since Menar had recited the prophecy. His hand strayed to his throat, where a bag of pearls lay covered up again. Ghrisz hadn't asked, but maybe he waited for an explanation now. Llesho didn't think that was it, though. The necklace belonged to the Great Goddess, his wife, and he was only a courier where it was concerned. Lady Chaiujin's gift of betrayal was no coincidence, however. And when it came to bitter lessons . . .

"Another cup, similar to the wedding cup of the goddess, but with a symbol carved into the bowl." As he described it his thumb stroked across the signet on his knife where Master Geomancer had hidden it. Ghrisz noticed the gesture but took it for a threat. With a jerk of his head he signaled Mgar, who stepped forward again to clamp a hand on Llesho's shoulder.

"A nervous habit," Llesho explained, moving his hand slowly from the knife. "I mean no harm."

"He'll give it back when we have decided your case."

Mgar reached for the knife but Llesho was there before him, ready to strike at the guardsman. Carefully, he lowered the blade to a defensive position while the spear burned its own smoking shape into the table. "I didn't come here to fight, but I won't give up the knife."

Tradition gave him an excuse to refuse. If not for the spell that held the Lady Chaiujin he would have given it over as a sign of good faith anyway. He trusted his brother, but not the lady trapped inside her box.

"If you were really the lost prince, you would have killed him," Ghrisz pointed out. Thebin training allowed for no other purpose between drawing the knife and sheathing it in the attacker.

"So I thought myself, early in my training. Master Den broke me of the habit of murder, however. Now I choose when to let loose my Thebin training and when to rely on my combat instructors and battle nerves. I won't hurt you. It would defeat my purpose in coming."

Ghrisz thought a moment before nodding his agreement, but made a sign with a finger resting on the arm of his chair. Llesho heard the snick of a sword leaving its scabbard, and then the prick of its point at his neck. He might kill one or two of the councillors nearest him, but Mgar would spit him before he could reach Ghrisz. Which was fine, since he didn't plan on killing anybody.

"About this cup," Ghrisz prodded.

"The lady who gave it to me had filled it with a potion to humiliate her husband and bring scorn down on my head in front of the Qubal clans. She succeeded in that small evil. In the form of a bamboo snake she later murdered her husband."

"It would seem the lesson was for the Harnishman, not for you." Ghrisz dropped his eyes to the spear on the table, letting his mind wander down the track that intelligence opened up to him.

"I learned it anyway."

"Oh?" That brought the prince snapping back to the point.

"I'm still alive. Chimbai-Khan isn't."

Ghrisz registered something of Llesho's dark memories passing in the back of his eyes. He saw more though: a young prince dead on his feet from exhaustion and carrying an unspeakable burden. He never stopped looking at the spear out of the corner of his eye, however. With the pretense of carelessness in the wave of his hand he gave Llesho permission to retrieve the weapon still spitting sparks on the table. Llesho took it up and slid it home, willing it quiet, and the light along its shaft dimmed.

Llesho thought his brother was on the point of accepting his identity but a woman who had remained silent until then spoke up suddenly. "May I ask the young stranger a question?"

Ghrisz gave the barest nod of permission, at which the woman rose from her chair and came around to stand at Llesho's side. She gave him a reassuring smile, as if to tell him that he had nothing to fear from her, but he knew better than to take any comfort from that table.

"If you are who you say, you will know who I am."

The face had changed with age and she no longer wore the robes of her office, but Llesho recognized her. Fortunately, he thought she recognized him as well.

"A priestess at my mother's temple, when she lived," he answered easily enough. He'd been too young to know more about her, but she smiled in spite of the grave nod with which she confirmed his answer.

"In that capacity, I must ask, delicately, as to your vigil-night. Were you able to find a way, in your servitude in far lands . . . ?"

"I did," Llesho stopped her as she had no doubt intended him to do, in a matter of great delicacy. "But I didn't recognize my gifts and for some seasons believed she hadn't come to me. I was wrong."

He thought he might have been able to tell the priestess about his dream travels to the gardens of heaven. The Goddess had comforted him with cool water and her own fingertips on his forehead. But they had an audience and some things, he knew, belonged to the temple alone. Fortunately, he'd figured out a lot of it with the help of his brothers and so could answer her questions both truthfully and without revealing the secret mysteries of his husbandly relationship with the Goddess.

The priestess may have understood all that passed behind his eyes, or she may have simply had a set of questions she asked all the royal princes who had passed their sixteenth summer. She didn't ask the questions he couldn't answer in a public hearing.

"Someone you knew did come to you then." It should have been a question, but she seemed to know the answer already.

"The Lady SienMa, with fruits from her orchard." He couldn't help the little smile at his own expense. Much later, Adar had explained to him the significance of that visit. At the time, it had seemed one with a disastrous night that had ended in the destruction of the governor's compound at Farshore Province and the flight of the household before Markko's southern forces.

"And now you understand your gifts?" The priestess pursued him with the persistence of his enemies, but he felt no greater threat from her than from any of the teachers who had tested him in the past. This was a path he knew well.

"Understand? Just enough to get myself in trouble, Master Den would say. Do I begin to have a notion what they are and how to use them? Yes."

Ghrisz sat forward at that to take part in the priestly interrogation. "And they are useful?" It was said the Goddess had passed him by, granting him no gifts but that of a normal life. Or so it should have been, if not for the Harn.

"I dream." Llesho found that wistfully wry smile creeping across his lips again. Ghrisz bristled at the diffidence of his answer, as if Llesho didn't appreciate his gifts. Only the priestess mirrored his expression with her own understanding of the cost of such heavenly favor.

"So you are the one," she said.

"I guess so."

"Two paths?" Ghrisz reminded them of the prophecy.

"The Way of the Goddess, or the way of evil." To follow the

path of the magician, Master Markko, that was. "I chose the Goddess."

"As do we."

Llesho accepted that with a nod. "The jewel mentioned in the final line remains unclear, however. Our mother had jewels—heirlooms and gifts—a few with historical or sentimental meaning. But nothing with the power to rally all of Thebin."

He didn't mention the tales of the sapphire princess but waited for his brother to answer instead.

Ghrisz did so with a proud smile of his own. "That jewel sits with you at this very table."

The girl-spy gave him a smug smile. "Our fighters call me the Sapphire Princess," she said. "Ghrisz says that the poetry of the title inspires soldiers to battle long after hope is lost."

Llesho saw what she meant by that. She had washed away the smudges on her face and arms that had disguised her in the doorway of the temple but still sported a bruise on her jaw, just above the scarf of beaten silk that wrapped her throat. Her arms bunched with ropy sinews when she gestured in the air. Even her gaze reflected her life of struggle in the conquered city. Her eyes were bright as sapphires and as hard, as if she walled her spirit away from the horrors of a hostage nation in the brilliant blue facets of her gemstone eyes. If they had been softer, her smile gentler, she would have reminded him of his mother.

"Ping!"

"Took you long enough! Are you sure he's the one?" she asked the priestess, though they all knew she was joking to cover her embarrassment at the emotion that gathered in the corners of her eyes.

"I thought you were dead!" Llesho stared hungrily at her through his own tears. "I thought they'd killed you."

"I thought the same about the rest of you." She shifted the scarf around her neck to show the mark of a Harnish knife, then covered it quickly again. "Mgar rescued me from the dung heap. And here you come, still alive yourself and with news of our other brothers safe as well. Which one of us is more surprised?"

"Can we trust this?" Ghrisz asked. It seemed no member of

that council was free of tears, but still the prince seemed to be afraid of hope. "Where are our brothers, if they are alive?"

"Nearby. Which leads me to why I am here."

"What do you need?"

"A way to bring a small band into the city undetected. Secret passages, hidden gates. A siege will kill thousands on both sides. But if we can slip into the city unseen . . ."

"The guards on the wall will spot you before you get close." Ghrisz stopped him before Llesho said more. "There's no cover to hide your approach even if we gave you what you want."

Llesho shook his head. "The only thing we need to hide is our strategy. Remember that line of the prophecy we skipped?"

Ghrisz went very still. "Five armies, like one hand," he recited.

It was Llesho's turn to be smug. Putting his hand up, fingers spread, he began to call the names of those he'd left gathering at his back. "Ten thousand Daughters of the Sword from Bithynia," he said, and folded in his thumb. "Ten thousand horsemen from the Qubal clans. Ten thousand more from the Tinglut. Twice that number from Shan." At the naming of each army he brought a finger in toward his palm. When just one finger remained raised, Llesho turned his gaze on his brother. "I had hoped to find the fifth in Kungol."

"You make me want to believe."

Ghrisz still doubted him, as a general if not as a prince, but they were out of time. "Choose," Llesho said, "as our father's son would choose."

"We can't muster more than five thousand in the resistance, but what I have I give to the coming battle."

Not to him, but Llesho bowed to acknowledge the offer. "Shokar returns with more of our own people among the forces of Shan. His troops will bring the Thebin count to its full tally." He bent the last finger into the fist he had made.

"Then I think we can help each other," Ghrisz agreed. "A wall, after all, is only as sound as the stones that build it. The Harn have little experience of such things, and choose not to learn. The artisans of Kungol, who were pressed into constructing this vast wall, were more practiced at building houses."

"And a house," Ping pointed out, "Is nothing but a wall on the outside, hollow on the inside to hold the people. When the Harn enslaved our people and forced them to raise their wall, they built what they knew."

Tunnels! His people had built what looked like a solid wall against the Harn's enemies, but inside, it was riddled with tunnels! Ping seemed extremely pleased about that, though she must have been toddling around on leading reins when the wall was begun.

"These cellars and tunnels are my palace," she explained, "I have explored every twisting li of them both below the city and within its walls. I know every secret way into the city and every secret way out. They are too few to bring all your armies through, but with sufficient distraction a small band can move easily into the city."

"Sneaking spies back and forth has been easy enough under cover of darkness or the coming and going of Harnish troops through the gates," Ghrisz commented. "Until now, however, we have lacked the army. You seem to have solved that part of the puzzle."

He smiled and Llesho curved his lips in a semblance of the same. Let his brother think that the battle they discussed would be the last. The priestess read him better than his brother or sister did. She wrapped her own fingers around his clenched fist. "Rest," she told him. "And don't give in to despair. A wife who has waited through countless lifetimes will have learned forgiveness above all virtues."

She expected him to fail, he thought, and tried to ease his conscience. Which could only mean she didn't understand the full consequences of his failure. Except that grief seemed to shadow her like a shroud.

He would have tried to reassure her, but his brother stirred just then, rose from his chair as a signal that talking was done.

"Welcome home, little brother," he said, and wrapped Llesho in his arms. It was the thing to do at homecoming, but Ghrisz's doubts made an awkward embrace.

"My turn!" Ping thumped her older brother, wedging herself

between them so that she could give Llesho a huge hug of her own. "I can't believe you're alive!"

A hug, a pat, a smile: one by one the councillors greeted him as they filed out, until he was alone with his brother and sister, and the priestess from the Temple of the Moon.

"Find him a safe bed and something to eat," Ghrisz asked her. He sent Llesho on his way with the promise, "You will have all our secrets when you are awake enough to take them in."

Llesho would have objected that there wasn't time, but Ghrisz needed time to absorb his change in fortunes. Sharing the secrets of a lifetime would not come easily. So he followed the priestess to an underground room with a warm lamp and a bed that was heaped with blankets, and didn't complain when someone put a bun and a cup of tea in his hand.

"You're safe here, even from your dreams," the priestess assured him. He figured he ought to question that, but he didn't plan on sleeping anyway. He needed to gather his thoughts for the next audience with his distant, desperate brother. It was time to talk strategy.

When they came for him again, he was ready.

Chapter Thirty-six

WITH a tumble of hooves over antlers, Llesho arrived in the yellow silk command tent of the mortal goddess of war. Fortunately his advisers who awaited him had seen him dream travel in his totem form before. Master Den looked up from his conversation in the corner with Bright Morning and Balar to give him a nod of greeting but otherwise made no comment on his precipitous arrival. At a table strewn with maps and crowded around by kings and princes and generals, the mortal goddess of war sat in the same chair he remembered from Farshore Province at the start of his quest. Then she had shown him a map and asked him what he knew of the blocks of color on it. Kungol, he remembered, had been gold, and the Harnlands a sea of green. Bithynia had been a question on the fringed edges.

Now he could identify each of those countries by a wound or a companion lost in crossing it. And the lady had a different question for him.

"Tea?" she asked, with a gesture at the pot that rested on a small table at her elbow. When Llesho respectfully accepted a cup from her hands, she continued with the business that concerned their gathered allies.

"Have you found the last of your brothers, holy king?" she asked. That was the first test of the prophecy which foretold their success. The next question spoke to the practicalities of conquest: "Will he join his forces with ours against the magician?"

"I have, and he will. However—" He knew that what he had to say next would inflame the khans who were his allies, and raised a hand to stop their protests before they were begun. "Prince Ghrisz was less than pleased to hear that we counted Harnish clans among our allies."

Mergen took this in with no more than a blink of his lashes, but Tinglut-Khan's face flushed a deeper shade of bronze. He took a deep breath to voice his indignation.

"Understand him, please," Llesho begged before words were said that could not, among kings, be withdrawn. "Of the clans, they know Harnishmen only as torturers and oppressors who murder for sport and wear the scalps of Thebin dead on their shirts."

"Thebin has no great cause to trust the Qubal ulus," Mergen-Khan reminded those at the table.

In the distant past, the Qubal had murdered a Thebin king for loving a daughter of the clans. Llesho wore that king's face, and sometimes he thought he remembered that king's death as one of his own. Sometimes he thought it was all his imagination.

"The clans have had no dealings with Thebin for many generations. Those ended badly, in treachery."

"And yet my brother Ghrisz, with caution, joins his forces with yours in the battle to come. His words come with a warning, but he is willing to judge by the actions he sees."

"With the spirits of my ancestors to guide me," Mergen pledged in the name of Chimbai-Khan, who had first promised aid when Llesho's forces had counted less than a hundred souls, "I hope to repair old wounds between our people. Friendship may be too much to ask, but we would be quit of this debt we owe for the death of your murdered grandfather."

That history, and not Llesho's uncertain memories of lives lived in the past, bound Mergen-Khan to him now. He accepted the khan's pledge as he had that of Chimbai, the Qubal Khan's murdered brother.

Tinglut made to speak up in his own defense, but Shou

answered his bluster with a twitch of an eyebrow. The Tinglut ulus had plotted with the governor of Guynm Province to make war against the empire. Only Shou's timely appearance, and the execution of that false official, had put a halt to the scheme. In the meantime, the Tinglut had aided Master Markko's Uulgar raiders in their attack on the Imperial City of Shan.

Thebin had no cause to trust him either. A king had to be cautious about the armies he invited into his country—they could be a lot harder to remove when the fighting was done. Tinglut wasn't the only worry in that regard. Shou's armies served at the will of the mortal goddess of war to preserve the kingdoms of heaven and earth and Mergen to repair his family's honor. He could trust them as much as one king can trust any other—to the extent it served their mutual need.

But the Apadisha made a sport of war, and Tinglut . . . Llesho determined to set the Daughters of the Sword in the field among the Tinglut forces. The two armies would no doubt watch each other, cutting off every move for advantage while they fought the common enemy. Later, his brothers would have their hands full getting rid of their allies, but that was a battle for another day.

That decided, Llesho drew a scroll from inside his coat and spread it on top of the maps on the table. It showed a rough drawing of Kungol and the wall with which the raiders had surrounded the city. The sketch had no marks to indicate the secret passages and ways in and out, but Llesho had committed them to memory and now he began to gesture here, here, there . . .

The morning had faded into afternoon before the battle plan had been laid out. When each leader knew his or her position and the task each army would accomplish for the taking of Kungol, they dispersed to pass the plan to their own generals and captains, who would in turn instruct their lieutenants. They would march for Kungol by sunrise on the following day.

The gates of heaven were another matter. Llesho had a plan of his own for that. He didn't think his advisers would approve, so he didn't tell them. There was nothing they could do anyway. He wouldn't be able to keep the news from his cadre—they had attached themselves to him again and refused to be moved on any order—but he figured they'd understand better than those who thought they could do it all for him and save him from the coming struggle. Persuading his healers to help might be harder, especially since he was using Master Markko's plan, or a part of it. He regretted what he had to ask, but knew he couldn't defeat the demon on the mountainside without them. When the war council broke up to prepare for battle, Llesho went looking for Carina.

Behind the hospital tent, Master Den had set up his great traveling washtub and his wringers and stretchers for cleaning bandages and bedclothes. He ordered his cadre to wait outside, assuring them that he meant to go nowhere, in dreams or the waking world, and promised not to put himself in danger. He didn't lie, exactly, since he expected no danger while in Carina's presence. That would come later. Kaydu didn't trust his innocent demeanor, but she conceded to his request with a stubborn bow of her head.

"We'll be listening, in case you find trouble where least expected," she vowed.

"I expect nothing less," he agreed. Then he entered the hospital tent to find Carina directing Adar and several apprentices in preparations for tending the wounded.

"Llesho! What can I do for you?" She stole a quick glance of greeting at him, but focused more sharply when she saw the grimness of his countenance. "What is it? What's wrong?"

"I need your help" he said. "I wouldn't ask, but I can't see any other way."

She read the desperation in the tense set of his shoulders and the lines around his hooded eyes. Sending away those who were folding cots with instructions to help with the bandage winding, she turned the full blaze of her attention on him.

"What do you want me to do?" she asked when only Adar remained between them.

"I don't trust anything else he's ever told me, but Master Markko was telling the truth about the creature that lays siege to the Great Goddess' gardens. I can't take this demon-king in a fair fight." Llesho's furtive glance toward her workbench gave away his reason for being here.

"I have no poisons strong enough to kill a demon, even if my oaths as a healer didn't forbid me to use them," she said.

"I wouldn't ask you to kill for me," Llesho assured her. It would have damaged something very deep about his belief in the goodness of the people he was trying to save if Mara's daughter had offered to do murder for him. He still needed her help, though, and he knew what he asked would test the limits of her loyalty.

"I think Master Markko was right about one thing: if I don't find a way to weaken the demon-king before we fight, he will kill me with one sweep of his claws. If I die before I defeat him, there is no hope for any of us." He knew he'd given too much away with that. He didn't count on surviving the encounter, but hoped to destroy the demon before he died of the wounds he would inevitably suffer in any encounter with so powerful an enemy.

Her face tightened with anguish for him. "The magician's plan serves himself, not the Goddess. I don't trust anything he said to bring you out of it alive."

"I have to do this. It's my quest." It would always come down to that: the ghost of his teacher at the bottom of Pearl Bay, sending him out into the world to free his people and save them from the end predicted in Lluka's nightmares. But nothing had ever said he'd be alive at the end of it.

Carina wouldn't look at him but stared at the herbs and medicines laid out on her workbench. "A potion to cause sleep, or a temporary illness is possible. Any draught strong enough to slow a creature from the underworld would kill a human being. How will you trick this king of demons into taking the poison from your hands without tasting it yourself?"

"Master Markko spent a season in his workshop making sure that I could sip his poisons and live, all for this very purpose. He planned that I would kill the demon-king for him. He said that I would rule beside him as his son, but I think that in my weakened state he planned to kill me and take his place alone at the head of his army of imps. That's why I have to deal with him first." And he'd be going after the more powerful foe already weakened in battle.

Adar's voice interrupted from the doorway. "He plans to open the way to the underworld with your blood and lead the armies of demons to cast down the gates of heaven. The demon will be looking to water the underworld with royal blood as well. You can't go up against either one of them alone. You've seen Lluka's dreams. It's not just your life at risk, but all the kingdoms of heaven and the mortal realm that will suffer if we fail on those mountains."

Outside, a voice rose in terrible screams and was quieted again. Lluka, growing more mad the closer they came to the time and place his dreams led him. Llesho shivered in anticipation of the battle to come, but let his brother draw his own conclusions from that terrible cry.

"What do you suggest I do?"

"I don't know." Adar went to the workbench, picked up a vial, another. "I just don't want you to die."

"I'll see what I can do. It would help to have that potion."

Tears streaked Carina's cheeks, but she handed Adar a pinch of an herb with a noxious odor and added a tincture of wine.

"Do you still have the Lady Chaiujin's cup?" Adar asked.

"Yes." Llesho unsheathed his knife and pried off the wooden signet. When he put it down on the workbench it began to grow of its own accord until the spell-carved box rested in front of them.

Adar opened the box and took out the cup with the spiral sigil at the bottom of the bowl. With a small brush, he painted the inside with the potion the two healers had concocted.

"Offer him this cup as a gift. He will doubtless make you drink from it first. If Master Markko has indeed hardened you against poisons, and if you only touch your lips to the tea, it will do little damage. But it's a very powerful draught. Don't drink more than a sip, however; you can't kill the creature if you are writhing in your own death agony." ·

Adar blew gently into the cup to dry the concoction that he had painted there. When it was done, he placed it back on its bed of earth and closed the box. "Try to handle the cup only from the sides, and keep your fingers away from the lip," he warned. "The poison can enter the body through the skin as easily as by swallowing."

"I understand." Llesho stared at the spell-box that held the cup for another moment. "But I don't know how to make it small again."

"It's a simple spell," Carina placed her hands on either side of the box.

"Master Geomancer needed my blood," Llesho told her, offering up the palm of his hand where a thin red line gave evidence of the setting of the spell.

"I won't hurt you." Carina sniffed, offended. "Besides, the spell has already been set. All I have to do is invoke it now. Put your hands over mine."

Llesho did, and slowly she brought her palms together with his hands tucked against her fingers, until the box was once again small enough to fit smoothly into the butt of his knife. As Master Markko used to do, they carefully cleaned the area with pure water and wrapped the bowl they had used for the potion in a clean towel for burying.

It felt wrong to ask such a thing of his brother or Carina, but he didn't know what else to do. "Thank you" choked in his throat. So he said, "I'm sorry."

"I know. I wish we could have found another way." Adar cocked his head as another desperate cry wavered in the thin air. "We'll take care of Lluka while you're gone."

Llesho gave a bow to acknowledge his gratitude to the healers, and his regret. He picked up his pack and left the red tent while his brother and the woman Llesho once thought he might love stood with their arms around each other watching him go. Like his brother Lluka, whose cries shattered the growing dusk, Llesho would find no comfort until the final battle was won.

Chapter Thirty-seven

HIGH in the mountains above Kungol, a single tree clung to the stone, shading the entrance to a cave. Scrub and underbrush grew like a filthy beard all around the rocky entrance, from which the smell of sulfur and rotting flesh tainted the clean mountain air. From the cave came the the sound of weeping, mingling with the mumbled grunts and growled curses floating like the stink on the breeze. Llesho thought he heard snuffling among those terrible noises. It had to be a dream, but Llesho didn't know how he had come to be in it.

"Pig?" He slipped a chilled hand inside his shirt, found the black pearl wound with silver still hanging from its silver chain. Not Pig, then . . . Llesho took a cautious step forward.

Out of the cave came a scream filled with horrific pain that rose in pitch as it went on, and on. It raised the hairs on Llesho's neck and curled his stomach in a tight protective ball in his gut. Something was dying—not easily—in that cave. He stepped back, looking for cover in the surrounding brush while the dark entrance filled with the snarling of a hundred angry voices.

A creature out of nightmares shambled into the light just as the screaming stopped. On first impression, he seemed to be short and squat, covered in a horny green hide that glistened with grease. When he stepped out from under the low roof of his den, however, he stood and stood, growing so tall that

Llesho had to crane his neck to look at him. He couldn't tell if the creature was always so tall and lived curled up in his cave, or if he—it seemed to be a he—had the ability to change his shape and size as he chose.

In the clawed fingers of one hand he dragged a human leg still dripping blood where it had been torn raggedly from the body of the creature's victim. Razor-sharp teeth protruded so far from the monster's jaws that the creature couldn't close his mouth around them. His lips remained stretched in a perpetual sneer made more terrible by the human meat that dangled from the pointed fangs. While he looked Llesho over, the beast lifted the leg to his mouth and took a great rending bite that snapped bones as easily as flesh. Bits of human meat and sinew flew as he shook the shreds from his fangs and from the back of his mouth came the crunching sound of teeth strong as stone grinding bone.

It wasn't the grisly snack that set Llesho to trembling, however, but its gaze. Instead of eyes, the awful creature looked at him out of two gleaming black pearls, the match of the ones he carried by a leather thong close to his heart. *Oh, Goddess*, he thought. *What powers do your stolen treasures put in the hand—or in the eye—of your most dreaded enemy?* But he kept this thought to himself.

"I'm glad to see you found me," the demon greeted him with a grimace of a smile. "I always enjoy company for lunch."

Llesho figured that wasn't an invitation, at least not for him. The thing was not alone: more than one pair of bright eyes peered back at him from the mouth of the cave. Harsh growls and hungry chitters accompanied the bobbing and shifting of the creatures. One of the things—an imp, which Llesho figured for about his own height if it ever straightened from its cringing crouch—tried to make a break for it. The imp was dragging something that slowed it down. Llesho realized, on stealing a quick glance, that it was a human torso, torn open and with its guts trailing after on the ground.

Twenty or more of the creatures poured out of the cave, following the dripping torso, and leaped upon the thief. It seemed to matter very little to them whether they took a bite out of the human body they had dismembered or out of their own brother imp who had stolen it. The creature's evil screams of pain and terror joined the vicious sounds of fighting and eating. Soon more screams rose from the center of that fray as the imps turned on each other in a frenzy of eating.

"I've come at a bad time." Llesho took a step back. He gave a little shake of his head, but his antlers weren't there. Still, time to go—

"You're not leaving us so soon?" With his stolen eyes, the demon-king cast an irritated glance over at the crawling knot of savage imps. His free hand reached out and broke off the tree that shaded the cave. Using his strong sharp teeth, he stripped it of branches for a makeshift club and quickly knocked his followers into an insensible heap with it. When he had regained a semblance of quiet that way, he turned the pearls of his eyes on Llesho.

"I thought you'd be dying to meet my guests. Or is that, 'I thought you would die and be meat *for* my guests?'" With that he made a swiping grab with his huge clawed hand.

Llesho jumped back, though not soon enough to have saved him if he'd brought his body along. But the demon-king's talons passed through him like a mist. He wasn't bleeding so it had to be a dream; until that moment, he hadn't been entirely sure.

"Ah, well, it doesn't matter, does it?" the demon gave a wistful sigh, gusting putrid breath in Llesho's direction. If he'd really been there, he'd be dead of the noxious gases the creature spewed before it added, "We'll be having you for dinner in the flesh soon enough."

The demon-king took another bite of the human leg he still carried, and another, licking the talons of his fingers when he was done. Then he crouched low on his wrongly-turning knees. "You cannot win," he said, in a reasonable tone made terrible by the contradiction of human flesh clinging to his teeth. "I have shown you the kindliest of my faces because I don't want you dying of fear in your dreams. That would deprive me of the pleasure of killing you myself, and that would never do."

"Pig!" he called, because he didn't know how he'd gotten here or where his body was on the other side of the dreamscape.

Even knowing that the demon-king couldn't hurt him, he stepped away from those knifelike claws and razor teeth. Back and back again until his heel came down on empty air.

"Later!" the demon-king yelled after him as he fell, a promise that their next meeting would go differently.

And then Llesho jolted out of a daze to catch his balance against a stumble in his horse's gait. Behind him, Shou's army had taken up a mournful Shannish marching song:

> *"As I march from the home I am leaving*
> *by the cottage door, holding our babe*
> *My sweetheart is quietly weeping*
> *For the sweet boy she sends to the grave."*

Next to him, Master Den was watching him curiously. "Where did you go this time?" the trickster asked. "I've been watching your empty eyes all morning."

Kungol had grown to fill the horizon. It was time to send his generals to lead their armies according to their plan. But her ladyship was watching him as well, and it was important that they know.

"I've seen Master Markko's demon, or what he wanted me to see. I think he was playing with me, like a cat with a mouse." He grimaced with the smell of death still caught in his throat. "I don't think I'll get away as easily next time."

He didn't mention the pearls that filled the demon's eye sockets, reminding him of a dream the other side of Pontus.

In the dream, he had walked among the Wastrels dead upon the grasslands, plucking pearls from the orbits of their eyes. In the waking world the stone monsters had taken their hearts and left the Goddess' pearls in their place. Either way his grief and horror had been the same. He'd thought the dream over, however. Now, it looked like he still had a part of the dream to face in yet another form. But at least he'd found where the black pearls of the Goddess had fallen.

> *"But the drums and the pipes now are silent*
> *and the tunic of red turns to rust*

*And the fields are now sown with the fallen
in the twilight, in blood, and in dust."*

The song cut too close to what he was feeling in the aftermath of his meeting with the demon-king, but her ladyship was quick to assure him, "Then we will strike at this demon. Your lady wife will have no complaint against your armies this time."

"I know," Llesho accepted her assurances rather than argue with a mortal god. It wouldn't work out that way. The demon resided in a pocket of the underworld intruding upon the mountain at the very place where the peaks touched heaven. Mortal armies might wander forever on that mountain and never find the contending forces out of realms that existed only in magic. That battle would be for him alone. But first, they had to take back the Holy City of the Goddess.

PART FIVE

THE GATES
OF HEAVEN

Chapter Thirty-eight

VIEWED from heaven, the Thousand Peaks Mountains began as a ridge of low hills in Farshore Province. From there they swept south, rising in a spine of jagged mountains that curved in a great crescent around Thebin's southernmost border. The Cloud Country, as their neighbors called Thebin, lay on a broad plateau high in the mountains, as if the ancient forces that had formed that awesome barrer had paused here on the roof of the world before their final effort: the six peaks whose glacier-crowned heads pierced heaven itself.

Llesho's heavenly ancestors, some said, had come down from those mountains to explore their handiwork and had stayed to aid and guide the people they found struggling at the foot of their great mountains. With their breath they gave the Thebin people the power to breathe the thin air. With their thumbs they created the great passes to the west in the mountains. Then they bid their people build a great Golden City and in it two towers, one to the Goddess, whose sign was the moon, and the other to recognize the earthy power of the sun.

When it was done, the king withdrew into his earthy palace and called the caravans for trade. The queen took her place among the priests in the temple built for her use, from where she might travel between the realms of heaven and earth. They had the mountains to protect them and the gaze of heaven to fill their hearts with joy. And they had no need of walls.

As a child in the palace, Llesho had been too young to sort fact from legend in the tales. His experiences since leaving Pearl Island gave him cause to wonder even now where that line should fall—or if there should be any line at all. Facing that hideous wall the Harn had forced his people to build around the fading Golden City, however, a baleful anger stirred in him for the crimes the Uulgar raiders had committed against his people and against the realm precious to the Great Goddess.

For himself that wall seemed not the devastation of his home but the setting before him of one more test. Another obstacle stood between him and the heavenly gardens that called him more powerfully than his city or his brothers or any earthly conquests. This time he was ready, with all his armies about him.

By some magic of his own, Master Den had provided yet again the appropriate wear for a king of Thebin going to war. Llesho had set the silver fillet of the king on his head and donned not his embroidered court coats, but genuine Thebin armor, the grown version of the child's armor that he had worn on parade before the Harn had taken all that away—the good and the bad. The armor was as uncomfortable as he remembered—a big part of the bad, that. The plates across his chest didn't shine as gloriously as Shou's, but those among his own people who had survived from before the raiders would recognize the challenge in the very fact he wore it.

As Llesho had hoped, word of rescue arriving in such numbers followed them through the dry and seemingly empty lands of abandoned farms and desolate villages. Thebin bandits and freedom fighters alike crept out of hiding to join them. Women and children, refugees all, fell in with the armies. They lacked the skills of a trained army, and their numbers made scarcely a ripple among Llesho's forces, but they were by their very presence symbols of the new resolve to take Thebin back from their oppressors in the name of their rightful king.

*   *   *

By the plan he had worked out with Ghrisz, the armies under Llesho's command marched nearly to the gates of the city in five long columns, each four soldiers across. When they had come close enough to read the grain in the wood that barred the gates, the first rank of kings and princes, gods and noble generals, with Llesho at their head, stopped. Their forces in the many uniforms of their own nations gathered with measured march around them, filling the whole expanse of land that opened out from the unwelcoming wall surrounding the city.

The raiders were cowards, preferring to make war on the unsuspecting. When the full reality of fifty thousand armed troops massed against them became more widely known the garrison would tremble with dread. Shokar had hoped that the display of might alone would bring the raiders to the point of surrender. Adar had expressed his doubts. He'd spent time as a prisoner of Markko's lieutenant and had seen firsthand the more urgent fear of their leader that kept the Uulgar clans facing forward. Llesho had seen that for himself in the South, when terror of their master had pushed Lord Yueh's men across the Golden Dragon Bridge that had been no bridge at all but a fierce and wily dragon.

Noise and a great show of ferocity would certainly weaken the raiders' resolve, Adar had conceded. Like any cornered beast, they might leap in unpredictable directions when pressed between their own deadly master and the forces arrayed against them. But leap they surely would. And so in the full light of Great Sun high overhead, they rode up to the gate under the watchful eyes of the captive city.

They were not surprised when a general of imposing stature, his chest decorated with locks of hair taken from his many victims, addressed them from the lookout post above the gate. "Take your rabble and go!" he said, "before my Master of the Crows has you for lunch!"

Llesho figured he meant Master Markko, who had poisoned the Uulgar khan and fed his body to a flock of crows which had themselves died in a great stinking blanket of soot-colored birds.

"My rabble has no intention of leaving until your wall is

torn down and Kungol is returned to its rightful king," Llesho answered him. "Tell your master that the lost king of Thebin has returned to reclaim the throne for his people. Open these gates and lay down your arms, or suffer the consequences."

"Thebin has no king," the general jeered. "The old king died on his knees, which is what the people of Thebin do best!"

Llesho wasn't sure if he meant the dying part or the kneeling part. Ghrisz had run them a merry race, however, something the Harnishman doubtless knew.

The general continued his bombast: "That's why Kungol is ruled by a khan more powerful than any mortal man!"

Llesho didn't let his anger show, but made his claim in a loud, clear voice: "Tell your master that the holy king of the Kungol people has returned. With him comes the emperor of Shan with his armies and the khans of the Qubal and the Tinglut with their armies and the Daughters of the Sword from Bithynia and the Gansau Wastrels out of legend. Tell him the mortal gods are knocking at his door, and the gods would see justice!"

The Harnish did not recognize the mortal gods, but one name among them must shake even these hardened warriors. "Tell Master Markko that the mortal goddess of war has ridden against him. Tell him she seeks satisfaction for deaths in the South and for the terrible end of all things he draws down upon all our heads. His armies will find only disaster on this field."

At mention of the mortal goddess of war, the man looked out over their company with a disdainful sneer. He drew a breath to sharpen the cut of his next insult, when his eyes lit upon the Lady SienMa. Llesho turned his eyes also to the lady. Terrible judgment set her icy white features in chiseled lines of marble, nothing living but the death in her eyes. The general trembled so that his sword knocked against the thick plaster of the wall behind which he hid.

"You think your master has terrified you with wonders," Llesho said, and raised his hand. "You have not seen wonders yet."

Master Den had slipped from the bare back of Marmer Sea Dragon, who had carried him in the form of Bluebell the giant horse. At Llesho's signal, the dragon took his natural form, rising in flight above the combined armies in a spiral of coils the color of a stormy sea. Higher and higher he rose, until he could be plainly seen inside the city walls. Then, with an elegant snap of his tail, he straightened to his full length. Without leaving his place at the northern gate his head looked down on the unbroken southern wall.

Llesho could hear voices from within the city walls rising in terror like the rumble of a storm. From his own troops there came not a sound or a stirring from their places. Marmer Sea Dragon had shown himself to the combined armies as part of field training so his monstrous appearance came as no surprise to them. It helped knowing the dragon-king was on their side, of course, but the Harnish general had no such comfort. He turned a shade of green that rivaled the dragon's scales and disappeared. A moment later a Thebin prisoner showed his face above the gate, no less terrified than the guard who commanded him. A little smile of triumph fought its way to his lips in spite of his fear. Dragons certainly made convincing allies.

"They want to know if you can make it go away."

Marmer Sea Dragon had made a lazy circle around the city, so that he faced back the way he had come. That was part of the plan, too. Llesho held his spear up over his head, so that the bladed head pointed skyward. He willed blue flame to shudder along its length. The flame arced overhead, snapping like lightning in the clear blue sky. The man fell back as the guard had done, but the dragon-king had seen the signal.

With a deep, powerful stroke of his wings, Marmer Sea Dragon lifted higher still in the air, until he was no larger, to the eye, than a butterfly. Then, as swiftly as a streak of lightning, he was gone, heading south. He would travel by magical routes to gather the other three worms promised in Menar's prophecy. Pearl Bay Dragon, Golden River Dragon, and Dun Dragon would return with him for the great battle with the demon for the gates of heaven. The taking of Kungol belonged to humans and their mortal gods.

The crack of light from his spear had been a signal to his troops as well. As they had agreed, the Daughters of the Sword divided into two columns, one heading east, one west to encircle the city in preparation for attack. Mergen-Khan's Qubal warriors did the same, matching the women warriors pace for pace. If the Apadisha's daughter decided to take on the winner in the coming battle, with Kungol her prize, Llesho had wanted his closest ally watching over her shoulder.

Closest save one. Llesho sheathed his spear and returned to the army he had come to see as his own. The emperor of Shan had led his forces from the heart of the empire across half the world to aid him in his quest. Now he would buy Llesho time— for his armies to get in place, and for Llesho himself to enter the city in secret by the hidden tunnels that Ghrisz had shown him. If they were very lucky, he might divert slaughter yet.

"Tell your general to come out," he shouted to the Thebin captive at the gate. "My champion challenges fair duel for your gate."

At that, and by agreement, Shou marched his great war steed forward. He had changed his sword for a long spear, but his armor shone as it had when Llesho had first met him on the field of battle on the outskirts of Shan Province.

"Come down and fight, or be ever called a coward!" To emphasize the call to single combat he struck a shivering blow against the gate, which shook under his assault.

In council, Shou had protested the archaic call to arms. "Why don't I just set fire to the gate?" he'd said, "If they don't come out to put out the flames, we can walk in through the ashes when it's done."

"It's not just about one battle," Menar had explained. As a poet he knew about such things. "We need the people inside the wall, who have been oppressed all these season by the Harn, to believe they have a chance to win if they fight. For that, we need to put legend to work in our cause."

"Then you need a legend to make your challenge," Shou had protested further.

Only ChiChu, the trickster god, had the nerve to laugh at that. "You are a legend; that's why it must be you!"

In all the faces around that map-spread table he had found no dissenting voice. And so Shou pounded on the well-made gate, drawing the attention of all who might view him from above, while Llesho faded quietly into the ranks, where he slid off his horse and quickly shed the armor that had already done its duty. Immediately his cadre surrounded him at the center of a protective circle of Imperial Guardsmen disguised in uniforms of a less prestigious service. They didn't want to call attention to the very figure they were trying to protect. Well accustomed to spycraft, Llesho slipped from his place at the center of the crowd to one off to the side where Bixei waited for him with a change of coat.

"Master Den usually sees to my wardrobe." Free of the heavy chest plate, Llesho rotated his shoulders in a few tight circles and took his first deep breath of the day. He had only a moment to enjoy his freedom before he slipped the short spear in its sheath over his shoulder and plunged his arms into the rough hooded coat.

"And you'll need this." Bixei handed him a small bag that held a few herbs for tea and the jade marriage cup that almost matched the poisoned one of the Lady Chaiujin. It was a rare treasure to use as a wayfare cup, but he didn't think the demon-king would have much experience with such things. With a nod of thanks he looped the bag over his belt, next to the sheath that held his Thebin knife. He kept the circlet of silver—he would need it in his confrontation with Master Markko—but he pulled the hood low over his brow. The coat would hide his identity as well as the weapon while they made their way to the Palace of the Sun, where Master Markko had set up his own evil court.

Around them, soldiers were moving out. "Are we ready?" Kaydu glided up beside him. Prince Tayyichiut had stayed behind when his uncle the khan had led his troops into position and he fell in line with Llesho's cadre as if he had always been there, which seemed to suit them all.

Llesho nodded. "Adar agreed to stay with Lluka, since his madness is growing." That was no surprise. Lluka now traveled bound so that he didn't hurt himself. Soon they would have to muffle his voice as well, or risk unnerving their own troops.

"Balar wished to stay with Menar to study the prophecy in greater depth," Kaydu reported. "Musician to poet, he said."

"And Little Brother?" Llesho asked. The monkey usually rode with the troops to battle, in a sling that hung from Kaydu's saddle. "With us as always," she said. "He is looking forward to seeing Master Markko fall almost as much as we are."

He seemed to have fooled his cadre, who gave no sign of any suspicion that his own battles would be longer, and lonelier, than he had reported to his council of war.

"Shokar will lead our Thebin forces," Kaydu added. "They'll be entering the city by the escape routes hidden along the wall, so we'll have reinforcements if we need them. All you have to do is not get killed."

"Sarcasm," he noted with a twist of his mouth. "I guess we're ready then."

Joining the crowd in apparent aimless wandering, the cadre with Llesho at its head worked its way closer to the wall, nearer to the hidden entrance that Ghrisz had sketched with a finger against a map. As Ghrisz had predicted, the guards on the city wall had gathered with drawn bows to watch the emperor of Shan challenge their general in single combat. They would expect the attack to come from the armies gathered below as soon as Shou abandoned his taunts and disappeared again into his own lines. Safe, as they must think, behind their defenses, they would assume the armies surrounding them intended a siege. And so they didn't notice when small groups of soldiers stationed here and there along the wall began disappearing inside.

Shokar led his troops, including two hands of Gansau Wastrels with him to represent the Dinha, to the northwestern corner of the city where resistance fighters in Ghrisz's command waited to sneak them in through a secret passage in the wall there. Llesho turned to the northeast. With his cadre, under Bixei's command, came a small band of mercenaries disguised in Harnish dress. They had pledged to regain their honor, lost, they believed, with the fall of Kungol. Their clan had sworn to defend the palace all those seasons ago and they meant to make good on that promise by recapturing it now.

Five thousand out of their fifty thousand in all found their assigned places along the wall, where Ghrisz's spies waited to sneak them into the city. Each band had its assigned task. And Llesho had his. Ghrisz hadn't wanted to risk Thebin's young king in the fighting but there hadn't been time for a debate: Llesho pulled rank.

His brother was waiting for them in the tunnels that riddled the Harnish wall. When the panel hiding the secret entrance slid out of the way, Bixei led his small band into the darkness, first to die if they had been betrayed. A ragged beggar with sharp, intelligent eyes waited for them with a torch in his hand. Mgar one of their own waiting to guide his brothers into the city. Llesho greeted him with a quick tilt of his chin.

"This way," Mgar instructed, and started moving the mercenary guardsmen farther down the tunnel.

Other resistance fighters waited with their own torches until they were all hidden inside the wall with Stipes the last to protect their backs. Someone in the dark slid the panel back in place, and Ghrisz stepped out of the shadows. He wore the usual castoffs that marked the oppressed population, disguise perhaps, though Llesho wasn't clear if the resistance had any better clothes if they had wanted them. Years of Harnish rule had been hard on all the people in the city, not least the oldest of her seven princes.

"We won't be entering the city here," Ghrisz said, and gestured for them to follow him. "We have tunnels that can get you closer to the magician. Or to one of our hideouts, if you've changed your mind. We can protect you there until the fighting is over—"

"You know that won't work," Llesho reminded him. "Somebody has to take on Master Markko. I've survived against him before, I can do it again."

"And what makes you think he won't kill you this time? I thought that was the point, at the end of the day? To kill a prince as a blood sacrifice to his demon lord?"

Llesho said nothing about the poisoned cup he carried in the spell-box hidden on his knife. Now that he had met the demon, he had begun to doubt that any of their plans would work against it. He didn't think his brother would appreciate the only answer he had to give, though—that his life belonged to his

Goddess to save or not as she pleased. He thought she might, this time. More importantly, he thought they would all die and their worlds with them if he didn't succeed.

He said none of this, but Ghrisz must have seen some of his determination in the flicker of torchlight.

"All right." He let out a disgusted sigh. "You'll want the raiders to have their eyes turned outward tonight. Your champion can't beat his chest all day out there. I assume you have your diversions as planned?"

"A full-scale attack on the outside of the wall will come soon." As the cadre's captain, Kaydu answered for them. "Shokar is bringing his forces into the city through the tunnels. When the raiders are fully engaged with the siege forces outside, we'll spring the trap. Shokar will take the gate and let in the army that will be waiting to enter on his signal."

Ghrisz nodded. With fifty thousand troops outside in addition to his own force and those Shokar was bringing through the tunnels, they should have no trouble defeating the Harnish raiders. They all knew the magician was the key, however. Markko could wipe the city flat with a storm like the one that had swept the Marmer Sea. He might command the demon-king to destroy the city if he chose. That's why Llesho had to get to him first.

"We'd better get moving, then. I'll be your guide myself." Ghrisz gave him a fleeting smile that disappeared as quickly as it had come. "Ping will meet you in the temple. I couldn't stop *her* either."

That didn't surprise Llesho. In his dream-walk, he'd found Ping waiting for him at the base of the temple tower and had it figured that she spent more nights than that one there. He followed Ghrisz down the long dark passage. He'd been in tunnels like this before, under the arena at Farshore, and following Shou through the secret passages under the palace in the Imperial City of Shan. With little concern for the weight of the great wall that towered above them, they made haste in the flickering light, while behind him the sound of his armies starting their attack thundered through the plaster.

Llesho tried to close his mind to the numbers who would

die in the diversionary battle. Master Markko's raiders had the
advantage of cover. Their arrows would be falling from above
like murderous hailstones into the midst of his troops below,
with only the shields of their swordsmen raised in a protective
leather shell over his own bowmen. The wall of shields would
protect them for a while, but his forces would break hopelessly
against the might of that great wall if Shokar didn't open the
gate.

All along the wall they heard the sound of fighting until
Ghrisz angled them down, to make their way underground
toward the center of the city. Bixei and his mercenaries had
passed out of hearing long ago, heading for their own exit point.
They would rejoin Llesho's group closer to the palace, in case
they had to fight their way through. For now, however, the goal
was to pass in small bands unnoticed through the city streets.

Here the tunnels were narrower and more roughly carved.
No plaster or beams held up the earth over their heads—nothing
but the dry stubbornness of the Thebin soil. For more than three
li they traveled that way, their shoulders brushing one side or
the other, with only a torch in Ghrisz's hand ahead of them
and one that Stipes carried behind to light their way. Narrow
conduits brought fresh air from the surface, and sometimes the
sound of shouting or running feet. Once Ghrisz pulled them
into a side tunnel to let a runner pass on his way to the front.

When they started moving again, the ground under their
feet began to rise. "This way." Ghrisz pressed against what
appeared to be a solid wall.

Llesho heard the slide of stone upon stone at ear level, then
a breeze tickled his face. A hidden door swung open into a
storeroom at the back of a tavern. The area was poor, the walls
of Thebin plaster long gone black with soot. A hallway crossed
in front of the storeroom, at the end of which a door stood open
to an alley stinking of piss and worse. From the other end of the
hall came the angry sounds of an argument in the public room.

"By ones and twos," Ghrisz said. He plunged his torch into
a bucket that sizzled and smoked as the flame went out and
pushed Hmishi and Lling into the hallway. After a few minutes

Stipes doused his own torch and with Kaydu followed them into the public house, arguing loudly with the two princes.

"More beer!" Ghrisz called, and the barman grabbed a club and shook it, bellowing, "Not tonight! If you are so keen to fight, take it to the gates! You'll find plenty of work for your fists!"

They had only just arrived and had done no fighting. Llesho figured the man was part of the plot and allowed himself to be chased from the pub.

Great Moon Lun had not yet shown her face but Han and Chen cast a dim light as they chased each other across the sky, cloaking the streets in layers of shadows. None of this was familiar ground for Llesho so he hunched ear-deep into his shoulders and ran, following Ghrisz, who knew where he was going.

Careening around a corner of broken plaster fallen in the street they were met by a squad of raiders rushing away from the temple in their direction.

"He's one of them!" shouted the leader, drawing his sword and pointing it at Ghrisz. Immediately his own cadre drew their weapons and the battle was on.

"Go!" his brother shouted amid the clang of sword against sword.

From its sheath at his back the short spear whispered, "Kill them!" in his ear, "Only cowards run!" But it had never spoken a true word to him in all the lifetimes he had known it. If he turned back to help here, Master Markko would gain valuable time against them. Just a few streets separated Llesho from the temple in the public square: from here he could see it rising in front of him, could figure out the way on his own.

He started to run, almost stopped at the grunt of surprised pain he heard behind him. Kaydu, that was. Little Brother screeched in rage, and suddenly his monkey voice deepened, bellowed louder than Llesho had ever heard it. He did turn then, just a quick glance, that took his breath away. Kaydu lay curled on her side, protecting a wound on her arm that bled slowly but surely onto the street. Above her Little Brother, in his uniform of the imperial militia, had grown to the height of a man. In his great hairy arms he had taken up her sword and he lay about him with it in perfect form. Enemy and ally alike fell back in amazement, but Little Brother recognized friend from foe and soon the street was slippery with blood.

Hmishi and Lling recovered quickly. Having traveled with Little Brother they'd had their own suspicions about him. Ghrisz had lived with fewer wonders but knew better than to insult an ally. "Go!" he said, and joined Little Brother in the attack. Llesho ran, dodged into an alley—

—and tripped over a beggar who snatched at his ankle from the dusty shadows. "Turn back! The monsters are coming!" the voice called to him, hoarse as if he'd been shouting for a long time. If he saw the things that Llesho had seen, that seemed likely. It didn't stop him, though; he turned onto the main thoroughfare, keeping close to the buildings collapsing in on themselves that had once been temples and markets and houses of trade and diplomacy.

The Temple of the Moon lay in front of him but so did another skirmish, between bands of Harnishmen, it seemed. Except that he was sure he recognized the fighting style at the center of the fray. Bixei, holding the way clear for him, or trying to. Llesho tried to zigzag around the fight, caught the blunt end of a short spear in the head and kept on moving while the ringing in his ears clashed with the sound of steel on steel.

Suddenly, moonlight so tangible he thought he might reach out and caress it poured like molten silver over its stepped sides. The sight filled him with so much yearning and pain and joy that for a moment he was paralyzed with the conflicting emotions. His mother had lived here, had held him on her lap and sung songs to him; had greeted dignitaries and priests alike with him tucked safely in her arms. His mother had died here, and her spirit still filled the temple with her death.

High atop her tower, two bridges of moonlight would reach out to him. Menar's prophecy itched at the back of his brain— two paths, it had said. Llesho knew which one he wanted to take, knew also that tonight he would go the other way. Not to the gates of heaven, where the Great Goddess awaited him, but to the Palace of the Sun, where Master Markko wove his poisonous webs.

Ahead lay the small side door he'd used as a child and later in his dream travels. As he approached, Princess Ping appeared from the shadows dressed in tattered rags as she had before.

"There isn't much time left. Give me your hand." She held out her own small, callused fingers and he took them, studying her eyes for something . . .

"The spirits," he began, a warning for her to stay out, to let him do alone what he had already done once.

"That's why I'm here." Ping gave him a mischievous smile. Lifetimes looked out of her eyes at him. "There isn't time— come on!"

She gave a tug on his hand and he followed her willingly, into the temple, to the staircase that had haunted him with its sorrowful spirits. This time when the ghosts crowded near, his sister spoke to them and they fell silent. Only a hushed whisper, as of ghostly clothing passing on the stairs, accompanied them. There was purpose in that unearthly tread; the higher they climbed, the stronger the sound of ghosts following on the stairs became.

Chapter Thirty-nine

AT FIRST the thought of so many Thebin dead at his back sent a chill of fear curling up Llesho's spine. Gradually, however, he allowed his awareness of their company to warm the spirit that curled at the bottom of his heart. His thoughts reached out to the temple's ghosts and they touched him, softly, as supplicants might kiss the robes of a priest who passed through the streets. They offered comfort and their own deadly protection, though he knew they couldn't travel beyond their own tower.

He felt the presence of his sister at his side, undisturbed by the spirits around them, and he knew she shared with him her easiness with their dead. He set the supplicant spirits aside with a promise, "Later," but his thoughts were for the living. Reaching out to them, he touched living minds.

The emperor of Shan sat his warhorse directing armies with a sword he clenched in his fist. With the emperor's ears Llesho heard the screaming of horses, the singing of arrows in flight from the Uulgar wall and the cries of his own followers as those arrows found their mark. Shou/Llesho raised his hand and a hundred ladders clattered against the Uulgar wall. Shannish soldiers climbed swiftly, dodging arrows—there were too many of them for the Harnish defenders. Llesho felt their fear and their determination as they climbed; some fell, and he staggered with the impact and kept on going. Others were reaching the top, drawing swords against bows and arrows that were no use for close-in fighting.

This was new, this living in the skins of his soldiers, of the newly dead and the soon to die. Was it some gift of the tower itself, or had his own mind expanded to meet his coming trial? Shou turned his emotions to stone, focused completely on the wall in front of him. In his mind, the emperor didn't waste men in a diversion to buy time for Shokar or for Llesho. He fought to take the wall, and if he had help from inside, fine, and if he didn't, then they'd take it any way they could—over the top or chipping away piece by piece until they had turned it into bloody rubble.

At his side the mortal goddess of war gathered messages from runners up and down the line. They could not hold long, but with a word, a command, they would, and did.

Somewhere in the Palace of the Sun a raider made a decision. He would send no troops outside the wall to engage the enemy. The wall would defeat them, or wear them down, he didn't have to make it easy for them. His master would see to their success; he just had to hold until the magician came out of his tower. A chill terror clutched at the man's gut at the thought of Master Markko, an image of his own superior officer gutted on a spit for failing in his mission. He *didn't* think, *reminded himself not to think* of surrender, of flight. The magician would know, would punish even the thought of failure . . .

Shokar moved silently in the shadows, by small gestures directing half his combined force of Thebin recruits and finely honed Gansau Wastrels up a secret stairway carved inside the wall to the left of the great northern gate. On the right, the rest of his troops did the same. Unaware of the danger rising at their backs the Uulgar bowmen continued firing down into Shou's army below. . . .

Willing his awareness to sweep over the city like a dragon, Llesho found Habiba astride his rearing white warhorse, urging a division of Shannish and Tinglut troops against the gate. Arrows flew perilously close all around him. One would have shattered his breast and exploded his heart, but her ladyship's witch held out his sword in a warding gesture and the arrow erupted in a shower of splinters over the pommel of his saddle. Habiba shook his head as if clearing it from a blow, then he raised his sword over his head and shouted a call to attack.

At the rear, Bright Morning rolled bandages with Master Den and Balar. Carina and Adar stole a moment for a frightened embrace while they gathered their salves and unguents and medicines to reduce the fever in grievous wounds. Lluka they had tied to a cot where he lay shivering in dreams of disaster and destruction that Llesho had no time to battle right now. But Menar held his brother's head and wiped his brow with a cool cloth, reciting healing poems over him from both Thebin and Bithynian apothecaries.

Llesho ascended higher into the tower but now he scarcely noticed the gathering storm of spirits following him. His dream vision moved on. Little Brother was nowhere to be seen, but Kaydu had a makeshift bandage wrapping the wound on her arm. She had joined his cadre to Bixei's mercenary forces and together they fought their way to the temple. When they tried to mount the haunted staircase, however, the voracious spirits drove them out again, half mad from the attempt. Kaydu set them about to defend the base below him, with Bixei to lead the defenders and Stipes as his lieutenant. She was a magician, the daughter of dragons, and would not abandon her charge to ghosts; Llesho felt her determination like a steady flame as she took one step and then another up the stairs. Hmishi joined her, his own heart calm. He had been where these spirits were, and had nothing to fear from them. Lling joined him, like hilt to blade he drew her into his calm, and together they climbed. . . .

Shokar's troops had reached the parapet above the gate and, with swords drawn, fell upon the archers, hacking and slaying. Llesho felt his brother's determination, his loathing for his own actions as he cut down men who had no time to draw sword against them. Bow and arrow were useless in this struggle. Archers threw down their weapons, reaching for their swords, but too late. The first rank were cut down with hand to scabbard, but the second turned the battle against the new invaders. The commotion was bringing Uulgar defenders from positions farther down the wall to aid their fellows at the gate, but that gave Shou's troops a clear shot with their ladders.

Not soon enough for the emperor on the other side of the wall, however. Llesho fell back against the tower wall that girded the stairs he traveled. With a gasp of surprise he gripped the scar below his shoulder where long ago an arrow from one of Lord Yueh's men had buried itself.

"What is it?" Ping asked. She moved his hand carefully, looking for some wound, but saw none.

"Can't you feel it?" he winced, sliding to the step with his knees up around his chin.

"I can't sense beyond this tower, not until we reach the top. I need the light of Great Moon Lun to read the city." Which told him something he'd begun to guess about her, too.

The spirits had grown silent in the tower, but the sound of battle reached them from closer now. There was fighting in the city streets and below them Bixei's mercenaries repelled a half-hearted attack on the temple. But the wounded lay on both sides of the wall, screaming, or too exhausted to weep into the mud of their own blood mixed with the soil of Thebin.

"Llesho, come back to me!" Ping was looking at him with desperate compassion. "What do you see?" she asked him again.

"Shou has fallen." Llesho's dream-vision found the emperor still on the battlefield, pale and bleeding in the arms of the mortal goddess of war. Her warhorse stood, steadfast as the mountains as his mistress took the emperor onto her own saddle.

Not even the gods had time to mourn their losses now. "Take him," Llesho heard the mortal goddess of war say, and felt the emperor's body eased into the arms of his Imperial Guard. It hurt so that he couldn't breath when they moved him. Llesho realized that the emperor must still be alive, but for how long?

"I think he may be dying." He rubbed his face, trying to clear his mind of the lingering effects of Shou's injury.

Ping nodded as if his words confirmed something that she had only guessed until that moment. "Let me help you. I can't stop it—if I were meant to, the tower wouldn't have given you the visions in the first place."

"That's enough," he assured her, comforted by the fact that she didn't doubt what he had seen and felt.

"Focus on me, and the staircase—direct your arms and legs as if you stood outside yourself. You can set the feelings at a distance." She put her hand on his shoulder and the pain faded. *Mother,* he thought. He knew that was wrong, but her power felt familiar in that way. His mother had been a priestess-queen, a goddess in her own way.

"Oh!" he realized. "I know who you are—"

"Your sister. Always." She meant more than this lifetime. His heart swelled within him. The sapphire princess indeed, and a stripling girl only in this world's eyes. He trusted her utterly to lead him unharmed to the queen's pavilion now. And he knew that, while he'd been born to be king for a little while, he'd never been meant to sit on the throne. Because his sister, Princess Ping, was going to be queen.

He levered himself up and, shaking off the reawakened ache of old wounds, he started up the stairs again. This time he kept his thoughts focused on the worn stone of the steps he ascended, and the rough walls of the tower at his shoulder.

He couldn't quite block out the spirit presence that gathered at his back. Ping took his hand again, however, and he accepted his living sister and her dead courtiers as a comfort and support for his coming battle. When they had reached as high as they could go it seemed that every life of every priest and priestess, of every queen and all her children who had lived and died in the temple, accompanied them in these last steps of his quest.

"I can't kill him," he said, a confession he hoped she'd understand. "There are innocents involved."

"We know," Ping said, denying nothing of her connection to the spirits of the temple.

Llesho stared out into the direction Marmer Sea Dragon had flown. "Reinforcements are on their way," he said, but his vision couldn't penetrate the gloom.

"Our odds of success improve."

"Thank you." For the trek through the temple and his new appreciation of her ghosts, he meant; for the confidence she placed in him and for witnessing his struggle with the magician.

"You're welcome," she answered all his thanks and stood aside for him.

Llesho stepped onto the pavilion atop the Temple of the Moon. Ping followed, lingering in the shadows. Across the public square, Master Markko stood looking back at him from the king's pavilion above the Palace of the Sun.

"You've come," the magician said. In the way of magic, the voice whispered in his ear as if Master Markko stood beside him. The magician glanced away. At that distance Llesho shouldn't have been able to see it, but he knew Markko looked toward the mountains where Great Moon Lun had begun her nightly ascent. Soon the rays of her light would pierce the eye of the needle and the bridge of moonlight would arc across the square. Already the light was striking the stone floor under Llesho's feet, glinting now off the spear at his back. He didn't dare take it with him into this battle, but unfastened the sheath and offered it, still covered, to his sister.

She reached out to accept it, but pulled her fingers away as sparks curled angrily along its length.

"I don't think it wants anyone but you."

Llesho accepted that and set the weapon that had caused so much grief throughout his lifetimes on the stones at her feet.

"I think I'm going to need it one more time," he said with a speaking look in the direction of the mountains, where an army of demons stood between him and the gates of heaven.

"I love you, brother. Don't forget that."

He was almost afraid to embrace her, but she grabbed him in a tight hug and thumped him to remind him that she was still Ghrisz's spy, and a soldier, whatever her rank or position might be when they had won.

"I love you, too," he said, then the time had come. The fabulous bridge of moonlight sprang into existence in the air between the temple and the palace. At first it was so thin and fragile Llesho could see right through it. Gradually, it grew brighter and more substantial, until it ran with silver light like rain.

On the other side, Master Markko set a cautious foot on the bridge. It passed right through and he tumbled backward rather than suffer the fate of his guardsman so few nights ago.

Llesho shook his head, surprised that the magician, having studied so much about the mysteries of Kungol, could know so little about this one. Then he set first one foot, then the other, onto the bridge of light and began to cross.

"I knew you were the one." Master Markko waited for him, hands at his sides and a smug grin on his face.

With a shrug, Llesho stepped down onto the stone flags of the king's pavilion. "Now I know it, too," he said. Mostly it had brought him grief through all his lifetimes. That hadn't changed in a thousand seasons and a thousand more.

Below he heard death stalking the armies who fought street to street. The city gates had fallen. Cries of horses maddened by fear mingled with the death cries of their masters and their enemies both. Hemmed in as they had never fought before, they plunged down the narrow chutes of the alleyways. The wailing of the spirits of the dead sounded the same to his new-found ear; it didn't matter to ghosts if they were friends or enemies.

Llesho felt it all and it rocked him back on his heels until he forced himself to remember Ping's instruction. As she had taught him, he focused on each step, each move of the magician waiting on the tower where his father once had ruled. The king's pavilion had seen many uses over time. As a husband, the king of Thebin walked the bridge of light to visit his queen, the high priestess, in her temple. In bloodier times, the people sacrificed their king to the setting sun here.

His father had been no warrior, had no army, but Llesho wondered what other tools the Palace of the Sun offered to one schooled in battle by the mortal goddess of war herself. *Power,* he thought, if he could figure out how to use it.

The tower fed him sensations from the battle below. The combined armies of his allies poured through the city. Off to the south the Qubal under Mergen and the Daughters of the Sword had attacked with grappling lines and ladders, swarming over the wall with their own war shrieks.

The Harnish raiders, who did not count women as soldiers, dropped their weapons in terror. Llesho focused, setting at a distance the Uulgar warriors' fear that the Daughters were not human at all but demons dropping from the skies to suck their spirits out through their eyes. Still he flinched as a sword flashed inches from the eyes of the soldier whose mind fed him the images.

The greater numbers of his own huge army left no doubt as to the outcome, except that the Daughters were making maps as well as corpses. Likewise, Tinglut-Khan had taken more than casual note that Shou had withdrawn to the surgery tent with wounds that left his survival in question. The wound on Kaydu's sword arm had begun to swell with infection. She didn't know it yet, but the arm was already dying and remained only to be separated from her body or take her with it into the underworld. Witches didn't have the power to heal their own wounds. He wondered if in shapeshifting she could repair the loss or if the eagle would never fly again.

Master Markko held a sword awkwardly in his hand, but not to fight with. "We could have done this differently," he said, true mourning in his voice. "I trained you like a son to stand against the creature out there—" his chin rose in the direction of the mountainside where the demon-king lay siege to the gates of heaven. "You could have defeated the monster. The gates would have opened to you."

"And then you would have murdered me and tried to take my place," Llesho pointed out. "I have no taste for sacrifice, particularly my own."

"Clever," the magician acknowledged. "But there is no other way. You've seen the dreams, I know you have. If the gates of heaven fall to the beast . . ." he shrugged, as if the truth of those dreams did not require speaking between them.

"And you see yourself as the hero of the tale?" Llesho circled slowly, his hands outstretched, empty of weapons. Focused on the challenger. He had trained for this and battles going on elsewhere faded from his awareness.

"Of course," Markko answered. "Who else has understood the power required to defeat the enemy? Who else has worked

so tirelessly throughout the seasons to acquire that power?''
Sparks rose where the magician stepped, and Llesho felt his
coat snap with the lightning that charged the air.

"Who else, indeed, would be so foolish to free a demon-king
and keep no reins on him?" Llesho let his hand fall to his side,
damping the energy that ran through the king's pavilion.

Master Markko brought the skills of a magician and the
powers of a young dragon to the fight, but the hidden might of
the Palace of the Sun ran in Llesho's veins and he tapped into
it now. Markko reached into the sky for a thunderbolt, threw
it. His face turned to shocked dismay when his blow disintegrated in the air, reaching Llesho as a breeze lightly stirring
his hair.

"You don't know who I am," Llesho mentioned casually. He
imagined shackles and Master Markko dropped his sword, tugging at the bindings that held his wrists.

"It won't be that easy," the magician promised. With a great
bunching of muscles under skin mottled with the scales of a
dragon he snapped the chain, unleashing his hands again to
conjure a ball of liquid fire, which he tossed in Llesho's direction.

"Catch," he said, and the ball grew until it claimed almost
all the space between the two combatants.

Llesho remembered talking to the storm with Marmer Sea
Dragon. He longed for the support of the dragon but made use
of his teaching in his absence. Calling down the gentlest of
storms, he extinguished the fireball with a soft, insistent rain.

The pavilion was slippery now. Master Markko moved more
cautiously, taking a new measure of his student, Llesho
thought.

"I didn't teach you that."

"No." Llesho raised a vortex.

The wind pushed the magician backward. Master Markko
seized on it and worked a conjuring to raise a greater storm.
Hailstones pummeled them and icy rain lashed the exposed
pavilion. Markko pushed back with the wind. Llesho skidded
toward the unprotected edge

"Gently, gently," Llesho answered the attack with a casual

seeming wave of his hand and the storm died down again. Sounds of battle from the street below rose in the sudden calm.

"It's time to put this to rest," Master Markko said. "I have much to do, and little time if I wish to ride the moonlight tonight."

Already the bridge of silver light was fading. Llesho realized he'd have time for his good-byes after all. His hand fell to his Thebin knife, but he didn't draw it. The Lady Chaiujin's cup—perhaps the lady herself—lay ensorcelled in the signet under his hand and he dared not risk the cup in this battle. The magician noted his hesitation and laughed at him.

"Simple tools for village butchers. No blade will cut me, no mortal hand can take a dragon's life. By now you know I hold within me that life which feeds my power. You can moan over your goddess all you want, but know when you die that she will bend her knee to me. She will show me her gardens and take me to her bed gladly because I will be the one to rescue all of heaven from the attack the demons press upon her."

"Your plan has several flaws," Llesho pointed out. "The first is a misunderstanding: the lady chooses her husbands, not the other way around."

Llesho began to move in the prayer forms that had marked the Way of the Goddess for him since he first stepped into the sawdust of a gladiators' training yard. Master Den had showed him the point at which prayer form became combat form and Llesho made the shift, struck at his opponenet with hands faster than the eye could follow. Master Markko staggered under the blow but regained his footing.

"Simple tricks, boy," he said, and reached for the earth below their feet. Shook it. Screams of terror rose from the square below as golden plaster shattered onto the street. Markko clutched at a pillar which threatened to fall and take him with it while Llesho fell to his knees, horrified at the trembling that went on and on below them. It was more than he thought he could do but he reached into the earth, thought of mines and wells and the dark caves that wound down through the mountains, and bid the earth be still. When the nauseating tremors subsided, a great yawning crack had formed in the tower where they stood.

"As I said, your plan has flaws. The second is that you have mistaken who I am when you call me a mortal man." Llesho moved into the form "Twining Branches," and conjured a gnarled old tree in his mind here atop the world of living men. He let the branches of the form wrap the arms of his enemy, so that Master Markko pulled and struggled but couldn't draw his hands away from his sides. "I am a god, beloved by she who reigns in the gardens of heaven, and you have no power over me."

"But you still hold my poisons in the blood and bone of your being," Master Markko growled at him, enraged at his unnatural captivity. He didn't need his hands to invoke his poisons, but Llesho stood upon the source of his power, in the growing awareness of his own identity. The magician's potions couldn't hurt him.

"The third flaw in your plan is that you judge all men by your own actions, or wishes. As it happens, I do not intend to kill you, though you must give up the powers that you have stolen." With that Llesho moved into the prayer form he had created, "Wind over Stone," and raised a gentle but insistent wind. It scoured them with a fine dust that seemed to wear away the surface magic like a false finish on a shoddy chest.

"It's time to put an end to this game." He raised his hand casually between them and called with a voice that seemed to fill the night, "Come air and earth and fire and water. Come gods and kings. Come powers of heaven and earth and the underworld. See this contest put to rest."

One by one the four dragons gathered in the sky under the wash of Great Moon's light. The color of their scales appeared and disappeared in the firelight of their dragon breath; green and gold and silver and the color of Ahkenbad's dust, as they hovered over the Palace of the Sun. Llesho worried that Marmer Sea Dragon would attack before he had a chance to set right the Jinn's mischief, but he waited with his fellow dragons, patient as his species was in the presence of the faster pace of human lives.

Master Markko recognized the dragon he had so mortally harmed, however. He struggled in terror against his invisible bonds but could not move as the stone that guarded the entrance to the king's pavilion slowly moved aside. Out of the staircase formerly held by the Uulgar guardsmen came the mortal gods. Master Markko hadn't known them for what they were, and he watched, agog, as first Master Den, then the Lady SienMa, then Bright Morning the dwarf, rose into the air to join the dragons in circling the king's pavilion.

Little Brother—in his tall form, almost human in looks, he was the Monkey God—bounded through the trapdoor with a screech of laughter to join the other gods in the sky. Two figures joined them. One Llesho had never met before was the mortal god of peace, and he bowed in homage to that most desired of the gods. The last alighted from the glittering silver back of Pearl Bay Dragon, who dipped low to present her great nose as a bridge to the king's pavilion. Llesho smiled when he recognized the newcomer—short and plump and still in the robes of the geomancer of Pontus. The god of learning grinned back at him, her feet hovering above the king's pavilion with the rest.

The Thebin princes followed, or those who could be spared from the fighting and the tending of the wounded and the mad. Ghrisz came first, blood smeared to his elbows and streaked across his face. Not his own blood, but his sweat dug channels through the gore. "Shokar leads the cleanup at the gate," he said, meaning the last of the fighting. "I have come as witness."

Next, Balar led Menar, the blind poet-prince, who made his way by memory as well as by the guidance of his brother. How they had come through the fighting unscathed Llesho couldn't figure, except by the will of the mortal gods themselves.

The kings were next to climb out onto the exposed tower: Mergen-Khan, with AlamaZara leaning heavily against his shoulder. The blood on her uniform was her own, but the wound had seen hasty treatment. Llesho worried more about the protective way Mergen wrapped an arm around her shoulder. What had he wrought in that pairing of armies that might grip Thebin in the closed fist of their association?

Sawghar followed, to represent the Tashek people, and Tinglut-Khan, whose lungs heaved like bellows. Suspicion furrowed the Eastern Khan's brow; he had no love of magic or his neighbors.

Ping, the sapphire princess, who owned the Temple of the Moon as only the queen and high priestess might, gathered up Llesho's spear and tripped lightly across the fading bridge of light to stand among the other heads of state. Llesho noted in passing that the spear remained quiet in her hand, as if now it didn't dare exert its influence in her presence.

His cadre, which now included Prince Tayy of the Qubal people, had not come up. He hadn't called their rank to join him but he wished they'd come anyway. Shou was also absent. Why was it that the good-byes he wanted most to make were the ones he would have no time for?

"I bear witness for the emperor of Shan," the mortal goddess of war said from her place in the gathering of magical persons. She nodded at the candlelit square in the floor of the pavilion where the stone remained pushed back. "The emperor would beg pardon of his Holy Excellence for his absence. He currently lies unconscious below.

Are you satisfied now? Has he sacrified enough for loving the goddess of war? Or won't it be enough until he's dead? He didn't say it, but she read the thoughts in his eyes. There was neither regret nor triumph in the answering look she gave him. *Necessity,* he thought, *a life against the absence of all life.* The Great Goddess herself prepared to end in a firestorm all the realms of gods and men and the underworld before she allowed the demon-king to defile her gardens. *How much would you give?* The Lady SienMa gave silent challenge with a little smile curling one corner of her blood-red mouth. She already knew the answer.

"Who are you?" Master Markko whispered under his breath. Eyes wide and shocky with terror, the magician had finally come to realize that perhaps he didn't have the whole thing figured out.

Llesho bent close so that he could whisper and still be heard by his enemy. He had no wish to astound the other mortals on that tower with his revelation. "I am Justice," he said. "Last of the Seven Mortal Gods. More terrible even than War." The gods already knew and nodded their approval—he'd finally got it right in their eyes. Menar, too, whose blindness had sharpened his hearing, showed no surprise.

The magician doubled over and beat his forehead against the stones in his frustration. "How could I not have seen? We are lost, lost!"

"No, we're not. It was never meant to be you." The answer to the first question seemed so obvious that Llesho wondered why it needed saying. "I didn't know myself." In his journeys his own identity had lured him forward like a riddle whose answer lay always just out of reach and he wondered how many lifetimes he had traveled searching for the part of him that had lain hidden until this moment. But now he had it. Prince Llesho, king of Thebin for a moment, but always the seventh mortal god, Justice. And Master Markko was just one more obstacle on his road to the gates of heaven. And in this place where the king's power rose, so near the gates of heaven that granted his divinity, not so great an obstacle after all.

"What are you going to do to me?" Markko covered his face with his hands, where the scales of Marmer Sea Dragon's son showed clearly in patches against the ridged tendons.

"What should have been done long ago." It didn't matter how the magician might beg or defy the powers arrayed against him. It didn't—couldn't—matter what consequences he would himself be required to pay. That, too, was justice.

"Do as you will; it won't save you from the coming storm." Brought down in the end as much by his visions as by the gods and kings arrayed against him, the magician issued his surrender like a challenge. "The dead can afford to be brave in the face of the end of the world."

Not death, or the end of the world as the magician might

imagine it. He didn't think the magician was nearly as prepared for the true fate in store for him.

Llesho reached for one particular pearl that hung at his neck. "Pig!" he called upon the Jinn who had been his guide through the dreamscape. "I would make a wish."

"I wish that you wouldn't." Pig appeared, his chains tinkling lightly as he moved. "How will I explain to the Great Goddess? How will I earn my way back into her gardens?"

Pig was very good at fulfilling the letter of a supplicant's desire, but in practice wishes often turned horribly against the one who asked them. Thus Master Markko, a second-rate conjurer with no dragon's blood had wished to be a true magician at the same time a young dragon, pining for the love of a human woman, wished to be human. The result of those two wishes might still bring down all the worlds of men and gods and the spirits of the underworld. Llesho could sympathize with the Jinn's present quandary. The Goddess he served would not be happy with a gardener who had brought her beloved husband to grief.

And then there was the matter of the battle still to be waged in the mountains, against the demon-king laying siege to the gates of heaven. How was Llesho to defeat the demon and his army of minions if Pig did something horrid and stupid to him over a wish? If the Jinn deliberately created an evil outcome for the wishes he granted, Llesho could have persuaded him, on pain of continued exile, to forgo his tricks on this occasion. But he didn't. He truly wanted to help each and every time. Llesho knew that. Things just didn't work out quite the way that he planned.

Pig begged again to be released from the wish. He clanked his chains for emphasis, to show what had happened the last time he'd granted a wish, "Please, Young God, what justice is there in rewards granted without toil?"

Therein lay the trick. A wish was a shortcut. And a shortcut, almost by definition, abandoned the way of the Goddess for the more convenient path that led ultimately to evil. This time, though, Llesho didn't think that would happen. This time, it was the only way. The way of justice. He thought his Goddess would approve.

"We have all toiled long toward this end, good Pig. And now it is time. I wish that you will reverse the wish you granted these two fools. Release Marmer Sea Dragon's son from the madness of this false magician, and free this false magician from the terror and pain of a young dragon trapped inside his body."

"Oh. Oh! Of course." In the way of Jinns, Pig had no power to reverse a wish once granted, no matter how ill-advised the asking had been. But a new wish could undo a small part of the damage, at least as it pertained to the individuals whose lives had been twisted together by their foolhardy requests. With a snap that singed the hair on the heads of the gathered company, Pig did as he was told.

A horrible scream of pain became two screams separating like the universe torn open, so that Llesho wondered what horror had resulted from his well-meaning wish. When the smoke had cleared, the haughty magician was gone. In his place huddled the shrunken shell of a man gibbering madly into his beard. In the sky above the king's pavilion, a young dragon writhed in an agony of muscles too long cramped into the shape of a man. The creature they had known as Master Markko had split in two again.

Marmer Sea Dragon raced after his son, wrapped his head in a tender wing and lifted him into the wind to ease his pain. In the streets below, where the sounds of battle had faded and died, new cries of panic and terror arose, but Marmer Sea Dragon led his son out over the empty plain where he might spit fire and roar out the years of his agony without doing any harm.

Pig didn't always know what effects his actions might cause. Llesho, fearing they had not seen the end of this one, waited for his own fate to make itself known. He waited a moment more. The Monkey God, who had traveled in their company as Little Brother, did a somersault in the air and added his own earth-shaking shrieks to those of the young dragon, but nothing happened. Or, well, nothing happened to Llesho.

"That's it," Pig said, dusting off his hands with a twist of distaste around his snout as his chains rattled. "Don't you have somewhere else to go?"

"What about—"

"Is this the man you fought on this tower?" Pig asked him.

Llesho looked at Markko, no longer a master at anything, curled in on his terror of all that had happened to him. "Not any more."

"Do you have any grudge to settle against the young dragon that he hasn't amply paid through his torment all these years?"

"Not at all."

Pig shrugged. "The consequences follow the wish," he explained. "Your wish wasn't about you, so the consequences weren't either."

Master Markko drooled out of the corners of his mouth. He would need tending and would eventually die as mad as he was right now. It was questionable, of course, if he'd ever been truly sane.

Marmer Sea Dragon's son would also need time and care. He would never again be that free and impetuous youth who had made a wish for love, but with his father's support he would survive. In the ages of a dragon's lifetime he would absorb the lessons he had learned in what, to him, would become just a blink of an eye. At least, he would if Llesho succeeded in defeating the first of Markko's mad magics—the demon-king conjured from the underworld.

"Justice has been served here," he concluded. Master Den and Bright Morning gave each other congratulatory glances at that, but the Lady SienMa watched him out of dark, sad eyes.

"It has been a long and terrible night," she said. "But your lady awaits you."

"I know." It was time to say good-bye to his brothers and to the kings who had lent their might to his struggle. When he came to the point of it, however, there was little he could say that would not reveal his own misgivings about the battle he still faced. Even if he survived his fight with the demon-king, Llesho knew that he wouldn't be coming back, not for a long while. Not until he sorted out all that had happened.

The Lady SienMa seemed to understand all that remained unsaid. "It always was that way," she answered with a tilt of her head that was a bow between the mortal gods.

"Shou—" He was afraid to ask the question.

"Will survive," her ladyship assured him. "Like our young dragon, Shou has finally learned the lessons he needed to find his path as emperor."

Llesho wondered if that meant Shou was finally ready to seek a wife, but he didn't intend to ask it of the lady in question. After the lady, his brothers came to him one by one. Balar hugged him as if he were still a child, and Menar touched his forehead to Llesho's crown. "Go in safety, brother," he whispered.

Ghrisz, who had known him only a short time since his return, clasped his arms as one warrior to another. "Don't leave me in the rear when the fighting has scarcely begun," he said. "We have an army that would ride to your banner even against the demons of the underworld."

"If I can, I'll find a way." He didn't think he'd have that chance, but the thought of an army to take against the imps that stood guard over their demon-king made his heart swell.

Ping said nothing as she set the strap of his spear across his shoulder, but she wept when he took the silver circlet from his head and handed it to her.

"Tell your husband to wear it well," he said. "Whoever he may be."

"Tell my brothers to have sons." She meant she would not marry, and though she didn't ask him to stay, he saw the wishing of it in her tears.

Ghrisz watched them both with a troubled frown. "What do you mean?" he asked. "Whatever else you are, Llesho, you are meant to be king of Thebin. Even I have realized that."

"I was, for a little while," Llesho answered him with a little shake of his head. It seemed so obvious to him. "Now I have other duties. Ping will make a good queen—the Temple of the Moon has already accepted her, now it's time her brothers did."

Ghrisz still seemed uncertain, but Llesho's good-byes had

taken more time than Great Moon Lun had allowed him. The silver bridge of moonlight between the towers shimmered and disappeared.

Marmer Sea Dragon tended the agonies of his son's return to his own flesh, but the remaining dragons turned their gaze as one to the place where, in her rise along the mountainside, Great Moon had spun her bridge of moonbeams between the realms of gods and mortals. One pediment, Llesho knew, rested before the gates of heaven, the other on the pavilion atop the Temple of the Moon. Where he wasn't.

"Looks like you missed your chance," Dun Dragon said, speaking of the silver bridge that had carried Llesho to the Palace of the Sun.

"There are other routes," Llesho answered, thinking of the dreamscape.

"Or you could hitch a ride. You've been inside my head before." With a lidded, inscrutable gaze, Dun Dragon rested a claw lightly on the stone of the king's pavilion. When Llesho climbed up, he hmmmed a slow curl of smoke from his nostrils. "Still haven't learned to say no, I see."

"Tomorrow," Llesho promised.

"I doubt that."

Llesho thought the dragon was probably right. "Do you know the way?"

"Some of us have always known the way."

Which led Llesho to wonder if there hadn't been a short-cut to saving the universe. Pig had taught him his lesson about shortcuts however. Better to have done it right. "Let's go, then."

Dun Dragon lifted him to his brow, between the dragon's horns. The cavern of bone pulsed with the light from the blue crystals embedded in the walls that Llesho figured must be some dragonish form of blood or life energy. The low pallet where Llesho had learned dream travel from the Tashek dream readers still rested in a rough corner, looking the worse for its adventures. It was the most comfortable place to sit, however, so Llesho did, curled cross-legged with a hand resting lightly on the bony wall for balance as Dun Dragon rose on a column of warm air.

"Remind me to get rid of this for you when we are done," he promised, meaning the pallet.

"Thank you."

With a powerful beat of his wings, Dun Dragon wheeled in the moonlit sky, heading for the mountains.

Chapter Forty

LLESHO had lost track of time during his confrontation with the magician, but he didn't think he'd lost that much. Dragons had a way of distorting the elements in their presence, though, time and place no less than the others. So he wasn't completely surprised when he looked out between the scales that covered Dun Dragon's forehead to discover the rays of Great Sun glittered off the icy crown of the mountains.

Almost there. Hidden deep within the brilliant flash of glacier, he made out two tall pillars of crystal. Between the pillars wound gates of silver set with drops of diamonds big as Llesho's head and pearls that caught the light and softened its sharp glint. The gates of heaven.

Dun Dragon circled above a dark mass seething on the edges of the glacier. Imps and demons climbed with jagged picks and lines made of the guts of their enemies. In one place they seemed to be making headway, but then a fight broke out in the midst of the creatures. Blood splashed on the pure mountaintop. Lines were cut and imps fell crashing from rocky cliffs to pick themselves up again, shake off the jarring fall, and begin again.

Dropping lower in the dragon's reconnaissance, Llesho saw again the cave where he had met the demon-king in his dreams. "That's it," he said, pointing to the entrance which now was decorated with the bones of victims, imp and creatures of every kind, including human. He didn't see the demon-king himself, but lesser demons and imps lounged around in front of the cave, quarreling among themselves, fighting over their terrible food and picking their teeth with the finger bones of children. Shadows moving just out of sight inside the cave raised Llesho's estimation of the force gathered against them.

"We are going to need help," Dun Dragon said.

Llesho wondered when his quest had suddenly become "we" but he didn't doubt the sentiment. "I wish Ghrisz were here," he said. He would have called on Shou, except the emperor lay insensible from his injuries below.

"Ghrisz for a start," Dun Dragon agreed. Opening his great toothed mouth he bellowed a dragon call so fearsome that Llesho cowered among the scales, covering his ears and praying to the Goddess to deliver him from his friends as well as from his enemies.

Above them on the mountain that cry was answered by a deep rumble. No creature, but the mountain itself gave throat to a great rending snap that cracked a tottering shelf of ice from the mass of the glacier. The avalanche gathered sound as it gathered speed, rolling unstoppably down on the imps and demons busy climbing and fighting on the mountainside. Burying the evil creatures in its icy snows, the avalanche continued down the mountain until it came to rest pressed up against the Harnish wall that circled Kungol. Without the hated wall, the southern end of the city would have been buried in snow. Even now the glacier threatened to break through into the streets.

"Not quite what I had in mind," Dun Dragon muttered. "But it will keep them until help arrives."

As he clung to the scales that protected the great beast's bony cavern, Llesho wondered what had possessed him to ally himself with dragons. Hadn't the destruction of the city of Ahkenbad taught him anything? Master Markko's attack on the dream readers had wakened the beast, but Dun Dragon, rising from that sleep, had shattered the city built on his back. Even when they meant well, dragons carried the seeds of destruction in their breath and in the beat of their wings.

"That is my city!" Llesho couldn't contain his outrage. "Hasn't Thebin suffered enough from its enemies? Do its friends have to knock the holy city flat for extra measure?"

"It was an accident." Dun Dragon's apologetic shrug nearly threw Llesho off his back. "Where I come from, mountains don't fall down so easily."

"It's not the mountain. It's ice and snow frozen against the mountain's side. If you shake it hard enough, the ice falls off, just like from a pitched roof."

The Gansau Wastes, where Dun Dragon had lived and then slept through the millennia of his lifetime, had neither high mountains nor snow to crust upon a rooftop. Llesho thought the dragon knew more of what he did than he was letting on, but couldn't figure out what the point had been. They'd eliminated a small part of the force sent by the demon-king to attack the gates of heaven, of course. But thousands more of the minions remained. Dun Dragon had already said it hadn't been his intention to bring down the glacier on Kungol's head. So what had he been trying to do?

The answers to his question were approaching on long, steady wing strokes. As they grew nearer Llesho recognized Golden River Dragon and Pearl Bay Dragon by the gold and silver of their scales. Marmer Sea Dragon had returned bearing a stranger on his back, a young man with hair the color of the sea and eyes with storms at their centers. Pearl Bay Dragon carried the lady SienMa, mortal god of war, and Master Geomancer, the mortal god of learning. On Golden River Dragon's back Master Den rode to battle with Little Brother, the Monkey God grown to the size of a man, at his back.

Peace and Mercy had no place in this battle, but Llesho felt the strength of his newly discovered rank fill him with purpose. He had more than a personal battle to fight. The realms of heaven, the mortal kingdoms, and even the underworld depended on what they did here. In the air, the four dragons with their riders circled, then suddenly Marmer Sea Dragon broke off, following the avalanche's fall.

With one clawed foot the size of a small hill he raked a gouge out of the landscape and with his sulfurous breath he roared out fire upon the snow. Gradually both snow and ice began to melt, running into the seam cut into the dry ground. As it filled, the seam became a lake on which dead imps bobbed in the steaming water.

Delicately, Marmer Sea Dragon raked his claws through the water, drawing out the dead monsters like a sieve. When he was done, the new lake shone clear as liquid sunlight next to the heaped dead. He then lifted into the sky, leaving the task of burning the dead to the armies who crept out when he had gone.

"We'll need their help," Dun Dragon's muttered explanation roared through the air passages in his head.

As they rose into the sunlight, he gazed out on the mountain where the demon-king's lair lay hidden at the heights. Low on the side of the towering mountainside, he caught sight of a solitary figure beginning to climb. Lluka, he recognized with the farseeing eye of a mortal god. Determined in his madness, the prince had escaped his brothers' loving guardianship. Whether he pursued a mad effort to join the battle against the demon-king or was drawn to the creature as a minion, Llesho couldn't tell. It seemed unlikely he would be in time even if he found his way between the worlds, however.

Llesho would have gone to him to save his life if not his sanity, but the demon-king had come out of his cave. Sunlight vanished into the dark gleaming pearls of his eyes, but he followed the sweeping flight of the dragons with small, tight movements of his neck and shoulders. A roar out of his awful mouth brought imps pouring from the cave.

"It's time," Dun Dragon said.

Dragons had the power of communicating mind to mind, as Llesho had experienced himself with Marmer Sea Dragon. This time, the dragons spoke by silent communication among themselves. Llesho didn't understand the thoughts that hummed through the cavern where he waited. He felt it tugging at his gut when the dragons reached a harmony of minds, however. It felt like some part of the universe had twisted out of true, taking his innards with it. When his ears stopped ringing, he heard the sounds of a human army crying out in a chaos of terror on the mountainside.

"You might have given them some warning," Llesho chided the dragon.

"That only makes it worse." Dun Dragon landed lightly on an outcrop above the demon's cave while Llesho wondered when he'd had the experience of moving an army before, and what had befallen those terrified troops. The answer might have given him a clue about what would happen to his own army out on that mountain in the crack between the mortal realm and the underworld that Master Markko had opened by accident long ago. Dun Dragon's tone didn't invite questions, however, and he had work to do.

Llesho climbed down the ridge that he'd once mistaken for a staircase on the right side of Dun Dragon's nose. When he reached the ground Dun Dragon lifted into the air, circling over-head with the other dragons in search of likely prey from among the imps attacking below. Nearby the other mortal gods had risen in the air under their own powers. Llesho hadn't figured out how to do that yet so he kept the stony ground under his feet.

Farther down the mountain, with the demon-king's cave between them, he saw Ghrisz, pale but standing and with his sword drawn. Ghrisz had seen him leave with Dun Dragon and so he was watching for him as he climbed down.

"For the god-king, Llesho!" he called, and the dragons lent him the power of their voices so that his words rang through the mountaintops like thunder. His own troops and those who had followed Llesho heard the call and set aside their terror as imps and minor demons poured out of the cave, where Master Markko had pierced the boundary between the worlds.

With a terrible, earth-shattering cry, the two forces of humans and imps fell upon each other, sword and shield against tooth and claw. The human soldiers had an advantage that their own battle frenzy drove them forward, against the foe, while imps and demons were as likely to attack their own as their human enemy.

The minions fully engaged, it was time for Llesho to con-

front the demon-king who threatened heaven. He shifted his
shoulder, stirring the cursed spear at his back, and checked his
belt for the bag of tea with the Lady SienMa's cup in it. Time to
release the tainted cup of the Lady Chaiujin: he removed the
signet from his knife and let it grow again until it returned to its
natural shape as an elaborately carved wooden box. Then he
opened it and took out the cup which Adar had painted with
the poison mixture. The cup went into the pouch with the tea
and the box went back on the butt of his knife. He was ready.

The next step, getting himself captured, was easy enough.
The tricky part was making it look like an accident. That was
less difficult then he'd expected. A stone gave way under his
foot, his ankle turned and he fell, skidding down the mountainside on his belly to land at the feet of a minor demon.

The creature looked up from tearing an imp apart to confront
the disturbance. "How did you get up here?" the demon mumbled around his fangs. Acids dripped from the corners of his
mouth as he talked, raising sizzling smoke as it hit the ground
between them.

"I flew up in the head of a dragon to kill your master," he
said.

"A likely story," the demon sighed, not believing a word of
it. He dropped the bleeding imp and dusted off his hands,
which only succeeded in spreading the blood. "Still, I guess I'd
better give you to the king. He'll want to question you before
we eat you."

Llesho tried to walk but his ankle wouldn't carry him. With
another exasperated sigh the demon grabbed him by the braids
of his hair and dragged him the little way to the mouth of the
cave from which imps continued to pour.

"You have a caller," the demon made the sarcastic introduction. "He says he's come to kill you."

"Does he have anything worth stealing?" The demon-king,
folded in upon himself like a paper crane to fit inside his own
cave, shambled into the light and peered at Llesho through the
stolen pearls of his eyes.

He made a gesture of command and his imps seized Llesho
by the arms, stealing the little bag of tea things and reaching for

the spear at his back. It burned their fingers when they touched it, however, and they quickly backed away, chittering and hissing angry threats at him.

When nothing else seemed to follow, however, one of the more daring of them snatched the empty silver chain from his neck. Pig was gone, freed when he released the dragon-king's son or simply traveling on his mistress' business in the dreamscape. Llesho hoped that he would return to his person and not to the chain which now wrapped the wrist of the demon-king as a bracelet. "Tasty," he said, licking his fingers of the last scraps of his imp-snack.

"What's this?" the demon who had brought him reached for the bag in which Llesho had gathered the Goddess' pearls.

"A charm to ward off demons," he answered, and used the powers of a god to channel the angry fire of the spear into the cord around his neck. When the demon touched it, blue light arced across the cave, throwing the demon against a wall and cracking his head open.

The demon-king considered the unconscious and bleeding heap of his minion. "Your charm seems more intent on protecting itself than its wearer," he pointed out. "And it strikes me that you've come ill-prepared either to storm my cave or to woo the lady in the gardens we all covet."

"Not so ill-prepared," Llesho pointed out. "I've brought an army."

The sound of battle came to them dimly through the stone of the mountain. The demon gestured for him to follow and imps jumped to surround him and push him deeper into the cave. He thought the demon-king would have him bound, but the creature flaunted his power. Surrounded by the creatures of the underworld, Llesho had no chance of escaping. Fortunately, escape was the last thing on his mind. As he had anticipated, the jade cups among his few possessions soon attracted the evil creatures who had stolen them, and their fighting drew the attention of their leader.

"Give me that!" With his sharp claws extended, the demon-king cuffed the imp who had opened the pouch. The imp scam-

pered out of the way but not before a claw had split his pointy
face from his temple to his long narrow chin.

Llesho kept his own features unconcerned when the demon-
king took out the cup the Lady SienMa had returned to him.
The trickster god had trained him well, however. When the
tainted cup of the Lady Chaiujin was drawn out, he made a face
of indignation and yearning.

"Does this cup mean something to you, young prince?" the
demon asked.

"Nothing," Llesho answered, with heat in his eyes.

"I see."

From outside the cave came the squeal of imps and the bellowing roars of the dragons, the clash of armies and the howls
of imps raised against the high piercing shriek of the wind
whistling with the speed of his movements as the Monkey God
mowed them down in rows with his hundred-yard staff. Inside,
however, the demon-king watched Llesho with no expression
in his stolen eyes.

"This wouldn't be where you draw your power, by any
chance?" he asked, holding up the Lady Chaiujin's cup.

"I don't know what you mean." He did, of course, and he let
the knowledge show in his eyes. Of what, however, he kept to
himself.

"I thought so." The demon-king gave him a triumphant
smile. "Bring us tea," he ordered. Imps dashed about to do his
bidding while he sat, still as the mountain, watching Llesho. So
wrapped in his thoughts had he become that he didn't notice
the new arrivals until they walked into his cavern and presented themselves below his squalid throne. Lluka cringed in
the company of a young man unsteady on his feet. Llesho recognized him as the passenger who had ridden to war on the back
of Marmer Sea Dragon, but he didn't know who he was.

"Bring me my tea!" The demon-king held out the poisoned
cup for the imp to fill while he looked the newcomers over. "I
know who you are," he said to Lluka. "You have troubled my
sleep for many cycles of the seasons now. It will be a pleasure
to put an end to the disturbance. As for you . . . familiar, but . . ."

"We've met." The young man crossed his legs and sat. He

made a graceful job of it, but from the quaking of his limbs, Llesho thought he couldn't have stood any longer if he'd tried. "Tea?"

"Not for you, little one. This is a drink for kings." The demon-king lifted his cup to drink, blood still dripping from his awful teeth. He watched Llesho as he did so; something in what he saw stopped him with a question.

"Or have you learned more from the tricksters who surround you than it seems? You'll drink first, I think."

Llesho had anticipated caution on the beast's part. He took the poisoned bowl with both hands, his expression one of gloating pleasure meant to entice the demon-king to drink deeply when it came his turn. For his part, Llesho did as Adar had told him, and barely sipped.

It hurt, but Master Markko had prepared him for that pain. He sat quite still, an eyebrow cocked, and waited for the demon-king to take his turn. The demon drank with loud slurping noises, tilting his head back so that he didn't lose a drop. When he was done he wiped his mouth with the back of his hand and turned his dark and gloating gaze on Llesho. Who smiled back, though the sweat had beaded on his brow and the pain had cramped his gut.

"What have you done?" The demon-king jumped up in a rage, but already the draught was coursing through his veins.

"I've poisoned you." Llesho confirmed what the monster already knew.

"But you poisoned yourself as well!" Sweat had formed on the monster's brow and Llesho didn't have to imagine the chill rattling the demon-king's bones. He shook with the same waves of hot and cold himself.

The demon-king flung down the cup in his rage, shattering it on the stone floor of the cavern. Quick as the flicker of a thought, an imp darted out of the darkness to snatch at the shards and dash out the yawning entrance to the cave. Llesho thought he saw something slither away from it, but his eyes were cloudy with sweat and with pain, so he couldn't be certain. He couldn't know the scream that followed was the imp dying either, but he felt the passage of the shard from one hand to another as if a thread that had tied the Lady Chaiujin's gift to his soul had broken.

"A word of caution could have prevented your own suffering!" the demon cried at him. He could make no sense of Llesho's actions. "Why would you allow yourself to be poisoned?"

"To save the gates of heaven," Llesho answered through teeth that had clenched shut. "To save the mortal realm."

"You must know human poisons can't kill even a minor demon." The beast paced as he ranted, his size shifting as he lost control of his folds. "No human weapon can kill a king of the underworld!"

"But it will make you suffer, at least for a little while—" He reached for the spear at his back, but the pain was too great. Wrapping his arms tightly around his belly, he toppled over while his muscles grew rigid, curving his back like a bow.

No, he thought, *not yet.* The demon-king was still alive, and though the poison would soon render him as helpless as Llesho was now, he'd told the truth; no human weapon could kill him. Llesho needed to use the cursed spear, the weapon of a mortal god.

"This is your fault!" The demon rose up to his great height and turned on Lluka, who muttered mindless incantations in the corner, wrapped as tightly around his own middle as if he had himself drunk from the poisoned cup. "Your visions brought him here! Your visions drove him!"

"Not mine," Lluka mumbled from his corner. "They were your dreams all along."

The demon-king seemed to grow more huge and terrible in his rage. He took a step, faltered as the poison tied cold knots in his gut. "They were my dreams! You had no right to invade my sleep and steal my dreams!"

Muscles rippled and snapped under his skin with the effect of the poison and his terrible anger. He had his back to Llesho now, who lay in agony on his floor. Llesho willed his hand to move, to reach for the spear at his back, and felt it slide away from him even as he grasped it.

The strange, shaking boy clasped the cursed weapon, wincing as the thing sizzled and burned the flesh of his palms. But he made no sound that might give away his purpose as he put the shaft firmly into Llesho's hand and closed Llesho's cramping fingers around it. It wasn't enough. He couldn't feel the weapon in his hand. It began to slip again. Then, with a slow smile and a nod to reassure him, the strange boy with eyes like the sea clasped Llesho's hand in his. Using his own trembling strength to secure the spear in both their hands, he crept along at Llesho's side.

Imps and demons all around them stopped in their tasks, casting nervous glances from the mouth of the cave where the sounds of battle still raged, to their monstrous king, whose color had paled and darkened by turns through shades of putrid green. They made no move to warn him as Llesho, with the strange boy at his side, dragged himself closer.

The demon-king snatched Lluka from his corner by one leg. "You are going to die for this!"

The poison stole the will from his wrongly jointed limbs, however, and writhing, the monster fell to his knees. "All you measly mortal creatures and the foolish gods who gather you like stones upon the board. You'll all die!" Bent over his poisoned gut, he reached for Lluka's other leg, to tear him in two.

Llesho staggered to his feet with the strange, silent boy at his side, and together they plunged the cursed spear into the demon-king's back. Cold fire ran like lightning up its length. The boy fell. Trembling with the effort of containing the shock, Llesho held on. But the monster still moved. Calling on previously unknown strength as the mortal god of justice, a strength greater than any mortal could summon, he plunged the weapon deep into the monster's heart.

"What?" The demon-king sighed on his last breath, and fell dead at Lluka's feet.

Suddenly, the madness cleared from Prince Lluka's eyes, leaving confusion in its place. "Where are we?" he asked.

Llesho heard him at the very edge of consciousness, but he wasn't able to answer. Didn't know what answer he would give if he could have spoken. The monster was dead, but what came next he didn't know, except that the strange boy who had helped him wasn't moving, and his own hold on consciousness was slipping away.

"Is it over?" Lluka tried another question. He likely didn't mean the battle, but the future that he had seen end in disaster so often in his dreams.

"Almost." He knew that voice, from long ago. Kwan-ti: Pearl Bay Dragon in her human form. A figure crossed at the corner of his eye and he saw her silver drapes glimmering like scales as she knelt at his side.

"Drink this," she said, and held his head while she fed him an antidote from the marriage cup that Lady SienMa had returned to him at the beginning of his quest. The draught in it was sweet and clear and pure as water from a mountain spring. Llesho drank sparingly, afraid that anything he added to his stomach would make the cramps and nausea worse. Kwan-ti's elixir soothed his pain, both of body and spirit, however. With each sip he found himself stronger and cleaner, as if some terrible stain caused by Master Markko's poisons was being purged from his soul as well as his body.

"Thank you," he said.

"We would have spared you if we could."

"I know. But it was my quest."

"And now it's time to rest." Satisfied that he'd taken enough, and that he would sleep for a while, she left him in Lluka's bewildered care.

"I don't remember much," Lluka whispered. "But I think I've done terrible things. I'm sorry."

"Not your fault," Llesho mumbled. He turned his head to watch as Kwan-ti knelt beside her next patient.

The boy who had helped him kill the demon-king lay unmoving, his eyes fixed. Tears gathered in Llesho's eyes; he recognized the bloodless look of a body growing cold with death in the healer's arms.

Kwan-ti brushed the stormy sea of his hair away from his chill brow. "Brave boy," she said, and took the stranger's hand in her own. "You learned your lesson and amended your errors as well as any creature might. Now rest."

"My son?" Marmer Sea Dragon joined them. He brought the

smell of blood and battle with him, more stinks to join the charred smoke of burning demon.

"Gone," Kwan-ti answered him. "Though he helped to save us all." As she spoke, the body of the stranger was changing, shifting slowly back to his true form. "Stories of the human king and the dragon-prince who fought together to defend the gates of heaven will keep him alive forever."

So, Llesho thought. *That's who he is.* Always at the center of Master Markko's thoughts, no one would know better than the dragon-king's son what disaster would come of the false magician's schemes. It was, after all, his own powers that had freed the demon-king to wreak his havoc.

But, dead? Too high a price to pay for an anxious heart and hasty word. Many had died in the battle to repair the damage of the wish he asked of Pig, the Jinn, however. In Justice, he couldn't rail against the fate of this young dragon-prince, as badly as he might wish to.

Marmer Sea Dragon roared with the terrible anguish of his dragon kind, so that Llesho feared his voice would shake the cave down on top of them, but soon the roaring gave over to weeping. He lifted the coils of his dead son into his arms and cradled him close to his breast, as if the beating of his heart could encourage the dead organ to resume its pulse in the other's chest. It didn't happen, of course. As the dragon-king started toward the door, he cast a glance at Llesho, who stared back out of half-lidded eyes.

"What of the boy-king?" he asked Pearl Bay Dragon in her human form.

Kwan-ti had risen to her feet again and wiped her hands on the crisp white apron of a healer that she'd tied over her shimmering silver robes.

"He lives," she said, and mused, thinking him asleep. "I wonder if he knows how close we came to disaster today? If the demon-king had managed to shed his royal blood here, we would all have died, more horribly than the monster did himself."

"Could he have killed the demon-king without the help of my son?" Marmer Sea Dragon asked. Llesho heard in that question the more pressing one: did my son give up his life for nothing?

Kwan-ti gave a little shrug, not indifference but, as she explained, "Maybe. Maybe not. At best, however, he would have fared no better than your son. And the consequences of that cannot even be measured."

Llesho wondered why that might be. The pearls, of course, but that seemed hardly an immeasurable goal. Pig might take them home in a pinch now that they had broken the siege, he thought. But he'd done what he set out to do. His Goddess, and his nation, were both safe now, whether he lived or died.

Marmer Sea Dragon didn't pursue his question, however. "I'm taking my son home now," he said.

"Won't you wait for the arrival of the princes?" Kwan-ti asked him. "They have much to thank you for, and will want to honor your son's bravery against the demon-king."

"Thank the princes for me in my absence. My son has paid for his mistakes; now it's time we both left such adventures to those for whom death stirs the blood."

"You do them an injustice," she chided her fellow dragon gently. "They started none of this. As for Llesho—"

"About the young god you need say nothing." Marmer Sea Dragon didn't look down at Llesho, but his words were meant to be overheard. "I have traveled with him, and have seen into the bottom of his soul. I know what this day has cost him."

There seemed nothing more to say then. Marmer Sea Dragon was determined to be gone before the princes and their sister could reach the cave which, freed of the demon who had lodged there, had entered the mortal realm again. And so he left, carrying his burden of sorrow close to his heart.

Chapter Forty-one

WHEN the dragon-king had gone, Llesho pulled himself to his feet.

"Not yet," Kwan-ti cautioned him.

The elixir had renewed his strength somewhat, but a poison strong enough to distract the demon-king could not be so easily thrown off. He still hunched over his aching gut. "One last thing—"

The fighting might be over, but he still had one task to complete. There it was, the corpse of the demon-king, rotting already as was the nature of that kind. It lay like a vast lake of putrefying flesh with its feet in the doorway and its head pressed up against the back of the huge cavern. Llesho climbed over an outthrust arm and made his way to the head, where two black pearls stared emptily out of the creature's eye sockets.

Llesho remembered a dream, long ago. Then it had been the eyes of the Gansau Wastrels that he plucked. He found it no less dismaying to take the jewels from the head of the monster, but knew what he had to do. They popped out easily enough; carefully wiping the slime off them with the hem of his coat, he added them to the pouch he wore at his throat.

"Come," Kwan-ti said when he was done. "If you are up to the walk, our people await you."

Llesho followed her slowly from the demon-king's cave.

Once outside, the healer gave a little snort and toss of her head. Transforming into her dragon form, she rose to join Dun Dragon and Golden River Dragon, who perched on the rocks above him. He noted the presence of the dragons with only a part of his attention, however.

He'd thought she meant a delegation from the forces that the dragons had brought to the mountain to fight the demon invaders. Instead he found the mountainside covered with all the combined armies that he had gathered from the far reaches of the world. Kaydu and Shou had remained behind in the infirmary—he remembered the shock of their wounds—but Habiba was there, and all the kings and generals who had accompanied him to Kungol. Sawghar, the Gansau Wastrel, who represented the dream readers of Ahkenbad and even the Thebin corporal, Tonkuq, who had sometimes fought at his side in the Harnlands. The mortal gods, all but the mortal god of learning, gathered at the fore of all that massed company. He'd seen Master Geomancer as she was in her mortal form, muttering to herself at the mouth of the demon cave when he'd come out. "There were shards here, I know I saw them," he'd heard her say, but he wasn't tracking well enough yet to figure out what shards she meant. She bustled after him, however, and took her place among the gods.

This time the Lady SienMa stood not at the head of gods and humans, but to the side, deferring to the mortal god of peace who smiled at Llesho with tears in his eyes. "A costly day," he said, meaning not this one battle. In the way that god spoke to god, Peace meant all the trials that had brought them here, from the attack on Kungol by Uulgar raiders and Master Markko's wish to be other than nature had made him, through all the wasted lives and destruction that led them here, to the death of the demon-king.

"The rift between underworld and the mortal realm—" Llesho held his breath, fearing the answer, that the damage was permanent and more nightmares were coming.

But the god gave him a reassuring smile and said, "Closed by the demons themselves, who feared the champion of the Great

Goddess might bring his war to the dead. For now, at least, the worlds of gods and men are safe."

That was good to know. "Thank you," Llesho said.

Peace answered, "I haven't earned your thanks yet, but I hope to, starting today. For a little while the Lady War will sit out the dance and Peace will have his turn at the floor."

"I trust there will be a place in this most peaceful of all worlds for a bit of mischief from time to time." Master Den pretended indignation at all this harmony. He carried Bright Morning the dwarf who, in turn, carried Little Brother. The Monkey God had returned to his small size—a good thing, Bright Morning declared, since the Monkey God would otherwise be forced to carry the god of mercy on his shoulders!

The company laughed a little too hard and a little too long at the joke, but that was okay. They'd narrowly escaped the end of the world, after all, and with fewer losses than they had any right to expect. Llesho mourned his dead, but few among their company had known Marmer Sea Dragon or would regret his son's passing as he did. He could see himself in the position of the young dragon-prince, had it not been for his teachers.

His brothers and his sister were there, including Lluka, who stumbled from the demon's cave as if newly woken from a daze. Adar took him gently by the arm and led him over to where Balar stood with Menar's hand on his shoulder. The wars had caused damage to mind and body, but Peace, he thought, would go a long way toward healing the worst of their wounds. From their midst came the warrior princes Ghrisz and Shokar, who would deny the title, as honor guard for their sister Ping, the sapphire princess, now their queen. Already she wore the robes of her office as high priestess of the Temple of the Moon. With her priests about her, she reminded Llesho of his mother so much that he didn't know whether to smile or weep.

"Ceremonies and celebrations can wait until we bury our dead and rebuild our country," Ghrisz said. "I know and accept that you will not be our king, but let us honor you before you leave us, at least."

Of his family only Ghrisz himself seemed particularly surprised that Llesho would not stay. They had seen him grow thinner and more distant from his mortal life with each li closer to the gates of heaven they had traveled and seemed to have known the outcome of his quest even before Llesho had. It hurt him that he couldn't give his brother even this one thing, but he'd kept the Goddess waiting far too long.

"Have your ceremony in my name," he said. "But I can't stay. I have a wife who misses me dearly, who I have longed to serve for more lives than I can count. I think I got it right this time, though, and I'm going home."

"You're not dying?" Ghrisz asked hesitantly.

He would have fought another war to prevent it, Llesho thought. He shook his head though. "I don't think so."

But he wasn't sure. He was so tired, so sick, both in his body from the damage of poisons and battles and in his spirit from the many things he had seen and done on his quest.

"Not for a long time, I should judge," Bright Morning agreed. "For most of us, however, comes a time of rest, to figure things out. Then a time of wandering. Then a time, perhaps, of coming home."

With the lifting of his madness Lluka had just begun to glimpse a future. While he still suffered from the memories of what he had done, and the horror he had lived with for so long, he wished his brother well with all his heart. "I hope my children's children see that day," he said, meaning the return of the wandering king.

But: "Us?" Shokar asked with a quizzical cock of his head in the direction of the god of mercy. This most grounded of the seven brothers had come to accept the presence of gods and magicians in his life. But to add one to his family seemed too much for a simple farmer-prince to accept. He hadn't been on the pavilion above the Palace of the Sun, and hadn't heard Llesho's true identity uncovered.

"Justice," Bright Morning told him, and from the shoulder of the massive trickster god he gestured to left and to right where the gods of war and peace and learning had gathered with the Monkey God and the trickster and the god of mercy to welcome their lost fellow to their ranks again. "Too long has Justice been absent from the world."

While his brothers stared from one god to another in amazement to find him among their ranks, Llesho answered Mercy's rebuke.

"The world must make do for a while with the aid of mortals."

"Rest," Bright Morning agreed. "And I think you have still a task to complete for the Goddess your lady wife. The world will be here when you get back."

"Indeed." Llesho set a hand to the pouch in which he had gathered the String of Midnights, the black pearls of the Goddess. He set his gaze on the gates of heaven, which he knew that only the husbands of the Goddess could see inside the ice of the glacier high above the demon-king's cave. It would be a long climb. If only he could sleep first . . .

"If I may—" Dun Dragon bowed his huge dragon head. "One last ride, for my lady, the Great Goddess?"

"Thank you," Llesho said, "for everything," and meant their first meeting as well as this last, the fulfillment of the prophecy, and the water flowing once again in the Stone River where Ahkenbad once stood against the thirst of a dusty desert. He was grateful as well for the offer of one last ride but, looking up at the huge creature, he knew he had to come to his lady wife on his own.

"Not this time," he said.

"And about time," Dun Dragon said, and meant: *good-bye, and you've done well.* "I'm glad I lived to see a young king learn to say 'no.'"

"So am I, old friend. So am I." Llesho made the heartfelt nature of his feelings known with a pat on the dragon's nose. Then, with all the gathered support of gods and men and dragons at his back, with all the five armies of the prophecy looking on, he started to climb.

The crystal pillars entwined with silver flashed with diamonds and pearls, with sapphires and garnets of the dawn. Llesho would have known them for home, however, if they'd been

made of ash and tied together with thongs of leather. Foot by
foot, handhold by handhold, he climbed toward his goal.

Although his battle with the demon-king had sapped his
strength, he found that as a god he pulled life from the ground
beneath his feet and the air which grew thinner with each step.
Mostly, he found the energy to go on in the sight of the gates
that waited for him. The first part of this last journey on his
quest taxed him no more than the steep staircase inside the
tower of the Temple of the Moon. He found that part an easier
climb, since no ghosts tormented him in his passage.

Gradually, however, the air grew too cold to breathe, and the
stone under his fingers became ice. He had come out onto the
glacier and he used his Thebin knife to dig his handholds as he
climbed. Only the hope that called from above him, the precious gates of heaven, kept him moving. It began to seem as
though he would never reach them, when, suddenly, he was
there. But he was still on the outside, in the eternal winter of
the glacier.

No gatekeeper stood to greet him, no gardener wandered down
a leafy path to say hello. All he saw beyond was more ice.
Llesho set his shoulder to the gates and pushed.

They didn't budge.

He pushed again.

They didn't move.

If he'd had the strength to fuel a temper he would have
pounded on the gates, but he had used up the last of it climbing
the mountain. Exhausted, he clung to the silver-turnings that
barred his way.

"My Lady Goddess," he called. "I've come, but I can't get
in."

No one came, and finally he fell asleep.

In his dreams he saw the Goddess, his wife, in all her glory,
which was beautiful and unearthly. He could not have
described the warmth of her, or the welcome he saw in her
arms, which were not arms as he had thought of them before.

"My lady," he answered her call, though no words passed

between them. She took his hands and led him forward and somehow the gates were meaningless and he had walked through as if the silver and jewels that barred his way did not exist.

The eternal dull light of heaven pressed down on them however, and the gardens had fallen to ruin as he remembered. Her pleasure at seeing him was equally dimmed by her uncertainty. "The String of Midnights?" she asked. "Have you found the pearls?"

"I have, my lady." He drew the leather thong over his head and into her cupped hands he spilled her pearls.

Her eyes of many colors tallied up the number and she turned to him, stricken down so near to hope. "There is one missing."

"Perhaps me?" Pig wandered out of a thicket, bound round with the silver chains that were the symbol of his disgrace. The Goddess put out her hand and Pig disappeared, shrinking down into the pearl that once had dangled from a silver chain at Llesho's neck. Now he wore no chains, however, and Pig lay expectantly on his lady wife's palm.

"The very one," she said. When she had them all in her hand she flung them into the sky, as far as she could throw. And when they had reached the highest point in their arc, they stayed there. Suddenly, the heavens darkened with a cloudless clarity. Where each pearl had stuck, stars bloomed in the shapes of the constellations: the carter and his cart, the weeping princess, the bull and the goat. At the top of the sky, most resplendent of all the stars, Pig the gardener took his hoe to the rich, loamy darkness. It seemed to Llesho that the Jinn looked down on him and winked, though he thought that must be the twinkling of the stars.

Night had returned to the gardens of heaven.

"Come, husband," the Goddess said as Great Moon Lun peeked over the gates of heaven. "You have been made to wait too long for your bed."

She took Llesho's hand and he let himself be led away to the bedchamber that had called to him across all the thousands of li of his quest. Soon enough he would return to the world as a mortal god with all of humanity to tend. For now, however, he had finally come home.